THE CRITICS LOVE IT!

"*THE PEKING MANDATE* IS HIGHLY READABLE"—*The New York Times*

"ONE OF THE MOST GRIPPING ADVENTURE STORIES OF THE YEAR"—*King Features Syndicate*

"THIS REMARKABLE FIRST NOVEL is . . . an engrossing adventure tale that deserves a wide readership. Highly recommended."—*Library Journal*

"THE ACTION . . . KEEPS THE READER TURNING PAGES. A solid and satisfying piece of espionage fiction."—*Washington Times Magazine*

"HERE'S A NOVEL THAT HAS EVERYTHING from espionage and smuggling to international intrigue, including romance and some gems of Chinese psychology."—*San Diego Union*

"A JOLLY ROMP . . . complete with bogus relics, daredevils, smuggled messages, forged wills, secret identities, and an earthquake."—*N. Y. Daily News*

THE BEST IN SUSPENSE FROM ZEBRA
by Jon Land

THE DOOMSDAY SPIRAL (1481, $3.50)

Tracing the deadly twists and turns of a plot born in Auschwitz, Alabaster — master assassin and sometime Mossad agent — races against time and operatives from every major service in order to control and kill a genetic nightmare let loose in America!

THE LUCIFER DIRECTIVE (1353, $3.50)

From a dramatic attack on Hollywood's Oscar Ceremony to the hijacking of three fighter bombers armed with nuclear weapons, terrorists are out-gunning agents and events are outracing governments. Minutes are ticking away to a searing blaze of earth-shattering destruction!

VORTEX (1469-4, $3.50)

The President of the US and the Soviet Premier are both helpless. Nuclear missiles are hurtling their way to a first strike and no one can stop the top-secret fiasco — except three men with old scores to settle. But if one of them dies, all humanity will perish in a vortex of annihilation!

MUNICH 10 (1300, $3.95)
by Lewis Orde

They've killed her lover, and they've kidnapped her son. Now the world-famous actress is swept into a maelstorm of international intrigue and bone-chilling suspense — and the only man who can help her pursue her enemies is a complete stranger . . .

DEADFALL (1400, $3.95)
By Lewis Orde and Bill Michaels

The two men Linda cares about most, her father and her lover, entangle her in a plot to hold Manhattan Island hostage for a billion dollars ransom. When the bridges and tunnels to Manhattan are blown, Linda is suddenly a terrorist — except *she's* the one who's terrified!

Available wherever paperbacks are sold, or order direct from the Publisher. Send cover price plus 50¢ per copy for mailing and handling to Zebra Books, 475 Park Avenue South, New York, N.Y. 10016. DO NOT SEND CASH.

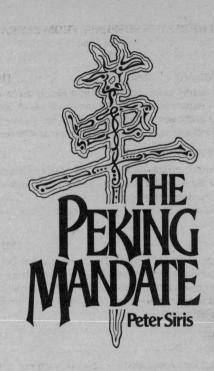

THE PEKING MANDATE

Peter Siris

ZEBRA BOOKS
KENSINGTON PUBLISHING CORP.

The author would like to thank the following sources
for permission to reprint material in this book:
Aria Music Co. for lines from "Too Young,"
copyright renewed 1979 by Aria Music Co.;
Chappell & Co., Inc. for lines from "It's De-lovely,"
copyright © 1936 by Chappell & Co., Inc.
and for lines from "At Long Last Love,"
copyright © 1938 by Chappell & Co., Inc.;
Delacorte Press for an excerpt from *The Future of China: After Mao*
by Ross Terrill, copyright © 1976 by Ross Terrill.

ZEBRA BOOKS

are published by

Kensington Publishing Corp.
475 Park Avenue South
New York, N.Y. 10016

First Zebra Books printing: January 1985

Printed in the United States of America

Author's Note

This is a novel, not a history book. It is entirely my creation. In order to present this story to Western readers who may lack in-depth knowledge of the People's Republic, it was necessary to use some historical events as well as certain real people; but most of the episodes in the book are fictional.

Because of the requirements of fiction, I would like to apologize to any individuals who feel that the characters and events unfairly reflect on them. I would like to extend special apologies to the people of China for taking liberties with their history, for rearranging the timing and location of certain actual events, for creating meetings that never occurred, and for involving fictional characters in real events. I hope that they will be able to look beyond the historical liberties and understand the deep respect I have for them and their country, and that in the future they will consider me a *lao pengyou* instead of a *yang guizi*.

Although this is a novel, I relied on the works of many other authors whose knowledge of the People's Republic far surpasses that of my own. I would especially recommend: *Comrade Chiang Ching*, a superb biography of Mao's wife by Roxane Witke; *The Future of China After Mao, Mao*, and *800,000,000: The Real China*, by Ross Terrill; *Red China Today* and *Red Star Over China* by Edgar Snow; *China: Alive in the Bitter Sea* and numerous excellent articles in the *New York Times* by Fox Butterfield.

Other very fine books and articles that were of considerable help include *Peking Diary*, by Lois Fisher;

Chairman Hua, by Ting Wang; *The Case of the Gang of Four* and *Teng Hsiao-ping* by Chi Hsin; *In The People's Republic*, by Orville Schell; *The Chinese: Portrait of a People*, by John Fraser; *The Silk Road*, by Jan Myrdal; *The Great Bronze Age of China*, by Wen Fong; *Chinese Fairy Tales & Fantasies* by Moss Roberts; *Folktales of China*, by Wolfram Eberhard; *In Search of History*, by Theodore H. White; *New Archaeological Finds in China*, by the Foreign Language Press; *20th Century China* and *China and Russia: The Great Game*, by O. Edmund Clubb; the individual volumes of Han Suyin's autobiography, "Journey to China's Far West," by Rick Gore, *National Geographic*, March 1980; "Skiing on a Chinese Peak," by Ned Gillette, *National Geographic*, February 1981; "China's Incredible Find," by Audrey Topping, *National Geographic*, April 1978; "An Ancient Chinese Army Rises from Underground Sentinel Duty," by Maxwell K. Hearn, *Smithsonian*, November 1979; and *Chinese Folktales*, by Louise and Yuan Hsi Kuo.

Special thanks must also be given to my friend Y. C. Wong, who guided me on my visits to the People's Republic; to Professor H. S. Ha, who taught me Chinese; to the Peking Language Institute; to Burt Siris, who supported me in both my business activities in the People's Republic and in my efforts to write this book; and to Elaine Winik, who imbued me with a love of history and knowledge.

My editor, Diane Reverand, extended herself to guide me. Finally, I owe a special debt of gratitude to my friend and agent Glenn Cowley. Glenn began to work with me when I could barely write. He advised and assisted me through all the drafts of this book. Without his guidance, patience, knowledge, and support, there would be no book.

A Note on Style

Most of the Chinese words used in this book have been transcribed according to the Pinyin system developed in the People's Republic of China. There are, however, several principal exceptions. The traditional spelling has been retained for familiar place names (China, Peking, Canton), famous historical characters (Mao Tse-tung, Chou En-lai, Chiang Kai-shek), Chinese names outside the People's Republic (Hong Kong, Kowloon), and also for a few specific words understood in the West by their traditional spellings (Tai Chi Chuan, Tsingtao Beer). Traditional spellings accepted in Hong Kong have been used for Cantonese words since Cantonese is an oral and not a written language.

Although Pinyin may at first look confusing, it should present few problems for the reader. In most cases, syllables begin with consonants, so Deng Xiaoping should read Deng Xiao-ping. Four letters seem to cause some difficulties. "X" as in Xiao should be pronounced "sh" as in sheep. "Q" as in Qing should be pronounced "ch" as in church. "Z" as in Zhang should be pronounced "J" as in John, and "C" as in cong should be pronounced "ts" as in cats.

Principal Characters

FOREIGNERS AND OVERSEAS CHINESE

Marc Slater: President, M. H. Schaffer Corporation

Linda Forbes: Buyer, Bloomingdale's Department Store

Samuel Tang: President, Far West Aviation Corporation

Beatrice Tang: Chairman, Chinese-American Cultural Committee

Sen Tailing: Managing Director, M. H. Schaffer, Hong Kong

Alexandra Koo: President, Empress Jade Imports

Leung Lilai: Military Official, Taiwan

Vance Stewart: President, Chinese American Tobacco

Wong Chuyun: Managing Director, Chinese American Tobacco

Frans Van Wyck: Managing Director, Royal Amsterdam Hotels

Aziz Rahman: Staff Assistant, Royal Amsterdam Hotels

Yamaguchi Yukio: Managing Director, Takamura Corporation

Avery Boswell: Deputy Managing Director, Gateshead & MacIntosh

Lord Henry Gateshead: Director, English Museum

Nicole LaFleur: Designer, Christian Dior

PRINCIPAL GOVERNMENT LEADERS: PEOPLE'S REPUBLIC OF CHINA

Mao Tse-tung: Chairman, Chinese Communist Party

Hua Guofeng: Premier, People's Republic

Chou En-lai: Former Premier (deceased)

Gang of Four
  Jiang Qing: Mao's Wife, Cultural Czar
  Wang Hongwen: Vice-Chairman, Politburo
  Zhang Chunqiao: Politburo Member
  Yao Wenyuan: Politburo Member

Conservatives
  Deng Xiaoping: Former Acting Premier (Currently
                           purged)
  Liu Teyu: Commander, Canton Military Region
  Hu Shengte: Petroleum Minister
  Kang Moruo: Director Arts and Crafts Corporation

Middle (Wind) Faction
  Ye Jianying: Vice-Chairman, Politburo and Defense
                        Minister
  Li Xiannian: Vice-Chairman, Politburo
  Wang Dongxin: Commander, Unit 8341 (Mao's Security
                            Guards)
  Wu De: Mayor of Peking

Other Chinese Characters
  Mao Yuanxin: Nephew, Mao Tse-tung
  Colonel Li: Commander, Red Guards
  Shen Mo: Jiang Qing's aide
  Chang Shuli (Little Chang): Guardian, National Archives
  Hu Meili: Daughter, Hu Shengte
  Kang Pingnan: Son, Kang Moruo
  Kang Xiaoma: Nephew, Kang Moruo
  Rong Yi: Personal Calligrapher of Mao Tse-tung
  Old Farmer Huang
  Hong Guoqiang: Director, State Farm 120
  Ren Daoling: Representative, China International Travel
                        Service

To Barbara,
for her friendship and love

Contents

THE PEKING MANDATE

1: The Helmsman

The crew of the Chinese trawler strapped the American-made Shark ground-to-air missile into the hoist and swung it toward the sampan bobbing in the brown waters of the Yangtze River. Leung Lilai, a heavily muscled Chinese, stood rigidly by the rail while the helmsman of the sampan guided the missile onto the deck. The rickety wooden boat listed sharply. "Is the cargo too heavy?" Leung asked, casting a critical glance around the shabby craft.

"We'll be fine," the helmsman replied as he secured the missile with strips of rope and then covered it with bales of cotton.

Leung tugged on the sleeves of his blue worker's uniform. He felt uncomfortable in the loose-fitting garments worn in the People's Republic. "What about patrols?" he asked.

"Thousands of boats will be riding the flood tide into Shanghai." The helmsman smiled his half-toothless grin. "No one will be looking for us, comrade."

"I am not a comrade."

"You are when you're in this country," the helmsman replied.

The helmsman signaled the fourteen other sampans under his command. All were fully loaded with weapons and ammunition. He did not know why these arms were needed in the People's Republic, nor why they were being carried from the river on sampans rather than transported into the harbor on freighters. But he was sure that Comrade Jiang Qing had her reasons. She was, after all, the wife of Chairman Mao.

As the helmsman tacked from the Yangtze into the more sheltered Huangpu River, he glanced at his passenger, who was peering through his binoculars at an oil refinery. Leung scribbled observations in a notebook and then stared at a shipyard in which a battleship was in the final stages of construction. "It must look much different from the last time you were here," the helmsman probed. "How long has it been?"

"Some years," Leung replied, continuing to take notes.

"But you were born in the People's Republic?" the helmsman asked, observing that Leung spoke with a classical Shanghainese accent.

"I was born in China," Leung corrected.

"Did you leave during the war or at the time of the Liberation?"

"I left when my home was captured." Leung ran his hands through his neatly cropped hair.

"That could have been by the Japanese or by the Communists."

"So it could." Leung trained his binoculars on a brilliantly lit chemical complex.

Before the helmsman could press on, a military patrol boat powered past, creating a wake that transformed the surface of the river into a continuing chop of a rolling sea.

The helmsman shoved the tiller to starboard as the patrol turned in a sweeping arc and stopped to inspect a smaller caravan of sampans off the bow. The rocking of the sampan forced Leung to grab hold of the gunwale. "What are they looking for?" he asked.

"Opium," the helmsman replied. "The smuggling has started again."

Leung's breath grew shallow as he considered the terrible irony—the drug that had enriched his family could now lead to his arrest. Even Jiang Qing would abandon him if his presence on the mainland were known.

The patrol boat turned toward the sampan. Leung crouched between two sacks of cotton. The patrol cruised along the sampan's starboard side. Except for his hands that worked the tiller, the helmsman stood motionless, staring at the soldiers. The patrol reached the bow. "What cargo are you carrying?" a soldier yelled.

"Cotton," the helmsman replied.

The soldier grabbed the railing. "Pull over for an inspection."

"Comrade Leung!" the helmsman shouted. Leung did not move. "Comrade Leung!" he shouted again. "Wake up and take the helm!"

Leung glared angrily at the helmsman as he jumped to his feet and took the tiller. "What the hell do you think you're doing?" he whispered.

"Trust me," the helmsman said. Then he walked to the bow.

"Tell the other boats to slow down," the soldier ordered.

"We can't stop. We must get to the Wuning Market."

"You will just have to be late."

"Comrade Jiang Qing will not be pleased." The helmsman pulled a letter from his pocket. "My cargo is consigned directly to her."

The soldier read the letter. "Comrade Jiang would not interfere with the People's Liberation Navy. She will not mind waiting one more day."

"Fine." The helmsman took out a pad and a pencil. "Then I'm sure you won't object if I report your name."

"Why should you do that?"

"Comrade,"—the helmsman bowed—"if my delivery is delayed, I do not intend to take the blame. Perhaps your position is more secure than mine, but I have no wish to deal with the wrath of Jiang Qing."

The soldier read the letter again. "All right," he said, climbing back to his own boat. "Be on your way."

Leung handed the tiller back to the helmsman and walked to the bow. He shivered as he gazed at the lights of Shanghai. The skyline hadn't changed physically since the Communist takeover. The Imperial Boulevard that the Europeans had called the Bund was crowded with traffic just as it had been when he was a child. The ornate buildings of French, British, German, Russian, and Japanese design still dominated the harbor, architecturally marking the boundaries of what had been each country's sovereign enclave in the treaty port. Even the promenade along the river was still jammed with strollers enjoying the pleasures of a summer evening. It was just as he remembered it. Yet everything had changed. It looked like the city of his birth, but it was alien territory, controlled by his enemy.

Leung spotted the riverfront mansion that had been his home, and the spires of the Customs House that had been controlled by his father. He wished he could fly across the water. Shanghai was the goal he had dreamed about during his exile. It was the gateway to the Middle Kingdom, the first step on his journey home. After twenty-seven years on a small island that called itself China, he was about to become the first of his people to set foot on the promised land.

The sight of the city of his youth made time slip away. Even with the disruptions of World War II, the years in Shanghai had been happy ones. His father was Chiang Kai-shek's director of customs, but his sideline was even more profitable: He was the leader of the infamous Green Gang that controlled opium and prostitution, trades acceptable to most of the upper class as a way of life contributing to the health of the masses. Leung had never questioned the source of his family's wealth. His own training by Chiang Kai-shek elite Blue Shirt military corps clearly delineated his life. He was to have taken over his father's position, which would have made him one of the most influential men in Chiang Kai-shek's KMT. Only one thing interrupted his perfectly planned career: The Communists won the Civil War.

Leung could still remember the day his father summoned the family. His father, so powerful and decisive, was disoriented and lost. He could not believe that the German-trained KMT, armed with American weapons, was being defeated by the rabble of peasant Communists. The family's land holdings were now worthless, but their store of antiques, jewels, and opium could be transported out of the country. The most valuable of the possessions were loaded onto the American-built, one-hundred-foot yacht that had been used to smuggle opium in better days. The boat was packed to the rafters. There was hardly room for the thirty relatives who crowded on board. Much had to be left behind. Leung's father wanted to make two runs to Taiwan, but there was no time. The Communists were at the edge of the city.

As they steamed out of the harbor, Leung had stood on the flying bridge. He could see red flags flying along the bank. Smoke billowed from the treaty port and from the neighborhood in which he had lived. The bandit Communists were destroying his way of life. He vowed to return.

It never occurred to him that it would take twenty-seven years, and that he would come home disguised as a coolie.

The sampan sailed into Suzhou Creek. Directly ahead was a floating city. Lines of boats, as many as ten abreast, were rafted together from either shore with no more than fifteen feet of navigable space in the middle. The current, funneling between the rafts, sucked the caravan into the narrow opening. Turning from their dinners, people on the outside boats hung their legs over the side and fended off the sampans. Children scampered to greet the new arrivals. "How are the waves on the Yangtze?" one shouted. "What are you carrying?" another called. "Where are you from?" a third yelled. It was fortunate they did not know the answers.

Leung smiled as he inhaled the aromas of fish and vegetables cooking on the backs of the boats. As a child, he had loved to come to the harbor. The fare of the boat people was simple, but he always imagined that all food tasted especially good when cooked in a sampan.

The caravan passed under a low bridge filled with families out for an evening stroll, workers on the night shift riding their bicycles, and young couples daring to hold hands only when they thought no one else was watching. A tall, blond Western woman hovered over the crowd taking photographs. When Leung raised his binoculars to get a better look, he was temporarily blinded by the strobe of her camera. Small circles of intense white light flashed in his eyes as he squinted at her. Before he could focus his eyes, she was too far away for him to see her features clearly.

The traffic on the river began to thin out as many boats stopped at busy markets, while others rafted alongside sampans from their native villages. The caravan did not stop. Its cargo could not be unloaded in such a public location. The deserted Wuning Market was far more suitable.

By 12:30 the current had changed. The helmsman turned up the throttle. The motor belched under the strain. Leung paced nervously as the speed of the tide increased. The debris in the creek flowed quickly past the boat, but it was the debris that made the headway; the Wuning Market was only two hundred yards away, but the boat appeared to be standing still. Finally, after what seemed like an hour, the caravan reached the market.

As the other sampans arrived, the helmsman shouted orders. They were behind schedule. The crew hurriedly removed the stacks of cotton and then unloaded the missiles and the oblong wooden crates containing submachine guns, bazookas, and ammunition. These weapons were destined to help Jiang Qing take control of China, but Leung hoped they would actually help foment a civil war that would permit his people to reclaim the mainland.

As the crew unloaded the guns, others carried smaller boxes from a truck back to the sampans. Leung's curiosity spurred him to disembark and take a look. Prying open one of the boxes, he found a delicately detailed figure of a rhinoceros cast in bronze. "Take the cover off its back," a sultry voice said in Mandarin Chinese. Leung looked up. An elegantly slim Chinese woman with jet-black, piercing eyes stood in front of him. Her dangling earrings and exquisite dark green jade pendant was an odd counterpoint to the loose-fitting Chinese worker's clothes she was wearing. Leung stiffly acknowledged her presence. "Alexandra, you look lovely. Is this the new peasant style from Paris?"

Alexandra Koo responded with a tense, thin smile. "You won't be joking when you open the animal's back."

Leung gasped when he looked into the cavity. Hundreds of pieces of green, white, and pink jade glistened in the reflections of the flares from the boats. "They're magnificent. Where are they from?"

"From a vault near the Qin Tomb. They're two thousand years old."

"They'll earn a nice profit," Leung responded as he fingered the cool surface of an extraordinary piece in the purest of pinks. He tossed the piece back into the rhinoceros. "What's in the others?"

"Half are filled with bronzes and jades, and half with statues that were buried in front of the Qin Tomb." Alexandra opened the cover of a coffin-shaped crate. Inside was a six-foot gray terra-cotta figure of a Chinese warrior in a carved, waist-length suit of armor. His fists were clenched as if he were holding the reins of a chariot. A scarf covered his neck. His hair was wrapped on top of his head and tied in a bun. His eyes and snarling lips were those of a man ready for battle.

Leung stared at the terra-cotta soldier, expecting the figure's chest to rise with a deep breath and its eyes to blink. "It's magnificent. How did you get it?"

"How I fill my half of this partnership is not your concern." Alexandra replied, brushing her long black hair over her shoulder.

"Can we get more?"

"There are seventy-five hundred in front of the tomb. You get the weapons and I'll get the antiques."

"Don't worry about the weapons. Two more shipments are ready."

"We must act quickly. Jiang Qing must have them before Mao dies."

Leung shook his finger. "Don't lecture me. I know my job."

The helmsman's approach cut into the palpable tension between them. He pointed to his watch. "We must get back to the trawler."

Leung turned to Alexandra. "I appreciate your help,

26

Comrade Koo."

"I am pleased to be of assistance." Alexandra bowed politely.

Excusing himself, Leung walked to the boats. Alexandra picked up the rhinoceros and ran her fingers through the shimmering, carved jades. She slipped three small pieces into her pocket. Then she packed the rhinoceros in its box and lugged it to Leung, who was standing in the first boat.

The crew cast off the lines and the caravan drifted toward the center of Shanghai. Leung stood at attention and gazed at the mixture of Chinese and Western buildings in the massive city that had once been his home. His return had been a teasing glimpse, a glimpse that only whetted his appetite to immerse himself in the Shanghai of his memories. He wanted to experience the city. He hungered to stay here and live in this, the real China. Clenching his jaw, he counseled himself to be patient. He would return again. If events went as planned, he and his people would come home to Shanghai as conquering heroes.

2: Petrol and Power

Marc Slater half-listened to the television as he sifted through the stacks of reports strewn on top of the massive semicircular Spanish desk in the study of his Beacon Hill town house. He selected the analysis of his company's recent acquisition of Pecos International Oil and settled into his leather-padded chair. Behind him were the framed cover stories from *Time* and *Fortune*, his sailing and tennis trophies, and the personal photographs with Kennedy, Johnson, Nixon, de Gaulle, and Mao.

In the ten years since becoming president of the M. H. Schaffer Corporation, Marc had transformed the company from a small producer of specialty chemicals into one of the world's largest traders of metals and minerals. He had opened offices in more than sixty countries, built an intelligence system said to rival that of the U.S. government, and acquired businesses in the fields of petroleum, construction, gold mining, and electronics. Yet despite these acquisitions, the basic business of M. H. Schaffer remained the buying and selling of metals and minerals.

Marc Slater's prowess as a trader was legendary. Although many thought him reckless, his risk-taking always rested on an uncanny sense of timing. He had bought millions of tons of Japanese steel two weeks before the American steel strike. He had cornered the market on copper one month before Chile closed its mines. He had taken a major position in wheat just as Russia was beginning the century's worst harvest. And in 1973, he had risked bankruptcy by signing long-term contracts with members of OPEC. His luck held. The Arabs declared an oil embargo, which raised the world price by ten dollars a barrel. He sat on commitments for almost a billion barrels at seven dollars below the new market price.

Many concluded that Marc Slater was born lucky. He was the sort of man for whom things always seemed to go right. When he tacked in a sailboat race, the wind shifted in his direction. When he chose sides in a power dispute, his side emerged victorious. And when he purchased a new company, its fortunes always improved. Even the press had taken to calling him "Lucky" Slater. Last week after he had announced a North Sea strike that promised to rival that of Alaska's North Slope, the *Wall Street Journal* had titled its headline "Lucky Slater Hits Pay Dirt Again."

Marc pushed back his chair and put his feet on the desk. He ran his hands through his brown hair. Baby hair, his wife, Carolyn, used to say because it was so soft. He glanced at his Rolex watch. Though it read 11:01, he knew that it was 10:55. Since his schedule always ran late, he set his watch ahead by six minutes hoping to fool himself. The ruse rarely worked. There never seemed to be enough time.

Marc walked to the burnished rosewood bar and poured a glass of chilled Pinot Chardonnay from the Slater Vineyards in Yountville, California. It was just time for his call from

Japan. He had established a precise daily phone schedule for his international vice-presidents in Teheran, Lagos, London, Rio, and Tokyo. These calls were the first phase in the intelligence system that enabled him to stay abreast of the constantly changing world markets.

Taking a sip of the delicate wine, Marc slid back the glass door to his terrace. The lights from the Prudential and John Hancock buildings cast a yellow aura on the bright evening sky. As he swirled the wine in his glass, he thought about Carolyn. Buying the vineyard had been her idea, and it had been one of her best. Some of their happiest times had been spent in the fields of the Napa Valley. It was their West Coast hideaway. Though others operated the vineyard, they always managed to help with the harvest. The earthly reality of cultivating forty acres of grapes was a wonderful counterpoint to the intangible reality of purchasing billions of dollars of minerals.

The throbbing bass of the stereo in David's room two floors below shattered the warmth of his memories. Ever since his mother's death, David had withdrawn. He would hide in his room for days at a time, watching television and listening to rock music. For six months Marc had tried to break down the barriers. Last week he had coaxed David into going sailing. That pleasant if slightly strained weekend led them to plan a trip to Martha's Vineyard scheduled for the next day. It was, Marc hoped, the beginning of a breakthrough.

The telephone rang. Marc hurried back inside. Certain that it was his Far Eastern vice-president calling, he answered in Japanese, "*Kombanwa* [Good evening]."

There was a momentary pause on the other end of the line. Then a heavily accented Germanic voice said, "Does anyone there speak English?"

Marc laughed as he recognized the voice of the American

Secretary of State. In a clumsy imitation of an Oriental accent, he replied, "I speak a rittle. Can I help you?"

"I'd like to make an appointment to service my Toyota."

"No probrem," Marc replied. "But I thought you drove a Mercedes."

"I did when I taught at Harvard, but then I joined the government. You know we public servants are notoriously underpaid."

"It's very sad. At twenty thousand dollars a shot on the lecture circuit, I don't know how you make ends meet."

The two men laughed comfortably together. Since their first meeting ten years before, when Slater was the representative of the business school and the Secretary was the representative of the Kennedy School to the now famous Harvard University Program on Technology and World Politics, they had become good friends and frequent allies, relying on each other for advice and assistance. They were a well-matched pair.

"I thought you were Joe Takada calling from Japan," Slater explained.

"How is Joe? I haven't seen him since Peking. Is he still trying to negotiate oil leases with the Vietnamese?"

"That was just one of his jokes. He wanted to give you something to worry about."

"I already have plenty to worry about." The Secretary's voice became serious. "Can you come to the White House tomorrow at ten?"

Marc's curiosity was tinged with disappointment. The Secretary's request meant that he would have to postpone his trip to the Vineyard, but there was no way that he could decline. "Of course," he responded, massaging his temples. "What's the subject?"

"I'll explain in the morning. See you at ten." With that, the Secretary abruptly hung up the phone. Marc knew it had to be China.

Few people had more knowledge of China. Marc had been born there, the product of an unlikely union between a Russian Jewish mother fleeing religious persecution and an American missionary father seeking to bring health care to the Chinese. They had settled in Yan'an in northwestern China and founded a hospital. With only three foreign families in Yan'an, Marc's upbringing was as much Oriental as Western. He learned to speak English and Chinese with equal fluency. Despite his "long nose" and "round eyes," he always considered himself of two nationalities.

When Marc was seven, Mao Tse-tung and the Communists reached the end of the Long March. Their successful escape from the well-armed Nationalists and five-thousand-mile trek through some of the most inhospitable land in the world had made them folk heroes in rural China. After they selected Yan'an as their capital, Marc's life became closely intertwined with their cause. He cared for the sick in his parents' hospital, taught English to the recruits, and served as a translator for the diplomats and reporters who shuttled in and out of the city. When the United States entered the war, he volunteered to become a courier. So adept was he at avoiding the enemy patrols that Mao personally nicknamed him the "blue-eyed spirit who runs like the wind."

Those days ended abruptly in March 1943. Northwest China was still covered with a blanket of snow as Marc made his way to Chongqing carrying documents to the American commander-in-chief, General Joseph Stilwell. He was fording a frozen river when he spotted the Japanese patrol. Bolting for cover, his feet skidded on the ice and he fell to his knees.

The first bullet burned as it tore into his shoulder. Two

more bullets penetrated his thigh. The world started to spin. He saw the Japanese soldier standing above him. The butt end of a rifle slammed into his head. Everything went black.

Marc gently rubbed the scar above the hairline. It was a souvenir he would never lose. He remembered awakening in a peasant's hut. A rural doctor was ministering to his wounds while a group of farmers debated how this brown-haired, blue-eyed *yang guizi* (long-nosed foreign devil) had come to be shot on their land.

Two weeks later the peasants had taken him to Chong-qing. There he spent six months in an American-run hospital recuperating from his wounds. One night, he was awakened by a man disguised as an orderly. It was Liu Teyu, one of the leaders of the Communist Army. Today, though more than thirty years had passed, Marc could still remember every detail of Liu's story. The American-made Chinese Air Force plane had circled his parents' hospital three times. Then, despite the large red cross painted on the roof, it dived directly toward the building and unloaded its bombs. Four separate explosions burst through the roof. Leaping columns of flame engulfed the frame. The walls collapsed. No one survived.

At sixteen, Marc had felt bitter and very alone, an orphan trapped in the midst of a civil and a world war. The fighting had escalated. Returning to Yan'an was impossible. The American army confined him to a barracks while others debated his fate. It was decided that he would be sent to live with his father's family in Boston.

The journey took ten weeks and covered 14,000 miles, but the cultural distance was even longer and more arduous. He had gone from being a long-nosed foreigner, living with the Communists in rural China, to being a Chinese-born immigrant in urban America, where the peasant Com-munists were the enemy. Everything he had loved and valued in China was hated and ridiculed in the United States.

His uncle, Endicott Slater, was a successful investment banker who had never understood his brother's decision to become a missionary. He took Marc into his home as a family obligation but always considered the boy to be tainted by his contact with the Communists. Endicott tried to wean Marc from this contamination by teaching him the virtues of free enterprise. Every night Marc had to read aloud from the *Wall Street Journal*. Endicott frequently interrupted to state his own views or quote from his favorite political theoriest, Henry Luce. Luce, too, had grown up in China as the son of a missionary, but had nothing but hatred for the Communists. With the weekly "Gospel According to Luce" in his hand, Endicott would preach that the Communists were destroying China and enslaving the Chinese. Despite his personal feelings for the people with whom he had lived, Marc recognized the futility of taking on his dogmatic uncle.

With the start of the Korean War, public opinion turned even more fiercely against the Communists. Foremost among the Red-baiters was Senator Joe McCarthy. At first Marc considered McCarthy a disturbing but ineffectual demagogue. After only five years in the United States, he could not begin to understand the fear that Americans harbored toward the Communists. The accounts of McCarthy's committee meant little to him, until the senator began to attack people he had known in China.

State Department officials were the first victims. Almost everyone who had served in China was interrogated. Marc knew they were not Communists. While some had been sympathetic to Mao, all had remained loyal to Chiang Kai-shek. In their visits to his home in China, not once had any of them indicated support for Mao. To the contrary, they were always concerned with how they could get the Communists to cooperate with the Nationalists.

It was a frightening irony that these dedicated officials were vilified as fellow travelers. Marc had heard McCarthy announce there was proof that Communists had infiltrated the State Department. The senator listed the names of men Marc knew and admired: Owen Lattimore, John Vincent, John Emerson, O. Edmund Clubb, John Service, Richard Service, John Paton Davies. A generation of Asian experts had been destroyed.

Even Teddy White, who had served as a correspondent for *Time* in China, had been subpoenaed. Marc felt a special closeness to White, who, like Marc's father, was a Harvard graduate from Boston. Whenever White visited Yan'an, he always filled the house with absorbing political conversations. Marc loved to listen to White and his father reminisce about their childhoods. It was a side of his father he rarely saw.

Marc had talked to White just after he testified for John Paton Davies. The committee had been like a lynch mob. They turned on White merely because he was Davies's friend, accusing him of aiding the Communists. The State Department refused to give him a new passport. White's experience greatly distressed Marc.

Although his uncle had been friendly with leading Republicans, his assistance was not enough to prevent Marc from being subpoenaed. It had been an uncomfortably humid summer day, made even more unpleasant by the heat from the lights of the television cameras. He was then twenty-three and was already working for M. H. Schaffer. Although he was accompanied by the noted attorney Bernard G. Post, Marc felt very much alone.

After the preliminary courtesies, McCarthy had begun his prosecution. "Mr. Slater, are you now or have you ever been a member of the Communist Party?"

"No."

"But you did live in their bandit revolutionary headquarters."

"My father operated a hospital in Yan'an for the Episcopal church."

"Please do not implicate the church with the Communists."

"I did not intend to."

"Did you know Mao Tse-tung, Chou En-lai, and the other Reds?"

"I knew most of them. These were the people who lived—"

"Please confine yourself to the questions, Mr. Slater. Now, did you serve as a courier for the Communists during the war?"

"I served as a courier for the Americans. The Communists were then our allies fighting against the Japanese."

"That's a treasonous lie."

"Not according to the diplomats who served in China."

"Are you referring to Davies, Service, Lattimore, and the other Communist sympathizers who sold out China to Mao and his hoodlums?"

"They are not Communist sympathizers and they did not sell out China."

"Let me remind you, Mr. Slater, that these men have already been exposed by this committee. The entire world knows that they are fellow travelers. Do you intend to challenge our findings?"

Marc had started to reply when his lawyer leaned over and warned him of the consequences. He hated the senator and wanted to defend his friends, but he realized that he had little choice. "I was not trying to challenge the committee," he aplogized grudgingly.

"Why did you continue to live in Yan'an?" the senator pressed on.

"I was just a young boy. I had to stay with my parents."

"Were your parents Communists?"

"Excuse me, senator," Post intervened. "I have statements from the Episcopal bishop, Henry Cabot Lodge, and Senator Saltonstall attesting to the patriotism of Mr. Slater's father. I further have affidavits from the deans at Harvard College and Harvard Business School, which Mr. Slater attended, stating . . ."

As Post continued, Marc felt a sense of numb relief. He was exhausted by the interrogation. He could hear his lawyer explaining that Marc had been too young to understand the political implications of communism. Marc resisted the urge to stop him. He had known the difference between the Communists and the Nationalists. He had supported the Communists because he believed they were stopping corruption, opium, and prostitution; increasing food production; and bringing hope to China. But he remained silent because he realized that speaking out would jeopardize his position in the United States.

Senator McCarthy returned to questioning him directly. "Mr. Slater, do you support the Communists in China?"

"I do not," Marc said, hating himself for buckling under.

The senator conferred with his aides and then turned back to Marc. "Because you were only a child when you lived in China, and because you have conducted yourself in a patriotic way since arriving in the United States, we will take no action at this time. But I warn you, if anyone reports that you are supporting the Communists, charges will be brought against you. Is that understood?"

Marc had been furious. He had wanted to shout, "Go to hell!" But he did not. He sullenly nodded his head. "It is understood." Those words separated him from what he valued most in his life.

For twenty-eight years he had maintained silence and had

been cut off from his friends and from the land of his youth. But since President Nixon had opened the door, everything had changed. He had returned fifteen times and had reestablished many of his former relationships. The Communists remembered his service and counted him as a *lao pengyou* (old friend). His company had obtained invaluable rights for the export of Chinese petroleum, and he had finally been able to reclaim in some measure the part of his life that he had buried when he left China.

Marc was upset that the request of the Secretary of State had interfered with the plans of his family. Spending time together was important to all of them. He especially did not want to disappoint David. Automatically he tapped Jill's number on the push-button phone. "Hello, Bunny."

"Hi, Daddy. Are you calling about tomorrow?"

"I sure am."

"And you're sorry but there's an emergency in Africa or China or someplace and you can't go. But David and I can take the boat and you'll meet us in Edgartown tomorrow night."

Marc laughed. "How'd you know that?"

"Come on, Daddy. I'm your daughter. I know whenever you call after eleven, it's always to cancel something."

Marc smiled, loving her for making it so easy. "I'm sorry. If there were any way to get out of it, I would."

"I understand. If I had an exam, I'd cancel, too."

"Thanks, Bunny. And I will meet you tomorrow night."

"We'll be waiting," Jill paused. "Daddy, I'll make the arrangements with David, but could you talk to him? He's pretty sensitive these days. It'd be really nice if you'd smooth things out."

"I'll go right now. I love you."

"I love you too, Daddy."

Marc wished that dealing with David would be as easy. He turned up the volume of the television to catch the weather forecast, hoping for rain. "The marine forecast for Massachusetts waters: west-southwest winds, ten to fifteen miles per hour. Chance of precipitation, less than ten percent."

"No such luck," Marc muttered. He did not know why, but it seemed that he was always looking for excuses when he dealt with his son.

About to talk to David, he was stopped by the ringing of the phone. This time it was Joe Takada. After briefly reviewing a problem with Indonesian oil, Marc discusssed his call from the Secretary of State. Takada said he had heard a rumor that Jiang Qing might attempt to take over the People's Republic. Marc asked him to find out what he could and then hung up the phone. If Jiang was planning a coup, she would have to be stopped.

He massaged his forehead. It was late and he was tired. He still hadn't talked to David and was sure that Jill had already broken the news about the change in plans. "Way to go, Marc," he cursed to himself as he hurried to the stairs. "You've blown it again."

Rock music was blaring as he knocked on the door. There was no answer. He turned the knob and peered inside. Lying on his bed playing a game of backgammon with himself, David petulantly stared at his father. "Can we talk?" Marc yelled over the sound of the music.

"It's your dime."

Marc stepped around a mound of laundry and turned down the stereo. "Son, I'm sorry about the sailing."

"You're always sorry."

"That's not fair. The Secretary of State asked me to come to the White House. What am I supposed to tell him?"

"We all have our priorities."

39

"Come on, David. You know that you and Jill are more important to me than anything else in the world."

"That's crap. The only thing that's really important to you is your damn company. You never have time for me."

Marc fought to control his temper. Standing up, he turned toward the wall that David had covered with a twenty-foot time line of Chinese history. His head was beginning to throb. "Suppose we take a week in the middle of August and sail to Maine?"

"Jill can't go. She has summer school."

"Then it'll be just you and me."

A smile flashed across David's face, but it was instantly replaced by an angry glare. "I'm not falling for that trick. I know what will happen—some business trip will come up and you'll have to cancel."

"All right, if a business trip does come up, I'll take you with me."

David looked up. "Really?"

"Sure. It'd be fun."

A smile struggled to emerge at the corner of David's mouth. "If you're not kidding, you know where I'd really like to go? China." David pointed to the time line. "I think I know almost as much Chinese history as you."

"I'll see what I can arrange."

David looked up. "Just you and me. Sailing or China? Right?"

"Right!"

David pushed the backgammon board aside and threw his arms around Marc's waist. "Dad, I love you."

"I love you too, son," Marc said as he stroked David's head.

The rosy-cheeked receptionist smiled broadly as she

opened the door of the Lincoln Continental limousine. "Welcome to Washington, Mr. Slater."

Stepping toward the entrance to the West Wing of the White House, Marc thanked the woman, who looked like his image of a former Midwest homecoming queen. Since Gerald Ford had taken office, the women in the administration had become far more wholesome, though not necessarily more attractive.

"The Secretary is finishing a photography session with a group from the Japanese Diet. He asked me to accompany you," the receptionist said as she led Marc along a green runner that looked like imitation grass and under a white awning. Although the entrance was at street level, it was called the West Wing Basement.

Marc felt a sense of anticipation as he followed the woman through a small, square sitting room filled with Secret Service men and cabinet officers' chauffeurs sitting on wood-trimmed couches. A short corridor opened into a reception area. A guard sat behind a long, narrow desk on the right. The receptionist handed him an envelope and then turned toward the two elevators with copper-colored doors. Marc stared at the rows of color photographs depicting the First Family playing golf, skiing, and entertaining guests. There was something very unpresidential about the Fords. After the pomp of the Nixons, it was refreshing.

They descended toward the subbasement. "Where are we going?" Marc asked, knowing the Secretary of State's office was on the first floor.

"The Secretary thought you'd be more comfortable downstairs," the receptionist said.

She led Marc to the end of the corridor and into a whitewashed, windowless conference room that was only slightly more hospitable. Inside were two computerized CRT screens on rolling typewriter desks, eight straight-backed leather chairs, and a long mahogany table. Three tele-phones—one black, one white, and one red—stood in the middle of the table. An electronic map of the world covered one of the cement walls; the others were barren except for the solitary photograph of the president that hung in all government offices. Inhaling the room's faintly musty odor, Marc wondered why this location had been selected.

"Would you like jasmine tea?" the receptionist asked with her winning Betty Crocker Bake-off smile as she extended a tray.

"Thank you." Marc smiled, watching the jasmine flowers float to the top of the cup. He was pleased that the White House remembered that he preferred Chinese tea. It was a small matter, but it was a nice touch.

The receptionist handed Marc a document stamped "Top Secret." Beneath the letterhead of the Central Intelligence Agency was the title "The Political and Economic Ramifica-tions of the Development of Petroleum in the People's Republic of China."

As Marc leafed through the tables, he realized that the CIA had reached conclusions that he had long known to be true: that the development of the petroleum industry in China could break the dominance of OPEC, strengthen the American economy, establish the People's Republic as a counterweight to the Soviet Union, and tilt the world balance of power in favor of the United States. Yet though he agreed with its findings, the report made him uneasy. Chinese petroleum was his turf. The last thing he wanted was government attention.

The door opened and the Secretary of State, the Director of the CIA, and two men whom he only vaguely knew entered the room. "Hello, Marc." The Secretary of State firmly shook his friend's hand. "How's my Toyota?"

"Toyota?" the Director of the CIA asked.

Marc smiled as he turned to the lanky, aristocratic Texan from Connecticut who had formerly served as the American ambassador to the People's Republic. He remembered fondly the mornings they had spent in Peking jogging through the courtyards of the Forbidden City, talking about their two favorite subjects, China and oil. "Our poor friend," Marc said, "can't make ends meet on his government salary and lecture fees."

"I wouldn't worry," the CIA Director assured. "I've heard he has already sold his ten-volume memoirs for twenty million dollars."

"What's your working title?" Marc asked. "*The Gospel According to Saint Henry*?"

"Unfortunately," the Secretary of State responded, "unlike the two of you, I do not own my own oil company."

"Shall we start a collection?" Marc asked.

"After the meeting," the Secretary said as he motioned for everyone to sit down. "Marc, I think you already know Warren Munash of the Central Intelligence Agency and Jack Knutsen of the National Security Council."

Marc greeted the other two men and then took his seat. The Secretary of State waited until everyone was settled, then placed his palms on the edge of the table and leaned forward. "So, Marc, how are things in the People's Republic?"

Marc paused, trying to calculate where the Secretary was heading. "You know China. Business there is frustrating. You need great patience."

"What do you think of PRC's oil prospects?"

Slater laughed as he held up the CIA report. "Why are you asking me? Your statistical types have just finished a comprehensive study, and—"

"Excuse me," Warren Munash interrupted, "but do you agree with our estimate that China has the third largest reserves in the world?"

"I'm sorry, but I'm not a geologist."

"Don't be so humble, Mr. Slater. The Secretary is always telling me that you are *the* expert."

Marc was taken aback by Munash's antagonistic tone. He could not afford to alienate the China specialists in the CIA. "I'm afraid that the Secretary is exaggerating my knowledge. I know the Chinese have substantial reserves, but I can't project their exact size."

"And you do agree," Munash pressed on, "that the development of this oil could change the balance of power in favor of the United States?"

Taking a Charatan pipe from his pocket, Marc tried to second-guess Munash. "I think," he replied, rubbing the bowl of his pipe, "that China will become a major producer of oil, and that whoever gets its oil will benefit greatly; but our friendship with the Chinese is very fragile, and I am by no means certain that the current government will accede to our wishes." Marc glimpsed a knowing gleam in the eyes of the Secretary of State. "Is there a problem with Hua and his government?"

"It's possible," the Secretary of State responded.

"What is it?"

"We're worried about Hua Guofeng. Hua's presence is essential for the stability of China. He's Mao's heir, the symbol of the legitimate government, but he's also very weak. With Deng purged, other forces may try to overthrow him."

"Do you have"—Marc paused, relishing the bombshell he was about to drop—"a specific date for Jiang's planned coup?"

"We know that your company has an excellent intelligence network," the Secretary replied. "We assume that

44

you knew about Jiang's coup and about the planned Russian invasion."

The reference to the Russians started Marc. His stomach clenched, but not a muscle in his face moved. Outward calm was a discipline he had learned in China. "I've heard vague rumors."

The Secretary stared intently at Marc, reading his friend's icy calm. "The Russians are planning to utilize Jiang's coup as a cover for invading China and capturing the Chinese oil and coal fields. If we are to stop them, we need your help."

"Why me?"

"Our regular agents are useless in China," the CIA Director replied. "Even if we could get them in, which isn't easy, they're never permitted outside the big cities and they're always followed by Mao's secret police. We need someone who can travel without arousing suspicion and enlist the support of Deng Xiaoping. Deng won't even talk to our people, but he respects you as a friend. He'll trust what you have to say. Can we count on you?"

Marc paused. "I'm not sure."

"Your company," Munash said, "has a virtual monopoly in Chinese oil. If Jiang and the Gang of Four take power, you lose everything. What more motivation do you need?"

"A lot more," Marc said.

The Secretary of State nodded to Knutsen, who crushed his cigarette and began to talk in a voice that had the twang of the Texas prairie. "Our operatives have informed us that Jiang plans to purge Deng's people and replace them with her supporters. Soon she'll control the Politburo. Then she'll get rid of Hua and appoint herself as Party chairman, Zhang Chunqiao as premier, Wang Hongwen as president of the National People's Congress, and Yao Wenyuan as deputy chairman."

"I get the message," Marc replied, picturing the Gang of Four.

"Good."

"Can Jiang and the others be stopped?"

"Won't be easy." Knutsen drummed his fingers on the table. "Jiang is arming Red Guards. They're her personal army."

"How's she getting the weapons?"

"We're not certain, but we do know there is a huge volume of ancient Chinese relics being dumped on the market."

"That explains the money," Marc said, knowing that Jiang controlled the antiquities, "but what about the weapons themselves?"

"With enough money and even the smallest thread of political legitimacy, anyone can buy arms."

"What can we do about it?" Marc said, surprised that he had used a first-person pronoun.

"We have agents in China working on Operation Jade Gate."

Marc started to laugh. The phrase "jade gate" carried a double meaning.

"What's so funny?" Knutsen asked in a tone indicating he had no knowledge of Chinese slang.

"Was that name selected by a Chinese?"

"Yes. Why?"

"Just curious." Had the name, Marc wondered, been chosen because a woman was centrally involved in the smuggling? Perhaps it referred to Jiang Qing, or perhaps to someone else. He smiled. He was almost certain he had deciphered one piece of the puzzle without their knowledge or help, but it was only a minor piece. "What can you tell me about the Russians?"

"Russian commandos have infiltrated China." Knutsen puffed on yet another cigarette. "Their objective is to perform acts of terrorism that look like the work of rival Chinese factions. They want to foment a civil war so they can invade China and capture the oil and coal fields."

Marc watched the heavy white smoke from his pipe drift toward the air vent and consume the wispier gray smoke from Knutsen's cigarettes. He knew their plan could work. He faced Knutsen, but his eyes studied the Secretary of State. "How exactly do you see my role?"

"We want you to convince Deng of the seriousness of the threats."

"Doesn't Deng know about the plans of Jiang and the Russians?"

"Not the specifics," Knutsen replied.

"Why didn't the people who told us also inform him?"

"They have their own hides to protect."

"What do they want?"

"A chance of winning. They don't want to be tried as traitors or spend the rest of their lives in prison camps."

"Fair enough."

"Our agents have documents describing the plans of the Gang of Four and the Russians. You must convince Deng of their authenticity and help him unite with Hua. By working together, they can control the Politburo."

"How am I going to do that? It was Hua who purged Deng last April."

"With your powers of persuasion," the Secretary chided, "it should be easy."

Marc smiled at his friend. "My father used to tell me, 'Beware of silver-tongued secretaries of state delivering florid praise.'"

"I'm just a humble immigrant."

Marc smiled. "You're forgetting. So am I."

"Convincing Hua shouldn't be that difficult," Knutsen continued. "Our reports indicate that Hua mistrusts both

Jiang and the Russians and might, under the right circumstances, consider reuniting with Deng."

As Marc listened, he wondered if he still could be the "blue-eyed spirit who runs like the wind." He cherished his memories of the adventures of his youth, but he was no longer a young man. He also had responsibilities. "If I accept this mission," he asked, "how would I get to see Deng?"

"Our people will arrange everything."

"Who are they?"

"Their identities will have to be kept on a need-to-know basis, but your principal contact is named Sen Tailing."

Knutsen's words send a jolt through Marc. "The managing director of my Hong Kong office is named Sen Tailing."

"It is the same man."

Marc was shocked by Sen's involvement. He knew Sen was a Party member, but he had always assumed that Sen's role was relatively unimportant. Hu Shengte, the petroleum minister, had originally introduced Sen as a bright but minor executive. Perhaps he should have realized that the Chinese government allowed only its most loyal cadres to risk contamination by working in a capitalist company. Since Sen had been very effective and M. H. Schaffer's business in China had increased substantially, Marc had never confronted the issue of his standing in the Party. Now he could no longer avoid the conclusion that Sen was a high-ranking official.

"Why did you pick Sen?" Marc's voice was guarded.

"We didn't. His name and yours were given to us by the people in the PRC. We had no quarrel with their choices."

Marc stared at the others as he contemplated the physical dangers. "Is Sen working with people in the Politburo?"

The Secretary of State smiled. "I'm afraid that information will also have to remain on a need-to-know basis."

"Don't tease me with this need-to-know nonsense, not when you are asking me to take so much risk."

"Risk?" The Secretary laughed. "Lucky Slater thrives on risk. Just ask the Arabs who sold you oil in '73."

"This is different. I could get killed."

"You could also save the friendship between the United States and China."

Marc nodded silently. It was no accident that the Secretary had become the world's most respected diplomat. He had an uncanny knack for getting to the heart of the matter. "How much time do I have to think this over?"

"We'd like you to leave by Wednesday."

Marc laughed. "You really play hardball, don't you?"

"No more than you would in the same situation," the Secretary said.

"Can you give me a few days to get my affairs in order?"

"Why this sudden hesitation? I thought you prided yourself on making instant decisions."

"I need a little time," Marc said, grappling with his conflicting emotions. His overwhelming reaction was to accept. He owed a debt to China, to the United States, and to the friends helping him to create a major oil business in the PRC. But he was reluctant to take the chance of becoming a dead hero. Perhaps this was not his fight. He was a middle-aged businessman, not an American James Bond. Whatever his debt to China, he also had an obligation to his children and to M. H. Schaffer. Yet as he examined the alternatives, he recognized that there were two Marc Slaters—the little boy who had grown up in the back hills of China and the man who had become a successful businessman in the United States. He was haunted by the idea that there was something the little boy had known in China that the businessman had to find out for himself.

"We'll make arrangements for you to leave a week from Monday," the Secretary said.

"You are assuming that I will accept."

"I have known you for ten years, my friend. You need to do this as much as we need you to go."

3: The Transformation

An hour before the plane was scheduled to depart, Marc Slater passed through the emigration checkpoint at JFK. Irritated that there had been no better connecting flights, he settled down to wait on a thickly padded couch in the Pan Am Clipper Club lounge, removed his brown tweed jacket, and loosened his tie. In a sea of pinstripe suits, Marc looked more like a university professor than a captain of industry.

He popped open the locks of his briefcase and pulled out a sheaf of market studies on the commodities that H. M. Schaffer traded. Foodstuffs and oil seemed fine, but the report from Steve Shulman, his vice-president for ferrous metals, disturbed him. He went to a phone and called Shulman. "Steve, this is Marc. What's happening with bauxite?"

"Not much," Shulman replied. "The market makes me nervous. Guyana is unstable. The Africans are having that civil war, and there are rumors that the Russians are dumping again. I think there's too much risk."

51

"Too much risk?" Marc scoffed. "What business do you think you're in? You get paid a half a million a year to stick your neck out and maybe get it cut off. There's too much opportunity in bauxite to sit on the sidelines. When I get back, I expect to see some new contracts."

"You will, Marc," Shulman said with resignation, knowing there was no way to fight Slater when he was on one of his pretrip rolls.

The public-address system blared the final call for Marc's flight. "Steve, I have to go. Can you switch me to Potruck?" Marc jotted some notes for his files as his vice-president for copper and tin came on the line. "Howard, what's happening with the deliveries of copper?"

"We're getting the shaft from our friends at Andean. They're furious that they have to fill our contracts at half the world price."

"When we signed at a twenty-percent premium, I didn't hear them complaining," Marc replied.

"Then they were hungry for the business. But now that the price has doubled, they're trying to back out. They've come up with a new ploy. They claim the Peruvian government won't give them an export license."

"Those s.o.b.'s! How much do we stand to lose?"

"Quite a lot. We presold the copper to Japan. If we have to cover from the spot market, it'll cost us almost forty million."

"Ouch. Do we have any options?"

"We can sue, but that won't help us now."

"What if we buy them?"

"I don't follow you."

"Go see Estridge." Marc referred to his VP of finance. "Tell him to make a tender offer for Andean at twelve points above the market price."

"Are you kidding?"

"Absolutely not. I looked at the company last year. It has reasonable earnings and good book value. Call Jim Posner, their president, and give him an ultimatum: Either we get our copper or we'll be forced to buy his company. I'd love to see his face when he hears that his copper empire is going to become a division of M. H. Schaffer."

"Do you really want to own Andean Copper?"

"It wouldn't be a bad investment, but it won't come to that—those boys enjoy their independence too much. After a few days, Posner will inform you that Peru has suddenly changed its position. If they ship, we'll call off the merger."

"And if they don't?"

"Then, my friend, you'll be the new president of Andean Copper."

"Thanks for the promotion, but I'd rather stay a trader."

"Then make sure that Posner falls for our bluff." The club attendant reminded Marc that it was 11:52. "Howard, I've got to run," Marc said as he packed his briefcase. He made one more call. "Hi, David," Marc said.

"What do you want?" David sounded depressed.

"Just calling to say goodbye. Remember, we're sailing to Maine when I get back."

"I'd rather go to China."

"Not this trip."

"But you promised."

Marc hesitated. He did not want his children to suspect the potential danger. "I'll be tied up in meetings."

"I'd stay out of your way. I'd be real happy visiting the Great Wall and the other tourist spots."

"There's not enough time to arrange your visa."

"Mr. Slater," the Clipper Club attendant said, "they're holding the plane for you."

"David, I'm sorry but I have to go. Why don't we settle on Maine for this summer and China for the next trip?"

53

"All right." David's voice was glum.

"I'll call you from Hong Kong."

"Goodbye, dad."

"I love you, son."

Marc took little notice of the takeoff or the trip announcements. His work absorbed his attention. Even the service of cocktails did not break his concentration. While others ate lunch and watched the first of the films, Marc dictated memos into a slim recorder to be transcribed in Hong Kong. He was determined to complete his office work while he was still in the United States. He did not like to deal with routine office problems once he arrived in the Orient.

The plane landed at Tokyo's Haneda Airport. The other Hong Kong passengers went to the transit lounge, but Marc passed through Japanese Customs, where Joe Takada was waiting. "*Konnichiwa!*" he greeted his Far Eastern vice-president. Takada bowed out of respect and friendship.

Marc followed Takada down a corridor leading to a deserted observation deck. "I assume," Marc said, "this hike means you've learned something."

"You assume correctly."

"Is it about the dumping of the archaeological relics?" Marc referred to information that Takada had telexed him in code two days before.

"No," Takada replied. "I haven't been able to trace the source. My information may have nothing to do with Jiang Qing, but it still strikes me as very odd. Do you know the Takamura Corporation?"

Marc smiled. "You mean Xenophobia Enterprises?" Takamura was a rightwing, militaristic company that had helped push Japan into World War II and now was a leading advocate of rearmament.

"I've learned," Takada said, "that they have paid the Russians two billion dollars for the rights to drill for oil in the Altay Mountains."

"That's impossible! The oil is on the Chinese side of the mountains."

"In an area that Russia has always claimed as its own."

Marc thought about the plans for the Russian invasion of China. "Are you suggesting that Takamura is aligned with the Russians?"

"I'm only suggesting that two billion dollars is a lot of money for the smartest trading company in Japan to throw away."

Marc slept fitfully on the flight to Hong Kong. Just before the plane began its descent, he picked up his suit bag and walked to the lavatory. There he changed into a pair of khaki slacks and a blue cotton safari shirt with epaulets, which had been custom-made by David's Tailors. He always liked to arrive in Hong Kong dressed as if he were a native.

Returning to his seat, Marc gazed at the brilliantly lit harbor. From the first time he had visited Hong Kong more than thirty years ago, he had been fascinated by this colony that was part Western and part Oriental, that permitted capitalism to coexist with communism, that thrived as an international trading center, and that offered unparalleled elegance together with wretched poverty. In the luxurious hotels it was as cosmopolitan as any city in the world. In the opulent international banking offices along Des Veoux Road, it was as capitalist as Wall Street. In its garment showrooms of Kowloon and its electronics shops on Nathan Road, it was as commercial as New York. Yet in the back alleys and in the farms and fishing villages of the New Territories, it was as Chinese as Canton; and in the many businesses that were owned by the People's Republic, it was as Communist as Peking. Hong Kong was a city that paralleled the duality which Marc was keenly aware existed in himself.

After the plane landed, Marc passed quickly through customs and was greeted by two junior executives from his Hong Kong office, waiting with the company's Rolls-Royce limousine. He was disappointed that Sen Tailing was not there to meet him, but he was certain that Sen had reasons for remaining in China. Ten minutes later, the Rolls pulled into the driveway of the Peninsula Hotel. A doorman, attired in a costume that made him look like a Chinese Philip Morris advertisement from the 1950s, politely ushered Marc from the car. "Welcome to the Peninsula, Mr. Slater. We are pleased you have returned."

"Thank you, Kam," Marc said, glancing at the spouting fountain colored red and yellow by the underwater lights. He was pleased to be back.

The night manager, an immaculately dressed Englishman, stepped briskly through the glass doors. "Mr. Slater, so good to see you again. Your suite is ready, just as you like it." He snapped his fingers. Two Chinese bellmen scurried up. "Bring Mr. Slater's luggage to the Moon Pearl."

Marc followed the manager into the spacious and ornate lobby. All the tables were filled with foreign businessmen, English colonialists, and wealthy Chinese, who had gravitated to the Peninsula to see and be seen. White-jacketed waiters hovered around, attending to their guests' every need. As always, the focus of attention was on the center aisle. It was the route through which all new arrivals were introduced to the social happening that was the Peninsula. Passing the first row of columns, Marc felt like a debutante coming into society. He nodded politely to three American importers and then stopped to greet Robert Kang, the president of the Hong Kong–Canton Bank.

"This is an unexpected pleasure." Kang stood up and shook Marc's hand. Since his bank handled Schaffer's Chinese business, he made it a policy always to be in the Peninsula when Marc arrived. "Join me for a drink?"

"Thanks for the invitation, but I've had a long flight and I'm off to Canton in the morning."

"That's a coincidence," Kang replied. "My sister and brother-in-law will be on the same train."

"Sam and Beatrice?" Marc asked. Samuel Tang was the president of Far Western Aviation, one of the largest defense contractors in the United States. His wife, Beatrice, was the chairman of the Chinese-American Cultural Committee as well as the sister of two members of the Politburo.

"Of course."

"It will be good to see them," Marc said, suspecting that he and the Tangs were traveling to China for the same reasons.

As soon as he entered the Moon Pear, Marc began to relax. The suite, with its vast living room and high ceilings, had been decorated in soft colors of light teak, pearl green, and midnight blue in order to convey an aura of serenity. Kicking off his shoes, he stepped to the window and gazed at the peak of Hong Kong across the harbor. Masthead lights on ferries and junks flickered like fireflies on the surface of the water. None of Hong Kong's blemishes showed. The Colony always looked magnificent at night through the arched picture window of a Peninsula suite.

Twenty-five hours of flying on planes and waiting in

airports had left Marc very tired. He picked a mandarin orange from a wicker basket of fresh fruit and leisurely ate the juicy sections. There was a knock on the door. "Come in," he called, thinking it was the hallboy bringing him the hotel's complimentary selection of luxurious European soaps.

"Mr. Slater?" a woman's voice asked in a distinctly American accent.

Standing in front of him was a young blond woman dressed in a blue silk blouse and a flowing magenta skirt, accented by a matching Indian sash. "Yes?" Marc said, walking toward her.

"I'm Linda Forbes." She paused to see if the name registered. It did not. "From Bloomingdale's?" Still no recognition.

"I'm delighted to meet you." Marc stared at the woman. In her late twenties, she was tall and willowy with a slightly open, inviting mouth that conveyed the wholesome good looks of an Iowa farm girl. Yet her greenish-gray eyes were different. They were narrow, almost Oriental, and intense, with a slight hint of mascara that came more from Park Avenue than from Main Street.

Linda smiled warmly. Her look was at once innocent and sophisticated. She opened her leather purse. "I have a letter for you."

Inspecting the envelope, Marc instantly recognized the handwriting of Sen Tailing. "Where did you see Sen?" he asked.

"In Canton," Linda replied.

Marc was surprised Sen would trust a stranger—but then, perhaps Linda was not a stranger. "Can I get you a drink?"

"Please, white wine."

Marc opened the refrigeraor and poured two glasses of

Chablis. "To new friends," he toasted. Linda smiled and walked to the window. Marc ripped open the envelope and withdrew the single sheet of paper.

Dear Marc:

Events are progressing faster than expected. The helmsman is quite ill. His wife and three of her friends locked him in the infirmary. Now there is no one to navigate.

There are major problems with oil. It often appears as if the sun is rising in the Northwest mountains.

Huge crates are being carried through the Empress's Jade Gate, but I've been unable to find their destination.

I am sending my friend Linda to help cheer you up. Please take care of yourself. Don't smoke too much. Remember, tobacco can be hazardous to your health.

Sen Tailing

Written in a hasty scrawl, the letter sounded strange and disjointed, as if Sen had been drunk. So this was the beginning, Marc thought as he tried to decipher Sen's code. The helmsman was certainly Mao Tse-tung. If his wife and her allies in the Gang of Four had imprisoned him in his hospital room, things would be more difficult than he had envisioned. Now there would be no one to stop them from issuing directives in Mao's name. The rising sun was Japan, probably the people from Takamura about whom Takada had warned. The Northwest, one of China's largest oil-producing regions, was the subject of a territorial dispute with the Soviet Union. The smuggling of arms and relics was obviously continuing. But who was the "empress"? He would have to be on his guard. And what of the reference to tobacco? He only smoked a pipe, while Sen, like most

Chinese, chain-smoked cigarettes.

Marc glanced at Linda. She was still politely staring at the harbor. He liked her for that. Massaging his neck, he felt, in the words of the Chinese saying, like an ant on a hot frying pan. There were too many parts to the equation. He would just have to wait until he saw Sen in Canton.

"How's the wine?" he asked Linda. He wanted to know more about her but decided to wait and see what she volunteered.

"Fine. What did Sen have to say?"

"He says that he's sending you to cheer me up."

Linda blushed. "Funny, he told me the same thing."

"Then what about dinner?"

Linda had already eaten, but she was intrigued by Marc. She smiled. "Why not!"

Marc and Linda walked the three blocks from the Peninsula to the Star Ferry that would take them to Hong Kong Island. After paying three cents for their first-class tickets, they followed a horde of Chinese and a smattering of foreigners down the gangplank and onto the boat.

As the ferry left the pier, Marc stood next to Linda and inhaled the pungent aroma of the harbor. Hong Kong was a city in which he felt very comfortable. It was his personal bridge that eased the transition between the United States and China. The place in which the American Marc Slater could recapture his Chinese heritage and the Chinese Marc Slater could reclaim his Western culture. "I love this harbor." He smiled at Linda.

"It suits you. You look like a taipan surveying his colony."

Marc placed his arm around her. "Sen was right. You're the perfect tonic for what ails me."

The ferry bumped clumsily into its berth. Marc and Linda

walked through the underpass below Connaught Road. There were many restaurants in which they could eat: the fancy European dining rooms in Hong Kong's luxury hotels; the wood-paneled private clubs that were always pleased to accept a businessman of Marc's stature; the floating eating palaces of Aberdeen; the seedy clubs featuring limited food and unlimited girls; or even the recently opened American chicken and hamburger franchises. But Marc had other ideas. "Do you mind a short stroll?" he asked.

"You're the tour guide." Linda smiled.

Marc strode briskly up the almost vertical narrow lane that inclined toward the peak. Linda had little difficulty keeping pace. They turned down a dark alley that reminded him of a scene from an old Clark Gable movie and walked to a dimly lit building marked #18. He opened the door and stepped into a storefront restaurant that had only eight tables. With paper lanterns covering the lights, dragons from New Year's celebrations still hanging from the walls, and a yellowing black and white checked linoleum floor, the decor could at best be called tacky. But the restaurant was immaculately clean and its eclectic decor was cheerful.

Liu Wan, the owner, stood near the door calculating a bill with his abacus. He was one of the very few pudgy Chinese Marc had ever met. He had a round face, puffy cheeks, and gleaming white teeth that shone whenever he flashed his infectious smile. Seeing Marc, Liu grinned broadly, bowed politely, and said, "Welcome, Slater old friend. You and your guest bring great honor to my humble restaurant. Wife, children," he called into the kitchen in Cantonese, "we have esteemed visitors from the United States."

Liu placed Marc and Linda at the largest table. His oldest son hurried into the room. He saw Marc, turned back into the kitchen, and came out wearing the Boston Red Sox cap Marc had given him on his last visit. The two youngest children ran in, jabbering in Chinese. "*Taitai* [wife]," the little girl said as she pointed to Linda.

Marc gave her a scolding look. He had been to the restaurant many times with Carolyn. "*Pengyou* [friend]," he told the girl.

Linda sat silently until the children turned away. "Are you married?" she asked.

"My wife died six months ago."

"You're still mourning?"

Marc nodded his head. "What about you? Is there a husband, perhaps a lawyer, waiting back on Park Avenue?"

"Greenwich Village. No husband."

"That must disappoint your poor gray-haired mother in Iowa."

"California. She's adjusted to it."

Marc smiled, liking Linda's toughness. "So how does a California girl adjust to the Big Apple?"

"Every weekend I take my surfboard to the Hamptons and pretend that it's Malibu." Linda poured a cup of tea. "And how does a China boy adjust to the Hub?"

"I eat my baked beans with chopsticks," Marc replied, resisting the temptation to ask how Linda knew about his background. He would learn more about her when he saw Sen.

Liu's wife came into the room drying her hands on a towel. Her face was lined by hard work, but her smile was warm as a Hong Kong summer day. She bowed to Marc with great respect. She could never forget the debt she owed him. Had it not been for Marc's intervention, her father would have remained imprisoned in China. "Distinguished guests," she said, "the chickens, fish, and pigs would have rejoiced had they known that they would have the honor of being served to you." Marc smiled as the wife herded her brood back into the kitchen. She did not even ask for his preferences. She intended to prepare a banquet of her finest dishes.

As Marc and Linda conversed with Liu, the children brought out plates of fried duck, rice birds, sweet-and-sour fish, moo shu pork, four delights vegetables, bird's-nest soup made from a real swallow's nest, and one dish that Marc could not identify. "What's in this one?" he asked.

"That's my speciality," the wife replied. "It's called the Dragon and the Phoenix. It's made from hawk and snake meat mixed with vegetables and herbs." She cackled. "It's supposed to give special potency."

"It's delicious, but a little premature." Marc winked at her.

The meal was the perfect introduction to China.

4: Fried Garoupa

The artist dipped his brush in the sienna paint and colored in the banks of the rice paddies on his canvas. The painting, entitled *The Foolish Old Man Who Moved Mountains*, depicted a wizened Chinese man carrying a boulder from the top of a mountain while his neighbors watched in mocking silence. The artist had taken the name and concept of the painting from an ancient Chinese folktale. In the tale, an old man wanted to move two mountains that blocked the water for his fields. Although more than seventy, the man started to carry away the mountains one rock at a time. His neighbors jeered, saying he was a foolish old man who would never succeed. But he smiled stoically and replied that he would move the rocks until he died; then his sons, his grandsons, and his great-grandsons would continue his work until the mountains had disappeared.

For the artist, the old man was the embodiment of China, ancient and tottering but determinedly inching forward, impervious to the rest of the world, unwilling to change, and yet impossible to subdue. It was this stoic Chinese determination that so fascinated him.

The Chinese had developed a remarkable knack for suffering extraordinary calamities and then emerging decades or even centuries later as if nothing had happened. The Mongolians and Manchurians had conquered China. Yet both were eventually absorbed, so that they, the victors, virtually ceased to exist. England, France, Russia, and Japan all inflicted embarrassing defeats on the Middle Kingdom. But in the end, China, without winning even one battle, managed to regain all its lost territory. Five hundred civil wars had been fought in the last century, with a death toll of eighty million. But the country itself somehow remained intact.

Nature, too, had been unusually cruel. The Middle Kingdom had been the site of the largest earthquake, the most severe famine, and the four worst floods in history. The number dead in these and other natural disasters was beyond comprehension. Perhaps it was one hundred million. Most likely it was more. Even the worst fire in history had occurred in China.

What distinguished China was that despite the signs of tragedies etched in the faces of the people, the country had emerged unscathed. Its population was by far the largest in the world, and it was in most ways that same Kingdom of the Han that the Qin emperor had established more than two thousand years before.

The artist, identified by his passport as Frans Van Wyck of Rotterdam, knew the Chinese had survived because of the way they looked at time. Unlike their enemies, who focused on short-term events, the Chinese thought in terms of centuries. No matter what the crisis, they believed they could outwait any enemy and outlast any tragedy. It was this patience that could doom Operation Kazak. Van Wyck's superiors in the Russian KGB thought they could destroy the People's Republic by fomenting a civil war and capturing the Chinese oil reserves; but he knew that no matter how effective his operation, China would survive. Long after the Soviet Union and the United States stopped contending for world supremacy, China would still be China.

Van Wyck sketched the weblike lines of age on the old man's face. Stepping back, he inspected his canvas in frustration. His selection and blending of colors were subtle and genuine. The composition of his painting was so balanced it could have been the work of a professional draftsman. Yet for all its admirable qualities, the most essential was missing. No matter how he tried to imitate what he saw, the artist seemed unable to capture the soul of the old man or the spirit of China.

Turning away from his work with a grimace, Van Wyck looked at his watch. It read 6:45. He had only half an hour to reach the river. Removing his smock, he walked into the bathroom and carefully washed his chalk white hands, giving individual attention to each finger. Then he rubbed on a rich pink cream. He had the smooth, unwrinkled skin of a youth of twenty, making him look more like a poet than a trained assassin. He gazed at his delicate features in the mirror as he applied another layer of lotion. He would be outside for many hours and did not want the powerful south China sun burning his sensitive skin.

Van Wyck changed from his painting clothes to a white shirt and brown suit. He opened his Italian man's purse and placed inside four tubes that looked like containers of oil paint, eight small wired disks, and several wads of cotton. Then he inspected the room. Everything was in place.

Fifteen minutes after leaving the Dong Fang Hotel, the

taxi in which Van Wyck was riding stopped in front of the Overseas Chinese Hotel in the center of Canton. "What time go back?" the driver asked as he handed Van Wyck his change. The Chinese liked to keep track of their foreign friends, so all cab rides had to include a time and place for the return trip.

"Eleven o'clock here," Van Wyck said. He stepped into the lobby of the new yet already dingy hotel and waited for the cab to leave. When he was certain no one was watching, he left the hotel, crossed Haizhu Square, and headed for one of the three bridges spanning the Pearl River.

Though it was only seven, the summer sun had already made the day uncomfortably warm. Van Wyck dabbed his forehead and the back of his neck with a freshly pressed handkerchief. He could feel the curious stares of the rush-hour workers riding in buses or pedaling bicycles in the opposite direction. Van Wyck meticulously replaced the handkerchief in his pocket as he turned onto Binjiang Road, the broad, tree-lined avenue running along the southern bank. To his right were modern, nondescript three- and four-story apartment buildings housing former boat people. A class of colorfully attired children, singing "The East Is Red," approached in single file. Van Wyck crossed to the promenade along the river, trying to remain as inconspicuous as possible.

Walking in the shade of a long, straight row of cypress trees, Van Wyck reached the deserted ferry wharf. A gray wooden launch, which had been floating aimlessly, steered toward him. As the launch caromed off the dock, Aziz Rahman, a half-Chinese Turk from Xinjiang Province, grabbed Van Wyck's arm and pulled him on board. "You look well," Rahman said with an open smile that belied his toughness. "The hotel business seems to agree with you." Van Wyck nodded politely as he settled himself under the boat's weather-beaten dodger.

The hotel business certainly did agree with him. It had solved the most serious problem facing Operation Kazak far better than he could have expected. Van Wyck had known from the beginning that it would be difficult for him to move his men and their materials around the tightly controlled People's Republic. Two of the Bureau's previous operations had failed because of just such logistic constraints. The contract offered by the Chinese Ministry of Tourism for the construction of fifty tourist hotels offered the perfect solution.

Through a company known as Royal Amsterdam Hotels N.V., which had been used as a cover for the Bureau's operations in Indonesia, Van Wyck submitted the lowest bid to the Ministry of Tourism. After a brief negotiation, he was awarded the contract and Operation Kazak was launched. Beginning construction at six sites, his company had already brought more than one hundred skilled KGB operatives to China. With the assistance of the Takamura Corporation, its Japanese partner, explosives and other materials were being stockpiled.

Van Wyck's nose flared in reaction to the stench of fish wafting his way. He looked up as Aziz Rahman took a bin filled with eight garoupa from the lazaret. Van Wyck crimped his nose as Rahman placed the fish beside him. "My friend," Rahman smiled, "I'm afraid you have no future as a fisherman. You clearly have no taste for the wonderful aroma of freshly caught garoupa."

"I prefer my fish cooked," Van Wyck replied.

"In Japan," Rahman said, "raw fish is a great delicacy, and in Kashi—"

"In Kashi," Van Wyck retorted, "you don't even have water, so please spare me your fish stories." Both men laughed together. They were a unique pair; this half-Chinese

Turk who was always making jokes, and this aesthetic Russian agent posing as a Dutch hotel magnate. Perhaps the only things they shared in common were their mutual trust and their ability to work together with perfect precision.

"Shall we prepare dinner?" Rahman asked as he grasped the first garoupa below the gills and held it under Van Wyck's nose.

"Just keep it away from my clothes. I don't want the stench following me all week," Van Wyck said, removing the four aluminum tubes and the eight wired disks from his bag.

Rahman began to whistle a Turkish folk song while Van Wyck carefully squeezed a red gelatinous substance into the fish's mouth. "What's that tune?" the Dutchman asked.

Rahman smiled and pressed his tongue into the gap between his front teeth. "You mean you don't remember 'He Who Has No Friends Must Dance with His Camel'?"

"Is it popular in Kashi?" Van Wyck asked as he placed a wire disk between the fish's jaws and tamped it down with a wad of cotton.

"It is among camels." Rahman held up the second fish.

Van Wyck worked intently as he finished the next five garoupa.

"I love the aroma." Rahman teased his friend by inhaling the fishy odor from his hands. "Care for a whiff?"

"Behave or I'll send you back to Xinjiang Province."

"Promises, promises. You know how I long to kneel on the sand of my homeland."

"And feel the yoke of Chinese oppression?"

The smile on Rahman's face disappeared. He was a fervent Turkic nationalist. "Not for long, my friend. Not for long," he said, placing the last of the fish back in the bin. Van Wyck closed his bag and scrubbed each of his fingers with a bar of Long March soap until the rancid smell of the fish had been washed away.

The launch continued downstream, passing two patrol boats, a ferry from Macao belching black smoke, fishing boats that could be smelled as well as seen, and countless river sampans carrying their goods to Canton. As it reached the entrance to Huangpu Harbor, Van Wyck peered through his binoculars. At the furthest pier in the busy port was the blue and red Union Jack of the H.M.S. *Wellington*. A smile tugged at his mouth. The British ship was exactly where it was supposed to be.

The captain slowed the launch and steamed in a wide circle. Van Wyck dipped his handkerchief in the river and mopped his brow to relieve the scorching heat. He was anxious for the mission to shift to the cooler climes of northern China.

A small sampan with a red sail and matching Chinese flag pulled abeam. Van Wyck and Rahman climbed into the cabin to conceal themselves. The first mate of the launch handed an envelope and the bin of fish to the seaman on the sampan. The seaman spilled the garoupa into a tub of other fish and leafed through the crisp stack of Hong Kong dollars in the envelope. Then he cast off from the launch, rendezvoused with four other sampans, and sailed toward the H.M.S. *Wellington*.

Ian Morrison, the quartermaster of the *Wellington*, stood on the pier reviewing his supply requisitions. The *Wellington*, a one-hundred-twenty-foot patrol boat, was making a goodwill visit to China. After two days in Canton, it was beginning a ten-day cruise to Hainan Island and then back to Hong Kong. As a gesture of friendship, the Chinese had agreed to supply fresh food at what they termed a reasonable cost. To Morrison, the cost, no matter how reasonable, was not worth having to deal with Chinese suppliers. Every type of food had a separate vendor. Just to purchase fruit, Morrison had to buy oranges from one man, lemons from a second, apples from a third, and pineapples from a fourth. For only ten days' supply of food, he had been required to give requisitions to more than thirty vendors. Equally annoying were the special arrangements he had been forced to make with the Bank of China. The British were being greatly overcharged by the Chinese government, which wanted to keep the profits for itself; so the vendors had to be paid in scrip instead of in cash. Morrison did not care who was making the profits, but he hated filling out all the bureaucratic forms. And now, less than an hour before departure, the fish vendor had not yet arrived.

Morrison paced the gangway as the sampans bearing the fish reached the dock. A disheveled fisherman ran up holding a collection of crumpled requisitions. Morrison's first inclination was to complain about the man's tardiness, but he realized it would be futile. Dealing with unreliable suppliers was part of the cost of maintaining the goodwill of the People's Republic. He checked the requisitions and, finding them in order, motioned for the Chinese to unload their cargo.

Van Wyck stared through his binoculars as the fish were weighed and the boatsman counted the chits, which he could redeem at the bank. After the fish were loaded on the *Wellington*, the sampans cast off and floated downstream. Their job was at an end. By the next morning they would be back in Hong Kong.

Van Wyck climbed back into the cockpit. He opened a black vinyl gym bag with the word "Shanghai" silk-screened on the side and withdrew a small electronic box. His legs shifted uneasily as he sat with the box on his lap. Beads of sweat rolled down his hairless chest and were absorbed by his now blotched white shirt. He stared at the buttons on the box. All he had to do was push and be done with the demolition. Then he could get off the river and go back to his painting. His fingers tingled as they hovered above the box. It would be so easy. He fondled the rubber cover on the button marked "start." His eyes gleamed as he gazed at the *Wellington.*

He paced to the bow, trying to repress the almost irresistible temptation. His plan called for action only after the ship had left the pier, and he never allowed himself to deviate from his plan. He was a consummate professional who never permitted emotion to interfere with his operations.

Van Wyck's feelings about professionalism were as intense as what others felt about God. It was his unquestioned faith. When he was given an assignment, whether to assassinate a politican or overthrow a government, he never questioned the justice of the ends or the morality of the means. His only concern was to accomplish the task with a minimum of effort and no continuing entanglements.

He had not always been so dispassionate. When he had first joined the Bureau, he had been an idealist who devoutly believed in his country and handled his assignments with a dedicated fervor. But after shooting the children during the raid on the Chinese oil refinery, his enthusiasm had waned. He had lost his zest for clandestine operations and had begun to doubt the righteousness of his cause. He had even asked to resign, but the Bureau had refused to release him. He had become embittered and then careless. While training revolutionaries in the Philippines, he had been shot by President Marcos's secret police.

Recovering from his wounds, Van Wyck had realized he would have to find some meaning in his work if he was to survive. He no longer believed in the mission of the Bureau, but he knew he could still take pride in his own performance. Ignoring the content of his assignments, he set out to achieve his objectives with perfect precision. While others debated the morality of sensitive projects, he devised strategies for implementation; and while others shunned the most dangerous assignments, he welcomed them as fresh challenges. In helping to depose the governments of Ethiopia and Afghanistan, he had become the Bureau's most respected operative.

Van Wyck's preeminent position had been affirmed when he was picked to direct Operation Kazak. Ten years before, he would have greeted this assignment with unrestrained joy; but now there was no emotional charge; there was only the intellectual challenge of a scientist undertaking a difficult experiment. He had to plan a complex operation that would foment a civil war and provide his country with a pretext for seizing the oil fields along the border. Operation Kazak was the ultimate test of his professionalism.

Van Wyck's lips broke into a smile as he saw the *Wellington* steam into the center of the harbor. He thought impassively about the quartermaster he had seen on the dock. He was probably a decent fellow. Most likely all the sailors were. But they were not his concern. With luck, some would be rescued. His eyes remained riveted on the *Wellington* as he carefully pushed the buttons in their proper sequence. Silently, he counted to five.

It started as a rumbling, like a late-afternoon thunderclap. Then an explosion. The superstructure shook. The conning tower collapsed, plunging the lookouts into the harbor. Acrid black smoke poured from the vents, blotting out the sun. A single tongue of flame surged toward the stern. The ammunition hold caught fire. Rapid bursts from hundreds of unmanned machine guns created the illusion of a full-fledged battle. The mortars ignited. Missiles tore through the roof, scattering burning debris through the harbor. Flaming sailors dived into the water. Nearby sampans started to burn. A thunderous explosion blew a gaping hole in the *Wellington*'s port side just below the waterline. The cruiser listed. Soon it would sink.

Van Wyck watched intently as boats rushed to rescue the British seamen. He felt no particular joy or sense of victory. Neither did he feel remorse. He merely felt the satisfaction that came from a perfectly implemented operation.

Three Chinese Navy patrol boats sped into the harbor to assist in the rescue effort. Soon others would arrive to investigate. It was time to leave. Van Wyck checked his watch. It was 9:42. Everything had gone according to schedule.

Fifty minutes later, Van Wyck knelt in front of the glass case and examined the extraordinary collection of miniature snuff bottles in the Friendship Department Store. He was fascinated by these bottles, which were painted on the insides through the narrow openings in their necks by craftsmen using brushes with only one hair. He had watched these artists spend months painting one bottle and had profound admiration for their intricate designs as well as for their almost unlimited patience. He had once tried this type of painting, but had quit in frustration.

Eight ancient Chinese warriors, each smaller than a fingernail, stared up at him from one of the bottles. Their faces, headdresses, and robes were individualized, but all had the identical look of determination in their eyes. The salesgirl handed him the bottle. Holding it delicately between his thumb and forefinger, Van Wyck gazed with admiration at the warriors. He turned the bottle around. On the back was an aristocratic general with a plumed helmet and a long wispy beard. His lips were pursed, his eyes intent, as if he were watching a battle. Next to his portrait, written in tiny characters, was a quotation from Sun Tzu: "For to win one hundred victories in one hundred battles is not the acme of skill. To subdue an enemy without fighting is the acme of skill." Van Wyck smiled as he clutched the bottle in his palm. Sun Tzu's maxim was one that he would be well advised to remember.

The Dutchman opened the jade cap and looked inside. It was incredible that someone could have painted so many complex figures through such a narrow opening. Awed by the unceasing dedication of the anonymous Chinese artist, he paid the salesgirl and walked briskly back to the Overseas Chinese Hotel. He was pleased with his successes. The attack had been executed perfectly. He had bought a beautiful work of art to commemorate the mission, and now he had the afternoon to devote to his painting.

Van Wyck climbed into the taxi. As the driver headed back toward the Dong Fang Hotel, Van Wyck stared through the refracted light of the humid summer sun at the people of Canton. On the sidewalk a toothless old peasant with deep hollow cheeks and a scraggy white goatee gazed at the convergence of traffic. Propped up by a wooden cane, the peasant stepped into the intersection and was immediately enveloped by an onrushing herd of bicycles. Van Wyck's taxi screeched to a halt, its horn blaring. The old peasant looked neither at the bicycles nor at the taxi. He just kept walking resolutely forward, one tottering step at a time. As the cab moved, Van Wyck stared into the man's eyes. Though sorrowful and tired, they were still determined and proud. The peasant reached the sidewalk, but he did not turn to look at his accomplishment or judge his progress. He just continued on his journey supported by his cane. The old man was much like China itself. Van Wyck snapped his eyes shut so that he could freeze the image of the peasant in his mind. When he arrived at the hotel, he would draw the man's face so that he would remember.

5: To Hang a Lamb's Head But Sell Dog Meat

Alexandra Koo, clad only in a pair of emerald-green silk bikini panties and a single strand of alabaster pearls with a dangling jade pendant, stood admiring herself in front of the full-length mirror in the bathroom at the Peninsula Hotel. Although she had passed the thirty-five years to which she would admit, her body was still pleasing to look at. Hardly an ounce of fat or a wrinkle of age disturbed the flowing lines of her soft fawn-colored skin. Slipping on a bra that matched her panties, she scanned the ten silk dresses in her closet. She felt in a provocative mood. For her entry into China, her Calvin Klein cobalt-green dress with the bateau neck and cap sleeves made her look the most alluring.

Alexandra pulled the dress over her head and tightened the rope belt. Then she attached jade hoops to her ears and slipped matching rings on six of her fingers. Holding up her hands, she watched the gems sparkle in the rays of the sun.

She smiled. Jade was her passion. It was almost her life. She was the largest exporter from China and always attired herself in jade jewelry as if she were the personification of her product. Even her clothes served merely to complement her jade. To everyone who knew her, she was the Empress of Jade.

Alexandra inspected herself in the mirror. She was more than pleased with what she saw. With her dark piercing eyes, her shoulder-length black hair, and her high cheekbones, her face had a sensual angularity that enhanced the air of mystery she so carefully cultivated.

There was a knock on the door. "*Qing, jin lai,*" Alexandra called. A young Chinese waiter wheeled in her breakfast. The boy fussed over the table until everything was perfect, as things usually were at the Peninsula, and then quietly departed. This leave-taking breakfast had become a ritual for Alexandra. On each trip, before boarding the train to Canton, she ordered an elegant meal of freshly squeezed orange juice, Scottish smoked salmon, Iranian caviar, Danish pastry, American coffee, and French champagne. Then she lounged in her suite, enjoying the spectacle of Hong Kong.

Pouring a glass of champagne, Alexandra watched the first rays of the sun bring the harbor to life. Myriad red-sailed junks carrying the daily provisions of the colony wended their way haphazardly, barely avoiding the dozens of ferries darting between Kowloon and Hong Kong Island and the more than fifty ocean freighters at anchor in the world's fastest-growing port. There was no city as beautiful as Hong Kong, and no hotel as fine as the Peninsula. The leave-taking breakfast afforded Alexandra her last opportunity to luxuriate in the pleasures that wealth could buy.

She lingered for another forty minutes. Then she walked to the dresser and opened one of her Louis Vuitton suitcases. On top of a layer of green silk blouses she neatly placed four reels of motion-picture film, her gifts to her friend and benefactress Jaing Qing. Alexandra knew that Jiang loved films, and that foreign films in particular represented forbidden fruit that she alone in China was permitted to taste. Jiang's favorite actress was Greta Garbo. She closely identified with the independent yet vulnerable women played by Garbo in *Queen Christiana, Camille*, and *Anna Karenina*, but she also enjoyed more recent movies. *The Sound of Music* had made such an impression on her that she was planning to produce a version in Chinese.

Films were such an appropriate gift for Jiang Qing because they had been so much a part of her life. As a young girl, Jiang, using the name Lan Ping (Blue Apple), had been a successful actress. Although she constantly denigrated her own movies, Alexandra suspected that she still thrived on their glamour. It was certainly this glamour that first attracted Mao. As one of tens of thousands of new arrivals in Yan'an in 1937, Jiang would have been just another anonymous recruit, but Mao had seen several of her movies and was intrigued by her seductive screen personality. Though still married to his third wife, he sought Jiang out. She soon because his mistress.

Now, almost forty years later, Jiang had chosen film and other entertainment as the arena in which to exert her authority. She had become the empress of culture in China, controlling all public communications and hence all public thought. It was a position she hoped would enable her to take command of the government.

Alexandra placed a well-manicured hand on the reels and smiled. It had not been easy to find American films featuring strong women or revolutionary themes, but she had chosen well and knew that Jiang would be pleased. She had picked

The African Queen and *Adam's Rib* because Jiang liked Katharine Hepburn. *The Grapes of Wrath* was selected because it was about impoverished American peasants and because it had been one of Mao's favorites during World War II. *Gone with the Wind* had been chosen because it was arguably the greatest movie ever made. Alexandra was proud of herself. She had spent years catering to Jiang's whims. Now their friendship was strong and her efforts were ready to pay off.

At breakfast, Marc Slater sat alone at a small table in the center of the lobby reading the *South China Morning Post*. Six hours of sleep had left him refreshed. He had enjoyed his evening with Linda Forbes and was looking forward to seeing more of her in China. He scanned the massive room just as Alexandra Koo stepped regally from the elevator. Alexandra paused, like an actress awaiting applause after her first entrance. Marc's eyes remained riveted on her.

Four businessmen hurried to greet her. They were clients, executives of companies she represented in China. So strong were her contacts that the fate of their businesses rested largely on her whim, a condition she rarely let them forget. She extended her hand and let it be kissed.

Marc recalled Sen's letter. Alexandra was the president of the Empress Jade Corporation. She was certainly ambitious enough to be involved in the smuggling. His expression remained impassive as he noticed Alexandra staring at him. Dismissing her entourage, she strolled toward him, stopping every few tables to allow herself to be greeted. "My dear Marc." She flashed her perfectly capped teeth.

"Hello, Alexandra," Marc replied formally. Her hand fluttered below his mouth. He had no alternative. People were watching. If he did not kiss her, she would lose face. He had enough problems without worrying about the revenge of a scorned empress. He touched his lips to the back of her hand.

"I must say this is a delightful surprise." Alexandra fingered the jade pendant dangling between her breasts. "I thought nothing could tear you from your boat during the summer."

"I'm just here for a few days." Marc covered himself.

"For an oil deal?"

"Something like that." Alexandra always seemed to know more about his business than he would have liked.

"Are you on the morning train?"

"The Eight-thirty Special."

"Perfect." She gently touched his arm. "Let's have a quiet dinner tonight in Canton?"

"I'm afraid I can't. I have to work with my people."

"Then meet me in my room after dinner. It's just possible that we have some mutual interests to explore."

"I'll do what I can," Marc replied, wondering what she had in mind.

"I'm saving you the first waltz on my dance card." Alexandra winked. Then she turned in a swirl of green silk and walked toward the door.

As Marc watched her leave, he remembered the way Carolyn had once described her: "She's a charlatan, but she's a real charlatan."

Linda Forbes rubbed the gold locket around her neck as she sat in the back seat of the Peninsula Hotel's ivory-covered Rolls-Royce limousine. She felt uneasy. Having tipped the doorman $20 to put her in the same car as Alexandra, she would now be facing the Empress one-on-one. Linda had spent three years preparing for this mission—two with a counterinsurgency team in the Philippines and one as a buyer at Bloomingdale's. This was her first direct operation, and she was by no means confident that she could hold her own against someone of Alexandra's experience.

To all appearances, Linda Forbes was an all-American girl, a fresh, open child of the California sunshine. She had at various times wanted to be a mother, teacher, tennis pro, and even an actress; but certainly never a spy. As a child she had taken no interest in China, short of begging her mother to take her to the local Chinese restaurant. Even in her teens, her prime concerns were the Beach Boys, the Beatles, the backyard swimming pool, and her red Mustang convertible. She was a bright student, but she preferred the beach to the library. She protested the war in Vietnam as much for social as political reasons and chose to attend U. Cal. Berkeley because she wanted to be away from home and near her grandmother, Margot Forbes, who lived in San Francisco.

Margot was a respected local artist and sometime poet who had moved to California with her husband more than thirty years earlier. As the only grandchild, Linda had always been very close to her grandmother. She thought she knew everything about Margot until the day, three months before her death, when Margot confided her real past.

She had moved to Paris after World War I to pursue her art. There she had become friendly with many Chinese Communists, including Chou En-lai and Deng Xiaoping. Liu Teyu, a massive Cantonese who was one-fourth European was working with them. Margot and Liu met and fell in love. When Liu returned to China, Margot followed him. They lived in Shanghai. Liu helped organize the local party, while Margot continued her painting.

During one of Chiang Kai-shek's crackdowns, Liu was

arrested and Margot was wounded. Party leaders informed her that Liu had been executed and warned that it was too dangerous to remain. An American acquaintance named Kenneth Forbes was returning home. He agreed to take Margot and her infant son with him. Everyone in the United States assumed that the boy was his.

Ten years later Margot learned that Liu was still alive. But she was already married to Kenneth Forbes, so there was no choice but to keep her silence. Over the next thirty years, Margot and Liu never communicated, but she had left instructions that a letter be sent to him upon her death.

The news stunned Linda. Her grandmother gave her diaries and letters that detailed not only her love affair with Liu but also her friendship with Mao and the other leaders of China. As Linda digested it all, she became possessed to learn what she could about the Orient and about her grandfather. She studied Chinese languages at Berkeley, Chinese culture at Harvard, and Far Eastern politics at Princeton's Woodrow Wilson School. She joined the Asian branch of the Agency and was trained for this operation. All that remained was for her to meet Liu.

Linda opened her compact and looked in the mirror. She had blond hair and the type of turned-up nose that plastic surgeons always try to imitate. What had happened to the Oriental genes? Some might have helped to shape her narrow eyes. It's impossible, she laughed as she applied her lipstick. But it was true.

Linda looked up and saw Alexandra standing beside the limousine. A young boy rushed to open the door. Alexandra tipped him a few coins. Then she sat down and smoothed the static electricity from her dress. "It's the carpeting," Linda said. "The same thing happened to me."

Alexandra turned and glanced at Linda, envying her youth. "Ralph Lauren?" She pointed to Linda's paisley silk shirt.

Linda smiled. "I see you know fashion."

"I have the same one in my closet in green."

"To match your jade?"

Alexandra beamed. "Everything matches my jade. It's my business. I'm Alexandra Koo. I'm the president of Empress Jade Imports in Peking."

"In Peking?" Linda asked. "But you look so Western and speak English so flawlessly."

"I live in New York five months of the year. My husband is a vice-president of Merrill Lynch."

Linda tried to look confused. She wanted to appear completely nonthreatening. "Why are you forced to stay in China seven months a year?"

"My dear, nothing forces me to stay in China. China is my home." Alexandra reached into her Gucci wallet, removed a business card, and carefully handed it to Linda with the side in Chinese facing up. Linda looked blankly at the card until Alexandra apologetically turned it to the side in English.

Linda glanced at the card and then at the green and red stripe on the wallet. The stripe was perfect for Alexandra, the green for the jade and the red for China. "It must be wonderful to live in Peking. I envy you."

"It is. What business are you in?"

"I'm the antiques buyer for Bloomingdale's. My name is Linda Forbes."

"You've picked a good store." Alexandra nodded politely. To her, department-store buyers were the meringue of American traders, all fluff and no substance. Impressed with the power of their pencils, they were willing to pay any price to get the right merchandise and thought that the Chinese would kowtow before the almighty American dollar. Still, this Linda seemed like a pleasant girl; and she was impressed with the jade, which at least showed that she had good taste. "Is this your first trip to China?"

"It's my second, but it's the first on my own."

"If you have patience, a desire to learn, and respect for the Chinese, I'm sure you'll do fine."

"Thanks for the advice," Linda replied, pleased that Alexandra seemed to be off her guard.

A stocky Chinese man climbed into the front seat. As the driver began the ten-minute trip to the railroad station, the man turned to introduce himself. His muscular biceps bulged from the sleeves of his sport shirt as he offered Alexandra the traditional Chinese greeting, "*Ni chi fan le ma* [Have you eaten rice today]?" Then he turned to Linda and stared intently without speaking.

Linda smiled. "Hi. I'm Linda Forbes. It's nice to meet you."

"*Ni hao ma? Wo jiao Leung Lilai*," he said in Chinese.

"He says how are you? His name is Leung Lilai," Alexandra translated.

"*Duibuqi. Wo de Yingwen bu tai hao. Wo yao jiang Zhongwen.*"

"He says his English isn't very good. He would like to speak Chinese." Linda appeared flustered, so Alexandra continued. "I told him you were an American and that you did not speak Chinese."

Leung scratched his head and laughed. "*Hao, hao. Wo cong Malaixiya lai. Wo hen gaoxing huijian ni.*"

Alexandra took on the burden of the conversation. "He says that he's from Malaysia and that he's very happy to meet you."

Linda replied that she, too, was pleased. Alexandra translated her words. Leung nodded his thanks. Then for an instant he and Linda stared at each other. "*Ni zuo shenma* [What do you think you're doing]?" Alexandra asked.

"Whatever do you mean?" Leung responded in Chinese.

"You're really cute," Alexandra scoffed in Chinese, "telling this girl you don't speak English. Didn't they teach you any at West Point?"

"It's just a game," Leung laughed.

"It's a pretty stupid one. This woman buys antiques. We could run into her all over China."

"Don't lecture me, Alexandra. I know what I'm doing."

"Then don't forget that we're not here to serve as play actors for wayward buyers." Alexandra could not restrain her bad temper. She liked to work alone and could not understand why Jiang had chosen this man from Taiwan as her partner. But all that really mattered was that Leung continue to provide the weapons. They would give Jiang the power to take control of China, and in return Alexandra would receive enough relics to make her independently wealthy.

"Tell the girl some story," Leung said in Chinese, "so she won't be so curious about our conversation."

Alexandra turned to Linda. "I told Mr. Leung that you were an antiques buyer from Bloomingdale's. He said that he hopes your trip is successful and wishes to help you in any way he can." Alexandra grinned at Leung. She would show him who could play games.

"Tell Mr. Leung," Linda said, "that I am grateful for his assistance. Perhaps he or you could suggest where I might find the best antiques."

Leung began to speak before Alexandra could translate. "See what happens when you play your stupid games? This woman is going to attach herself to us like a flea to a dog. Tell her we'll find her antiques in Canton. She'll be happy and we'll be rid of her before we get to Peking."

"Mr. Leung," Alexandra said, "reminded me that there are almost no good antiques left in Peking, because the warehouse has been temporarily closed. He thinks the one in Canton has the best stock, and he would be pleased to direct you there when we arrive."

"Thanks," Linda replied. "That's how I got fouled up last time. The government trotted me around the country. They wouldn't let me buy a thing until I got to Tianjin, and there I found nothing but junk. Please tell Mr. Leung I'm happy he clued me in."

"*Ta shuo xie xie ni* [She says thank you]," Alexandra translated.

"It's tough being in a strange country." Linda smiled at the others. "I'm just lucky to have met you at the start of my trip."

Alexandra relaxed, realizing she would have no problem getting rid of Linda. "We're pleased to help you in any way we can."

"And if I can do something for you in New York or at Bloomingdale's, just ask." Linda smiled. So far, so good.

The Rolls-Royce stopped in front of the passenger terminal. Linda stepped out and turned toward the harbor. She wanted a moment alone. Her head was beginning to throb. She looked up at the tropical sun and took a deep breath. Alexandra and Leung were more than worthy adversaries. She had to be careful not to make them suspicious. An old Chinese proverb came to mind: "A visible spear is easy to dodge, but it is difficult to defend oneself from an arrow shot from a hiding place." For the moment she could see their spears and they could not see her arrows. Still, it might not be enough of an advantage.

Linda bought a morning newspaper and looked quickly at the headlines. She saw Alexandra pointing in the direction of the ticket office. As she walked toward the Jade Empress, she chuckled at the suggestion that the Canton warehouse had the best antiques. Although she had been with Bloomingdale's for only one year, even she knew that the

6: Comrade Ren

HONG KONG

The 7:30 A.M. temperature was already twenty-nine degrees Celsius as Comrade Ren Daoling of Luxingche, the China International Travel Service, started to review the applications for the morning train to Canton. As was common during the summer, the train would be half empty. Few overseas Chinese and even fewer foreigners seemed willing to leave the comfort of their air-conditioned offices for the blistering heat and oppressive humidity of southern China.

As Ren reviewed the applications, he reflected that the Year of the Dragon had not been a good one for the People's Republic. In January, Chou En-lai had died. The loss felt almost personal to Ren. Chou, the premier of the People's Republic, had been China's second most important man and its diplomat to the world. Yet Ren did not grieve because Chou had been such an important political figure. He grieved because Chou had been a good man, a person to be admired. Chou was simple and unassuming. He lived modestly, required no special extravagances, and never demanded the spotlight. His was a life that all Chinese wanted to emulate. Ren's father used to say, "Mao is the father of China, but Chou is the father of each of us. We must all respect Mao, but we all love Chou."

Though Ren had not always been a man of politics, the events of the last year had convinced him to act. Like most Chinese, he had thought that Mao would die before Chou. Then Chou would have become the Party chairman and Deng Xiaoping would have become the premier. But with Chou's death, everything had changed. Mao had appointed the little-known Hua Guofeng to succeed Chou. Hua was not a veteran of the Long March. He had served in Peking for only a short time, and most of his previous experience had been as the governor of Mao's home province. Although Ren accepted the choice of Chairman Mao, he had no answer for the American who had asked how the inexperienced governor of a small southern state could become the leader of a nation as powerful as China.

Ren had still believed that Deng would inherit Chou's legacy, until the events of April 5 forced him to change his mind. On that day workers in Peking had gone to Tian'-anmen Square to lay wreaths honoring Chou around the Monument to the People's Heroes. As workers eulogized Chou, the crowd became unruly. Violence erupted. An army barracks was burned. Government offices were ransacked. Thousands were injured. The *People's Daily* said the disturbance had been instigated by the capitalist-roader Deng Xiaoping, a charge Ren knew to be false. No violence would have occurred if the mourners had not been provoked by Jiang Qing and the Gang of Four.

Chou was dead, Hua was unknown, Deng was purged, and Mao was about to die. The only strong political force seemed to be Jiang Qing. She wanted to lead China into a second cultural revolution, a prospect that greatly disturbed

Ren. The first had badly disrupted the country, and a second might have even more disastrous consequences.

Ren recalled with great sadness the events of the Cultural Revolution. He had been a middle-school student when the movement started. Swept up by Mao's call to action and Jiang Qing's oratory, he joined the Red Guard. At first it was exciting, a chance for his generation to lead their own crusade. Parading around with red armbands, they closed schools, burned deviationist books, and removed rightists from positions of responsibility. His father, a minor party official, cautioned that events were getting out of control. But Ren and his friends refused to listen.

The commander of the Ren's Red Guard unit began to campaign against deviationist teachers. Ren's mother, a professor of literature, was one of the first targets. As the mother of a Red Guard, she had to be above reproach. Ren had led his comrades in the search of his own home. Under his parents' mattress, he found the incriminating evidence. It was the foreign counterrevolutionary novel *Les Miserables* by Victor Hugo.

The branding of his mother as a rightist brought disgrace to Ren's family. His father was expelled from the party. His brother lost his supervisory position in the bicycle factory. His sister was divorced by her husband and returned to their home. And he himself was regarded with suspicion by his comrades. Even though he had helped to expose two leading party cadres, Ren was eventually expelled from the Red Guards.

Ren hated his mother for what she had done. He and his elder brother baited her. Her deviationist tendencies had destroyed the family. With no other alternative, she and Ren's sister fled from home in the middle of the night. It was Ren's last contact with either of them.

The past ten years had brought many changes. Ren had

grown into a man. He regretted what he had done, but it was too late to reverse the excesses of his youth. He had finally read the book that had destroyed his family and found nothing that was treasonous. He would never forget the destruction that it had helped to cause. He was determined not to let Jiang Qing drive the People's Republic into another insane revolution.

Ren remembered a poem that Mao had written to Chou:

Loyal parents who sacrificed so much for the nation
    never feared the ultimate fate.
Now that our country has become Red,
    who will be its guardian?
Our mission, unfinished, may take a thousand years.
The struggle tires us, and our hair is grey.
You and I, old friend, can we just watch our efforts
    being washed away?

Ren checked his watch. Only forty-five minutes remained before the departure of the morning train. He looked at the stack of applications. Marc Slater's was on the top. Ren touched the envelope wedged between the pages of a book and wondered what was on the microfilm he was to deliver.

Ren had known Slater for four years and had escorted delegations on which the American was a representative. To him, Slater was the best of the foreigners. Even though he was an influential businessman, Slater was never rude nor overbearing. While other foreigners demanded special favors, he always waited patiently for his turn. While others treated Travel Service personnel as if they were coolies, he never talked down to people. And while others required special Western comforts, he always accepted Chinese services as they were offered.

Ren looked up. The morning travelers were beginning to

surround his desk. He placed Slater's papers at the bottom of the pile and looked back at his applications. Those of Samuel and Beatrice Tang, highly influential Chinese-Americans, were joined by a paper clip.

Ren had met the Tangs many times. Except for their Oriental faces, they looked like Western tourists. Sam was a balding, round-faced yet trim man in his early fifties. His dark skin and sharp features indicated he had once come from the impoverished Hakkas of southern China, but he now appeared very prosperous. He wore a dark blue suit, white shirt, and conservative striped tie. He carried a fine leather attaché case. In his lapel he wore a pin with the flags of the People's Republic and the United States, the symbol of the National Council for U.S.-China Trade.

Beatrice, about the same age, was a light-skinned, aristocratic Chinese from Shanghai. Her smile was open and friendly, but her eyes were dark and intent. Around her neck she carried Nikon and Polaroid cameras. She was known for giving children photographs of themselves. It always caused great excitement. Ren smiled as he handed Sam the two applications.

An attractive Chinese woman approached the counter. She stared at Ren with a supercilious expression. Beads of sweat formed on his forehead. He inconspicuously wiped them away with the back of his hand. The woman known as the Jade Empress always made him feel ill at ease. Ren hurriedly found Alexandra Koo's application and checked the details. Alexandra placed her palms on the counter and inclined her body forward so that she could observe his work. He turned away, stamped the passport, and handed her the papers without looking up.

"I'm not finished." Alexandra pointed to a young woman standing beside her. "I'd appreciate it if you would help my friend," she ordered.

Ren looked at the blond foreigner. Although he did not think Western women were attractive, there was something special about this one. She had an intelligence in her eyes and a gentle compassion in her smile, as if she understood his discomfort. "What's her name?" he asked.

"It's Linda," Alexandra replied, "Linda—ah—"

"Forbes," Linda assisted.

"Forbes, that's right," Alexandra confirmed. "Please give her special treatment. This is only her second trip to China."

As Ren looked through his applications, he heard Linda say to Alexandra, "I'm so grateful to you for getting me this personal service."

"No thanks are necessary," Alexandra told Linda. "My friend Comrade Ren will take care of everything. I'll see you on the train."

The Jade Empress walked toward a bank of phone booths while Ren reviewed Linda's application. "Excuse me," he said. "I must have misunderstood. I thought Mrs. Koo said that this was only your second trip to China."

"Mrs. Koo just assumed I was a neophyte."

"But you have been to China many times."

"Please don't divulge my secret." Linda stared at him with a softly electric smile. "Alexandra enjoys being helpful. She would lose face if she learned that I was not a newcomer."

"Your secret is safe," Ren laughed. "I'm pleased to see that you have learned some of our culture."

As Linda walked away, Ren turned to the application of Lord Henry Gateshead. Though Ren had never met the director of the English Museum, Gateshead's name was familiar because the noble house of Hong Kong was known as Gateshead & MacIntosh. Ren was eager to see the man whose name adorned everything from elevators to bananas, but when he called Gateshead's name, he was answered not by an English gentleman but by a young Chinese from the

Peninsula Hotel. The Chinese reported that the Englishman did not like the heat and had decided to remain inside the air-conditioned limousine until it was time for the train to depart. Ren gave the application to the Chinese, resisting the temptation to ask how someone who did not like the heat would fare in Canton during the summer.

Four Japanese approached Ren's counter. Although he had not yet seen their papers, he assumed they worked together, because the Japanese always traveled in groups. Ren thought this system of sending delegations was far superior to the Western system of sending single individuals. While the Japanese could help each other, the Westerners had to be experts in every phase of business and make decisions on their own. Ren did not understand why Westerners were forced to work alone or how they could compete against their better staffed Japanese adversaries.

Ren found the applications of the four men. All were representing the powerful Takamura Corporation from Osaka. Two, Sakuri Gentaro and Yasuda Yoshimasu, were in the oil division; one, Iohora Shu, was with the construction division; and the last, Yamaguchi Yukio, was the managing director of all the corporation's activities.

The four stood in front of the counter talking in loud and animated voices that distracted Ren from his paper work. Three were short and wiry, perfectly fitting the Chinese stereotype of the Japanese, or, as they were called behind their backs, the Island Dwarfs. The fourth looked like a sumo wrestler. He was far more than six feet tall, with broad shoulders, powerful arms, and a middle-aged stomach that rolled over the top of his gold belt bucklet. "*Ohayo gozaimasu*," the large man greeted in Japanese. "Yamaguchi, Sakuri, Yasuda, Iohara, *dozo* [please]."

Although at least one of the Japanese probably spoke Chinese, Ren knew they would make no concessions toward finding a common language. The Japanese still acted as if they were the conquerors of China; and despite the recently signed Treaty of Friendship, much of the animosity from the Anti-Japanese War still remained. Ren handed Yamaguchi the applications but made no attempt to start a conversation.

He turned to the applications for the Yugoslavian Choral Society, the Australian-Chinese Friendship Association, and the Nigerian National Basketball Team. Once in Canton, these groups would be assigned to other representatives, but for now they were his responsibility. Then he completed the visas for six individual travelers. Only one application remained. "Marc Slater," Ren called out as he scanned the waiting room.

The American, wearing white linen slacks and a cranberry sport shirt, greeted him in Chinese. "Comrade Ren, how are you?"

"Fine! It's good to have you back in China, old friend," Ren said as he handed Marc the visa papers. "How is your wife?"

Marc's blue eyes peered at Ren with a stinging intensity as he replied. "She died last spring."

Shocked, Ren searched for the appropriate words, but all he could find was "I'm sorry. I am so very sorry."

"Thank you, old friend," Slater said. "Your consolation comforts me."

They talked for a few minutes, and then Slater turned to leave. Ren took the book out from under the counter. "Mr. Slater, perhaps you'd like a book to read on the train."

Marc stared in confusion at the Chinese characters on the cover. "I don't know if my Chinese is good enough."

"Please leaf through it. I brought it just for you."

Marc spotted the envelope sticking out from between the pages. He glanced around the room. No one was watching.

He casually slipped the envelope from the book. "What shall I do with it?"

"Someone will contact you at the hotel in Canton."

"Thank you, comrade," Marc said, hurriedly cramming the envelope into his pocket. "I'll see you on the train."

"Take care of yourself, my friend." Ren's voice sounded nervous. "There are many people who want what you have."

7: The Hong Kong— Canton Railway

HONG KONG TO LOWU

As the train emerged from the main tunnel, Marc Slater put on his sunglasses and stared at the raucous confusion of Kowloon. On either side of the tracks were row after row of recently constructed but already crumbling tenements and factories. Old women clutching infants hung laundry to dry on the fire escapes, while their grandchildren operated sewing machines in stifling garment lofts. On the inadequate roads, the traffic was so congested that pedestrians, bicycles, and carts drawn by animals easily outdistanced automobiles.

The train approached a bay. Fishermen in rickety wooden sampans were returning with their morning catch. On the far shore was a small farming area with a few cows, an acre of rice paddies, and an old chicken coop. Beyond the farm, two modern factories were being built. Marc glanced wistfully at a lone water buffalo grazing next to a construction crane. In the competition for space, the water buffalo was doomed.

Marc opened the *Asian Wall Street Journal* and started to review his investments. Since this would be his last opportunity to read a Western newspaper until after his return, he methodically studied the tables of stocks and commodities. He loved the competition in the stock market and enjoyed outperforming everyone else. He owned more than twenty stocks, and in almost every instance he was far ahead of where he had begun.

He had just started to look at his OTC stocks when he heard a man with a thick southern accent ask, "How's the market treatin' you?"

He looked up and saw two Marc Slaters staring back at him from the lenses of Vance Stewart's mirrored sunglasses. "Not too bad, Vance," he replied to the six-foot, five-inch American who was president of Chinese American Tobacco, or, as it was commonly known, CAT.

"Are you heavily invested?" Stewart asked. A cigarette dangled from the side of his mouth.

"I'm pretty well bought up. What about you?"

"Don't like the market, 'cept for my own stock." Stewart brushed his flaxen hair away from his sunglasses. "I like to put my money in something I can touch, like tobacco land."

"Land's too dull. I like the intellectual stimulation of the market."

"Cut the BS," Stewart laughed, placing his hand-tooled cowboy boot on Marc's seat. "You just like to make more money than everyone else."

"I suppose you're in business to lose money," Marc said, thinking about the three thousand dollars he had won from Stewart last year playing backgammon on a flight to Peking.

"I don't mind coming out ahead," Stewart replied, flicking his ashes onto the floor. "Give me a chance to improve my fortunes?"

"Sure," Marc replied, understanding Stewart's challenge.

Marc's eyes followed as Vance left to get the backgammon board. Although Stewart still looked the part of a *bon vivant*, he had aged a lot in the past year. Flab had started to settle around his formerly trim waist. His hair was thinner, his sideburns greyer. Lines of age filled his brow. There might be problems in the tobacco business. Marc recalled Sen's words, "Tobacco can be hazardous to your health."

With the guidance of his politically savvy managing director, Wong Chuyun, Stewart had transformed CAT from a small tobacco trader into an agricultural conglomerate with interests in soybeans, citrus fruits, and it was rumored, marijuana and opium as well. But tobacco was still the core of CAT's business. With the support of Jiang Qing, CAT had obtained a virtual monopoly over the trade in China, a country that smoked three times as many cigarettes as any other. It seemed unlikely that Vance would risk his monopoly for Chinese relics, but there was no telling what hold Jiang Qing might have over him. Sen was not the type to issue indiscriminate warnings. As Marc watched Vance approach, he hoped that Sen's advice did not also apply to playing backgammon.

Vance placed the board on the table between them. Deciding on stakes of five dollars a point, they arranged the pieces and started to play. With the aid of a 3-1 opening followed by double sixes, Vance moved his pieces aggressively forward. "What do you do with your stocks when you're in China?" the tall southerner asked.

"Today's my last look," Marc replied as his less lucky rolls forced him to move defensively and await his opportunity. "The stocks belong to the Western part of my life. Once I get to China, I forget about them."

"And what happens?"

"Usually the stocks go up," Marc laughed. "My decision-making actually seems to improve when I'm not around to outsmart myself."

"Lucky Slater never loses," Vance said as he filled five bars in a row and twisted the cube to double the bet, "except perhaps at backgammon."

"You haven't lost too many times," Marc probed, accepting the double. "Every time I open the *Journal*, I read about another of your acquisitions."

"They're fun to play with."

"Any you can let me in on?"

"CAT needs no partners."

"No Western partners." Marc tested Vance with a vague reference to Jiang Qing.

"What does that crack mean?" Stewart asked as he rolled double fives and was forced to leave an opening.

"Nothing," Marc said as he hit Vance's piece and closed out the board.

"One more?" Vance asked as he set up the next game.

"All right," Marc said, knowing Vance would be furious if he refused a rematch. "But this is the last one. I want to finish my work so I can enjoy myself when I get to China."

"You really have a thing for China, don't you? You speak the language, eat the food, collect the art. I mean, you really seem to love it."

"I should," Marc smiled. "I was born there."

"I was born there too, but I detest the place. If I didn't have so much business to protect, I'd never go to the damn mainland."

Marc had no desire to refute Vance, whose attitude was similar to that of most Westerners born in China. Vance had grown up in the International Concession of Shanghai in which almost everyone he knew was a Westerner, the only exception being the servants in his house and the workers in his father's office. He looked down upon the Chinese and had made no attempt to understand their culture. It was his loss. "I like visiting China," Marc said. "It's like going home."

"Where? Back to the caves of Yan'an with the Communists?"

"It's where I grew up." Marc sat motionless with the dice in his hand, sensitive to the direction the conversation was taking.

"Come on, Marc." Stewart tugged on his arm. "Didn't mean to break your concentration."

Marc lit his pipe. Sen's warnings were still with him, but the smoke felt soothing. He rolled the dice, obviously distracted. After two more moves, Stewart seized the advantage. "I double you."

"I concede." Marc gazed at the game with relief. "Let's play later."

"Look, Marc," Stewart said, "sometimes my mouth works a bit faster than my brain. I'm just sorry if I started to sound like McCarthy."

"Thanks." Marc slapped Vance on the back. "Let's have a rematch in Canton. Perhaps I can win enough to pay for my trip."

Stewart laughed. "No way, my friend. Now I've got your number."

Marc walked quickly down the aisle of the rattling car. He needed a moment to himself. He passed Lord Henry Gateshead, the slightly paunchy Englishman whose family had founded the largest British trading company in the Orient, sitting with an attractive European woman. He had read that Gateshead was planning to build a new wing onto the English Museum. It was perhaps more than a coincidence that the Englishman was visiting China at the same time as vast amounts of relics were being dumped on the world market.

Sam and Beatrice Tang were sitting next to each other reading a newspaper. "Hello, Marc." Sam patted the seat. "Come join us."

"I'll be right back," Marc said as he pointed toward the lavatory.

Avery Boswell, the deputy managing director of Gateshead & MacIntosh, was dozing in a row by himself. Marc stared at Boswell and then looked back at Lord Gateshead. Even though the Englishman was no longer involved in the management of the company, it seemed odd that the deputy managing director would be sitting separately in the same car. A chill tickled the hairs on the back of Marc's neck. Too many things were out of place.

As he reached the end of the car, his eyes met those of Ren Daoling. Smiling to conceal his discomfort, he tapped the envelope in his back pocket. "Don't worry," he whispered without stopping.

Opening the steel door, Marc walked into the alcove. The train bounced along the rails, making that unique grinding sound that can be produced only by the meeting of fifty-year-old locomotives with eighty-year-old tracks. The morning air, though hot, was refreshing as it blew against his face. He stared blankly at the hills of the New Territory. Ramshackle villages, new white apartment buildings, and rice paddies rushed by.

He turned toward the dining car and entered the coach filled with Australians and Nigerians. He felt a gust of warm wind on his back. Somebody was following. Glancing at the floor behind him, he saw a pair of khaki slacks draped over the top of a man's black sneakers. It was probably just another thirsty passenger. He crossed through another alcove and into the coach filled with the Yugoslavians. The footsteps were still there. He quickened his pace, trying to ignore the man behind him.

The train entered a tunnel. Marc looked into the window. In the reflection, he saw a blue, long-brimmed baseball cap on the head of a wiry Chinese. Their eyes met. The man smiled mysteriously. There was a gold tooth in the center of his mouth.

Marc hurried into the dining car. Sitting at an open table in the center, he was grateful for the security of the commotion around him. The man with the gold tooth sat near the door. Marc called for the waiter. In the far corner he saw Alexandra Koo. The muscles in his neck began to throb. She was sitting with Linda Forbes. He turned toward the window, pretending not to see them. Was it possible that Linda was working with Alexandra? His breath felt short as he tried to remember if he had said anything that would have given him away. A hand touched his arm. Marc jumped. "Your tea," the waiter said, clearing a place.

Gazing at the jasmine flowers in the cup, Marc sipped his tea and tried to compose himself. He was probably overreacting. The fear of the unknown was always worse than the reality.

"Hello, Marc." Alexandra Koo stepped next to him. "You look lousy."

"Thanks for the compliment." Marc glanced over Alexandra's shoulder at Linda. She nodded silently. He could detect no meaning in her expression.

"Mind if we join you?" Alexandra slid into the next chair. "This is my friend Linda Forbes." Linda hesitantly took the seat across the table.

"I was introduced to Miss Forbes in the hotel." Marc's tone was cautious. "It's nice to see you again."

Linda stared into his eyes. "The pleasure is mine."

"You never did tell me," Marc said, "what you are doing

going to China at such an inhospitable time of the year."

"Linda is a buyer for Bloomingdale's," Alexandra responded as if she were still translating for two people who did not speak the same language. "I'm taking her under my wing."

"That sounds like a nice safe place to be." Marc probed for more information about their relationship. "What are you buying?"

"Antiques and artifacts," Alexandra replied.

"Also jade," Linda said. "Now that I've seen how beautiful Alexandra's are, I want some for myself."

"I'll take care of you." Alexandra placed her hand condescendingly on Linda's shoulder. "Marc is in the metals and minerals trading business."

"Everyone knows Lucky Slater," Linda said, brushing back her blond hair to show off a pair of gold earrings with inlaid rubies. "I bought these when M. H. Schaffer acquired my shares in Pecos International Oil."

"My friend is quite an enterprising capitalist," Alexandra said.

"Perhaps you could use her in your business. Why don't you make her a junior partner and let her handle your arts and crafts clients?"

Alexandra turned her chair so that she partially blocked Marc's view of Linda. "I prefer to work alone."

"Just a suggestion." Marc stood up. "Now if you'll excuse me, I promised Samuel Tang that I'd help him review a development proposal."

"I'll let you go this time"—Alexandra clutched Marc's hand—"but don't forget the waltz."

"I'll try not to. Nice talking to you, Linda. I hope to see you again."

"I hope so too," Linda said. As Marc turned and walked away, Linda noticed that a Chinese man wearing a baseball cap was staring at him. "What's that about a waltz?"

"It's a private joke," Alexandra replied.

Marc entered the alcove. The Chinese man hurried after him. "Could you excuse me for a minute?" Linda said. "I forgot to give Mr. Slater a letter from one of my vendors. They're old friends."

"Give it to him later."

"I'd better go now. It'll just take a minute."

"Isn't it a little early to be shopping for antiques?" Alexandra's voice took on a hard edge. "Slater is way out of your league."

Linda forced a laugh. "Do you think I'm interested in Marc?"

"I know you're interested. But let me give you some advice. There's no way that you can stand the heat. The competition is too strong."

"Like you?" Linda asked, glancing toward the door.

"If I want."

"Look, Alexandra, I just want to deliver this letter. I have no intention of trying to cut you out."

"My dear, you couldn't if your life depended on it."

"Please! I'll be right back." Linda turned quickly toward the door.

Marc had reached the alcove between the third and fourth cars. There was a sound behind him. He turned. The Chinese man with the blue baseball cap stood glaring at him. Without a word, the Chinese pulled a stiletto and lunged at his chest. Marc deflected the thrust. He kicked the Chinese in the side. The man screamed and dropped the knife. Marc reached for the door. The man recovered and struck Marc's arm with a piercing chop. Marc cried out in agony. Dazed, he staggered against a wall. The man with the gold tooth rushed at him. Marc spun and kicked him in the back. The man fell to the floor. Marc tugged on the door. The latch jammed. Glancing over his shoulder, he saw the Chinese moving toward him, knife in hand.

Marc waited in judo position, his eyes riveted on the shining blade. He felt emotionally attached to the man who was trying to kill him. His breath was rapid and uneven. Thus far he had been lucky, but the attacker was armed, younger, and more experienced. The Chinese lunged at him. Marc jumped to the left. The knife missed its target, but the man's fist slammed into Marc's jaw. He fell to the floor. A knee crushed the air from his throat. He coughed as he watched the man raise the dagger. Everything was in slow motion. He stared into his attacker's eyes. They were wide open yet expressionless. A stream of saliva flowed from the man's mouth. Marc flailed his arms as the dagger plunged toward his chest.

There was a scream. It was not Marc's voice. The knife continued downward, but the arm guiding it suddenly became limp. The fingers released their grip one knuckle at a time. The knife dropped to the floor. The Chinese fell on top of him. Marc lay under the motionless man, his mind unable to keep pace with the furious action. He heard a voice. "Marc, are you all right?"

The inert man started to roll over. Marc looked up. Linda Forbes was trying to drag the Chinese off him. "Linda! What happened?"

"I saw him attacking you." Linda was shaking. Her face radiated panic. "I hit him in the neck. I guess I got lucky and knocked him out."

"I'm the one that got lucky," Marc said, struggling to his feet. Blood, oozing from a cut above his eye, trickled down his cheek. He stared at the man and then at Linda, desperately wanting answers. Who was the mysterious attacker? And how had Linda just happened to be there? One thing was certain—from the way she was trembling, Marc knew she had never done anything like this before.

Linda wiped her brow. "We've got to get rid of him before he comes to."

Marc bent over and grabbed the man's arms. The sun reflected off the gold tooth in the center of his mouth. A door opened at the far end of the alcove. There were voices. Marc rolled the body down the stairs. It came to rest against the outside door. He pulled Linda toward him so that they blocked the view of the stairs. Linda threw her arms around his waist and hugged tightly. She started to sob.

Three Chinese entered the alcove and stared curiously at the Western couple. There was a small pool of blood on the floor. Sliding his foot over the pool, Marc lifted Linda's face and kissed her. The men laughed, muttered something in Cantonese, and walked on.

Marc lingered a moment with Linda in his arms. She was regaining her composure. He gazed into her eyes. His blood was smeared on her cheek. He looked down at the body. The man with the gold tooth was starting to stir. He pressed his heel into the man's throat, choking out the air. "Let's get him out of here!" Marc said, flinging open the outside door. Bracing themselves on the side handles of the train, Marc and Linda kicked the man from the bottom step. Marc leaned forward and watched the body disappear in the rapidly receding distance. Now he would never know the man's identity. He felt very vulnerable. It was a feeling he did not like.

Marc carefully scanned the alcove. Signs of the struggle were all around: the open door, a scrap of clothing, the Chinese man's sneaker, and the blood on the floor and on their faces. There was more than enough to incriminate them. "Do you have a handkerchief?" Marc asked, closing

108

the outside door.

Linda pulled a red bandanna from her purse and moistened it with spit. Though her hands were still shaking, she carefully cleaned Marc's face. She couldn't wash away the blood on his shirt, but luckily its cranberry color muted the stain. Marc mopped the blood from the floor; tossed the sneaker, the bandanna, and the scraps under the train; and inspected the alcove. Most of the evidence was gone. He felt more at ease. "Stay here and cover for me," he whispered to Linda.

"I can't. I told Alexandra that I was just going to give you a letter. If I don't get back soon, she'll be suspicious."

Marc stared at her. Perhaps she would give him one final answer. "Does the term 'Jade Gate' mean anything to you?"

Marc could feel only the slightest tremor as Linda pulled away. "Are you looking for a Chinese whorehouse?"

"Is there another meaning?"

Linda walked to the door. "We'll talk in Canton."

"Linda," Marc called. She turned and faced him. Her smile was soft, but her eyes were intently serious. "Thank you."

Alone in the alcove, Marc dusted off his linen pants. He needed a moment alone. He could not go back to his car. There were too many people who would ask questions he was not prepared to answer. He heard voices. Before he could turn away, Beatrice Tang entered the alcove. "My God! What happened?" She rushed to him.

"The train lurched," Marc replied, brushing a splotch of dirt off his shirt. "I fell forward and hit my head."

"Are you all right?"

"Just a little shook up."

"Then let's get a cup of tea." Before he could reply, Beatrice took his arm, and dragged him into the dining car. Finding all the tables occupied, she propelled him to the far end where four Chinese peasants were raucously playing a game, the object of which was to avoid the number selected by the others. "*Saam, saam, saam, yut* [Three, three, three, one]," the Chinese called in Cantonese as they thrust the appropriate number of fingers toward the center of the table.

"You old woman, you sons of whores!" The peasant who had shown one finger laughed as he raked in his winnings. "I fooled you again." The peasant took a peanut and dropped it through the wire mesh of a wooden box. A chicken cackled. "As long as these fools keep playing, there'll be plenty of food for both of us, *heya*," the peasant said to his chicken, and then took a swig of beer.

"Don't you have any manners?" Beatrice asked shrilly as she stood by the table. "Can't you see that the barbarian is injured? He is a special friend of China and should not be forced to stand while you cackle like chickens and gossip like fishmongers."

The Chinese hurriedly cleaned the table. They knew that Chairman Mao insisted that foreigners receive preferred treatment in matters of comfort. Gathering their boxes, the peasants bowed obsequiously and continued to stare.

"Stop gaping," Beatrice ordered. "You look like hungry garoupa. If you don't shut your mouths, someone will put hooks in them. Show our old friend some respect."

Marc smiled at Beatrice as the Chinese scurried away. "I always thought you were so demure, but now I see another side."

"My soul is from the hills of China."

"What about mine?"

"Yours, my friend, is that of a *yang guizi*."

Marc laughed at the word from his past. "I'm still a long-nosed foreign devil?"

"Of course—but one who is about to gain control over Chinese petroleum, so I wouldn't complain."

Marc eyed Beatrice suspiciously. His request for a monopoly on the export of Chinese oil was supposed to be a secret. If she knew about that, there was no telling what else she knew.

"That cut above your eye looks nasty. *Fogei*," she called to the waiter in Cantonese, "bring us two cups of tea, a glass of water, and a napkin. Is tea all right with you?" she asked Marc in English even though she knew that he understood her Chinese.

"Fine." Marc glanced distractedly at Linda. Seemingly quite composed, she was talking with Alexandra. He wanted to be with her. There was so much about her he needed to know.

"Are you thinking about the accident?" Beatrice asked.

"No. It's more a business problem," Marc responded as he tried to decide who could have sent the man who had attacked him.

"I'm sure your problem is difficult, for I know you'll solve it. After all, you have Sen Tailing to help you."

Marc was surprised to hear Sen's name. He had thought that Beatrice and Sen hardly knew each other. Was Beatrice's comment a signal that she and Sam knew about the project? "Sen is a great help," Marc responded, "but my problem is related to a copper deal in Zaire."

"I know nothing about copper, but Sam has sold planes to Mobutu. I'm sure he'd be pleased to help. For now, why don't you relax."

"Thanks. I'm glad to know you and Sam are around if I need you."

"We're behind you all the way."

Beatrice's words repeated in Marc's brain like a record stuck in a groove. Was she being polite, or was she speaking literally?

The waiter brought the drinks. Beatrice dipped the napkin

in the water and dabbed it on Marc's cut. "Don't worry. With Sen negotiating for you and with Sam and me supporting you, there's no way you can fail."

Marc counseled himself to be patient. For the moment, there was nothing else to do. The attacker was gone. Linda was talking to Alexandra, and Beatrice would tell him of her involvement when the situation warranted. He took a deep breath. "I suppose you're right about relaxing."

"Good. Now perhaps we can forget about Zaire and get down to some really important matters."

"Like what?"

"Like why you haven't invited us sailing on your lovely sloop."

"I'm sorry." Marc's smile broke some of the tension. "I thought that you and Sam only travel by plane."

"Then what am I doing on this damn railroad?"

"You are going to China so Sam can sell the PRC airplanes, which they can use to start direct flights from Hong Kong, so that no one will ever again have to travel on this wretched train."

8: The Forgery

Rong Yi ran his hand over the throbbing bruise on the back of his head; the lump had grown as large as a ripe lichee nut. Groggily he opened his eyes and tried to get his bearings. He was lying on a sagging mattress in a musty cubicle, which, from the sound of cackling chickens and baaing sheep, seemed to be in the countryside. He propped himself up on the bed and inspected the tiny room. The only other furniture consisted of a desk and rickety chair opposite the bed. There was also a sink and toilet in a partially enclosed alcove next to the door. The wooden floors and cement walls had both turned dingy gray. A faint odor of mildew emanated from the corners.

Rong placed his feet on the floor and tried to stand. His legs shook. Waves of nausea swept through him. He steadied himself on the bed till his head had cleared and he had recovered his balance. Gingerly he walked to the room's only window and looked outside. There was an enclosed circular courtyard ringed by four barns, which were connected by tall wooden fences. A heavily rutted dirt road led past the barns into the mountains. The rays of sun penetrated the thick cloud of dust blowing off the desert. Rong pulled up on the window, but it would not budge. He inspected the frame. Nails had been hammered in place to keep it from moving. He crossed the room and opened the door. A Red Guard stood in the narrow corridor. "Good afternoon, comrade," the soldier greeted him.

"Good afternoon. Where am I?"

"I am sorry, comrade, but I cannot answer any questions. Please get back into your room. I will get Colonel Li."

Rong started to protest. The guard stepped forward, pulled the door shut, and locked it from the outside. Rong's head pounded as he staggered back to his bed. He was in the midst of a confusing nightmare he could not comprehend. He lay down and tried to reconstruct the events that had brought him here. He had been working in his studio when a Red Guard arrived with a letter from Yao Wenyuan, one of the Gang of Four. The letter said that Yao needed to see him on a matter of special importance. The guard had driven him into the country. As they climbed into the hills surrounding Peking, Rong had asked about their destination but received no response. He reminded the guard of his position as Mao's calligrapher and warned him of the consequences if he received no answer, but the guard remained silent. When he continued to press for a response, the guard raised his gun and slammed the butt into the back of Rong's head. The next thing he could remember was waking up in this dingy cell of a room.

The intensity of the pain increased. He could not understand why he was being held captive. He had been a loyal member of the Party for more than forty years. He had risen to become the director of the Peking Institute of Art, China's most prestigious school of calligraphy, and he had served as the private tutor of many of the leaders of the Republic. Now he was one of the very few with direct access to the Chairman. Since Mao had become ill, Rong had served as his personal scribe, writing documents that appeared to be in the hand of the Chairman himself. His position should have made him untouchable.

The door opened and a stocky man in his thirties, with cropped hair, entered the cubicle. A long, thin scar ran from beneath his ear across his neck, as if someone had tried to slit his throat with a knife too dull to penetrate his skin's leathery toughness. His eyes were icy gray, his gaze impenetrable. A leather briefcase dangled from his shoulder. The cut of his clothing revealed that he was a high-ranking officer. "Good morning, comrade. I am Colonel Li. How are you feeling?"

"A bit sore"—Rong rubbed the bump on his head—"and very confused."

"I'm sorry about your head. My aide is young and not used to dealing with someone of your position. Please excuse him."

"I'd like to know why I'm being held prisoner."

"You are not a prisoner. We are holding you for your own protection."

"Protection? Protection from what?"

"From those who would stop you from completing our special project."

"What project? Your aide mentioned a request from Comrade Yao?"

"Actually the request is from Chairman Mao and Comrade Jiang Qing."

Rong's eyes narrowed with suspicion. Chairman Mao had summoned him to his hospital room several times during the last week. If there had been a special project, Mao would have mentioned it then. The imprisonment just did not make sense. "Why did Chairman Mao not send for me directly?"

"This project is too important to be discussed in a hospital. We must be assured of complete secrecy."

Li's explanation sounded plausible, but Rong was wary. "Why must this project be so secretive?"

Colonel Li opened his briefcase and removed two sheets of rice paper, a bottle of ink, and a calligrapher's quill pen. Then he withdrew a letter and handed it to Rong. "We want you to copy this in Mao's own hand."

Rong put on his glasses and started to read.

LAST WILL AND TESTAMENT CHAIRMAN MAO TSE-TUNG

ACT ACCORDING TO THE PRINCIPLES LAID DOWN

Though I am dying, the struggle between Marxism and the running dogs of imperialism must continue. We have fought the KMT and the revisionists and have won every battle. But the fight is not over. We must continue to act according to the principles laid down until the revolution of the proletariat has conquered the world.

To ensure a continuation of our revolutionary leadership, it is my wish that the much esteemed Comrade Jiang Qing become the new chairman of the Communist Party. Comrade Jiang is the one person I can trust to follow the principles that I have laid down. Under her leadership, the People's Republic will have a glorious future.

Mao Tse-tung
July 20, 1976
Peking

"What is this document?" Rong Yi asked.

"It is the last will of Chairman Mao."

"I have already drafted a last will for Chairman Mao. That will appoints Hua Guofeng to lead the People's Republic and actually contains a warning against Jiang Qing."

"The Chairman has changed his mind."

"I will not write anything in the Chairman's hand without a direct order."

"I think you should reconsider."

"I will not."

"Please understand. I don't want to force you to act against your conscience, but this will is vital, and I have my orders."

"Who are they from?"

"They are from Comrade Jiang Qing."

"Jiang Qing is not Chairman Mao."

"She is his wife and his closest confidante."

"She may be his wife, but she is no longer his confidante."

"I don't want to argue. You are a learned teacher and a veteran of the Long March, but I have been ordered to have you copy the new will. It is a small task, but if you refuse, things will not go well for me."

"I am sorry, but that is your problem, isn't it?"

"Ah, yes, but my problem is also your problem"—Li's voice held a hint of impatience as he stared coldly at Rong—"because I have no alternative but to convince you to change your mind."

"My position is firm."

"Why don't you look outside while you consider your decision."

Rong peered through the window and saw a young sheep standing alone in the courtyard. Colonel Li waved his arms. One of the wooden gates was thrust open. Three white Chinese tigers stalked into the ring. The first tiger caught the scent of the sheep and began to circle his prey. The sheep started to run. Before he could reach the wall, the second tiger sprang, clawed the back of the sheep, and implanted his long incisors in the animal's flabby midsection. The sheep let out a piercing bleat as its crimson blood gushed onto the tiger's ivory coat. The third tiger attacked, severing a vein in the sheep's neck. The sheep squealed and then toppled over as blood foamed out of its mouth. Rong felt the food in his stomach heave up into his throat and penetrate to the inside of his nostrils. He gasped for air and turned from the window. Colonel Li continued to stare as the three tigers gnawed at the hide of the dead animal. "Please keep watching," Li ordered. "These tigers are fascinating. Look how hungry they have become after five days of fasting."

Rong glanced at the bloody sight as one of the tigers buried his head in the carcass and chewed on a chunk of flesh. The second devoured the hindquarter, while the third tore the remaining flesh off the stomach. "Why are you subjecting me to this?"

"Obligation to duty is an interesting phenomenon," Li said as a truck with a makeshift plow drove into the courtyard and scooped up the dead sheep. Roaring, the tigers charged at the mechanized animal that was stealing their dinner. "In the abstract, it is easy to stand by one's principles; but if the stakes are high enough, the decision becomes more difficult." The tigers nipped at the dead animal as the truck drove out of the courtyard. Three men with whips cajoled them into a cage filled with fresh meat, after which the gate was pulled closed. The courtyard was now empty. Only the bloodstained dirt and the scraps of bone and sinew from the sheep marked the violence that had just occurred. "Take our disagreement. I want you to write the will. You refuse. It is a classic confrontation between two men trying to uphold their duty. If we both stand by our positions, we will remain at an impasse. It is my responsibility to change the stakes in a way that will permit you to reevaluate your primary obligation."

"I am afraid that I do not understand your meaning."

Colonel Li pointed to the courtyard. "Everything will soon be clear."

An old blind woman was pushed into the ring. Rong gasped. "What are you doing with my wife?" The woman stumbled and then recovered her balance. Using a long stick for guidance, she found her way to the back wall. When she heard the sounds of the tigers feasting on their dinner, her face became ashen as she trembled in fear and confusion. She nervously shifted her stick from side to side as she rushed away from the wall. Stepping in to a rut, she lost her balance and fell forward. As she lay on the ground, more stunned than injured, blood trickled from a cut above her eyebrow.

"I am just trying to prove that all duties are relative," Li replied.

"How could you harm her? She has nothing to do with this struggle."

"None of us have anything to do with this struggle. We are all just pawns. But in the end, it is the pawns that suffer."

"But she is an old woman."

"And I am a young man. Her life is near its end, but mine is still before me. Would you have me sacrifice my future so that you and your wife can live until the next time someone wants you to write something with which you disagree?"

"I cannot write the will, because I know it is a fraud."

"Don't you understand, old man? As long as Chairman Mao is alive yet unable to write, and as long as you are the only person qualified to be his scribe, someone will try to torture you until you give in. I have no qualms about letting my starving tigers feed off your wife, and if necessary off your oldest son and his family, who are in one of the barns. If you decide to hold out, you are going to have to watch while your entire family is eaten by the tigers."

"You are a barbarian and a traitor."

"No, old man, I am just a man, like you, who has his own obligations. I wish there were another alternative, but I must have the will. I cannot debate this issue any longer. I'll count to ten. If you have not started to write by then, I'll signal my soldiers to bring in the tigers. Ready?"

Rong tried to form a protest as Colonel Li started to count. He looked at his wife shifting her cane in panic. Her face was wrenched in a silent scream as she fled from the sound of the tigers. Then he looked at the impassive expression on the face of the colonel. He knew that Li would have no compunction about killing his family.

Rong's father and grandfather had been calligraphers. For ten generations his family had been among China's leading artists. Now his eldest son, recently appointed director of the Canton School of Art, was carrying on the tradition. But there was far more than tradition to protect. There were people: a second son, two daughters, twelve grandchildren. Far more than communism, Mao, or even the People's Republic, they were his life. He really had no other choice. He walked to the desk, opened the bottle of ink, and took the quill pen in his hand.

Colonel Li patted him on the back. "You are making the right decision, old man." Then he walked out of the room.

Rong Yi sat staring at the blank piece of paper. For the first time in his life, he cursed his talent. As he lifted his pen to write, he grieved that he had been too weak to watch the murder of his family. He tried to console himself with the thought that no one would believe the new will, but he knew he was only fooling himself. In China, people believed everything written in the hand of Chairman Mao Tse-tung.

9: Across the Border

Linda Forbes busied herself repacking her travel bag until everyone else had left the train. Opening her compact, she stared at herself in the mirror. Her face looked drawn. Lines of tension fanned out from the corners of the eyes. She applied a light pink blush to her cheeks and smiled. Her face always looked better with a little makeup.

Her hands trembled as she looked at the bracelet on her wrist. One of the charms was an antique gold hairpin that her grandmother had given her. It was supposed to symbolize the magic in a Chinese folktale called *The Bank of the Celestial Stream.* In the story, a fairy was being pursued by an evil man trying to kidnap her. As she ascended through the clouds, the fairy pulled a pin from her hair and drew an imaginary line across the sky. The line became a broad river that her pursuer was unable to cross, and the fairy was saved. Linda ran her fingers over her charm, hoping it would magically protect her. "Come on, girl," she said as she grabbed her bag and headed toward the door. "Time's awastin'."

121

Linda stepped onto the siding at the Lowu Railroad Station. Although the tracks continued, the train from Hong Kong could go only as far as the border. To get to Canton, she would have to walk across a small bridge, go into China where the station was called Sumchun by the PRC, and board the People's Republic Railroad for the remainder of the journey. Someday, when direct service commenced between Hong Kong and Canton, the two stations would cease having any function; but for now, Lowu was the end of one line and Sumchun was the beginning of another.

Linda followed myriad Chinese and some fifty foreigners across the no-man's-land of the green steel bridge. She gazed at the prominent red sign that in English and Chinese said, "Welcome to the People's Republic of China." A sense of anticipation gripped her body. This was it, the main event. It was her sixth visit in less than a year, but she doubted there would be a seventh. Forces in China were mobilizing and Mao was near death. The Gang of Four would not wait long to take military action.

Linda saw Alexandra talking with two guards at the end of the bridge. One was ushering foreigners into the newly decorated lobby of a large whitewashed building, while the other was directing Chinese down a long and grungy alley already filled with hordes of people and animals waiting for the first stage of customs. Alexandra glanced down the alley and then followed the foreigners. "Alexandra! Excuse me," Linda called. "Why are those people going through the back door?"

"They are Chinese, traveling people's class. While you enjoy first-class service, they must carry their luggage, bring their own food, wait in long lines, and take a second-class train. It would not be right to submit our foreign friends to such inconveniences, but we Chinese can stand the discomfort."

"Then why are you traveling with us?"

"I would gladly travel with my comrades; but because I have an American passport, Chinese customs must treat me as a foreigner."

As Linda started to extend her condolences, a chicken cackled, flew out of its box, and ran headlong across the platform toward Alexandra. The Empress of Jade retreated, flinging her arms futilely. "Don't come near me, you stupid bird," she ordered in Mandarin. The disobedient chicken bobbed up and down, pecking at the hem of her skirt. "Get away from me, you cackling turd." Alexandra stepped back and toppled a wheelbarrow.

The peasant who had recently won the numbers game in the dining car ran up and grasped the chicken by the neck. "One thousand apologies, honorable lady," he said to Alexandra in Cantonese. "My chicken does not understand Mandarin. I hope it did not upset you."

"Fool! I suppose your bird does understand Cantonese."

"No, actually the bird understands only the language of the Hakka people." Linda forced herself to suppress a smile.

"Don't play me for a fool. Do you think I'm some long-nosed foreign devil?"

"No, honorable lady. I did not mean to offend you. It is obvious to me that you are one of my people."

Alexandra caressed her jade pendant, trying to decide if the shabbily dressed peasant was being sarcastic. "If you don't want that bird of yours fried in the wok of the Red Guard, I suggest you put it back in its box and take it down the alley where it belongs."

The peasant bowed politely. "You are too kind to me."

Alexandra turned and brusquely strode into the white-washed building. Linda started to follow. As she stepped forward, the chicken flapped its wings and tried to break free. The peasant lunged for the bird and jostled Linda with his arm. Linda stumbled. The peasant grabbed her around the waist. "*Deui m'jeu*," he apologized in Cantonese. Linda smiled quizzically, pretending not to understand. The peasant grasped the bird and then whispered in Chinese, "That's one dangerous Jade Gate." Linda stared at him with great surprise. "If you want to learn about the relics, meet me at six on the small island at the far end of Liuhua Park." The peasant resumed his normal speaking voice. "Oh, honorable foreign friend, please excuse my unfortunate clumsiness. I vow to keep my disobedient bird under control." He bowed politely and hurried toward Chinese Customs. Linda watched him disappear into the crowd. She had expected to be contacted by someone, but the man with the chicken had surprised her.

Entering the customs building, Linda climbed two flights of stairs and stepped into a large waiting room filled with comfortable old couches. She stared at the photographs of China's deities: Mao, Marx, Lenin, and Stalin. Although Stalin had supported the People's Republic, she did not understand why the Chinese still included him. She would have selected Chou En-lai, but she knew that Chou had been too modest to permit his picture to be hung in every room in China. Besides, Mao would not have wanted the competition. Since the other deities were Caucasians, there was no one to challenge Mao's leadership.

Linda turned and saw Marc Slater talking to a tall and somewhat gangling American businessman. Dressed in a neatly tailored safari suit from Abercrombie & Fitch, the businessman looked the perfect stereotype of the American white hunter, a blond Farley Granger. "Hello, Marc," she called as she walked toward them.

"Nice to see you again, Linda." Marc smiled. His eyes twinkled.

"You've been holdin' out on me," the tall man said with an accent that oozed southern-fried charm. "Who is this sweet young thing?"

"This is Linda Forbes from Bloomingdale's. Linda, this is Vance Stewart."

"Colonel Vance Stewart," the southerner corrected.

"Of the People's Liberation Army?" Linda asked.

"You've heard of me," Vance laughed. "Is this your first trip to China?"

"It's my second. What about you?"

"Mah dear, I guess you don't realize that you're dealin' with one of the most experienced China hands in the entire U.S. of A. I was comin' to this country long before you were born."

"That long?"

"Longer. I started very young. I can tell you anythin' you want to know about China: the best people's commune, the best hospital for accupuncture, the cheapest hand laundry— anythin'."

"How about the best place to eat in Canton?"

"I like the Dong Fang Hotel. It's the only place in town that knows how to make sweet potato pie and grits."

"Sweet potato pie and grits? What about Chinese food?"

"I'll stick to southern fried food. It's what I was raised on."

"Cut the bull," Marc laughed. "The only South you have ever known is south China; and as for that oozing accent, it comes from watching old Civil War movies in Hong Kong. I've heard you in your room practicing your Rhett Butler."

"Don't believe a word this Yankee says. He's always been jealous of me. He's still trying to figure out how a little ole tobacco salesman could go into China before normalization; while he, a personal friend of Chou En-lai, had to stay in Hong Kong and send his messengers."

"I'll concede on that. I still don't know how you kept

125

getting visas."

"Perhaps the Chinese liked my good looks and my southern charm."

"Perhaps certain of Mao's relatives also liked your gifts. What are you bringing this time?"

"Unlike some people, I don't need to shower the Chinese with gifts," Vance retorted. "I seem to recall that when you came to China with Nixon, you brought half of the Library of Congress."

"Don't mind him," Marc told Linda. "He's still bitter that Nixon didn't select him for the delegation."

"I don't need to spend my time attending fancy banquets in the Great Hall of the People in order to build my business."

"Of course you don't. Not when you have a monopoly on the tobacco trade, and Mao, the Marlboro man of China, smoking three packs a day. Every Chinese kid dreams of the day when he can have one of your cigarettes dangling from his mouth."

"Are you in the tobacco business?" Linda asked.

"Vance *is* the tobacco business. He's the CAT of Chinese American Tobacco."

"You must have seen my ads with Mao astride his horse— 'Return to Mao Burou Country.'"

Linda laughed. "Sorry I missed it."

"Now I'm thinking of doing one with Jiang Qing. Got any ideas?"

"How about a Chinese Virginia Slims with Jiang and the slogan 'You've come a long way, baby'?"

Vance laughed and put his arm around Linda. "Not bad for a girl."

Linda pulled away. "A woman."

Marc smiled, liking the way Linda was handling herself. He winked at her. "Vance, I think she's got your number."

"She's just flirtin'. Aren't you, honey?"

"Not exactly."

"Don't tell me you're actually interested in China boy over there?" Vance said. Linda's cheeks reddened. "Honey, take it from ole Colonel Stewart, you're makin' a terrible mistake. Our friend Mr. Slater is about to find himself very alone in the PRC. All of his allies have been purged. It seems that Mao didn't appreciate their giving away China's natural resources to the shark of American capitalism."

"Nobody's giving anything away. Unlike some people, we're trying to build the economy of China."

"What does that crack mean?" Vance's eyes bore in on Marc.

"Come on, Vance. Everyone knows the history of CAT. For one hundred years your company has stayed alive by bribing the winning side in every Chinese power struggle."

"It sure beats bribing the losing side."

"You haven't won this one yet." Marc clenched his fist. "Even a CAT has only nine lives, and you've just about run out of your allotment."

"China boy," Vance scoffed, "thinks because he was raised with the Communists, he's the only person qualified to do business in the country."

"And Colonel Stewart thinks a little money under the table will get him anything he wants."

Linda was completely engrossed in the battle of wits when a Chinese voice called out, "Forbes, Stewart, and Slater— please come to customs."

Linda looked up. The crowded room was now empty. Without a word, both men smiled at each other. Then they turned, and each took one of Linda's arms.

Avery Boswell, a lanky, fair-skinned man in cotton slacks

and a short-sleeved dress shirt, placed his two suitcases on the counter in front of the customs inspector. Although Boswell was quite young, the puffy bags under his eyes and the furrows intersecting his forehead belied his age. His dress was casual, as befitted a China trader, but his bearing was formal and erect, like that of a Prussian soldier. His smile seemed forced as the ends of his lips extended into a snarl.

Boswell shifted uneasily while the inspector opened the leather suitcase. "Just personal possessions?" he asked.

"That's all."

The inspector closed that bag and opened the aluminum one. It contained an array of tubes filled with liquids and powders. "What are these?" the inspector asked.

"They're for a hotel-construction project."

The inspector studied one of the tubes. "This is for building hotels?"

"It's for use on the project." Boswell tried to appear nonchalant.

"I am sorry to ask again, but specifically for what use?"

"They are for demolition," Boswell replied impatiently as he wiped a bead of sweat from the corner of his eye.

Since he was not authorized to permit the importation of explosives, the inspector summoned his supervisor.

"What seems to be the problem?" the supervisor asked as he approached.

Boswell intercepted him. "Your man is giving me a hard time."

"Please excuse him. He is just doing his job."

"I am Avery Boswell. Does that name mean anything to you?"

"Of course, Mr. Boswell. You are a respected old friend."

"Excellent. Now as to my demolition materials"—Boswell tried to sound forceful—"I am bringing them at the request of the Hotel Corporation. My client is constructing fifty hotels, which are essential if China is to strengthen its foreign friendships. Do you want me to go to Peking and tell them that you delayed the project by harassing me at the border?"

The supervisor studied Boswell. It would not go well for him if the Englishman complained. His wife had already been criticized for deviationist activities, and he did not need another problem on his record. He looked at the inspector with an expression of disapproval. If the inspector had made the decision on his own, it would not have become his concern; but the inspector was never one to take chances. Knowing he had no other choice, the supervisor stamped Boswell's visa and closed the suitcase. "Please enjoy your trip."

"Thank you," Boswell replied, and left the customs area. When he reached the stairs, he lit a cigarette and inhaled the smoke deep into his lungs. He had taken a big risk.

Boswell stopped at the bank to change his money. Since *Renmenbi* could not be taken out of the country, the bank at the border was the first and last stop for every foreign visitor. For Boswell, who entered China every week, it was an expensive annoyance. In addition to wasting time, he had to pay a five-percent fee whenever he exchanged Chinese currency.

Stuffing his wallet full of ten-yuan bills, the largest denomination available, Boswell walked down a flight of stairs and entered a large, sunny reception room filled with foreigners from the train. A waiter handed him a glass of Tsingtao beer. He took a sip. The beer was light, smooth, and slightly tangy, like the finest German brew. It was the perfect antidote for this hot summer day.

A bell rang. Blue-jacketed Travel Service personnel herded the guests into a dining room next to the tracks. Ceiling fans whirred above the round, neatly set tables draped with white cloths. Boswell spotted an attractive young woman with large round eyes and auburn hair sitting alone in the back. Threading his way between tables, he took the seat opposite her. "Good afternoon. I am Avery Boswell at your service," he said with an antiseptically pure Oxford accent that made him sound like an acting student perfecting his first recitation of Shakespeare.

"I'm pleased to meet you," the woman said in sweetly accented English. "I am Nicole LaFleur."

Boswell filled his plate with dishes of eggplant and chicken, asparagus and shrimp, and steamed fish. "Are you enjoying your meal?" he asked, staring at the soft, full breasts that filled Nicole's clinging lavender cotton blouse.

"It's delicious," Nicole said. "Quite a wonderful welcome for a foreigner, don't you agree?"

"I come here every week," Boswell said, "so the novelty has worn off."

"Every week," Nicole said as she stuffed a pancake with moo shu pork. That's very exciting. This is only my first trip."

"What will you be doing in China?"

"I work for Dior in Paris. I am here to design a line of belts, shoes, bags, and scarves—all coordinated with an Oriental motif."

"If I can be of assistance, please call on me. I am the deputy manging director of Gateshead and MacIntosh."

Nicole looked up with surprise. "Then you must know Lord Henry."

"Lord Henry who?"

"Lord Henry Gateshead. His family founded your company."

"I know that," Boswell stammered, "but how do you know him?"

"I met him on the train from Hong Kong."

Boswell scowled as he searched for the English lord. The

last thing he needed was some old fossil from London upsetting his plans. How could his elaborate intelligence system have failed to alert him? He pulled out a cigarette and struck a wooden match. It broke in half, scarring the tablecloth. Boswell crushed it with his glass. "Damn matches."

"Don't you know Lord Henry?" Nicole asked.

"I've never had the pleasure."

"Let me introduce you. Lord Henry," she blithely called out, waving to Gateshead standing in the doorway. The short and slightly balding man was wearing a gray pinstripe suit, a white shirt with a gold collar pin, a silk navy-blue tie embroidered with miniature crests, and a neatly folded white monogrammed pocket handkerchief. Although his clothes were clearly unsuited to the heat of southern China, he looked quite dapper. Lord Gateshead smiled broadly when he saw Nicole. He combed the back of his hair with his hands as he walked eagerly to the table.

Boswell rose as the Englishman approached. "Lord Gateshead, it is an honor to meet you. I am Avery Boswell, the deputy managing director of Gateshead and MacIntosh in Hong Kong."

"I'm pleased to meet you, Mr. Boswell. I've heard many fine things about you." Lord Gateshead turned to Nicole. "It's a pleasure to see you again, my dear." He softly kissed the back of her hand. "May I join you?"

"By all means." Nicole smiled pleasantly.

"*Elle est très jolie. N'est-ce pas?*" Gateshead said in schoolboy French.

"Quite so," Boswell replied, trying to assess whether the Englishman would interfere in his activities.

"What brings you to China on this trip, Boswell?"

"I plan to discuss trade agreements in coal, tea, and computers, and to negotiate the opening of five new ports for

131

our shipping company."

"I hope you don't require the assistance of the British navy."

"I'm sorry, Lord Gateshead, I don't follow."

"It was an oblique reference to the Opium War. The last time we wanted to open five Chinese ports, we forced England to declare war on China."

"I'll try to avoid war," Boswell joked. He lit a cigarette. Lord Henry's comments had triggered an idea. His objective was to create unrest. If something happened to Gateshead, England might be provoked into acting. It would not be war, but it might be enough to topple Hua Guofeng's already shaky rule. He had to find a way of involving Gateshead. A kidnapping was possible. But first he needed Van Wyck's approval.

"If it would not be too much of a bother," Lord Gateshead asked, "I would appreciate learning more about your activities."

"I'd be honored to discuss some projects, but others I must keep confidential. Even though you are a director, I cannot violate the trust of my clients. I hope you understand my position."

"I understand it entirely, and I respect your loyalty. Perhaps we can consider some of the less confidential matters at another time."

"It would be my pleasure," Boswell replied, relieved that Gateshead had been so understanding; the lord's ancestors would surely not have been as easy to dismiss. Boswell watched Lord Gateshead gazing down the plunging neckline of Nicole's dress while she poured a cup of tea. He wondered whether his life would have been different if he had lived at the time of George Gateshead, the first *taipan* and the founder of the noble house of Gateshead & MacIntosh, instead of at the time of this foppish descendant. Perhaps if he had come of age in an England that still ruled the oceans and offered unlimited opportunities to its enterprising youth, he would have been able to look beyond the social injustices and convince himself that capitalism could survive. But he had come of age during the final decline of the British Empire, and he was certain that his choice, though difficult, had been correct.

At the end of the banquet, the passengers boarded the train for Canton. Samuel Tang sat at the window, gazing at the verdant countryside of southern China. Unlike western China, which is a vast desert, or northern China, which is cold and inhospitable, and even unlike Peking, which is filled with the ever-present dust from the Gobi Desert, southern China is a luscious paradise of semitropical vegetation. From the train tracks to the gently sloping mountains in the distance, endless rows of symmetrical green rice paddies at midgrowth alternated with brown irrigation ditches, giving the land the appearance of a never-ending army in perfect formation.

The train crossed a bridge spanning one of the many rivers intersecting the countryside. The well-worn dirt footpaths paralleling the tracks were filled with workers loaded with hand tools, buffaloes pulling plows, and children playing on their way home from school. Toward the horizon, intricately cultivated, terraced fields were sculpted to the peaks like a succession of winding green staircases.

Sam watched the workers harvesting rice with wooden foot-powered threshers. He felt great pride in the progress made by the People's Republic. When he visited China in 1948, he had seen a country of opium-sotted, war-torn, impoverished peasants. Now he saw a country freed from the ravages of war and opium, in which no one was rich but in which everyone had enough food, good health care, a place to live, and, most importantly, a purpose in life. Although he was a consummate capitalist who found it difficult to support communism, he was also a Chinese who could take satisfaction in the advances of his people.

Yet thinking about Mao's goal of industrializing by the year 2000, he realized how much still had to be accomplished. In many ways China was very primitive. Farmers used tools that had been obsolete in the United States for more than a century. The stark contrast between the wooden foot-powered threshers on Chinese farms and the fully automated reapers on American farms symbolized the vast gap that had to be closed. Still, if the PRC could eliminate hunger and opium in its first quarter-century, why could it not industrialize in the next? Sam was thrilled by the prospect of lending his skills. For most of his life, he had been cut off from his people; but now he was welcomed as a valued friend.

Throughout his career, Sam had thrived on challenge. He had graduated from MIT at the age of nineteen and had received his doctorate from Cal Tech before he was twenty-two. Then he had joined Far West Aviation, where he directed the development of the American Eagle Fighter plane. In advancing to become president of the company, he had built the first commercial jet and all of NASA's top-secret Scarecrow spy satellites. For thirty years the frontier of space had excited him. Now he wanted more. Helping to industrialize a country of almost one billion people was a challenge unlike any ever faced by a Chinese-American.

With Chou dead and Mao dying, new leaders would have to direct China, and they caused Sam great concern. Hua Guofeng had been anointed by Mao; but his primary experience had been as the governor of a province, and there was no evidence that he was capable of leading such a massive country. More disturbing was the presence of Jiang Qing, the empress of the socialist revolution. Jiang practiced the politics of personality and hate, and sought revenge for even the pettiest of reasons. Sam had heard that she once forced a worker to stand barefoot in the cold for failing to heat her room, that she closed a shipyard because its noise prevented her from sleeping, and that she razed a forest because it blocked her view. She had allied herself with the radicals. If they were permitted to gain control, they would stop industrial development, purge competent officials, and end the emerging friendship with the United States.

It was up to Sam and his allies to stop her. Their plan was good, as were some of their people. Sam was especially pleased to have Marc Slater on his team, even if Marc did not yet know they were working together. But other operatives caused him concern. Because of the decades of conflict between the United States and China, there were few experienced agents. Rookies, like Linda Forbes, would have to be relied on for several of the key slots, and this increased everyone's risk.

Closing his eyes, Sam recalled his first parachute jump. He remembered the simultaneous feelings of panic and exhilaration as he floated through the air. He was out of control, yet he was free. He was risking death, yet he felt completely alive. His face broke into a broad smile. Why was he always happiest when he was taking huge risks?

"Sam is such wonderful company," Marc Slater said to Beatrice Tang, who was sitting to Sam's right.

"He's very tired. Leave him to his dreams."

"You're makin' a mistake," Vance Stewart warned. "Don't you see Sam's smile? Any man who dreams with that kind of smile should be immediately awakened and chastised by his wife."

Beatrice looked at Sam. His eyes were closed and his face still had that expression of enigmatic pleasure. She laughed gently. "My dear Vance, I'll gladly permit Sam any fantasies he desires; but I can assure you that at this moment his thoughts are far away from sex. Sexual ecstasy is softer. Sam's expression is too electric. Don't be fooled by his smile. Watch how the lines of his eyes flare to his temples and how his eyebrows arch toward the bridge of his nose. Can you feel the intensity? That's not the look of sexual pleasure. That's the look of a man trying to conquer some new challenge."

As Marc watched the Tangs, he envied Sam's luck in having a woman who understood him so well. It had been that way with him and Carolyn. She had been his closest friend and confidante. Now there was a gaping void. There was no shortage of attractive women willing to cater to his every whim. But he needed more. Besides mutual respect and friendship, he wanted a woman who could provide a spark, a magic.

Marc looked at Beatrice and Vance. Both were still lost in their own thoughts. "You're quite a woman," he said to Beatrice. "Not only do you understand Sam, but you have actually managed to silence Vance. I don't know which is the greater accomplishment."

"Understanding Sam isn't that difficult; and as for Vance, I'd never try to silence him. His conversation may be off-color, but it's usually quite charming."

"Off-color? Surely you can't be talkin' about me?"

"My dear Mr. Stewart, I heard stories about your legendary sexual proclivities long before I came to China."

"Where did such malicious stories originate?"

"From you, of course. Your reputation for sexual achievement is exceeded only by your reputation for bragging about your sexual achievements." Beatrice and Marc laughed as Vance blushed slightly.

Sam opened his eyes at the sound of their laughter. "What's going on?"

"Absolutely nothing," Marc replied. "We're merely discussing Vance's reputation for sexual prowess."

"A fascinating subject," Sam said. "Perhaps we could hear the story of the Bulgarian Women's Volleyball Team or Vance's mass initiation of Chinese flight attendants into the Mile High Club."

"My favorite," Marc said, "is Vance and the Red Guard in the Temple of Heaven. It's so awe-inspiring. It's virtually a religious experience."

Beatrice's face turned beet red. "He's kidding, isn't he? In the Temple of Heaven with a Red Guard? You really didn't, did you?"

"Of course not," Vance laughed. "It was on top of the Great Wall, not inside the Temple of Heaven."

"Was that your attempt to reenact Genghis Khan's rape of China?"

"Don't mind Marc," Vance retorted. "He's just jealous of my success with the ladies."

"Success? Your success is confined to your fantasy relationships with the pictures in that magazine you tried to bring through customs."

"Did you try to bring in another *Playboy*?" Beatrice asked. "I think you're just trying to provoke a reaction."

"The *Playboy* is for market research," Vance replied.

"Market research? For what market?"

"For my new venture. I plan to bring pornography to China."

"You must be kidding."

"I'm absolutely serious. It'd be a fantastic business. On the surface the Chinese are so damn prudish. Men don't get married until they're about twenty-eight, and, if you accept the word of Mao, there is no premarital sex. The Communists want us to believe that their men have no sex drive. Well, that drive may be repressed in revolutionary fervor, but it's still there. I love to watch the Chinese when they see the pictures in the magazine. They're embarrassed, but they always look."

"You're perverted," Sam scoffed.

"Perhaps, but I'll guarantee you that beneath the stern Communist morality are five hundred million horny men. China is still caught up in the ethos of its revolution. The generation of Mao will do anythin' the Party says, but that generation is dying. New generations will demand more. No civilization has ever survived without prostitution and pornography. China won't be the first."

"Are you serious?" Slater queried.

"Of course. Pornography satisfies a basic human need. One day these people are goin' to hunger for sexual fantasies; and when that day comes, I'm goin' to be ready with whatever they want."

"While you're bringing back porn," Sam chided, "why don't you also bring back opium?"

Vance winced at Sam's remark and tried to deflect the conversation. "Opium isn't the business for me. It's too much of a conflict with tobacco. But I promise you that someday the Chinese will relearn the habit. Then opium will be everywhere. They can no more keep opium out of China than they can keep marijuana out of the U.S. of A."

"Are you really willing to ruin China just to make money?"

"Come on, Sam. Stop being so all-fired holy. I have no intention of ruinin' China. I'm offerin' a product. If the Chinese want to buy, that's their concern. I won't make moral judgments, but I refuse to pretend that the People's

Republic is a paradise on earth. The PRC is filled with men who have the same drives as those in every other country. The Communists may have repressed one generation, but they'll never repress the next."

Marc stared at the self-satisfied smirk on Vance's face, trying to guess if he was serious. Despite his reservations, he had to accept the logic in Vance's arguments. He had already noticed a decline of the revolutionary spirit and an increase in the demand for consumer goods. Perhaps pornography would be next. For several minutes no one spoke. Finally Vance stood up, walked down the aisle. "Son of a bitch!" Sam muttered.

"Don't let him get to you," Marc advised. "He's all talk."

"He's a bastard, as is his whole dung-ridden family." Sam's voice sounded distant. "His family and mine go back a long way. We've been fighting each other for more than a century. It was his ancestors who shanghaied mine from China." Sam paused and shook his head. "I'd watch out for Stewart."

"Because he's selling opium or because he's working with Jiang Qing?" Marc asked.

"I see you already know."

"Just a calculated guess." Marc paused and lit his pipe. "What I don't know is what you're doing here."

"Selling airplanes."

"Like I'm buying oil?"

"Exactly, my friend."

"And I assume that I cannot ask about your assignment."

"Not just now."

"Is there nothing you can tell me?"

Sam smiled. "Just know that I'll be there for you—and that, as they say in China, I won't forget to wrap our plans in silk before it rains."

10: The Sound of Music

Colonel Li followed Shen Mo, Jiang Qing's personal assistant, into the screening room. In the reflection of the film, he could see Jiang sitting in a high-backed swivel chair behind an electronic control console. On the screen, an Englishwoman was warbling to seven enraptured children in the countryside beneath majestic, snowcapped mountains. Although the colonel had never been outside of China, he assumed that the mountains were somewhere in Europe. He shifted uncomfortably as he waited. He had performed his assignment perfectly, but with Jiang Qing there was always uncertainty. She was so mercurial.

"This song will be over in just a minute," Shen whispered.

Colonel Li stared curiously at the strangely dressed figures. This was the first Western film he had ever seen. Before the revolution he had been too young and his family too poor to attend the cinema, and now Chinese theaters showed only films produced by Jiang herself. Although he had enjoyed *The Red Detachment of Women* and *The*

140

White-Haired Girl, he would have liked to see something other than stories about heroic women fighting against capitalist oppressors. He tried to listen to the words, but his English was too limited and his mind too preoccupied with the envelope in his hands. It was his passport to ultimate security.

Li thought about the old calligrapher. Rong Yi had served the Party for many years and had deserved a better fate, but there had been no other way. This was his opportunity. He would not spoil it with sentiment.

As the figures on the screen laughed and embraced, Jiang Qing pushed a small red button in front of her seat. Fluorescent ceiling lights blinked on and the frolicking Austrian family disappeared into the screen's shimmering metallic whiteness. Jiang swiveled around and smiled politely. "Comrade Li, I'm pleased to see you."

"The honor is mine." Li bowed.

"Did your research go well?"

"Perfectly."

"And the artist?"

"I'm afraid he was forced to retire, but I'm sure you will be pleased with his last work."

Jiang opened the manila envelope and studied the parchment inside. Colonel Li watched as she made inaudible comments to herself. She did not look well. Her complexion was pallid and her cheeks were becoming jowled. Although she was still attractive, she was no longer the beautiful film actress who had captivated Mao. Jiang placed the document back in the envelope. "You've done well," she said.

"I am pleased to be of service."

"If I'm not mistaken, you're from Tangshan, aren't you?"

"I am." Colonel Li tried to control his expectation.

"There is an opening for director of the Tangshan Municipal District." Jiang offered the bargain that his

141

friends had previously sealed for him. "Would that be of interest to you?"

"I would be honored to assist Chairman Mao and the People's Republic in any capacity that you request."

"If you do well and continue to serve me, there may be a governorship of Hebei Province available."

A feeling of joy surged through Colonel Li. A governorship! It was more than he had hoped. He wiped the smile from his face. It was not appropriate for him to appear too pleased. "I am your loyal servant."

"We will not forget what you have done," Jiang continued as the colonel bowed his head with the humility that the occasion required, "but perhaps this small pouch will give you some indication of my gratitude."

Colonel Li opened the pouch. Inside were three pieces of dark green jade with ancient figures etched upon them. "They are from the Han Tombs," Shen Mo said. "They are almost two thousand years old."

"Please remember that you can depend on us. We won't dismantle the bridge after crossing the river," Jiang said, echoing an ancient Chinese proverb as Colonel Li admired the stones. Then she swiveled back around and pressed the small red button. The room instantly became dark and the frolicking Austrian family magically reappeared.

Jiang Qing smiled as she watched Julie Andrews romp with the children. In her hands she held the key to control of the People's Republic. When Mao died, everyone would learn that she was his chosen successor. Thoughts of gaining ultimate power occupied her mind. She took no notice of how well the children on the screen had learned their lessons.

11: Dong Fang Binguan

Marc Slater stared out the middle window on the driver's side as the Chinese copy of a Mercedes-Benz minibus motored toward the massive expanse of four-story buildings housing the Chinese Export Commodities Fair—or, as it was commonly known, the Canton Fair. On the first floors were mazes of exhibition halls featuring samples of all Chinese products. Silks, carpets, tractors, jade carvings, model hydroelectric power plants, tea, computers, seafood, mining equipment, medicines, and even petroleum were presented in elaborate displays. On the upper three floors, set on either side of boulevardlike hallways, were hundreds of conference rooms, each filled with clusters of tables and chairs and glass-covered cabinets containing the two essentials for doing business in China: ashtrays and teapots. Ten months a year these floors were empty and the exhibition halls were visited only by schoolchildren and tourists. But for one month starting each April 15 and October 15, the buildings came to life as the Chinese welcomed a controlled invasion of merchants from throughout the world.

The fair was a marvelous spectacle, brilliantly stage-managed by the Chinese, who loved to watch greedy foreigners drooling over the prospect of finding nine hundred million new customers or a supply of labor so inexpensive that they could easily undercut their competitors. From the time of the first Hongs, it had been the only door in China open to foreign businessmen.

Months in advance, invitations were sent to selected merchants, informing them when they could come and how long they could stay. Except for the oldest of foreign friends, none was permitted to visit the rest of the country or to come into contact with the average Chinese worker. It was a system designed to keep the people free from barbarian influences.

The day before the opening, the most favored of the businessmen arrived at the Dong Fang Binguan, the East Wind Hotel. The same people reappeared every six months, falling into their standard cliques as if they had never left China. A United Nations of international traders, they drank together, discussed world politics, and complained about the problems of dealing with the Chinese.

The next morning, after the playing of "The East Is Red," the traders were treated to the industrial smorgasbord of China. In each of the conference rooms, delegates representing the regional branches of every Chinese trade corporation waited with their products. Customers were free to wander into any room, inspect the samples, and negotiate contracts. It was a tantalizing opportunity for even the most established capitalist.

Shopping was fascinating, but buying was often impossible, or, as the Chinese would say, difficult. In many fields, goods were sold out by the end of the first morning, offering only those who had run fast enough to make the first appointments a chance to place orders. Delivery times were often quoted in years; and when the Chinese wanted to discourage their foreign friends, prices could double within a morning. Still, despite the difficulties, the fair remained an enticing lure to foreign merchants.

The minibus passed through a guarded gate and into the parking lot of the Dong Fang. Marc walked up the stone steps into the hotel and squinted to adjust to the change in light. The cavernous lobby was unfurnished. Long, narrow, and dimly lit, it had the appearance of a darkened subway platform. Welcoming banners with quotes from Chairman Mao hung from the walls. The business cards of guests were displayed on a bulletin board. A large red poster written in English listed the daily activities. Today's outings featured visits to a people's commune and an ivory factory, while tomorrow's offered a boat ride on the Pearl River and an excursion to the Conghua Hot Springs. Marc smiled as he thought about the springs. It was among his favorite spots in China.

The passengers from the train were crowded around a rectangular bullpen on the left, contesting for what they thought would be the choicest rooms. Although everyone's assignment had been predetermined, the Chinese did nothing to discourage the frenzied competition. The Nigerians, unaware that in China anything modern was rarely preferable, demanded rooms in the new wing. They argued until the manager graciously acceded and registered them in rooms to which they had been assigned for more than a month. As they walked away, Marc wondered if they would still be pleased when they saw the shabby condition of their accommodations. He was grateful that he was no longer subjected to such inconveniences.

"Slater old friend." The room manager bowed politely. "I

have assigned you to a room on the sixth floor of the old wing." He handed Marc a card that read #638. This was M. H. Schaffer's permanent room. The company paid $11 a day to guarantee its availability even if no one from Schaffer was in the hotel. "I hope you will find it comfortable."

"I'm grateful for your assistance," Marc replied, pleased that such a small sum of money could guarantee him the best room in Canton.

Turning the knob, Marc opened the door. No key was required, because rooms in Chinese hotels were rarely kept locked. He flicked the switch for the white, dish-shaped lamp dangling from the ceiling. Everything was as he had left it, dingy but clean. The two single pine beds, their varnish peeling, were neatly made. The white cotton bedspreads were rolled up by the footboards. The mosquito netting, which hung from hoops attached to the ceiling, were rolled into the shape of inverted cones, tied with sashes, and tucked behind the headboards. No one could sleep in southern China without using the netting. The ever-present Chinese fan was on top of a rickety wooden table that stood between two soft cushioned chairs. A red Thermos of hot water painted with a picture of the Great Wall rested on a wooden cabinet. A varnished desk with a surface too bumpy for writing was placed next to a curtained glass door leading to the balcony.

Marc whipped aside the double-layered white curtains and stepped outside. Ringed by the quadrangle of the hotel, the wonderfully intricate courtyard was like a miniature park. Palms, cypresses, and banyans interspersed with ponds stocked with golden fish created a pastoral setting. Below his balcony, three boys, dressed in blue workers' uniforms, sat studying. To their right, two girls played badminton. A path wound through a garden and across a stone footbridge toward a marble veranda filled with foreigners talking business or taking late-afternoon naps.

Marc saw Alexandra Koo sitting on the terrace next to a stone lantern. A well-dressed young Chinese girl, wearing a blue flared skirt and a white silk blouse, approached. She was, Marc decided, one of Jiang Qing's aides. The two women moved to a deserted corner and talked privately. Marc wished he could eavesdrop.

He stepped back inside and placed a cassette of progressive jazz on his tape deck. Opening a bamboo box, he sprinkled four pinches of tea into a porcelain cup. As he filled the cup with hot water, he watched the dried tea leaves and jasmine flowers expand, almost coming to life as they formed patterns like those in a Chinese watercolor. He studied the tea for a moment before permitting it to steep. Unlike Western tea, whose potent caffeinated taste instantly dominates a cup, Chinese tea has a delicate flavor that becomes more sophisticated over time. The teas, he thought, were much like the women. Western women tended to be strong, passionate, and direct; while Chinese women tended to be softer, more mysterious, and usually more complex. For those with sufficient patience, Chinese women offered a uniquely subtle beauty.

There was only one problem. Because of the desire to restrict foreign influence, women in China were forbidden to have affairs with Westerners. Even spending time together was difficult. Once in a while someone broke the rules, but the results were always bad for both sides. It was a pitfall Marc knew he had to avoid. Picking up the phone, he called Linda. "Hi," he said. "Do you want to take a walk?"

"I'd love to, but I can't right now. I'm going jogging."

"I'll join you."

There was a pause. "How about a rain check? I'm just on

147

my way out."

"You can't leave. There's an old Chinese rule that once you save somebody's life, you are eternally responsible for them. I'm now your ward. You can't leave me alone in the hotel."

Linda laughed. "I'll be back in half an hour. Until then, don't open your door or talk to anyone."

There was a click on the line. Marc smiled as he put on his jogging clothes. Nothing appealed to him more than a challenge.

Linda, wearing purple nylon shorts and a lavender polo shirt, pulled her hair into a ponytail and clipped it with a red barrette. She rotated her neck in a circle, feeling the knots of tension dissolve. After touching her fingers to the floor, she swung her leg onto the desk to stretch out her thigh muscles. The limberness of her body pleased her.

She started down the hall, but before she could reach the elevator, the quiet of the Dong Fang was interrupted by a lurid wolf whistle. She stopped abruptly. Vance Stewart, his safari shirt half unbuttoned, stood in the doorway of his room with a glass of bourbon in his hand and a Cheshire-cat grin on his face. "What have we here?"

"I'm going jogging."

"It's too hot." Vance held out his glass. "Have a bourbon instead."

"Perhaps when I get back."

"I hate to drink alone."

"And I hate to jog alone, but sometimes we all must suffer."

"Please stay. I could be very helpful to you."

Linda was intrigued by Vance's offer. "I'll be back in half

an hour."

"And we'll have dinner?"

The door to room 638 opened. Marc Slater, dressed in a pair of navy shorts and a crimson Harvard T-shirt, stepped into the corridor. "She can't because I asked her first."

"You're a snake in the grass." Vance turned to Linda. "I'd watch John Harvard if I were you."

Linda smiled. "I can take care of myself. Now if you'll both excuse me . . ."

"I'm going with you," Marc said. "Why don't you join us, Vance?"

Stewart laughed. "I don't want to destroy my business. The more people get into runnin', the less they smoke. I can't afford to set a bad example for all my loyal customers."

A short, wiry Chinese man with dark, intense eyes and long hair that was heavily slicked down walked from the elevator. "Evenin', Lawrence," Vance called to Wong Chuyun, the managing director of Chinese American Tobacco. "Care for a brisk five-mile jog?"

Wong pulled a cigarette from the pocket of his brown safari suit. "No, thank you," he replied. He greeted Marc and introduced himself to Linda.

Linda looked nervously at her watch. She had only twenty minutes to find the peasant with the chicken who had met her in the station. And she had to meet him alone. She could not get rid of Marc now, but perhaps when they reached the park, she could find a way. "I hate to break up this tête-à-tête, but I have to get back so I can telex New York."

"I'm ready," Marc said, and they turned down the hall.

"I'll keep your drink on ice," Vance called as the elevator closed.

*   *   *

"What was that all about?" Wong asked.

"What was what all about?" Vance said, pouring another bourbon.

"Look, Vance, this is the most important trip we've ever made."

"So?" Stewart drank his bourbon.

Wong took a long drag. "I know that you like to drink, that you enjoy young women, and that you relish baiting Slater. But on this trip you're going to be on your best behavior. No liquor, no women, and no games. *Ni ting de dong ma*?"

Stewart stared indignantly at Wong as he raised his glass to his lips. "Who do you think you're talkin' to? I'm the president of CAT. You're the managing director of one lousy branch. I can fire your ass anytime I want. I own the company, and you, my rice-eating friend, work for me. Where do you get the balls to tell me how I should behave?"

"I know you own the company." Wong calmly measured his response. "I've devoted my life to CAT. I've never undermined your authority, but I'll not stand here and be told that I'm just a disposable employee in a do-nothing branch. Without my family, there'd be no CAT. When your grandfather made a deal with the wrong empress, who forged the alliance with the Dowager? And when your grandfather wanted to stay aligned with the dynasty, who arranged the contracts with the republican warlords? Who set up the opium deal with the Japanese during World War Two? Who reached the pact with Mao in 'forty-eight, courted Jiang when she took power, and arranged for you to be the only American who could enter the PRC? For three generations my family has helped CAT avoid every political crisis in China. If you want to fire me, that's your prerogative. But if you do, I won't have any trouble finding someone, like Marc Slater, who'll accept me on my terms."

"Come on, Lawrence." Stewart buttoned his shirt. "You're over reactin'. I'd never try to do business without you. We're a team." He patted Wong on the shoulder. "We need each other. I just don't like being threatened."

"Neither do I, my friend."

"Then I was wrong. I'm just tired from the trip. But you must know that workin' together is more important than anythin' else."

"If you want to work with me, it's no alcohol, no women, and no games on this trip. *Ni ting de dong ma?*"

"How 'bout if I promise to watch the booze, be cautious with the women, and stay away from Slater? Will that satisfy you?"

Wong was not comfortable with Stewart's response. He had made strong commitments to Jiang Qing and was worried that Stewart would not be able to hold up his part of the bargain. But it was too late to back out. He had to let his partner save face. "Your word is good enough for me."

"Good." Stewart flashed his Cheshire-cat smile. "Then let's drink to our partnership. How about a cup of tea? *Ni ting de dong ma?*"

Linda and Marc jogged from the hotel, across Renmin (People's) Road, and into Liuhua Park. Marc waved at the guard in the ticket booth, who politely smiled back. People entering the park were supposed to pay twenty cents, but an exception was made for foreign joggers because the Chinese respected physical exercise and did not want to embarrass the joggers, who rarely carried any money.

They ran to the lake, along a path bordered by yellow, red, and purple orchids that grew wild in the midst of verdant tropical ferns. Tall palm trees lined the route. Their reflections glistened brilliantly in the still water, like pictures painted on a mirror. Elderly women cast mesh nets for fish while their grandchildren played on the grass. A young couple floated peacefully in a wooden rowboat. Linda felt secure as she listened to the rhythmic pace of Marc's stride. "I'm glad we have the chance to be alone." Linda smiled warmly. "I want to thank you for rescuing me from Vance."

"You wanted to thank me?" Marc laughed, noticing that Linda was easily keeping pace with him. "It should be the other way around. You saved my life on the train."

"It was nothing."

"It was something to me. It's the only life I've got."

"I was just lucky to be in the right place at the right time."

"But you weren't there by accident, were you? You told Alexandra Koo something about a letter."

Linda blushed. "That was a ruse. I just wanted to talk to you."

"Why?" Marc asked, hoping she would tell him of her involvement.

She patted him on his rear and smiled. "Because I like your legs."

"And that's all you can tell me?"

Linda paused. "All right. I like your eyes, too. They're kind and sensitive. But that's the last of my compliments, at least until I get to know you better."

"My ego appreciates the massage, but that wasn't what I was referring to." Marc's voice became serious. "Tell me about the Jade Gate."

Linda looked away. "That's the second time you've asked me about it."

"And I still haven't gotten an answer."

"If I find out what it is, you'll be the first to know."

"You know we're working together."

"We probably are. But I can't violate my instructions, not even for you." Linda glanced at her watch. There were only five minutes left until her meeting with the peasant. She had to find a way of getting rid of Marc. She slowed down. "I've got a stitch."

"OK, we'll walk."

"You keep running. I'll meet you back at the hotel."

"No. I'll stay with you."

"I'm supposed to be protecting you, not vice versa."

"Exactly." Marc put his arm on Linda's shoulder. She shivered. "And if you stay in the park, who's going to protect me on the way back?"

She stared at him, wanting to be with him and yet knowing she had to be alone. "You're a big boy. You can take care of yourself. Besides, I have some things that I'd like to think over."

"I'd like to share what's bothering you."

"Please," Linda entreated. "Not this time."

"You're not making it easy to get to know you."

"I'm not trying to."

"Never let it be said that I'm not one to take a hint," Marc replied. Then he turned and jogged back down the path.

Linda cursed herself as she ran across a covered bridge surrounded by a floating garden of white flowers and dark green lily pads. She was annoyed that she had been forced to push him away. She hoped she could make it up to him later. She watched a group of old men practicing *tai chi chuan* and marveled at the precision of their agonizingly deliberate movements. These perfectly disciplined dancers in their martial-arts ballet could have handled a situation like hers and not lost their composure; but she did not have their patience or self-control. Despite her grandfather and her training, she was still a Westerner.

Reaching the far side of the lake, she ran onto the next

chain of islands. The setting sun, reflecting through the humid summer air, emitted an orange hue. She wiped the sweat from her forehead. It felt good. She enjoyed sweating as she ran. It relaxed her. The sweat was her body's way of purging itself of its poisons, and today there were many to expunge.

She jogged onto the last of the islands. The man she had met in the station was not there. She hoped he would arrive soon. Finding a seat beneath the drooping branches of a banyan tree, she rested in the tranquility of the park. Across the lake was a huge billboard with a painting of two Red Guards holding a cowering landlord at gunpoint. The caption read, "Chairman Mao says, 'Political power comes out of the barrel of a gun.'" It was just like Mao, Linda thought, to place a stark reminder of military power in such a pacific setting.

Two of the men who had been practicing *tai chi* strolled onto the island, sat down on the bank, and dangled their feet in the lake. Linda watched uneasily, worried that their presence might frighten off the peasant. She debated leaving, but decided to follow the instructions she had been given. She inched closer to eavesdrop on their conversation.

"Two years of digging and they finally found these pits in front of the dung-ridden mound filled with thousands of life-size sculptures of that bastard's entire army." The old man described the recently excavated tomb of the Qin emperor. "The pox-ridden emperor forced hundreds of thousands of workers to labor for thirty years to sculpt those statues, and for what? After he died, his tomb was ransacked and not one of the statues lifted a hand to protect his possessions. A pox on all emperors for being so foolish." The old man laughed and stroked his wispy goatee.

"I can't believe," the second man said, "that the man who united China, universalized the Chinese language, and built the Great Wall would have been foolish enough to believe that stone figures could protect his treasury."

"Is your head filled with congee? The stupid tyrant arranged his soldiers in battle formation to defend his possessions for eternity; but any rice-eating peasant could have known how to rob his grave."

"*Si shi er fei* [Things are not always what they seem]." The second man nodded to Linda. Although he looked twenty years older than the peasant in the station, it was the same man. She smiled, realizing that the discussion was being staged for her benefit.

"What in the name of pig's intestines are you talking about?" The first old man spit into the lake.

"The statues were an elaborate trick. The emperor knew his grave would be robbed, so he placed copies of his treasures inside his tomb just as he placed copies of his soldiers outside. The real treasures are buried in secret vaults near the tombs."

Linda gasped. Such vaults could contain relics of immense value.

"That's water-buffalo shit. My elder son is the deputy assistant supervisor of diggers. He'd have told me if they had found such vaults."

"Perhaps he does not know. It is possible that whoever discovered these vaults has kept their existence a secret, because they intend to smuggle the treasures out of the country."

"Have you been smoking old rope?" the first man asked. "To dig up a Qin treasure chest and smuggle it out of the country would be impossible unless you had the backing of someone very important."

No one had to fill in the name for Linda.

"But it is possible," the peasant asserted.

"Just like it's possible for a hunter to catch a rabbit by

waiting for it to run into a tree and kill itself. You've been in the sun too long."

The old men put on their shoes, bowed politely, and walked away. Linda had to act. Their information gave her an advantage, but it also heightened the pressure to move against Jiang Qing and Alexandra Koo. She stood up and jogged back to the hotel, hoping that Marc would be there.

Feeling refreshed, Marc Slater stepped out of the shower and stared at his body in the mirror. Though he weighed five pounds more than he would have liked, he was in excellent shape. He might no longer be the blue-eyed spirit who runs like the wind, but he could still handle a five-mile jog. He suspected that Linda was meeting someone in the park. There could be no other explanation for her actions. Despite her denials, he was certain that she was involved with the Jade Gate. When she returned, he would have to press for answers.

There was a knock. Wrapping a towel around his waist, Marc opened the door and peered outside. Sen Tailing was standing in front of him. A tall, well-built man in his mid-thirties, Sen looked the part of a prosperous executive in his neatly tailored business suit and expensive chrome glasses. Sen greeted his employer. "Am I coming at a bad time?"

"Absolutely not. I was hoping to see you." Marc opened the door.

Sen pulled it back almost shut. "You might want to put on something besides the towel." He nodded to his left.

Marc looked into the hallway. A young woman wearing a pale blue silk blouse and a navy pleated skirt blushed and glanced toward her feet. She was very tall for a Chinese, almost statuesque. The lines of her body flowed in soft curves from her graceful shoulders, through her reed-thin waist, and down her firm, slender legs. Her hair was pulled back and tied in two long braids that extended to the middle of her back. Marc stood motionless, staring at her from behind the door. He heard Sen's voice. "Are you going to change and invite us in?"

Marc hurriedly put on his clothes, speculating on the identity of the woman. She was neither Sen's wife nor his mistress—he knew both of them. He combed his hair, splashed on cologne, and greeted his guests.

"Marc Slater"—Sen escorted the woman into the room—"I'd like to introduce Hu Meili."

The young woman smiled warmly as she extended her hand. Her bright, intelligent eyes pulled Marc magnetically toward her. "I'm very pleased to meet you." Her voice was lilting, her English accent almost British. "My father has told me so much about you."

"Your father?" Marc asked, wanting to touch her.

She smiled. Her high cheekbones and firm, narrow chin gave her face an appealing angularity. "Hu Shengte."

Hu Shengte was a member of the Politburo and China's leading petroleum expert. He was also one of Marc's oldest friends. They had met in 1936. A hero of the Long March, Hu had taken Marc under his wing and instructed him in the art of war. Almost four decades later he had helped Marc to obtain lucrative petroleum contracts. The new oil agreements had been based largely on their friendship. "So you're Meili?" Marc said, seeing her father's face in her eyes.

The young woman blushed again. "I hope you're not disappointed."

"I am honored to meet the daughter of my *lao pengyou*."

Meili lifted the Thermos. "Would you like some tea?"

"Please." Marc watched as she sprinkled the leaves in the cup and poured the water. There was a graceful rhythm to her movements. She bowed respectfully as she placed the cup in his hands. "How is your father?" he asked.

"He is fine. He is looking forward to seeing you tomorrow."

"Tomorrow?"

"Meili is to take you to a special meeting," Sen replied.

"Where?" Marc asked, unable to take his eyes from the young woman.

"You are to join the tour to the Conghua Hot Springs." Meili smiled delicately. "It would be best if you booked the most expensive room. It only costs eighteen dollars."

Marc smiled. "I'm not worried about the money."

"He would like you to bring the envelope you received this morning."

"Of course," Marc replied, pleased to be rid of that obligation. "Sen, are you going to be with us?" he asked.

"I have to go to Peking to arrange the trip to see Deng."

"All right," Marc said, wondering whose orders Sen was following. "But before you go, do you think you could translate your letter? I picked up most of the clues, but I'd like you to confirm them." Marc was anxious to see if Sen would stop him from speaking in front of Meili. The more Sen allowed him to say, the higher her position. Marc walked to the window so that he could see both of them. "Correct me if I'm wrong. Jiang Qing is holding Mao in his hospital room, and only those who support her have access to him." Sen nodded his agreement. "Takamura has made a deal with Russia for Xinjiang oil and is now supplying the Russians with weapons." Sen nodded again. "Operation Jade Gate is being directed by Alexandra Koo. Linda Forbes is one of those trying to stop her."

Sen smiled. "You learn fast, my friend."

"Stewart and Wong are dealing in opium with Jiang Qing."

"You have the makings of a first-grade spy," Sen said.

Marc bowed respectfully. "You are a good teacher."

"Why don't we go somewhere to eat," Sen suggested. "Meili and I would like to review some documents with you."

"Perfect," Marc replied, grabbing his jacket. Suddenly he recalled he had a previous engagement with Linda. Lifting the phone, he called her room. There was no answer. She probably had not returned from running. He jotted a note. It was unfortunate he could not bring her along. It would be fascinating to see her and Meili together. They were the best that both cultures had to offer.

12: The National People's Archives

PEKING

Chang Shuli—or Little Chang, as she was called by all who knew her—began her final inspection of the National People's Archives before leaving for the night. Walking the fifteen corridors, she carefully checked the locks on the battleship-gray steel cabinets that gave the archives the appearance of an American high-school locker room. Inside these innocuous chests were the most important documents in China. So vital were the contents that only members of the Politburo, Mao's personal staff, and Little Chang were ever permitted inside.

Finding everything in order, Little Chang began to lock the outside door. There were three closures: a combination padlock on the top, an electronic lock in the middle, and a restricted cylinder on the bottom. As a measure of extra control, only Chairman Mao and Little Chang were able to open more than one. If neither was available, people from three different branches of government were needed to gain access.

Little Chang signed out with the guard in the hallway. Upon taking the job, she had been surprised that only one man was assigned for protection, but Chou En-lai had assuaged her concern. "In a world of believers," he had said, "no one need fear the heretic."

Certain that the archives were secure, Little Chang crossed massive Tian'anmen Square toward the National History Museum, where she was to attend a leadership-development class. She and her husband, Sen Bao, had been among the one hundred Party cadres selected to participate. For both it was a signal honor, open only to those who were being groomed for the highest levels of bureaucracy.

Though Little Chang was only thirty, she had already attained a position of considerable importance. She and her husband, a manager of the China Corporation for the Promotion of International Trade, were happy together, loved each other, and managed to earn more than two hundred and fifty dollars a month. They had a fine apartment in a modern building, two new bicycles, a private telephone, and a color television set. Now perhaps they were also going to have a child. Life was as good as she could ever have wanted.

Little Chang had already reached the museum when she realized she had forgotten her notebook. She checked her watch. There was still time to return to the archives. Rushing through the square, she scolded herself. It was not like her to be so careless.

Taking the elevator to the fourth floor, she walked to the archives. The hallway was empty. The guard had probably gone to the bathroom. She reached for the padlock at the top of the door. It was missing. She looked around in confusion. Could she have forgotten to attach the lock? No!

She might have forgotten the notebook, but never the padlock. She checked the other locks. They were open. The door was ajar. A ray of light filtered through a crack. She was certain that she had turned out the lights.

How, she asked, could anyone have broken into the archives? She had left only ten minutes before. It would have taken more time than that to locate three officials to open the door. Besides, they would have put their names on the still blank admittance sheet; the punishment for failing to sign in was severe. Yet someone was definitely inside.

Little Chang stood frozen as she peered through the crack. She had to remain composed. It was her duty to protect the archives. She wanted to summon the guards but was afraid that the intruder might escape if she left her post. She felt as if she had been personally violated.

Two lights shone from the back, but she could not hear or see anyone. She closed the door and tiptoed down the first corridor. There was a crash. She jumped. Her heart beat furiously. A vein in her neck throbbed. She tried to keep her wits. The intruder had only dropped a vault box. The next six corridors were empty. She crept to the eighth and heard a voice coming from the back. No one was in the ninth, tenth, or eleventh. Her concern increased. The most important papers were stored in the last rows. She stopped at the twelfth. Now she could hear the voice. It was a woman's. She pressed her body against the lockers and peeked into the thirteenth corridor. It was empty, as was the fourteenth. She was finding it difficult to breathe. The only row remaining was the fifteenth, and it held the country's most highly classified papers.

She peered into the rear corridor. There was a woman about five foot five, dressed in a neatly tailored gray Zhongshan suit, standing at the far end. Little Chang wanted to yell for help, but she stopped herself. The woman looked familiar. She crept to the far end of the fourteenth corridor. She did not have to check the name on the lockers to see which was open. It was the private vault of Chairman Mao.

Little Chang inched around the corner. At first she could see only the woman's hands. They were long and slender with perfectly manicured nails. There were rings of gold and jade on several fingers. She watched silently as they sorted a stack of papers and removed a manila envelope with three red wax seals. She gasped. The red wax was the Chairman's private color, and the envelope contained his last will and testament.

A flame flared. Little Chang pulled back. She smelled the smoke. The odor was perfumed like melting paraffin, not acrid like burning paper. She edged forward until she could once more see the hands. The right held a marble chop covered with soft red wax. She watched as seals were stamped on another envelope. The hands shoved the original will into a briefcase and then placed the newly sealed document in the vault. Suddenly it became clear. There was only one person who could have obtained the combination and borrowed Mao's personal chop.

A lump formed in the hollow of Little Chang's throat. Jiang Qing was the most powerful woman in China and one of the few people with access to Mao. If she accosted her, Jiang would claim to be acting under Mao's orders, as perhaps she was. Although Little Chang had heard that Mao and his wife were now estranged, she could not risk challenging Jiang by herself. She needed allies who would know that she was telling the truth.

Creeping from her hiding place, Little Chang ran toward the entrance. There was a sound behind her. She turned. Jiang Qing stood at the end of the room, her hand clenched into a fist. "Stop right there, comrade." Jiang strode toward her. Little Chang tried to control her trembling body. She had to escape. Using all her strength, she tugged open the door.

"I order you to stop." The words reverberated in Little Chang's ears as she fled into the hallway. She looked for the guard. No one was there. She reached the stairs. Mao's wife was behind her. Starting to sprint, she slipped on the newly waxed floors. She grasped the bannister for balance. Jiang screamed something, but Little Chang was too frightened to hear the words. She reached the landing on the third floor. The hall was empty. Jiang's screams sounded louder. She reached the second floor. Only one more to go, then she could disappear into the evening crowds. She glanced over her shoulder. Jiang was still pursuing.

Little Chang bounded down the last flight, covering three steps with each stride. She dashed into the massive entrance hall. Three of Jiang's bodyguards stood in a circle talking, while the building's guard sat near the door, aimlessly gazing out at the summer evening. Little Chang did not even consider trying to adopt the pretense of casualness. She continued sprinting. By the time the guards looked up, she was almost at the door. Jiang Qing reached the landing and shrieked, "Stop her! Stop the traitor!"

As the guards turned toward Mao's wife, they were temporarily distracted. Little Chang seized the opportunity. She pointed to the front door, yelled, "Stop the traitor!" and escaped into Tian'anmen Square before anyone could recover.

Sprinting into the engulfing darkness, Little Chang could hear the commotion behind her, but was too panicked to look. She pushed through the evening crowds and ran down an alley past the Great Hall of the People. Thousands of black Red Star bicycles were neatly chained to iron racks.

She spotted the leather carry bag attached to the seat of her bike and fumbled with the lock, momentarily forgetting the combination. The lock popped open in her hands. She stared at it in surprise and then glanced over her shoulder. Still no sign of the pursuing guards. Strapping the chain around her waist, she pulled the bicycle from the rack.

As she pedaled furiously down Chang'an Avenue, Peking's largest boulevard, a sense of impotence began to consume her. Though she was a respected member of the Party, no one would ever accept her word against that of Jiang Qing. Frightened and confused, she turned toward the Western District. She had to find her husband. He would know what to do.

Flinging open the door of their apartment, she called Sen Bao's name. There was no answer. She remembered he would be in class for two hours. She could not wait. Two police cars pulled up in front. She knew they were searching for her. She had to run. There was no time to pack anything or call anyone. She could not even leave a note. The police might find it. She had to remain free so she could tell her story to someone in power.

She fled out the back door. For two hours, she wandered the streets. Then she walked to Tian'anmen, hoping to find her husband. He was there, talking with two friends. She started toward him. Just then, three Red Guards approached. They pulled Sen to the side and began to interrogate him. Sen looked confused. The guards were angry. Dissatisfied, the interrogators forced Sen into a jeep and hurriedly drove away.

The muscles in Little Chang's face started to spasm. She felt lost and alone, but she would not permit herself to cry. She would have to wait until morning before contacting help. Now she had to make herself invisible. Hiding in Peking was not easy. As in all Chinese cities, life was organized around the block association. A person seeing someone who did not belong would contact the local party cadre. With such supervision, she could not sleep on the street or stay with a friend. Neither could she stay in a hotel or leave town; hotels required government-requested reservations, and travel required an approved visa. She had no idea what to do.

Little Chang glanced uneasily at every soldier and policeman as she walked to Wangfujing Street, the heart of Peking's shopping district. Thousands of evening shoppers jammed the busy sidewalks and spilled over into the narrow roadway. Taxis and limousines sounded their horns but had no impact on the horde. A crowd was standing in front of the brightly lit windows of a department store. Little Chang wedged her way into the pack, hoping to find anonymity. Bodies pressed against her. She felt faint. The people were staring at a new model of a washing machine, which they would never be able to afford. Little Chang had always dreamed that she and Sen could buy such an appliance as they advanced to the top levels of the Party. Now she saw her dream slipping away.

Shen Mo ushered Colonel Li into a small conference room in the Great Hall of the People. Neat rows of couches and easy chairs, draped with loose-fitting beige slipcovers and white embroidered doilies, lined the four walls. In front of them were glass-covered teak coffee tables, each with two white teacups, a blue cloisonné ashtray, a black cigarette case, and a box of wooden matches. The teak-paneled walls were covered with photographs of Chairman Mao and with a large mural of Tian'anmen Square stitched in needlepoint. The mural looked so realistic that at first glance it appeared to be an oil painting.

Colonel Li's eyes scanned the room. Three other men were already there, sitting silently on separate couches. One was the police chief of Peking, the second was the commander of the Peking Garrison of the People's Liberation Army, while the third was the deputy director of Unit 8431, the thirty-thousand-man force of Mao's private bodyguards. Although he did not know them well, they were men he would not want as enemies.

Shen Mo distributed the photographs of a woman. Colonel Li studied her face. She was young, perhaps less than thirty, and quite attractive, with short straight hair, a small delicate nose, and soft round cheeks. Her large, almost Western eyes conveyed an aura of determined pride. According to the notation on the back, she was a Grade 9 Party cadre, a position of considerable importance for one so young.

Zhang Chunqiao, Wang Hongwen, and Yao Wenyuan walked into the room and took adjacent seats in the front. Along with Jiang Qing, they comprised the Gang of Four. Zhang, at sixty-one, was tall and thin with a heavy beard, dark glasses, and a long, distinctly un-Chinese nose. An intellectual who had gained prominence during the Cultural Revolution, he had been considered a possible successor to Mao. Wang, the thirty-nine-year-old vice-chairman of the Politburo, had a dark, almost mysterious look. A former industrial worker who had risen rapidly during the Cultural Revolution, Wang had long narrow eyes and a perpetual expression of having just smelled something bad. Yao, the forty-five-year-old party theoretician, was a short, round-faced man with wide, gleaming eyes. Except for his slightly receding hairline, he had an almost cherubic look, one that contrasted sharply with the bitter vituperation that spewed from his pen.

Jiang Qing, appearing overwrought, stepped to the center

of the room. "Comrades"—her voice quivered with anger—
"study this woman. Her name is Chang Shuli, but many
know her as Little Chang. She is a dangerous traitor who
would fart in the face of the devil himself. Until this evening,
she worked as the guardian of the National People's
Archives." Colonel Li stared in disbelief. Something had
gone wrong with their plan. "This woman was bribed by
Deng Xiaoping and the capitalist-roaders to remove
important documents from the archives. I caught her
breaking into Mao's private vault, but she escaped. We must
apprehend her."

"And when we do?" Colonel Li asked.

"When slashing weeds, you must pull out the roots or the
rice will die," Jiang said. Then she turned abruptly and left
the room.

Shen Mo ushered out the four guests individually, making
certain there was no communication between them. Jiang
Qing, Colonel Li thought to himself, was a master at keeping
her supporters off-balance.

At ten o'clock, the crowds began to disappear. Little
Chang wandered aimlessly. Rings of pain encircled her
throbbing forehead. Stopping in front of a clothing store,
she stared at her reflection in the window. Her eyes were red,
but her face was the color of a dried husk. "You're a
disgrace," she lectured her mirror image. "Does the field
mouse cry when it smells a cat? Pull yourself together. The
rice is not yet harvested."

Little Chang turned from the window. Except for factory
workers on the night shift, the street was deserted.
Pretending to be on her way to work, she started toward the
industrial district. During the next eight hours, she walked
more than twenty miles, passing virtually every factory in the

city. By dawn she found herself in the northwest of Peking.

The Beixi Fanguan was just opening. Famished and aching, she went into the dingy restaurant, took a seat in the back, and ordered a bowl of chicken congee. She sipped the watery rice gruel, trying to stretch out her breakfast until it was time for the offices to open. She ordered a second bowl and lingered another forty minutes. People in the restaurant were staring at her. She had no choice but to leave.

She walked to the Long March Luggage Factory, produced her Party membership card, and announced that she needed to use the phone. Given her rank, no one objected. She dialed the number of Wang Shante, the deputy director of the General Office of the Central Committee. A voice answered, "*Wei* [Hello]?" She was in luck. It was Wang himself.

"Comrade Wang, this is Comrade Chang Shuli."

"Yes, Comrade Lin," he replied.

"Excuse me. I said this is Comrade Chang Shuli from the archives."

"How are things in Qingdao?"

"Qingdao? I live in Peking. Don't you remember me?"

"Of course I've heard about the treasonous actions of Chang Shuli. I'm sure she won't try to contact me. She must know that anyone she talked to would immediately report her to Comrade Jiang Qing."

Little Chang tried to still the trembling in her legs. "Are all my friends being watched?"

"Certainly we will catch her and her traitorous allies. Thank you for offering to help. I'll inform Comrade Jiang Qing of your concern." Wang hung up the telephone.

There had to be others who would talk, Little Chang counseled herself as she walked to the Maxam Toothpaste Factory. She needed someone strong enough to stand up to Jiang. She dialed two more numbers. Both of her friends claimed they were in meetings. For the next five hours she kept trying, but in every case the result was the same. She had become a leper.

Exhausted, Little Chang considered giving up and striking a bargain with Jiang. There was only one more alternative, her brother-in-law, Sen Tailing. Although Sen was a Party cadre, he worked for an American trading company. Because of his unique status, it would be difficult for Jiang to harm him without incurring international repercussions. Little Chang was certain that Sen would talk to her. The only problem was how to contact him. He was staying at the well-guarded Peking Hotel. It was likely that the police would be watching his room and listening to his telephone. Still, there had to be a way.

Little Chang tried to think of alternatives, but found it difficult to focus her mind. Fatigue was overcoming her. She needed sleep. Her legs led her into Beihai Park and up a path to the top of the hill overlooking the lake. Just off the path was a large boulder surrounded on three sides by evergreen trees. She crawled over the boulder, nestled herself into a narrow crevice, and closed her eyes for a short nap.

13: Conghua Hot Springs

Marc Slater turned on the spigots and watched as hot water from a mineral spring and cold water from a mountain stream poured into the massive tiled tub that was nine feet long, six feet wide, and four feet deep. Then he turned and walked the sixty feet to the far end of the room. He had followed Meili's instructions and ordered the most expensive suite. Though the hotel had become somewhat shopworn, it was easy to see why it had once been a favorite retreat of Chiang Kai-shek and his warlords.

A stack of documents rested on the desk. Marc tried to read but could not concentrate. The huge suite, with its separate areas for sleeping, sitting, working, and bathing, made him feel intensely lonely. Pacing to the balcony, he gazed at the verdant river valley far below. The last time he had visited the springs, Carolyn had been with him. They had taken a weekend from the Canton Fair and had spent most of the time luxuriating in the tub that was part swimming pool and part health spa. It had been one of those

171

special but all too rare occasions when they had been able to give each other their undivided attention.

After thirty minutes, the bath was finally filled. Marc eased his body into the steaming tub. His legs fluttered uneasily as he tried to adjust to the space. He knew how to scrunch his body into the constricted dimensions of an American tub and how to float in a swimming pool, but this was too large for one technique and too small for the other. It was, he decided, better suited for two people. He crawled around the perimeter until he found a position in which his head could rest on the side while his body floated free. The water, shot from underwater jets, bombarded the aching muscles in his back, gradually dissolving his tensions. It felt wonderfully soothing.

While he relaxed, Marc imagined that Meili was beside him. Since meeting the exquisite daughter of his old friend, he had been unable to get her out of his mind. He could feel her deftly massaging his neck. He ran his hands over her body. Her skin was silky smooth. She turned to him with an open, inviting mouth and softly kissed him. The water welded them together in an embrace.

He opened his eyes and grabbed the side of the tub. His fantasy had left him unnerved—he did not like feeling aroused when it could only lead to frustration. A relationship was impossible. Thinking about her would only jeopardize his position in China. He stepped out of the bath and got dressed. Pouring a cool glass of beer, he stretched out on a couch and opened a report on Chinese oil production.

He had finished less than ten pages when he heard scraping on a mesh screen. Meili was standing outside. She looked lovelier than he had remembered. Her hair dipped in front of her forehead and flowed over her shoulders in long dark waves, making her seem older. Marc raised the screen.

Meili placed her hands on the frame and lithely vaulted over the sill. Marc smiled at her agility. "You could have come through the door." He extended his hand.

Meili grasped it and shyly looked away, but she did not let go. "I could not take the risk that someone would see me."

The standard blue worker's uniform hung seductively on her limber body, making Marc want to undress her. "Would you like a beer?"

"We have no time." Her voice sounded musical. "We must get you to the meeting and then back to the hotel by dawn."

Marc collected his papers and followed her out the rear window. A narrow dirt path ran along a ridge. Reaching a clearing, Meili stopped and looked around. No one was there. She pulled aside a small tree. A hidden passage was revealed. She handed Marc a flashlight and held the tree as he ducked into a long tunnel. A quarter-mile later, they reached the far side of Conghua Mountain.

They walked silently through a thinly wooded forest. With only the moon and the dim beam of her flashlight for illumination, Meili was very surefooted. Marc hurried to keep pace. The night was alive with sounds. Frogs croaked in baritone voices from the banks of a stream. Small field animals scampered in search of food. Birds called to each other from the branches of flowering trees, while crickets, hidden in the underbrush, provided the percussion. "It's beautiful here." Marc finally spoke.

"I love the countryside." Meili slowed her pace as she watched the reflection of the moon on the lake in the valley below. "In Peking the dust hides the moon, and the people destroy the silence. Do you have such beautiful land in Boston?"

"How do you know where I'm from?"

Meili turned and continued walking. "I learned it either from my father or from you at our last meeting."

"Yesterday?"

"No. We met two or three years ago in Peking."

"I'm embarrassed that I don't remember," Marc said, surprised that his usually flawless memory had failed him.

Meili gently flicked her hair over her shoulders. "I was much younger then and looked much different. Besides, I didn't talk to you except to translate."

"I wish—" The shriek of fleeing birds shattered the quiet of the summer evening. Small, panicking animals chattered nervously as they scurried past the figures on the path. Meili grabbed Marc's hand. She was trembling. "Stay still," she said. Marc stopped and listened. The sounds of the countryside seemed strangely alien. Thirty years ago the wilds had been his home, but now he felt out of place.

There was a roar. A mountain lion the size of a Great Dane prowled into the clearing. His golden coat gleamed in the moonlight. Flashing his long pearl incisors, he growled as he stalked to the path. Marc instinctively retreated. The cat pawed at the ground as he stared at the two figures who had invaded his turf. Meili fumbled for her gun. The cat growled again, showing the insides of his powerful jaws. Meili stood frozen. The mountain lion advanced, his muscles rippling with every motion. Marc grabbed a branch lying at his feet. The cat sprang forward. Marc hurled the branch into its face, scraping its eye. The cat screamed and rubbed its face with its paw. Marc grabbed another branch. The cat growled, wanting revenge. Marc pushed Meili away and stepped back toward the woods. The cat bounded toward him. Evading the thrust of the branch, it opened its massive jaws and tore the stick from Marc's hands. Then it lunged for Marc's leg.

There was a shot. The cat screamed as it clawed Marc's jeans. Two more shots. Blood gushed from its mouth. Its body twitched. Marc pulled his foot free. Blood covered his shoe. Meili took aim and fired into the center of the lion's temple. The animal moaned and then collapsed.

For a minute, no one moved. "I think it's dead," Marc said, bending over the inert animal. Meili stood motionless, the smoking gun still in her hand. "Are you all right?" Marc asked.

"I'm fine."

"You did well," Marc said, realizing that since he had begun his trip, he had been rescued twice.

Meili took out a handkerchief and cleaned the blood off Marc's shoes. He bent down and touched her shoulder. He wanted to hold her but knew it would be wrong to do so. "I'll do that."

Meili's eyes glowed softly. "You are my guest. You must let me take care of you."

Sitting down next to her, Marc remembered an incident that had happened long ago. "It seems"—he ran his fingers through her hair—"that you are a warrior just like your mother."

"In China, many women are warriors."

"Your mother once saved my life."

"But you also saved hers. She has often talked of your bravery in killing the Japanese who tried to rape her."

Marc wondered how much more this young woman knew about him. "There were many who were brave during the war."

"But they were fighting for their country."

"It was my country too. I was born in China and would have lived the rest of my life here if my parents hadn't died."

Meili bowed politely from the waist. "Please accept my apologies. My English is not very good. I meant to indicate that your bravery was greater than that of others because you chose to remain here."

Marc blushed. "It is you who are the hero. I'll be forever in your debt for killing the mountain lion."

"Excellent," Meili smiled. "It's a great comfort to be under the protection of the blue-eyed spirit who runs like the wind."

Marc gently touched her cheek. He bent over, undecided whether to kiss her. Meili turned away. "We must go. The gunfire may have attracted attention."

The moon had risen halfway through the sky by the time they reached the cave. Meili flashed her light three times and then led Marc into the opening. At the far end, she pulled open a dark screen. A flood of light filled the passageway. Shielding his eyes, Marc peered into a hall filled with technicians operating shortwave radios, computers, and radar consoles. He was stunned. He'd known he was going to some sort of headquarters, but he had not expected to see an elaborate communications center in the wilderness of south China. He looked questioningly at Meili, but she continued walking toward a door at the far end of the hall.

Hu Shengte stepped in front of the door and waved to Marc. Short and trim with a square, firm jaw and black glasses, Hu looked much older than he had six months ago. His once black hair, brushed back from his heavily lined foreheard, was now almost white. Dressed in a charcoal-gray Zhongshan suit with a Mao collar, Hu smiled and bowed toward his guest. "*Selate lao pengyou, ni hao ma* [How are you, Slater old friend]?"

Marc bowed. "*Wo hen gao xing kanjian ni* [I'm very happy to see you]."

"Your journey went well?"

"Thanks to your daughter."

"She's becoming a fine woman, almost consolation for her not being a son."

Meili smiled dutifully, trying to conceal her displeasure. Her father was of the old school that still considered it a disadvantage to have a daughter. Although girl children were no longer abandoned on mountaintops, neither had they achieved real equality.

"You have trained her well," Marc said.

"Because she brought you here safely?"

"No, because she didn't kill you for that remark. Do you know what my daughter would have done if I had said the same thing?"

Hu smiled. "I am pleased to say that Chinese girls still respect their elders and remember the dictum of the Sages, 'A silent girl is a virtuous one.' My young beauty will make an especially good wife. She is smart, her teeth are good, and she is not bad to look at. Don't you agree?"

"Someone will be very lucky," Marc said, wondering if Meili was still a virgin. Given the mores in the People's Republic, it was quite likely.

Hu laughed and slapped Meili on her rump. "If only she were a little more humble, finding a husband would be easy."

Meili cast her eyes to the floor. "I will try to show more humility."

"Do you know she wants to be a doctor?"

"My father was a doctor," Marc said.

"But he was a man and a barbarian." Hu's voice conveyed his pride in his daughter. "For a Chinese girl to have such aspirations is very rare."

"She is a nightingale among pigeons," Marc replied.

"That saying was banned during the Cultural Revolution."

"Are you going to report me?"

"It's not worth the effort," a voice said in almost unaccented English. "This long-nosed foreign devil is a lost cause." Marc smiled as he saw Kang Moruo walking toward him. Kang, the fashion plate of the Politburo, was wearing a neatly tailored, light gray, cashmere Zhongshan suit. He was a handsome, dapper man, with a bushy head of hair, white straight teeth, and large twinkling eyes.

Marc had known Kang, the brother of Beatrice Tang, since their days at Harvard. Unlike other Communist leaders, whose fathers were peasants or workers, Kang was the son of the most successful merchant in China. He had studied in the United States and in Europe; spoke English, French, and four dialects of Chinese; and was respected as one of the finest administrative minds in the country. A member of the Politburo responsible for several trade corporations, he was regarded as one of China's top experts on the West. Had it not been for the wealth of his family, which made him undesirable to the more radical elements, Kang would have become one of the top leaders of China.

"Shall we?" Kang ushered Marc toward the door. "General Liu is waiting inside."

As Marc's eyes adjusted to the dimly lit room, he saw Liu Teyu sitting at the end of the table. He had known and admired the vice-minister of defense for more than thirty years. Long Way Liu as everyone called him, had gained renown for having led his troops on an extra two-thousand-mile detour to Tibet during the Long March. When asked why he had taken this route, Liu was said to have replied, "To defeat one's enemies, one must practice misdirection and diversion." Marc bowed respectfully to the general. In the years since the Long March, Liu had managed to weather every political storm and had emerged as one of the country's strongmen. As commander of the Canton Military Region, he now controlled the second largest army in the People's Republic.

The general stood up. He was a broad, powerfully built man with arms like tree trunks. Though in his seventies, his

complexion was remarkably unwrinkled. His thick eyebrows and sideburns had turned white, but the rest of his
hair was dark. A cigarette dangled from his lips as he spoke
with a heavy Cantonese accent. "I am told that your journey
has been like a date pit. Both ends have been pointed, this
end by the mountain lion and the other end by that
unfortunate incident on the train."

"My joss has not been good." Marc stared quizzically at
the general.

Liu motioned toward the chairs as he poured four cups of
tea. "I believe you have a microfilm for me."

Marc handed him the envelope from Ren. He wanted to
ask about its contents but knew it would be inappropriate to
do so. Liu would tell him when the time warranted.

"I assume that you are perplexed by our operation," Liu
continued.

"I am, but first I'd like to learn what you know about the
man who tried to kill me."

"Old friend, I'm surprised at your impatience. I remember
when you trusted your friends and had the spiritual reserves
to control your anxieties. Is this directness what living in the
West has taught you? Do you think we, who protected you in
the war, would now let you be harmed?"

Marc bowed his head. "*Laodaye*," he addressed Liu, using
the term of highest respect for one who is older, "I am just a
foolish barbarian who has forgotten the value of your
excellent teachings. I do not know why you waste your time
giving me counsel. It is like playing a piano to a cow."

The others laughed at Marc's use of the Chinese
colloquialism. "Perhaps you have not become completely
Westernized," Liu responded. "I think, with practice, bright
blue will be able to outshine blue—or as you say in the West,
the pupil will outshine the teacher."

"Thank you for your gracious consideration." Marc

sipped his tea.

"We have some information that we want you to convey to Deng and Hua, but the source must not be divulged."

"I understand."

Liu handed Marc a stack of papers. "We have reports that Jiang Qing is planning to kill off her opponents until she has gained control of the Politburo. The first target will be Deng himself. According to our information, the attack will take place within the next ten days."

Marc stared uneasily at the round-faced general. "Can we stop her?"

"Not if she remains the fox followed by the tiger."

"I don't understand."

"It is an old Chinese fable. A fox was captured by a tiger. The fox said, 'You can't eat me, because the gods have made me the leader of all animals.' The tiger did not believe him; but the fox said, 'Follow and see if any animal dares to stand its ground.' The tiger agreed and walked directly behind the fox. Every animal they saw fled in panic. The tiger was amazed, and agreed that the fox was the leader of all animals."

"And Mao is the tiger behind Jiang," Marc affirmed.

"As long as Mao backs his wife," Hu stated, "and Hua is too frightened to stop him, Jiang Qing has an excellent chance of seizing power. You, old friend, must convince Deng and Hua to unite against her."

"I'll do what I can," Marc said as he studied the faces of the men in the room. He owed much to them and was honored that they trusted him. Convincing Deng and Hua would not be easy. He hoped he was up to the task.

"Old friend,"—Liu leaned toward Marc—"if you are to succeed, you must remember what it is to be Chinese. You must think and act the way you did during the war. You must try to forget what you have learned in the West and become once again the blue-eyed spirit who runs like the wind."

"I'm surprised that you recall my Chinese nickname."

"I hope you can remember why it was given to you."

"Of course I can, but I'm older now, and no longer as fast as my feet."

"Then, old friend, you will just have to be faster in your mind."

14: The Chain

Sitting in the dining room of the Dong Fang Hotel, Lord
Henry Gateshead gazed at photographs of new Chinese
archaeological excavations and dreamed of his future
successes. At fifty-one, Gateshead had had an undis-
tinguished career as director of the English Museum and a
member of the House of Lords. Everyone considered him
well meaning yet largely ineffectual. But China would be his
opportunity. He would change his reputation here.

It was only natural that Gateshead would seek his success
in China. His ancestors had opened the country for the
British; his family fortune had been based on trade with
China; and the two collections that had made the English
Museum preeminent in Oriental Art had both been donated
by his forebears. He expected the tradition would work for
him as well.

Lord Gateshead's family had been traders in the Orient
since the start of the nineteenth century. At the time England
had been facing financial collapse. It had bought tons of

teas, silks, and spices from China; but since China had bought nothing in return, England had to pay in silver, thus depleting its treasury. There had also been a crisis in the British textile industry. Its export market in India had dried up when the Indians ran out of money. To save its treasury from bankruptcy and its economy from ruin, England had to find a product that China would want to buy from India. In that way a balanced triangular trade could be established and all three economies could flourish.

British leaders knew that opium was their only alternative. Through the East India Company, they had acquired a monopoly over the fields in India; and although they could not bring themselves to condone the trade officially, they were willing to expand production so others could smuggle the drug into China.

George Gateshead, the grandfather of Lord Henry's great-grandfather, was a merchant seaman in the Far East. Seeing the new opportunity, he established the firm of Gateshead & MacIntosh, purchased his own ship, and aggressively began to trade opium. His sales expanded faster than anyone could have imagined. Within twenty years he had made millions of pounds and became an important political force in London.

So effective were George and the other traders that by the 1830s more than half the men in Canton had become addicts. To stem the epidemic, the emperor of China ordered his aides to seize all shipments and force all captains to sign declarations stating that they would never transport opium. George convinced the captains to reject the demands. Their refusal meant that British ships could not trade in Canton, and this changed the issue of debate from opium to free trade and national rights. George's allies in Parliament then convinced the government to compensate the merchants for what had been confiscated. The resulting three-million-pound obligation linked England directly to the future of opium.

Both the British and the Chinese had too much at stake to permit a compromise. An armed conflict became inevitable. China called it the Opium War. England called it the Trade War. Despite the terminology, it was brief and one-sided. A few thousand British troops armed with guns fought tens of thousands of Chinese armed with bows and arrows. The British fought by theories of modern warfare, the Chinese by theories of ancient war magic. The war magic failed.

The peace treaty gave England everything it wanted: a huge indemnity that more than covered the cost of the war; sovereign enclaves called "treaty ports" in five Chinese cities; and the colony of Hong Kong, which became the base for the opium merchants. Freed from the restrictions of the Chinese, George Gateshead expanded his trading activities, built factories and office buildings in Hong Kong, and then returned to London, where he became a leader of Parliament.

His son Philip succeeded him as president of Gateshead & MacIntosh. Philip was a colorless man who did not like ships, hated fighting, and fared poorly in the climate of Hong Kong. He was also a snob who disliked all Chinese and socialized only with Europeans. Yet, ironically, he developed a love for Chinese art. Like an emperor receiving tribute, he demanded gifts of porcelain vases, jade statues, ivory carvings, and cloisonné ware from his customers. The Chinese, wishing to secure special advantages, contributed some of their most valuable antiques. It was these pieces that formed the basis of the family's fabled art collection.

Even more significant than the pieces collected by Philip were those obtained by his son Angus, Lord Henry's great-grandfather. Angus was a rogue and a reprobate whose only interests were women, gambling, and drinking. Exiled to Shanghai at an early age, he ignored the company's trading activities there and instead devoted himself to investing in his favorite pleasures. To everyone's surprise, sin in Shanghai proved to be among the company's most profitable investments. Foreigners with no home life and wealthy Chinese flocked to Angus's brothels, gambling houses, and opium dens, which were among the finest in the Orient.

While Angus's businesses flourished, hostilities between Chinese and foreigners increased. The foreigners were frustrated because they were still blocked from trading in most parts of the country, while the Chinese were angry because foreigners controlled their customs service, their mail delivery, and five of their ports. Except for those working as servants, Chinese were not allowed to live in treaty ports. Signs reading "No Dogs or Chinese Permitted" were common in most of the foreign enclaves.

Although noted for their patience, even the Chinese had limits. Anti-foreign violence began to spread. Bread was poisoned, British ships were seized, French priests were murdered, and riots erupted. The Europeans demanded revenge. In 1860 the Second Opium War began.

The Manchu dynasty still trying to quash the Taiping, was no match for the European armies. The Chinese had already agreed to surrender when the Europeans arrived at the Summer Palace near Peking. The palace was a sight unique in the world: eighty miles of park across which were dispersed baroque palaces, forests with herds of deer, lakes filled with golden fish; ornate temples; two life-sized lions made of gold; and endless storehouses containing enough jewels, relics, pottery, and paintings to fill half the museums in Europe. It was more than the finest example of Chinese civilization. The Summer Palace was the treasure chest of China.

The allied soldiers were not connoisseurs of art. They were

semiliterates who resented being in China. Like a plague of locusts, they decimated the palace. In one day, two thousand years of Chinese treasures were looted or destroyed. As a final gesture, the British commander, Lord Elgin, ordered the palace burned to the ground.

Even those treasures that had not been destroyed would have been lost had it not been for Angus and his vices. Knowing the value of the looted antiques, Angus met the returning soldiers and offered them women, liquor, opium, and the opportunity to gamble in exchange for their booty. In one month of servicing the troops, he procured the finest collection of Oriental art ever seen in the West.

Lord Henry sipped his tea as he pictured the gilt-framed paintings of George, Philip, and Angus that hung in his study in Gateshead Castle. They had peered down on him for forty years, dominating the opulent hall built with profits from their trade with China. Even at work, he could not escape their overpowering presence. The English Museum was respected only for the collections of his ancestors, which were now housed in its Gateshead Gallery of Oriental Art.

Lord Henry's dream was to acquire a collection of artifacts that would rival those of Philip and Angus. For more than twenty years, he had been stymied. The Communist, trying to build their republic, had little time for archaeological excavations. But in the last decade, things had changed. The Communists renewed their interest in their past and began to dig on an unprecedented scale. Lord Henry had diligently followed their progress. Now he hoped to convince them to sell him their finest relics.

Avery Boswell pulled open the double glass doors and entered the dining room. The large room contained more than fifty tables, each covered with long white cloths stained from years of spilt tea. Most of the tables were round and set for eight or oblong and set for twelve. The Chinese liked to encourage their guests to eat in large groups. Today there were few diners. During the summer, guests preferred the garden restaurants in the city.

Boswell noticed Lord Henry Gateshead sitting alone in the far corner. Dressed in a dark pinstripe suit, a white shirt with French cuffs, and gold cuff links, Gateshead looked completely out of place. Boswell disliked everything Gateshead represented, but he was intrigued by the thought of using the Englishman as a pawn. He suspected Van Wyck would not approve, but he could not resist the temptation. He stiffly threaded his way toward the Englishman's table. "Lord Gateshead, good-day."

Gateshead looked up from his book. "Good-day, Boswell."

"May I join you?"

"Please do."

Boswell took a seat across the table.

"Tea?"

"Thank you," Boswell replied as Lord Gateshead poured.

"It's Twinings Earl Grey from London." Lord Gateshead smiled. "You should have seen the expression of the chap inspecting my luggage. I suspect that he had never before seen anyone bring tea into China and thought I was a bit daft. But for fifty years I have been devoted to Twinings, and I see no reason why travel should force me to change my habits."

"I'm in complete accord," Boswell replied, remembering a passage that Marx had written on the decline of the British aristocracy.

"Do you mind if I smoke?" Lord Gateshead asked as he took out a gold cigar cutter and neatly snipped off the end of a panatela.

"Please do."

"Would you care for one?" Gateshead extended a brown leather case with four cigars tucked into separate pockets. "They're from Havana."

"I'll stick with my Players." Boswell lit one of his cigarettes.

"How are your negotiations faring?"

"Quite well," Boswell said, trying to inflate his importance in front of Gateshead. "I'm meeting with the governor of Guangdong Province, who's planning to build a highway from Canton to Hong Kong. I'd like to see a central role for some of the companies we represent."

"Excellent." Gateshead puffed on his cigar. It had an elegant aroma. "It's strange that I know so little about your business. It's like talking to a doctor about one's kidneys. You live with them all your life and yet you are completely baffled by the explanation of how they work."

"Have you never been involved in the business?"

"Only on the board of directors of the parent company. I don't have the time to follow operations. But I do know you have made quite a reputation for yourself."

"I am grateful for your confidence," Boswell said, averting his eyes from Gateshead. He was becoming everything that he wanted not to be, a rich and successful capitalist, and was petrified he might get to like it. The Party would tolerate only so much opulence. He had made his choice fifteen years ago when he had joined the cell at Oxford. It was too late to back out now. The slightest slippage and he could be exposed. His only alternative was to strive for success within the structure of the Party. He lit another cigarette and thought of his mission. "Tell me, Lord Gateshead, what brings you to China?"

"I am here to visit some of the newest archaeological excavations. Are you acquainted with any of them?"

"Only vaguely." Boswell hoped that Gateshead did not intend to quiz him. He detested relics of dead imperial civilizations.

"The three most spectacular are the Qin Tomb in Xian, the Han Tomb in Mancheng, and Genghis Khan's capital of Khanbaliq in Peking. It is my hope to acquire the finest pieces from each of these sites." Lord Gateshead stared at the two-inch gray ash from his cigar. "With such acquisitions, I would be able to assume my place alongside my more illustrious ancestors."

"Glory to the British Empire." Boswell raised his teacup. *In its last imperialist gasp,* he added silently. Boswell thought about his plan to kidnap Gateshead. "I have a feeling you may return from China far more well known than anyone else in the history of your family."

"That's a jolly good dream." Gateshead arched his bushy eyebrows. "Perhaps you can remember me in your prayers. Help often comes from most unlikely places."

Frans Van Wyck closed his tubes of paint and hung his smock neatly on a hanger. He was in no mood for seeing Avery Boswell, but he knew that he could not indefinitely avoid one of his own operatives. He was not pleased that Boswell had been assigned to work for him. The Englishman was far too amateurish for his taste, constantly ranting about China's deviationist position with an emotionalism that was dangerous and unprofessional. Van Wyck's plans had no room for such philosophical nitpicking. There was a knock. "Come in, Mr. Boswell," Van Wyck called, straightening his tie.

"Good afternoon, Mr. Van Wyck," the massive Japanese said as he walked into the room.

"*Konnichiwa, Yamaguchi san,*" Van Wyck greeted his ally

from the Takamura Corporation in Japanese. He liked working with Yamaguchi and greatly respected his professionalism.

"You were expecting someone else?" Yamaguchi asked.

"Yes, a man named Boswell who works for Gateshead and MacIntosh."

"Is he one of your crew from Oxford?"

Van Wyck stared at Yamaguchi with great surprise. The Bureau had recruited a small contingent of operatives from Oxford more than fifteen years before. All were now in sensitive positions with the British government or with multinational corporations. Only two of the more than three dozen had ever been exposed. So how had this Japanese businessman learned of their existence? "I'm not sure where he went to school."

"Perhaps I was mistaken," Yamaguchi replied, even though both men knew he was correct. Standing up, he paced to the easel near the window. "Did you paint this?" Yamaguchi asked.

Van Wyck nodded. "I'm working on it. But I can't quite get it to express the feeling I want."

"It's quite interesting. What do you call it?"

"*The Chain.*"

"*Wakarimasen.*" He confessed that he did not understand.

"It's from an old Chinese folktale. Do you see the cicada on the branch of the tree? It's the beginning. The cicada is so concerned with sipping the dew off the leaf that he is unaware of the mantis crouching and twisting behind him. The mantis, for his part, is so obsessed with the cicada that he does not see the oriole stretching its neck to attack; and the oriole does not see the boy with the slingshot preparing to kill him. All three animals are so intent on what is in front of them that they do not notice the danger behind."

"Are you the boy with the slingshot?" Yamaguchi asked.

"I am the artist."

"And the artist sees everything?"

"The artist sees what he paints, and hopes that he has seen all that there is."

"Excellent."

"And what does the businessman do?" Van Wyck asked.

"The businessman"—Yamaguchi paused to sip his tea—"accumulates capital and then buys the artist."

There was a knock on the door. Avery Boswell walked in carrying his aluminum suitcase. He greeted Van Wyck, who made the appropriate introductions. The three men stood uncomfortably making small talk. Sensing that Van Wyck wanted to confer privately with Boswell, Yamaguchi politely excused himself. After he had left the room, Boswell asked suspiciously, "What's that Japo doing here?"

"He's an associate on one of my projects."

"Is he a Communist?"

"No," Van Wyck said, turning toward his easel.

"Then I'd be cautious. Do you know how vital it is for us to correct the deviationist tenden—"

Van Wyck dipped a brush into his palette. "Boswell, I don't give a damn for your doctrinaire politics. My only concern is with my mission."

"I cannot agree with your approach. When I was in Moscow for political orientation, I had a fascinating discussion with Comrade Tikanov. He postulated that—"

"Tikanov's theories are of little interest to me."

"I think you are making a mistake. Comrade Lenin said—"

"I also don't give a damn about Lenin, unless he can wire a bomb."

"That's treasonous."

"You may be right."

"Do you know what would happen if your superiors in the

Bureau knew of your attitude?"

"Absolutely nothing. The Bureau and I have made an accommodation. I am not a theorist. I am a craftsman, a carpenter for its missions. The Bureau wants its ends achieved and knows I'm the best it has. It doesn't try to make me a model Communist. Perhaps it even understands that the traits that make me a good craftsman also make me a lousy Party member. Its only concern is that I achieve my objectives efficiently and effectively."

"Your attitude could place you in a most precarious position. There are many who care about political purity. If just once you fail—"

"I'll be killed with my men. So you see, this really is not any of my concern." For several minutes Van Wyck painted in silence. "Did you come here for a specific reason, Mr. Boswell?"

"I brought you the explosives as you requested," Boswell said, placing the suitcase next to Van Wyck.

"Thank you." The Dutchman cleaned his hands and opened the suitcase.

"Did I tell you about the problems I had in customs?" As Boswell prattled on about his difficulties, Van Wyck inspected the explosives his men so urgently needed. The Japanese were delivering the munitions for the operations in Shanghai and Peking, but Boswell's were the only supplies available in Canton.

"I had lunch with Lord Gateshead, the director of the English Museum."

"Is he related to the Gateshead that founded your company?"

"It was one of his ancestors."

"That's a problem."

"To the contrary, it's an opportunity. Suppose Lord Henry Gateshead were kidnapped and an unreasonable ransom—such as the return of Hong Kong's New Territories—were demanded. England would be forced to take action and the People's Republic would be discredited. By kidnapping one inept English lord, we would be able to hasten the destruction of Hua's government."

Van Wyck picked up a paintbrush and snapped it in half. Spinning on his heels, he faced Boswell. Though he was three inches shorter than the Englishman, his physical presence easily dominated. He stared at Boswell with his piercing blue eyes, furious that the Englishman never seemed to be able to follow orders.

"Well, what do you think?" Boswell asked.

Van Wyck fought to control his temper. He was the artist, not the mantis or the cicada. He could not let Boswell get to him. It was completely unprofessional. Calmly he measured his words. "Your plan is interesting, but Comrade Bulganov has approved specific operations and I will not add new ones without his approval."

"Please ask Bulganov," Boswell entreated.

"I will. But until I get his approval, I want no kidnapping. Is that understood?" Boswell nodded. Van Wyck walked to the front of the room and opened the door. "If there is nothing else, Mr. Boswell, I'd like to finish my painting."

The Hong Qi limousine passed through a white iron gate guarded by four soldiers and approached the imposing red villa that served as Jiang Qing's vacation retreat. Built by a merchant who had been south China's leading opium distributor, the villa had been designed to look like the palaces of the Forbidden City. There were four central buildings set around a square, white stone courtyard. A two-tiered, yellow tiled imperial roof, supported by red columns, covered the structures. Below both tiers were ornate painted friezes depicting scenes of Chinese mythology.

Alexandra Koo stepped from the limousine and started to ascend a carved marble stairway that was draped with vines of climbing bougainvillaea. Shen Mo, one of Jiang's aides, greeted Alexandra and led her into a series of lush tropical gardens.

The women chatted as they walked past a reflecting pool covered with pink-tinged lotus blossoms. Alexandra inhaled the delicate floral aromas and listened to the screams of cicadas and the chirping of summer songbirds. It was all quite beautiful. Being the wife of Chairman Mao, she decided, certainly had its compensations.

Alexandra stepped to a ridge overlooking a valley filled with a kaleidoscope of orchids. In the midst of the lush beauty, Jiang Qing stood behind a Japanese camera mounted on a tripod. Jiang was wearing a neatly tailored yellow shirtwaist dress of heavy silk crepe de chine that high-lighted her narrow waist and extended below her knees in a style reminiscent of American fashions of the 1950s. Although past sixty, her body was still supple and graceful. Her short hair was parted in the middle and attractively brushed back from her forehead. She wore a strand of pearls with a jade pendant around her neck and rings on six of her fingers. In many ways she more closely resembled an aging film star than a militant revolutionary warrior.

Choosing an orchid with magenta and purple flowers, Jiang meticulously arranged the petals for the next photograph. A soft breeze rustled the leaves. Jiang smiled. Though she seemed content, lines of tension filled her face. Looking up, she saw Alexandra and waved. "Comrade Koo, my old friend, it's so good of you to come to see me."

"It's an honor to be invited." Alexandra stepped through a bed of sweet-smelling jasmine.

194

"You look lovely." Jiang clasped her hand. "Is that a new dress?"

"No, it's something I had in my closet," Alexandra replied, thinking about the four-hundred-dollar check she had just written to Saks Fifth Avenue."

"It becomes you marvelously."

"I'd be delighted to bring you one on my next trip. Size six?"

"Don't go to any trouble," Jiang responded, knowing that Alexandra would ignore her advice. "How about a cup of tea?" Jiang walked to a gazebo shaped like a miniature pagoda and offered Alexandra a wicker chair. "My friend, I'm very pleased with your deliveries."

"We completed another last night in Fujian."

Jiang smiled. Fujian was an area firmly under her control. "What goods were included?"

"Mortars, artillery guns, and bazookas."

"Excellent, we will soon have need of them. I will arrange a trip to Xian so that you can inspect the next cache of relics."

Alexandra nodded politely. "I appreciate your consideration."

A servant placed a pot of tea on the marble table. Jiang poured two cups. "It's chrysanthemum tea. Very good for the eyesight. I'll give you some before you leave."

"Thank you," Alexandra replied.

"I've become very devoted to herbal medicine. I used to have chronic trouble with my urinary system. Nothing helped, not even antibiotics, until I started taking lotus stalk. Now I feel much better." Jiang picked a flower and offered it to Alexandra. "This is a white day lily. It's one of my favorites. It's so fragrant, and it's wonderful for the complexion."

"I'm pleased to see you look so well. I know things must be very difficult."

"They are," Jiang said, suddenly sounding drained. "Mao is deteriorating rapidly. His face is drawn, his speech is unclear, and his mind is fading. He just stares into the distance with a look of resignation."

"I'm sorry."

"It's much harder than I thought it would be. We had such a good life together, especially during our first years in Yan'an. We lived in a small cave while we fought the Nationalists and the Japanese. Mao liked to work late into the night. After I finished my duties, I'd come into the part of the cave that served as his office and bring him a bowl of noodles. I'd sit and listen while he talked about his dreams for China, and I'd ask questions. Mao was my teacher. No matter what problems were weighing on him, he'd always find time to educate me. Sometimes we'd talk until we saw the first rays of the sun. Then we'd make love, get up, and begin our work for the day. I'd forgotten how happy we were in those early years."

"Why?"

"I suppose the demands of our lives put too much pressure on our relationship. Each year the struggles became more difficult and running the country more complicated. As I emerged from Mao's shadow, the responsibilities of my work forced me to be away from home. There was almost no time for us to be alone. Eventually a bitterness developed."

"I'm sorry."

"Since Mao has been ill, we've become close again, but now I'm afraid it's too late."

Alexandra tried to grasp the real reason for Jiang's confessions. Jiang and Mao had not lived together for three years. It was difficult to believe that either had the energy to rekindle their long-cooled passion. Mao was consumed with dying, and Jiang with taking his place.

Jiang sipped her tea. "If Mao could live for only six more months, we could join together and lead the revolution. Then he could appoint me his successor and the People's Republic could be assured of having a stable government. But Mao will not outlive the summer; and when he dies, those old men in the Politburo will be on me like a pack of wolves. Though they know that I'm the only person capable of leading China, they're jealous of my position in the public eye, nervous that I will expose them as lazy and inefficient bureaucrats, and threatened by the thought of having to follow the dictates of a woman. For all their talk about equal rights, they still think a woman is supposed to do nothing but raise children and cook meals. How can they have forgotten how we fought to liberate this country?"

"Forget them. They're old men. It's easier to move rivers and mountains than to change their attitude. But don't worry. Your friends are strong. We can defeat those old water buffaloes."

"I hope you're right; because if we lose, we'll be destroyed."

Alexandra looked up. Jiang Qing had picked a petal off the day lily and placed it on her tongue. Her eyes suddenly looked very old and tired.

15: A Jog in the Park

The first rays of the morning sun shone into Little Chang's eyes and startled her. Her short nap had lasted fourteen hours. She felt grubby. Her neck and face itched from mosquito bites. The back of her pants and work shirt seemed glued to her body. Her mouth tasted as if it were filled with cobwebs. The muscles in her spine throbbed with pain. She crawled to the opening between the trees and nervously looked around. No one was there, at least not yet; but they would find her soon enough.

There was a cawing sound behind her. A bird with a long black beak flew out of a clump of bushes and arched toward the sky. She dropped to her knees, glancing about to see what had frightened it. Nothing appeared. There was a sharp rustling noise. Stalks of yellow goldenrod vibrated in the morning breeze. She stood motionless, terrified she would be spotted. She could not remain a fugitive much longer. Her only chance was to find Sen Tailing.

She hurried down the hall, staying on the least traveled

198

paths. A tall young woman in red nylon shorts and a pink shirt came running toward her. Little Chang started to retreat but then stopped. The woman had blond hair and Western features. There was no need to be concerned.

The runner continued up the hill. "Hello," the woman said in English.

Little Chang sensed that the woman was trying to be friendly, but she could not reply to her words. "*Duibuqi. Wo bu hui jiang Yingwen*," she said, indicating that she could not speak English.

The jogger gazed at Little Chang as if she were planning to speak. Then she smiled, said goodbye, and continued running into the park.

Watching the woman disappear, Little Chang felt very alone. She wished she could run home to her husband, crawl into bed, and hide under the covers; but she knew she could not. She forced herself to continue. There had to be some way to penetrate the defenses of the Peking Hotel.

Little Chang walked tentatively onto Changyangmen Street. She hunched her shoulders and dropped her head to avoid the stares of the early morning workers, any one of whom could have been a policeman or a Red Guard. Feeling naked on the still empty sidewalks, she hugged the western wall of the Forbidden City and waited patiently beneath the shadows of the palaces until rush-hour traffic began to build. Then she plunged into the masses of buses, bicycles, and pedestrians flooding Chang'an Avenue. She started to feel more relaxed. There were so many people in the center of Peking that any one individual was completely inconspicuous. It was ironic that in the park she had sought to disappear by keeping to the least traveled paths, while in the city she sought to disappear by keeping to the most traveled streets.

Little Chang threaded her way toward the Peking Hotel.

Turning into the semicircular driveway, she saw a contingent of soldiers blocking the front door. She watched as they inspected every Chinese attempting to enter the building. There was no way to get past them. She walked to Wangfujing Street and looked for another entrance. Every door was covered by soldiers. There was no way for her to get to Sen Tailing.

Starting back to Tian'anmen Square, she saw two of her coworkers crossing the street. Her first impulse was to ask for assistance; they were lower-level cadres who owed her favors. But she could not risk contacting them. They had much to gain by reporting her and much to lose by helping her. She turned away and jumped onto a street car. Others climbed on behind, sandwiching her in the anonymity of the morning rush.

The streetcar stopped in front of the offices of the Telephone and Telegraph Company. Little Chang hurried into the building. This might be her last opportunity. She could feel the sweat gushing from her pores as she dialed the number of the Peking Hotel. "*Wei*," the operator answered.

"I'd like to speak to Sen Tailing."

"Please wait a minute." There was a click on the line.

A man came on the phone. "You want to speak to Sen Tailing?"

"Yes."

"Who are you?"

"I—ah—I am Assistant Manager Li from the Minitmetals Corporation," Little Chang said.

"Comrade Sen cannot be reached at this moment. Give me your number. I'll have him return your call within ten minutes."

"I'll call back."

"That may be difficult. Please give me your number."

"One minute, I have to answer my manager's phone."

Little Chang put down the receiver and rushed from the building. Jiang Qing's people had her completely isolated. She turned despondently back toward Beihai Park, now only half-caring whether anyone saw her. She reached an intersection and turned right. "Hello again," a voice said in English. Little Chang looked up. The blond Western woman smiled at her and then continued running toward Tian'anmen Square.

16: Slater and Van Wyck

CANTON AND SHANGHAI

Exhausted from his trip to the hot springs, Marc Slater strode onto the marble veranda of the Dong Fang Hotel, dropped onto a black aluminum chaise longue, and drifted to sleep. "Are you awake," a soft voice whispered twenty minutes later. Marc opened his eyes. Meili was standing above him. Her hand rested on the frame of his chair. He wanted to reach out and touch it, but there were too many people around.

"This is a delightful surprise." He stared into her eyes and smiled.

She blushed but did not look away. "I'm sorry to disturb your nap, but there has been a change of plans. My father would like you to fly to Shanghai in the morning. There is something he wants you to see."

"What is it?"

"I can't tell you now."

Marc leaned forward and smiled. "Are you coming with me?"

Meili laughed. "Did you think I would leave you to face the wilds of China on your own? My father has assigned me to be your official guide."

"Please thank him for me."

"I already have."

"What time is our flight?"

"Yours is at ten A.M. I must leave tonight to make preparations. A car will meet you in front of the Peace Hotel at nine A.M., the day after tomorrow, and bring you to our rendezvous."

"Are you sure that you don't want to travel with me?"

Meili cast her eyes away from Marc. "What I want really does not matter. Like you, I must be concerned about my responsibilities." She bowed deeply and turned to leave the veranda.

Marc watched as she walked away. Her carriage and stride were those of a ballet dancer. Even in loose-fitting work clothes, she excited him. He wanted to go after her. Standing up, he saw Alexandra Koo approaching. He tried to escape. "Marc," Alexandra called. Her footsteps were getting closer. "Marc." There was no way to avoid her. He stopped and turned toward her. Alexandra was wearing dangling jade earrings with a matching skirt and blouse. She smiled at him. "I hope I didn't interrupt anything. You seemed very engrossed in your business."

Marc stared at her suspiciously. "There are many pressures."

"But this one's a little young, and a comrade to boot."

"She's a representative of the Petroleum Corporation," Marc responded, wondering how he had alerted Alexandra to his feelings for Meili.

"And I'm the Dowager Empress."

Marc smiled. "I always knew there was something regal about you."

Alexandra placed her hand on her hip and stared at Marc with her jet-black eyes. "I'm only looking out for your welfare."

"Don't lose any sleep over it."

"I won't, but you should. You are a *lao pengyou*. You have worked for years building your relationships. If you play your cards right, you can trade oil and minerals as long as you want. But there's one thing the Chinese will never forgive, not even from their closest foreign friends. Just remember what happened to that French diplomat."

Marc thought about the man, who had been expelled when he tried to marry a Chinese woman. "I can take care of myself."

"For your sake, I hope you're right."

It was past 10:30 A.M. when the CAAC (Civil Aviation Administration of China) Boeing 707 crossed the coastline and turned north. Marc glanced out the window at the rocky islands below. He did not know why Hu Shengte had arranged the stopover in Shanghai, but he was pleased to have the opportunity to spend more time with Meili.

Unlocking his briefcase, Marc opened the document that Hu had sent him from the Petroleum Corporation. After three years of negotiations, the corporation had finally approved his proposal to jointly build a new oil refinery at the Karamay fields in Xinjiang Province. Two months ago, the news would have been cause for celebration: Even though Karamay was two thousand miles from the nearest port, it was a productive field with ample untapped reserves. But now, because of the political uncertainties and the threat from the Russians, it was far too risky a site for development.

Marc smiled at Hu's sense of timing. By delaying his

204

decision, Hu had saved him from committing more than a half-billion dollars to a project that might be doomed to failure. But he had also offered a tempting carrot: If the Russians and the Japanese could be stopped, Schaffer would be able to obtain an even more powerful foothold in Chinese petroleum.

Marc lit his pipe, thankful that the CAAC did not yet have the same restrictions as its American counterparts. He wished he knew more about the Russians. The intelligence reports from Liu Teyu indicated that they had been responsible for the sinking of the British ship in Huangpu Harbor, the destruction of two railroad bridges in Manchuria, and the bombing of a Party headquarters in Sichuan. But as yet there was no news as to their identity or their future targets.

The only solid lead was that they were allied with the Takamura Corporation of Japan. Although the right-wing, nationalistic Takamura was diametrically opposed to the Russians on philosophical grounds, they shared the common goal of a weak and divided China. The Russians wanted to remove the threat to their eastern borders and remain the dominant force in international communism, while Takamura wanted to expand Japanese hegemony in the Far East and open new markets for its goods.

If there was a weak link, it was the Japanese. The Russians were professionally trained operatives with vast experience in clandestine operations, but the Japanese were merely businessmen, no more experienced than he. It was through them that he could get at the Russians. All he needed was a lead.

"*Ni yao bu yao cha* [Do you want tea]?" A round-faced flight attendant with a flat nose and a sweet smile interrupted his thoughts.

"*Qing gei wo yi bei.*" He gratefully accepted a cup of tea.

The attendant poured the still steaming brew. "*Xiexie ni.*"

"Where did you learn Chinese?" a blond man in the next seat asked.

"I was born in China." Marc looked at the man's impeccable clothing and perfectly manicured nails. "Do you speak any?"

"*Yi dian dian,*" the man said modestly.

Marc laughed. "That's a very Chinese answer for a foreigner."

"This foreigner has always been intrigued by China."

"As has this one," Marc replied, noticing that though the man looked young, his eyes were aged and hollow.

"Please excuse me." The man removed a business card from his wallet and handed it to Marc. "I'm Frans Van Wyck."

Marc offered his in return. "I'm Marc Slater."

"Of M. H. Schaffer?" Van Wyck asked without reading the card.

"The same."

"I'm honored."

Marc was pleased by the recognition. "You have me at a disadvantage. I know nothing about your company."

"We operate a few hotels in Holland and Indonesia. Recently we were awarded a contract to build fifty hotels in the People's Republic."

"That's a pretty impressive undertaking for a small company."

"We have a very strong partner, the Takamura Corporation of Japan. Perhaps you have heard of it?"

The name sent a jolt through Marc. "I know Takamura well," Marc replied as he carefully placed his tea back on his tray. Takamura was a vast and highly diversified conglomerate. It was most unlikely that this Dutch company was in any way related to its alliance with the Russians. But with no other contacts, anything, no matter how tangential, might be of use. "Why did you choose the Japanese?"

"We needed someone with experience, and Takamura came highly recommended," Van Wyck said.

"What exactly are they doing for you?" Marc asked.

"Surveys, engineering, general construction. They're operating like a contractor."

"Demolition?"

Van Wyck took a sip of tea and then wiped his mouth with a handkerchief. "That too. Why do you ask?"

"I'm fascinated with the construction procedures in China. My company is about to build an oil refinery and we're going to need a contractor."

"We've just started, but our experience thus far is very positive."

"Where do you get your materials?"

"Almost everything comes from China, except appliances and the like, which are Toshibas, built in Taiwan." Van Wyck smiled, enjoying the role of hotel magnate.

"Has the government given you any static about them?"

"Not here. They consider Taiwan one of their provinces. But we had to transship the goods through Japan so that the Taiwanese government would not know their ultimate destination."

"So everything else comes from China?"

"That's right. In the contract the Chinese stipulated that we use domestic products whenever they were available."

"That sounds like the Chinese," Marc said.

Van Wyck forced a smile. "Doing business here is a world unto itself."

"I've spent many years in China," Marc said politely. "If there's anything I can do to help, please feel free to call on me."

"That's a generous offer," Van Wyck said. "I may take you

207

up on it."

The deputy manager of the Shanghai branch of the Chinese Hotel Corporation greeted Van Wyck on the tarmac and ushered him into a waiting limousine. He wanted to talk with the Dutchman about the construction schedule for the White Cloud and North Sea hotels. Shanghai's existing facilities were always overbooked, and these new hotels were needed to accommodate the increased demands of the city's foreign friends. The Shanghai branch had originally wanted to build its own facilities, but the government had refused to give it the capital. Now it was forced to rely on the services of this Dutch company.

Van Wyck distractedly answered the questions of the bureaucrat; he had far more important things on his mind than the schedule for hotels that would never be built. The limousine reached the harbor and turned down Zhongshan Road. Van Wyck's eyes scanned the boulevard that the Europeans had called the Bund. The harbor of Shanghai was beautiful. The massive, ornate structures along the boulevard had been built by Western powers from their profits in the opium trade. But now that these powers had been banished, the sculptured walls, marble lobbies, and gilded balustrades were all decaying.

The limousine stopped in front of the Peace Hotel, once the finest in the Orient. The deputy manager had arranged for Van Wyck to occupy a top-floor suite facing the harbor. The Dutchman smiled. Capitalism did have some advantages. He thanked the bureaucrat and went directly to his three-room suite. The rooms were spacious with high ceilings, elaborately carved furniture, and fully paneled dressing areas. In the living room was a glass cabinet filled with sculptures of jade, ivory, and cinnabar. Van Wyck opened the cabinet and inspected the pieces. There was nothing that could compare with Chinese craftsmanship. The design was never original, but the workmanship was always magnificent.

He went into the bedroom and placed his suitcase on the king-size bed. Its prerevolutionary mattress sagged from too many years of use. Stepping into the bathroom, he washed his hands and face. The paint was peeling in large strips. Missing quarry tiles had been replaced by slabs of white plaster. Perhaps he would complain. Everyone was very solicitous of his needs. They thought that he would soon be able to offer them jobs with incentive compensation.

Van Wyck unpacked his easel and placed it on the balcony. He watched as ferries and sampans scurried around the score of oceangoing ships at anchor. Except for the red flags on the boats and the flat terrain in the background, he could have been in Hong Kong. Opening his paints, Van Wyck felt comfortable in this luxurious though shopworn suite. It was certainly far superior to the small cubicles in the Red Star Hotel to which the Russian technicians were always assigned. The telephone rang. Van Wyck answered it with a customary greeting: "*Wei.*" He listened for a minute. "Good. Then it's all set for tomorrow. I'll meet you at noon, and I'll deliver the package to the Mongolian in the morning." He jotted some notes in a diary. "I need one more thing. There's an American named Marc Slater staying here. I want him followed."

By the time the first rays of the sun began to sparkle off the surface of the harbor, Van Wyck had already been awake for two hours. He had wanted the time to paint and relax. The Dutchman walked to the balcony and glanced at the spacious promenade overlooking the river. At least two thousand Chinese were practicing *tai chi chuan*. Although no one seemed to be leading them, they conducted their silent martial-arts ballet with geometric symmetry, like a company of trained dancers. New workers arrived and within seconds were perfectly attuned to the timing of the movements. Van Wyck sipped his tea and marveled at the ability of the Chinese to submerge their individuality to the demands of the group. In Russia such conformity could be achieved only through force. This capability of working together gave the Chinese an inner strength that would make them difficult to subdue.

A squat man with cropped hair and heavy Mongolian features walked past the exercisers to the stone embankment bordering the river. He lit a cigarette, dropped it on the ground, and crushed it with his foot. Van Wyck left his room, crossed Zhongshan Road, and strode quickly through the esplanade. He stood silently for five minutes gazing at the factories on the far side of the river. Then he turned toward his contact.

"Van Wyck," a man called in English. The Dutchman stopped. Marc Slater, wearing shorts and a sport shirt, was walking toward him.

"Good morning, Slater," Van Wyck said, turning away from the Mongolian. "What are you doing here?"

"Getting a little exercise. You ever tried *tai chi*?"

"I don't really understand it."

"It's not difficult." Van Wyck feigned interest as Slater described the ancient Chinese ritual. "Why don't you join me tomorrow?"

"Perhaps I will."

"Six o'clock sharp, by the monument. Then we can have breakfast."

"I'll be there," Van Wyck said, although Slater's suggestion made him ill at ease. He was not certain why the

American was interested in him.

"See you tomorrow." Slater waved as he jogged toward Zhongshan Road.

Van Wyck glanced to the right. The Mongolian was still standing at the embankment. He waited until Slater had entered the Peace Hotel, then he turned north along the esplanade. The Mongolian walked toward him. As they passed, the Mongolian whispered, "There's a big delivery tomorrow night at the turn of the tide." Without indicating whether he had heard these words, Van Wyck continued walking. He was pleased that he would have to wait only one more day.

17: The Fugitive and the Jogger

PEKING

The day had slowly started to brighten as Linda Forbes jogged into Beihai Park. The wet leaves gave the park the aroma of mildewing fertilizer and made Linda feel as if she were running on a plate of soggy noodles. Rotating her neck, she tried to shake the cobwebs from her brain. She was still hung over from last night's fourteen-course banquet hosted by the Arts and Crafts Corporation. The food had been marvelous, but the Maotai had done the damage. Despite pleas that she was not a drinker, they kept filling her glass with the clear liquid, making toasts, and calling "*Ganbei,*" the Chinese expression for bottoms up. Now she was paying the price for Chinese hospitality.

Linda shortened her stride as she started up the hill. For the second day in a row, she would be visiting factories, actively playing out her cover as a buyer for Bloomingdale's. Though she enjoyed the role, she was worried about the smuggling. Leung Lilai had gone to Fujian to receive a shipment of arms. She had wanted to follow him, but Fujian was off limits to Westerners.

Reaching the top of the hill, Linda stopped to stare at the city magnificently stretched out below. There was a noise behind her. She turned uneasily. Through a cluster of bushes adorned with magenta flowers she saw a disheveled young Chinese woman. It was the same one she had seen the day before. "Hello again," Linda smiled.

The woman stepped from her hiding place. Her blue work clothes were covered with clumps of dirt. Her hair was matted and greasy. Her large eyes were puffy and red. Her face radiated desperation and fear. "Excuse me, are you all right?" Linda asked.

"I have the most difficult of problems," the young woman blurted out in Chinese. "The Red Guard is searching for me. I cannot talk with my friends. I need to find someone who can help me."

"Please calm yourself," Linda said in English. She could not risk divulging her knowledge of Chinese to someone she did not know.

"It is a matter that could change the future of China." A tear rolled down her cheek. "If only you spoke Chinese, you could tell Sen Tailing."

"Sen Tailing!" Linda exclaimed at the mention of Marc's assistant.

"Sen is the brother of my lover," Little Chang said, referring to her husband. "He will know that I am not a traitor and that she was the one who stole the papers from Mao's private vault."

Turning away, Linda tried to conceal her look of shock. Sen was her friend and ally. There would be little to risk by talking to him and much to lose if the woman was telling the truth. She turned to the woman, whose large, almost Western eyes stared imploringly. "Don't be discouraged," she consoled in Chinese.

213

"Ni ting de dong!" the woman shouted, and grabbed the American's arms, realizing her outpouring was understood.

Linda freed one arm and placed a finger to her lips. "Yes, I understand, but you must not tell anyone."

The woman shook her head. "Please try to find my brother-in-law. He's at the Peking Hotel."

"I know." Linda touched the woman's shoulder. "Sen is a friend."

"It is the joss of the gods," she sobbed.

"What's your name?"

"Chang Shuli, but I am known as Little Chang." The woman wiped her eyes. "My friend, what is your name?"

"Linda Forbes."

"Lin-da-fol-be. With all my heart, I am grateful for your help."

Running back to the Peking Hotel, Linda saw nothing but Little Chang's terrified expression. She had to find Sen. His room was number 1527, just down the hall from hers. She knocked on his door. A radio was playing, but no one answered. She telephoned from her room. Still no response. She left a message with the operator and slid a note under his door. Then she went downstairs for breakfast.

She had just finished a glass of juice when a soldier approached. Dressed in the uniform of Mao's private bodyguards, his stocky physique and erect posture conveyed an aura of authority. "Miss Fol-be,"—his English was heavily accented—"please come with me."

The guard spun around and marched from the room. Linda nervously searched her mind as she followed him into the old wing of the hotel, now closed to guests. She did not know what he wanted, but it did not seem possible that her identity had already been discovered.

The guard opened the door to a small, windowless room and motioned her to a couch with red cushions. Linda sat stiffly, her knees pressed together. The guard remained standing. "Cigarette?" he asked. Linda shook her head. "Tea?" He poured before she could reply. The cup rattled in its saucer as she tentatively lifted it to her lips.

"Please excuse the interruption." The guard's voice was artificially polite. "You were looking for Sen Tailing. I'd like to know why."

Little Chang's face flashed through Linda's mind. She tried to maintain her composure. "Sen is a friend of mine. I thought we might eat breakfast together."

"And that was the problem which was so critical?"

Either the operator had given the guard her message or he had read the note slipped under the door. "I'm a newcomer to China. Many things confuse me. I needed Sen's advice. Why? Is there a problem?"

"Nothing that concerns you." The guard lit a cigarette. "But it would be better if you sought advice from someone else. Do I make myself clear?"

"I understand," Linda replied, becoming certain that Little Chang was the cause of the inquisition.

The guard opened the door. "I apologize for any inconvenience. I hope I am not forced to trouble you again."

Linda tried to keep a steady pace as she walked back to the new wing. She had to learn more about Little Chang and then report her information to someone who could help. She wished she could find Marc Slater. The guard could never stop her from talking to an American. She walked toward the elevators. "Miss Fol-be," a voice called. She turned abruptly. Comrade Lu of the Arts and Crafts Corporation rushed up and bowed. "I am pleased to see you. We were becoming concerned because of the lateness of the hour."

Linda gasped as she looked at her watch. It was 9:05. She

had arranged to meet Lu at 8:30. "I'm sorry. I must have lost track of time. Let me get my briefcase and camera," Linda said, thinking that there would still be time for a quick phone call. "I'll be down in two minutes."

"I will be pleased to accompany you." Lu extended a hand toward an open elevator. "We can talk about our agenda on the way."

"Thank you for being so considerate." Linda forced a smile as she fought to control her frustration. There was nothing she could do about it, at least not now.

"Everything is planned," Lu said. "We will spend the morning and lunch at the cloisonné factory, the afternoon at the lacquerware center, and dinner at a banquet hosted by the Peking Jewelry Branch."

"When will we get a chance to rest?" Linda asked, trying to decide how to go about contacting someone with her news.

"You are young and we have much to accomplish," Lu smiled. "You can rest tonight when we return to the hotel."

Linda felt like a trapped animal. There was no way to cancel the appointments without arousing suspicion. She only hoped that Little Chang could elude the people hunting her and remain free until she returned.

At 9:00 P.M. Linda rushed back into the lobby of the Peking Hotel. During the long day and the interminable banquet, her mind had been preoccupied with thoughts of Little Chang. She only hoped it was not too late to help. "Excuse me," she said to the young clerk behind the front desk. "Is Marc Slater registered?"

The clerk searched through a stack of index cards while Linda paced nervously. "I'm sorry. Mr. Slater changed his reservation. He is not expected for two days."

"Do you know where I can reach him? It's very important."

"I do not have that information," the clerk replied. "Perhaps the Petroleum Corporation can help you. The host corporation always knows the location of its foreign guests. Why don't you call them in the morning?"

"I can't wait that long," Linda replied. There was one other alternative. She had been told to use it only in an emergency, but this certainly qualified. "Could you check Mr. and Mrs. Samuel Tang?"

The clerk again searched through the cards. "The Tangs are expected at eleven-thirty tomorrow morning."

Linda turned from the desk in frustration. She had to find another way. Taking the elevator to her room, she opened the back of her leather passport case and removed a scrap of paper with the home phone number of her grandfather. She could feel her palm sweating as she reached for the receiver. She had rehearsed this first conversation many times. "Comrade Liu," she would say, "my name is Linda Forbes." She would pause. "My granddaughter," he would say, his voice tinged with delight. "You don't know how much I've longed to hear from you."

"Is someone there?" the operator's voice crackled through the earpiece on the phone. Linda slammed the phone back in its cradle, concerned that she had almost made a foolish mistake. What if Liu had never received her grandmother's letter? What if he had no idea that she existed? What if he refused to see her or to listen? What was she going to tell him anyway—that she met a frightened girl in the park who told her that someone had stolen something out of Mao's private vault? Linda laughed at her own words. He'll think I'm nuts.

Wishing that she had not given up smoking, she poured a cup of tea. She could not relax. There were no other

217

alternatives. She had to take the chance. Picking up the phone, she gave the number to the operator. "*Wei*," a man answered in Chinese.

"Comrade Liu?" Linda asked in her best Pekingese accent.

"I am sorry but Comrade Liu is out of town," the man said. "Could you tell me who you are and why you are calling?"

"This is—" Linda hung up the phone. What could she say? "Please tell Liu that his illegitimate granddaughter called"? It was ridiculous. There was no way she could leave a message.

18: Marc and Meili

As the car turned off the main highway that led northwest from Shanghai, Marc Slater sat alone in the back seat listening to the unending monologue of the driver. In the two hours since they had left the hotel, Marc had heard two new recipes for cooking carp and an interminable story about the visit of President Nixon to the driver's commune. No matter how often he asked, he received no answer as to their destination. Although he trusted Meili, he would have felt more comfortable knowing where the driver was taking him.

The car drove between two fieldstone pillars spanned by a wooden sign that read, "Welcome to the South Wind People's Commune." This commune, like thousands of others in the People's Republic, was a self-contained, cooperatively owned community that resembled a rural county in the United States. South Wind had almost thirty thousand residents, three-fourths of whom lived in one of its five towns. In addition to the primary occupation of farming, the commune also produced garments, agricultural implements, and power stations. Because it was virtually self-sufficient, its residents rarely had the need or the opportunity to leave its boundaries.

Marc looked out on a group of young boys playing basketball in front of a row of single-story white buildings with brown tiled roofs. "Damn!" he said under his breath. Visiting a commune always meant sitting through boring presentations by the Party leaders. He could no longer count the times he had listened while these men had exhaustively detailed their victories over exploitative landlords, disease, and hunger, and their increases in production under the sage guidance of Chairman Mao. "How could she have done this to me?" he muttered. "I'll be here all day."

The car turned away from the offices of the commune and onto a dirt road. "Where are we going?" Marc asked, curious to know why he was not being subjected to the official greeting. The driver did not reply as he maneuvered the car through groves of flowering fruit trees, coming to a stop in a clearing surrounded by a cluster of small hills. Written at the top of the highest ridge in letters ten feet high was Chairman Mao's slogan "Each Pig Is a Fertilizer Factory."

Marc stepped outside and looked around. No one else was in sight. He heard the car starting to move, turned, and saw its taillights speeding in the direction from which they had come. As the sound of the motor became fainter, Marc felt very alone. He picked an apple and cleaned it on his sleeve. Where, he wondered, was Meili, and why had she selected this location? He gnawed at the fruit as his eyes searched the hills.

Two minutes later, Aziz Rahman rode through the

entrance to the South Wind People's Commune. Pointing to the tire tracks of Slater's car, Rahman instructed the driver to turn. A worker stepped forward waving his arms. Three others, following orders from Meili, directed the car toward the stucco buildings that served as the center of the community. Rahman grimaced. The official greeting could cause him to lose track of Slater.

A committee approached the limousine. "We welcome you. I am Comrade Ling, the Party secretary of the South Wind People's Commune. *Ni chi fan le ma*?" he asked, extending the traditional polite greeting in Chinese, Have you eaten rice today?

"I'm pleased to meet you. I'm Comrade Yuen from Peking." Rahman extended the bogus card that identified him as a deputy director of the Ministry of Foreign Affairs.

"My commune is greatly honored. I regret that we were not informed of your arrival so that we could have provided a proper greeting."

"The oversight was mine." Rahman tried to appear cordial as he invented a story to justify his visit. "My office has just been informed of the visit of President Giscard d'Estaing of France. I am here to plan the itinerary."

"The South Wind People's Commune would be honored to be the host of such a special foreign *lao pengyou*."

"Your hospitality is most appreciated," Rahman said as he saw the car that had carried Slater turn from a dirt road. Only the driver was inside. "Please excuse my haste, comrade, but we are on an exacting schedule. With your kind permission, I would like to tour the commune."

"Of course," the secretary replied. "As soon as we finish lunch."

"Lunch is not necessary," Rahman said.

"Comrade, I implore you not to reject our humble hospitality."

Realizing that it was a matter of face and that there was no way he could refuse the Party secretary's offer, Rahman replied, "I would be honored to join you for a bowl of rice."

Marc was so engrossed in his own thoughts that he did not hear the footsteps until they were almost upon him. Startled, he looked up. Meili, wearing a floral print blouse beneath her blue work clothes, smiled shyly as she bowed. "Mr. Slater, my honored guest, I am pleased to see you. I apologize for not being here when you arrived."

Marc stood stiffly, controlling his desire to touch her. "I wasn't waiting long."

Meili brushed her bangs away from her eyes. Her long dark hair was neatly tied back in a ponytail. "I hope your trip went well."

"Quite well, but it's better now."

Meili turned away. "We have little time. Please follow me."

As Meili started to jog up the hill, Marc watched the fluid rhythm of her body. They trotted stride for stride over a hill and through a valley of orchards. Reaching the top of another ridge, Marc stopped. Half a mile away was the massive Yangtze River. Four thousand miles long from its headwaters and now almost six miles wide, the silt-laden river looked like a vast brown carpet laid between east China's fields of wheat and rice.

Meili climbed down a steep embankment. "In here," she said, disappearing into a wall of rocks. Marc hurried after her. He found an opening and crawled into a cave illuminated by a thin ray of light emanating from the far end. Trying to maintain his balance on the moss-covered rocks, he inched between the sheer walls, rounded a bend, and found himself standing in a circular cathedral sculpted by nature. A brilliant stream of light flooded through an opening two hundred feet above and sparkled off the crystal-clear surface of a pool of water embedded in the rocks. He stepped onto a ledge honed smooth by millennia of erosion and watched a mountain spring cascading into a river far below.

"Do you like it?" Meili touched his shoulder and then backed away.

A tingling sensation rushed through his body. "It's magnificent. How did you find it?"

"I used to come here all the time."

Meili slid her body onto the smooth rock and stretched out her legs. She extended her hand to Marc. He softly touched her fingertips. "I didn't know your father lived near Shanghai."

"He didn't." Meili's smile faded. "I was sent here when my father was purged. The South Wind People's Commune was my rectification camp."

Marc knelt beside her. "It must have been very difficult for you."

"It was terrible." Meili splashed the icy water on her face. "I was separated from my family and treated like a pariah. People tormented me and accused my father of being a traitor. When my mother died in Manchuria from malnutrition, I almost fell apart. I know we Chinese are supposed to be self-reliant and that the ideal is to be a peasant, but I hated harvesting rice. Every day I would come to the grotto and pretend that I was back in Peking with my family, studying to be a doctor. I needed that fantasy to survive."

"I understand." Marc gazed into her sad yet determined eyes. The struggles of the Cultural Revolution had left her far stronger than he would have suspected.

"I apologize for prattling on."

"Don't." Marc touched her long, graceful neck. "I'd like to hear more."

"It was wrong to dwell on the past," Meili said. "But I have never brought anyone to this grotto before. It's always been my private place."

"I'm glad I'm here."

She turned to him with a smile that illuminated the cave and tenderly kissed his cheek. He took her face in his hands. Her lips quivered. Her eyes made him feel chilled. He wanted to pull her down on the rock and press his body on top of her, but fought the urge. She was at the same time inviting and forbidding. He touched his lips to her mouth. His body trembled. She gently placed a finger to her lips. "Please don't tell Chairman Mao about my decadent barbarian habits."

"Your secret is safe with me."

"We are taking a great risk."

"We can over—"

Meili shook her head. "No promises now. There is too much uncertainty to predict the future."

"But—"

"Please, we have to go. The boat is waiting." Meili turned abruptly away and headed back to the entrance of the cave.

It began to pour as Marc and Meili reached the banks of the Yangtze and climbed aboard a small motor launch. Drenched, Meili gave instructions to the captain and then led Marc into the grimy cabin, reeking of motor oil and fish. She opened a hatch. "I'm sorry for the accommodations. I am sure they are nothing compared to those on your boat."

Marc smiled, surprised that she knew so many details of his life. "When you come to the United States, I will take you sailing."

"I hope to have the opportunity," Meili said as she removed her blue jacket. Her sopping-wet blouse clung to the soft contours of her body. Marc's eyes honed in on the

224

smooth lines of her trim waist. She untied her ponytail and shook out her hair. A drop of water ran from her forehead down her nose. Marc had an almost irresistible impulse to sip it.

He lit his pipe. It tasted good, and puffing on it made him feel less wet. The faintly nutty aroma overpowered the odor of oil and fish as it filled the cabin. Meili laughed. "I am certainly glad that I brought my own private incense maker."

Marc brushed lightly against her. "I'm always at your service."

The launch steamed upstream. Rain pelted against the hatch, making a sound like spring silkworms chewing on mulberry leaves. "Do you want a cup of tea?" Meili asked as she dried her hair with a towel.

"There are other things I'd like more."

"And there are comrades staring at us." Meili stepped to the small alcohol stove and poured two steaming cups.

Marc laughed. "Why does everything in the People's Republic seem designed to frustrate me?"

"Perhaps because you have forgotten your Chinese patience." Meili lightly touched Marc's neck as she handed him the tea.

"You sound just like your father."

Meili's eyes smiled at Marc's. "I have tried to follow his example, but I think he would not be pleased by all of my actions."

"Then we will not mention them to him."

Marc and Meili spent the next hour engrossed in conversation, until a seaman summoned them to the deck. Marc looked out the porthole. The rain had let up and they had docked alongside a flat rock in a horseshoe-shaped cove. On all sides were wide fields of rice paddies. Yet, strangely, all were fallow and no workers were in sight. Marc glanced suspiciously at Meili. In a country with chronic food shortages, it did not make sense that such fertile land would remain uncultivated.

Meili climbed up the companionway. One of the seamen was already ashore. "We'd better hurry," she said as she jumped off the boat. Marc followed, his curiosity piqued by their mysterious destination.

The seaman led the way as they jogged along the muddy path. After ten minutes, the path turned back toward the harbor, where a fleet of sampans and barges were docked. Marc watched as large crates were unloaded from boats and placed in waiting trucks. "What's going on?" he asked.

"You'll see soon enough," the seaman replied, leading them up a hill toward a cluster of trees. He stopped next to a large banyan. "Can you climb?" he asked Marc.

"If you'll give me a hand up."

Marc stepped into the basket formed by the seaman's hands and pulled himself onto the lowest branch. The seaman handed him a pair of binoculars. He peered through them, scanning the horizon. Next to the harbor was a staging area with jeeps, trucks, and pieces of field artillery. Beyond the staging area were barracks and warehouses, and beyond them was an antiquated airfield. "Is it a People's Liberation Army camp?" he asked.

"No," Meili replied, "it's Jiang Qing's private arsenal."

Marc looked angry but not surprised. "And the weapons?"

"All smuggled. Many are American."

Marc noticed an airplane. "Damn! I don't believe it, but I'd swear that there's an old American jet on the runway."

"There are twenty more in the arsenal," the seaman said.

"Where did Jiang get them?"

"Most were captured in the Korean and Vietnamese wars," Meili replied.

"How did they get the planes to fly?"

"Jiang Qing smuggled in spare parts from all over the world."

"She seems quite well organized."

"She is a formidable adversary," Meili responded.

"So it would appear," Marc said, climbing down from the tree. Though he had not been able to view the entire arsenal or learn whether this was the only one controlled by Jiang, he had seen enough to realize that Mao's wife was building a powerful fighting force.

"A pox on the long-nosed foreign devil," Aziz Rahman cursed Marc Slater, as still another cadre from the South Wind People's Commune toasted the long life of Chairman Mao. Almost two hours had been consumed at this never-ending banquet, and he was now completely frustrated.

"More pigs' livers and spinach?" the secretary of the commune asked.

Rahman's stomach growled, belching the food back to his throat and giving stern warning that it would not accept another serving. "I think I've had enough."

"How about some pickled jellyfish?"

"Not right now, thank you." The hospitality of the commune had become oppressive. Rahman realized that it had been a mistake to introduce himself as an official of the Ministry of Foreign Affairs. If he had posed as a Red Guard, he would have been able to search for Slater without being subjected to their courtesies.

"You'll enjoy this," the secretary announced, plunging a ladle into a tureen. "It's one of our specialties, sea cucumber and pork rind soup."

Rahman forced a smile. It was against his religion to eat pork. He had eaten the pigs' livers for the sake of appearance, but another dish was well beyond the call of

227

duty. He looked at his watch and shook his head. "It's late and I unfortunately have to return to Peking."

"What about your tour of the orchards?" the Party secretary asked.

"You have shown me such hospitality," Rahman replied, "that I am certain the president of France will be more than satisfied."

Everyone at the table stood up as the Party secretary escorted Rahman into the parking lot. "Our humble commune has been honored by your presence. You may be certain that we will work diligently to prepare everything for the visit of our honored foreign guest."

Rahman thanked the cadre, climbed into his car, and instructed the driver to stop at the first turnoff on the main road. He was annoyed that he had lost the track of the American, but Slater had to return sometime and he was prepared to wait. He opened a window. The pigs' livers gurgled in his stomach. He controlled himself until he had passed the gate of the commune, then he hung his head outside and proceeded to throw up everything he had eaten.

The launch docked along the pier at the South Wind People's Commune. Grabbing her still wet jacket, Meili turned to the stairs. "I'll see you tomorrow in Peking," she said to Marc.

"Wait a second." He stood facing her, wishing that one of the seamen were not standing in the cockpit. "Where are you going?"

"I'm staying here. I have some work to do."

"What about me?"

She kissed her finger and then touched it to his cheek. "You, my friend, are going for a boat ride."

"What about the car that brought me here?"

"It seems," Meili said in English, "that I am not the only one who wants to see you. Someone went to all the trouble of following you this morning from Shanghai."

"Who?" Marc asked. His eyes showed his concern.

"We do not know, but he is still waiting near the commune."

"Can you find out who it is?"

"We will try. But it would be safer if you returned to the city by boat. It may take a few hours, but your friend is likely to have considerable difficulty following you on the river in his limousine."

19: Little Chang's Last Hope

Sleep had been impossible. Linda Forbes paced the floor of her room until 7:00 A.M., then grabbed a thick novel and went to the dining room. Choosing a table near the entrance, she lingered over her breakfast for an hour and a half while she searched for someone she knew. But no one appeared.

Returning to her room, Linda canceled her morning appointment with the Peking Jewelry Branch. Then she phoned Comrade Lu at the Arts and Crafts Corporation and explained that she had to reach Marc Slater on an urgent personal matter. Lu said he would try to help.

More than two hours passed before he called back. "I've been unable to locate Mr. Slater." Lu's voice was terse. "The chief of the international trade section of the Petroleum Corporation is at a meeting, and no one else is empowered to tell me what I wanted to know."

"Thank you for your efforts," Linda replied, certain that something was wrong. If no one would divulge Marc's whereabouts, it was because he was either on a secret mission or in great trouble.

It was almost noon. Perhaps the Tangs had arrived. They were now her only chance. She picked up the telephone and asked for their room. She was in luck. "*Wei*," a woman's voice answered.

"Mrs. Tang, this is Linda Forbes from Bloomingdale's." Linda tried to keep a formal tone just in case someone was listening.

"How nice to hear your voice, Linda. What can I do for you?"

"I wanted to tell you how much I admire your bronze drum." Linda used the code as she had been instructed.

"Like the one in the Forbidden City?"

"Exactly. Do you know where I can purchase one?"

"Let me check. I'll get back to you in half an hour."

Twenty-five minutes later, Linda Forbes entered the Forbidden City and hurried through a stone courtyard so massive that it dwarfed the thousands of Chinese gathered inside. Beyond the courtyard, the Hall of Supreme Harmony, the Hall of Perfect Harmony, and the Hall of the Preservation of Harmony, stretched majestically in single file. Gazing at the ornately painted walls, Linda tried to imagine what these palaces must have been like during the dynastic New Year celebrations when legions of men carrying pennants and orchestras playing stone chimes and gilt-bronze bells had heralded the appointments of the emperors. A group of schoolchildren in blue outfits with matching hats and red scarfs mounted both sides of the central stairway of the Hall of Supreme Harmony. Between them was a panel of carved clouds and dragons that had served as the route over which the emperor's chair had been carried.

Linda followed the children. As she reached the top of the stairs, she heard a voice behind her. "Are you still interested in the bronze drum?"

She did not turn around. "I'm sorry to inconvenience you, but I didn't know if we could talk freely in the hotel."

"Your precaution was wise. What's the problem?"

"Someone told me that documents were stolen from Mao's private vault."

"I wouldn't worry. Peking has more rumors than it has flies."

"I think this one is true. I met a woman named Little Chang."

"The guardian of the National Archives?" Beatrice gasped.

"Do you know her?"

"She is Sen Tailing's sister-in-law."

"That's what she said. Do you think she has actually seen something?"

Beatrice laughed. "If she hasn't, then Jiang Qing has half the Red Guards in China wasting their time. There hasn't been a search like this since Lin Biao tried to flee the country after the failure of his coup. Do you think you can locate her again?"

"I'll try."

"Good," Beatrice said. "I want you to find out everything she knows."

"What about my other assignment?"

"Someone will take over from you until this is finished. Little Chang is far more important. Call me as soon as you have spoken to her."

As Beatrice walked away, a surge of excitement welled up

inside Linda. She was the only link to Little Chang. She thought of Marc and her grandfather. If she succeeded in this assignment, both would be proud of her.

Returning to the hotel, Linda changed into her red shorts and pink shirt. Posing as a jogger would give her the best cover for remaining in the park until she found Little Chang. She circled the block to make sure no one was following and then ran toward the Forbidden City. A platoon of Red Guards marched under the huge portrait of Chairman Mao hanging between two red signs that proclaimed, "Long Live the People's Republic of China" and "Long Live the Solidarity of the Peoples of the World." Linda assumed that they were among those searching for Little Chang. She tried to appear nonchalant, but it was not easy.

She ran through the gate of Beihai Park and up the hill. Little Chang was partially hidden by a grove of trees. Linda stepped off the path. "Did you find Sen Tailing?" the young woman asked in Chinese.

"He wasn't in the hotel, and his room is being watched."

"There has to be a way to get to him," Little Chang's voice cracked.

"Why don't you tell me what you know," Linda entreated.

"That would put your life in danger."

"Do you have another choice?"

Little Chang pulled at her hair in frustration. "What can you do? You are nothing but a long-nosed barbarian."

Linda stared at the woman. "What if I could tell your story to Liu Teyu?"

"He would believe me." Little Chang grasped Linda's arm. "But how do you know him?"

"That doesn't matter. What matters is that I can find him."

Little Chang was still not convinced that Linda could help, but she had no other options. "Last week"—her voice quivered—"I saw Jiang Qing remove Chairman Mao's will from his private vault and substitute a forgery, which, I assume, names her and her Gang of Four as Mao's successors."

"Oh, my God!" Linda exclaimed.

"Jiang saw me, but I escaped. She informed the Red Guards that I was the one who had broken into the vault. Without other witnesses, it is my word against hers, and most people will believe Jiang."

"I believe you." Linda struggled to remain calm. She had to transmit Little Chang's desperate secret to Beatrice Tang and her grandfather. "I'll get help and come back for you."

With a look of sudden panic, Little Chang grabbed Linda's hand and pointed to the path behind her. Linda turned and saw six Red Guards approaching. Her legs trembled. She could not be seen in the company of Little Chang. "I'll meet you here at sundown," she said. Then she slipped between the trees and sprinted toward the lake.

Four soldiers reached the rim of the hill and moved to intercept her. One shouted in Chinese for her to halt, but she feigned ignorance and continued running. He fired a shot. She stopped. He hurried toward her with his gun raised. "*Bu yao pao*! [Don't run!] *Bu yao pao*!"

Linda's body shook as the soldier pressed his rifle into her ribs. He looked no more than sixteen, and his eyes reflected the confusion he felt in arresting his first foreigner. Raising her hands over her head, Linda pleaded, "Please don't hurt me. I am an American. I don't speak Chinese."

The Red Guards stared at Linda with intense curiosity as they debated her fate. Ordinarily they would have released her; but since she had been seen talking with Little Chang, they decided to bring her to headquarters. Surrounding her, the guards marched toward the gate of the park. Linda breathed deeply to calm herself. She had to keep a clear head if she was to escape from this trap. Her only hope was to maintain the pretense that she did not speak Chinese and pray that Little Chang had the presence of mind to confirm it.

20: An Evening Cruise on the Yangtze

SHANGHAI, PEKING, AND CANTON

Sitting in the theater of her villa, Jiang Qing watched as the scruffy English captain on the screen steadied the compressed-air cylinders while the missionary spinster filled them with dynamite. The captain connected his makeshift detonators and placed the cylinders through holes cut in the bow of the rickety launch. "They are very daring to use their boat as a floating torpedo," Jiang said, "much like we were against the Japanese."

Alexandra Koo smiled. The selection of the film, *The African Queen*, had been an excellent one. "I think they make a good team," Alexandra said.

"You can't be serious." Jiang glared at Alexandra through the darkness. "The woman is the hero. The man was nothing but a drunken slob before she emboldened him."

"Of course," Alexandra replied, wanting to avoid a confrontation.

"Westerners cannot accept women as warriors. In your movies the women are always hiding helplessly from the enemy while the men do all the fighting. It was much the same in China before I took control of culture. But my films and operas have changed things. They are truly revolutionary because they portray women as the equals of men."

"They are wonderful dramas." Alexandra tried to calm her hostess.

A door opened. "Excuse me," Shen Mo interrupted. "Mrs. Koo has a call from Mr. Leung in Shanghai. He says it's important."

Pleased for the excuse, Alexandra bowed politely, followed Shen into the study, and answered the phone. She smiled as she took down the list of weapons scheduled to arrive in Shanghai the next evening: 90 mortars, 5,000 hand grenades, 1,000 rifles, and 40 missiles. With these deliveries, they would soon be able to obtain more relics. Alexandra thought about her grandfather, who had been driven penniless from China. "The poor," he used to say, "are always three generations younger than the rich." It was about time that someone in the Koo family had the opportunity to come of age.

It was ironic that the future of the Koo family was once again dependent on the shipment of foreign weapons and the goodwill of a Chinese empress. Once before the Koos had been presented with such an opportunity. That time they had failed.

Alexandra's great-grandfather, Koo Kang, had been China's finest naval commander. Though his fleet was destroyed in the Sino-French War in 1884, the Dowager Empress appointed him her chief admiral and instructed him to build the strongest force in the Orient. For several years he made impressive strides. Then, as the memories of the loss to France dimmed, the empress changed her priorities and used her funds to rebuild the Summer Palace. Koo protested that China would be defenseless without Western arms, but his pleas were ignored.

Koo had to wait only two years to prove he had been correct. In the Sino-Japanese War, the Japanese, armed with Western weapons, easily defeated the troops of the empress. The rout at the hands of the Island Dwarfs was a crushing blow to the Chinese. A scapegoat was needed. Koo was selected as the symbol of defeat and ordered to kill himself. Alexandra still felt intense bitterness about her great-grandfather. He had been killed not because he performed badly but because he had been right.

Alexandra stared at her jade pendant. It was the one treasure her family had taken from China. Now there were debts that had to be settled. China owed her the suicide of her great-grandfather. Although she was as much of a vassal to the Communist empress as her grandfather had been to the Dowager Empress, she had had no other choice. She needed Jiang to help obtain the riches that were her due. She would not leave China without them.

Beatrice Tang, dressed in a pair of brown slacks and a neatly tailored matching tweed jacket, opened the door to Marc Slater's room. "May I come in?" she asked. Her voice sounded strained. Her eyes looked tired.

"Hello, my friend," Marc smiled. He was glad to see Beatrice. Before leaving the South, Liu Teyu had confirmed that Beatrice and Sam were two of his principal contacts.

"Have you talked to Sen Tailing?" Beatrice asked.

"I've been waiting for him," Marc replied.

"He has a serious family problem." Beatrice's mouth hung in a pout. "His sister-in-law, Chang Shuli, has been accused by Jiang Qing of stealing papers from Mao's vault in the

238

National Archives."

"I can't believe it."

"Neither can I. I think Jiang Qing is trying to silence Little Chang because she knows something of critical importance."

"What?"

"I'm not sure. But one of my people is working on it."

Striking a match, Marc puffed on his pipe. He did not know how much Beatrice would confide in him, but he had to ask. "It is Linda Forbes?"

Beatrice nodded silently. "How did you know?"

"I found this note under Sen's door." Marc handed Linda's letter to Beatrice. "When are you going to see her?"

"I expected her this afternoon." Beatrice shook her head. "She went to see Little Chang but never returned."

"Half the Red Guards in the country must be looking for Little Chang. If they find Linda with her, it could be very serious."

"I'm sure she's all right." Beatrice poorly concealed her concern.

"Damn! I hate waiting around for things to happen to other people."

Beatrice touched Marc's shoulder. "I don't want to sound like a mother hen, but there's really nothing you can do."

Marc laughed at himself. "You'd think that after years of living in China and years of gambling fortunes on minerals contracts, I'd be able to function better with uncertainty. But I never seem to learn."

Working by the light of battery-powered beacons, Frans Van Wyck wrapped the red wire leading from the radio transmitter around the positive terminal on the detonator and tightened the screw until the connection was firm. He placed the detonator in a plastic container filled with a gelatinous explosive and gingerly enclosed the device in an inverted Styrofoam cone resembling the buoys that fishermen use to mark their lobster pots. After attaching an antenna to the top of the cone, he wired the device to a drum of gasoline. Then he and Aziz Rahman placed the devices in two ancient sampans tied to the stern of a launch. When he had finished, Van Wyck rechecked his work. He was pleased. The design and wiring were clean and precise. The bombs were securely in place. They were ready to leave the deserted pier near Shanghai.

Rahman opened the casing and checked the motor. He was still annoyed about losing Slater's trail. "I just can't understand what happened to that pox-covered barbarian," he said. "I followed him to the commune, but then he disappeared like beef off a peasant's plate."

"Don't worry about it," Van Wyck replied. "We'll take care of him when we get back."

Rahman started the motor while Van Wyck cast off the lines. The launch towing the sampans turned from the secluded cove into the Yangtze River and sailed toward the southern shore of a small island shaped like a bent thumb. A channel between two stone breakwaters led to a large protected habor. Stopping the launch at the narrowest point of the channel, Van Wyck and Rahman climbed into the two sampans.

After checking the connections on the explosives, they dropped the mushroom anchors overboard and drilled a series of holes below the water line. The sampans filled with water. In less than ten minutes, both rested on the bottom, forming an invisible explosive chain across the width of the channel. Only the inverted cones bobbing in the currents and the bubbles from the crabs, who had come to inspect the intruders, hinted of their existence. The Dutchman smiled.

"Just twenty hours more and these things could create quite a show."

Rahman laughed. "We'll have Chinese New Year in July."

Linda Forbes had just finished her breakfast when she heard the commotion in the hall. She walked to the front of her cell and watched as Colonel Li strode down the corridor to where Little Chang was imprisoned. The colonel greeted the young woman with a voice that exuded soothing rationality. Little Chang's response was nervous and high-pitched. The colonel's voice grew harsh and distinct as he demanded answers. Little Chang stuttered, trying to justify her actions. The colonel pressed on. "Who have you talked to since you left the archives?"

"No one."

"What about the American girl?"

"No. She was just jogging through the park."

"Don't lie to me. Paper cannot wrap up a fire."

"I swear—"

Linda heard a loud scream, followed by muffled sobs. A throbbing knot formed in her chest. She tried to take a deep breath. Her lungs felt clogged. She was trapped in the center of a maelstrom. She prayed that Little Chang would protect her identity.

There was another panicked scream. Linda winced, feeling Little Chang's pain. The screams became more intense and desperate. Linda fled to the army cot in the back of the cell. She could do nothing to help. She pulled her knees to her chest, hunched her shoulders, and covered her ears, trying to blot out the woman's agony.

Three hours later, a flood of light gushed through the corridor. Colonel Li and two guards approached her cell. "*Ni hao ma*?" the colonel asked politely. Linda stared blankly into his eyes.

"The colonel asks if you are well," a guard said.

"Please tell the colonel that I do not speak Chinese."

The guard translated.

"*Hu shuo ba dao*! [Nonsense!] *Wo zhidao ni hui jiang Zhongwen. Wo zhidao ni shi Xiao Chang de lao pengyou.*"

"The colonel says that he does not believe you. He knows that you speak Chinese and that you are an old friend of Little Chang."

Tears welled up in Linda's eyes. She had to find a way of convincing them to release her. "Please believe me. I did not talk to the Chinese woman. I am an American. I work for a department store. I don't understand anything that is happening. I just want to go home." The words and the tears gathered speed. What had begun solely for effect took on its own momentum and became a torrent.

Colonel Li spat on the floor and said to the guards in Chinese, "Look at this capitalist barbarian. It is a disgrace to see how she throws away her face. But I will not be tricked. Make sure that she confesses."

A telephone rang. A guard answered it and bowed to the colonel with great respect. "Comrade Jiang Qing wishes to speak with you." Distressed, Linda watched the colonel rush to the phone. Jiang Qing's personal involvement did not bode well for her.

"This is a great honor, Comrade Jiang," the colonel said in a voice too soft for Linda to hear. "Thank you for your kindness. . . . That's correct. Chang Shuli says she spoke with no one, but we found the American with her." The colonel stared at Linda. "Yes. Linda Folbe. She says she is a buyer for a department store. . . . Of course, I'll wait."

Colonel Li forced a smile as he paced nervously. "Yes, Mrs. Koo. I'd say no more than thirty. . . . Yes, I'd say quite tall." The colonel squinted at Linda. "Blond, the color of a wheat field in the noon sun. Yes." Colonel Li looked annoyed. "If that's what you want. Of course, I'll wait."

Colonel Li hung up and stalked back to Linda's cell. "We won't have to listen to your lies any longer." He paused while the guard translated. "Someone is coming who knows who you are and what you are doing in China."

It was just past dusk when Yamaguchi Yukio stepped onto the launch, docked in a cove along the Yangtze River. "What's the problem?" he asked.

Frans Van Wyck bowed politely. "I'm sorry to inform you that the weapons are being carried on the *Kobe Maru*, a Japanese ship."

Yamaguchi repressed his desire to smile. The *Kobe Maru* was owned by the Matsuyama Corporation, his company's toughest competitor. For him to be concerned with its fate would be like the cat crying for the mouse. Still, it was appropriate for him to maintain appearances. He ran his hand across his brow. "That makes things most difficult."

"Do you want me to cancel the mission?"

"No. You have put too much work into it. I made a firm commitment and it would be wrong of me to back out now."

"Is there anything I can do?"

"Perhaps, when we negotiate the terms of the petroleum contracts, you could remind your superiors in Moscow of the sacrifices of my people."

"I would be pleased to do so. And perhaps you could convey my condolences to your friends at the Matsuyama Corporation."

Yamaguchi did not change his expression. To do so would have made them both lose face. He respected the Dutchman and appreciated his Oriental subtlety. "I'll tell them that you are as distraught as I am."

"It's because we both want the same ends." Van Wyck bowed his head toward Yamaguchi. "With your most considerate permission . . ." Van Wyck's men cast off, and the launch sailed to a small cove near the breakwater. The anchor was dropped. Van Wyck checked his detonators. Then he poured himself a cup of tea and waited.

The moon had already passed through more than half the sky by the time the masthead lights of the *Kobe Maru* became visible. As the freighter approached a green flashing light, Van Wyck clicked on his stopwatch and then removed the remote-control detonator from his gym bag. Tenderly he fondled the rubber knobs on the black box. His eyes were riveted on the Japanese freighter, as if it were the object of his affection. His fingers tingled as he watched it turn into the breakwater where the sampans had been sunk the night before. He closed his eyes as he pressed the buttons. A smile of satisfaction crept onto his face.

There was a deep rumbling beneath the starboard bow of the *Kobe Maru*, followed by a muffled boom that sounded like an exploding depth charge. The ship lurched to the right as a spout of water showered scraps of the sunken sampan onto the deck. A flaming stream of gasoline climbed the hull. A second explosion thrust the bow violently into the air. Fire reached the cargo holds and ignited the mortar shells. The ammunition burst in continuing crescendos, transforming night into midday. Van Wyck turned his launch back toward Shanghai. His work was over. Tomorrow he would treat himself to the sculpted ivory warrior he had been admiring.

Vance Stewart sat up in his bed in Canton's Dong Fang Hotel when he heard the knocking on his door. He squinted at his watch. It was 5:15. He had been up late drinking and was in no mood to greet the day. Wrapping himself in his robe, he opened the door. Wong Chuyun, dressed in a beige safari suit, stood in front of him, nervously puffing on a cigarette. "Do you know what time it is?" Stewart complained.

"Jiang Qing wants to see us immediately."

"That's not my problem. It's your job to handle her."

"I'm sorry but Jiang insisted that you come as well."

"What the hell does she want with me?"

"I don't know," Wong said as he selected Stewart's clothes, "but her aide said that if you don't show, the opium deal will be canceled."

"That bitch!"

Vance dressed quickly and hurried to the limousine waiting in front of the hotel. Alexandra Koo was sitting inside. "Good morning, Alexandra." Vance politely extended his hand.

"Vance," she smiled, "so nice to see you."

"Do you know why we've been summoned?" Vance asked.

"A Japanese freighter carrying Jiang's weapons was sunk last night."

"What does that have to do with Wong and me? We're tobacco merchants."

Alexandra laughed. "My dear Vance, it's too early to play games. I know about your opium deal." Vance glared at Wong. "Don't blame him. Jiang consulted me first. I told her you'd make an excellent partner."

"And what do you expect from me for your unselfish act?"

"How about some civilized behavior? I lost ten million dollars when that shipment blew up."

"It wasn't my doin'."

"Nor was it mine. Jiang's allies in Shanghai were supposed to protect it. But they screwed up. And now we have to bear the brunt of her rage."

The limousine reached Jiang Qing's villa. Shen Mo

opened the door. "Jiang is in one of her states," Shen said. "She complains of stomach pains and sharp flashes. She is also highly suspicious. She blames that movie you brought for bringing bad luck on the Japanese freighter. I wouldn't refer to it if I were you."

Shen led them into a sparse meeting room. Jiang Qing, dressed in a Red Guard uniform, walked through the open door. Without greeting her guests, she picked up a wooden pointer. "We are at war." Her voice was strained. "Deng Xiaoping and his capitalist allies want to seize control of the country. They will do anything to achieve their ends. Last week they blew up a British ship and stole some of Comrade Mao's most important papers. Then last night, they bombed a Japanese cargo ship. Had I not personally called the prime minister of Japan, we might be at war right now."

Jiang sipped a cup of herb tea. "Deng knows that the people love Comrade Mao and me. He won't rest until I am destroyed. Then he will transform China into his own private capitalist empire. I cannot sit still while everything that Comrade Mao and I have struggled to achieve is destroyed. We must strike while there is still time."

Vance stirred uneasily. He agreed with many of Deng's policies, but the success of his business was dependent on Jiang's support. To maintain his monopoly on tobacco and opium, he would have to do her bidding.

"Deng is staying at a villa near Tangshan." Jiang's voice was suddenly calm. "He is meeting with two of the most perfidious traitors in the country, Liu Teyu and Hu Shengte, as well as with an American agent named Marc Slater." Vance looked up in surprise at the mention of Slater's name. "These people must be removed. My position is precarious. If something happened to them and if it were traced to me, I would be undermined and Deng would become a martyr. But if Deng and his allies were disposed of by someone who was trying to kill Slater, then their deaths would be thought of as an accident, unrelated to me."

"Why would anyone want to kill Slater?" Vance asked in English.

"Perhaps because he is attempting to gain control of opium."

"Slater wants oil. He has no interest in opium."

"And you?" Jiang responded in Chinese. "What do you want?"

"I want to work together for our mutual benefit."

"There is an old saying, 'When the lips die, the teeth immediately feel cold.' I am your lips. Without me, your tobacco-stained teeth will freeze."

"*Women dong* [We understand]," Wong interrupted.

"Mrs. Koo's associate, Leung Lilai," Jiang continued, "will work with you. I am confident that he will help you eliminate our problems."

"Are you asking us to kill Deng and the others?" Stewart protested.

Jiang smiled. "If that's what's needed to save China."

"Do not worry," Wong replied. "You may count on Mr. Stewart and me."

"I knew I could." Jiang bowed politely and left the room.

Stewart grabbed Wong's arm and pulled him into the corner. "You son of a bitch! I'm not going to be involved in any killing."

"You don't have to be. I'll find others to handle the work."

"How could you have given in to her blackmail?"

"Because she holds the cards. Without her, our business is finished."

"But is it worth killing people?"

"Come now, my friend," Wong said, "do you think your great-grandfather never killed anyone? Do you think no Chinese ever died in our factories? And do you think the

247

special concessions we've obtained have come without a price? Don't be naïve! To protect our monopoly, we've had no choice but to break the law. The only difference this time is that instead of sloughing off the dirty work on me, you're stuck in the middle."

"What if I refuse to help?"

Wong lit a cigarette. "Do you seriously think Jiang would let you leave the country with what you now know?"

Vance clenched his fists. "I'll protest to the American ambassador."

"And Jiang will claim that you are a spy."

"She can't do that to me!"

"Are you willing to risk your life testing her?"

Stewart angrily rubbed his heel into the floor. "I'll burn your ass when we get back to Hong Kong."

"My friend, when we get back to Hong Kong, we'll either be in control of the world's largest supply of opium or we'll be ruined. Either way, your vengeance won't matter."

21: The Road to Tangshan

PEKING, TIANJIN, AND TANGSHAN

Lord Henry Gateshead stepped into the cabin and inspected CAAC flight 32 with relief. There were no red slipcovers on the seats, no quotations from Chairman Mao above the lavatories, and no pictures of Marx and Lenin on the bulkhead. Except for the instructional signs in Chinese and the flight attendants attired in loose-fitting blue work clothes, flight 32 had the same functional neo-Seattle decor of all 707s. Although Gateshead would have preferred a British Viscount, there was something comforting about unadulterated American technology.

Lord Gateshead found his seat and watched as passengers filled the foreign section in the front of the plane. A six-foot-five American and a well-dressed, wiry Chinese sat in the row behind him. Nine overseas Chinese in polyester suits filled the first three rows. An elegant Chinese woman with long black hair and dark piercing eyes entered the plane. She was wearing a flowing green dress and a magnificent jade pendant. The woman spoke briefly to the tall

American and then took the seat across the aisle from Lord Gateshead.

After the foreigners were settled, the local Chinese were permitted to board. Since the CAAC charged a substantial fee for overweight, the Chinese arrived laden with elaborately tied boxes and fully stuffed shopping bags, which they crammed into every available crevice. One man had to be packed into his seat by two of his friends. Gateshead hoped the man would not need to visit the lavatory during the flight.

A round-faced flight attendant handed Gateshead a plastic bag filled with candies that looked like saltwater taffy. As he unwrapped one, a melodious voice greeted him warmly. "*Bonjour*, Lord Henry."

He looked up smiling. Nicole LaFleur was standing in the aisle wearing a clinging dress that showed off her attractive figure to the fullest extent that good taste would permit. "Good-day, Nicole," Lord Gateshead said. "Would you like to join me?"

"*Enchantée.*"

Gateshead inspected the Frenchwoman. "Are you enjoying your visit?"

"It's been wonderful. This country is fascinating." Nicole laughed and toyed with her wavy brown hair. She prattled on predictably for several more minutes, then looked apologetically at the Englishman. "I'm sorry if I'm boring you."

"You're not boring me." Gateshead arched his bushy eyebrows.

"But you've been to China so many times."

"Sometimes I feel as if I have," Lord Gateshead said. "When I was a boy, I would dream about joining the other Gatesheads in the Orient. But unfortunately my father died and I was forced to assume the responsibility as head of the family. There was no time for the frivolity of being an adventurer in China. So although I feel as if this is my homecoming, it is actually my first visit."

"I'm glad you finally made the trip." Nicole gently touched Lord Gateshead's arm. "Besides your dreams, what brings you here now?"

"I am trying to purchase archaeological relics." Alexandra Koo inclined her head toward Lord Gateshead. "In the last decade the Chinese have uncovered the most spectacular finds imaginable: the Han Tombs, the Mongol capital of Khanbaliq, the Tomb of the Qin Emperor, the Caves of Turpan, and countless other treasures. There are jades, bronzes, terra-cotta statues, pottery, silks, and jewelry of every imaginable type. The opportunities are unparalleled."

"Weren't many of the antiquities in your museum acquired by your ancestors?"

"'Acquired' is a delicate way of putting it," Lord Gateshead smiled. "Our two primary collections have had a somewhat checkered heritage. But when I see the benefit they provide, I realize that the ends were definitely worth the means. Without them, we in the West would never have been able to gain the understanding of China that we now possess."

For the next hour Lord Gateshead and Nicole talked about the archaeological excavations. Across the aisle, Alexandra Koo hurriedly scribbled notes in an expensive leatherbound portfolio.

The CAAC flight attendant announced that the plane would shortly begin its descent into Peking. "I think that I'd better get back to my seat," Nicole said. She stood up and turned with a soft swirl. Her hand brushed against Gateshead's face. He blushed as he watched her. She was charming, and not at all too young.

As Lord Henry turned back, his eyes met those of the

woman across the aisle. "Good-day, Lord Gateshead. Allow me to introduce myself. I'm Alexandra Koo." The woman's elegant accent had a hard edge, like that of a street kid who had spent years in finishing school.

"Pleased to meet you."

"I believe we have some business to discuss." Without an invitation, Alexandra stood up and moved to the seat that had been occupied by Nicole.

Lord Gateshead stared at her condescendingly. "Business? I am sorry but I cannot fathom your meaning."

"I'm referring to the jade suits, terra-cotta soldiers, and gold-inlaid pottery that you were just describing. I can obtain any relic you want."

"I dislike being rude, but that does not make sense."

"Do you know the *Young Girl Holding Gilt-Bronze Lamp* from the Han Tombs?"

"Of course. It is a magnificent piece."

"How much is it worth?"

"At least a half-million British pounds."

"It will be in your hotel tonight. If you want it, telex payment to my bank. Here's my card."

The woman's directness made Lord Gateshead uneasy. "But how can you obtain these relics?"

"I have my methods." Alexandra paused. "By the way, I'm going to the Han Tombs tomorrow. If you're interested in jade funeral suits or any other pieces, I might be able to work something out."

Lord Gateshead stared suspiciously at Alexandra, wondering how much of what she said was true. There was no relic he coveted more than the jade funeral suits from the Han Tombs, but he was reluctant to do anything that would jeopardize the contacts he had spent years developing. "Do you mind if I talk to some of my friends in the Bureau of Archaeology?"

"I do indeed!" Her dark eyes bore in on him. "If you tell anyone about our discussion, I'll make sure that you leave China without any relics."

"I do not understand any of this. Couldn't you just—"

"This isn't a good place to talk. Wait till you've inspected the gilt-bronze lamp, then call me." Alexandra moved back to her seat.

The Englishman sat staring at her business card. Her story seemed preposterous, but he could not dismiss it out of hand. He wanted the relics more than he had ever wanted anything. If there was even the slightest possibility that she was not a fraud, he had to take the chance and trust her.

As the plane approached the Capital Airport, Vance Stewart walked to the lavatory. This was his third trip to the bathroom in the two-hour flight. He placed a hand on the back of a seat for balance as he reached the rows occupied by the nine men Wong had summoned from Hong Kong. He nodded politely and then turned away, thinking how ill at ease they looked in their polyester suits. Technically they were listed as production specialists for Chinese American Tobacco, but Vance suspected the only thing they knew about cigarettes was how to smoke.

Stewart locked the door and tried to relieve the terrible cramping in his stomach. For three days constipation and nausea had fought to a stalemate. Ignoring the "No Smoking" sign, he lit a cigarette and filled his lungs. The smoke numbed his nerves, but it did nothing to erase his unpleasant reality. How, he asked himself, had he gotten into such a mess? He was no god damn commando. He didn't even like guns. He was a good ole boy who enjoyed his luxuries and was willing to play the game, just like every other American businessman in the Orient.

253

It was all Wong's fault. Wong was supposed to protect him from becoming directly involved with Jiang Qing; and up until now, he had managed it very effectively. Why then had he slipped up? Vance did not want to consider the obvious answer. He longed to be home in North Carolina, or at least in Hong Kong, but he saw no way of getting out of China. Everything about Jiang's plan was ridiculous, except that it was real and it scared the hell out of him.

The muscles in Marc Slater's lower back creaked from tension as he bent over to touch his toes. Linda Forbes had still not returned to the hotel. It was not a good sign. Given the tightly regulated security in China, the only logical explanation was that she had been caught in the trap that had snared Little Chang. Marc was furious at Beatrice. She had made a serious error sending someone as inexperienced as Linda to deal with a woman who was the target of Jiang's witch-hunt. Marc felt responsible. If he had been in Peking instead of in Shanghai with Meili, he would have stopped her.

There was a knock on the door. "Come in," Marc called, hoping it was Beatrice with good news. Meili stepped into the room. "Good morning," she said in a softly melodious voice that made Marc feel strangely chilled.

"*Ni hao ma*?" Marc greeted her.

"May I come in?"

"Is it all right?" Marc asked tentatively, aware that a Chinese woman in a foreigner's room could cause a scandal.

"Don't worry. I'm here on the instructions of my father."

"I'm glad."

"About what? That I'm here, or that I'm here on business!"

Marc felt the warmth of Meili's eyes. "I'm pleased both for your companionship and for your guidance."

"Spoken very diplomatically, like a mouse trying to referee two fighting cats." Meili dropped her limber body into a cushioned chair. "You seem very upset this morning. Is it the American woman?"

Marc looked up in surprise. "How did you know?"

"Mrs. Tang told me."

"I hate waiting around without being able to do anything."

"Are you and she—" Meili stopped herself in midsentence and cast her eyes toward the floor.

"She's just a friend," Marc responded, uncertain why he felt compelled to answer a question she had not asked.

"It was very rude of me to pry. Please accept my apologies."

Marc smiled. "None is necessary."

Meili walked to the window and stood silently facing him. "I know you are very concerned about the American, but my father is waiting for us in Tianjin. He wants to review our strategy with you tonight, because he has scheduled a meeting tomorrow morning, in Tangshan, with Deng."

"When do you want to leave?"

"Right now."

"Before lunch?" Marc asked, relieved that he would at last be doing something. "What about my ravenous appetite?"

Meili leaned forward. Her moist lips were delicately parted. Tenderly they touched Marc's, seeking to explore, yet shyly pulling back. He placed his arms around her and pulled her toward him. Her supple body folded into his. "Will that satisfy your hunger?" she whispered softly.

He smiled and touched her silky black hair. "Perhaps for lunch. But I'll make no promises about dinner."

She touched his lips. "We have a saying, 'The wise man

eats his rice one grain at a time. The fool wolfs down his bowl in one mouthful.'"

He kissed her hand and asked, "But who is happier?"

"In the People's Republic"—Meili turned away—"it is irrelevant to ask who is happier. Happiness is not really a Chinese concept."

Linda Forbes stared blankly ahead as the cordon of Red Guards entered a battleship-gray, single-story building that housed the prison offices. She tried to prepare herself for dealing with Colonel Li. The colonel frightened her, but she had to remain strong and find a way of getting out. If Little Chang was dead or permanently imprisoned, then she was the only one who could report on Jiang's forgery of Mao's will.

Standing by a window in the spartan office, Colonel Li motioned for her to sit on a slatted wooden chair. "I'm very busy today," he began in Chinese while one of his guards translated. "I don't have time to play around wasting spit on you. If you confess your connection with the traitor Little Chang, we can resolve this matter and send you home."

Linda fought the temptation to accept the colonel's suggestion. "I couldn't talk to the Chinese girl because she didn't speak English."

"Stop playing games. Do you think I am a gardener trying to grow peonies in the desert?"

"I'm not playing games." Linda tried to keep her voice from quivering.

"Don't lie! If you are innocent, why did you flee from my troops?"

"They were chasing me with guns. What was I supposed to do, stand there and let them shoot me?"

"You were seen with Little Chang. I will keep you here

until you confess the truth."

The side door suddenly opened. Alexandra Koo paraded into the office in a flurry of green silk and jade, like a model on a runway. Linda hurriedly tried to collect her thoughts. If Alexandra had discovered her real identity, she was lost. Placing her hands on her hips, Alexandra turned to Linda. "Well, young lady, Colonel Li tells me you are a spy."

"A spy?" Linda nervously wiped her forehead. "That's impossible."

"The colonel has evidence."

"He can't." Linda started to sob.

"He claims you were seen in the presence of a traitor."

"I was just jogging in the park," Linda cried. "Please, Mrs. Koo, you know who I am. Tell the colonel that I am only a department-store buyer who knows nothing of politics or China."

Alexandra stared condescendingly at Linda and then turned to Colonel Li. "This is your spy?" she scoffed. "This foolish woman is the conspirator who wants to destroy the People's Republic? Comrade Jiang appreciates your diligence, but this woman is hardly a threat to anyone, except perhaps to herself. You have no more to fear from her than a tiger does from an ant."

The colonel shifted uncomfortably. He did not like being upbraided, especially not by an overseas Chinese woman. "What should I do with her?"

"It doesn't matter. Letting her go is like farting, but killing her is like squashing a bedbug."

"Which would Comrade Jiang prefer?"

"There's no point provoking an incident with the United States. Why don't you fart and be done with her."

As the car motored from Peking to Tianjin, Meili

entertained Marc with a delightful narration of Chinese folktales. She tantalized and enchanted him. He felt himself being swept up by a desire that he knew could do nothing but cause him trouble. Stirring uneasily, he lit his pipe. He felt guilty, as if he were betraying both Meili's father and Linda. And he felt angry for feeling guilty. He wanted Meili. And right now, that was all that mattered.

The car stopped in front of a twenty-five-room villa in what had been Tianjin's foreign settlement. Built by British traders, the villa had gained fame during the Boxer Rebellion, when Herbert Hoover, then a mining engineer, directed the defense of the International Concession from its walls. Later it had been taken over by the Japanese. But since Liberation, it had served as a guest house for Politburo members visiting the city.

Meili conducted Marc to the living room, where Hu Shengte was sitting on a worn but elegant red brocaded couch. Dressed in a blue silk lounging suit with the Chinese character for long life embroidered on the breast pocket, Hu greeted Marc. "Did my daughter treat you courteously?"

"Perfectly," Marc said, hoping his eyes did not reveal what was developing between them. "You should be very proud of her."

"I am, but I wish she were a boy. She's got the mind and spirit of a man, and unfortunately lacks the discipline to be a proper Chinese wife."

"Perhaps the role of women in China is changing?"

Hu's face became like that of a death mask. "That's what her mother used to say. You remember my wife?" Marc nodded silently. "She was so strong-willed. Did I ever tell you how she stood up to Lin Biao when I was purged? Right in front of half the Politburo, she told him to stop biting people's cocks off! Can you imagine? She was such a special woman. But those bastards let her starve and didn't even get her a doctor. They had malaria in their hearts." Hu fell silent. For several minutes neither man talked. "She always wanted Meili to be a doctor. My daughter would have made a good one, had it not been for those vultures and their Cultural Revolution." Hu lit a cigarette. "I'm getting old, my friend, and bitter. I feel like a skinny fish swimming against the waves." Hu rang a ceramic bell. A waiter carried in a bottle and two glasses. "Chivas on the rocks?"

"I hope it's twenty-five-year-old Royal Salute."

"This is the People's Republic. I'm afraid twelve-year-old will have to suffice."

Marc laughed. "You should have been a capitalist."

Placing a finger to his lips, Hu whispered, "I am, but don't tell anybody."

Marc raised his glass and made a traditional Chinese toast: "When you drink with an old friend, even a thousand glasses are too few."

"Ganbei!" Hu drained his glass in one gulp. Then he removed a stack of reports from his briefcase. "I have some news I think will please you. I have just received the results from the test well in the Bohai Gulf." Marc felt an anxious tingling in his neck. "At a depth of three thousand feet, we should be able to produce one thousand metric tons of oil per day." Marc struggled to maintain a placid expression. "The oil has an excellent specific gravity as well as low paraffin and sulfur content." Marc smiled in spite of his resolve. The results were far better than he had ever expected. They even compared favorably with those from Prudhoe Bay, and it was much easier to drill in these temperate and sheltered waters than in the Alaskan tundra.

When Marc had first suggested the Bohai Gulf project, he had been opposed by virtually all his board of directors. They had argued that M. H. Schaffer was in no position to pioneer an oil field with unproven reserves. He had pointed

259

to favorable seismic studies and suggested that the company might be able to gain a commanding position in Chinese oil. The board had continued to have reservations and would have rejected the project had he not demanded a vote of confidence in his leadership. No one had been willing to oppose him, but several had indicated that they would hold him responsible for any failures. Marc had not minded crawling out on a limb, but he was much happier knowing that the limb was filled with high-grade crude.

"I wouldn't commit any funds to drilling," Hu said, sipping his scotch, "until we have dealt with the Russians."

"Is there something new?"

"You know about the bombing of the two ships?" Marc nodded. "It looks like the Russians are also responsible for the destruction of key railroad bridges, which has isolated most of east China. Jiang Qing is furious. First she lost her weapons on the Japanese ship, and now her strongholds are without rail transportation. She's been ranting about getting even. When you add Hua's anger about the burning of that school he helped build in Mao's hometown, you realize that it won't take much more pressure to start everyone shooting at each other."

"Are we in a position to stop them?"

"Right now"—Hu massaged his eyes—"we don't stand a chance."

Linda Forbes felt elated as she stepped out of Colonel Li's jeep and strode into the lobby of the Peking Hotel. She had made it! She was free. Her identity was still a secret, and Alexandra Koo still considered her to be nothing but a bubble-headed buyer.

Entering the elevator, she pushed the button for the fifteenth floor and let her body droop against a wall. Her jogging clothes felt as if they were growing right on her body. Her hair was oily and knotted in snarled clumps. She longed to spend the day soaking in a hot bath, but she had to find Beatrice Tang.

Beatrice sounded as relieved to hear her voice as she felt to be out of jail. The Chinese-American woman hurried to Linda's room; there was no time for another meeting in the Forbidden City. Linda's voice cracked as she described her encounter with Little Chang, her arrest, and her imprisonment. Beatrice's eyes stared at her sympathetically. Only when Linda explained that Alexandra Koo had been responsible for her release did a thin smile cross Beatrice's lips. "Were you able to learn why Jiang Qing wanted to silence Little Chang?" she asked.

"Little Chang saw Jiang substitute a forged last will and testament in Mao's private vault."

"I expected as much," Beatrice replied as she evaluated Linda's story.

"We have to do something," Linda pleaded.

"I'd like you to go to Tangshan in the morning," Beatrice said. "Marc Slater will be there, meeting with Deng Xiaoping and your grandfather."

Linda raised her eyebrows, surprised that Beatrice knew of her relationship to Liu. "Will they allow me to report to them?"

"I'm not certain," Beatrice responded. "You're a woman and a foreigner. But Marc will arrange to get your information."

"Does my grandfather know who I am?"

"I don't know. But I'm sure that by the time you return from Tangshan, you will have found a way of telling him."

Linda smiled at Beatrice as she thought about Liu, the Chinese she had been longing to meet, and Slater, the American she wanted to get to know. For the first time in three days, she felt hopeful.

Colonel Li snapped to attention as he instantly recognized Jiang Qing's voice on the other end of the phone. Jiang sounded forceful but not angry as she explained her wish to assassinate Deng Xiaoping. Because the colonel was originally from Tangshan and knew all the local Party cadres, Jiang Qing wanted him to direct the operation. Li was more than pleased to be of further assistance. With the forgery of Mao's will, the arrest of Little Chang, and now the planned attack on Deng, he was becoming increasingly indispensable.

After talking to Jiang, Colonel Li contacted his allies in Tangshan. He could not tell them of his objective, but he had to be certain that they would do nothing to interfere with his plans. Then he requisitioned an ample supply of machine guns, bazookas, mortars, and hand grenades from the Red Guard arsenal north of Peking. His troops transported the weapons to an empty grain warehouse south of Tangshan while he went to the Peking Hotel, where Stewart, Wong, and the men from Hong Kong were waiting. Li was surprised that Jiang had chosen these foreigners for such an important assignment. He would have preferred a detachment of Red Guards. But he had learned long ago not to question her judgment.

Li and the others arrived in Tangshan at dusk. Before checking into the Tangshan Guest House, Li stopped at the grain warehouse to inspect his munitions and organize his men. Each man was given a specific task, and all except for Stewart received Red Guard uniforms. Despite his initial skepticism, Colonel Li was pleased with his troops. Even Stewart's reluctance to participate did not disturb him. He mistrusted the American and had assigned him to only the most minor of roles. No matter what happened, Stewart would never be in a position to harm the operation.

"Come join me for a brandy," Lord Henry Gateshead entreated as he entered the elevator of the Peking Hotel.

"All right, but just a short one," Nicole LaFleur replied as the elevator ascended to the fourteenth floor. The Chinese had developed a very sensible system for handling their foreign guests: They segregated them by nationality and surrounded them with attendants who were specially trained in the languages and customs of each country.

Lord Gateshead politely ushered Nicole into his room. While he stopped to clean two glasses in the bathroom, her eyes were immediately drawn to a statue resting on the desk. No more than sixteen inches high, it was the kneeling figure of a young girl in an ancient flowing robe. Her left hand held a bronze lamp that was almost half her size, while her right hand draped over the top, forming a funnel to keep the room free of soot. Nicole stared admiringly at the piece. Although there were occasional patches of blue-green corrosion, most of the surface was a brilliant, gilded gold. "I love your statue," she called out.

Lord Gateshead rushed from the bathroom. "It's incredible!" he exclaimed. "Look at her face. It's so natural and sensitive. Look at the delicate detailing of the robe and the perfect quality of the gilt bronze. It's a masterpiece!"

Nicole was overwhelmed by his enthusiasm. "Is this the first time you've seen it?"

"I've only seen it in photographs." Lord Gateshead carefully traced its outline without daring to touch. He had been very wrong to dismiss Mrs. Koo as a charlatan. She obviously had some powerful contacts in the Cultural Relics Administration Bureau and could prove to be a most important friend. "This is the *Young Girl Holding Gilt-Bronze Lamp* from the tomb of Princess Dou Wan of the Han dynasty. It's almost two thousand years old and is one of the most valuable relics ever excavated in China."

"Where did you get it?"

Gateshead suspected that Alexandra's plan to sell him the antiques was not strictly legal, but he wanted them more than he had ever wanted anything. There was no reason to confide in Nicole. "One of my staff purchased it," he replied, wondering if there would still be time for him to arrange the trip to the Han Tombs.

22: Kailuan Mine #6

Early the next morning, Marc Slater sat in the back seat of a gray Toyota on his way to the meeting in Tangshan with Deng Xiaoping. He was greatly relieved that Linda had managed to elude the Red Guards and most anxious to hear the information that was too explosive for Beatrice to repeat over the phone. The car reached a ridge overlooking a gnarled plain that could have been mistaken for the north of England. Mammoth coal-processing plants covered the horizon. The soot from their smokestacks had already obliterated the sun. For one hundred years the Kailuan Mines had been the most productive in China. Despite the construction of new thermal electric power stations and despite its huge oil reserves, the country continued to rely on these mines that made China the world's third largest producer of coal.

The Toyota turned onto a badly worn road marked by a sign that read "Kailuan Mine #6." In the gully below was a red brick processing plant, surrounded by a cluster of mine shafts that looked like mouseholes in a wheat field. Even from a distance, the engulfing decay was apparent. The windows of the factory were covered with colonies of lichens that had rooted in the decades since the last cleaning. The footpaths and rusting machinery were protectively webbed by forests of weeds growing out of the coal dust, and all of the shafts, save one, were boarded up. Kailuan #6, which had fueled the ships and businesses of the International Concessions as well as the heavy industry of the People's Republic, was now dormant. The only sign of life was a solitary soldier standing guard on the balcony of the administration building.

After parking the car in the open mine shaft, the driver led Marc through a series of tunnels toward a gray, cracked wooden door. The driver opened the creaking door. Marc shielded his eyes and stepped into a large, brightly lit room. To his surprise, the room reflected none of the mine's decay. Instead, it was filled with Chinese technicians operating modern communications equipment, not unlike the cave near the hot springs.

Stepping forward, Hu Shengte greeted Marc and led him into a room furnished with groups of couches set around glass-covered wooden coffee tables. The powerfully built figure of Liu Teyu was sprawled out on a couch, while a midget of a man paced the floor. The man waved his arms in the air and turned his thumbs down in a sign of rejection. Then he cleared his throat and hurled a wad of phlegm into the center of a spittoon four feet away.

"Good shot," Liu called out, clapping his huge hands.

Deng Xiaoping bowed to accept his applause and then bounded over to greet his new guests. With his cherubic smile, twinkling eyes, and perpetually moving limbs, he looked like a windup doll. Those who did not know Deng were frequently disarmed by his appearance, but anyone

who had ever dealt with this man recognized his extraordinary acumen.

Deng's genius was quite different from that of the other
Chinese leaders. Unlike Mao, he was not a philosopher who
could mold the minds of a billion people; and unlike Chou,
he was not a man whose moral principles set standards for
others to follow. Deng was often coarse and opportunistic,
but the quality that set him apart was his unique ability to
manage organizations without being paralyzed by the
philosophical correctness of every action. It was a refreshing
and much-needed quality in China.

Marc smiled, remembering the scandal that had ensued
when Deng had said, "It doesn't matter whether it's a black
cat or a white cat. As long as it can catch mice, it's a good
cat." Such pragmatism had gained him a fanatical following
among bureaucrats and military leaders, but it had made
him highly vulnerable to the machinations of the ideologues
who surrounded Mao. Now, only three years after his
rehabilitation, Deng had again been purged. It was quite a
change from the Great Hall of the People to the back room
of an abandoned mining office. Marc would have wished
better for his old friend.

Meili entered the room. Marc glanced at her and nodded
politely. Deng motioned for his guests to sit down. "I was
sorry to hear about Carolyn. She was a fine woman and a *lao
pengyou*."

"*Xiexie ni* [Thank you]." Marc bowed respectfully,
averting his eyes from Meili. "Life must also be very difficult
for you."

"Sometimes I feel like a bee trapped in a house, but mostly
I'm just bored. At least I'm not waiting on tables or working
in a factory like I was the first time I was purged, during the
Cultural Revolution."

"What are you complaining about?" Hu Shengte asked.

"You made out well compared to me. I was sent to Mongolia as a shepherd. China's oil output dried to a trickle while I froze my ass off with a flock of sheep."

"How about my brother?" Liu Teyu asked in his singsong Cantonese accent. "He was managing the Yellow River Hydroelectric Project, which was to supply irrigation and power to one hundred million comrades. So what did our friends do? They sent him to the Gobi Desert to be a camel driver."

Marc listened while the others told stories about the injustices they had suffered. Beneath their sarcastic humor was a profound bitterness. During the Cultural Revolution, schools had been closed while teachers were sent to grow rice; technical programs had been suspended while scientists were taught to weave rugs; and hospitals had been emptied while doctors were forced to herd water buffaloes. The Great Proletarian Cultural Revolution had been far more than the tragedy of a country turned against its most able citizens; it had also been a tragedy of the individuals whose lives had been uprooted and often destroyed.

Deng slammed his fist into a pillow. "I get so damn mad at Mao when I think of the colossal waste. How could the man who built the People's Republic let those kids in their toy uniforms destroy the country? How could he sit silently while they humiliated men who had been his friends from before the Long March?"

"Mao just lost control," Liu said. "He became worried that his power was slipping and initiated the Cultural Revolution to forge a direct link to the people. But once the Red Guards began to flood the country, he was like a man trying to hold back the Yellow River."

"What's your point?" Deng lit a cigarette.

"Mao may once have been a great man, but in the last decade he's lost control of the government. Who do you think is running the country today? Mao? Mao is a corpse. Hua? Hua is a joke. He just poles the boat with the current and tries not to disgrace himself. The Politburo? It's pitiful. With Chou dead and you purged, there's no one to stand up to Jiang Qing and her radical helicopters." Deng grimaced at the reference to the quickly rising young radicals. "If we don't act soon, we'll have another cultural revolution, or perhaps a Russian invasion."

"I don't buy it," Deng replied. "Brezhnev may snipe at us along the border, but I can't see him risking war."

"I don't think our American friend would agree with you."

"With due respect to Mr. Slater, Americans tend to think of the Soviet Union as a fire-breathing dragon." Marc shifted uneasily.

"This time they're ready to act. We've been informed that KGB operatives have already infiltrated our country and undertaken acts of sabotage that look like the work of rival Chinese factions." Liu laid documents in front of Deng that detailed all of the Russian actions.

Deng leafed through the papers. "Bastards," he said as he bounced up and spit in a brass spittoon.

"To stop the Russians," Liu said, "we first must stop Jiang. And for that we need your help."

Deng laughed. "I'd love to destroy the woman who has made me a leper in my own country, but unfortunately I'm not the man for the job."

Liu stood up, towering over the diminutive Deng. "You're the only one with the power to stop Jiang."

"Maybe once, but not now. Have you been around this country? Have you seen the billboards and wall posters depicting me as a capitalist-roader? Have you listened to the radio and watched television? Next to the KMT and the Russians, I am presented as the greatest threat to the People's Republic. Party officials may respect me, but to the masses I'm an enemy of China. Jiang has done her job well. While I was building the economy, she was seizing control of communications. Now no one can stop her from telling the country that I am a tool of the imperialists."

"You still have many friends," Liu said. "They will listen if you stand up against Jiang."

"With your evidence they'll think I'm out for personal revenge. The country will become polarized. There'll be no one to stop the Russians." Deng stepped in front of Liu and pointed his finger like a professor giving a lecture. "Before you do anything, you need the support of Hua."

"Hua is a fool."

"Ah, yes, my friend; but he's a legitimate fool."

Liu wrapped his hands around the bottle of beer. "Mao was senile when he anointed Hua."

"Let me see." Deng smiled like a leprechaun. "You are suggesting that I, the capitalist heretic, tell the people of China that their god is senile, his wife is a traitor, and his successor is a fool. What are you smoking in that cigarette of yours? The people will crucify me."

"Don't you think you're exaggerating?"

"Let me give you an analogy. Do you consider yourself a Christian?"

Liu nodded. He had converted as a child and had studied in missionary schools. "My other faith still comforts me."

Deng smiled. "Good. Then how would you have reacted if Judas Iscariot had announced that God was senile, Jesus a fool, and Mary a prostitute?"

"I might have questioned him. But do you have any better ideas?"

Deng walked to the window and sipped from a cup of lukewarm tea. A heavy silence filled the room. "Since this is strictly a Chinese matter," Marc said quietly, "I know that it's not my place to talk."

"You were born in China and have the heart of a Chinese," Deng said.

Marc bowed his head. "Your words honor me."

"They are deserved. Please speak your mind."

"I wouldn't presume to show off my carpentry in front of an expert carpenter, but I do know that we need Hua's support; and I suspect that in order to get it, we must obtain concrete evidence of Jiang's treachery."

"A smoking gun."

"What?"

"Do you remember when your Congress was trying to impeach President Nixon?" Deng asked. "No one would vote until they had found incontrovertible evidence of Nixon's guilt. They were looking for what they called a 'smoking gun.' If we are to get Hua's support and then convince the people, we must find a Chinese smoking gun with Jiang Qing's fingerprints. You find me such a gun and I'll move against her."

Marc did not want to lose the chance to gain Deng's participation. He thought about Linda and the evidence she had obtained from Little Chang. "There may just be such evidence," he said.

Deng's deep-set eyes stared intently. "What is it?"

Marc hesitated. He was concerned about Linda and worried that he had spoken too quickly. "I'm not positive, but I'll know very soon."

Deng rubbed his square, heavily lined forehead. "I hope you're right. We're running out of time. Without something explosive, we have little chance of stopping Jiang Qing."

Marc lit his pipe as he walked along the path away from the administration building. Deng had asked him to leave so that he could confer privately with the others. Marc was pleased for the break. He stared at the horizon. The late-afternoon sun glowed bright orange through the clouds of coal dust. He stepped from the path and walked across an open field toward a small stream. "How can you go for a walk without your official guide?" a lilting voice called from behind him.

Marc saw Meili waving at him. "Please excuse my indiscretion." She ran toward him. Her body moved with grace and ease. Her hair billowed in the wind. He extended his hand. Her eyes looked away as they touched. Her skin was soft. Her fingers long and delicate. They walked in silence, each lost in thought, yet each feeling the electricity that bound them together.

The stream flowed quietly. Meili kicked off her shoes and dangled her feet in the cool water. She smiled at Marc. Without a word, she removed his shoes and began to massage his feet. Her young hands rubbed firmly, unlocking the tension in his shoulders and neck. Marc lay back, closed his eyes, and felt the anxieties of the day flow from his body. Meili dipped a handkerchief in the stream and spread it across his face. Then she softly kissed him. Marc opened his eyes. Meili was astride him. Her back arched smoothly skyward. Her face glowed in the reflection of the sun. She was as beautiful as any woman he had ever seen. "Lie still," she whispered as her fingers manipulated the tired muscles in his neck.

He reached up and caressed her hair. It was soft and silky, like her skin. She placed her lips against his hand. He touched her small, firm breasts. She shivered. He pulled her to him. Her body throbbed. Her legs wrapped around his. She opened the top button on his shirt and smothered his chest with kisses. He lifted her face in his hands. Shyly she looked away. He kissed her cheek. She turned back to him, her soft, moist mouth invitingly parted. Their tongues tantalized each other. "I want to emerge from the clouds into the sunlight of the mountain peak"—Meili whispered the phrase she had once read in an ancient Chinese pillow book.

Marc smiled tenderly as he gently rolled on top of her. He felt as if he were reexperiencing the pure passion of first love. He pressed his body down on top of her, seeking to drive away the air that separated them. Whatever reservations he might have once had were now drowned in the desire he felt for Meili.

Colonel Li and his men spent the day searching for Deng. After six hours there had been no clues. Most people were surprised that Deng might be nearby. His home was in Sichuan, on the other side of China. The others returned to the guest house, but Colonel Li continued to search. Despite his frustrations, he did not want to let this opportunity slip away.

The sun was setting as the colonel stopped for gas. An old man driving an overheating mining truck pulled up to the rusting pump. The colonel walked over and offered a Great Wall cigarette. The old man smiled. His teeth were spotted like the hide of a leopard. "I'm looking for Deng Xiaoping," the colonel said. "Have you seen him?"

The old man puffed silently on his cigarette. "This is my first cigarette in many months. I had to give up smoking when my wife became ill and money became short." The colonel offered the pack. The old man walked to a fruit stand. "The harvest has been very poor this year."

Colonel Li purchased a melon and five apples and gave them to the man. "Revisionist pig," he muttered to himself, though he could not really blame the man for bartering for his information.

"I am very grateful for your consideration." The old man

flashed his leopard-skin smile as he climbed back into his truck.

"What about Deng?"

"He's a capitalist-roader. At least that's what the wall posters say."

"I'm in no mood for games. Tell me what you know or I'll inform your party unit that you bribed a Red Guard officer with false information."

The man inclined his head toward Li. "My humblest apologies. Your kindness distracted me from my duties. I have not seen Comrade Deng, but I believe a search of the coal mines would be a useful experience."

It was dusk by the time Marc and Meili got back to the administration building. Hu Shengte was waiting for them. Marc felt young and ill at ease, like a high-school student bringing a date home late from the prom. Although Hu had no way of knowing what had happened, the mere fact that they were walking alone in the countryside was a violation of the principles that guided relationships between Chinese and foreigners.

Pressing his twisted lips together like those of a giant newt, Hu glared at his daughter. Meili blushed and stepped away from Marc. Hu's eyes chastised her as he silently pointed to an adjacent dormitory. She cast her eyes to the ground and said nothing as she hurried inside. Hu looked at Marc with an expression of disdain. "You, who claim to be my friend, how can you have done this?"

Marc shivered under Hu's icy stare. "Your daughter offered to accompany me so that I would not get lost."

"And what of her honor and her face?"

Marc wanted to tell Hu that he loved Meili, but he knew that he could not do so. He would never accept a relationship between his daughter and a barbarian. It could destroy both Hu's standing in the government and his own work in China. "I'm sorry. I did not think."

Hu stood rigidly. His face was motionless. "You're like a weasel wanting to eat swan's eggs. You expect your rice to be here without having to shed a drop of sweat for it."

"We were only out for a walk."

Hu interrupted with a wave of his fist. "Building a friendship is as hard as growing a flowering tree. It can wither and die because of a moment's carelessness. Please consider if a walk is worth that price." Then he turned abruptly and went inside to lecture Meili.

Marc stepped well out of sight of the dormitory, picked up a stone, and threw it against the boards of a closed mine shaft. He felt isolated and angry. Whether Hu had been referring to their personal friendship or to the emerging relationship between the United States and China, his threat was not one to be taken lightly.

Marc did not like the egocentricity that permeated China. Nor did he like being condescended to. He had known Hu Shengte more than forty years. They had fought together during the war, worked together to develop China's oil industry, and supported each other on many occasions. No one had been a better friend to China than Marc. But the fact that he had lived half his life in China obviously counted for nothing. The Chinese had erected an artificial barrier between themselves and everyone else. Their country was the Middle Kingdom between heaven and earth. They were the chosen people and everyone else was a barbarian. When they called someone a *lao pengyou*, they meant that he was better than most foreigners. But they never would accept him as their equal.

Marc thought about his daughter, Jill. He would not have been upset if she had become involved with one of the leaders of the People's Republic, so what right did Hu have to chastise Meili for becoming involved with him? Western logic was on his side, but he knew that convincing Hu to change his attitude would be, as the Chinese say, as difficult as drawing blood from a peeled turnip.

Closing his eyes, Marc took a deep breath. He had to control his anger before facing his friends. If he had learned anything living in China, it was the importance of disguising his feelings. Perhaps at another time, with less at stake, he would try to talk to Hu about Meili; but for now, he could not afford to jeopardize his position as a *lao pengyou*.

23: The Suits of Jade

MANCHENG

As the Hong Qi limousine bounced over the poorly paved
road on the one-hundred-and-fifty-mile trip from Peking to
Mancheng, Lord Henry Gateshead dreamed about the relics
he intended to obtain when he arrived at the Han Tombs.
With the help of the remarkable Mrs. Koo, he now had the
chance to unlock the riches of ancient China. He had called
upon all his contacts to get the directors of the Institute of
Archaeology to agree to this visit. Originally they had
wanted him to wait; but he had been unwilling to risk
missing his appointment, and they had been reluctant to
embarrass their foreign guest.

The car reached Lingshan, a craggy mountain no more
than six hundred feet high. The rocky surface, once covered
with weeds, was now cluttered with piles of stones and dirt
from the excavations. In its bowels were the magnificent
tombs of Prince Liu Sheng and his wife, Dou Wan.

Cai Yunwen, the deputy manager of the Institute of
Archaeology, greeted Lord Gateshead and then led him on a

path that wound its way up the rugged cliff. Unaccustomed to physical exercise, Gateshead's muscles ached and his breathing became strained, but he refused to stop. He felt like a pilgrim approaching Jerusalem.

Cai escorted him into a darkened tunnel that led more than one hundred fifty feet inside the mountain. "This," he announced, "is the tomb of Prince Liu Sheng, the stepbrother of the famous Emperor Wu Di. Although Wu Di expanded the Empire and opened the silk route, he was a greedy man who viciously exploited the working classes." Gateshead gazed at the sheer stone walls and tried to imagine the splendor of the man for whom so many had labored. "Prince Liu," Cai continued his prepared lecture, "who died in what you call 113 B.C., was the most decadent member of the royal family. He enslaved thousands to dig these two massive tombs and fill them with pottery and jade as well as weapons and horses."

"Horses?" Lord Gateshead asked.

"There is a large stable in which the prince buried his horses and their chariots."

"That seems an unfortunate waste of good animals."

"Indeed," Cai replied.

The tunnel opened into a massive entrance hall carved from the rock. To the left were the stables, and to the right were the prince's storehouses. Gateshead had expected Mrs. Koo to be waiting, but the only people in sight were a group of workers cataloging pottery and lacquerware. Gateshead inspected the pottery. The workers bowed politely. "We are honored to be visited by such an eminent foreign guest," the foreman said as Cai translated.

"The honor is mine." Gateshead studied the relics. The pottery and the lacquerware were more beautiful than he had imagined. He could easily see them in their own gallery. "Liu Sheng's treasures are magnificent."

"They merely expose the extravagances of the feudal ruling class and demonstrate the oppression suffered by the working people," Cai replied.

Having heard the party line before, Lord Gateshead turned from Cai and searched once more for Mrs. Koo. Without her, this would be nothing but an interesting tour; but with her it would be the first step in his plan to make the English Museum preeminent in Oriental artifacts. "Are you looking for something?" Cai asked.

"No. I'm just enthralled by the magnitude of what I see."

"Excellent. Then I shall show you more." Cai ushered Gateshead past the well that provided water for the spirits and to the stone gateway that led to the inner tomb. He opened the door to the central chamber. Inside was a collection of bronzes that rivaled anything Gateshead had ever seen. There were wine vessels, ornate cooking pots, plates, and incense burners as well as sculptures of horses, chariots, and dragons.

Gateshead lifted an incense burner that looked like a mountain resting in a bowl. Made of bronze with brilliantly inlaid hairlines of gold, the piece was a rendering of one of the Three Isles of the Immortals of Taoist myth. In its undulating peaks were miniature sculptures of men and animals as well as representations of trees and plants. "I admire your taste," Cai said. "That's the finest piece yet uncovered."

Lord Gateshead gazed wistfully at the incense burner, imagining it exhibited in his museum. He bent over and lifted a *hu*, a large wine vessel decorated with gold and silver inlays in scroll-like configurations. "That's also quite beautiful," Cai advised.

"What's your opinion of the statue of the girl holding the gilt-bronze lamp?" Gateshead tested.

Cai looked at his guest with surprise. "How do you know

about that?"

Gateshead sensed that he had made an error in judgment, but he could not retreat. "Your department sent me a photograph at the time of the excavation. Why do you ask?"

"Our institute recently donated that gift to our Great Helmsman."

Gateshead tried to maintain his composure as he thought about the statue in his hotel room. He had no doubt that it was real. "Are you positive that it was given to Chairman Mao?" he asked.

"Of course. I personally made the presentation to Jiang Qing."

Gateshead nervously fingered his cuff links. If his statue was the original, then Mrs. Koo had to have obtained it from Jiang. That made her more powerful than he had thought. "And it's the only one of its kind?" the Englishman asked.

"We do not mass-produce two-thousand-year-old relics." Cai sounded annoyed. "Why are you so concerned about this one statue?"

"I had hoped I might be able to purchase it for my museum."

"That would be quite difficult," Cai said, anxious to change the subject. "Why don't we continue our tour. In the rear of the tomb, we have the encircling corridor, the bathroom, and, of course, the burial chamber."

Lord Gateshead stifled a smile of anticipation as he thought about the opportunities offered by Mrs. Koo. "With a stable, a well, and a bathroom, the spirits of your princes lived rather luxuriously."

"And that is why China will never again have royalty." Cai noticed his guest's perplexed expression. "Of course, in your country I am sure that royalty is not nearly as reprehensible."

Lord Gateshead nodded politely. This was not the right time for a discussion of political ideology. Cai approached two Red Guards standing in front of a large door and presented his papers. The young guards seemed strangely cool to the deputy manager. Without an acknowledgment, they opened the gate to the burial chamber.

Lord Gateshead took one step inside and stopped. His mouth dropped open. A tingling sensation rushed through his body. It was the same feeling he had experienced as a six-year-old boy when he had visited the crown jewels in the Tower of London for the first time. In front of him was a work of art more spectacular than any he had ever seen. Lying on a table was the form of Prince Liu completely encased in a suit of jade. Twenty-five hundred pieces of shimmering green polished jade had been sewn together with thread of solid gold to form a gemstone suit of armor that completely covered the prince's body. The suit rested on a brick-shaped jade pillow adorned with two dragon heads.

Gateshead was unable to speak. He coveted the suit as the centerpiece of his museum. A guard whispered something to Cai. "I have a phone call," Cai said. "Do you mind being left alone?"

"I am not alone," Lord Gateshead replied, staring at the jade. In each corner of the wafer-thin squares, a tiny hole had been drilled through which the gold string had been threaded. It must have taken skilled master craftsmen decades to create such a masterpiece.

"In ancient times, our people were very superstitious." A silken woman's voice cut through the awesome stillness. Gateshead turned to find Alexandra Koo standing like an apparition in the doorway. In the pale light of the chamber, her green silk dress blended with her jade jewelry to give her the same eerie hue as the suit of armor. She looked like the ghost of the mistress of the long-dead prince. "Jade"—her voice echoed off the walls—"was not only considered to be beautiful and to symbolize virtue, but it was also thought to prevent decay of the human body. What do you think? Can the jade armor still guarantee immortality?"

"I suspect that the promise of immortality was, as you suggest, merely an ancient superstition," Lord Gateshead responded cautiously.

"But what about your own immortality?"

"Mine?"

"Of course. Why else would you be willing to spend fifty million dollars to acquire Chinese antiques?"

Lord Gateshead held his body rigid. "How did you know the amount?"

"It's not important," Alexandra laughed. "But I don't think that we should spend everything here. Fifteen million dollars would seem to be appropriate. That would give you a collection of twenty-five bronzes, including the incense burner you were admiring; fifty pieces of pottery and lacquerware; and the jade suit with its matching pillow."

The financial terms were much better than Gateshead could have hoped. He considered the jade suit to be priceless, but museums would pay more than thirty million dollars. The bronzes, lacquerware, and pottery should be worth another twelve million. But the political aspects concerned him. "How do you have the authority to sell me these relics?"

"I brought you the lamp, didn't I?"

"But these are so much more valuable. The jade suit is—"

"Please excuse my abruptness, but I can't spend my day listening to crows eat grains of rice. Do we have an agreement?"

"Couldn't you tell me how—"

"Did you ask your ancestors how they smuggled opium or obtained the relics from the Summer Palace? You want to

282

build your museum. I control the relics. Is there really anything else you have to know?"

Lord Gateshead stared silently at Mrs. Koo. Although he knew that what he was doing was illegal, he had no intention of pressing her further. Once he accepted the statue of the girl with the lamp he had discarded the right to quibble about morality.

24: The Search for Deng

Vance Stewart stood at the entrance to the Tangshan Guest House and watched as Wong Chuyun, Leung Lilai, and Colonel Li, wearing Red Guard uniforms, climbed into their jeeps and prepared to resume their search. Vance was not upset that they were leaving without him. He did not share the others' zest for killing Deng and Slater. He did not even care whether they succeeded. Their failure would hurt his business, but CAT would survive. There was no company strong enough to take its place.

Leaving the hotel, Vance walked into Fenghuangshan Park. Although it was well before seven, the park was filled with workers practicing Tai Chi. Avoiding the exercisers, he reached a playground where Chinese were playing basketball. As he watched the men trying to master the American sport, he thought of his days at Duke when basketball had been the center of his life and everything else had been much less complicated. A ball rolled toward him. He picked it up and bounced it a few times. The Chinese beckoned him onto the court. He dribbled toward basket, stopped, and jumped as high as he could. As his lanky frame stretched toward the hoop, he flicked the ball off his fingers. Swish, he said to himself as he imagined the sound that the ball would have made if there had been a net.

The Chinese invited Vance to join their game. With his height it was easy for him to score baskets, but running proved more difficult. The cigarettes that provided his livelihood had destroyed his stamina. After fifteen minutes, his legs were cramping, his lungs were gasping for air, and his mouth was craving refreshment. He thanked the Chinese and headed for the hotel, hoping it served beer for breakfast.

"Good morning." Linda Forbes waved as she approached Sen Tailing's table. She had arrived at the guest house late last night. "Did you talk to Marc?"

"He hasn't called."

"I wish we knew where to reach him." Linda tried to hide her disappointment.

"Don't worry. He'll contact us today," Sen reassured.

"I hope so." Linda forced a smile. A waiter approached the table and stood patiently behind her. "Will you order me a bowl of shrimp congee, a pot of tea, and three pieces of toast?" she asked.

"Of course." Sen gave the order to the waiter even though he knew Linda spoke Chinese.

As the waiter placed Linda's rice gruel on the table, Sen saw Vance Stewart standing in the doorway. Stewart's presence disturbed him. He could not understand what a tobacco trader was doing in a mining center, and he did not want to have to explain Slater's absence. Sen turned his back to the door. There was too much riding on the meetings with Deng Xiaoping to have someone as persistent as the owner of CAT asking questions. Sen waited for Stewart to pass so that he could excuse himself and go back to his room.

"Good mornin'! This must be mah lucky day!" the southerner boomed. Sen stared at his bowl of congee.

"It's nice to see you again, Vance," Linda said from across the table. Sen looked at her. She was smiling.

"Mind if I join you?" Vance asked, taking a chair. "As I live and breathe, Sen Tailing! This really is an ole homecomin'!"

"Good morning, Mr. Stewart," Sen said politely.

Stewart took a napkin and wiped his forehead as he smiled at Linda. "Excuse my perspiration. I've been out in the park, shootin' hoops." The waiter approached the table. "Sen, be a good guy and order me two eggs over easy with sausage and a bottle of beer." Sen translated Stewart's request. "So now, what brings you both to this garden spot of China?"

"I'm here to look at a cloisonné factory," Linda replied.

Stewart laughed. "In Tangshan?"

"Yes. What's wrong?"

"All the good cloisonné factories are in Peking. The Chinese probably opened a new one here and, figuring you were a novice, decided to stick you with its inferior products. Don't you agree, Sen?"

"I know very little about arts and crafts," Sen replied cautiously.

"Don't buy too much here. You'll get much better merchandise in Peking."

"I appreciate your help," Linda said.

"No problem." Stewart took a bite of his eggs and then lit a cigarette. "And what about you, Tonto? Where's the Lone Ranger?"

"What?"

"Where's Marc?"

"He's visiting a coal mine," Sen replied.

"Give him my love." Vance sipped his beer and then smiled at Linda. "I've got a great idea. I've got nothing to do this morning. Why don't I go with you to the cloisonné factory?"

A shrimp caught in Linda's throat, making her cough. "I don't know if it's allowed."

"Sure it is. And don't worry your pretty little head—I promise to stay out of your way."

Sen watched Linda trying to conceal her discomfort. He turned to Vance. "Why don't you let Miss Forbes go by herself? I think she feels self-conscious having someone looking over her shoulder."

Vance ate a forkful of eggs and then cleansed the taste with a drag on his cigarette. "Fair enough, but how about dinner tonight?"

Linda searched for an excuse. "I'm not sure when I'll be back."

"The Chinese always bring you home by six. I'll meet you back in the hotel and take you to some of the hot spots in Tangshan."

Linda had no desire to spend an evening with Stewart, but she could not risk making him suspicious. "What hot spots did you have in mind?"

"How about the People's Revolutionary Club featuring the Bing Family? They're a Chinese version of the Osmonds."

"I think I'll pass."

"The East Is Red Nightclub is supposed to be very decadent."

"I'm not into decadence."

"All right," Vance smiled, "then I've got the perfect place for you. The Defend Mao Tse-tung Disco. They've got a real hot act called Sergeant Pepper's People's Liberation Army Band. They're very in."

Linda laughed, realizing that there was no way for her to continue to decline Vance's invitations. "I'll leave everything in your hands. You find the hot spot and I'll meet you later."

Marc Slater sat at the end of a long, ornate teak conference table trying to read some of the documents that had been transcribed from the microfilm he had smuggled into the country. Although Hu Shengte had been coolly gracious this morning, Marc knew that he was walking on thin ice. He cursed his weakness for allowing himself to become involved with Meili. She affected him like the noon sun in July at a time in his life when he would have been much better off with the shade of a late fall afternoon.

Marc glanced at the three Chinese at the other end of the table. They were almost hidden in a dense cloud of cigarette smoke as they pored over the reams of information in front of them. Finally Deng broke the silence. "The intelligence reports about Jiang and the Russians are fascinating," the diminutive Chinese said. "Unfortunately, there is almost no concrete proof. We still need hard evidence before we go to Hua."

"We could intercept one of their shipments of Western weapons at the time of delivery," Hu suggested tentatively.

Deng laughed. "With thousands of miles of coastline and few ships, that sounds about as fruitless as a hen pecking at a closed clam."

"Perhaps I can come up with something," Marc suggested.

"Where are you going?" Deng asked.

"To find a woman." Marc winked at him.

Linda leaped across the room when she heard the phone ring. "Hello?" Her voice was breathless.

"Linda, this is Marc. Are you all right?"

Linda smiled as she detected a tone of expectancy and excitement. "I had an unfortunate encounter with the Red Guards, but now I'm OK."

"I'm glad," Marc said. "Beatrice informs me that you have some critical news for us."

"It could change everything."

"What is it?"

"Not on the phone. I think I should deliver it in person."

Marc wanted to see Linda and hear her report, but he was hesitant about inviting her to the mines. "Let me talk to the others. I'll be right back."

Linda nervously paced the floor, waiting for Marc's return. She was anxious to unload her bombshell and eager to meet her grandfather, especially under these circumstances.

"Linda?" Marc's voice sounded tentative when he returned to the phone. "I don't think this is the appropriate occasion. The men here are concerned about working with a foreigner they've never met."

"Did you tell them who I am?"

"I told them that Beatrice Tang had sent you and that your information was absolutely essential."

"But did you tell them my name?" Linda asked, wondering why her grandfather would not see her.

"I didn't think that was necessary." Marc sounded slightly annoyed. "Would it be possible for you to give your information to Sen?"

"Of course. But I'd really—"

"Please do it my way," Marc interrupted. "I'll send a car right away. Tell Sen it will be a woman named Hu Meili. She'll be in a gray Toyota."

"All right," Linda said, feeling a twinge of jealousy at the mention of the name of the young Chinese she had seen with

Marc in Canton.

"I'll see you late tonight or early tomorrow morning."

"I'll be looking forward to it." Linda tried not to sound disappointed. "May I ask a favor? If the opportunity arises, could you tell the others where Sen's information came from?"

"Of course," Marc replied, not understanding why Linda was so insistent about receiving personal credit.

Wong Chuyun and his men from Hong Kong had spent the morning searching the Kailuan Coal Mines, but they had met no one who knew of Deng's whereabouts. Wong felt discouraged as he reached the Protect the East Eatery, a ramshackle wooden restaurant that also functioned as a country store. He ordered the only dish on the menu, Four Flavor Chinese Noodles served with a large lump of fried dough. Although the food was greasy and not particularly tasty, Wong had not eaten all day and anything would have been better than going hungry.

After finishing, Wong began to chat with the old peasant who operated the restaurant. He told of their search and asked if the peasant had seen anything out of the ordinary. "*Aiya*"—the peasant's eyes brightened like the shiny kernels of a lichee nut. "Yesterday this big car, like the cadres in Peking drive, came here. Inside were a People's Liberation soldier and a young woman with clothes that looked like they were made of silk." The peasant held up his horny hands. His thumbs were thick as yams. "She was no coal miner." He laughed and winked at Wong. "She bought all of my meat, five fish, a huge basket of fruit, and enough vegetables for a banquet. Then she paid for everything with money—not with coupons but with real money. *Aiya*, I haven't seen that much money since we sent the KMT scurrying to Taiwan Province."

"Where did the car go?"

"Life is very difficult. The mind fades when the stomach is empty."

Wong reached into his pocket and handed the man three crisp ten-yuan bills. The toothless grin flashed once again across the man's face. He was old enough to remember the workings of capitalism. "I don't know where they went, but I'm sure that it was close by, because the woman came back early this morning. This time she was driving a gray Japanese automobile."

"Do you think she'll return again?" Wong asked.

"Will the fox call on the chicken at New Year's time? People always have to eat."

Wong smiled and thanked the old man. He was pleased to finally have a lead, even if it was tenuous.

For four hours, Wong waited, but none of the passing cars resembled the one that the peasant had described. He had almost decided to return to the guest house when the old man started to shout. Wong looked up the road. A gray Toyota was traveling toward Tangshan. Inside were a PLA soldier and a young woman. "That's it," Wong said as he jumped into his jeep and ordered the driver to start the motor. The Toyota was his only lead and he could not afford to waste it.

Forty minutes later, Wong went tearing through the lobby of the Tangshan Guest House. He had to find his people and then get back to his jeep before the girl from the gray Toyota was ready to leave. He ran to the second floor and knocked on Colonel Li's door. There was no answer. Impatiently he tried Leung's room, but it, too, was empty. He climbed two flights of stairs and pounded on another door. "Vance?" A muffled sound came from inside the room. "It's Wong. Hurry and open the door."

Dressed in a kimono that he had borrowed from the Osaka Royal Hotel, Stewart looked half asleep. "What is it, Lawrence?" he asked. His breath reeked of scotch.

"I have a lead to Deng. Find Li and the others." He spoke rapidly with a directness uncharacteristic of a Chinese. "Tell them to get the personnel carriers and the weapons. I'll send a driver back for them. Do you understand?"

"My English is just fine," Vance snapped.

Wong turned, ran downstairs, and hurried outside. The Toyota was still there. Reaching the jeep, he looked back into the hotel. The girl from the Toyota was walking out the door. Behind her was Sen Tailing. Wong's eyes met Sen's. Both men stared silently at each other. Wong had known Sen for many years, but they were more business rivals then friends. Wong turned away first. Although he knew that Sen was a direct link to Slater and hence to Deng, he was furious that he had been caught in plain sight. Now Sen would be wary. It would be difficult to follow the Toyota without being detected. He somehow had to allay Sen's suspicions without losing his only lead. "Drive around the block," he ordered. If he was correct, the Toyota would return the way it had come.

Wong's jeep remained half a mile behind the Toyota as they drove back into the country. As they neared the restaurant, Wong ordered the driver to accelerate. The jeep sped past a small village and traversed a sharp S-shaped curve. Suddenly the taillights of the Toyota appeared in the distance. Wong slapped his thigh and smiled. His gamble had paid off.

The Toyota turned down a road marked "Kailuan Mine #6." The driver of the jeep doused his lights and followed cautiously. The administration building came into view. The jeep stopped. Wong climbed out of the car and ordered the driver to return to Tangshan for the others. Then he walked toward the mine.

Linda ran the brush through her long blond hair for the ninetieth time. She had already showered twice and tried to read her book, but nothing relieved her anxieties. Although she trusted Sen, she wished that she could have delivered the news about Jiang Qing. She would certainly have been invited if she had told Marc that Liu was her grandfather, but telling him would have been highly inappropriate. Acknowledging her would have to be Liu's decision.

A young Chinese floor boy entered the room and handed her a small box. She thanked him and opened it. Inside was a red orchid, the color of blood. She searched for a note but could not find one. She pressed the flower to her nose. There was no scent. Still, it was beautiful. She closed her eyes and smiled. It was probably from Marc, she decided. A ringing telephone disturbed her reverie.

"Hi, good-lookin'," a cheerful voice on the other end greeted her.

"Hello, Vance." Linda tried not to sound disappointed.

"You better get a move on if you're goin' to get to that factory."

"Oh, God. I didn't realize it was so late. I'll talk to you later."

"Did you get the flowers?"

"I'm sorry, Vance. Did you send them? There was no card."

"Who did you think they were from, Marc Slater?" Vance laughed. "I'm the only man in China sportin' enough to send orchids."

"They're beautiful, and I promise that next time I'll remember."

"I'm a good friend for you to have. Stick with me and

you'll be much more than just a department-store buyer. You'd like that, wouldn't you?"

"I'm very happy at Bloomingdale's."

"No you're not. You may fool the others, but I know that you're a very ambitious young woman," Vance said. "We'll talk later. I've got some ideas for you."

Linda put on a navy-blue silk blouse and a matching Ralph Lauren paisley skirt. She looked at herself in the mirror and smiled. One advantage of posing as a Bloomingdale's buyer was that the Agency had been forced to give her an extraordinarily large clothing budget. Even in China she had to look her part. She took the elevator to the lobby and walked quickly to the front door. Fortunately, Vance Stewart was not in sight. If he had been there, it would have been difficult for her to explain why no cadres were waiting to take her to the factory.

She reached Wenhua Road and continued past the massive Exhibition on Class Education Building. Although she was hungry, she did not stop. She wanted to find a restaurant far from the hotel, where no one she knew could see her. She turned into a side street and approached the East Is Red Restaurant. There were twelve tables, and eleven were filled with Chinese eating noodles and drinking beer. Linda walked up to the manager, who stared at her with great surprise. His restaurant was almost never patronized by foreigners, and this was certainly the first time that a foreign woman had come alone. Linda pointed to her mouth and then to her stomach. It would have been far easier for her to speak Chinese, but a cover was a cover. The manager looked around the restaurant. Many of the patrons were staring at Linda. He pointed toward Wenhua Road and tried to wave her away, but she did not move. The manager's cheeks started to redden. He turned around and shouted to his wife, "Clean that dung-covered table for this whore of a long-nosed barbarian."

Linda smiled politely and followed him to the back of the restaurant. He handed her a red piece of paper filled with black calligraphy. The men at the two surrounding tables laughed as she read the menu. "Stupid bitch," one called out in Chinese, "she can't tell the difference between Peking Duck and Tangshan Dog."

Linda pointed to the characters for roast duck. "The barbarian has made a lucky guess," the manager laughed. "She missed all of my dog specialties and selected the duck."

The men leered at Linda, who tried her best to ignore them. She picked up a pictorial magazine and thumbed through the pages. "Hey, long-nose," a man with a goatee called. "I like your lips. Do you want to kiss me?"

The manager searched through a cabinet and took out a tarnished knife and fork. He cleaned them on his apron and then placed them in front of his foreign customer. Linda smiled politely and pointed to a jar filled with chopsticks. "I bet she wields them like a tree trunks," a man in a gray jacket joked to his comrades. Linda stared at the man. His hair, coated with oil, gleamed in the light.

The manager's wife carried in the duck. Using sign language, Linda asked for a beer. Then she picked up her chopsticks and started to eat, trying not to appear too dexterous. "Look at her use those trees," a man with an eye patch said. "She's not bad. Besides, she has nice breasts."

"I'll take her long legs," the man with the goatee said. "I'd love to have them wrapped around me."

Linda ate quickly, trying to pretend she did not understand their taunts. When she had finished, she handed the manager a ten-yuan bill. He looked at her in confusion. The Municipal Administration had not yet given him a special price list for foreigners. He did not want to cheat the woman, but it was certainly appropriate to charge her more than the eighty-five cents that his comrades paid. After all, she required special service as well as the knife and fork. He wrote out a receipt and then stuffed the ten-yuan bill in his pants. "Thank you." Linda smiled politely and stood up.

"You can't leave now." The man with the eye patch stepped in front of her. "I want a chance to look at your pubics. I bet they're blond, just like your hair."

The man with the goatee filled the aisle between the tables. "I'm sure they're silky smooth. Tell me, do you comb them with a brush?"

Linda looked nervously around the restaurant. There were no other foreigners in sight, and none of the men looked like high-level cadres. The wife of the owner scurried by and disappeared into the kitchen. No one made a move to help her. "Excuse me," Linda said in English.

"I bet it tastes like honey inside your jade gate," the man with the eye patch said.

Linda shifted uneasily as she watched the men. The man with the gray jacket blocked her retreat. She had had enough. "Out of my way, you cowardly abortion of blithering baboons," she ordered in Chinese. "You're like a pack of shit-eating dogs following a bitch in heat! Put your eyes back in your head or I'll scratch them out!"

The men stood motionless, except for their mouths, which gaped open. Other customers tittered to each other in whispers that sounded like damp firecrackers. Linda pushed between the men and walked to the door.

"Hey, foreign tiger girl," a man called. "Come back tomorrow."

Marc Slater, Deng Xiaoping, Hu Shengte, and Liu Teyu

sat spellbound as Sen Tailing detailed the story of Little Chang and Jiang Qing's forgery of Mao's will. When he finished, the silence in the room was like that in a deep cave. The sounds of chairs creaking and men puffing on cigarettes could be heard distinctly and yet seemed very remote. Deng jumped out of his chair and paced around the table. "Where did you get this information?" he demanded.

"I heard it from an American sent to me by the sister of Kang Moruo."

"One of your people?" Deng asked Marc.

"I think that Linda Forbes is—"

Liu thrust his mammoth hands onto the table. "What's her name?"

"Linda Forbes." Marc smiled, remembering his promise.

Inhaling his cigarette until his lungs were full, Liu puffed up his cheeks and slowly emitted a long, wispy stream of smoke. He screwed up his face so that his wrinkles took on a pattern that Marc thought resembled a freeway map of Los Angeles. "That nervy, interfering woman," Liu said.

"Is there something I should know about this American?" Deng asked.

"Does the name Margot Kappel mean anything to you?"

"The American artist who lived in Paris after the First World War?"

"Yes."

"She was a beautiful woman. You were just lucky she was so tall; otherwise I would have taken her away from you." Deng smiled.

"When water buffaloes fly," Liu gibed.

"I was surprised that you left her to return to China."

"I didn't exactly leave her." Liu's sunken eyes stared toward the window. "She came with me to Shanghai."

"I never knew," Deng laughed. "I'm not surprised you kept her secret."

"I loved her very much. Do you remember the massacre of April 12, 1927, when Chiang Kai-shek turned traitor and tried to annihilate our party?" The others nodded. "Someone," Liu said, his voice tinged with bitterness, "told Chiang that a cell meeting of party leaders was taking place at my house. He sent two battalions to stop us. We were all downstairs when the soldiers stormed through the door. Hearing the commotion, Margot hurried up to the living room. One of the Green Gang shot her in the leg. Then the soldiers rushed to the basement and arrested the rest of us.

"We were all in jail together, under the control of the Green Gang and its leader, Leung Keqing. One by one our leaders were tortured and then shot. I was sharing a cell with Chou En-lai. At three the next morning, one of Chiang's lieutenants came by to inspect the cells. He had been a student of Chou's at the Whampoa Military Academy. Although he could not help the rest of our officials, he felt a special allegiance to his former teacher. Paying off the guards, he sneaked us out of the prison. Chou and I were the only leaders who survived.

"My house was guarded by soldiers, and Margot had been taken to the hospital, so I fled underground with Chou. The next day it was reported that I had been shot. Thinking I was dead and realizing that her life was still in danger, Margot linked up with an American who helped her flee to the United States."

"I appreciate the history lesson," Deng replied, "but what does this have to do with the American girl, Linda Forbes?"

"When Margot fled, she had an infant son. My son. He was adopted by an American named Forbes. Linda Forbes is his daughter and my granddaughter."

"Oh, my God!" Marc gasped.

"Before she died, Margot wrote and told me about Linda."

"You should be proud of her," Marc said.

"Of course I am," Liu boomed. "Leave it to my flesh and blood to find the famous smoking gun that will hang Jiang Qing."

Wong Chuyun had been waiting for almost two hours when he heard the sound of approaching cars. He ran to meet Colonel Li. "Everyone is inside," Wong panted from too much smoking.

"What about guards?"

"There's one on the front balcony, one in the mine shaft, and two in the rear. There are many men inside, but they don't appear to be armed."

Colonel Li nodded his approval. "Have you checked out the site?"

"I've found several good places for our weapons on the high ground." Wong pointed to three small hills. "I think we should also have one man behind that mine shaft and another on the back road."

Colonel Li nodded his agreement. Then he ordered the six men he had brought with him to move to their positions. He would have to wait until Leung arrived with the rest of the weapons before attacking.

Hurrying through the lobby of the Tangshan Guest House, Linda Forbes saw Vance Stewart standing in a corner talking to a Chinese man. Though the man was facing away from her, he looked familiar. Linda circled through two side rooms until she reached a small alcove. She could hear Stewart explaining something. The Chinese turned toward her. He was Leung Lilai, Alexandra Koo's partner. Could Stewart be allied with them as well? She edged forward as Leung said, "Tell Li I'll have the weapons at the mine by eight."

What weapons? What mine? Linda asked herself. Perhaps it had something to do with Marc's meeting with Deng. She had to summon help, but the only way out of the alcove was through the corridor. She waited impatiently, hoping for her chance. Suddenly Stewart and Leung turned and walked toward her. She would have to look for another opportunity to find Sen. She stepped quickly out of the alcove. "Linda!" Stewart seemed surprised. "What are you doing here?"

"We have a date, remember?"

"How could I forget! I was just coming to find you. Do you two know each other?"

"I had the pleasure of meeting Miss Forbes on the train from Hong Kong," Leung replied.

"It's nice to see you again, Mr. Leung," Linda replied, recalling that Leung had pretended not to speak English. "Your English has improved."

Leung appeared embarrassed. "I've been studying quite diligently."

Linda was annoyed with herself for making Leung lose face unnecessarily. It would be better to get away from him before she said something else she regretted. She tugged on Stewart's arm. "Vance, when are we going to the disco?"

"Disco?" Leung asked.

Vance smiled his Cheshire-cat grin and winked at Leung. "I promised to take this young lady on a tour of the hottest night spots in Tangshan."

25: The Partnerships

Frans Van Wyck sat at his desk in the Peking Hotel studying the plans that Aziz Rahman had proposed for the attack that evening on the United States Liaison Office. The only official American presence in China, USLO was the perfect target for his operatives.

Van Wyck knew that Jiang Qing and her Gang of Four allies were disturbed by the increasingly friendly relations with the United States. To them, the United States was not only the leader of the capitalist world but also the country that had armed the KMT, fought against the People's Republic in Korea and Vietnam, and established threatening military bases on Taiwan. On many occasions, Jiang had advocated the severing of all relations. So that there would be no doubt that the attack was the work of the Gang of Four, Van Wyck's operatives would dress in Red Guard uniforms and place wall posters on Chang'an Avenue criticizing the capitalist-roaders.

Van Wyck had scheduled the operation for an evening on

which the American ambassador was hosting a banquet for Samuel Tang. Samuel's brothers-in-law would be in attendance. If all went according to plan, he would be able to kill two of the Politburo's leading conservatives, discredit Jiang Qing, and rupture relations between the United States and China, thus depriving the People's Republic of whatever intelligence information the Americans might be providing. It was the type of operation he most enjoyed: simple, disciplined, and effective.

There was a knock on the door. Avery Boswell, dressed in a Hong Kong safari suit, entered the room and greeted Van Wyck. "Would you object if I closed the window and turned on the fan?" The Englishman grimaced as if he had just smelled something unpleasant.

"Of course not," Van Wyck replied. "What's wrong?"

Boswell dipped his handkerchief in a glass of water and dabbed his forehead. "It's the air. I can't stand the dust."

Van Wyck smiled as he thought about his plan to put Boswell on the team going to the Gobi Desert. "Have a cup of tea."

"Thank you." Boswell removed three manila envelopes from his briefcase. "I have the maps you wanted, but getting them wasn't easy."

"I didn't expect it to be." Van Wyck inspected the maps of the pipelines in the Junggar Basin, the coal regions in Manzhouli and Yichun, the oil fields in Daching, the hydroelectric installation in Jilin, and the legation section in Peking. "These are excellent," he said. "Your work is most appreciated."

Boswell hovered over Van Wyck's shoulder. "Why did you want the legation section?"

Van Wyck described the plans for the operation against USLO.

Boswell placed his hand on Van Wyck's shoulder and smiled admiringly. "I'm grateful to have the opportunity to learn from you. What's my role in the action against the Americans?"

Van Wyck laughed. "I need men who can disguise themselves as Red Guards. Do you think a six-foot, blond-haired, blue-eyed, sallow-skinned Caucasion would pass?"

"But your appearance is much the same as mine."

"And I am staying in the hotel."

Boswell looked disappointed. "There must be something I can do."

"You've done a lot. In fact I've already written to Comrade Bulganov commending you."

"I'm grateful, but please understand how important this operation is to me. All my previous work has involved industrial espionage. My progress is being blocked by my lack of military expertise. If you insist on using me as nothing but a courier, I'll never be able to advance to the levels at which the Bureau formulates policy."

"I have no intention of restricting your activities," Van Wyck said, knowing that Boswell would continue to pester him for a military assignment until he relented. With three attacks planned during the next ten days, he had no time to discuss the Englishman's future. He had to find a way of keeping him occupied. "Do you remember your suggestion that we kidnap Lord Gateshead?"

"Of course."

"I have received official approval from Moscow."

Boswell's face broke into a broad smile. "That's wonderful. I promise you won't be disappointed."

"I have every confidence in you. Take three men and whatever weapons you need. But before you do anything, I want to see a detailed plan."

"I'll have everything ready by this afternoon," Boswell responded with the eagerness of a schoolboy.

Avery Boswell sat with Lord Gateshead at a small table in the bar in the Peking Hotel. In the five hours since receiving authorization, he had devised his plans, presented them to Van Wyck, and made contact with Gateshead. Now it was only a matter of hours before the kidnapping. "Lord Gateshead, if you'll excuse me, I have to meet one of my clients."

"Certainly," Lord Gateshead replied. "I'm pleased we had this opportunity to talk."

"The pleasure is mine." Boswell bowed politely. "I'm just glad that I was able to obtain the extra invitation for the banquet hosted by the Ministry of Machine Industry. It should be quite a gala. A car will pick you up in two hours. We'll meet at Beihai Park, if that's all right."

"You've been most considerate," Gateshead said as Boswell walked away.

Gateshead lingered at the table, sipping his tea and reading his reports. "*Bonjour*," a sweetly accented woman's voice said. Gateshead looked up. Nicole LaFleur's blouse was opened provocatively one button more than it should have been. Her large round eyes smiled at him. She seemed extremely inviting, especially since he had seen nothing but Oriental women for the last week. Women, he thought, were much like food. It was fascinating to sample foreign delicacies, but his stomach was much happier with a thick slab of roast beef and Yorkshire pudding. Nicole was not roast beef, but she was *boeuf bourguignon*, which was close enough.

"I haven't seen you for a while." Nicole smiled as

Gateshead rose to greet her. "How has your trip been going?"

Though anxious to share his success, Gateshead knew he had to be circumspect. "It is far better than I could have dreamed."

"I'm pleased for you."

"Thank you." Gateshead evaluated his opportunities. "I would be honored if you would join me for a bottle of champagne in celebration."

"I'd be delighted."

He pulled out a chair at his small table in front of the bar. A waiter brought two glasses and a bottle of Daxiangbin, a Chinese champagne. "A toast"—Nicole held up her glass—"to the English Museum and its new Oriental wing."

"And another to the fairest woman in Peking." Gateshead clinked their glasses and sipped the champagne, which tasted like very sweet 7-Up. "I am sorry that it is not Moët et Chandon."

"I find it very interesting." Nicole smiled politely. "Besides, it's the thought that counts."

As Lord Gateshead clasped Nicole's hand, he heard the swish of silk and felt an unmistakable presence hovering above him. Alexandra Koo, attired in a flowing celadon dress and dangling jade earrings adorned with carved tigers, stepped between him and Nicole. "Good evening," she said in a haughty voice.

Gateshead stood up and extended his hand. "Mrs. Koo, this is an unexpected pleasure. May I introduce Miss Nicole LaFleur from Paris."

Nicole shook hands with Alexandra. "I'm pleased to meet you, Mrs. Koo."

"Thank you." Alexandra stared at the Englishman. "I'm glad to see you in the company of such a lovely young girl."

Lord Gateshead ignored her cattiness. "Would you like to join us?"

"I'd just like a word with you, in private." Alexandra slipped into the Englishman's chair. "Do you think your young friend could leave us for a few minutes?"

Lord Gateshead struggled to control his anger at the affront. He stared silently as Mrs. Koo ordered the waiter to bring another glass.

Nicole kissed him on the cheek. "If you'll excuse me, Lord Henry, I'd better go finish my work. Call me when you're finished." She placed her hand on Alexandra's shoulder. "It was nice meeting you, Mrs. Kong."

"Koo."

"Whatever." Nicole promenaded out of the bar to admiring glances.

"Lord Gateshead, if you don't mind . . ." The Englishman turned back to the table. Alexandra raised her glass. "Shall we drink to our partnership?"

"Of course." Lord Gateshead took a sip.

"What's troubling you?" Alexandra asked.

"If you don't mind my saying so, I think you could have been a little more gracious."

"To that tart?"

"Miss LaFleur is a gifted young woman. She is a designer for Dior."

"She seems to be working her designs on you."

Gateshead shifted uncomfortably. "I do not appreciate the innuendoes."

"And I do not appreciate my business associates placing themselves in potentially vulnerable positions."

"Vulnerable? That woman knows nothing about my business."

"Then what were you celebrating?"

306

Lord Gateshead smiled uneasily. "I thought that a little champagne might put her in the mood, if you understand my intentions."

"I understand that she is an attractive young woman in her twenties, and you are, shall we say, closer to Robert Morley than Robert Redford. Do you remember John Profumo?"

Lord Gateshead bristled silently at the insult. He resented the reference to the former British defense minister who had been disgraced for divulging state secrets to a call girl who passed them on to the Russians. Nicole had done nothing to merit Alexandra's wrath. "I find your comments out of line and quite tasteless," he said.

"You're entitled to your opinion, but I'm not willing to risk my entire plan so that you can recapture your lost youth." Alexandra stood up. "Besides, you have far more important commitments. I've just arranged a short visit to the Qin Tombs in Xian."

"Frightfully good!" Lord Gateshead's eyes beamed.

"I thought that would make you forget about your little strumpet," Alexandra smiled.

Lord Gateshead stared at Mrs. Koo. She had no right to be so cheeky. She needed him and his money as much as he needed her. But this was not the time to quibble. The Qin Tombs were the ultimate prize. He was willing to make any reasonable sacrifice to obtain its relics. "When are you planning to leave?"

"There's a special transport at nine. I'll pick you up in one hour."

"Tonight?"

"Is that inconvenient? Do you have a more pressing engagement with your young friend?"

Lord Gateshead considered his plan to attend the banquet with Boswell and his desire to spend the rest of the evening with Nicole. Although the former sounded interesting and the latter inviting, neither could compare with the opportunities offered by Mrs. Koo. "Not at all," Lord Gateshead said. "I'd be honored to accompany you to Xian."

"I somehow suspected"—Alexandra winked at Lord Gateshead—"that you were the kind of English gentleman whose devotion to duty takes precedence over lust."

26: The Mandate of Heaven

Jiang Qing sat in the living room of the golden-tiled Ming dynasty pavilion that had been her home for most of the past twenty-seven years. She had been forced to move out during her separation from Chairman Mao, but once he entered the hospital, she had returned and was determined to never leave.

Jiang had been posing for more than two hours while Mok Hongda, the country's most renowned portrait artist, worked on the painting that was to depict her official ascension as Mao's successor. The work contained only two figures, she and Mao. Mao was sitting sideways, bending deferentially, and touching her arm; while she was sitting erect and facing forward. In her hands, she held a parchment with the characters. "You, Comrade Jiang Qing, are the only one qualified to assume my post as chairman of the Communist Party of China."

Jiang nervously brushed her bangs off her forehead with her bean-thread fingers. She was in no mood for posing. She

309

was still concerned about her unpleasant meeting with Wang Dongxin, the commander of Unit 8341, Mao's elite private guards. Though she disliked Dongxin, she needed the support of his highly trained forty-thousand-man force. Organized into an independent armored regiment, two guard divisions, and three battalions specializing in anti-aircraft, engineering, and communications, Unit 8341 not only protected Mao and the Politburo but also staffed the administrative office of the Central Committee and handled much of the spy work in China. Whoever gained its loyalty was in an excellent position to control the government. She had to find a way of convincing Dongxin and his uncommitted Wind Faction to support her. "That damn radish," she muttered. "His outside may be red, but his inside is bleach white."

"Excuse me, comrade, did you say something?" Mok the artist asked.

Jiang looked up. "Ah, yes. I said I wanted to see how you are doing."

"But, comrade, you inspected my work twenty minutes ago."

"Everything must be perfect," Jiang said, staring at the painting.

"Are there aspects that displease you?"

"Just a few," Jiang replied. "My cheeks are too puffy and my eyes too small. There are too many wrinkles on my neck. Leave a few for character, but remove the rest. I want to be seen as a strong and determined leader."

"As you wish."

"I also don't like the green and black plaid of the cushions."

"But those are the colors of Chairman Mao's study."

"I appreciate your attention to detail, but I look much better in blue and red, and this is my official portrait."

"It shall be as you request."

"Excellent." The door opened and Mao Yuanxin, the son of Mao's dead younger brother, entered the room. "Nephew," Jiang called, "come see what Comrade Mok and I are painting."

Greeting his aunt, Yuanxin smiled as he crossed the floor. He knew that Jiang's remark was more than just egotism. As the czar of culture, she had been actively involved in every aspect of the creative process. In plays and operas, she wrote much of the dialogue, assigned the roles, and directed the actors; while in films, she supervised everything from camera angles to editing. Even symphonies and paintings bore her imprint. Composers and artists often revised their works many times to satisfy her exacting standards. All creative works of the last decade had been crafted to conform to her personal taste and political viewpoint. Perhaps that was why only four model operas, two ballets, and two symphonies had been performed since the start of the Cultural Revolution.

"Do you like it?" Jiang asked.

Yuanxin stared skeptically at the canvas. "It is very well done, but I do not understand why you are facing the front while our Teacher is looking to the side." Yuanxin used the name Teacher as Mao preferred to be called. He disliked the terms Great Helmsman, Great Teacher, Great Supreme Leader, and Great Commander applied to him by Lin Biao during the Cultural Revolution, suspecting that those who shouted his name the loudest were, in his own words, "waving the Red flag in order to defeat the Red flag."

"This is my first official portrait," Jiang said. "Paintings of our Teacher hang in virtually every room in China."

"But is it proper that our Teacher defer to you?"

"My husband will never defer to anyone. He is the greatest leader in history. But China cannot always live in his memory. If I am to defeat the capitalist-roaders, I must establish my own legitimacy."

"Honored elder aunt, I did not mean to seem critical. I only wanted to understand so that I could learn from you."

"Your attitude pleases me," Jiang said as she poured Yuanxin a cup of tea. "Now tell me about my husband. Did you see him today?"

"I left him less than an hour ago," Yuanxin replied. Since Mao had returned to the hospital, Yuanxin had functioned as his personal secretary, controlling his uncle's schedule and taking notes at all meetings.

"How did he seem to you?" Jiang asked.

"He is weak and his trembling has become more severe," Yuanxin said, referring to the Parkinson's disease that had afflicted Mao for more than three decades. "When I entered his room, he was lying in bed, staring glassy-eyed at the ceiling. He looked like a beached whale."

"That is a harsh thing to say about the Great Helmsman." Jiang knowingly used a term that both Mao and Yuanxin disliked.

"I am sorry, honorable elder aunt. I am just trying to be accurate. Since our Teacher can no longer move on his own, he has gained more than forty pounds."

"I thought he could still walk."

"When he has visitors, he forces himself to shuffle across the room so that they will not suspect the extent of his weakness. But he is unable to do that more than once or twice a day. His body has become very stiff and brittle. He even needs an attendant to help escort him to the bathroom."

Jiang glanced out the window at the walls of the Forbidden City. "Are there other signs of deterioration?"

Yuanxin gazed sympathetically at his aunt as he pictured Mao's broad, unwrinkled face that once had been so animated. "His face is almost always expressionless. He never laughs nor shows emotion. Only his eyes reflect the painful frustration of being trapped in a body that no longer works. He has lost much of the use of his hands. Writing is impossible, as is using chopsticks. I must feed him many of his meals. And when he smokes, I have to remove the cigarette after every puff."

"It must be very hard for him," Jiang said, thinking of better times.

"For a man used to ruling, it is almost impossible. This morning I gave him a cup of tea. He clasped it in both hands, but he was shaking so badly that he spilled most of it on his gown."

"What about his mind?" Jiang asked.

"His memory is slipping. There are times when he's completely lucid, but then something happens. He'll begin to mutter and suddenly it's like he's living in the past. He'll dictate memos to Chou En-lai as if Chou were still alive."

Jiang wiped her eyes with a silk handkerchief. "Your news deeply saddens me. It's difficult to believe his health has faded so rapidly."

"Honored elder aunt, please sit down." Yuanxin pulled out a chair.

"Thank you, but working people don't sit or bury their heads when they cry. They cry standing."

Yuanxin repressed a smile as he remembered the film from which Jiang's last line had come. His aunt had incorporated speeches from many of her movies into her normal conversation. "I'd like to talk to you in private," Yuanxin said.

"You"—Jiang pointed to the artist. "Go outside and smell the flowers." She paced impatiently as Mok left the room. "All right, nephew, is it something about me?"

"Not exactly. It is something about the entire country and the *Tian Ming*," Yuanxin said, referring to the Mandate of

Heaven under which governments in China were said to rule

"What of the Mandate?" Jiang asked uneasily.

"Our Teacher has had nightmares of a coming *Ge Ming*."

"A revolution?" Jiang used the definition of the word adopted by the Communists.

"No. It is the ancient *Ge Ming*, the Withdrawal of the Mandate. Our Teacher fears that the government he created will soon be at an end."

"Mao scorns all Confucian teachings."

"Perhaps not any longer. He has begun to think of himself as an emperor. Each day he asks me to read him the stories of the fall of other dynasties."

"But surely this government is in no danger of losing the Mandate of Heaven," Jiang insisted. "Mao has not lived debaucherously. He has been humble, pious, and dutiful, thinking only of the welfare of the people. He has not made unreasonable demands, imposed usurious taxes, or forced people to labor building useless monuments." Jiang listed the conditions that had caused the Withdrawal of the Mandate during imperial times. "Mao has been a virtuous leader. We have nothing to fear."

"I agree with you, honored elder aunt." Yuanxin poured two cups of tea. "But these are the concerns of our Teacher."

Jiang massaged her temples. She did not believe in Confucian teachings, but she knew that many still did. If they thought Mao's Mandate was being withdrawn, she would have little chance of succeeding him. "I think my husband is just frightened of dying."

"It is far more than that," Yuanxin said. "He keeps talking about imperial omens and natural disasters."

"But there have been no peasant revolts or natural disasters."

"What of April fifth?" Yuanxin asked, referring to the terrible incident during Chou En-lai's memorial service.

Jiang's eyes narrowed with annoyance. "That was just a demonstration orchestrated by the capitalist-roaders. It ended with Deng's purge."

"Then what of the meteor?" Yuanxin asked. Three months earlier, the largest meteor ever seen by man had landed on China.

"One rock is hardly enough to herald the Withdrawal of the Mandate."

"Our Teacher fears that there will be other natural disasters."

Jiang walked to the window. "I fear the strain of age is pulling at my husband. Our government is strong. Our country is secure. Nothing can threaten our Mandate of Heaven."

"I pray you are correct, honored elder aunt," Yuanxin said in a voice tinged with uncertainty.

Veering away from the administration building of the Kailuan Mines in Tangshan, Colonel Li wound through the deserted shafts. It had taken him two hours to survey the territory around Mine #6. The only route of escape was the main road, stretching between highways on the north and the south. It would be easy to trap Deng and the others. Li inspected the fully loaded ammunition cartridge of his revolver. He wished there had been a better way of removing Deng. Killing was so unsubtle, so un-Chinese. He knew the capitalist-roaders could destroy the People's Republic, but he still had qualms about Jiang Qing's leadership. It would have been far better if Mao could have continued in power. Since his death was inevitable, the only viable choices were Jiang and Deng. And he had already cast his lot.

Li approached the encampment where Wong and two of his men were talking Cantonese. He listened to their singsong speech. The language of the South, with its nine tones and sharp accents, was grating on his ears. In Cantonese, even lovemaking sounded like hungry peasants fighting over a squawking chicken.

The Cantonese were quite unlike the rest of the Han people. Although they made excellent merchants and revolutionaries, they were loud, not particularly subtle, and quite uninhibited. Perhaps it was their climate, their diet of rice, and their extra years of contact with the West. Whatever the reasons, the colonel was uncomfortable working with them, especially with this group, all of whom were capitalists from Hong Kong. But the choice had not been his, and he was not about to risk challenging the wishes of Jiang Qing.

Twenty minutes later Leung arrived with the personnel carriers and the weapons. Colonel Li deployed his troops. Five men were assigned to the main road; four, including Leung, were sent to guard the rear exit; while Wong and another man were ordered to position themselves as lookouts near the administration building. All were provided with walkie-talkies.

It was almost 8:00, the Hour of the Snake. Pacing the perimeter of a small clearing, Colonel Li checked with his operatives. All were ready. He lit a cigarette and tried to relax. The night seemed strangely ominous. Two rabbits scampered by. Birds fled from their nests, shrieking eerily as they ascended into the sky. His nerves were tightly wound.

"Colonel Li," a voice cackled over the walkie-talkie. "This is Wong. There are two people walking toward us."

"Who are they?"

"It's Slater. He's with the Chinese woman from the Toyota."

"What are they doing?"

Wong laughed. "She's kissing him."

"That bitch!" The colonel released the "speak" button. "Something has to be done about these revisionist women who disgrace the country by throwing themselves at wealthy imperialists." Li spat a foul taste from his mouth.

An aide summoned Marc back into the conference room where Deng Xiaoping sat reviewing the documents he had presented. Despite the evidence against Jiang and the Russians, Deng was reluctant to act precipitously. Jiang Qing was immensely popular, and he was still an outcast in his own country. Stubbing out one cigarette, he lit another.

"Keep smoking that way," Hu Shengte said as he entered into the room, "and your girl friend will soon be tasting another man's fruit."

"With Comrade Jiang Qing determined to kill me"— Deng placed his hand to his throat and pretended to choke himself—"why should I fear a pack of cigarettes?"

"At seventy-two, my friend, you should take better care of yourself."

Liu Teyu laughed as he poured a glass of beer. "Don't worry about Deng. He can survive anything: the Long March, the KMT, the Japanese, two purges, and sixty cigarettes a day. He's so tough that he makes Mao seem like a leaf tossed in the wind. I have it on good authority that his father was part water buffalo and part elephant."

"If that's the case, how'd I end up so short?"

"Perhaps your mother was part house cat and part frog."

"You've found me out!" Deng laughed. He opened a bottle of beer and motioned for the others to sit on the couches. "Now that the biology lesson is over, do you think you vultures could help advise this frog as to how we should proceed?"

"Our first step," Hu Shengte suggested, "should be to

contact Hua. Once he learns of Jiang's plans, I'm sure he'll side with us."

"Why?" Deng rebutted. "We've nothing to offer in exchange."

"Nothing? With our support, Hua can continue as the leader of China."

"Are you serious?" Deng's intense eyes bore in on Hu. "None of us likes Hua's policies or respects his leadership. How long do you think we're going to stand by and let him parade around as chairman?"

"I don't understand. You're arguing against our own position."

"I'm just being realistic. Do you think Hua is a plucked chicken waiting to be dropped into a pot?" Deng quoted a Chinese aphorism. "He may be inept, but he's no fool. He knows that there'll be no place for him in our government. So what incentive does he have? He's like a man trapped in a cave with a tiger in front and a snake behind. No matter which way he walks, he'll eventually be killed."

"But he must realize that the People's Republic needs our leadership."

"How can you be so naïve?" Deng curled his lower lip. "Don't you realize that Jiang and Hua sincerely believe that only they can save China?" Since the Liberation, a vast gulf had existed between the right-wing pragmatists and the left-wing ideologues. For twenty-seven years they had fought bitterly against each other, each side convinced that only it could lead the country.

"We must plan our strategy with utmost care," Deng said, "seeking to use the best of our intelligence in order to divide our enemies. We can't approach Hua directly or confront Jiang with the forgery of Mao's will. We must find a subtler way of using our knowledge."

"You sound like Sun Tzu," Marc suggested, referring to

the military theorist of the fifth century B.C.

Deng smiled, "Do you think Mao is the only Chinese ever to have read *The Art of War?*" Mao took most of his military strategies from the classic book. "You are forgetting that our friend General Liu followed Sun's teachings two thousand miles into the Heavenly Mountains."

"I could never forget the lessons taught me by Long Way Liu." Marc bowed his head respectfully.

"What then do you remember of Sun's teachings?" Deng asked.

Although it had been years since Marc had read the book, the lessons drummed into him as a youth were still fresh in his mind. Sensing he was being tested, Marc began deliberately. "Sun believed the best generals were the ones who could break the enemy's resistance without fighting. He theorized that wars were won not by massive force but by finesse, infiltration, and foreknowledge. He advocated battle plans based on deception and indirection in order to lure the enemy into fighting at a time and on a terrain that would guarantee victory."

"Not bad," Deng said, "but how would you apply these teachings?"

Marc paused before answering. "With regard to the forgery of Mao's will, I think indirection would be appropriate. Instead of challenging Jiang, I think we should try to remove the forged will from the archives."

"Perfect," Deng laughed. "I can see her now when they open the empty vault." He contorted his face in a look of feigned horror. "If we're lucky, she'll fly into one of her famous rages and incriminate herself."

"The same strategy might also work for the relics," Marc said, feeling increasingly confident.

"We can only do that," Deng said, "if we can make use of another of Sun's prerequisites—spies." Sun advocated spending lavishly on spies so that the best generals could learn the plans of their opponents and thoroughly prepare their own troops.

"I think Beatrice Tang has a lead on the smuggling," Marc said. "If she can find out what relics are involved and where they are being shipped, we can have the Arts and Crafts Corporation produce copies, which we can secretly substitute for the originals. When the buyers discover they've received fakes, not only will they refuse to pay, they might protest loudly enough to undermine Jiang's credibility."

Deng strutted behind the couch like a victorious fighting cock. "You have learned your lessons well, my friend. I must remember your devious nature when I am negotiating against you."

"I would never be devious with you."

"A magician can fool an audience, but not the gong beater standing behind him."

"And you are the gong beater?"

Deng smiled. "Of course. That was another job I held during my rectification."

"Before we congratulate ourselves"—Hu's expression was intensely serious—"we still should consider what we intend to do about the Russians. Do we have any leads on their identity?"

There was a silence in the room as the men stared uneasily at each other. Not one seemed to know anything about the Russians, and all realized that identifying expertly trained commandoes would not be an easy task. "I have," Marc said, "what they call in the United States a 'long shot.' I don't know the identity of the Russians, but I suspect they're working with the Takamura Corporation."

"That's impossible," Hu said. "the People's Republic and Takamura are very close friends."

Marc felt uneasy challenging Hu, but he did not want to

back down. "Are they the same friends who encouraged the Japanese invasion, and the same friends who controlled half the industry in Manchuria?"

"That's in the past. Now the People's Republic and Takamura are working together on many important projects," Hu stated.

"I've been informed," Marc said, "that Takamura has paid the Russians two billion dollars for the right to drill for oil in the Altay Mountains."

"That's ridiculous. The oil is on the Chinese side of the border."

"In a region that the Soviet Union has always claimed as its own."

"Are you suggesting that the Japanese would help the Russians to invade China?"

Marc stared nervously at the others. He could detect no sign of their positions. "That's exactly what I'm suggesting."

"You're creating a typhoon in an oyster shell." Hu's tone was harsh. "Perhaps it's because you and Takamura are competitors."

Marc recalled Hu's angry reaction over the incident with Meili. He tried to keep his voice steady. "I resent your implication. Do you think I'd let my business interests interfere in a situation like this?"

"I'm no longer certain what you'd do!"

Marc felt as if he were digging himself into a bottomless pit. He had to choose his words carefully without giving ground. "I have been your friend for forty years. I've never lied to you and wouldn't start now."

Deng raised his hands in the air. "I think we should relax. It's clear the pressures are affecting us all." Opening a bottle of beer, he poured four drinks. Marc drained his glass. His heart pounded as he waited to hear the reactions of Liu and Deng.

"I think," Deng said cautiously, "that we owe our friend Mr. Slater the benefit of the doubt. Although we now have some major projects with Takamura, I don't think we can yet trust an Island Dwarf. They would eat the donkey that turns the millstone for them."

Liu nodded his agreement. Despite the Chinese penchant for civility, it was difficult for him and Deng to disguise their disdain. The Chinese had always considered the island people to be vastly inferior, but twice in this century Japan had conquered China. During the Anti-Japanese War, the island people had inflicted untold atrocities on the Middle Kingdom. Their soldiers had tortured children, raped women, and mutilated old men. They had ransacked Chinese treasures, destroyed entire villages, and burned the food that peasants had needed for survival. Because the Communists had been the only Chinese to pursue the enemy, they had borne the brunt of the most vicious actions. None of the men at the table would ever forget the suffering inflicted by the Japanese.

Deng ran his hands through his thinning hair. "There is only one way to find out if the Island Dwarfs are working with the Russians."

"What's that?" Liu asked.

"Appeal to their greed. The Japanese have no loyalty. They are like old silkworms gobbling up big leaves—they'll grab for anything they can get. We must offer them something so valuable that they'll betray the Russians and side with us."

"What did you have in mind?"

"The lifeblood of Japan, the ultimate vulnerability of the Island Dwarfs—oil." Deng turned to Hu. "I want you to contact Takamura. Inform them that we have decided against working with M. H. Schaffer and that we are now in a position to offer them a twenty-five-year exclusive agreement at thirty percent below the lowest OPEC price."

Marc stared at Deng, concerned about how far his friend would push the ploy. If Takamura accepted Hu's offer, his company could lose its position in Chinese petroleum. He lit his pipe and told himself to relax. There was nothing he could do. If he spoke up for his own business interests, it would seem as if Hu's earlier accusations had been correct.

"I'm sorry to give away your oil rights," Deng said to Marc, "but there are no other alternatives."

"We are old friends. We must be willing to take risks in order to help each other."

Samuel and Beatrice Tang climbed the marble stairs of the imposing fieldstone house, built by the manager of one of England's largest trading companies. A butler opened the front door and ushered them into a large entrance hall decorated with glass cases filled with blue-and-white Ming vases. Beatrice smiled. Her brothers had been fortunate. Their father had been the first important capitalist to support the Communists. Although the government had confiscated their properties and businesses, it had permitted them to keep their personal possessions.

The Tangs followed the servant into a living room decorated with opulently carved rosewood furniture. The floor was covered with a magnificent peach-colored, white-fringed Oriental rug with a plum-blossom motif derived from traditional Chinese porcelain. The subtle colorations and the lack of a border indicated that the rug was of very recent design. Two Chinese silk tapestries, one called *Morning Scene at South Lake* and the other *Tall Tree, Bamboo, and Stone*, hung on the walls. Bronze relics were prominently displayed on the end tables.

Kang Moruo tugged at the sash on his red silk smoking

jacket as he stood to greet his guests. "Younger sister, worthy brother-in-law, I am honored to have you visit my humble home."

Beatrice and Sam took seats on the turquoise brocaded couch while the butler served a sweet Chinese wine. "A toast." Beatrice held up her glass. "To our family, may it grow and prosper."

"And to our countries," Kang replied. "May our dinner at the Liaison Office provide the first step in our renewed cooperation."

Kang's wife, still known by her milk name of Golden Flower, stepped into the room with a distracted air. She bowed silently to her guests and took a seat in the corner. She was beautifully dressed in a blue silk shift with a necklace of pearls, but her face was lifeless and her heavily lined eyes looked like little black peas. She had been ill for a long time. Eight years in a rectification camp for the crime of being the daughter of a landlord had sapped her strength and broken her spirit.

Beatrice went to the corner and gently stroked Golden Flower's hair. "You look well, honored sister," she said with great sympathy. Golden Flower closed her eyes and sat motionless.

"My wife," Kang Moruo said, "has been tormented by nightmares for almost a month. My little petal, why don't you go upstairs and rest."

"I can't sleep," Golden Flower's voice rasped in a whisper. "The river is up to its banks. I must carry more sand or we will all be washed away." It was 1931 in her nightmare. She was once again a young girl sitting helplessly in a large manor house, watching as thousands of peasants frantically built dikes to hold back the Yangtze River. The crest advanced like a never-ending army. It tore through the dikes, carrying everyone with it, inundating the fertile lowlands that provided food for tens of millions of people. As the gorged river receded, dysentery, cholera, and famine decimated the survivors. Four million people were killed. In her own family, only her father, who was in Peking, and her amah were saved.

"This is not 1931," Kang stated, "this is the People's Republic. We can control our rivers."

"It will be much worse this time." Golden Flower's voice sounded like the crackling of dried leaves. "The waters will wash away more than just land and people. They will wash away the Mandate of Heaven."

"Stop acting like a child," Kang lectured. "Our country is strong. Besides, there have been no portents."

"What of Chou En-lai?"

"One man's death can hardly be taken as a sign from heaven."

"And Mao?"

"Mao is still alive."

"But he is very ill. And what of Zhu De?" Golden Flower's voice sounded as bitter as an unripe melon as she asked about the founder of the People's Liberation Army.

"Zhu will live another ten years."

"You are wrong. Zhu Mao is almost dead." Golden Flower spoke as if Zhu De and Mao Tse-tung were one man.

Her slip reminded Sam of the early years of the Communist Party, when Mao and Zhu had been so inseparable that the foreign press had referred to them as "the Red Bandit Chieftain Zhu Mao," and to their army as "the Zhu Mao Army."

"My little petal," Kang said, "those are just dreams. Our leaders will survive."

"I think not. I see many portents of death."

Sam shook his head as he watched Kang shepherd Golden Flower out of the room. He prayed that her words were the ravings of a madwoman and not the visions of a seer.

Avery Boswell crouched behind a black limousine at the bottom of the semicircular driveway of the Peking Hotel and waited for Lord Henry Gateshead. He had intended to meet Gateshead in Beihai Park, but he wanted to be certain that there would be no problems. He had never before planned such an operation. Even though Van Wyck would undoubtedly criticize him for taking unnecessary risks, the experience was too heady for him to miss.

Boswell checked his watch. It would not be long now. The driveway was filled with cars waiting to take foreign guests to banquets. In China banquets always started between 6:00 and 6:30 and lasted exactly two hours, creating unusual traffic jams at the hotel before and after dinner. Boswell saw one of his operatives in a pale green Shanghai car. He searched for Lord Gateshead. Where is that old fossil? he asked himself, shaking out his legs to relieve the tension.

Gateshead emerged from the hotel carrying a small suitcase. "What's that fool doing?" Boswell muttered as he rushed to the entrance. "Lord Gateshead," he shouted. "I'm so glad I intercepted you. My meeting was over early. We can ride to the banquet together."

"Boswell old man,"—Gateshead looked slightly embarrassed—"something has come up. I'm sorry but I will be unable to attend your banquet."

"You what?" Boswell stammered. "But that's impossible. Do you know the trouble it took to get you an invitation?"

"I apologize for the inconvenience."

"Inconvenience? Do you know how much face I will lose when you fail to arrive?"

"Mr. Boswell, I have already apologized twice. I am dreadfully sorry but I have more important obligations. Please try to understand."

"Where are you going?"

"I do not think that it is any of your concern."

"Of course it is." Boswell's voice had a sharp edge. "You are a director of the company I represent. I have arranged a banquet at which you were expected to make a speech. I must know where you are going."

"Of all the unmitigated gall!"

Alexandra Koo stepped between the two men. "Excuse me, Mr. Boswell, but Comrade Jiang Qing has requested a special audience with Lord Gateshead. I'll have him back in Peking tomorrow night. Until then, I'm certain that you can justify his actions to your people."

"Jiang Qing? Why would—"

"Lord Gateshead, our car is waiting." Alexandra opened the door of a limousine. The Englishman turned and climbed into the back seat. Boswell stood seething in front of the hotel as the car drove away. He knew Gateshead was an incompetent fool, yet the Englishman had somehow managed to ruin his perfectly planned operation. His future in the party was dependent on this kidnapping. Van Wyck would never let him lead another mission. And without military experience, he would never advance to top policymaking levels. He still had forty-eight hours left to get Gateshead. When the Englishman returned, he would be waiting.

Kang Moruo sat in his living room with Samuel Tang, waiting for his eldest son, Pingnan. It was 6:30. They should already have been at the Liaison Office for dinner, but as usual Pingnan was late. It must have been something at the hospital, Kang decided. He wanted to involve his son in Party affairs, but he understood Pingnan's devotion to medicine. Politics had wreaked havoc with the young man's career. Pingnan had received his medical degree in 1966, but just as he had become licensed, the Cultural Revolution began and he was sent to Inner Mongolia to work as a "barefoot" doctor. Instead of using his surgical training, he had spent eight years growing rice and working as a medic. Since his rehabilitation, Pingnan had thrown himself into his work in order to compensate for the wasted years. He worked sixteen hours a day and took no interest in politics.

Kang had almost decided to leave when the front door opened and Pingnan rushed into the room. His face was drawn. Large bags sagged under his eyes. "You are thirty minutes late," Kang said.

Pingnan bowed respectfully to his father and uncle. "I'm sorry. We had an emergency."

"What was it this time, an appendicitis?"

"No, far worse. It was terrible." Pingnan cast his eyes to the floor.

"You must learn to not let your patients upset you so much."

"This will upset you as well. I am sorry to be the one to tell you."

"Tell me what?"

"Comrade Zhu De is dead."

There was a painful silence in the room as the men stared at each other. First Chou, now Zhu, two of the three men who had made the revolution, dead within six months of each other, and the third, Mao, virtually a corpse. The portents were ominous. Sam shivered as he thought about Golden Flower's visions. Perhaps she was prescient, not insane. Perhaps there would be a *Ge Ming*, a Withdrawal of the Mandate. The social omens were all apparent: the deaths of the leaders of the revolution, the planned coup of Jiang Qing, and the massing of the Russians along the border. Only a dramatic natural omen was missing.

Sam walked to the window and looked toward the heavens. The once clear sky had become covered by slate-gray thunderclouds. A faint rumbling began beneath his feet. He grabbed the sill and looked nervously around the room. The rumbling stopped. Perhaps it had been a small earthquake or only his imagination. Samuel ran his fingers through his hair and shook his head. He was a scientist and an engineer. He did not believe in portents or omens.

27: The Earthquake

TANGSHAN AND PEKING

"I'm sorry they had to close the bar," Vance Stewart said as he placed his arm around Linda Forbes.

"You polished off all their Maotai," Linda replied. The evening had been less unpleasant than expected. After a few drinks, Vance had become quite charming. But now she wanted to return to the guest house.

Vance lit a cigarette. "I have a bottle of Jack Daniel's in my room."

"It's a little late."

"Late? It's the middle of the day." Vance started to sing: "The night is young, the sky is clear, and if you want to go walking, dear, it's delightful, it's delovely, it's DeSoto."

"What are you singing?"

"It's a combination old ballad and DeSoto advertisement."

"What's a DeSoto?"

Vance laughed. "You can't be that young!"

"I'm twenty-eight."

"Too young to really be in love." Two Chinese stared at Vance, who responded by singing louder. "They say that love's a word—"

"Come on, Vance." Linda stopped suddenly. She heard a rumbling and felt the sidewalk start to vibrate. It was like standing in the basement of Bloomingdale's when the subway roared underneath. "Is it an earthquake?"

"Or merely a shock," Vance sang in response. "Is it the good turtle soup, or merely the mock?"

"Vance, please stop. I felt an earthquake!"

"Was it my singin'?"

"Be serious."

"OK." Vance tried to wipe the inebriated grin off his face. "It could have been a quake. China has more rumbles than California. But don't be alarmed—they're only large enough to excite the tourists."

"Is the hotel safe?"

"If you're worried, you can share my bed."

"I'm not *that* worried."

"Then how 'bout a drink to settle your nerves?" Vance held open the door to the guest house.

"I'm really tired."

"Too tired to learn how I intend to make you rich?"

Linda was intrigued. It was the second time Vance had referred to her future. "All right, but first I want to see if Sen was able to set up an appointment for me in Tianjin."

"I don't think you'll be seeing Sen," Vance grinned. "He's gone to visit the coal mines. It might take him a long time to get back."

Linda stared anxiously at Vance, feeling the four bottles of beer churning in her stomach. Vance could have known about the mines only if one of his people had tailed Sen. If Sen had not reached his destination, then Marc and the others would still be ignorant of the forgery. She had to find

331

out what had happened. "Do you mind if I check his room?" she asked, trying to keep her voice steady.

"Of course not." Vance smiled as Linda knocked on Sen's door and waited for an answer that did not come.

Vance led Linda to his room, which smelled of stale cigarette smoke. He opened the window and turned on the fan. Snapping a Frank Sinatra cassette into his tape deck, he poured two bourbons. He handed one to Linda and lightly kissed her. She did not turn away. There was too much she needed to learn. "Have my comments about your future piqued your curiosity?"

"They have."

Vance stretched out on the bed. "You're runnin' around tryin' to buy arts and crafts, right? And you're makin' twenty-five or thirty a year?"

"Something like that." Linda sat in a straight-backed desk chair.

"Suppose I could get antiques, real antiques—Ming vases, ancient bronzes, jade sculptures, things like that. Interested?"

"Of course," Linda said, thinking about Koo and Leung.

"We could be partners. You could go back to New York and sell to galleries and collectors. We could make millions."

Linda tried to remain calm. "How can you get these antiques?"

"Do you remember the man I was talkin' to earlier, Mr. Leung? He's got a deal with the government. But there are always a few extra pieces that can fall off the truck, if you get my drift?"

Linda walked to the window, uncertain how to respond to Vance's offer. If she accepted, he might lead her to the smuggled relics. Two days ago she would have jumped at the opportunity. But now she had to be cautious. "It sounds interesting," Linda said.

"We'd work real well together." Vance walked over and nuzzled Linda's neck. "You turn me on."

"There's something in my room I'd like you to see," Linda said, hoping Vance would get too drunk to pressure her. "I'll be right back."

He kissed her and grinned. "I knew you were a smart one."

Linda hurried down the hall. She scribbled a note and slipped it under Sen's door, then went to her own room and called the hotel operator. There were no messages. She felt lost. Things were happening too fast for her control. She removed a small stiletto from her suitcase and placed it in her purse.

Marc Slater puffed impatiently on his pipe as he paced across the conference room to the darkened windows. The black paper shades made him feel claustrophobic. He glanced furtively at Meili, wishing Liu Teyu would leave the room. Stepping to the door, he ran his hand over the knob. He wanted to go for a walk, but he had promised to stay inside for two hours while Deng escaped through the tunnels that connected the deserted mine shafts. Deng had taken this precaution after hearing a rumor that Jiang Qing was planning to assassinate him. "Is it time yet?" Marc asked.

Liu checked his watch. "Patience, my friend, just ten more minutes."

Marc opened a report on Chinese coal production. Gazing blankly at the first page, he relit his pipe. So much was happening, yet he could do nothing but act as a decoy. As a youth in China, he had learned to be patient; but as a businessman in the United States, he had developed a preference for making decisions and taking action. Although he knew he should follow Chinese rules, he could not force himself to adapt.

Placing the report in his bag, Marc checked his courier pouch. Inside were three letters from Deng dealing with the smuggling of relics, the forged will, and the need for unified action against Jiang and the Russians. Marc had been asked to carry these letters as a precaution.

Liu signaled that they were ready to leave. Marc followed the others to a waiting limousine. Two soldiers ushered Liu into the back seat. As Marc approached the limo, Meili touched his arm. "We're going in another car."

Marc watched as cawing flocks of crows rendezvoused in midair and flew wildly in all directions. The night seemed perilously alive. Meili climbed into the driver's seat of the Toyota and started the motor. Marc crawled into the back. "Where are our guards?" he asked.

"There are none," Meili responded. "I hope you're not disappointed."

"How did you arrange it?"

Meili's eyes shone in the rearview mirror. "Let's just say I have my ways."

Marc smiled and stared at Meili's graceful neck. She was a special woman who would be a prize in any culture. Every time he looked at her, his determination to possess her increased. Now they finally had the chance to be alone. He had no idea what would happen, but at least he would be able to deal with the reality of the woman. "I'm coming up front," he said.

"Wait until we're on the road by ourselves."

The limousine made a U-turn and headed away from Tangshan. Meili followed in the Toyota. "Where are we going?" Marc asked.

"Back to Peking."

"But I thought it was in the other direction."

Meili laughed. "You know we Chinese never take the direct route."

Wong Chuyun, stationed behind a mine shaft, watched the cars turn around. "They're heading toward Leung," he said into the walkie-talkie.

Colonel Li peered through his binoculars at the taillights of the cars. "Leung, when they get to you, I want them stopped."

"Will do."

"Wong, I'm bringing my men down. As soon as the little shrimps are out of sight, we're going in for the shark."

Colonel Li drove his jeep to within two hundred yards of the administration building. Silently, his men grabbed their weapons and moved toward their target. "What's going on inside?" he asked Wong.

"Inside, not much," Wong responded, "but out here, everything is very strange. The field animals are going crazy, running around and screeching. It's creepier than a back alley in Kowloon on a Saturday night."

Colonel Li ignored Wong's protestations. "What about the guards?"

"No problem. There are just two in front and one on the far side."

"Cover them," the colonel said. "But don't do anything until you hear my signal. He checked his gun and then looked back at the building. It seemed to be swaying. He turned off the motor of his jeep, but it continued to vibrate as if it were still running.

Linda checked the stiletto in her purse before entering Vance's room. She felt better having it for protection. He was sitting on the bed, still drinking bourbon. He stood up and handed her a refill. "Have you thought about our new partnership?"

She sipped her drink. The bourbon burned her throat. "It's tempting."

"But what?"

"Well, first, I don't know if it's legal. And, second, I don't know if I want to give up my job at Bloomingdale's."

Vance smiled and waved his arm in an arc. "Not to worry. Do you think I'd be involved in somethin' that wasn't completely aboveboard?"

"Of course not," Linda said, suspecting the truth.

"And as for your job, you could handle our project on the side—until, of course, it becomes too lucrative."

"Sounds interesting, but there's a lot I'd like to know."

Vance pulled her to the bed. "I'll tell you anythin' you want. I'm putty in your hands." He laughed. "That's hardly an original line, is it?"

"I've heard better."

"How about 'Blow in my ear and I'll follow you anywhere'?"

Linda shook her head. "That's not much of an improvement."

"I may not be very original, but I'm very sincere. Try thinkin' of me as a large, gentle lapdog." He ran his fingers through her hair.

Linda repressed her desire to pull away. "Where do you get these antiques?" she asked.

"I thought you were goin' to trust me."

"I am, but that doesn't stop me from being curious."

"Or beautiful." Vance kissed her lips. His breath reeked of alcohol.

"I think that's enough."

"Enough?" He slid his hand adroitly onto one of her

breasts. "I'm offerin' you millions and all you're willing to give up is one kiss. I think I deserve a little more." He put his other arm around her and plunged his tongue into her mouth. Linda wriggled under his grasp. She was wary of provoking him. "Not now, Vance!" She shoved her hand against his chin. His head snapped backward.

"Why'd you do that?" He moved toward her, looking like a hurt child. "Don't you know I want you?" She eluded his grasp and retreated toward the bathroom. He grinned as he closed in on her. "I like your spirit, and I know you want me. Why don't we stop the games. If we're goin' to be partners, I can't think of a better time to get to know each other."

Linda fended him off with her arms. "I think I'd better leave now. Maybe we can start on the right foot tomorrow."

Vance draped his six-foot-five frame over her like a cheap suit. He reached a free hand under her skirt. Linda shoved her knee into his groin. "You bitch!" Vance coughed and doubled over.

Realizing she could no longer control the situation, Linda fled to the door. Her purse opened. The stiletto fell to the floor. Vance picked it up and pushed the button. The blade thrust forward. He stepped toward Linda. "What's this?" he asked with a drunken grin as he touched the tip of the blade to her chin. Suddenly the room began to shake.

Sen Tailing and Hu Shengte arrived at the Tangshan Guest House and rushed to Sen's room. Deng had instructed them to return to Peking. They had little time to waste. Sen opened his door. The note from Linda was lying inside. He read it to Hu, then rushed to the phone and dialed Linda's room. There was no answer. "I'll bet she's with Stewart." He asked the operator for Stewart's room number. "It's two floors up," he said to Hu. They ran to the stairwell. As they reached the first landing, Sen felt a rumbling beneath his feet and saw the stairs start to sway.

The limousine carrying Liu Teyu traversed an S-shaped curve and ascended a hill. Leung gave the order to open fire. Rapid bursts from a machine gun blew out the tires and riddled the body of the car. A bullet plunged into the temple of the guard. The man grabbed his head, emitted a muffled sob, and slumped against the door. The driver struggled with the wheel. The car swerved and then careened into a ditch. Liu was flung from his seat, hitting his head on the door. Bullets extinguished the lights. The driver jammed the car into reverse. It lurched back onto the road. The Toyota rounded the curve. One hundred feet ahead was the darkened mass of the crippled limousine. Meili slammed on the brakes. The Toyota skidded, went into a tailspin, and slammed into the limousine.

Marc braced his hands on the dashboard to cushion the shock. Meili's torso was thrust forward. Her head slumped over the steering wheel. Marc pulled her to him. Her eyes were glassy and her mouth slack, but she was still conscious. He looked up. Smoke was rising from the hood of the limousine. He dragged Meili into a ditch and crawled back to the limousine. Opening the back door, he saw Liu lying unconscious on the floor. Blood flowed from a deep gash in his head, but the old general was still breathing. One guard was dead, the other unconscious. Marc took a gun from the dead man, then placed his left arm under the general's shoulders and lugged him to the ditch.

A partially closed mine shaft was less than twenty feet away. Marc ripped off two boards and pulled Liu and Meili inside. The earth started to tremble. Marc's first thought was that the shaft was about to cave in. He looked outside. The ground began to sway and the hills heaved like the stomach of a potbellied man suffering from indigestion. Clumps of earth dropped from the roof of the shaft. The rumbling became more severe. The road seemed to lift and then drop. A wooden beam creaked. Marc dragged Meili and Liu to the front of the shaft. Suddenly the limousine exploded. Marc shielded his eyes as fire engulfed the car. There was a clattering above him, like a train speeding through a tunnel. The supporting timbers splintered and gave way. Marc was buried in a casket of dirt and rocks.

Reaching the end of his two-mile trek through the tunnels of Kailuan #6, Deng Xiaoping climbed through a trapdoor and into a car waiting in a field. Gunfire erupted in the distance. Deng felt a pang as he stared back at the administration building. Though he was too far away to see anything, he knew that he was the planned target of the attack. "Damn Jiang!" he cursed, fighting the urge to return to help his men. Though he wanted to fight, his first obligation was to the People's Republic and to those depending on his leadership. He could not allow himself the luxury of risking his life in such a minor skirmish. "Let's get out of here," he ordered, but his eyes remained riveted in the direction of the shooting.

The car vibrated as it ascended a hill. The road undulated like a wave on the ocean. The earth belched. Trees toppled. The driver slammed on the brakes. Deng and the others ran for safety. The road shook like the tail section of a small plane in a typhoon. There was a deafening explosion. Deng fell to the ground. The earth rose up and dropped like a roller coaster. Then it opened its yawning mouth and digested the land above it.

Somewhere underground, two of the massive slabs that

form the surface of the earth grated against each other. Expanding and then contracting, the crustal rocks tried unsuccessfully to find a fit. The uneasy balance that had existed for generations along the boundaries finally gave way. Rocks bumped and pulled apart, plunging one edge below the other. The surface of the earth shook violently, responding to the battle being waged in its innards. Radioactive gases with pressures thousands of times greater than all of the bombs ever produced surged from the core and exploded between the plates of the earth. A gaping hole ripped open along the fault line as the center of the world split apart. The earth, it appeared, was withdrawing its Mandate.

Linda grabbed the bureau to support herself in the violently shaking room. Vance dropped the stiletto and tugged at her arm. "Let's get out of here." His voice was panic-stricken. "The building is goin' to collapse!"

Linda followed him into the hallway. It tilted like the room in the fun house she had visited as a child. Vance dropped her hand and steadied himself on the wall. He was having difficulty maintaining his balance. "I should have listened to my mother." He forced a frightened smile. "She always told me never to drink before an earthquake."

"Come with me," Linda said, pushing herself toward the stairwell. The vibrations became more severe. The building lurched. Linda was thrown to the floor. There was a thunderous boom, then a terrifying cracking sound as massive wooden beams snapped in two. A gust of wind blew against Linda's back. She turned around. The quake had bisected the hotel, leaving a four-foot chasm between the two sides. Vance had disappeared.

Linda stood paralyzed as the other half of the hotel started to crumble. Bricks and plaster toppling from the roof created an avalanche of debris. The top three floors, wrenched from their foundation, vomited beds, desks, and petrified guests into the chasm. Clouds of dust gushed from below. There was a deafening creak. The ceiling sagged.

Propelled by instinct, Linda crawled to the stairwell. A window, thrust from its casing, hurtled toward her. She grabbed for the banister, tripped, and rolled down a half-flight of stairs. Panicking guests shoved from behind. A woman lay wailing on the floor, covering her child with her body. Linda wanted to help, but the stampeding crowds flung her down to the next landing.

At the third floor, the guests became a ruthless mob as they struggled toward the narrow exit. The tremors of the quake had abated, but the deadly rumble of the crumbling hotel terrified everyone. Two men pushed Linda out of the way as they lunged past. People fought with each other, but no one seemed to be getting anywhere. Linda realized she would never escape by the stairs. She wedged herself into the third-floor corridor and ran to a room facing the street. The windows were broken. Glass was everywhere. It was too far to jump.

She ripped the covers off the bed and tied two sheets together. Then she fastened one end to the frame where the window had been. Praying they would hold, she climbed onto the ledge. The air was filled with dust and flames. The screams of a million Chinese were drowned out by the sounds of crashing buildings. She guided herself hand over hand until she reached the bottom of the second sheet. The remains of the hotel were beginning to spill into the chasm. The muscles in her shoulders and along her sides throbbed as she dangled from the end of the sheet. Her arms felt as if they were being ripped out of their sockets.

People below screamed at her. She looked down. The

ground was still ten feet away. She could feel the knot starting to slip. It was now or never. She closed her eyes and took a deep breath. Then she let go. She moved in slow motion as she dropped to the ground. It was like doing a backward swan dive into a swimming pool. Hands, arms, shoulders reached up for her, trying to break her fall. She would not stop. Someone grabbed her feet, flipping her head toward the pavement. She closed her eyes and pressed her chin to her chest. The piercing jolt of impact racked her body. Her muscles twitched once and then became still.

One hundred miles west of the epicenter in Peking, the two flatbed trucks carrying Aziz Rahman and his operatives inched along Dongbei Road. A policeman stopped traffic for two farmers and a herd of pigs. Rahman impatiently drummed his fingers as he watched the slow-moving animals. Unexpectedly, the pigs began to squeal and charge wildly in all directions. The two farmers vainly chased their panicking animals. There was a momentary opening in the road. "Drive on," Rahman ordered. Whatever had frightened the pigs was an ill portent for his mission.

The earth started to rumble. Buses stalled. Some people stood uneasily beside their bicycles, but others ran in panic into the street. Rahman ordered the driver to turn down one of Peking's back roads, known as *hutongs*. The driver leaned on his horn as the trucks squeezed next to a crumbling produce stand. The vibrations became more intense. A panicking chicken darted back and forth across the road. As the truck approached, the chicken turned like a kamikaze and ran headlong into the front grill. Slabs of plaster and rock tumbled from the roofs. People flooding from the buildings stared apprehensively at their homes and then ran for what they hoped would be safety. "Keep going," Rahman urged. Whatever else happened, he could not leave two trucks filled with weapons in the center of Peking.

The *hutong* seemed to lurch. There was a crashing sound. The building on the corner collapsed as if demolition charges had been planted inside. The building next to it started to fall, touching off a chain reaction that spread up the block. Stepping out onto the shaking road, Rahman looked at his munitions and ordered his men out of both trucks. He climbed into the driver's seat of the rear vehicle. As his men scattered, he gazed at the buildings and prayed that none would tumble on him.

Frans Van Wyck lay on his bed in the Peking Hotel, reading *Crime and Punishment* for the fourth time. He heard a dim rumbling and felt the building start to vibrate, but he was not alarmed. He had experienced much the same feeling in his flat in Moscow when the subway passed underneath. The vibrations became more pronounced. Automobile horns blared from the street. Van Wyck got out of bed and walked toward the balcony. The room started to sway. He grasped a chair to steady himself. There was a jolt. The desk slid away from the wall, knocking him to the ground and pinning him in the corner. His ankle twisted beneath him and cracked. He grimaced in pain, but then started to laugh. After all his dangerous missions, the irony of being injured by a piece of furniture was absurd.

As the earth began to shake, Leung Lilai crawled into a ditch and pressed his body to the ground. The undulations made him feel as if he were on a storm-tossed sea. Of all the dangers he might face in this land of his enemy, he had never thought of the possibility of being trapped in an earthquake.

Three of the men from Hong Kong were sprawled in the ditch in front of him. Suddenly the earth was rent apart. A crack ripped open like the seam on a pair of pants. One man dropped into the bottomless abyss. The other two screamed in panic as they tried to crawl away from the fissure. Leung lay stoically motionless. He was just as frightened, but he would not allow the earth the satisfaction of seeing his fear. Even in death, dignity and discipline had to be maintained. The earth belched again. The crack opened wider and raced toward him. His men disappeared. There was no time to move.

Wong Chuyun crouched behind a small mound and watched the spasming earth. A cloud of poisonous smoke gushed from a mine shaft. Wong steadied his hand and lit a cigarette. Tobacco had been so much a part of his life, it seemed appropriate to have one last smoke. There was nothing he could do to improve his chances of survival. The convulsions uprooted trees and tossed pieces of machinery into the air. The walls of the administration building were split apart. The roof shifted and then collapsed, slab by slab. There was an explosion. Wong did not know if it had come from the building or the earth. A fire erupted. The building, built eighty years before in accordance with the highest British standards, toppled in a heap. A dense cloud of coal dust filled the air. Wong coughed the smoke from his lungs. Breathing was difficult. A wall of dirt cascaded down from the mound. There was no place to escape. He shielded his hand and let the soil cover him.

Colonel Li stumbled as he ran up a hill toward an open field where he hoped to find safety. He tried to stand, but the earth was shaking too turbulently. He crawled toward a ridge. A violent tremor sent rocks and clumps of dirt rolling in his direction. He grabbed his knees and pulled himself into a ball. Then he closed his eyes and prayed to a god in whom he did not believe.

Although the earthquake had lasted only a few minutes, it seemed as if hours had passed. Colonel Li crawled out of the pile of dirt and inspected his injuries. Except for the bruises on his back and a bump on his head, he was fine. He looked at the administration building but could see nothing through the haze of coal dust. He had to find out what had happened to the others.

Climbing around the mounds of dirt, he saw a fire raging in front of him. The administration building was gone; there was nothing but a pile of burning debris. A muffled voice came from inside one of the mounds. Li started to dig. It did not matter who was trapped inside. The disaster of the earthquake had far transcended all thoughts of politics. He shoveled feverishly with his hands as the voice became weaker. He had to reach the man while there was still air. He called out. There was no response. He worked faster, not knowing where the man was buried. Suddenly he saw a hand. Burrowing his body into the hole, he felt the shape of a head. He cleared away the dirt. It was Wong. His face had turned blue. The colonel pressed his mouth to Wong's. Wong coughed, took a tentative breath, and then opened his eyes.

Sen and Hu passed the second-floor landing in the guest house and were carried along with the panicking horde. Hu stumbled, but the pressure of the encircling bodies kept him from falling. Sen reached for him but was swept away by the irresistible thrust of the crowd. Two men collided at the exit,

345

blocking the door as they fought to reach safety. Others pressed against them. Movement became impossible. A woman toppled to the ground, creating a logjam of prone bodies. Death screams propelled the crowd forward as the ceiling started to drop. Fire leaped up the stairs. Sen pleaded for calm, but he could not even hear his own voice. Frightened men pushed from behind as more bodies fell. The tidal wave of terror left him no choice. He crawled over the carpet of bodies and ran out into the street.

The scene in Fenghuang Road was as horrible as any he could imagine. Thousands of people stood helplessly screaming as one after another of the buildings collapsed. Overturned cooking pots and ruptured gas lines ignited the rubble, transforming the evening into a glowing oven as bright as midday. Sen searched for Hu. People were still pouring out of the guest house, but many more were inside. Flames climbed to the roof. An aftershock jolted the foundation. The building swayed once and then disappeared into the chasm. Sen turned away from the heat of the flames with great sadness. He saw Linda lying motionless on the pavement. He lifted her in his arms and carried her into the park.

A sharp throbbing pain from his legs shot through Marc's body. He opened his eyes. It was pitch black. He was trapped underground, but at least he was alive. He tried to move his left hand. It would not budge. A sharp object pressed into his bicep. His other arm was pinned under his body. His legs were trapped in casts of earth. He struggled onto his side. His skin felt as if it were being pricked by thousands of small pins. He shook the muck from his face and moistened his lips. A clump of dirt dropped into his mouth. He drew mucus from his throat and spit. The dirt turned to mud on the inside of his gums.

There was a creaking sound above him. He shivered. It would not be long before the rest of the shaft collapsed. He had to get out. But what of the others? They had to be nearby. "Meili! Liu!" He mashed his fingers into the dirt as he listened to the silence. "Meili! Liu!" he called again. "Please, God, let them be alive!"

Twisting onto his back to get his bearings, he shook out his body, one bone at a time. His joints ached. Huge bruises covered his arms and legs. Blood oozed from a cut on the bridge of his nose. A bump on his head the size of a golf ball throbbed louder than his heart. Shooting pains surged through him, but nothing was broken.

"Meili! Liu! Please answer!" he called in frustration as he explored the perimeter of the hole. From his waist down, he was locked in place, but his torso had room to move. He squirmed forward. It was the only direction in which he could go. He hoped it was toward the opening. Perhaps Meili and Liu were in front of him. If they were behind him, they were certain to be dead.

Wriggling like an earthworm, he emerged into a small open space. He searched for a route of escape. The stone walls were intact—the shaft had apparently withstood the quake. The air was stale, but it was not poisoned. He wet a finger and felt a soft breath against his knuckle. He was safe, at least for the moment.

"Meili, Liu, can you hear me?" he pleaded in frustration. The silence was deafening. He crawled ahead over stones and piles of dirt. A rock scraped his leg. He groaned as warm blood trickled toward his feet. A wall of dirt blocked his path. He searched for the top. There was less than two feet of leeway. Using his hands as a guide, he slithered through on his belly and dropped into an open cavity on the other side. "Meili! Liu!" he yelled. There was a muffled murmur. "Is someone there?" he called.

"Marc!" A faint voice filtered through a mound of dirt.

"Meili, are you all right?" Marc screamed, crawling as fast as he could toward the sound of her voice.

"I can't move," Meili moaned.

Marc placed his shoulder against two large boulders and pushed them away. "I'll be there in a minute," he screamed.

"I can't breathe." Meili's voice became fainter.

"Just hold on. You'll be fine," Marc urged as he burrowed through the dirt. His hands touched Meili's ankle. "I'll get you out," he said, feverishly shoveling dirt from her legs.

A huge beam blocked his path. Two feet thick, it had been one of the supports for the shaft. He could feel Meili's blouse underneath it. He pulled out his hand. It was wet. He touched it to his lips. It tasted of blood and dirt. His body tensed in an awful, silent sob. "I'm going to move this beam," he said, trying to keep his emotions from showing. In a fury he searched for the ends of the column. One was wedged into the ceiling. The other, more than twenty feet away, was buried under a rock slide. "I'll dig you out," Marc called, even though he knew that thirty men could not have moved the beam.

"Please, come here," Meili moaned.

Marc wept as he pictured Meili's crushed torso. He crawled toward her head. Reaching out, he touched her soft, straight hair. He pulled his body next to hers and delicately caressed her cheek. "I love you," he said, touching his hands to her lips.

"Please kiss me," she whispered in a barely audible voice.

He bent over in the darkness and tenderly placed his lips on hers. She was sobbing. He tried to fight back the tears, but could not. "I wish I could see you."

"I can see you," she murmured. Her breathing was uneven. "I merely have to close my eyes and you are there, my blue-eyed spirit who runs like the wind." Marc buried his head and kissed her long graceful neck. "I love you so much," she said. Her body spasmed.

He touched her neck. There was no pulse. He threw himself to the ground and embraced her. Lying silently next to her, he caressed her hair. Suddenly a grating sound echoed through the cave. Clumps of dirt crashed from the ceiling, filling the shaft with dust. Marc coughed. It was becoming difficult to breathe. He had to escape. Tenderly he kissed Meili. "I love you," he whispered. Then he raced forward on his hands and knees, hoping to find safety.

28: The Rubble

PEKING AND TANGSHAN

The fires from the surrounding buildings filtered through clouds of dust to illuminate Fenghuangshan Park with an eerie haze. Linda Forbes opened her eyes and saw Sen Tailing standing beside her. "What happened?" she asked, rubbing the throbbing bruise on her shoulder.

"I found you lying unconscious in the street and carried you into the park," Sen said, sitting down next to her. "Are you all right?"

Linda shook out her legs. Her head ached. Her clothes were ripped and her arm badly scraped. Otherwise she was fine. She gazed around the park. Thousands of people had converged on the open ground. Some were dead, others critically injured. She reached out and touched Sen's hand. Though foreigners and Chinese were not supposed to have physical contact, Sen did not pull away. This was a night on which all rules could be suspended. "I'm a little shaken," Linda said, "but very glad to be alive."

"You gave me quite a scare," Sen said.

"Are you sure it was me and not the earthquake?" Linda forced. "My God! It was awful." She closed her eyes and started to weep.

"I was there too." Sen put his arm around her. "But now we're safe."

"I was in Vance Stewart's room when the quake hit," Linda said, wiping her eyes. "We ran into the corridor. The building started to sway like a willow tree in a hurricane. There was a deafening crack. The hotel split in half. I looked back, but Vance had disappeared into the chasm. What a horrible way to die."

"It's too late to do anything about it now," Sen said, stroking Linda's blond hair.

"I know." Linda cleaned off her cuts. "I'm just grateful that I got myself out of there. For a while I thought I was going to die in the stairwell. There were so many people fighting to get out. No one was moving. I ran into a room on the third floor, tied bedsheets together, and let myself down. I had to jump the last ten feet. I guess I hit my head."

"You were very smart," Sen said. "Few made it out of the stairwell. Hu Shengte and I were both trapped in there."

"Where is Hu?"

Sen shook his head. "He was behind me. We had almost reached the door when the crowd went mad. He never came out. Then the building collapsed."

Linda turned to Sen. "Is there any chance—"

"None."

A mother and father carried their two children into the park and laid them on the ground, not far from Linda. Their bodies were caked with blood. Both were dead. Linda covered her face. "It's such a horrendous nightmare." Suddenly she opened her eyes and grabbed Sen's arm. "What happened at the mine?"

"Your news shocked everyone," Sen replied. "Deng said it

351

was the smoking gun needed to stop Jiang."

"But what happened to them in the earthquake?"

Sen shrugged. "I don't know."

"They have to be all right," Linda said. She had come too far not to meet her grandfather or see Marc again.

"I'm sure they are." Sen tried to sound convincing.

"But if they're not"—Linda looked at Sen—"we may be the only ones who know about the will."

"It's possible."

"Can we get back to Peking?"

Sen pointed to the fires raging outside the park. "Not easily. The city has been decimated. My car has been crushed. There are no buses or trains. It'd be miles before we could even find a road that's passable."

"We'll just have to walk."

"It's over a hundred miles."

"Then we'd better get started," Linda said as Sen helped her to her feet. She stepped gingerly on the now quiet earth. Her legs trembled. She felt dizzy. Sen extended his hand for balance.

They walked toward the destruction of what had once been Tangshan. Every building on Fenghuang Road had collapsed. The main street was now a burning pile of rubble. Bodies, some dead and some badly injured, were scattered everywhere. People ran through the streets searching for their relatives. Others dug feverishly toward muffled voices beneath the debris. It reminded Linda of pictures of Hiroshima after the atomic bomb. A little girl clutching a doll gazed into a pile of smoldering ashes and screamed for her mother. Linda buried her head in her hands and sobbed.

"Why don't we go back to the park and sleep?" Sen said. "It's the middle of the night."

"I'll be all right," Linda replied. "If we stop now, we'll

never get out of Tangshan."

Linda and Sen wedged their way through the crowd. What had once been a broad boulevard was now clogged with chunks of buildings, toppled buses, and people aimlessly searching for their families. A breeze fanned the fires, making the city feel like an inferno. There was an explosion. Blue flames, like those from the bottom of a rocket, thrust into the sky. A row of old houses sagged and then collapsed in a thunderous cloud of dust. Linda coughed and shielded her mouth with her blouse.

They walked in silence for another hour through the neighborhoods in which workers lived. Here the destruction was even worse than in the center of the city. The ancient buildings had toppled so quickly that few had escaped. A young boy with his head cracked open stuck out of a pile of debris. Two rats gnawed at his neck. The stench of death was overpowering. Linda's legs wobbled. She grabbed Sen's hand, bent over, and retched violently.

It began to rain. Linda looked at the sky and let the drops wash the stench of vomit from her mouth. She was exhausted. Her entire body ached. The rain fell harder, turning the rubble into tombs of mud. They passed a park filled with crowds of survivors. The people were clustered in groups, comforting each other. Although virtually everyone had lost relatives, there were few tears and no panic. Instead there was the restraint and stoicism that had marked Chinese behavior for centuries. Sen took Linda's hand and led her to an open space on a bank between two rice paddies. "I want to keep going," Linda insisted.

"Let's just take a short rest," Sen replied.

"But I'm—" The world around Linda began to spin. She sat down and placed her arms to each side for support. The specter of the crumbling guest house haunted her. She dropped her head to her chest, and, without realizing it, collapsed on the ground.

Colonel Li approached the burning pile of rubble that once had been the administration building. "Is anyone alive in there?" he yelled. There was no response. Stepping over a fallen tree, he walked to the far side and yelled again. No matter what the political disputes, the men trapped inside were Chinese. He could not leave them to die. There was a rumbling beneath the rubble. The debris shifted. "Can't anyone hear me?" he pleaded as the flames leaped toward him.

"They're all dead," Wong Chuyun said, limping toward the colonel. Though he was coated with dirt, Wong's injuries seemed minor. "That thing collapsed like the walls were made of sand. No one could have survived."

"Was Deng inside?"

"I never saw him come out."

Li ran his hands across his eyes. He was pleased that he had not been forced to kill Deng. "Perhaps it's for the best," he replied.

"The job is done," Wong said. "That's all that matters."

There was a loud explosion up the road. Continuous gunfire erupted, as if two squads were engaged in direct combat. The nighttime sky was lit by hundreds of tracer bullets, looking like backward shooting stars as they ascended to the heavens. The colonel dropped behind a fallen tree. "Do you think it's our men?" he asked Wong, who had crouched next to him.

A man came running toward them. It was Jack Woo, one of those from Hong Kong. Colonel Li stood up and called to him. "Woo, what's going on?"

"It's one of our personnel carriers exploding," Woo

354

replied. "But two of the others are all right."

Li breathed a sigh of relief. He was pleased that he would not have to fight Deng's troops. Even with most of his weapons intact, the earthquake had destroyed his zest for combat. "Have you seen any of our men?" he asked.

"I saw the Chuk brothers by the bottom of where that hill used to be." Woo pointed to a landslide. "And Fish Eye Ching was crushed in the collapse of the administration building. I think the two Tams are still alive, but the rest seem to have disappeared. The earth looks as if it had been mixed up by an eggbeater."

"What about Leung and his men?" Wong asked.

"They were almost a mile up the road," Colonel Li replied. "I heard them shooting at Liu and the American before the quake, but I don't know if they survived."

"Things can't be as bad up there," Wong said. "I'll find them."

"I'll follow you after I finish up here." Li handed Wong a flashlight. "We must make sure that Liu and Slater are dead."

"Why?" Wong asked. He had always respected both men. Slater was more than an acquaintance, and Liu was a Cantonese like himself. "If Deng is dead, why do we need to kill anyone else?"

"Liu is a leading conservative, and Jiang ordered us to kill Slater. I don't want to be the one to tell her that we let them get away."

Marc tripped over a rock and stumbled forward as the dirt from the collapsing ceiling filled the cavity behind him. He wiped the tears and dust from his face and then scrambled ahead on all fours. Although he could not see the route of escape, he could taste the wisps of fresh air seeping into the shaft. His path was blocked by a wall. Like a caged animal he tore at the dirt, searching for the entrance. He reached his hand into a crevice. The dirt felt damp. He burrowed through the wet earth. Jagged rocks shredded his clothes. In the distance he could dimly hear the sound of falling rain. He pushed a stone. It rolled forward. A blast of wind slapped his face. He pulled his body through the hole.

The night was pitch black, but he could feel the rain falling on his back. Rolling over, he grabbed his arms and started to shiver. He had made it! He was out of the shaft. He was alive! He turned around and stared back into the hole. Meili was still in there, trapped under the beam. He felt angry and helpless. "God damn! It's not fair," he said, slamming his fist into the ground. There was a rumbling inside the shaft. Dust gushed out of the passageway as dirt and rocks collapsed. "Meili! I'm sorry!" he moaned as he pounded his head into the wet earth.

"Is someone there?" a voice called out.

"Liu?" Marc crawled toward the sound. "Are you all right?"

"I think my leg is broken."

In the darkness Marc examined Liu. The old general's leg was swollen and bleeding just above the shinbone. Marc ripped off a piece of his shirt, let the rain dampen it, and wiped off the general's blood. Then he ripped another piece and bound it tightly around Liu's leg.

Liu lay back on the ground while Marc worked. "Have you seen Meili?"

"She's dead." Marc choked on his words.

"In the mine?"

"Crushed by a beam."

"I'm sorry. She was a very special woman."

"Too special to die." Marc muffled a sob. "I couldn't get

her out. I tried to move the beam, but it was too large. I sat there, unable to do anything while she died."

"Don't blame yourself," Liu advised.

"How about blaming that bitch Jiang Qing?" Marc paced angrily in a circle. "If she hadn't sent those people to kill us, we never would have ended up trapped in that blasted shaft."

"Sit down, my friend." Liu propped himself up on his elbows. "This is not the time for mourning, nor is it the time to begin a personal vendetta against Jiang Qing. If we are to survive, you must heed the advice I gave you when we met in the South and learn to think like a Chinese."

Marc walked away and stood by himself. The rain had stopped and a three-quarter moon had emerged from behind the clouds. Huge piles of dirt and rocks lay strewn around the countryside. Landslides had torn away many of the hills. Hardly a tree remained standing. The land looked like it had been eaten by an army of giant steam shovels.

Leaning against a large boulder, Marc thought about Meili. Liu was right. He could not continue to mourn. He had to accept her death. Their relationship had been doomed from the start. Perhaps this was the only way it could have ended. But she had aroused passions that he had not felt since before Carolyn died. At least he knew that he was still capable of loving and giving. For now he would try to think like a Chinese. But he would not let Meili's death go unavenged; he would settle accounts with Jiang Qing. He turned back toward Liu. In the distance he saw a figure carrying a flashlight. "Someone's coming," he whispered.

The man made his way along what had been the road. He shone his flashlight into the ditch. The limousine and the Toyota lay on their sides, welded together in a charred clump. Marc could see that the man was carrying a gun. The man walked toward the fissure. He knelt down and peered into the opening to see if it had digested his friends. Then he inspected the damage around the mine shaft. "It's Wong Chuyun, the managing director of CAT," Marc said. "What the hell is he doing here?"

"Perhaps he was one of the people who tried to kill us."

"That's ridiculous. He's a tobacco merchant."

"Who happens to be allied with Jiang Qing."

"That may be, but he's a friend."

"Then why is he carrying a gun?"

"I'm a foreigner. He won't hurt me. It's you they're after. I'll lead him away and then come back."

"Don't come back. My men will find me in the morning."

"If they're still alive." Marc crawled behind the shaft. He did not want to believe that Wong and Stewart were involved in a plot to kill him. "Hello, is someone there?" he called as he walked out on the other side.

Wong shone the light into his eyes. "Don't move, Marc."

Marc squinted into the beam, feigning ignorance. "Who's there?"

"It's Wong Chuyun."

"Wong?" Slater walked forward holding out his hand. "I don't know what you're doing here, but I'm really glad to see you. Is Vance—" Marc stopped. He saw the gun pointing at him. "What's that for?"

"I'm sorry, Marc, but there are orders to kill you."

Marc laughed. "OK, I'll lower my price on the Turkish cavendish by two cents a pound."

"I'm not joking." Wong shook his gun. "Stop right there."

"What the hell are you talking about?"

"You are to be killed as a cover for the assassination of Deng."

Marc realized that Wong did not know of Deng's escape. "But Deng was killed in the quake. What better cover do you need?"

Wong shone the light away from Marc's eyes. "I made that point to the colonel, but he reminded me of our orders."

Marc leaned against the collapsed mine shaft. His only chance was to appeal to Wong's greed and political astuteness. "Then tell him you didn't see me. I'll make it worth your while."

"What can you do for me?"

"You're betting your company that Jiang Qing is going to win."

"CAT has an excellent record for selecting the victorious side."

"That may be, but what if you're wrong?"

"We'll find another way. Don't you know the CAT has nine lives?"

"Why waste one?"

"What do you mean?"

"If I could convince the other side to give you tobacco contracts, then you'd have a hedge. No matter who won, you'd be ahead."

"It's more than just tobacco."

Marc could feel Wong nibble at his bait. "Then I'll make sure you get the opium as well."

Wong shone the light into Marc's face. "Why do you think I'd be interested in opium?"

Marc shielded his eyes. "Let's not play games." A flashlight shone in their direction from the ridge of a hill. Wong and Slater stared as the light approached. "You'd better make up your mind before he gets here. What's more important to you, the political machinations inside China or your own business?"

"I could ask you the same question."

"Do you want to debate philosophy or guarantee the future of your company?"

Wong distractedly surveyed the surroundings with the beam of his flashlight. The other figure was getting closer. "Get out of here. If the colonel sees you, I'll have no choice but to kill you."

Turning quickly, Marc passed the other side of the mine shaft where Liu was still lying, and hurried up the road.

29: The Politburo

THE FORBIDDEN CITY

Kang Moruo sat in the back seat as the limousine inched through the stunned crowds in Tien'anmen Square. He was still shaken by the impact of the earthquake. The United States Liaison Office in which he had been eating had withstood the tremor, but some of the guests had been hurt. Beatrice Tang had been hit by falling debris and had sustained a broken leg. Fortunately, his son had been there to apply a splint and take her to the hospital.

Remembering his wife's vision that the Mandate of Heaven would be withdrawn, Kang stared blankly at the main entrance to the Forbidden City. The portents were irrefutable: the deaths of Chou En-lai and Zhu De, the treason of Jiang Qing, the planned invasion of the Russians, and now the earthquake. Yet despite the omens, Kang did not want to believe that the end of the People's Republic was at hand.

The limousine stopped in front of Zhong Nanhai (Central South Sea) Park. This westernmost entrance to the

Forbidden City now served as the official residence of the leaders of China. A guard found Kang's name on the list of those invited to the special meeting of the Politburo and signaled for the imposing red gate to be opened. Kang gazed at the ornately painted pavilions that had once housed the imperial families. The limousine passed the palace that had been the home of Chairman Mao since the liberation. It had always seemed strange to Kang that the man who had led the people's revolution should have chosen to live in a palace built by an emperor.

The car approached Huairen Hall, a large pavilion that served as the headquarters of the Politburo. Kang watched the bustle of activity in front of the building and wondered how the new government would fare during its first emergency. He wished that his allies were not off meeting with Deng. It never occurred to him that they could have been trapped in the earthquake that had rocked Peking.

Entering the sparse meeting room that served the Central Committee during emergencies, Kang saw that most of the others had already arrived. Unaware of the extent of the devastation, they stood in small groups exchanging stories of how they had survived the quake, which they assumed had been centered near Peking. Kang poured a glass of Maotai and joined the circle of moderates.

Hua Guofeng stepped to the front of the room. He looked tired and a bit nervous. Kang took a chair at the far end of the table and watched the others arrange themselves by cliques. Soon everyone was seated except Jiang Qing and her allies. All eyes shifted between Hua and Jiang, wondering how long the affront would continue. Hua picked up three large books and dropped them to the floor. Their thud silenced the room. Jiang looked up. "Ah, Comrade Jiang." Hua feigned politeness. "We would be honored if you would join us."

"Of course, Comrade Hua, please excuse me." Jiang walked to the head of the table and waited impatiently until someone brought her a chair.

Hua stared chastisingly at Jiang, but he did not object to her usurpation of such a strategic seat. He had far more important problems to consider. He waited until the others had stopped talking, then he began in his twangy country accent. "I have been informed that tonight's earthquake registered 8.2 on the Richter Scale and was as strong as the Nanshan quake in 1927 that killed over two hundred thousand people." The Politburo members stared at each other with great concern. No one had conceived that the quake had been so severe. "The epicenter was in the city of Tangshan."

Kang glanced anxiously around the room. If the epicenter was more than a hundred miles away, one of the most populous regions of China could be completely devastated. Kang placed his head in his hands and rubbed his eyes. Liu, Hu, and Deng were all in Tangshan. He had no way of knowing if they had survived, but he was certain that their deaths would end any hope the moderates might still harbor of gaining power.

"Our information is very sketchy." Hua's voice penetrated Kang's thoughts. "There is no communication with Tangshan or even with Tianjin. We will have to wait until morning before making a more complete assessment, but the preliminary indications are that this could be the worst natural disaster in history." Hua looked uncertainly around the room. "Does anyone have any suggestions as to how we should proceed?"

"You are supposed to be the premier," Jiang Qing scoffed. At recent meetings of the Politburo she had used every opportunity to provoke Hua. "Don't you think we are entitled to the benefit of your wise leadership?"

"I believe in asking for everyone's opinion," Hua replied.

"Why? Because you have none of your own?"

Ye Jianying, the pudgy, balding defense minister, broke in before the argument could continue. "If we are to restore order, we must work together. I would like to immediately mobilize the People's Liberation Army and move all available troops to the north."

"What about the Red Guards?" Wang Hongwen, the vice-chairman of the Politburo and one of Jiang's Gang of Four, asked.

"The Red Guards are too undisciplined."

"You are prejudiced because you run the Ministry of Defense and are too old to understand the people," replied Wang, who was thirty years younger than most of the others in the Politburo and forty years younger than Ye. "If you ever left your capitalist offices and visited the country, you'd know the Red Guards enjoy support and respect while the army is thought of as incompetent and bourgeois."

"I will ignore the insult."

"As you ignore the demands of the people."

"As the minister of defense, I have the authority to deal with all emergencies, and I intend to start by using the army."

"That is a decision you will regret."

"I think not." Ye turned toward Hua. "In addition to restoring order, we must deliver medical care. I suggest we bring available medical personnel to Peking. I'll commandeer nonessential vehicles to carry them to Tangshan. We must also evacuate people from buildings still in danger of toppling, not only in Tangshan but throughout the quake area. Even large hotels like the Peking and the Minzu should be emptied. The army can set up cities of tents."

"Do you really intend to make our foreign friends live in tents?" the minister of trade asked.

"It's better than having a hotel fall on top of them."

"They will resist moving."

Ye smiled. "Not if we put them in the Forbidden City. With the backdrop of the palaces and the service of the hotel personnel, our foreign friends will be very content pretending that they're imperial princes."

"Why should we even waste spit talking about foreigners?" Yao Wenyuan, the theoretician of the Gang of Four, asked. "They are an affront to our country."

"They are our guests," Vice-chairman Li Xiannian said. "It is the way of our people to treat all guests with honor and respect."

"Even if they act as a seditious influence?"

"Can we table our political differences and discuss the earthquake relief?" Hua asked. "What should we do about food?"

"There will be serious risk of disease and starvation if we don't act immediately," Ye asserted. "We must obtain supplies of rice and wheat from around the country. I think the most feasible plan is to bring the food by boat to Tianjin and then by truck to Tangshan. I'll assign construction crews from the army to repair the port and open the roads."

"Our harvest has been below production," the minister of agriculture said. "We have little surplus."

"Then everyone will have to eat less."

"Excuse me." Kang spoke tentatively, aware that there were few conservatives to support him. "If the destruction is as serious as it seems, shouldn't we get help from other countries?"

Leaning across the table, Jiang Qing extended a clenched fist and quoted a Chinese proverb: "The ugly affairs of a family should not be talked about in public."

"Comrade Jiang, this is not a petty personal dispute." Kang spoke very deliberately. "Thousands of lives are at stake. I am certain our allies would be pleased to assist us."

"And pleased to expose our weaknesses? I will not permit the capitalists and the imperialists to humiliate us."

"What is the value of keeping our outside face strong if our insides are crumbling?" Kang responded with his own proverb.

"Asking for help is not the Chinese way. Chairman Mao has lived by the code of *ziligengsheng*. His teachings of self-reliance have enabled us to defeat the Japanese, the KMT, and the imperialists. Whatever the cost, we must remain self-sufficient and meet this emergency on our own."

Jiang Qing walked to the back of the room and poured a cup of tea. Yao followed and the two started to talk. Hua looked helplessly at Ye and Li. "Comrade Jiang," Li said, "we would appreciate it if you would return so that we can decide how to help the people of China recover from the quake."

"The people of China do not need any help. They are strong. They will survive as they always have."

"Then why are we all so concerned?"

"Your concern is just a ruse to permit the infiltration of capitalist-roaders into positions of power and to distract the attention of the country from its most important goal, which is the continuation of the revolution of the proletariat."

Defense Minister Ye laughed in frustration. "When will you ever stop these political polemics?"

"When my friends and I have rid this government of senile old men, country bumpkins, and capitalist-roaders."

"Shall I take that as a threat?"

"Take it as a prophecy, from Chairman Mao."

30: Old Farmer Huang

TANGSHAN

Old Farmer Huang sat motionless on a rock, staring at the smoldering ashes of what had once been his home. His donkey paced nervously across a dirt road. "They're all lost," the farmer moaned, though only the donkey could hear him. His eldest two sons and his grandson, as well as his wife of forty years, his son's wives, and his infant granddaughter, had all been trapped in the burning pyre. No one had escaped.

"Why didn't I listen to you when you tried to warn me?" Huang asked the donkey gnawing on a tuft of weeds. The animal had heard the nervous scampering of field mice and seen the panicked flight of flocks of crows. Feeling the first uneasy vibrations of the earth, the donkey had screamed out. Huang had come to see what was wrong. In the ten years they had been together, the donkey had never interrupted his sleep, but on this night the animal had been jumping about like a bee trapped inside a house. Huang had patted his donkey's mane, but the animal reared in the air and urinated on his foot. "What's wrong with you? Are there tigers around?" Huang had asked. The donkey's voice cracked as it brayed in terror. "Stop it!" Huang screamed, but his voice had been drowned out by the rupture of the earth.

It was over so quickly, and yet it had lasted a lifetime. The first violent tremor threw him to the ground, leaving him stunned. He looked up at the house in which he had lived for more than sixty years. The structure, built of wood and mud, collapsed in a heap, trapping his family inside. He tried to stand, but the quake knocked him back down. While he watched, the cooking fires, kindled by the thatch from the roof, consumed his home as if it had been a pile of dried leaves.

Huang closed his eyes which were bloodshot from hours of staring at the fire. He had done what he could. He had carried buckets of water from the pump and beaten the fire with a blanket, but his efforts had not retarded the flames. His mind was haunted by the image of his eldest son burning like a torch as he struggled to escape from the rubble. Huang had tried to save him, but had been unable to penetrate the inferno.

"What have I done to deserve this?" Old Farmer Huang tilted his head toward the sky. He thought of his youngest son, working in the Kailuan Mines, and wondered whether he, too, had been killed. Only his daughter, serving with the army in Manchuria, was certain to have survived. "What a curse," the old man said, "to be left without any sons."

The old farmer was unable to understand why the gods had brought their wrath upon him. He had always been a believer. Despite the attempt of the government to eliminate the worshiping of spirits, he never missed a New Year's or a harvest offering. He painted red-colored eggs for all special events in his family, lit joss sticks every week, and kept the altar in his home filled with oblations. So why had the spirits killed his family and destroyed his home?

Marc Slater, guided by the light from thousands of fires burning out of control, staggered along the road. It had been more than an hour since he had left Wong among the mine shafts. His legs felt leaden and his body throbbed as if it had been squeezed in a vise. He was beyond exhaustion, but he refused to stop. He knew that he had to find help and then return for Liu. He reached the crest of a hill just as Old Farmer Huang dropped to his knees and began to beseech the gods. "Oh, spirit of the earth and mountains, why have you done this to me?"

"Old man," Marc said in Chinese, "are you all right?"

Old Farmer Huang stared at the heavens and responded to what he thought was the word of God. "How can you ask me that? My family is dead. My house is a pile of ashes."

"I'm sorry." Marc walked toward the man.

Old Farmer Huang heard the footsteps and opened his eyes. "*Aiya!*" he screamed in fright. He shook his head from side to side, but the wrinkles on his face remained motionless, as if carved of stone. "Get away from here, you fornicating, evil, barbarian God! What have you done with the Chinese spirit to whom I was praying?"

"Take your heart out of your throat," Marc entreated in Chinese. "I am not a spirit."

"You do not fool me by speaking the language of my people. It is a trick that the evil spirits of the sky have used for thousands of years."

"I did not come from the sky. I came from the Kailuan Mines."

"*Aiya!*" The old man sneaked behind his donkey and held his hands in position to defend against an attack. "Then you are a spirit of the underworld, from inside the earth!"

"I am a man." Marc opened his shirt. "Do you not see the blood on my skin? Do you think spirits can bleed?"

"Spirits can fool humans."

"Why would I want to fool you? I, too, was caught in the earthquake. Some of my friends died when a mine shaft caved in."

"How did you survive?"

"The fates were good to me."

"Perhaps because they knew of your evil powers."

Marc massaged his eyes in frustration. He could see that the old man was too traumatized to listen to reason. He would have to find someone else to help him with Liu. He walked to the far side of the road. The old man pushed the donkey forward and blocked his path. "Please let me pass."

"Go back to your mines."

"I can't. I must find someone who can help my old friend Liu Teyu."

"Long Way Liu?"

"Yes. Do you know him?"

"I fought with him during the Long March."

"Then help him." Marc extended his arms toward the man. "Liu's leg is broken. It will take both of us and your donkey to carry him to safety."

"Is this a trick?"

"No!" Marc shook his head and tried to control his temper. "I am a foreigner, not an evil spirit. Please come with me."

The farmer draped his arm over his donkey. "What do you think?" he asked the animal. The donkey said nothing as it chomped on the grass.

"Old man, this is your last chance. If you do not come with me, Liu's death will be on your conscience."

Huang buried his head in his hands. Then he turned back to Marc with a look of resignation. "Perhaps I should come with you. My family is dead. My life is unworthy and unimportant. Even though you are an evil spirit, there is little more for me to lose. I cannot risk letting Liu die."

"Thank you," Marc said, feeling as if he wanted to collapse.

"There is one condition," Huang said. "You must walk ahead of me. I want to be able to see you in case you try one of your tricks."

"Agreed," Marc replied. "We'll need your wagon." He walked to a cart lying on its side in a ditch. The farmer stepped next to him. Marc's muscles strained as they flipped the cart onto its side. Some of the boards had splintered, but it was otherwise intact.

Old Farmer Huang took hold of the donkey. The animal reared. "Don't be nervous." The farmer stroked the donkey's mane as he coaxed it into the rigging. "We're going to save our old friend." Huang slapped the donkey. The animal stepped forward, but the wheels stuck in the ditch. Marc lifted the rear end of the wagon while Huang tugged on the bridle. The donkey plodded ahead and pulled the wagon onto the road.

The old farmer stopped for a moment and stared sorrowfully at the smoldering embers of what had once been his home. He looked to the heavens and prayed that the evil foreign spirit would bring him back safely from the mines. Then he pulled on the reins and started up the road.

Liu Teyu was lying behind a mine shaft. His leg was swollen and he was in considerable pain, but he was still conscious. "What are you doing back here?" he called to Marc.

"Did you think I'd leave you?"

"I heard the Red Guard colonel order his men to go after

371

you. I was worried that you might have been captured."

"Me, the blue-eyed spirit who runs like the wind, captured?"

"I knew it!" Old Farmer Huang grabbed the reins of his donkey. "I knew you were an evil spirit."

"Who are you and what are you talking about?" Liu asked.

"Excuse me, honorable general, I am Huang. I have a farm not five *li* from here. I fought with you during the Long March. I was known as Coal Mountain Huang. Perhaps you remember me?"

Liu squinted through the darkness, but could not recognize the man. "Oh, yes, of course."

"This long-nosed barbarian told me that you needed help. I came as quickly as I could, though I knew he was an evil spirit."

Liu smiled. "The long-nose is bad as they come."

The old farmer backed away. "Stop joking," Marc said. "This guy actually thinks that I'm a devil from inside the earth."

Liu laughed. "I know many who share his opinion." Then he beckoned to the old man. "My friend, this foreigner is no devil. He is a *lao pengyou*. He fought with me back in Yan'an."

"In Yan'an?" Old Farmer Huang asked with surprise. "How did a barbarian get to Yan'an?"

"He was born in China. His family ran a hospital in Yan'an. I'm sure you remember it."

The farmer stared suspiciously at Marc. "Then his speaking Chinese is not a trick and he is not an evil spirit?"

"He has the heart of a Han."

The farmer clapped his hands. "I knew it all the time."

Liu grasped Marc's arm and pointed to the crest of a hill. They watched in silence as three men carrying flashlights inspected the area where the attack had taken place. The searchers fanned out and started to flank their position. It was just a matter of time until they were seen. With no weapons, they were defenseless against the armed men. The donkey stepped back and kicked a rock. The beam of a still distant flashlight danced toward them. Liu propped himself up. "Marc, you had better get out of here."

Marc's aching body urged him to stay, but he knew that he would be captured unless he moved. "What about you? We can't just leave you here."

"I'm going with you."

"How are you going to get by the guards with a broken leg?"

Liu looked at the old farmer. "Coal Mountain Huang, can you pretend that I am your younger brother?"

"I wish I could, but even our evil-spirited friend knows that I am younger than you." Old Farmer Huang smiled knowingly at Liu. With Marc's help, he lifted the general into the cart and covered him with a blanket. Then he turned the donkey around and started up the road.

Marc quickly distanced himself from the others. A man with a flashlight jogged toward the cart. It was one of Wong's operatives from Hong Kong. The man pointed his gun at the old farmer. "Identify yourself!"

"I am Coal Mountain Huang, a farmer from over the next hill. What do you want with me?"

"We are searching for a barbarian."

"What use do I have for fornicating barbarians?"

"Have you seen any?"

"I have seen the gods of the earth fart. I have seen mountains topple. I have seen my sons killed and my home destroyed. That is all I care to see." The farmer slapped the reins against the neck of the donkey. "I am going home to bury the dead so that the spirits of the underworld do not haunt my family for eternity."

Marc watched as the flashlights of the other two men

began to move toward the cart like small boats seeking a port after a storm. He was apprehensive, fearing one of the men from Hong Kong would recognize Liu. The first man inspected the back of the cart with his flashlight. "Who's this?" he asked, lifting the blanket.

"He's my elder brother," the farmer replied.

"Are you certain that he is not Liu Teyu?"

"Who is Liu Teyu?"

"He is a general of the People's Liberation Army."

Old Farmer Huang walked to the back of the cart and stared down at Liu. "Tell me the truth, elder brother. Have you been disguising yourself for these seventy-five years? Have you been sneaking off from the wheat fields during the day to go fight wars?" Liu kept his eyes closed and pretended to be unconscious. "I'm sorry," the farmer said to the man with the flashlight. "My brother has broken his leg and lost a lot of blood. He cannot tell me if he has been fooling me all these years."

"Stop treating me like an idiot." The man waved his arm at the farmer.

"How else would you treat a man who tries to tell you that your brother, with whom you have labored in the fields since the time of the dynasty, is really a leader of the army? Has the quake dented your mind?" The farmer pulled his donkey forward.

"Don't move! We'll see what my friends have to say."

"I am going to take my elder brother to the hospital." The farmer spit on the ground. "He is the only member of my family still alive. I will not let him die. If you want to stop me, you will have to shoot." The farmer slapped the flank of the donkey and walked off.

The man with the flashlight pointed his gun at the man in the cart. Liu did not move. "To hell with these peasants and their god damn country," he said as he turned away and walked back to his friends.

31: Breakfast in the Forbidden City

From the vantage point of a stretcher lugged by People's Liberation Army soldiers, Frans Van Wyck surveyed the minor cosmetic damage in the lobby of the Peking Hotel. He had argued with the soldiers when they arrived at his room and insisted on carrying him downstairs. He had only a broken ankle and some bruises and easily could have found his way out on his own. But they had been ordered to evacuate the hotel and were unwilling to take any chances with him.

Van Wyck gazed at the parking lot jammed with thousands of foreigners. There were clusters of Americans, East and West Europeans, Asians, Africans, Arabs, and overseas Chinese. Many were still in their pajamas, making the scene look as if someone had raided a slumber party at the United Nations. Although a few lay on the ground, most stood in groups, nervously recounting how mirrors had

375

broken, cabinets had toppled, and furniture had careened around their rooms during the quake.

Van Wyck smiled as he observed the destruction around him. He usually disliked anything that interfered with the precise schedule of his plans, but the earthquake was the perfect complement to his operation. The quake would disrupt the stability of the country and spread panic among the people. Hua's already shaky government would have to devote its energies to burying the dead and digging out of the rubble. The army and the Red Guards would have to assist in the reconstruction, making it difficult for them to respond to an invasion. Everyone would be too busy to get in the way of his operatives.

The quake would also feed the superstitions of the Chinese. To them, it was far more than a geological event; it was an omen that their government was doomed. If he acted quickly, he could use this paranoia to his advantage. Given everyone's fatalistic panic, this was the time to hammer the final nails into the coffin of the People's Republic.

Van Wyck's leg began to throb. "Damn!" he muttered under his breath. It was difficult to be a saboteur if you couldn't walk. His men were good and his preparations were complete, but he hated missing out on the kill. He inspected his ankle. It had swollen to twice its normal size and become discolored. For now he had no choice but to rely on his lieutenants.

Van Wyck saw Boswell walking toward him. Since Rahman had not yet returned from the mission against the Liaison Office, Boswell would have to do. There were two new assignments he wanted implemented before dawn. He called Boswell's name.

The Englishman forced a smile. His blond hair was disheveled and his normally sunken eyes were hollower than usual, but he was otherwise unharmed. "Are you all right?"

he asked, kneeling next to Van Wyck.

"I'm fine. It's just a broken ankle."

"I had a terrifying experience. The chandelier in my room started to sway. I jumped out of the way just as it crashed onto the bed. I crawled against the wall. The furniture slid across the room and almost—"

"Have you seen Rahman?" Van Wyck interrupted.

"No." Boswell looked away, hoping Van Wyck would not ask about Gateshead.

"Get me a sheet of paper and a pen," Van Wyck ordered.

"Right away." Boswell hurried to a desk being used by hotel personnel and returned with the items Van Wyck had requested.

A People's Liberation Army soldier motioned that it was time to go to the hospital. Van Wyck held up two fingers, indicating that he would be ready shortly. Then he quickly scribbled a note in code. "Wait here for Rahman," Van Wyck instructed. "There's going to be an aftershock in the next couple of hours. I want Rahman prepared for another mission."

"Can I go with him?"

Van Wyck saw the anxious look on Boswell's face. There was so much confusion in Peking that Boswell's presence was unlikely to present any risk. "All right, provided you follow Rahman's orders. Understood?"

"Understood."

The soldiers loaded the stretcher onto a flatbed truck already filled with other foreigners. As they drove down Chang'an Avenue, Van Wyck stared at the streets of Peking. The contrast with the tumult at the hotel was striking. The people sat quietly in parks and intersections smoking cigarettes, fanning themselves, and gossiping as if nothing had happened. Disciplined civil-defense teams cleared the rubble in the *hutongs* while traffic flowed smoothly on the main thoroughfares.

Following a caravan of three-wheeled bicycles serving as ambulances, the truck drove down a side street and passed through a pair of green steel gates. Inside was a magnificent building with a curving green tiled roof adorned with sculptures of mythical animals. Written in bold red letters across the front was the slogan "Long Live the Unconquerable Thought of Mao Tse-tung." This was the facility now known as the Capital Hospital. Built in the 1920s with money from the Rockefellers as Peking Union Medical College, the institution had also been known during the Cultural Revolution as the Anti-Imperialist Hospital. However, just before Nixon's first trip to China, the Chinese had renamed it Capital Hospital so as not to insult the Americans.

After the truck had stopped, the PLA soldiers lugged Van Wyck up a staircase past hundreds of injured Chinese who filled a stone courtyard. Patients with broken bones and deep gashes quietly waited in an hour-long line that stretched into the Chinese section of the building, beneath a sign that read "Serve the People." The line separated to permit the foreigner to pass. The soldiers climbed another flight and entered the freshly painted foreign section where there was no waiting line. They carried Van Wyck into a modern examination room. A nurse X-rayed Van Wyck's foot and gave the film to an orderly for development. Two other foreigners with cuts and abrasions were placed on examination tables. They were in far better shape than most of the Chinese, who would have to wait for hours.

"When are you going to get to me?" a man asked in German.

The doctors nodded politely and continued working.

"If you don't treat me soon," the man insisted, "I'll be forced to complain to my embassy." A nurse nudged him back onto the table and applied a cool towel to his forehead. The man flung the towel on the floor. "That's not helping me! It's my arm that's broken!"

The nurse bowed politely, picked up the towel, and put it back on the man's forehead. Van Wyck smiled. Nothing, not even the rude impatience of foreigners, could ruffle the composure of the Chinese. With such self-control, perhaps China could survive an earthquake.

As soon as the buildings stopped shaking and the danger subsided, Aziz Rahman and his men returned to their trucks. The Chinese in the *hutong* gathered around, seeking direction from Rahman's men still dressed as Red Guards. At first the attention made Rahman uncomfortable; but once he realized that the Chinese were deferring to his leadership, he mobilized a force to liberate his trucks from the debris.

While the rubble was being moved, the women and children were herded behind the trucks. The local Party cadre divided the street so that everyone had a place to sleep away from buildings still in danger of falling. Old women placed their grandchildren under wooden tables while they stood guard over the few possessions their families had salvaged.

Two hours after the quake, a path had been opened enabling Rahman and his trucks to reach Chang'an Avenue. Everywhere workers were clearing the city. Although there was little news about the quake itself, the radio broadcast that more than thirty thousand volunteers were already working in Peking and that Premier Hua had developed a massive reconstruction program involving more than five million people. The Chinese, who handled most tasks with deliberate slowness, had mobilized quickly to cope with the impact of a disaster.

Stopping at the Peking Hotel, Rahman searched for Van Wyck. He pushed through a mass of agitated foreigners fighting over access to overseas phone lines until Boswell intercepted him. The Englishman described Van Wyck's injuries and then handed Rahman the letter. The Dutchman wanted him to place bombs around the television station and the telephone company; the bombs would explode during the aftershocks. Rahman smiled. He appreciated the way Van Wyck tried to seize every opportunity. With the city still in chaos, disrupting communications was a masterstroke.

It was almost five in the morning when the People's Liberation Army car carrying Frans Van Wyck turned onto Chang'an Avenue. The car passed the Peking Hotel. "Where are we going?" Van Wyck asked.

"We have been instructed to take you to a new residence," a soldier replied.

"Why me?" Van Wyck stared uneasily at the guards.

"It's not just you. All our foreign guests are being moved."

Van Wyck watched as spotlights illuminated a yawning crack extending down the side of the Great Hall of the People. He smiled: It was an omen certain to disturb the Chinese. The car drove through the main gate of the Forbidden City and stopped in front of Wumen, the Gate of the Midday Sun. The soldiers helped Van Wyck to his feet and handed him his crutches. "Can you walk on your own?" one asked.

"I am, as Chairman Mao says, self-relient," Van Wyck replied.

The soldier laughed. "Where did you learn such excellent Chinese?"

"From reading the *Little Red Book*."

The soldier laughed again and slapped him on the back, almost knocking him over. "You are a true *lao pengyou.*"

Van Wyck thanked the soldiers for their courtesy and then tested his crutches. The moisture from the long rain and the bumpy surface of the ancient bricks made walking difficult, but he pushed ahead toward the bridge that spanned the moat of the Imperial Palace. A cordon of soldiers guarded the gate. They inspected his papers and then let him pass.

Van Wyck stepped through Wumen and into the magnificent courtyard that had been designed by the emperors to overwhelm anyone visiting the Forbidden City. The usually austere court was now filled with thousands of olive-drab tents. In the center were hundreds of dining tables being serviced by white-jacketed waiters. A guide approached and led Van Wyck to a tent in the southeast corner. Inside he found all his belongings, including his easel and his paints, neatly packed in his suitcases. He smiled as he thanked the guard. If he had to be incapacitated, he could think of no place where he would rather spend his time.

Van Wyck lay down for a short nap. The ground started to shake. There was a deep, booming sound from inside the earth. Crawling out of his tent, he pressed his palms to the trembling courtyard. There was another explosion, but this one did not come from inside the earth. Smoke and flames billowed from the direction of the central television station.

When the aftershock ended, Van Wyck hobbled to the dining area to eat breakfast. Sipping a cup of tea, he saw Boswell striding determinedly toward him with a gleam in his eyes. The Englishman smiled as he took a seat. "I assume everything went well last night," Van Wyck said.

"It was, so to speak, smashing." Boswell laughed. "I'm grateful you gave me the chance to participate. It certainly will help my standing."

"Of course, but what of the operations?"

"Your friend Rahman is an artist with explosives. The television station looks like it was attacked by a squadron of bombers."

"And the phone company?"

"We could not get there before the aftershock, but we did wire the entire building. If the earth decides to move one more time, it's going to be very difficult to make a phone call anywhere in northern China."

At 9:00 A.M., Wang Hongwen finished his private meeting with Hua Guofeng and stormed angrily out of the Hall of Benevolence. "That stupid country bumpkin," Wang cursed. "He hears the wind and immediately expects the rain." Wang had never liked Hua, especially since Mao had chosen Hua over his ally Zhang Chunqiao and himself. Wang had once been the number two man in China, but first Deng, then Zhang, and now Hua had been pushed ahead of him. Although he was young enough to wait his turn, he was wary about the direction of Hua's government. Hua could easily reunite with Deng and eliminate any chance Wang might have to become the leader of China. There was no alternative but to remove Hua.

Raising his umbrella, Wang walked quickly through Zhong Nanhai. There was something comic about a man as limited as Hua attempting to cope with the destruction of the earthquake. It was like watching a person trying to wrap a cloud with a piece of paper. The problem was that, through his stupidity, Hua was capable of destroying the People's Republic.

The pavement of Zhong Nanhai Park started to tremble. A group of bicycles toppled like a row of dominoes. Wang grabbed a bronze dragon to steady himself. The vibrations increased, but they were much less severe than those of the first aftershock. Wang looked toward Mao's home. There was an explosion. A cloud of acrid brown smoke rose from beyond the palace walls. The aftershock had not been strong enough to set it off. It must, Wang assumed, have been the demolition of a building that had been battered in the main quake.

Regaining his footing, Wang hurried toward the Ming dynasty pavilion that was Mao's home. A cordon of soldiers stood in front of the four glass doors marking the entrance. Ascending the white stone stairs, Wang walked between the massive red pillars holding up the pavilion. The People's Republic needed such pillars to survive. Wang and his allies were not yet strong enough to take power. They had to rely on Mao's continuing support.

It was not that China could not function without Mao's guidance; in many ways it had been deprived of the Chairman's leadership for the past several years. Rather, the country could not survive without his imperial presence. Once Mao died, there would be turmoil. The generals would try to seize control, and the bureaucracy would turn against the workers. Elderly officials, out of touch with the ideals of the revolution, would increase their salaries, build fancy houses, and adopt foreign values. They would take mistresses and become corrupt. The party would become ossified. And China would be back where it was at the time of Liberation.

Wang understood the machinations of power and was not about to permit the old men to push China back onto the capitalist road. He and his generation had struggled through the Cultural Revolution. It was their turn to lead the country. It was ironic that their success was dependent on the survival of the most revered member of the original revolutionary generation.

Shen Mo, Jiang Qing's aide, greeted Wang and ushered

him into Mao's study. The room was cluttered with stacks of books, so much a part of Mao's life. Despite his continual attacks on the universities, Mao was an intellectual. Running the government had never been his prime concern. He saw himself as a teacher, not a politician. He hated bureaucratic infighting, and instead preferred to spend his time writing, planning, and serving as the helmsman for his people. Mao seemed happiest when he could take his books, leave the capital, and spend months at a time in the countryside, thinking about the future and recapturing his peasant roots.

It was during such a hiatus that Wang, then a textile worker and the leader of the radical January Storm in Shanghai, had first met Mao. The two developed an instant rapport. The Chairman had gone to east China to decide how to wrest control from the increasingly powerful bureaucracy. Wang, a leader of the new generation of disenfranchised Chinese, became a devoted disciple. After three months of contemplation, Mao emerged with the blueprint for the Cultural Revolution, and Wang became one of its staunchest supporters.

During the past decade Mao had often fled from the responsibilities of the capital to people's communes, where he could work with his hands and contemplate the future. Less than two years ago, he had gone to the South, leaving control of the government in the hands of Chou En-lai and Deng Xiaoping. For eight months, he had remained in seclusion, refusing to communicate with anyone in Peking.

Wang smiled as he thought about the contrast between the People's Republic and the countries of the West, with their pervasive media. There the heads of state had to be constantly available. They had no opportunity to devote themselves to serious study and thought. Perhaps that was why those countries were in a continuing state of decline. It was not easy to divorce oneself from the daily operations of the government, but it was essential. He would not forget to do so when he became the leader of the People's Republic. He walked to Mao's cloth-covered scholar's desk with its wicker chair, looked around, and then sat down. He felt comfortable in Mao's chair. Perhaps one day it would be his.

"Isn't it a little premature to be trying it out for size?" a catty voice snipped through the silence of the room. Wang looked up and saw Jiang Qing approaching him. She was wearing a white silk blouse and blue bell-bottom jeans. The jeans were a variation of a French design that she had personally introduced into China.

"Just taking some weight off my feet," Wang replied as he stood up. "How are you feeling this morning?"

"Not well. I'm having a recurrence of my liver ailment."

"I'm sorry."

"I appreciate your concern," Jiang said. "If you will excuse me, I'll take my morning medicine and check on the preparations for breakfast."

Jiang turned with a flourish and strode out of the room. Watching her go, Wang saw Zhuang Zedong standing in the living room. A former world table-tennis champion and a national idol in China, Zhuang was one of Jiang's lovers. "What's he doing here?" Wang asked Shen.

"He heard that Comrade Jiang was ill and came to show his concern."

"In Chairman Mao's house?"

"It is time for us to eat breakfast," Shen said, turning away.

Wang spat into Mao's brass cuspidor and then followed Shen into the dining room. Jiang was already seated at the head of the table. She has certainly fit back in here quickly, Wang thought to himself. After Mao had kicked her out, Jiang had moved outside of the Imperial Palace. For a while she had been persona non grata. Mao had refused to see her without an appointment, and she had been forced to submit all requests, even those relating to their children, through an intermediary. But now that Mao was ill, Jiang had reassumed her role as mistress of the Empire.

Even though Wang, as vice-chairman of the Politburo, outranked Jiang, he politely took a seat to her right. Jiang always sought to place herself in the center of power, but this was not the time to complain. Wang knew that time was on his side. He was thirty years younger than most of the members of the Politburo. The future belonged to him. All he had to do was avoid being purged and wait. Now, however, he needed Jiang. She could give him the one thing he lacked, an indisputable link of legitimacy to Chairman Mao. Although she and Mao had not lived together for several years, the people of China did not know of the rift. She was still the wife of the Chairman—a unique role that ensured her a special authority at the time of his death. Until the People's Republic was once again stabilized, Wang could not afford to alienate her. For the moment, he was more than willing to let her have her way on insignificant issues.

A waiter brought out four white porcelain bowls, each filled with a different mushy-looking porridge. There was a broth with floating shrimp and mushrooms cut to resemble flowers, a congee filled with chicken and shallots, an oatmeal adorned with jasmine blossoms, and a sweetened puree of walnuts. Because of her delicate digestion, Jiang preferred these mild-flavored, soft-textured dishes.

Shen Mo led Yao Wenyuan and Zhang Chunqiao into the dining room. Yao greeted Jiang and then sat next to Wang. Zhang, whose current ranking in the Party placed him second to Hua, gave Jiang an annoyed look before he, too, sat down. Mao Yuanxin, Mao's nephew, walked quietly into the room and took a seat next to Zhang.

"I'm glad you could come," Wang began. "I had a very disturbing meeting with Hua Guofeng this morning. He looks and sounds like a nervous wreck. The earthquake has left him quite confused."

"That's the way he always is," Yao said.

"He's much worse today."

"Worse?" Yao laughed. "He's so incompetent, he has to walk around with a hole in the seam of his pants." Yao referred to the practice of dressing Chinese children in open-backed pants to make it easy for them to go to the bathroom.

Wang reported that the morning's news about the quake was far worse than even the most pessimistic projections. It appeared that more than half a million had been killed, two million had been injured, and at least twenty million had been left homeless. The only consolation was that the quake had occurred during the summer. Had it taken place during the winter, many more would have frozen or starved to death. Now at least the people could live off the food in the fields while they rebuilt their homes. Wang then detailed Hua's plan to mobilize the entire country.

"It's all a trick," Jiang interrupted.

"How can it be a trick?" Zhang Chunqiao asked. "Look at the severity of the quake."

"I'm not trying to minimize the damage," Jiang replied. "My heart is with the people of Tangshan. But I'm concerned that besides the real problems, Hua is looking for an excuse to build up the forces against us. With Chou dead and Deng purged, the right is powerless, but we are getting stronger. Hua will grasp at any straw to undermine our power."

"How can he do that?"

"By rehabilitating Deng and the other capitalist-roaders for his rescue efforts, and by moving Liu Teyu's troops from the South so they can be in position to act against us."

"I agree with Comrade Jiang," Wang said. "We must

watch Hua very closely. He's very threatened by us."

"Hua," Yao said, "would be threatened by a frog jumping on his foot."

"Do you know," Wang said, "he even blames us for the attack on the TV station."

"That's ridiculous," Jiang replied. "We control the station. We wouldn't sabotage it."

"I tried to explain that, but it's very difficult to reason with him."

"What did he say about the explosion at the telephone building?" Zhang asked.

"What explosion?" Wang asked.

"We've lost all phone service to the area of the quake, Manchuria, and Shanghai, including our three largest arsenals."

"Shit!" Jiang said. "It had to be the work of Deng and his people."

"We must be careful," Yao warned. "They blew up the ships and the railroads. They destroyed the agricultural center in the Chairman's hometown. Now they're trying to blame us for their own sabotage. These are very devious people. They'd try to sneak the sunrise past a rooster if they thought they could get away with it."

"I think," Wang said, "that we should meet with the Chairman. We must make sure that he supports us on all issues."

"Excuse me," Yuanxin interrupted. "I am not certain that today would be the appropriate time. Our Teacher was awake all night. He was very upset about the earthquake, or as he called it, 'the crocodile blinking his eyes.'"

"The crocodile was from a folktale that Comrade Mao's mother told him as a child," Jiang smiled, remembering earlier, better times.

"Our Teacher," Yuanxin continued, "was very depressed

about the future of the People's Republic. He said that the earthquake confirmed his vision that the Mandate of Heaven was about to be withdrawn."

"Our Chairman," Yao interrupted, "is sounding more like an emperor every day."

"That is his right," Yuanxin replied.

"There is no time for bickering." Jiang glared angrily at the others. "We must be united. We cannot allow Comrade Mao to waver. Nor can we permit Deng and his capitalist-roaders to take the power from us. We have worked too hard to turn the people's revolution back to the bureaucrats."

"Then we will just have to make sure," Wang replied, "that Mao gets no opportunity to communicate with our opposition."

"And how do you suggest we accomplish that?"

Wang walked to the back of the room and sat at the other end of the table so that all attention was focused on him. "We must isolate the Chairman so that no one can see him without our approval. Yuanxin, you must remain in the hospital at all times so that you can control all of Mao's visitors. We'll check everyone with direct contact. The new calligrapher, the interpreters, the guards, and even the hospital personnel. They must all be our people. If we have the slightest doubt about anyone's reliability, we must replace him. Finally, we must meet with the Chairman as often as possible. His mind is slipping and he vacillates daily. We must get him to sign documents stating that we should run the country. Then we must publish the documents in our newspapers and broadcast them on our radio and television stations."

"While he's still alive?" Yuanxin asked.

"If necessary," Wang said, lighting a cigarette. "Deng and his allies dominate the bureaucracy and the army. Our prime base of power is the media. If we're to have any hope of success, we most bombard the people with whatever propaganda we can produce. We must keep Hua's name out of the papers and ours in the limelight."

"But what of Comrade Mao's own wishes?"

"The tiger is dying. If we don't act now, the old monkey will seize control of the mountain."

32: Transfusion

Marc Slater rolled over on his bruised shoulder and winced in pain. Every bone in his body seemed to ache. His mouth tasted of dirt. He opened his eyes and gazed at the ruptured earth. The gray skies of morning cast a sickening pall on the destruction in the countryside. Rivers of dirt, carrying boulders and uprooted trees, carved paths down the hills and coated the wheat fields in the valley.

Propping himself up on his arms, Marc stared at an old Chinese man leaning fast asleep against his donkey. Everything seemed strange and alien. For a moment he was unsure of where he was or how he had gotten here. Then slowly, like the recollection of a nightmare, pieces of his memory were jogged into place.

Marc remembered that Liu Teyu was injured and that Wong Chuyun and his men were still pursuing them. He forced himself to his feet. His legs trembled. Tentatively he walked to the cart in which Liu was lying. The general was asleep. His face was ashen. Beads of sweat glistened on his fevered brow. His leg was badly swollen and discolored. Marc removed the general's shoes. Liu stirred but did not awaken. Marc had to find a doctor and get them something to eat. He went over to Old Farmer Huang and tugged on his arm.

"*Aiya!*" Huang exclaimed in fright.

"Are you all right?" Marc asked.

"Fine. Fine," Huang said. "I was just resting for a minute."

"Thanks for taking the last watch," Marc said. Huang had stood guard since five. "I couldn't keep my eyes open any longer."

The old farmer smiled. "I am used to watching over the general. Did I tell you I served with him during the Long March?"

"You did," Marc smiled. He suspected that there were over forty million people in China who now claimed to have been among the one hundred thousand on the Long March. "Someday you'll have to tell me of your experiences."

Huang looked over and saw Liu sitting up. "Ah, general, it's good to see you awake," he said. "I was just going to tell the long-nosed foreign devil about Luding Bridge. Do you remember the battle?"

"How could I forget?" Liu said in a barely audible voice. "It was the most important battle of the Long March. If we had not crossed the river, our army would have been crushed. We would never have been able to escape from the grip of the KMT and liberate the country."

"I was one of the soldiers who stormed the bridge," the old farmer said with great pride.

"Coal Mountain Huang, you are a true hero," Liu said. Although he had met thousands of men, each of whom had claimed to be among the first to cross the river, the truth was irrelevant. There had been similar heroism in hundreds of battles not only against the Nationalists and the Japanese but also against the floods and the starvation that had plagued China. Like so many others, the old farmer had chosen a public incident to depict his private struggle. "Without you, my friend, Mao, Chou, and the rest of us would have died with our backs to the Dadu River."

"I am greatly honored by your words," Old Farmer Huang said, "but I am unworthy of such compliments."

"Nonsense," Liu replied. "It was men like you—peasants, factory workers, and coal miners—who made our revolution. Without you, there would have been no one for Mao to lead."

"And without leaders, we would have remained unorganized peasants, exploited by the landlords."

"Shall we say we helped each other?" Liu replied, contorting his face in pain.

"Are you all right, honorable old friend?" Huang asked.

"I'll be fine. It's just my broken leg."

"We will find you a doctor," the old farmer said. "Can you hold out until after breakfast?"

"Of course."

"Good," Huang laughed. "I am told that people have two meals a day in the land of the Golden Mountains." He referred to the United States with the term that the Chinese had used since the California gold rush. "I would not want our foreign friend to go hungry in the Middle Kingdom."

"Don't worry about me," Marc said. "I can wait until we get to the hospital."

"The comforts of our foreign friends must always come first," Huang insisted. Then he walked into the fields to scavenge for food.

As the old farmer disappeared behind a hill formed by a rockslide, Marc doused his jacket in a creek and wiped the clotted blood off Liu's leg and forehead. "How are you really?" Marc asked.

"Don't worry about an old man like me," Liu said. His eyes darted from side to side like those of a man in a state of delirium. Dizziness overcame him. He lay back on the cart.

Marc unbuttoned Liu's shirt. There were disturbingly large purple splotches below Liu's rib cage. Marc ran his fingers around the general's torso. Two ribs were broken, and there seemed to be internal bleeding. Despite Liu's assurances, Marc was worried.

The farmer returned twenty minutes later carrying a collection of twigs, roots, and weeds. He washed them in the creek, built a fire, and, using a piece of tin as a pan, cooked the concoction. It smelled vaguely like burning leaves. Marc crimped his nose. "I know it doesn't look so appetizing," the old farmer said, "but when I was on the Long March, we used to count ourselves lucky to have roots and weeds for dinner. Sometimes things got so bad that we had to eat dirt. The specialty of our chef was called 'yellow dust stew.'"

Marc took his plate and started to chomp on what passed for breakfast. His stomach gurgled. Knowing he needed nourishment and unwilling to insult the farmer, he forced himself to eat. It wasn't as bad as he had thought it would be. It was fresh and crunchy with a slightly nutty flavor. Only the inedible small twigs posed difficulties. Marc sucked out the pulp and spit the rest away. Oh, for a thick, juicy sirloin steak, he thought to himself.

"I am told that in the land of the Golden Mountain, people are so rich that everyone has bird's-nest soup at every meal." The old farmer laughed. "I'm sorry I could not feed you the soup, but at least we've eaten the bird's nest."

"The nest was delicious," Marc said respectfully, marveling that the old farmer could carry on after having lost his entire family. It was a quality of the Chinese that he had always envied. "Can you watch the general for a few minutes?"

The old farmer scratched his head. "I doubt he will be running anywhere."

Marc jogged to the Kailuan Mines. He stopped next to the shaft in which Meili had been killed. The aftershocks had closed the passageway he had dug in his escape. Kneeling down, he shut his eyes and prayed for Meili. He felt too numb to cry. Drawing a heart in the dirt, he wrote their names inside in Chinese characters. Then he bound two sticks together and placed them on top of the mound. When the danger subsided, he would return and give Meili a proper burial.

Marc stood up and walked over to the charred wreckage of the Toyota and the limousine. The two cars lay mingled together, covered with mounds of dirt like a horrible piece of avant-garde sculpture. On his hands and knees, he searched through the ditch until he touched something soft. His leather travel bag was still intact. He brushed off the dirt and pulled open the zippers. The letters from Deng were still inside, as were his passport, pipe, and tobacco. Marc smiled. He was pleased that Wong and the others had not found the bag. The letters could be critical to his mission, especially if Deng had survived the quake; and his passport was essential for him to move around in China. Marc lit his pipe and inhaled the mellow aroma as he walked back to the campsite.

The others were waiting when Marc returned. The old farmer tugged on the reins of his donkey, and they began to traverse what had once been a road. Fallen trees, rockslides, and other debris blocked the path, forcing frequent detours. For more than an hour they continued in silence, each lost in his own world.

The procession stopped when it reached the place where the old farmer's home had once stood. Huang stoically inspected the badly charred rubble. There was no trace of his family who had been trapped inside. He knelt next to his brick chimney and promised to return. Graves still had to be dug for the adults so that the spirits of his family could find eternal peace. Then, since the souls of children were not fully developed and hence could not be buried in the family grave, he would also have to find a crevice in which to place the body of his granddaughter. The old farmer prayed silently, without tears or maudlin outpourings. Then he stood up and led the others toward a village at the bottom of a valley.

As they approached, Marc saw teams of people clearing the rubble. Huang walked toward a mud and wood house at the end of the main street. A cooking fire was burning in a pit outside. Huang smiled as he picked his teeth with a twig. "Now you can have your soup," he said to Marc.

"What about a doctor for Liu?"

"Patience, my friend. Patience."

The door of the house was open. Inside, a woman knelt on the floor in front of a Buddhist altar. "*Ohm, Futu, ohm Futu,*" she chanted as she fingered a necklace of beads. Huang stopped the donkey and approached the woman, who continued her chant: "*Ohm, Futu, ohm Futu. . . .*"

He knelt behind her and chanted, "Third Cousin Li, Third Cousin Li."

"*Ohm Futu . . .*" the woman continued.

"Third Cousin Li, Third Cousin Li," he chanted more loudly.

The woman turned around and faced him. "You old fool, I heard you the first time. Why do you keep calling me? Don't you know that a person gets tired of hearing her name called over and over?"

"And what of a god?"

"What do you mean?"

"Don't you think that Buddha gets tired of listening to

you call his name all day?"

"That's different. I call Buddha to show my devotion."

"And I call you for the same reason."

"But Buddha can bring me salvation with his blessings."

"And you can bring me salvation with your soup."

The woman stared perplexedly at Old Farmer Huang. "I cannot understand your riddles, Cousin Huang."

"There are no riddles. I am traveling with two friends. One is a barbarian and the other is General Long Way Liu."

"Fool. Your mind must have been killed in the quake. What would the great General Liu be doing with you?"

"He was injured in a mine shaft. I am taking him to see a doctor."

"Why would the general of our southern armies be in the North?"

"Why don't you ask him yourself?" Huang said, pulling Third Cousin Li toward the cart. He pointed with pride to the ashen-faced man. "This is Comrade Liu Teyu."

Liu put his finger to his lips and shook his head. "Old friend, my presence must remain a secret. Please do not call me Liu Teyu. Call me elder uncle."

"He cannot call you elder uncle," Third Cousin Li scoffed. "We are his people. We know all his relatives."

Liu forced a polite smile. "Even an elder uncle by marriage from Canton?"

Third Cousin Li tugged on Huang's arm and pulled him away from the cart. "Stop with your masquerade. How am I supposed to tell if this is Liu Teyu? I have never seen his photograph."

"I am telling you the truth," Huang insisted. "Do you think I would put face powder on a pig and try to convince you that it was my sister?"

"Enough of your proverbs," the woman ordered. "I can cope with an earthquake and with the visit of both a barbarian and one of the leaders of the Liberation, but I cannot cope with any more of your stories. I will make you some food while you put the general on the *kang*."

The old farmer and Marc carried Liu into the room and placed him on the brick platform that was used as a bed at night and a worktable during the day. During the winter, burning coals heated the bricks beneath the platform so that the *kang* was comfortable for sleeping. The old farmer turned to the door. "I'm going get a barefoot doctor."

"Don't trouble yourself," Liu said. "The doctors have too many other problems today without having to come and tend to an old man."

"But you are in considerable pain."

"As soon as we eat," Liu said, "you can take me to the hospital, if it's not too much of an inconvenience."

"Inconvenience?" The old farmer laughed. "I would carry you on my back up Mount Qingkang if that's what was needed to make you well."

Third Cousin Li served a bowl of eggdrop-and-bean-curd soup, a plate of fried noodles, and a cup of tea to each of her guests. Marc gulped down the soup and then attacked the noodles mixed with vegetables and soy sauce. The food was warm and nourishing. Liu and Old Farmer Huang seemed equally satisfied with the meal. Although Liu was in obvious pain, he finished his soup and traded stories with Huang about the Long March. Suddenly, Liu turned white. "Are you all right?" Marc asked.

"Just a little dizzy," Liu said.

"Have a sip of tea." Marc handed him a cup.

Liu raised the cup to his lips. His hands started to shake. The cup crashed to the floor, shattering into pieces. Liu's body trembled, but his eyes remained dull and expressionless. Streams of sweat rolled down his cheeks. He reached out for Marc, gagged, and toppled backward onto the *kang*.

Marc grabbed his wrist. Liu's pulse throbbed at twice its normal pace. Marc slapped Liu's face. There was no response. "Where's the hospital?" Marc demanded.

"It's in the central village of the commune, about twenty *li* from here," Huang responded.

"We need a car. If we have to use your donkey, the general will die before we reach the hospital."

Old Farmer Huang turned and dashed out the front door.

Sen Tailing waved his arms vigorously from side to side as a truck approached. It was the first vehicle in the last ten minutes coming from Tangshan. Because of the emergency, both sides of the road were filled with bumper-to-bumper traffic going the other way. Ambulances, jeeps bringing soldiers to aid in the reconstruction, and trucks carrying relief supplies clogged the road. Soon some of these vehicles would return to Tianjin, taking the wounded to hospitals and picking up more supplies, but Sen did not have time to wait. He had to get his information to the conservatives in Peking.

Sen and Linda Forbes had already walked more than twenty miles. They had started at dawn, but it had been two o'clock before the road became clear enough for traffic to pass. For two hours Sen had been trying to flag down a car, but no one had stopped.

The truck from Tangshan drove onto the dirt shoulder. Sen stepped out of the way and continued to wave. The driver honked his horn, shifted to low gear, and swerved onto the road. As the truck accelerated past, Sen looked into the open trailer. It was tightly packed with prone bodies covered with blankets. "Damn," he said. "Why don't they stop for us?"

"Why don't you let me hail the trucks for a while?"

"This is my country," Sen replied. "It's my job to find us a ride."

"Come on," Linda said, getting up. "Let's walk a little." Her ribs and her head ached from her ordeal at the guest house, but the waiting frustrated her.

Sen turned back to the road and waved at a truck. He took his Party membership card from his wallet and shook it at three passing ambulances. "Damn you! Can't you tell a Grade Eight Party cadre when you see one?"

"Grade Eight," Linda smiled. "I'm impressed. It sounds like someone has big plans for you after they bring you back from Hong Kong."

"What makes you think I would leave Schaffer and return to the People's Republic?"

"The Party would never send a Grade Eight to work for a foreign business unless it was grooming him for a ministry."

"Did you learn about the inner workings of the CCP at Bloomingdale's?"

"I read a lot."

Sen waved at another truck. "Then tell my friend George Bush that he has taught you well."

Linda smiled at Sen. "It appears that now we are both standing naked."

Sen laughed. "Perhaps that is why no one has picked us up."

Linda walked to where Sen was standing. "I'll bet you a Peking-duck dinner that I can get us a ride within five minutes."

"You're on," Sen said, sitting down. He was convinced she would not succeed, but was pleased for any excuse that would get him off his feet.

Linda stood on the side of the road and watched several jeeps and ambulances pass. An old truck, with two men inside, motored slowly toward them. Linda stuck out her leg and slowly lifted the hem of her skirt above her knees.

"What the hell do you think you're doing?" Sen demanded.

"I saw this in an old Clark Gable movie."

"It is stupid and degrading."

"It worked for Claudette Colbert."

"That's enough!" Sen ordered as Linda uncovered the bottom of her thigh.

The truck slowed down and then stopped. The worker riding shotgun jumped out and walked over to Linda. "We must have died and gone to heaven," he shouted back to the driver. "The Middle Kingdom doesn't have any women of the pillow with large white twin lotus peaks and jade terraces the color of wheat fields."

Linda smiled at the man. "I need to go to Peking."

"We don't have to go to such trouble," the man said. "I know a farmer's hut a mile or so up the road. It's not as luxurious as Peking, but it's good enough for us to try the Red Horned Unicorn and the Winding Dragon, unless of course you have some special barbarian postures you'd like to show us."

"I'd love to show you some of my favorite barbarian pillow postures, but I don't think my friend would like it." Linda pointed to Sen. "He's a Grade Eight Party cadre."

"Fucking cadre," the man muttered under his breath.

"Excuse me," Linda said. "Did I hear you say something about a May seventh Rectification Camp in Mongolia?"

The man kicked a stone with his feet. "I said that we could drive you to Tianjin."

"And I said that I needed to go to Peking."

"Please," the man entreated Sen. "I have no papers to go to Peking. I must return to Tianjin to carry more food supplies. If I don't show up, my unit will put me on report."

"Tianjin will be fine," Sen said.

The man walked over to the truck, spit on the ground, and conversed with the driver. Then he opened the door of the cab for his guests and walked to the back of the truck.

"Young lady," Sen said to Linda as he stepped on the running board, "I hope that's the last of your tricks."

"Why? Can't you risk losing any more dinners?"

"Dinners I can risk. It's the revolution that bothers me."

"What revolution?"

"The one that will occur if you keep pulling up your skirt."

While Old Farmer Huang drove the tractor over the mountain road, Marc sat on the flatbed grain trailer and applied another damp towel to Liu's feverish brow. The general's pulse thudded irregularly. Marc moistened Liu's lips, but there was nothing he could do to really help. He just prayed that they would reach the hospital before it was too late.

A cluster of whitewashed buildings with brown tiled roofs came into view. The hospital was on the far left. Printed on its walls in large red characters was the slogan "Serve the People, Cure the Sick." The health quotations of Chairman Mao, written on scrolls of brown, yellow, and pink parchment, hung from long strands of rope stretched between stone columns. Beneath the quotations, rows of people waited on brown wooden benches. Most wore blood-stained bandages. The doctors were working quickly, but they could not keep pace with the influx of injured. It reminded Marc of his parents' hospital after the first of the Japanese attacks.

Huang parked the tractor and ran up to one of the barefoot doctors. Although they received only one year of medical training, the barefoot doctors were usually able to cope with most of the common injuries at the commune. But the devastation of the quake had taxed their capacities. "My uncle has a broken leg," Huang said. "Where should I bring him?"

"I'm sorry," the barefoot doctor replied, "he must wait his turn." Marc walked over to where the two men were talking. The doctor eyed him nervously. Was it possible, the doctor wondered, that the old farmer had been speaking of this barbarian when he had referred to his uncle? Realizing that it would be inappropriate to have a foreigner sitting in front of the hospital, the doctor said, "Come inside quickly. We will treat you right away."

"Why are you taking the foreigner?" one of the injured peasants shouted. "I've been waiting three hours."

"Chairman Mao," the doctor stated, "said always serve foreigners first. If they are friends, they deserve special treatment; and if they are enemies, we should get them out of the way so that they don't contaminate our people."

"I'm not the patient," Marc said in Chinese. "It's Huang's uncle who is ill."

The peasants, surprised to hear a foreigner speak their language, smiled and nodded.

"I am sorry," the doctor said. "We can treat you because you are a foreign friend, but Chinese must wait their turn."

"But you do not understand!" Marc said.

"I understand only that I have hundreds of patients and almost no staff to handle them."

"This man will die!" Marc said.

"As will many of my other patients. Why should I make an exception in the case of the old farmer's uncle!"

Marc stared uncertainly at the doctor. He realized the man had no authority to change the rules, and he was unwilling to divulge Liu's identity without the proper precautions. "I'd like to talk to the director of the village," Marc insisted.

The doctor ordered one of his aides to find the director. "God damn shit-eating, long-nosed foreign devils," he muttered as he strode back to his hospital.

Marc intercepted the director of the commune and introduced himself in Chinese. "We welcome you to the Yellow Mountain People's Commune." The director's voice was coolly polite.

"Thank you," Marc replied formally, trying to size up the man. "You seem surprised to see a foreigner."

"I've met barbarians before, although your Chinese is better than most," the director said. "What country are you from?"

"The United States."

The director did not look pleased. "You are our first American visitor."

"I hope there will be more," Marc probed. Before revealing Liu's identity, he had to be certain of the director's loyalty. "The United States would like to build its friendship with the People's Republic."

"That is good," the director said. "The time has come for the People's Republic to have more foreign friends, but that cannot be the reason why you had me summoned to the hospital."

"Perhaps we could talk in private," Marc said.

"As you wish."

"You said that you wanted the People's Republic to have more foreign friends. May I assume then that you do not agree with Comrade Jiang Qing and the other leaders of the Cultural Revolution?"

"I do not mean to appear rude"—the director shifted his feet—"but we are facing monumental problems. Do you think it would be possible to discuss politics later?"

"This is quite important. Please humor me."

The director spit on the ground. "All right. I do not

particularly care for Comrade Jiang."

"Good," Marc smiled. "I'd like you to look at my friend. He is not from your commune, but he needs a doctor."

The director followed Marc to the trailer. As he stared at the unconscious body, a flickering glimmer of recognition lit up his eyes. His shoulders twitched as his gaze became riveted on Liu's face. "Your friend looks familiar."

"It is possible."

"Perhaps he is traveling in the wrong direction."

"He often loses his way."

"Yes, but he still looks like a leader of men."

Marc nodded. "Before he became unconscious, my friend asked that his presence be kept secret."

"I am sure he has good reason to do so."

"Would it be possible to say that he is a business associate of mine from Hong Kong?"

The director looked at the hordes of people waiting for medical treatment and then stared back at Liu. "Bring this man a stretcher," he called to the barefoot doctor. "He is an overseas Chinese guest. We must treat him immediately."

Marc and the cadre followed while two stretcher-bearers carried Liu into the hospital. Liu was placed on an empty table in a sparse operating room. The only electric instruments were a single floodlight dangling from the ceiling, a polygraph to test pulse, and a small oscillating machine for the acupuncture needles. Marc was neither surprised nor disturbed by the rudimentary level of medical technology. The operating room was quite similar to the one in his parents' hospital.

A barefoot doctor wrapped a tape around Liu's arm and checked his blood pressure. It was 50/10. His pulse was thudding at more than one hundred twenty beats a minute, and his hands and feet were ice-cold. The doctor elevated Liu's badly swollen leg and attached an IV tube to his arm.

After examining the leg, the doctor inspected the bruise on Liu's belly and the swelling on the left side of his abdomen. "He's in shock," the doctor said to Dr. Ma Ke, the Peking-trained surgeon who had just entered the room. "My diagnosis is a broken leg and internal bleeding."

Dr. Ma ordered the barefoot doctor to test Liu's blood type while he examined the broken ribs. He inserted a hypodermic needle into Liu's stomach. It quickly filled with blood. He ordered his nurses to prepare the patient for surgery and to get six pints of his blood type.

Marc shifted nervously. "Is it a ruptured spleen?" he asked.

Dr. Ma stared at Marc and then at the director, who nodded to indicate that Marc's presence was appropriate. "Are you a doctor?" Ma asked.

"I used to be a sort of barefoot doctor."

"Can you help prepare someone for acupuncture surgery?"

"I think so," Marc said, hoping he could remember the procedures that his father had used.

"For his sake, I hope you can."

Marc went to a sink in the corner and scrubbed his hands. A nurse helped him put on the white gown, cap, mask, and gloves required for surgery, and then escorted him back to the operating table. A barefoot doctor had already drawn three lines around Liu's rib cage and abdomen. Marc opened a bottle filled with an iodinelike liquid and painted broad swaths over the lines. Then he raised the steel frame on the operating table and draped it with a sheet so the patient would be unable to observe the operation.

While Marc was working, the nurse implanted acupuncture needles behind the right knee, between the first two toes of the left foot, under the left armpit, above the left eye, and behind the right ear. Then she attached wires from the tops of the needles to the oscillator. During the operation, the machine would vibrate slowly, enabling the needles to deaden the nerve endings. Marc tried to help the nurse, but his assistance was of minimal use. It had been many years since he had played doctor.

Dr. Ma nodded approvingly at Marc as he stepped to the table. "A little rusty perhaps, but I have seen worse."

"Is there anything I can do?" Marc asked.

"If you have Type O blood, your friend might be able to use a few more pints."

Marc was pleased to give blood. For him it was a routine procedure. When he was a boy, his father used to take his blood every two weeks to augment the supply in the hospital. Marc lay down on a table across the room and watched as the barefoot doctor inserted a needle into a vein in his arm. Then he closed his eyes and, for the first time in hours, let himself experience the exhaustion and pain that racked his body.

Marc felt a twinge as the doctor withdrew the needle. "Lie there for a while," the doctor instructed. "The loss of two pints of blood will weaken you."

Marc looked over to the operating theater. The other doctors were already cutting Liu's abdomen while a nurse was massaging his temples. Perhaps he could help. He did not want to stay on the table, haunted by his thoughts. He propped himself up on his elbows and stepped gingerly to the floor. His legs shook and he felt light-headed. Starting to swoon, he grabbed the table and braced himself.

The dizziness passed, and he walked to the operating theater. Blood was gushing from Liu's abdomen. A nurse drew as much as she could into a syringe, but she made little progress against the hemorrhaging spleen. Marc stared at Liu with great concern. "Is there anything I can do?" he asked.

"Go massage his head," Dr. Ma said without looking up from his work. Without the use of a general anesthetic, massaging was necessary to augment the acupuncture.

Marc went to the head of the operating table and stepped in for the nurse. As he rubbed Liu's temples, he watched the general's mouth and eyebrows. Although Liu was unconscious, his facial muscles moved as the doctor continued to operate, indicating that he was feeling something. The doctor sank the scalpel deep into Liu's stomach. The old general's mouth jerked open. The straining muscles in his neck became clearly delineated against his leathery skin. "You'll be all right," Marc said hopefully as he massaged harder to relieve the pain.

The nurse kept removing the blood, but the hypodermic needles were no longer filled. Dr. Ma clamped the last of the blood vessels leading to the spleen. A nurse mopped Ma's forehead with a washcloth while he removed the ruptured spleen and placed it in a white metal bowl. Then, after the blood had been sponged from Liu's abdomen, Dr. Ma stitched up the wound.

Marc continued to massage Liu's temples as he watched Ma closing the cavity. He looked back at the general. Liu opened his eyes and smiled. "He's awake," Marc pronounced.

A nurse went to the back of the room and returned with a plate of sliced fruit. "Would you like an apple?" she asked.

Liu nodded. She cut a small piece with a knife, stabbed it with a chopstick, and placed it in Liu's mouth. The general chewed the fruit while the surgeon continued to stitch his stomach. Marc stopped his massaging and stared in amazement at his old friend. "Come on, my foreign barefoot assistant," Dr. Ma said. "Keep rubbing until I finish sewing."

"How's my long-nosed friend doing?" Liu asked.

"Not too bad," the doctor replied. "If you'd leave him here

for a few months, I could make a first-rate medical technician out of him."

"Sorry," Liu replied. "He was supposed to be in Peking yesterday. I have no idea why he's here playing doctor to an old man like me when he should be delivering messages."

A tear formed in Marc's eye as he rubbed Liu's temples. "Tell me, old friend, how do you suggest I get to Peking?"

Liu crinkled his eyes as he winced in pain. He took a deep breath and then looked back at Marc. "What kind of a question is that for you to ask? It's less than one hundred miles, hardly a distance of concern for the blue-eyed spirit who runs like the wind."

33: The Army of Stone

XIAN

Twenty miles to the east of Xian, the car in which Alexandra Koo and Lord Henry Gateshead were riding entered a long, flat valley ringed by rugged mountains. At the far end of the valley, standing strangely alone in the midst of thousands of acres of neatly cultivated cornfields, was a circular hill with groves of pomegranate trees covering its surface. The hill bore no organic connection to its surroundings. More than 6 miles in circumference and yet only one hundred and twenty feet high, it looked from a distance like an imitation mountain in a toy-store display of electric trains. Lord Gateshead was not surprised by its appearance. He knew that the hill had been constructed two thousand years ago to cover the massive tomb of Qin Shi Huangdi, the first emperor of China.

In establishing the first Chinese Empire, Shi Huangdi initiated sweeping changes that made his dynasty a turning point in history. He replaced the feudal slave-owning system with a centralized government, standardized weights and measures, codified laws; and created a uniform system of writing characters. He also constructed a vast network of roads, completed the Great Wall, built the longest inland waterways in the ancient world, and developed systems of irrigation still in use. With the possible exception of Chairman Mao, he was the most significant figure in the history of China.

But it was the emperor's death rather than his life that fascinated Lord Gateshead. Craving immortality, Shi Huangdi had constructed a tomb the size of a small city, reputed to be the most spectacular memorial ever built. More than seven hundred thousand workers had labored for thirty years on the shrine, which had a perimeter of almost four miles. Inside the burial chamber, the emperor had re-created the entire Chinese Empire. There were replicas of cities, miniature mountains, flowing rivers made of quick-silver, heavenly constellations with pearls representing the stars, and a sun filled with whale oil that would burn forever.

To defend the tomb, craftsmen had sculpted seventy-five hundred life-size stone replicas of the emperor's palace guards with their chariots and horses. These sculptures were armed with real weapons and buried in perfect battle formation in three large pits in front of the tumulus. From a distance they looked like the most powerful army China had ever seen, but the soldiers of stone proved to be inept defenders against ememies of flesh. The roofs of the pit, raised eight feet above the ground, formed a path that led the attackers to the tumulus. Less than a decade after the emperor's death, the tomb was ransacked by marauders.

Lord Gateshead hoped some of the relics were still buried under the massive mountain. But even if the mausoleum had been desecrated, the discovery of the soldiers was sufficient to make the Qin Tomb one of the greatest archaeological finds in history. Since he had first read of these statues three years before, he had been captivated by the thought of seeing this army of stone. He wanted to purchase at least twenty figures so that he could house them in battle formation in their own wing of the museum.

A representative of the Cultural Relics Administration Bureau greeted Alexandra and Lord Gateshead in front of a small gray guardhouse. After handing them aprons and sleeve guards to protect their clothing, he led them down a path toward the three pits containing the army of stone. Alexandra and the representative chatted with each other, but Lord Gateshead had no interest in talking. His thoughts were riveted on the six-hundred-foot-long, ten-foot-wide, and fifteen-foot-deep yawning chasm of Pit #1 just in front of him. It was in this pit that six thousand of the figures were buried.

Gateshead steadied himself against the dirt walls as he climbed down to the first of the pit's eleven parallel trenches. Stopping, he stared silently at the sight in front of him. There, like the warriors in the Greek myth of Jason and the Argonauts who had sprung from dragon's teeth sown in the earth, was a forest of two hundred torsos growing out of the ground.

Gateshead felt his pulse quicken as he watched teams of Chinese workers scraping dirt caked for millennia off newly excavated figures. Although many of the weapons had been stolen, the army was still intact. Standing at attention in straight rows or kneeling to fire their bows and arrows, the soldiers seemed as ready for battle as they had when they were buried, two thousand years ago. Gateshead stared at the statues thrust out of the ground and tried to imagine that he was an ancient general preparing for war.

Stepping into the pit, he gazed admiringly at the impressive beauty of the individual sculptures. Each was a unique human figure with individualized facial structures, hairstyle, clothing, and expression. He wanted to reach out and touch the statues. Awed by the magnitude of what was in front of him, he found it difficult to maintain his proper British reserve.

"Is it as you expected?" Alexandra asked.

"It is more spectacular than I could have imagined."

"If you are interested, I can arrange for you to acquire some of these figures."

"I am more than interested," Gateshead replied. "My only regret is that the tomb itself was ransacked. If the emperor constructed all these statues to defend it, its contents must have been beyond compare."

"What makes you believe that the riches of the empire were destroyed?" Alexandra asked as she led Lord Gateshead away from the representative of the Cultural Relics Administration bureau.

"I've read the reports of the ancient historians."

Alexandra's eyes gleamed as she stared at the Englishman. "Perhaps Shi Huangdi purposely tried to mislead the historians."

"I am afraid that I am missing your point."

"The Qin emperor was a military genius, but he was also a very suspicious man who was terrified of dying. Didn't he send his navies throughout the world to find a magic elixir that would guarantee his immortality? And didn't he build secret passageways throughout his palaces so that none of his subjects could have the opportunity to kill him?"

"So I have heard."

"Does it seem to you that a man who was so cautious with his life would be so careless with his spirit? Do you think that the man who conquered all of China in less than two decades would have trusted stone soldiers to defend his soul?"

Gateshead stared quizzically at Alexandra. "Are you suggesting that the tomb was built as a ruse to fool the emperor's enemies?"

"The thought is deliciously perverse, isn't it?" Alexandra smiled wryly as she fingered the jade pendant around her neck.

Lord Gateshead rubbed his chin. "I find it difficult to believe that there really is a second tomb. I have reviewed every report from the Cultural Relics Administration Bureau and I have never seen any reference to the excavation."

"Perhaps the Cultural Relics Administration Bureau has not yet been informed of the discovery."

"How could that be?"

Alexandra ran her jade-ringed fingers through her long black hair. "It is possible that someone prefers to keep the excavation a secret."

"I find that highly irregular."

"Come now, Lord Gateshead, shall we stop pretending to be so naïve."

"Naïve?" Gateshead arched his bushy eyebrows. "You are asking me to believe that you have discovered what could potentially be the greatest archaeological find in history, and that you and your people have been able to keep the news of this discovery from every archaeologist in the world." -

"That's correct."

"Would you not agree that I am entitled to be skeptical?"

"Was your great-grandfather skeptical when he bought the relics stolen from the Summer Palace?"

"That was more than one hundred years ago."

"And last week when you bought the relics from the Han Tomb without any thought for the Cultural Relics Administration Bureau, where was your British skepticism then?"

Gateshead stared uneasily at Alexandra. "That was different. The existence of those relics was public knowledge. You merely helped me with a financial transaction."

Alexandra put on her sunglasses. "It appears I'm wasting both my time and yours. If you'll excuse me . . ." She turned abruptly and started to climb out of the pit.

Lord Gateshead shifted nervously as he watched her walk away. He was disturbed by the implications of her alleged discovery. Although his ancestors had acquired relics by illegal means, he questioned whether he could do the same in the middle of the twentieth century. He knew that Alexandra was aligned with Jiang Qing. But no matter who was involved, any acquisitions from this newly discovered tomb would be closely scrutinized not only by museum directors throughout the world but also by political leaders in England. If the People's Republic protested his actions, he could be humiliated and forced to give up his position. On the other hand, if the relics were as Mrs. Koo had represented, they could be the most spectacular archaeological finds ever uncovered. They could help him to achieve a success that would rival that of any of his ancestors.

Lord Gateshead studied the army of sculptures. They stared patiently back at him with the same stony expressions that they had maintained for the past two thousand years. He looked at Mrs. Koo standing on the ridge. The opportunities she offered were too great for him to decline without further investigation. There was no reason for him to make a decision at this juncture. He would let her take him to the site of the tomb. Once he saw the relics, he would know what to do.

34: On the Road Again

Two days had passed since Liu Teyu's operation. Marc Slater had decided to wait until he was certain that Liu was recuperating—not just because Liu was a friend, but also because, with the possibility of Deng's death, Liu's strong presence was essential. Fortunately the old general had made an excellent recovery. Almost from the time he regained consciousness, Liu had talked of nothing but his plans for stopping Jiang and the Russians. But his broken ribs and low white blood count forced him to remain in bed for another week, so Marc agreed to return to Peking and take messages to the general's key aides and to Hua Guofeng.

After eating breakfast, Marc rode out of the commune on a used bicycle he had purchased the night before. There had been no spare automobiles, but even if one had been available, Marc still would have selected the bike. The two-wheeled vehicle gave him the flexibility to traverse roads that might be impassable for a car, and also to avoid government checkpoints that might prove troublesome. His visa authorized only a two-day visit to Tangshan, and he was worried that an ambitious soldier might arrest him because he was over the time limit and outside of the city limits.

Marc turned north along the access road for a new railway line. Not only did the route keep him away from most of the traffic, it was also forty miles shorter than the main highway through Tianjin. As he rode through several small villages, workers stared at him in surprise. The last thing they expected to see after the earthquake was a long-nosed barbarian riding a bicycle.

Marc stopped for water at a well and ate a piece of chicken that had been prepared at the commune. A pungent aroma wafted from the road. Marc crimped his nose as he recognized the distinct odor of a "honey wagon." Because China had a severe shortage of chemical fertilizers, workers were assigned the task of collecting all human and animal wastes. In a country of almost one billion hungry people, anything that could help grow crops was essential. The man pulling the cart stopped next to a pile of horse manure. He took out a small tin shovel, scraped the manure off the road, and dropped it into a wicker basket on his cart. Marc remembered that as a boy, he had often collected the waste in his parents' hospital. He wrapped his chicken and put it in his basket. He had suddenly lost his appetite.

Marc made slower progress than he had hoped. The heavily damaged roads forced him to make numerous detours, and by early evening he had only reached the village of Bright Cloud. His stomach growled as he searched for a restaurant. The only one in town was a ramshackle storefront imposingly named the Defend Mao Tse-tung Eatery. As he approached the entrance, he saw a large man in a white apron shaking a poor peasant while a crowd of bystanders shouted insults at both combatants. When the people saw Marc, they immediately became silent. The man in the apron released the peasant. "What's going on?" Marc asked a worker.

"This beggar tried to sneak out of my restaurant without paying," the man in the apron answered.

"But I didn't eat anything," the peasant protested to Marc.

"He sat in my restaurant for almost two hours drinking my water and flavoring his bread with the fragrance from my kitchen. The village cadre is placing pressure on me to reduce my expenses. Do you think it is fair for him to come into my restaurant and steal the smell of my food?"

"There's no fee on your menu for smelling food. Why should I pay you?"

Marc felt embarrassed as he noticed the villagers staring at him. They had decided that he should be the judge. "Do you have any money?" he asked the peasant.

"Only a few fen."

"Give them to me," Marc said. The manager smiled, suspecting that Marc would see his point of view. Marc took the coins in his hand and shook them next to the manager's ear. "Do you hear the sound?"

"Of course," the manager replied as he prepared to collect his money.

Marc handed the coins back to the peasant.

"What are you doing?" the manager shouted.

"I'm just trying to be fair," Marc replied.

"Fair? What sort of a trick are you playing?"

"It's no trick. He smelled the aroma of your food but didn't eat any. Now you have heard the sound of his money but didn't get any. It seems like an equal exchange."

The man in the apron scowled at Marc and then started to laugh. "You have fooled me after all!"

"How's that?" Marc asked.

"I assumed that since you were a long-nosed barbarian,

you would give me a proper capitalist answer. But that jingling of the coins is from an old Kazak folktale."

"I didn't intend to fool you—only to settle the dispute," Marc smiled. "To make amends, why don't I treat everyone here to dinner?"

"How will I explain all the extra money to the village cadre?" the manager joked.

"Tell him a busload of barbarians came from Tangshan to smell your food."

"All right, foreign devil." The manager bowed and held open the door. "Tonight, you can smell whatever you want for free. But anything that goes in your mouth—*aiya*, that will cost you."

Linda Forbes walked to a table in the center of the massive Imperial Palace courtyard. Taking a seat, she gazed blankly at the setting sun shimmering off the red walls of the Forbidden City. The one-hundred-mile trip from Tangshan had taken two days. Although the truck had brought them to Tianjin, where Sen had been able to obtain a car, driving on the earthquake-damaged roads had been almost impossible. They had been forced to take detours through fields and wait for hours as the vast convoys carrying relief supplies received priority. They had slept in rice paddies and had eaten almost nothing since the quake. Upon reaching Peking, Sen had gone to see Kang Moruo, but she had been too exhausted to join him. Her head ached and the muscles in her body felt limp. All she wanted to do was sit quietly and eat her dinner.

Linda distractedly ordered four dishes. Her mind was bombarded by images of the crises facing China. What had happened to her grandfather and Marc? Where was Alexandra Koo, and what could be done to stop the forgery of Mao's will? She poured herself a glass of beer, drained it in one gulp, and poured another. She needed to force herself to concentrate on something more trivial than the future of China.

Watching the waiters light the candles, Linda eaves-dropped on the conversations around her. To her right, four English tourists talked about their struggles in the earth-quake. Although none had been injured, they treated the episode as a great adventure, the kind that would become continually more heroic as they recounted it to their children in years to come. It was, Linda sadly reflected, an experience she would never be permitted to share. Her work for the Bureau demanded complete secrecy.

Four Japanese who worked for the Takamura Corpora-tion took the table to her left. As they started to eat, Frans Van Wyck hobbled up on his crutches. He conversed with Yamaguchi, the tallest of the Japanese, and handed him an envelope. As Linda watched, Sen Tailing sat down next to her. "Do you know that man?" Sen asked, pointing to Van Wyck.

"I've seen him before, but I don't know who he is. Why?"

"Just curious," Sen replied. He knew that Takamura might offer the only link to the Russian commandos, but he had not been authorized to divulge the information to Linda.

"Did you find out anything from Kang?" Linda asked.

"He's spent the last three days touring the earthquake site with Hua Guofeng. Reconstruction has already started, but there is an incredible amount to accomplish. They think the death toll could reach eight hundred thousand, half in Tangshan alone."

"That's awful," Linda said. She tried to grasp the magnitude of the numbers, but all she could see was the dead boy in Tangshan being gnawed by the rat. "What about our friends?"

"I will give you the easiest first." Sen sipped his beer. "Beatrice and Sam are safe. They are here in the Imperial Palace. Deng also survived the quake, but he is still stranded near Tangshan."

"What about my grandfather and Marc?"

"No word."

"Damn!" Linda pounded her fist on the table. "It will be tough trying to do anything without their help."

"I know," Sen replied. "Liu's southern armies are especially critical. They are our only real counterweight to Jiang's Red Guards."

"What can we do if they're—" The word caught in Linda's throat.

"Don't worry." Sen tried to sound hopeful. "They'll be all right. They're both fighters."

"You're a good man, Tailing." Linda touched Sen's hand. "Have you heard anything about Little Chang?"

Sen shook his head. "It looks like we are both missing members of our families."

"What about Alexandra Koo and the relics?" Linda asked.

"The day of the quake, Mrs. Koo went to Xian with Lord Henry Gateshead, the director of the English Museum."

"She must be trying to sell him some of the relics from the Qin Tomb."

"That was Kang's assumption as well," Sen replied.

Linda pulled on the ends of her hair. "Everything about this mission feels like it's slipping away."

"Don't be discouraged," Sen responded. "Here we may be in luck. Kang Moruo's brother, Kang Momin, is the governor of Shaanxi Province. He has had his son, Xiaoma, following Mrs. Koo for the last three days. Xiaoma was able to track their path to a cave in the mountains where Mrs. Koo is storing the relics she plans to smuggle out of the

421

country. Xiaoma is not sure he can stop her, but at least it's a first step."

"That's terrific," Linda smiled. Despite her exhaustion, she could feel the adrenaline starting to flow. "When can I go there?"

"You have been through a harrowing ordeal. Don't you want a day to rest?"

"Not when Alexandra's in Xian. I'd leave tonight if I could."

Sen laughed. "How did you get to be so headstrong?"

"I get it from my Chinese grandfather," Linda smiled. "So when do I leave for Xian?"

"Kang is making the arrangements. He has to go with Hua to Tianjin in the morning. He'll contact us when he returns. With luck, we'll have you on a plane the day after tomorrow."

It was late afternoon on the next day by the time Marc Slater reached Tong Xian, a small city on the outskirts of Peking. The day was hot and very dusty. Marc had been riding since sunrise. Now his legs ached and his mouth felt as if a family of raccoons had been nesting on his tongue. He stopped his bike in front of a small restaurant and ordered a beer. The bottle was warm, but the brew was still refreshing.

Ordering another bottle, Marc stepped out to the street and watched as teams of workers demolished a block of badly damaged houses. He crossed into a park. A cluster of people stood in front of a long glass case. Inside was that day's edition of the *People's Daily* neatly tacked on a bulletin board. He edged forward and began to read the paper. All the news related to the earthquake, and Jiang Qing's name appeared in every headline, as if she were the only person concerned with reconstruction. In the center of the front page was a letter from Mao commending the work of Jiang and the other members of the Gang of Four. Marc drummed his fingers against his leg. It was not difficult to guess who had been the letter's real author. He scanned the page for a reference to Hua Guofeng, but the premier was not even mentioned.

Marc stepped in front of the second page. His body became rigid. The muscles around his heart constricted. He gasped as he read the headline: GENERAL LIU TEYU KILLED IN QUAKE. Wedging his way to the front of the crowd, he intently read the rest of the article. The paper reported that Liu had been killed while visiting the Kailuan Mines. The information could only have come from Wong and the others who had tried to kill them.

Marc started to laugh. Others stared at him. He covered his mouth. The news was perfect—it played right into his hands. As long as Jiang Qing and her people thought Liu was dead, the old general would have a chance to secretly plan his revenge. Marc might even use the news story to his advantage by convincing Hua that Jiang had tried to assassinate Liu. Whatever happened, he would have to act quickly. Liu's presumed death would set off a power struggle. The longer Liu waited to reappear, the greater the risk that someone else might seize control of his armies.

Marc's eyes scanned the biographical data on Liu as he read to the bottom of the article. There in the last three lines was a group of characters he readily recognized. "Marc Slater, an American capitalist, was also killed in the Kailuan Mines." Marc shivered in the ninety-degree heat as he read on. "Slater, born in China, was once an old friend of the People's Republic. During the years in Yan'an, he and his parents operated a hospital that served the people. But since fleeing China, Slater had become a wealthy capitalist who was trying to exploit this country's natural resources."

"That bitch!" Marc said as he reread Jiang Qing's handiwork. After all he had done for China, he deserved a better eulogy. He had seen many stories about his life, but this was the first time he had seen a notice of his own death. It was an eerie feeling that made his skin crawl. He wanted to rip the article off the board and tell the people standing beside him that he was alive. But it would be futile. Tens of millions of people had already read that he was a corpse.

He turned away from the paper and walked into the park. The news of his death was a reality, one that could work to his benefit, yet one that could have very serious consequences. It would only add to his case against Jiang Qing. His presence in Peking the next morning could shock Hua and the others into believing that Jiang had planned the attempted assassinations. But he also had to deal with the repercussions when the information was reported in the United States. Jill and David would be grief-stricken. His company would be in turmoil. Its stock price would plunge and the board of directors would have to find someone to replace him. Finally, those who had sent him to China would be distressed by the failure of their mission. Marc was willing to let the price of his stock decline and leave the White House in a state of uncertainty, but he did not want his children to suffer under the mistaken assumption that they were now orphans. By the time he reached Peking, he would have to decide whether he could accept the consequences of remaining a corpse.

Linda Forbes sat quietly in a corner of the passenger terminal, waiting for the morning flight to Xian. The news of the deaths of her grandfather and Marc Slater had left her despondent. It was almost as if her past and her future had died simultaneously. She had spent the last eight years preparing for this mission so she could help her grandfather. She had come close to seeing him in Tangshan. But now he was dead. She felt as if she had been robbed of her own heritage. Marc had no link with her past, but he figured prominently in her plans for the future. She had met him only a few times, but from the first night in Hong Kong, she had known he was the man for her. Yet now he, too, had been snatched away from her.

Sen and the Tangs had been very supportive. They had said that the obituary was a propaganda trick and that Liu and Marc were still alive. But she knew they were just trying to buoy her spirits. Every newspaper in the country had reported the deaths. They would not have made such announcements without irrefutable evidence.

Beatrice had suggested that she let someone else handle her mission so she could have time to deal with her grief. But Linda did not want to dwell on her loss. She preferred to lose herself in her work. It would help her to forget. Both Liu and Marc would have wanted her to continue. They had given their lives for the People's Republic. She was unwilling to see everything they had worked for destroyed by Jiang Qing.

Linda looked around the terminal. A Chinese Turk and a neatly dressed European on crutches were standing at the ticket counter. The European was the same man that Sen had asked about two nights before in the Forbidden City. Linda picked up her travel bag and walked to the counter.

"Comrade Rahman, you are booked on flight 21 to Lanzhou, flight 1409 to Urumqi, and flight 1802 to Kashi," the airline clerk said as he handed him his tickets. Then he looked at the European. "Can I help you?"

"I'm just here to see off my associate," the man replied.

Linda stepped to the counter. "Is the flight to Xian still on time?" she asked, trying to eavesdrop on the conversation behind her.

She did not hear the clerk's answer. All she heard was the Turk saying, "We'll contact you after we set up everything for the Altay Mountains and Dzungarian Basin projects."

"Fine," the man with the crutches replied, "but don't forget you're supposed to be planning the construction of hotels in Urumqi and Kashi."

The Turk laughed. "By the time I'm finished, the cadres in Xinjiang won't be able to tell me from the American Conrad Hilton."

"You have learned your capitalism well, my friend," the man with the crutches laughed.

The conversation was meaningless to Linda, but she was certain that Sen would be able to decipher the plans. She waited for the men to leave. Then she hurried back to the waiting room and transcribed what she remembered of the discussion. After sealing the envelope, she found one of Kang's aides and instructed him to take the letter to Sen. For the first time in days, she felt useful. She hoped that Liu and Marc would have been proud of her.

35: The Treasure of Black Horse Hill

NEAR XIAN

Linda Forbes dabbed the sweat off of the nape of her neck as she strolled along the path surrounding the lake at the Huaqing Hot Springs. She looked at Black Horse Hill, searching for a sign of Kang Xiaoma, the nephew of Kang Moruo. For the past four days, Xiaoma had followed Alexandra Koo and Lord Gateshead from the hot springs, up Black Horse Hill, and then down to the cave on the far side of the mountain. Linda impatiently checked her watch. She was anxious to see what Alexandra had discovered in the cave. She clasped the walkie-talkie in her purse. "Where are you, Xiaoma?" she whispered with annoyance. This was her operation. She wanted to be on the mountain helping instead of standing impotently beside the ancient imperial springs.

Passing a circular gazebo with a green tiled roof, Linda approached a large pavilion filled with people drinking tea and beer. Huaqing had first been opened to the average worker after the Liberation, but its 109 degree therapeutic mineral waters had been a favorite of the imperial families for more than three thousand years. Emperors whose dynasties had been centered in Xian had built palaces and gardens around the springs. Although the palaces had been destroyed, the new buildings had been designed with the same imperial decor. The ornately painted red walls, the curving dragon-backed roofs, and the marble boat attached to one of the pavilions made the hot springs look much like a miniature version of Peking's Summer Palace.

Taking a seat by the lake, Linda stared at the reflections of rose bushes and weeping willows on the surface of the murky green water. She wished that Marc were there to experience the beauty with her. She still could not believe that he was dead. Forcing her mind away from Marc, she ordered a cup of tea and stared at the intricate sculptures of the marble boat. Her walkie-talkie started to beep. She signaled Xiaoma and received instructions. After checking to see that no one was following, she walked through a moon gate and past a lotus pond where a boy was trying to catch frogs with a fishing rod. Just past the pond, she found a path lined with evergreens and cypress that led to the top of Black Horse Hill.

Xiaoma was standing next to a monument built into the rocks. He was tall for a Chinese and elegantly slim. His straight black hair was fashionably long and, like all members of the Kang family, his blue worker's uniform was hand-tailored and made of expensive fabric. "Welcome to the Capture Chiang Pavilion," he announced as Linda approached.

"Are you my tour guide?" she asked.

"I am indeed," Xiaoma replied in the code to which they had agreed. "It is an honor to be able to show you the site where the traitor Chiang Kai-shek was captured by his own troops."

As Linda paced up the hill, she thought about the truly extraordinary event that had occurred here forty years before. The troops of Chiang Kai-shek's Northeast Armies, furious that Chiang was fighting the Communists instead of the Japanese, mutinied and arrested Chiang in the middle of teh night. They held the Generalissimo captive for several weeks until he agreed to join with the Communists in a united front. Although the front remained a shaky alliance, it strengthened the Chinese war effort and gave the Communists much-needed credibility.

Linda's legs ached as she stopped at the peak of Black Horse Hill and gazed down into a long open valley on the far side of the mountain. In the center of flowing fields of grain stood the tumulus of Shi Huangdi.

The path down the far side of the mountain was steeper and far less traveled than the one they had ascended. Xiaoma climbed over two stone walls as he worked his way down the intricately terraced fields. A man stepped out from the mouth of a cave. He was old and thin, with a long scraggly beard and sandals on his feet. Xiaoma exchanged some words with the man and then introduced him to Linda. "This is Hong Dun, but you can call him Goat. He is our spelunker."

Linda nodded politely. Goat laughed and winked at her. He handed her a flashlight and then hurried into a darkened cave. She tried to keep pace as he crawled through narrow passageways with the dexterity of a ballet dancer. He had spent most of his sixty-five years in these caves and he traversed them as easily as she could cover the hallways of her apartment.

For fifteen minutes they walked through a maze of connecting tunnels. Suddenly Goat stopped. Linda shut off her flashlight and tiptoed to where he was standing. A ray of light was coming from a vast cavity hollowed out of the mountain. She followed the others as they crept closer. Large wooden crates covered with magnificent pieces of pottery, bronze, and ivory filled the cavity. She took another step and emitted a slight gasp. In the center of the cave, guarding a casket, were the four largest bronze figures she had ever seen. Each was at least twenty feet high and more than four feet wide. They could be nothing but the bronzes of Shi Huangdi. According to legend, the emperor had melted the weapons of his enemies to cast eleven of these massive statues, each of which was said to weigh more than 260,000 pounds. None had ever before been unearthed.

Alexandra Koo and Lord Gateshead stepped between two of the giant figures. Dwarfed by the statues and tinted green from the hue of the bronze, they looked like actors in a bizarre science-fiction movie. Goat waited until two of Koo's assistants began to lug a crate across the dirt floor. Then he scampered up to a ledge overlooking the cave. Linda steadied her breath as she crawled next to him. In front of her was the most spectacular collection of ancient relics that she had ever seen. She pounded her fist silently into the ground and smiled. This was the chance she had been waiting for. Now she finally could stop Alexandra.

"All right," Alexandra said, "let's get on to the bronzes."

"That's acceptable to me. We've covered everything else," Lord Gateshead said as he inspected one of the figures towering above him. In the last three days, he had agreed to spend more than thirty million dollars for a collection of relics from the cave.

"The price for one bronze statue is three million."

"Three million!" Lord Gateshead responded. "That's

outrageous! I think a million would be far more appropriate."

"For the largest bronze statue ever uncovered?"

"There are ten other copies."

"Shall we stop playing games, Lord Gateshead? You know as well as I that the piece is worth at least ten million."

"You may be correct, but you must realize that there has to be a discount for, shall we say, tainted goods."

"There is nothing tainted about these figures."

"Then give me official certification from the government."

"Right now it would be quite difficult"—Alexandra glared at Gateshead—"but as soon as my people gain control, we can provide it to you."

"In that case," Lord Gateshead said, lifting an emerald-studded ivory goblet, "perhaps it would be better if I returned after your people have done whatever you plan to do."

"But I thought you wanted to buy the relics now."

"And I thought you wanted to sell them."

"Then we should be able to reach an agreement."

"We should. But you fail to understand that your time pressures are more severe than mine. I can return next year, but I suspect that you have to have the money now."

"I'm in no great rush."

"Excellent! Why don't we wait six months. Then I can open a bank account in China and pay you directly. It will save us the trouble of sending the money to Switzerland."

"Switzerland is no trouble. They transmit the funds immediately to our account in the Bank of China."

"Excuse me, Mrs. Koo. I am committed to spending fifty million dollars, but I refuse to be put on the rack for each negotiation. Your people need my money to help you take control of the government. If you win, the relics are inconsequential. If you lose, they are useless. I know you

Orientals pride yourself on patience, but I also know that you have to dispose of these relics before Mao dies. I can wait, but you cannot. So you decide. You can sell me two statues at one million each or we can forget the entire arrangement."

Alexandra walked to the far end of the cave. She was not pleased by Gateshead's newfound aggressiveness. "All right, you can have two for one million each." She affixed a yellow tag that read "English Museum" to two of the statues. "But I promise you that after we take control, you'll find it much tougher to negotiate with me."

"By the time you take control, Mrs. Koo, I will have spent all of my money, so I am not particularly worried."

Linda watched as Koo and Gateshead completed their negotiations and made arrangements for the delivery of the relics. All the purchases were to be moved within the week. That left her little time to implement her plan. She intended to substitute newly made copies for the ancient relics. With luck, Koo would leave Xian convinced that everything was satisfactory. Only when the goods reached Hong Kong would the fraud be discovered. By then, so many people would have handled the relics that it would be impossible to identify where the switch had occurred.

Koo and Gateshead walked to the mouth of the cave and took one final look at the relics. As soon as they had gone, Goat climbed off the ledge and crept toward the bronze statues. Two soldiers were guarding the front of the cave, but none was inside or at the back entrance, most probably because only Goat knew of its existence. While Goat positioned himself in front of the door, Linda and Xiaoma located the relics with the yellow tags. Xiaoma wrote descriptions of each piece in a notebook, after which Linda took photographs with her Polaroid camera. Goat stared in disbelief as he watched the pictures develop.

There was a noise outside the cave. A beam of light shone through the entrance. Goat climbed into a crevice in the wall, but Linda stood frozen. Footsteps came toward her. She heard voices. Someone tugged on her arm. She turned slowly. Her feet seemed glued to the floor. Xiaoma pulled her to the ground. She pressed her body against the casket of Shi Huangdi, experiencing a strange mixture of fear and excitement.

The guards entered the cave and shone their lights off the walls. "Everything all right in here?" one called out.

There was silence. "Who did you think would answer?" the other asked. "One of those bronzes?"

"I know it's strange, but I keep expecting Shi Huangdi to respond."

"He's been dead for two thousand years."

"So they say. But I look at the stone statues from the pits and then I come in here and see all his personal possessions and I half-expect to see the top of the casket open and the emperor step out."

"You're talking like a fool."

"I'm not the only one. Little Stalin and Red Dawn both claim they've heard the emperor's ghost."

"They must be teasing you. There's nothing here. I'll show you," the other guard said, walking toward the casket.

Linda trembled as she felt the guard approach. Another two steps and he would see her. She had to do something. With all her strength, she pushed against the casket. The box creaked as it shifted on the dirt floor. The guard stopped. Linda pushed the casket again. "Is someone there?" The guard's voice cracked as he drew his gun.

"I am the spirit of Shi Huangdi!" Goat's booming voice echoed off the roof of the cave. Linda almost burst

433

out laughing.

The two guards nervously shone their flashlights in search of the elusive voice. "What do you want of us?" one asked.

"Leave me in peace," the voice ordered.

"You can't be Shi Huangdi!" the guard challenged.

"If you are sure, stand there and watch as I turn your friend to stone." The guard fired three shots toward the sound of the voice. "You can't shoot me!" the voice blared, "I am a disembodied spirit."

The two men shook with fear as they scanned the walls and the ceiling. "Let's get some help," the first guard suggested.

"Who would believe us?" the other replied.

"I'm getting tired of waiting," the voice called. "Perhaps I'll have to turn *both* of you to stone." Linda pushed the casket. "I'm coming out now!" the voice called.

The two men turned and fled from the cave. Goat crawled out of his hiding place near the ceiling, smiling with satisfaction. "It sounds like you've tried that before," Xiaoma said.

"I like my privacy," Goat replied.

"Do you think they'll tell anyone?" Linda asked.

"I hope so," Goat said. "Our work will be much easier if people believe the cave is haunted."

36: The War in Xinjiang

Flight 21 flew west-southwest from Peking, crisscrossing the wandering path of China's Great Wall. Twenty thousand feet below were the yellow loess plateaus of Shaanxi, Ningsha, and Gansu. To the north were the barren steppes of the Gobi Desert where endless miles of colorless flat gravel created the monotony that had terrified travelers for centuries. The Yellow River bent north into the Ordos Loop and then extended southward toward Lanzhou, the industrial and commercial hub of northwest China. Beyond Lanzhou lay the vast regions of Xinjiang, Tibet, and Qinghai which occupied forty percent of China's land area but contained less than two percent of its people.

Aziz Rahman gazed out the window at the oil refineries, chemical factories, and aluminum smelters of Lanzhou. In order to build the economy of interior China and dominate the local minority groups, the People's Republic had stocked the city with hundreds of thousands of Han Chinese. The Hans now controlled most of the important economic and political posts. With the steadily increasing pace of resettlement, they would comprise a majority within the next decade.

In Lanzhou, Rahman boarded a small Russian-built jet for the eleven-hundred-mile flight to Urumqi, the capital of the Xinjiang Uygur Autonomous Region. Heading northwest, the plane passed over the territory of the eastern Tibetans and the Koshot Mongolians and entered Xinjiang, the vast, undeveloped land of the Turkish-speaking, Islam-worshiping Uygur, Kazak, and Kirgiz tribes. Composed of rugged mountains and unending deserts, Xinjiang was harsh and inhospitable. With less than four inches of rain a year, little of the land was arable. Rivers that flowed from the mountains dried up as they reached the arid steppes. It was a land of desolation. Yet it was one with a fabled past and a strategic future.

The Silk Road had run the length of Xingiang. For centuries, traders from the West had traveled through the province to buy silks, teas, and spices in China. With the advent of modern transportation, the importance of the Silk Road declined. Xinjiang drifted into the political and economic backwater, ignored by both Russia and China, its powerful neighbors.

The nomads of Xinjiang were not distressed at being relegated to such an inconsequential position. Too distant to be controlled by any government, they roamed easily over the vast steppes of East Turkestan, herding livestock and growing food in the narrow green belts, much as their ancestors had done. They showed allegiance to no nation and thought of themselves only as Turks.

The political split between China and Russia in 1962 wrenched Xinjiang unwillingly into the twentieth century. Its eighteen-hundred-mile border with the Soviet Union, large oil deposits, and ample land for growing grain along its western edge made the province strategically critical. Peking needed the oil and grain and wanted to keep the Russians on the other side of the Himalayas. It could not let Xinjiang slip away. To secure its position, it expanded its military forces, resettled Han workers, and invested large sums building new factories.

The increasing encroachment of the Hans greatly distressed Rahman. He was a Kirgiz Turk who had always dreamed that the Turkic tribes on both sides of the border would unite to form the Republic of East Turkestan. For a while it had seemed that the Chinese would grant them some form of independence, but time was running out. Now his people had to act. The only way to obtain their liberation was, as Chairman Mao would say, through the barrel of a gun.

Rahman and his people had chosen to align themselves with the Soviet Union. He did not particularly trust the Russians, but they were united in their dislike of the Chinese. The Soviets supported the Vietnamese, the Indians, and anyone else who could threaten China. They had helped the Mongolians establish their own independent homeland. There was no reason why they could not do the same for the Uygurs, Kazaks, and Kirgiz.

The Russians had been building their influence with the Turks for most of the century. During World War II, Xinjiang had functioned virtually as a Soviet protectorate. Afterward, one hundred and twenty thousand Turks secretly received Russian citizenship. When the rift between the People's Republic and the Soviet Union broke into the open, the Russians provided a base for Turkic nationalists. More than sixty thousand, including Rahman's family, migrated across the border and formed the Alliance for the Liberation of East Turkestan. The Russians assisted the alliance with money, equipment, and technical support. Rahman was trained as an agent by the KGB and sent back into Xinjiang to help organize revolutionary cells. Now, after ten years of preparation, his people were ready to act. With the instability in Peking, they finally had a chance to overthrow the yoke of Chinese imperialism.

As the plane landed in Urumqi, Rahman stared with a feeling of disgust at the city in which he had grown up. Urumqi had once been an attractive Turkic trading center of eighty thousand people; now it was an ugly Chinese industrial metropolis of more than one million. Blast furnaces, coal-processing plants, fertilizer factories, and sterile East European-style government offices had overwhelmed whatever charm had once existed. Rahman was pleased that he was only stopping to change planes.

The small piston-driven plane took almost three hours to fly from Urumqi to Kashi. Below were Tien Shan (the Celestial Mountains) and the nine-hundred-mile-long Taklimakan Desert. So desolate was the Taklimakan that its name in Rahman's native language meant "Once you get in, you never get out." Only as the plane neared Kashi did Rahman see the string of verdant oases, extending to the border, that provided the wheat and fresh fruits on which the diet of his people depended.

The orange sun was setting over the dusty yellow sky as Rahman rode in the car belonging to the Xinjiang branch of the Chinese Hotel Corporation. The car turned onto East Brigade Street, the poplar-lined boulevard that led to the center of Kashi. In the distance he could see the one-hundred-foot-high concrete statue of Chairman Mao peering down, like a messiah, from the highest hill in the city. It would, he vowed, be the first of the monuments to be removed.

Rahman spit into his hands and washed the grit from the air off his teeth. He was exhausted from the long plane ride, but there was no time for rest. Tomorrow was Sunday, the only day when the Hotel Corporation would not require his presence at official functions. Even if he left early that evening, it would still not be easy to reach the border, complete his mission, and return to Kashi before the start of work on Monday morning.

Sitting in his office, Kao Yangxu lit a cigarette as he reviewed the plans for the construction of a new jade factory in Hotan. Kao was the regional director of the Arts and Crafts Corporation. Ordinarily this would have been a post of minor significance; but in western Xinjiang, where jade, rugs, and handicrafts were three of the largest industries, Kao was a person of considerable influence. He controlled three hundred factories employing more than thirty thousand workers and supervised a region that stretched for one thousand miles along both the Silk Road and Genghis Khan's original mail route.

Yet for all his power and prestige, Kao was very dissatisfied with his life. He was a native of Shanghai, who loved the ocean and thrived in the cosmopolitan culture of the world's largest city. He had never been able to adapt to the dust, the violent changes in temperature, the lack of rain, and the isolation of Kashi. He missed his wife and two children, and found it difficult to work in an environment populated by Turks. Like most people, he preferred to live among his own kind. But the decision had not been his. The Red Guard had accused him of being a capitalist-roader. He had been given a choice of being sent to a rectification camp or to Xinjiang. After eight years in the Autonomous Region, he was not certain he had made the right decision. Like so many other victims of the Cultural Revolution, Kao lived for the day when he would be rehabilitated.

Kao's secretary informed him that Kang Moruo was

calling from Peking. He nervously lifted the phone. He had met the director of his corporation only once, but he knew that the personal attention of such an important party leader could mean either that the news was very good or that it was very bad. "*Wei*," he said tentatively.

"Comrade Kao"—Kang's voice was smooth and richly melodious, reflecting his upper-class background—"would you be interested in being reassigned to Shanghai?"

Kao grabbed the receiver with both hands. "I will do whatever the Party requires of me," he replied, trying to conceal his eagerness.

"I have a confidential matter that I want you to look into. If you discharge it to my satisfaction, I will arrange to have you transferred."

Kao paced nervously around his desk, trying to force his thoughts away from his family and Shanghai. He interrupted several times to ask questions as Kang described the Turk whom he was supposed to follow. He would need trusted associates to assist him, but the task did not appear to be especially difficult.

"Remember," Kang said, "report back directly to me and inform no one of our discussion. Is that clear?"

"Perfectly," Kao replied. He hung up the phone and opened the bottom drawer of his desk. Inside was a bottle of Maotai that he reserved for special occasions. He cleaned the dust off his glass, poured the clear liquor, and toasted his homecoming.

At 7:00 P.M., Aziz Rahman left the Welcome Guest House and walked through the streets of Kashi. The area surrounding the newly built government offices was almost deserted. But near the homes of the Turkic workers, crowds gathered to enjoy the pleasures of the balmy summer night.

A group of musicians, playing stringed rababs and pounding on homemade drums, sang folk songs about the Silk Road. A tune about an old man and his goats stuck in Rahman's brain as he hurried past the recently demolished original walls of the city. The Chinese had no respect for Turkic history or tradition. Rahman walked through a field filled with domed adobe tombs that looked like brown anthills. A car was waiting at the far end. Inside were Kamal, Nur, and Ruzi, three of his lieutenants.

Ruzi drove northeast toward the border of the Soviet Union. Mulberry trees, cultivated to feed silkworms, lined the road. Beyond the trees, extending toward the mountains, were hundreds of what appeared to be large mole holes. These were *karezes*—horizontal wells dug beneath the surface of the earth, often for more than five miles. Through these *karezes*, water was drawn from the mountains to irrigate the populated oases. In a land with four inches of rainfall and a thousand inches of evaporation, the *karezes* were essential for survival.

As the car ascended into the foothills of Tien Shan, the air became crisp and cool. Rushing rivers cascaded down the mountains. The road leveled off into a broad valley. A cluster of circular tents called "yurts" stood in the center. In the surrounding pastures, herds of goats, sheep, and horses grazed silently. The car stopped. Rahman, Kamal, and Nur jumped out and ran toward the yurts. After they were out of sight, Ruzi turned the car around and drove back to Kashi.

Kao Yangxu drove along the narrow mountain road. Tracking Rahman had not been easy, but with the help of four associates, radios, and a little luck, he had been able to pick up the trail. The headlights of a car shone in his eyes. He pulled onto the dirt shoulder to let it pass. He had been following more than a mile behind Rahman, but this was the only other car he had seen since leaving Kashi. As the two automobiles squeezed by each other, Kao stared at the driver. "Damn!" he exclaimed. It was the car that had brought Rahman, but now there was only one man inside. Rahman and two of the others had disappeared into the mountains.

Kao motored slowly through a narrow pass, searching for the missing passengers. He entered a broad valley, in the center of which was a settlement of yurts. He pulled off the road and waited. If Rahman left by car, he would still be able to trail him. But if the Turk left on foot or horseback, Kao would stand no chance. The mountains were too rugged.

Rahman and the others slept for three hours. At 3:30 A.M., an old woman awakened them with a breakfast of fresh melon, curled fried wheat noodles called *sangza*, and a hard bread that had to be dipped in tea before it could be eaten. After finishing, the three men mounted their horses and rode toward the border. Rahman smiled as he gazed at a magnificent thousand-foot-high sand dune outlined in front of majestic snowcapped mountains. He was glad to be home and anxious to begin his operation.

The wind picked up. Sand swirled violently, stinging eyes and faces, but Rahman and the others continued riding. After four hours, they reached the staging area. There, in a ravine tucked behind groves of cottonwood and spruce, was an encampment of more than a hundred Turks. Beyond the encampment was a collection of jeeps, tanks, and armored personnel carriers. Rahman greeted each man by name; he had personally selected everyone for this mission. He inspected the Korean War-vintage weapons that had been provided. Though old, they would suffice.

After distributing the People's Liberation Army uniforms and rifles, Rahman reviewed the plans for the bogus attack against the Russian village of Turugart. By noon, everything was ready. His contingent of Turkic Nationalists had been perfectly transformed into a battalion of the People's Liberation Army.

The main route into Russia went through Turugart Pass; but since there were small garrisons on either side of the border, Rahman selected a back road used by Turkic nomads for thousands of years. The battalion slipped across the border without being noticed and motored to the northern shore of Chatykrel Lake. The village of Turugart was less than a mile away. Rahman halted his troops and gave the order to attack.

A Russian in the lookout tower took photographs as Rahman's Chinese troops separated into three columns and flanked the town. Russian artillery opened fire. The shells sailed far over the heads of the attackers. Dead bodies lay scattered on the ground as Chinese tanks reached the main square. A Russian with a movie camera hid in an alley recording the events as the Chinese shot salvos into the school and town hall. Another Russian snapped pictures as mortars tore massive chunks out of the wall of the village hospital. Russians fired machine guns from a fortified barricade on the main street, but none of the bullets endangered Rahman's soldiers. They were purposely shooting high.

It was over in less than an hour. Every building in the village was leveled. None of the Turks were wounded. Rahman viewed the wreckage with satisfaction. The attack had gone perfectly. Now he would have to await the repercussions. He ordered his troops to retreat.

Three hours later, the soldiers had changed back into their peasant garments and the weapons were safely hidden in the ravine. Eight men were assigned to guard the equipment. The rest scattered into the countryside. Some returned to their families in the hills of western China; others crossed back into Russia. Rahman inspected his weapons one last time. Then he, Kamal, and Nur rode back to the valley, where Ruzi would be waiting to take them to Kashi.

Two days after the attack on Turugart, Hua Guofeng sat behind the simple teak desk in his sparsely decorated office listening while Kang Moruo argued that the Russians were planning to foment a civil war in China. Although both were members of the Politburo, Hua did not particularly like Kang, who, as a well-educated, wealthy, urban aristocrat from Shanghai, represented everything that Hua was not. Hua had been born out of wedlock, had never received a formal education, and had spent most of his life fighting for what he wanted. Even though he was now the second most important person in the People's Republic, he still felt ill at ease around his more cosmopolitan colleagues.

"Comrade Kang"—Hua spoke with a thick southern accent acquired during his years of living in Mao's home province—"I have read these reports, but I find it difficult to believe that the Russians could be responsible for everything you claim."

"The evidence is there." Kang spoke with the perfect diction that was the product of his years studying with a personal tutor.

"All I see are your allegations." Hua's large, square face showed no emotion.

"Allegations?" Kang tugged on the sleeves of his white silk shirt. "There are specific details about the attacks on the British and Japanese ships, the destruction of the railroad bridges, and even the burning of the agricultural school that you helped to build."

"And where did you get these details, from the American CIA?" Hua leaned back and placed his sandaled feet on the desk. He was wearing a faded gray worker's uniform.

Kang picked a French licorice mint out of a small tin and dropped it into his mouth. "That does not necessarily make it invalid."

"I'm not certain that you are the most impartial observer."

"What do you mean by that?"

"If I accept your view that the Russians are planning to attack, then my only alternative is to side with the United States. Your brother-in-law, I believe, is the president of one of the largest American defense contractors. It would appear that you have a considerable personal stake in my decision."

"I resent your accusation," Kang bristled. "I would never put the financial interests of my family above that of my country."

Hua smiled. "I did not suggest that you would. But these capitalist contacts might have a subtle effect on the way you look at evidence. If you learn anything more concrete, I will consider it. But for now, I think we should table the discussion of the Soviets."

Kang grimaced as he removed another stack of documents from his leather briefcase. "If you won't accept what I have to say about the Russians, will you at least look at the evidence against Jiang Qing and the Gang of Four?"

Hua nodded silently as he started to read the documents that accused Jiang of plotting a coup to take control of the government. He knew that Jiang was ambitious. She tried to dominate and disrupt the meetings of the Politburo; she often directly challenged his authority, calling him a country bumpkin or worse; and she exercised such tight control over the media that all news stories reflected only her point of view. Hua was still furious that she had blocked all reports of his efforts to rebuild after the quake, but he could not believe that she would be reckless enough to oppose both the wishes of Chairman Mao and the leadership of the Party.

"What do you think?" Kang asked.

"Once again, you are hardly an impartial observer," Hua said. "Jiang and her people represent the Left. You and your supporters represent the Right. It is my job to avoid the extremes and steer a middle course."

"And what do you propose to do when Jiang produces a forged last will for Chairman Mao?"

"I cannot believe she would stoop so low."

"Can you believe that she would try to assassinate Deng Xiaoping, Hu Shengte, and Liu Teyu?"

"Absolutely not."

"And what if I can introduce you to someone who has proof of both the forgery and the attempted assassination?"

Hua pulled his feet off the desk and leaned forward. His large, penetrating eyes bore in on Kang. "Who is this mysterious witness?"

"He is an American named Marc Slater."

"That's impossible. Slater was killed in the earthquake. I read the report of his death in the *People's Daily*."

"And who controls the *People's Daily*?"

Hua stood up from his desk. "Stop playing games with me. You'll have to find something more incriminating than the incorrect reporting of the death of one American capitalist to convince me that Jiang is plotting against my government."

"How about the incorrect reporting of the death of Liu Teyu?"

Hua placed his hands on the desk and glared intently at Kang. "That's impossible."

"Mr. Slater was with him two days ago."

"I find that difficult to believe."

"All I ask is that you listen to what he has to say."

Hua inhaled slowly on a cigarette as he evaluated Kang's offer. He recognized that Kang was merely serving the interests of Deng and the other members of the right wing, and that they were no more closely allied to him than were Jiang and the Left. But if Slater had evidence that Liu was still alive, he had no choice but to listen. "All right. Bring him tonight at seven."

"Not here," Kang said. "It is essential that no one learns he is alive until he has talked to you. Then it will be your decision."

"Is Marshal Ye's home acceptable?"

"Absolutely," Kang replied.

"Then I will see you at seven," Hua said, crossing the room and holding open the door.

After Kang had left, Hua poured a cup of jasmine tea and rested his head in his hands. He had begun to doubt his ability to lead the country. The only time he felt content was when he got out of Peking and worked directly with Party leaders in the field. He often wished he were back in Hunan running the provincial government. The destruction of the earthquake had sapped much of his strength, and now he had to find the personal reserve to cope with the increasing bickering in the Politburo. The right and left wings were openly hostile, not only to each other but to him as well. There was not much to choose from: Jiang, the shrew, on one side; and Deng, the manipulator, on the other. Both wanted to dominate the government and neither was willing to compromise for the benefit of the country.

Hua wished there had been a strong center behind him; but with the exception of Defense Minister Ye and Vice-Chairman Li, most leaders had chosen to support the extremes. His only legitimate claim to power was that he had been anointed by Mao. He needed Mao's continuing support if he was to have any hope of holding the country together.

He picked up the telephone and dialed the direct line to the Chairman's hospital room. Mao's nephew answered. "Comrade Yuanxin, this is Premier Hua. I would like to see Chairman Mao this afternoon."

"I am sorry, comrade," Yuanxin replied, "this would not be a good day."

"That's the answer you gave me yesterday."

"I am only following the orders of the doctors. Our Teacher is not well. He has been instructed to rest and avoid all discussions of government."

"But Comrade Jiang Qing has seen him."

"She is his wife."

"And Comrades Yao, Zhang, and Wang—what are they?"

"They saw our Teacher for only ten minutes, and then just to give him a gift."

"I, too, have a gift."

"I am sorry, comrade premier. Perhaps you can see him tomorrow."

Hua hung up the phone in disgust. Since Yuanxin had moved into the hospital, Mao had become inaccessible. Hua knew that Mao was dying, but he did not believe that the Chairman was too ill to see him. If Jiang and her allies were the only ones with access, there was no telling what concessions they could wring out of him on his deathbed. Hua somehow would have to find a way to counter their influence.

He paced to the window and looked out at the Forbidden City. He had to compose himself before his meeting with the Russian ambassador. He did not know why the man had demanded to see him, or what Brezhnev could have written in the private communication, but he hoped that the information did not cause any further difficulties for his government.

At 3:00 the door opened and Defense Minister Ye escorted the Soviet ambassador into the room. The ambassador, a middle-aged man who looked badly in need of a shave, was dressed in an ill-fitting brown suit, a white shirt, and a brown tie. Hua offered him a chair. He refused. He appeared somber as he quickly dispensed with pleasantries. "My government," he said with uncharacteristic bluntness, "officially protests the attack of the People's Liberation Army against the town of Turugart."

Hua and Ye stared at each other in shock as the ambassador withdrew a stack of photographs from his briefcase. Ye put on his thick black reading glasses.

"As you can see"—the ambassador laid the pictures on the desk—"your soldiers crossed the border and made an unprovoked attack against a peaceful settlement. Almost every building in Turugart was destroyed and more than two hundred of our citizens were killed." The ambassador pointed to a photograph of dead bodies strewn across the village square. "Comrade Brezhnev is greatly disturbed by these actions. He has advised our delegate at the United Nations to lodge an official protest and he has instructed me to inform you that the Soviet Union will not sit idly by while its citizens are wantonly murdered by your bloodthirsty soldiers."

Hua gazed at the ambassador in a state of great confusion. "There has been some sort of mistake."

"Do you call the deaths of two hundred of our citizens a mistake?"

"These deaths are a great tragedy, but your news is the first that I have heard of this incident. Xinjiang is far away and there has always been unrest along the border. Perhaps the attack was the work of Turkic Nationalists."

"Then why were they wearing the uniforms of the People's Liberation Army and using your armored equipment?"

"The uniforms could have been stolen," Defense Minister Ye said. "And the tanks in these pictures were manufactured by your country."

"They were given as gifts to the People's Republic during the Korean War. Surely, comrade, you can't really be suggesting that we would arm Turkic Nationalists so that they could murder our people."

"Please accept my apologies. Our government deeply regrets every aspect of this incident."

"My government demands an immediate public apology."

"You will have it," Hua said.

"We further demand that the traitors responsible for this action be arrested and executed."

"We will find the people and deal with them severely."

"Secretary Brezhnev instructed me to warn you that failure to take appropriate action or the incidence of any further incursions along our border will be met by a direct military response."

"We understand the position of your government," Hua said. "Please be assured that there will be no further difficulties."

"Thank you, comrade," the ambassador said. He placed his photographs back in his briefcase and left the room.

Hua stared at Ye in confusion and bewilderment. He remembered his discussion with Kang and wondered if he had been wrong to dismiss the accusations so readily. "Who is the stupid ass who could have ordered this?" Hua demanded.

"I don't know," Ye replied, "but I wouldn't be surprised if it was those camel-dung-eating Turks."

"Why would they attack Russia?"

"They'd do anything to stir up trouble."

"Another attack like this and we will be at war." Hua gazed at the ceiling. "And it will be a war that we have no chance of winning."

*　　*　　*

"What's going on there?" Kang Moruo barked into the phone over the static of the connection. "I asked you to follow Rahman. What happened?"

"He slipped away." Kao wiped the sweat from his brow. "I'm sorry."

"Sorry is not sufficient." Kang's voice was icy. "The Russian ambassador just lodged a protest with Premier Hua claiming that our soldiers attacked a Soviet village called Turugart."

"Turugart! Rahman was on the road to Turugart when I lost him."

"What do you know about the village?"

"Only that for the last five years it's been deserted."

"Deserted! Damn!" Kang said. "The Turks must have staged the attack."

"Why would they do that?"

"Perhaps to create a pretext for a Russian invasion," Kang replied.

"Can we stop them?" Kao asked.

"Only if we know what they're planning," Kang answered. "It is essential that you stick to Rahman like a flea to a dog."

"You can depend on me." Kao tried to sound forceful.

"I have no other choice."

"Comrade, there is one other thing. A foreign barbarian arrived in Kashi today and reported directly to Rahman. His name is Avery Boswell."

"Boswell?" Kang could not hide the surprise in his voice. "Do you know him?"

"He is the deputy managing director of Hong Kong's largest trading company, Gateshead and MacIntosh."

"I know, and that is what troubles me." Kao spoke very deliberately. "Do you know much about Western names?"

Kang laughed. "I attended college in the United States."

"Is Gateshead a common name?"

"Not very. Why?"

"There is only one other English barbarian in all of Kashi, and his name is Gateshead."

"Lord Henry Gateshead from the British Museum." Kang confidently supplied the information.

"Yes," Kao replied. "He's here to buy some of the fifteen-hundred-year-old silks recently excavated from two of our oases."

"Well, that solves your problem. I'm sure Gateshead and Boswell are working together."

"That's what I suspected at first"—Kao's voice was tentative—"but now I don't think so. I saw Boswell standing in the hotel lobby. When Gateshead walked through, he ran and hid like a scared chicken. He has also been asking questions about the Englishman's schedule. Today, when Gateshead toured the silk museums, two of Rahman's men followed him."

"Shadow the foreigners at all times," Kang said, having no idea how Gateshead was involved. "One of them is bound to make a mistake. If we're lucky, they'll help us trap Rahman."

Avery Boswell clung tightly to the reins as his horse cantered down a trail that led to the Russian border. He had come to Kashi with Van Wyck's plans for two new bogus attacks and had convinced Rahman to let him participate in the first.

A mortar shell exploded in the center of the village less than a hundred yards ahead. The horse reared and then stumbled. Boswell lurched forward, grabbed the animal's neck, and thrust his knees into its flanks. The horse angrily tossed its head but did not slow down. Boswell tugged again on the reins. He was supposed to have remained behind the others, but his horse was headstrong and he was a poor rider.

An artillery shell whistled overhead and landed on the ridge far above him. Boswell spurred his horse toward the battle. Although he knew that the guns were manned by Rahman's own soldiers and aimed away from the attackers, he was still nervous. Despite the planning, it was always possible that one might inadvertently shoot in the wrong direction.

Boswell rode down the main street of the village named Murgab. Dead bodies were strewn everywhere. Boswell knew that the men had not been killed in the fighting; they were spies who had been shot and placed in the street prior to the attack. He slowed his horse and watched the staging of the battle. The ingenuity of Van Wyck's plan fascinated him. The Chinese had already publicly apologized for the attack on Turugart. Given the current unrest, little additional provocation would be required before the Russians could invade China and capture the Chinese oil and coal fields.

After Murgab was leveled, Rahman and his men returned to their base. Trotting behind the others, Boswell thought about his own private operation, the kidnapping of Lord Henry Gateshead. Although he had not yet received specific approval from Van Wyck, he had decided to act. With only two English-speaking Westerners in Kashi, it was only a matter of time before Gateshead became aware of his presence. Then the lord would start asking questions, which he would be unable to answer. His only choice was to remove Gateshead before it was too late.

It was almost sundown when Kang Moruo drove past the soldiers guarding the gate of the country home of Marshal Ye. Ye's primary residence was in Zhong Nanhai, but he had kept this house in the Western Hills as a place to escape from the pressures of government. Kang pulled the car behind the building and opened the trunk. Marc Slater, dressed in the clothes of a Chinese peasant, uncurled his body and stepped onto the pavement.

Marc shook out his legs. He was tired of being a corpse. For the last two days, he had been forced to hide while Kang set up the meeting with Hua. He wished that he could talk to his children, but he knew he would have to continue to pretend he was dead until he had succeeded in bringing Hua together with Liu.

Kang led Marc through a back door and into the study, where Hua and Ye were waiting. "Good evening, Mr. Slater," Hua said with great formality.

"I'm glad to see you, *lao pengyou*," the jowly, balding Ye smiled as he greeted the American whom he had known since the end of the Long March. "I must say, you look quite healthy for a corpse."

"The reports of my death have been somewhat exaggerated."

"I have received numerous requests from your government, your family, and your company for information about your death. Would you like me to inform them that you are still alive?"

"I think it would be better to wait until you have heard what I have to say."

While Ye poured four cups of tea, Marc reported on his experiences with Liu. Then he offered the letter from Liu inviting Hua to a secret meeting at the Yellow Mountain People's Commune. Hua read the letter and then turned to Marc. "It looks like Comrade Liu's calligraphy, but I cannot be certain."

"Comrade Liu was very badly injured. His hand was very unsteady when he wrote this letter, but I can assure you that it is legitimate."

"Would you excuse us for a minute?" Ye asked.

While the others remained in the study discussing the letter, Marc stepped into the living room. A telephone sat on a table. Marc touched the receiver. He wanted to call Boston. It would take less than a minute to relieve the misery of his family. They had done nothing and did not deserve to suffer. He lifted the receiver and then put it back down. With the meeting between Hua and Liu still pending, he could not take the risk. The line could be tapped. People in the telephone company might report the call to Jiang Qing. He would have to find another, more subtle way of contacting his children. Until then, he would have to be patient. Hua summoned Marc back into the study. "It shall be as you request. A helicopter will be here tomorrow to take us to the meeting. I just hope for your sake that everything is as you have presented it."

Marc bowed respectfully. "Deceiving you would be as dumb as trying to raise a tiger under my quilt."

"That's little consolation," Marshal Ye laughed. "I know many men who have awakened the morning after their wedding to find just that between their sheets."

Early the next morning, Lord Henry Gateshead stepped off a propeller-driven plane in the Urumqi airport. Despite the unpleasant dust, his trip to Kashi had gone quite well. Now he was about to visit the desert oasis of Turpan, which, though five hundred feet below sea level, has been one of the most thriving trading posts along the Silk Road. It was in Turpan that archaeologists had recently excavated two exquisite collections of ancient silks from the Tang and Shang dynasties. Because the climate of the region was so dry, these silks had been preserved in almost perfect condition.

It had been five days since he had left Xian. Gateshead

hoped that Alexandra Koo had encountered no difficulty in shipping the relics. The antiquities from the Han and the Qin tombs, coupled with those he hoped to acquire in Xinjiang, would give the English Museum the finest collection of Oriental relics outside of China.

"Lord Gateshead." A thin man in a worker's uniform bowed deeply. "I am Comrade Ruzi. This is my associate, Comrade Nur. It is our pleasure to escort you to Turpan."

"The pleasure is mine," Gateshead said, handing Ruzi his suitcase. "I have long wanted to visit the oasis."

"I can assure you," Ruzi smiled shyly, "that this will be a trip you will never forget."

Marc paced to a corner of Kang Moruo's study and distractedly lifted a blue and white Ming vase. He stared at the dragons glazed into its surface but saw nothing. His thoughts were centered on the reaction to the news of his death. Samuel Tang had informed him that the stock of M. H. Schaffer had dropped more than eighteen points in the last two days, a loss of half a billion dollars in the value of the company and more than sixty million dollars of his own net worth. Playing dead was an expensive proposition. Still, it was nice to know that the amorphous collection of forces known as Wall Street placed such a huge value on his life. When he returned home, he intended to use the decline as a tool to prod his sometimes unruly board of directors.

Marc wished he could invisibly transport himself back to Boston. He would love to watch his executives competing for control—the knowledge he would gain could be of great value in his future dealings with each of them. Still, no matter what happened now, everything would be stabilized upon his return. Of more lasting concern was the impact of the news of his death on his children. He was pleased he had thought of a way of contacting them. The phone rang. Marc lifted the receiver. "Ready on your call to Japan," the operator said.

Marc heard Joe Takada answer. "Mr. Takada," he said, suspecting that someone might be tapping the phone, "I am Comrade Ma from the Chinese Petroleum Corporation."

"Comrade Ma?" Takada blurted as he recognized Marc's voice. "Ah, yes. I'm surprised to hear from you."

"I have been reviewing some of our contracts with your company. I am concerned whether the death of your president will affect them adversely."

"Our company is very strong. We intend to honor our agreements and even hope to expand our business in the future."

"We would be pleased to consider your wishes, but we are still saddened by the loss of Mr. Slater. He was a good man and a *lao pengyou.*" Marc enjoyed delivering his own eulogy.

"Thank you for your consideration," Takada said. "I am certain that your sentiments will be of great comfort to his co-workers and family."

"Do you intend to visit the United States in the near future?" Marc had to be circumspect.

"I am not certain. Why?"

"My government would appreciate it if you would extend its deepest sympathies to Mr. Slater's family."

"Should I extend your condolences to the executives of our company?"

"It would be inappropriate for us to appear to be too friendly with a capitalist corporation, but Mr. Slater's family is a different matter."

"I understand your position, and I may just be leaving for Boston sooner than expected."

"My government is very grateful for your assistance. But

please keep all communications as confidential as possible."

"You may rely on my discretion."

Marc smiled as he hung up the phone. He had made the right choice. Takada would deliver the news to Jill and David with utmost tact. It was asking a lot to have only one person in the company know that he was alive; but if anyone could cope with the information, it was Takada.

Marc slumped down on the couch. He was exhausted. He closed his eyes and tried to relax. A picture of Linda Forbes flashed through his mind. He was anxious to see her. Perhaps when all this was over, they could go somewhere together.

The telephone rang again, interrupting his reverie. "Is Comrade Kang there?" a Chinese voice asked over the cackle of a connection far worse than the one to Japan.

"Kang is out," Marc replied. "Are you Comrade Kao from Kashi?"

There was a moment's hesitation. "How did you know?"

"Comrade Kang told me to expect your call," Marc said. "He requested that you deliver your report to me. What have you been able to learn?"

"I once again followed Rahman toward the border, but I lost him in the Pamirs. The damn Turks are like goats. They are far better suited to the mountainous terrain than we are."

Marc smiled, pleased that Kao took him to be a Chinese.

"In one of the valleys," Kao continued, "we found an encampment that had probably serviced one hundred men. Tire tracks led to Murgab, a town on the Russian border. We followed the tracks; but when we reached Murgab, it looked like a war had been fought there. What disturbed me was that Murgab, like Turugart, has been deserted for more than five years."

"I will relay your information to Comrade Kang."

"There's something else," Kao exclaimed before Marc

could hang up. "One of the English barbarians, Lord Henry Gateshead, has disappeared."

"What do you mean?"

"Early this morning Gateshead flew to Urumqi. Two of my people were supposed to drive him to Turpan, but somebody stole the distributor on their car. By the time they arrived at the airport, Gateshead was gone."

"No one can just disappear in the People's Republic," Marc insisted.

"Out here they can. With all the open space, there's very little security. And the Turks seem to enjoy causing trouble."

"What makes you think Turks are involved?"

"People at the airport saw the English barbarian leaving with two Turks. Their descriptions match those of two of Rahman's lieutenants."

"Is there any trace of Rahman and the others?"

"Rahman is still here, but Boswell and two of Rahman's people flew to Urumqi last night. One of my sources saw them passing through Shawan on the road to Karamay."

"Damn!" Marc muttered in English. Karamay was one of China's leading oil-producing centers. He remembered the warning he had received from Joe Takada. "Have you seen Rahman with any Japanese?"

"There were two Japanese on the plane to Urumqi."

"Do you know their identities?"

"I think they're with the Takamura Corporation."

"Find out what you can about them. I'll convey our conversation to Comrade Kang. I'm sure he'll be pleased."

"My only interest is to serve my country."

And also perhaps to return to Shanghai, Marc thought to himself.

37: The Reversal of the Verdict

Mao Yuanxin walked out of Mao Tse-tung's hospital room and hurried through Tian'anmen Square. In the last week Chairman Mao had been obsessed with the earthquake. He demanded constant reports on the rebuilding effort and continually dictated letters informing Hua and the other government leaders of his suggestions. To Mao, the quake was far more than a geological event; it was a symbol of the Withdrawal of the Mandate. The deaths of Chou En-lai and Zhu De, the meteor that had fallen three months ago, and now the earthquake—all were irrefutable signs that the dynasty he had founded was drawing to an end; only his death was lacking. Yuanxin had tried to reason with his uncle, but Mao refused to listen. As his health declined, he was becoming more rigid and fatalistic.

The streets of Peking were still clogged with homeless workers. Considerable progress had been made in reconstruction, but with a series of aftershocks and seven days of rain, many of the damaged structures were ready to collapse.

Yuanxin stared at workers repairing the yawning crack in the side of the Great Hall of the People. He could not let Mao's talk of the Withdrawal of the Mandate affect his judgment. He was Mao's primary link to the world. If Mao's mind became clouded by superstitions, his people might lose their chance to take control of the government.

Yuanxin passed through the entrance to Zhong Nanhai and walked to the Ming dynasty palace in which Mao lived. Shen Mo greeted him at the door. "I am here to see Comrade Jiang," Yuanxin announced.

Shen blushed and turned her eyes away. "I am sorry but Comrade Jiang is indisposed."

"At ten in the morning? Who is it this time?"

A smile curled to the ends of Shen's lips. "She is not with anybody. She is not feeling well. She was very upset by the earthquake and the difficulties in the Politburo. She took some pills to help her sleep. I found her on the floor and carried her to bed."

"Do you think you might be able to awaken her?"

"I'll try." Shen bowed respectfully and called on an intercom to another of Jiang's assistants, stationed in front of her bedroom. "Comrade Jiang Qing will see you in a few minutes," Shen announced, motioning toward the living room. "May I get you a cup of tea?"

Yuanxin wiped his brow. The day was already quite hot. "I'll take a beer," he said. Tea would not fortify him for the discussion he had to face. Shen walked to the bar, opened a dark green bottle, and handed it to Mao's nephew.

Yuanxin nervously paced across the crimson Oriental carpet as he reviewed his last discussion with Chairman Mao. He had never seen his Teacher so vindictive. When he told Mao that Jiang wanted to visit, the Chairman's eyes had narrowed angrily. "I will not see her," Mao had said. "She is too ambitious and too much in love with herself. She is like an ox let loose in a vegetable garden, poking her nose into other people's business and lecturing everybody." Yuanxin had argued that Jiang was Mao's constant supporter and friend, but the Chairman would not listen.

Debating with Mao was one thing; explaining the Chairman's attitude to the mercurial Jiang was something else entirely. Since Yuanxin had moved to the hospital, his relationship with his aunt had deteriorated. He was the messenger who had to tell Jiang that her husband would not see her. Jiang always demanded explanations, and he could not tell her that Mao had called her an ox and a busybody, so he invented stories. His words rarely satisfied her. She often flew into rages, accusing him of sandbagging her and blaming him for Mao's attitude. It was the last thing he would ever do. He had been raised by Mao and Jiang. Besides Mao, Jiang was his only relative. He would soon have to rely on her as his patron.

Yuanxin took a deep breath as he tried to decide how to deal with his aunt. Today of all days he had to avoid arousing her ire. She had to be rational when he informed her of the drastic changes in Mao's attitude. If they did not act at once, everything they had worked for could slip away.

"Good morning, younger nephew," Jiang said as she entered the living room. She was wearing a pair of white silk slacks and a navy silk blouse.

"Good morning, honorable elder aunt. I hope you slept well."

"How can I sleep when my husband is so ill?" Jiang lit a cigarette and coughed. "I think I should go see him as soon as I finish breakfast."

Yuanxin turned toward the kitchen as he sipped his beer. He did not want to look at his aunt. "This would not be a good time."

"What do you mean?"

"Why don't you wait a day or two?"

"Until he has become a corpse?"

"The doctors say he will soon be fine. Unfortunately, his condition has temporarily worsened. They suggested that visitors might tire him."

"I will call the doctors and order them to change their minds."

"I don't think that would be a good idea."

Jiang stepped in front of Yuanxin and grasped his arms. "What are you trying to hide from me?"

"Nothing."

"Don't fart and tell me it's perfume."

"Honorable elder aunt, you have been like a mother to me. I would never do anything that would hurt you."

"Then why won't you let me see my husband?"

"It is not me."

"Then who is it?"

Yuanxin hunched his shoulders and glanced at the ceiling. "It is our Teacher himself. His mind has been slipping. He has become very crotchety. He says that right now he does not want to see you."

"What kind of nonsense is that?"

"Foolish nonsense." Yuanxin tried to placate her. "I told him that you were his most stalwart friend and supporter."

"And how did he respond?"

"He said that since he has been incapacitated, you have not shown sufficient consideration for his health and his position; you have been working to promote your own career rather than attending to his needs."

Jiang gazed out the window at the Forbidden City. "That's ridiculous! I was only doing as Comrade Mao suggested. It was he who encouraged me to take an active role in Party affairs, he who urged me to move against the capitalist-roaders, and he who groomed me as his successor. Don't you remember when he said, 'The man must abdicate and let the woman take over'? Who do you think he was talking about, the Dowager Empress?"

"Please try to understand, honorable elder aunt. Our Teacher is not well. I am sure his medication is affecting him. I will ask again tomorrow. I am sure he will consent to see you."

"I'd like to get to the bottom of this now," Jiang said.

"As would I." Yuanxin shifted uneasily. "But I fear we have far more serious problems to consider."

"Such as?"

"Our Teacher has begun to dwell in the past. He keeps talking remorsefully about Chou En-lai."

"As it concerns me?"

"Somewhat." Yuanxin's voice was tentative. "He said that he envied Comrade Chou's marriage, that Chou and Deng Yingchao were a true team, while he is cursed with a wife who wants to be an empress."

Jiang Qing scowled. "That's sheer foolishness. I was exactly the wife that Mao wanted. I let him mold me in his image."

"I tried to explain that," Yuanxin replied. "But our Teacher's concerns go much farther than you or Chou's marriage. He is jealous that the people think of him as a disciplinarian and as a cold Buddha, while they think of Chou as a kind and understanding father figure."

"Chou was a weakling," Jiang said. "It was Mao who kept the movement alive. Had he not started the Cultural Revolution, the Great Leap, and the Antis campaigns, Chou and his bureaucrats would have taken the country back onto the capitalist road."

"I argued that way as well, but our Teacher said he has made many errors and there is not much time to correct them. He questioned whether our group could follow his teachings and adequately govern the country."

"Of course we can rule China," Jiang scoffed. "Who else is there?"

Yuanxin turned away. "Our Teacher suggested that he might have been wrong about the verdict and that it perhaps should be reversed."

Jiang pounced at him. "Are you talking about April fifth?"

Yuanxin sadly shook his head. During the beginning of April, memorial services for Chou En-lai had been held in Tian'anmen Square. Each day people had gathered to recite poems, make impromptu speechs, and place wreaths around the Monument to the People's Heroes. On the evening of April 4, Wang Hongwen ordered that the wreaths be removed. The next morning the crowds became enraged. They shouted, "The era of Shi Huangdi is gone," equating Mao with the Qin emperor, and then became violent. Government buildings were ransacked, cars were burned, and people were killed. One of the dead was the grandson of Zhu De. The next day Mao rendered the verdict that the incident had been caused by Deng Xiaoping. He denounced Deng, stripped him of his Party posts, and appointed Hua premier.

Jiang Qing glared angrily. "Chairman Mao cannot reverse the verdict."

"Honorable elder aunt, you of all people should know that our Teacher can do whatever he wants."

"But the thought is just absurd. With everything that Deng has done to establish revisionist policies, how could he possibly be rehabilitated?"

"Our Teacher is very worried about the impact of his

death on the future of the People's Republic. Just this morning he quoted the old saying 'Each person has only one death, but it can be light as a feather or heavy as Mount Tai.' Then, staring at me with resignation, he said, 'Mine, I fear, will be heavy as the mountain. I must prepare the country before I go to the clouds.'"

"We cannot permit that to occur," Jiang said as she rang for Shen Mo. "Get me Zhang Chunqiao." Shen bowed and left the room.

Jiang stared silently at a photograph of herself and Mao studying at a table in their cave in Yan'an. It was her favorite picture, because it captured the essence of their relationship: Mao the teacher and she the student. For forty years she had defined her identity as his wife. Now she would not only have to function on her own but would also have to find the reserves to assume his role as the leader of China. The challenge frightened her more than she had ever let anyone know. But she could not show her weakness, nor could she let her dying husband steal control of the government from her.

The intercom buzzed. Jiang lifted the telephone and greeted Zhang Chunqiao. "Yuanxin," she began, "informs me that Comrade Mao's condition has worsened. I think that we can no longer afford to delay."

"I am in full agreement," Zhang replied.

"What's happening with the man from Chinese American Tobacco?"

"Wong Chuyun will reach Shanghai with the weapons tomorrow morning."

"Excellent." Jiang's eyes gleamed. "Once they arrive, I think we should mobilize all our forces."

"Shall we cut off the petroleum?" Zhang asked.

"Absolutely! Only areas under our control should receive oil."

"Do you think we should move Chairman Mao again?"

"I was just going to suggest that," Jiang said. "The more we change his room, the harder it will be for Hua and the others to get to him."

"What's happening with Yuanxin's troops from Shenyang?" Zhang asked.

"I want Yuanxin to move two tank divisions to the capital," Jiang replied. "We need a strong military presence in case events occur quicker than expected."

Yuanxin looked at Jiang with surprise. "Excuse me, honored aunt, but is that necessary?"

"Do you think that Mao in one of his senile reveries could suddenly decide to rehabilitate and then endorse Deng?"

"It's possible."

"We've worked too hard to take any chances. We must remain alert. When the wolves are on the prowl, it is best to guard the sheep."

38: The Switch

Linda Forbes twirled an imitation pearl in her hand as she watched a master craftsman implant a piece of colored glass cut to look like a ruby in a brass imitation of one of the gold crowns found in the cave on Black Horse Hill. She nodded approvingly and then went over to a long bench where other workmen were using substandard jade to copy ancient carvings. Since the start of the project, she had been surprised by the speed and dedication of these usually deliberate Chinese craftsmen. Kang Moruo and Kang Momin had mobilized more than two hundred workers in eight different factories. In three days they had already copied more than two-thirds of the relics.

Linda marveled at the ingenious techniques devised by the Chinese. Copper, brass, and nickel had been used in place of gold and silver. Colored glass, fake pearls, and imitation diamonds had been cut to resemble the original gems. Molds had been sculpted, cast in bronze, and then dipped in corrosive acids to give the appearance of aging. Pottery and terra-cotta had been fired at extra-high temperatures for long periods of time so that the pieces would crack and the paint would peel; while wood, soapstone, and lacquerware carvings had been treated with special chemicals. None of the replicas was good enough to trick an expert, but almost all were sufficient to fool the workers and customs inspectors who would be handling them.

Linda checked the pieces being produced against those on her manifest. The relics were scheduled to be moved the day after tomorrow. She and her people needed twenty-four hours to lug the rest of the pieces to the cave and make the substitutions. Anything that was not ready by the morning would have to be excluded. She walked over to Kang Xiaoma, who was talking on the telephone. "How are things progressing at the bronze factory?" she asked.

"Everything is finished except the statue." Xiaoma's voice was unusually soft and cultured. "But we may have problems."

"Such as?"

"First we have to get it up the mountain. We are casting it hollow, but even so, it will weigh four tons. To carry it by hand, we'd have to divide it into one hundred pieces and then weld everything back together in the cave."

"With enough men I think we could manage it," Linda said.

"Perhaps, but then how do we move the original? It's supposed to weight two hundred and sixty thousand pounds. That's a hundred and thirty tons."

"Oh, what a tangled web we weave." Linda laughed and touched her forefinger to her temple. "We've made everything so complicated that we've missed the simple solution. If we can't move it, then neither can our friend Mrs. Koo. She'll also have to break her original statue into pieces. I'd bet whatever equipment she's going to use is already in the cave, so we merely have to carry our pieces up to the cave and then use her equipment to make the switch."

"That's not bad thinking for a foreign woman," said Xiaoma, intending it as a compliment. "Now we just have to hope that we finish casting our pieces on time."

"We won't even have to do that," Linda said. "Since our pieces are lighter than the originals, we'd be better off substituting only part of the statue. That way no one will notice the change in weight. If we pick carefully, we should be able to deliver a jigsaw puzzle of old and new pieces that won't fit together. Gateshead will have a hemorrhage, certain that Alexandra was trying to cheat him."

"I'm glad I'm working with you," Xiaoma said respectfully. "I'd hate to be the enemy of anyone with such a devious mind."

Linda smiled and turned back to her work.

Early the next morning Linda walked into the lobby of the Renmin Hotel to wait for Kang Xiaoma. She was dressed casually in jeans, a cotton shirt, and jogging shoes. She planned to spend the day carrying the fake relics into the cave on Black Horse Hill. In less than twenty-four hours they would be on their way to the English Museum in place of the real antiques. Her only regret was that she would not have the chance to see the expression on Alexandra Koo's face when the treachery was discovered.

"Good morning, Miss Forbes." Alexandra Koo's voice cut through the silence of the lobby. Linda had managed to avoid the Jade Empress for the entire week, but on this most critical day, she had let down her guard. She had thought Alexandra would still be asleep. It was foolish of her. She should have been more careful. She turned toward the voice.

Alexandra was attired in a flowing green silk dress

accessorized with dangling earrings, eight rings, and a large pendant, all made of jade. Even in the back hills of China, she looked like a Madison Avenue socialite off for a day of shopping at Saks. "Alexandra, what a nice surprise." Linda forced a sweet smile. "I still haven't had a chance to thank you for helping me out of jail in Peking."

"I was pleased to be of assistance," Alexandra replied. "I hope you've been keeping your skirts clean."

Linda pointed to her jeans. "I've been keeping my skirts off."

"You hardly look the part of a Bloomingdale's buyer. What are you decked out for? A formal tour of an antiques warehouse?"

"I'm supposed to be going to the countryside to see some of the relics from the Qin Tomb." Linda paused, but Alexandra showed no reaction. "They said it was very dirty in the excavation and told me to dress casually."

"Don't tell me that you're now buying relics?"

Linda shook her head. "I'm just going as a tourist."

"You'll find it fascinating." Alexandra lit a cigarette. "By the way, have you seen Marc Slater?"

It was the trap Linda had been waiting for. As a department-store buyer, it was unlikely that she would have heard that Marc had been killed. "I haven't seen him since Canton. What about you?"

"I hate to be the bearer of bad news, but he was killed in the earthquake."

"Killed?" Linda forced herself to look shocked. "That's terrible! He seemed like such an interesting man. I'm sorry for you."

"For me?" Alexandra asked.

"I thought you liked him?"

"My dear, I have a husband in New York. Marc was an old friend, an overseas dalliance, if you will. By the way, where were you when the earthquake struck?"

Linda shifted nervously. Alexandra was testing her, but she had no idea how much the Jade Empress knew. Both Leung and Stewart had seen her in Tangshan. If they had told Alexandra, her cover might be blown. She had no choice but to play along and hope that Alexandra either had not talked to them or had no way of linking her with Deng Xiaoping. "I was in Tianjin. It was the most awful experience I can ever remember," Linda said, trying to look shaken. It was an easy piece of acting. She had no difficulty re-creating the torment she had suffered. "I thought I was going to die. I still don't know how I survived."

"You were very fortunate," Alexandra said. "Others were not so lucky. Do you remember that man Leung from Malaysia who rode in the car with us?"

"Of course," Linda replied, trying to maintain her composure.

"He was killed."

"I'm sorry. He seemed like quite a nice fellow."

"Vance Stewart is also dead."

"My God! The southerner from the tobacco company? That's horrible."

"He mentioned that he had seen you."

Linda tried to steady her breathing. She had to go with the truth and hope that Alexandra could not put the pieces together. "We had breakfast in Tangshan the day of the quake."

"What were you doing in Tangshan?" Alexandra moved in on Linda.

"Touring a cloisonné factory. But its products were really second-rate, so I returned to Tianjin. I'm lucky the cloisonné was so bad. Had it been better, I might have stayed in Tangshan and been killed." Linda summoned her strength and stared directly at Alexandra. "You were right about one thing. Peking has the best antiques."

"How can you say that when you are in Xian?" a heavily accented man's voice said in English.

Linda saw Kang Xiaoma approaching, "Hello, Xiaoma." She smiled broadly, happy for the excuse to disengage herself from Alexandra. "I would like to introduce—"

"It's nice to see you again, Comrade Kang," Alexandra said in a slightly impolite voice.

"The honor is mine, Mrs. Koo." Xiaoma bowed.

"Miss Forbes, if you will excuse me for a moment, I have to leave a message at the desk. Then we can leave for the Qin Tombs."

Alexandra watched Xiaoma walk off. "You're coming up in the world."

"What do you mean?" Linda hoped she sounded sufficiently innocent.

"Xiaoma is the son of Kang Momin and the nephew of Kang Moruo."

"Who are they?"

Alexandra smiled slyly. "As if you didn't know!"

Linda could feel her legs trembling. "I don't."

"They are famous writers of sayings on fortune cookies."

"Look, Alexandra, I'm sorry if you're still angry at me for the inconvenience I caused you in Peking, but I resent your condescension. All I know is that Kang Xiaoma is the deputy manager of the Xian branch of the Arts and Crafts Corporation."

"And you don't know that his father is the governor of Shaanxi Province and his uncle is the director of the China Arts and Crafts Corporation?"

"You're kidding!"

Alexandra shook her head. "Your naïveté strains the imagination."

"I'm sorry about that," Linda replied.

"If I were you, I'd be careful about the games I was playing. Sometime, somebody is going to stop falling for your act."

The car in which Linda and Xiaoma were riding passed the pits where the stone soldiers of the Qin emperor were being excavated and continued toward Mount Li. A small dirt road led past the tumulus. The car bounced along, navigating its way through the deep ruts. The road led into a narrow valley ringed by steep cliffs. At the far end a dozen water buffaloes grazed aimlessly, while a group of men played cards. Xiaoma stopped the car and greeted them. They conversed for a few minutes. Everything seemed in order.

Three trucks motored toward them. Taking the relics from the trucks, workers from the Arts and Crafts Corporation packed them in strong hemp bags and draped them on the backs of the water buffaloes. Then Xiaoma divided the men into three groups and detailed the route to the cave.

While Xiaoma remained behind, Linda walked with the first group. The day was extremely warm. Dust from the yellow loess plains, whipped by the wind, clouded the air and made breathing difficult. The buffaloes set a fast pace on the rocky slope. Though Linda was in good shape, the animals were far better suited to the mountainous terrain. She struggled to keep up. One of the men handed her a bottle of warm beer. She took a swig and let the beer wash the dusty cobwebs from her throat.

They walked for more than two hours along a narrow, rutted path that led around the back of Black Horse Hill. Goat was waiting for them two hundred feet above the back of the cave. Further down the mountain, guards were patrolling the front entrance. Goat helped them unpack and then led them down the last portion of the winding path.

Checking off the relics against those on her manifest, Linda carefully laid each piece in its proper position for packing later that afternoon. The men brought three more loads from the water buffaloes and then headed back down the mountain. While Goat returned to the top of the hill, Linda waited alone in the cave. It was a dark, eerie place haunted by the spirit of an emperor who had been dead for two thousand years, yet Linda could remember few times when she had felt so alive.

It was well past four in the afternoon when Xiaoma reached the cave. "That's the last of it," he said, reviewing the replicas. "I've sent the animals and the rest of the men back. The ten of us"—he pointed to the men in the cave—"should be able to finish."

"I count eleven," Linda said.

"It's late," Xiaoma said. "We have to get you back to the hotel."

"I'm not made of paper. It's not so easy for me to get blown away," Linda said, quoting a Chinese saying.

Xiaoma pulled her aside. "Please be reasonable. We could be here all night."

"I can stay awake as long as any of you."

"It could be dangerous."

"I'm not here for the mineral springs."

Goat stepped up and winked at Linda. "Let her stay. She's a good warrior. Besides, I can use some help with my cooking."

"Cooking?" Linda asked.

"Our friend Lao Hu"—Goat pointed to an old man—"is supposed to bring the guards their dinner." He removed a bag filled with white powder from his belt. "I thought we might add a little spice to help them relax."

"Is that opium?" Linda asked.

Goat smiled his yellow-toothed smile. "It's an ancient Chinese herbal recipe, guaranteed to make anyone who uses it forget everything of concern in the world."

"You are most considerate," Linda said.

"We wouldn't want the guards staying up all night worrying about their relics, now would we?"

Early the next morning, Alexandra Koo stopped the hall porter. "Excuse me," she said, "have you seen Miss Forbes, the American in room 522?"

"Not since yesterday morning," the porter replied.

"I searched for her last night," Alexandra said, "but couldn't find her. Could I look in her room? She's an old friend of mine."

"Certainly." The porter opened Linda's door.

Alexandra stepped inside. The bed was neatly made. Yesterday's activities announcement still lay on the floor. Wherever Linda had gone with Kang Xiaoma, she had not returned.

Alexandra called the front desk. "I'd like to know if an American named Linda Forbes is still registered in the hotel."

There was a pause on the other end of the line. "Yes, Miss Forbes is still in the hotel. In fact, I believe she is now eating breakfast."

Lighting a cigarette, Alexandra walked to the dining room. She peered around the door and saw Linda sitting alone, wearing the same clothes she had on the day before. Alexandra crushed her cigarette. Something was very wrong. Foreigners in China never spent a night away from the hotels in which they were registered. Linda would have needed clearance from someone in a position of power, and such clearance would never have been given to a mere department-store buyer.

Alexandra scratched her neck with her long, neatly manicured nails. The coincidences involving Linda were becoming increasingly difficult to explain. She phoned Peking. Shen Mo answered Jiang Qing's private line. "I need a favor," Alexandra said. "Find out what you can about an American named Linda Forbes. She was the one who was arrested with Little Chang. She claims to be a buyer for a department store."

"I will do it at once," Shen responded.

"Also, contact Colonel Li. Tell him that an error may have been made with the American. She is now in Xian, but she should be returning to Peking. When she reaches the capital, I would like her arrested."

"On what grounds?"

"Treason or subversion would be fine. I just want her out of my hair."

"How's the corpse this morning?" Samuel Tang smiled at Marc Slater as he strode into the exquisite living room of Kang Moruo's house.

"Not bad, considering," Marc replied, running his hands over the lapels of his blue cotton Chinese worker's uniform.

"Your obit made the front pages of both the *New York Times* and the *Wall Street Journal*," Sam said, taking a seat on the brocaded couch. "I'm having copies flown in. I thought you might enjoy reading it."

"I think I'll pass."

"I wouldn't if I were you. It's a rare opportunity."

Marc shook his head as he poured a cup of tea. "It's macabre."

"Don't tell me you're not interested in your own immortality. No one builds a multibillion-dollar corporation and then risks his life on this sort of mission without some fleeting thought of his place in history."

A slightly embarrassed smile tugged at the ends of Marc's lips. "Well, maybe I do think about it every once in a while."

"And if your obituary were sitting right here . . ." Sam tapped his palm on a hand-carved teak table.

Marc laughed. "I might glance at it, if there was nothing on TV."

"Speaking of newspapers," Sam asked, "did you see today's edition of the *People's Daily*?"

"Was there another feature story on me?"

"Sorry to disappoint you. But it did have a lead editorial extolling Jiang Qing and the Gang of Four as the most able leaders in China. The editorial said that they were the only ones certain to 'act according to the principles laid down.'" Sam shook his head as he quoted the dictum used by Mao to define the loyalty of China's leaders.

"Who wrote that? Jiang herself?"

"The by-line read Mao Tse-tung."

"That's ridiculous," Marc replied. "Even in his least lucid moments, Mao could never think that Jiang and her Gang of Four were the most capable leaders in the country."

"You'll get no argument from me."

"If Jiang is using Mao's name to promote herself, why doesn't he object?"

"I'll give you three reasons." Sam ran his fingers through his thinning straight black hair. "Either Mao is crazy, or in a coma, or"—he paused—"he's already dead!"

The front door opened. Kang Moruo assisted Beatrice Tang down the steps from the hallway. She hobbled across the living room on her crutches. Her leg, broken during the earthquake, was still in a cast. Handing the crutches to Sam, she smoothed the wrinkles out of her print silk dress and dropped onto the couch. "How are you doing?" Marc asked.

"I'm getting speedier on these things all the time," Beatrice said as she removed two sheets of yellow paper from her purse. "I've just come from the Liaison Office. They gave me two coded messages." She put on her reading glasses. "The first is an intercept of a British transmission. Lord Henry Gateshead has been kidnapped by a group calling themselves the Peoples' Revolutionary Guards. As a ransom, they demand the return of Hong Kong's New Territories."

"That's ridiculous," Sam scoffed. "How can they expect England to trade two million people and twenty billion dollars in land and buildings for one ineffectual lord."

Beatrice laughed. "Sam has always had a warm spot for the Gatesheads. They're illegitimate cousins."

"That has nothing to do with it," Sam said, silently rebuking his wife. "It's the Chinese. I can't believe they're so stupid. Don't they understand that even if Lord Henry is nothing but a fop, the English are going to have to take some action to protect their citizens?"

"What makes you think the kidnappers are Chinese?" Marc asked.

"Who do you suggest?"

"How about the Russians?"

"It's strange that you should mention the Russians," Beatrice said as she tried to shift her leg. Sam helped prop it on a coffee table. "My other message deals with them. One of our satellites has spotted a heavy concentration of Russian troops moving along the western border of China in the vicinity of the Dzungarian Gate."

"Where's that?" Sam asked.

Marc paced to the window. "I bet it's in Xinjiang Province, near Karamay."

"How did you know?" Kang asked with surprise.

Marc smiled knowingly. "Because the pieces of the puzzle are falling into place. Karamay is the site of a highly productive oil field that the Russians have always coveted. All they need is a pretext for their invasion."

"Are you suggesting a fake attack like those near Kashi?" Kang asked.

Marc paused and lit his pipe. The Panda brand tobacco had a sharp bite and a slightly bitter aroma, but it was the only one available. "That's just what I'm suggesting."

"Do you think we can stop them?" Beatrice asked.

"Stop them?" Kang retorted. "Xinjiang is a wasteland of desolate mountains and arid deserts. How the hell are we even going to find them?"

"Finding them may be easier than we think," Marc said. "We're not looking for a group of local natives, we're looking for a strange entourage that, besides Gateshead, includes Avery Boswell, Van Wyck, Japanese from the Takamura Corporation, and a bunch of Turkic Nationalists."

"How do you suggest we search one million square miles?"

"We won't have to," Marc smiled, "because I think we know where they've been and where they're going."

"How did you get so prescient?"

"It's actually quite simple. We know the Russians are massing on the border near the Dzungarian Gate and that they want the oil fields in Karamay. Any mock attack will have to take place in this area." Marc took out a piece of paper and sketched a rough map of the province. "We also know that Gateshead was kidnapped in Urumqi and that Rahman's men were seen afterward on the way to Karamay. If they're going to lead the attack, they've got to pass through the oil fields and take the road to the border." Marc drew a large "X" on the map.

Kang nodded admiringly. "Let's say you're right. How do we get an armed force out there to stop them?"

Marc ran his hands through his soft hair. "We must

convince Hua to accept our plan."

"And if he won't?"

"Once the forgery of Mao's will and Jiang's other tricks are exposed, he'll have no choice but to side with us."

"By then it may be too late." Kang nervously lit a cigarette. "It could take us a week to mobilize men and weapons and get them to Xinjiang. By then, we could find ourselves in a full-fledged war with the Russians."

Marc stared at the spare but elegant Oriental garden in the courtyard behind the house. "Sam," he asked, "didn't you tell me you were planning a demonstration of your weapons for the People's Liberation Army?"

"It's supposed to take place ten days from now."

"Could you get them here sooner?"

"My people are just waiting for the Chinese."

"If we had your planes and equipment with a few well-trained men ready to go, we'd have a little leeway with Hua. We could send people to Xinjiang to track down the Russians, and then, as soon as we get Hua in our camp, we can fill your planes with men and send them west."

"It's fine with me," Sam said, "but I don't think Hua will buy it. We're hitting him with so many things now, I'm sure he's numb."

"What about Defense Minister Ye? He's more moderate. Maybe we could convince him?"

"Without telling Hua?"

"Without telling anyone."

"We'd really be putting our necks on the line." Sam wiped his brow.

"It would be far worse if Russia dismembered half of China."

"I'll try to set up an appointment with Ye," Sam said. "But if this stunt fails, none of us may ever leave the People's Republic."

"Don't worry," Marc laughed. "You're dealing with Lucky Slater."

Sam patted Marc on the back. "Looking at your track record on this trip, I think I have every reason to worry."

The cool night wind blew off the loess countryside. Stepping from the maintainance shed onto the tarmac, Alexandra Koo tightened the belt on her Burberry trench coat. Five trucks, filled with the relics that Lord Gateshead was purchasing, stood waiting next to a fence marking the outside boundary of the Xian airport. A Boeing 707 taxied from the main terminal almost a mile away.

Originally, Alexandra had planned to ship the relics by train to Shanghai and then by boat to Hong Kong, but the disruptions caused by the earthquake and the increasing tensions within the People's Republic had made her change her mind. Time was now the enemy. She could not take the risk that the relics would still be inside China once the coup started. Although she trusted Jiang Qing, these antiquities were her only insurance against the possibility that Jiang might lose.

Alexandra had talked to Jiang earlier that day. The apprehension in her friend's voice had been unmistakable. Jiang had said that Mao would not live out the week. She was already mobilizing her troops. She asked Alexandra to make one last purchase of weapons. Alexandra was pleased to do so, but first she needed the money from Gateshead. Jiang had pulled strings to arrange for the plane. It had been carrying relief supplies to Tianjin, but she had diverted it for one day. With all the crises of the last week, Alexandra would not be able to relax until these goods were in the hands of Gateshead's people in Hong Kong.

Two men wheeled a makeshift ladder up to the plane. The

captain presented himself to Alexandra. His instructions were to fly to Canton and then directly on to Hong Kong. Alexandra had decided to fly the first leg and then return to Peking by CAAC in the morning. The men loaded the crates into the cargo hold. Alexandra smiled as she checked the wooden boxes. When she had seen Linda Forbes that morning, she had been concerned that the relics had been tampered with, but at the cave, they had been exactly as she had left them.

Alexandra pulled the collar of her trench coat around her neck. Perhaps she had been wrong to suspect Linda. It was possible that Linda's connection with Little Chang and appearance in Tangshan and Xian had all been coincidences. There were no specific acts that could be traced to her. Whatever the truth, it was now too late to do anything. She felt much better knowing that Linda was safely out of the way.

Exhausted but pleased, Linda Forbes disembarked at Peking's Capital Airport. Her mission had been accomplished with perfect precision. The fake relics were on their way to Hong Kong. When they were unpacked and inspected, someone would have a rude awakening. Gateshead would refuse to pay for the forgeries; and without his money, Jiang Qing would be unable to purchase additional arms.

Passing through the checkpoint, Linda headed for the baggage claim. In the distance she saw Sen hurrying toward her. It had been a long time since she had seen a friendly face. She broke into a broad smile and quickened her pace. She felt close to Sen. They had struggled together through the earthquake and had shared the secret of the forged will. Sen was also her only living link to Marc. "You're really a sight for sore eyes, my friend," Linda said.

"I'm very glad to see you as well." Sen's eyes twinkled as he bowed respectfully. "I've got some wonderful news for you."

"I hope it's half as wonderful as mine. Our operation in Xian went perfectly. We have thirty million dollars' worth of antiques hidden in a cave and our friend, the Jade Empress, has two hundred and eighty crates of fakes." Linda's eyes sparkled. She was overjoyed at being able to share her success with a friend. "How does your news compare with that?"

"Your success is beyond comparison," Sen said, "but I think you will be equally pleased with my report."

"Stop teasing me and tell me what it is."

"I'll tell you in the car. There are too many people here. I can't take the risk that someone might overhear."

Linda gave Sen a fake pout. "All right. I'll get my luggage and meet you out front."

After a ten-minute wait at the baggage claim, Linda found her suitcases and hurried to meet Sen. "Excuse me, Miss Forbes," a heavily accented voice said in English.

She stopped instantly. Three men in Red Guard uniforms stepped in front of her. Her hands began to tremble. She could not believe what was happening. "Colonel Li!" she stammered.

The colonel's deep-set eyes stared menacingly as he bowed politely. "I am sorry to interrupt your journey"—he paused so that one of the soldiers could translate his words into English—"but I am afraid that we have some unfinished business to discuss."

Linda felt herself breaking into a cold sweat. "I don't understand."

Colonel Li toyed with the long scar that bisected his leathery neck. "There are a few questions we would like to ask."

"Please, I'm just exhausted." She was certain that they had discovered her real identity, but she had no idea where she had slipped up. "Can't it wait until morning?"

"I am afraid it can't."

Linda saw Sen ascending the stairs. She raised her voice so Sen could hear her. "Do your questions concern that young woman you arrested me with? I told you last time that I had no connection with her."

Colonel Li shifted uncomfortably. It would go badly for him if he caused a scene with a foreigner in the airport. "Miss Forbes, you are making this unnecessarily complicated. It would be advisable for you to come quietly. When we get to my office, we can discuss this matter in private." The colonel nodded to his two men, who positioned themselves on either side of Linda and began to escort her from the terminal.

"Are you arresting me?" Linda tried to form a protest. Her voice cracked. "I am a foreigner. I have my rights. I will go to my embassy."

"Please be quiet, Miss Forbes. The more you talk, the more difficult things will become." The colonel's tone was icy calm, but the ends of his lips quivered angrily. "I would not like to have to use force."

Linda glanced away from the colonel and saw Sen nodding at her. His calm expression made her feel a little better. She did not know if he could help, but at least this time someone would know where she was. "All right," Linda said as the Red Guards pushed her down the stairs. She gazed at Sen, hoping he would follow and then save her. Taking a deep breath, she tried to regain her composure. It's just a bad dream, she told herself. In the morning everything will be fine. She forced a smile. She did not believe her own words, but she had to keep up the pretense. She could not let the Red Guards make her lose face.

39: Two Old Codgers and a Country Bumpkin

Lighting a cigarette, Deng Xiaoping paced in front of a map of China in the oblong conference room in the central offices of the Yellow Mountain People's Commune. Six adjoining tables, three long and two abreast, and thirty brown wooden chairs filled most of the floor area. Despite the thirty chairs, only five men were in the room.

Befitting his role as premier, Hua Guofeng sat at the head of the table directly under his own portrait and that of Chairman Mao. To his side, at the near left corner of the table, sat Li Xiannian, the sixty-nine-year-old vice-chairman of the Politburo. As the chief economic planner in the People's Republic, Li was regarded as a moderate and pragmatist; but he was firmly aligned with Hua. In the middle Liu Teyu, still bothered by his broken leg and ruptured spleen, sat facing Hua with his feet stretched across three chairs. Deng Xiaoping had selected a chair at the far end, but since the start of the meeting more than three hours before, he had rarely left his feet.

In the back of the room, Marc Slater sat alone. Initially Hua had objected to Marc's presence, but Liu and Deng had both argued that he should be permitted to attend. Marc had arranged for the meeting and had firsthand knowledge of the assassination attempt on Deng and Hua, the troop movements and commando activities of the Russians, Jiang's smuggling of weapons, and the forgery of Mao's will. Aware that his position as a foreigner made him highly vulnerable, Marc had tried to remain as inconspicuous as possible.

Deng placed his palms on the table and stared at the motionless Hua. He and Liu had painstakingly made the case against Jiang Qing and the Russians. Using documents, tapes, and satellite photographs, they had pleaded and cajoled, trying to win Hua to their side. Li Xiannian had inched toward compromise, but the premier had refused to give ground. Deng pursed his lips. A large vein on the side of his head throbbed. "All right," he said. "What more do you need to know?"

"I think I should talk to Chairman Mao," Hua said in his dull, ponderous voice.

"Who are you kidding?" Deng scoffed. As the discussion had progressed, he had become increasingly short-tempered. "Mao is so senile, he won't even know who you are. I heard he was ranting yesterday about Lin Biao. Lin's been dead for fourteen years."

"He probably meant that we should be watchful of others who would follow Lin's line."

"You can't really believe that!"

"I do," Hua replied.

Deng lit another cigarette. "Did you see that ridiculous editorial in today's *People's Daily*? Do you think Mao really believes that Jiang Qing is the only one who will act according to the principles laid down?"

"I'm sure he meant to say that Comrade Jiang was a loyal and valued leader of the People's Republic."

"You sound like a horny man being seduced by a syphilitic whore." Deng blew smoke rings toward the ceiling. "You're determined to get laid even if it kills you."

Liu raised his hands toward the antagonists. "Why don't we all relax?" the massive general suggested. "Then perhaps we can lift this discussion out of the gutter."

"I am not about to be seduced by anyone," Hua insisted. His broad face remained expressionless. "I merely want to talk things over with our Great Helmsman."

"And how do you propose to see Mao?" Deng pumped his arms like a marching windup doll as he strode down the side of the table. "Yuanxin has Mao so heavily guarded that no one can see the Chairman without his nephew's permission."

"But I am the premier of the People's Republic. I am next in line for succession."

Deng laughed. "Until Jiang Qing produces her forged last will."

"You have a fanatic dislike for Jiang, perhaps because you blame her for your purge," Hua said, "but I don't think she'd be that treacherous."

"They why did Mao's calligrapher disappear after leaving for a meeting with Yao Wenyuan?" The diminutive Deng shook his finger at Hua. "And how do you explain that the guardian of the National Archives caught Jiang breaking into Mao's private vault?"

"Jiang said it was the other way around."

Deng pounded his fist on the table. "Why would the guardian of the archives do something stupid like that?"

"Perhaps she was working for you. She is the sister-in-law of the assistant to your capitalist friend." Hua pointed at

Marc, who stirred uneasily but remained silent. This was not the time to defend himself.

"That's bullshit!" Deng said as he stormed to the back of the table.

"If this guardian is right, why doesn't she present some evidence to defend herself?"

"Because," Deng said, "once she was arrested by the Red Guard, she disappeared off the face of the earth."

"Then what makes you believe her?"

"For one thing, she was a middle-level cadre who had nothing to gain and everything to lose. Both she and her husband were advancing in the Party. They had never aligned themselves with any faction. It just wouldn't make sense for them to become involved in such treachery."

"That's not enough to convince me," Hua responded.

"We also have someone who met with the guardian and heard her story."

"Who is your mystery witness?" Li Xiannian asked.

"She is an American woman named Linda Forbes."

"An American?" Hua's usually monotonous voice sounded irritated. "Why should I believe an American? All Americans hate Jiang Qing."

"Because this one"—Liu spoke in a soft yet powerful voice—"is my granddaughter." Hua and Li stared at Liu in shock. "If you question her veracity, you must also question mine."

Hua pushed back his chair and stood for a minute silently facing the wall. When he turned back to the others, his eyes looked strained. "Jiang Qing is not my enemy. I don't want to talk about her anymore. I'd like to change the subject."

"I don't understand you." Deng clasped his hands behind his neck and pressed his arms against his ears in frustration. "You're willing to tackle the problems of the earthquake—in fact, you've handled them exceptionally well. But you run, like a chicken being chased by a wolf, from any discussion of Jiang Qing."

"Jiang is Mao's wife. We all owe Mao complete respect and support."

"Jiang is Mao's mattress." Deng used the phrase originated by Nikita Khrushchev twenty years before. "She is the last person whom he would want to see leading the People's Republic."

"No, she's not." Hua stared blankly at Deng as he slowly shook his head. "You are!"

"Why does it have to be a choice between Jiang and me?" Deng's voice reflected his exasperation.

"I may be a country bumpkin," Hua said with a slight smile, "and I may not have your connections in the Party, but credit me with some understanding of how the world works. There is no doubt in my mind that if I side with you, you will eventually take over."

"Me?" Deng screwed his face into an expression of comic disbelief. "I am a nobody. I've been kicked out of Peking and purged from my Party posts. I'm even unemployed."

"You're Lazarus," Hua scoffed. "You've risen from the dead before, and you wouldn't be here now if you did not intend to do it again."

"But it's your government. If you keep me purged, there is nothing I can do but watch the grass grow."

"Stop treating me like an imbecile." Despite the strength of his words, Hua continued to speak in a monotone. "If I want to keep control of my own government, my only hope is to maintain a careful balance between you and Jiang. If I join forces with you, how long do you think I'll last? A year? Maybe two?"

Deng spit into a large brass bowl in the corner of the room. "That's longer than Jiang will give you."

"With the support of Comrade Mao, I hope to fend off

490

both extremes and lead China on the middle road according to the principles laid down."

"Mao is virtually a dead man."

"I'll still take my chances with him."

"Even if it means throwing the country into a civil war?"

"I think, old friend, you are becoming a little melodramatic," Li Xiannian said. Although Li supported Hua, he and Deng had worked closely together for many years.

"You're right." Deng's eyes twinkled. "There is no reason to be alarmed just because Jiang has mobilized her troops in Shanghai and transferred two of Mao Yuanxin's tank divisions from Shenyang to Peking."

"Are you certain of that?"

"As certain as I am that the Hour of the Snake follows the Hour of the Dragon."

Li wiped his face with a damp washcloth. "Can this be verified?"

"You two run the government. You shouldn't have any difficulty," Deng said, taking another swig of beer. The room was becoming uncomfortably warm. "By the way, while you're at it, why don't you also check on the troop movements of the Russians? I believe you'll find them massed in considerable strength in the Dzungarian Gate. Our intelligence indicates that they plan to capture the Karamay oil fields."

"That's capitalist propaganda," Hua scoffed.

"It would not hurt to check," Deng replied. "Even capitalists are sometimes correct."

"I am not worried," Hua said. "We are well armed in that region."

Deng laughed, "We are like a minnow trying to battle a shark."

"Comrade Hua and I," Li said, "recognize the strength of the Russians and the ambition of Jiang Qing, but we cannot take precipitous action based on nothing but your allegations and a stack of evidence supplied by the American CIA. We would like some time to verify what you have told us. After we have completed our investigation, we can meet again."

"I appreciate your desire for caution." Liu placed his hands on the sides of his chair and shifted his body. A sharp pain shot through his ribs. "But if we don't take action now, it may soon be too late."

"Do you have something specific in mind?" Li asked.

Liu's voice was strained. "We can't let the Russians continue to threaten us. We must do something now to keep them at bay. I suggest we test one of our new hydrogen bombs and then launch one of our reconnaissance satellites. I'm sure the Russians will get the message, especially since our atomic-missile facilities are in Xinjiang, the very province they plan to invade."

"All right," Hua said, pleased that he could finally do something. "I'll accept your suggestions. Li, call Defense Minister Ye. Have him order the bomb test for tomorrow and the satellite for the next day."

"Before you go," Liu said to Li, "I have a further request. I'd also like approval to transfer one of my battalions to Xinjiang to defend against the Russians and one to Peking just in case Jiang stages a coup."

"What guarantee do I have," Hua asked, "that you won't use the troops against me?"

"You have my word!" The hard edge of Liu's voice cut through the room.

"But these are complex times."

"Look, son!" Liu addressed the much younger premier of the People's Republic. "No one, not even Chairman Mao, has ever questioned my word. From the time of the Long March, everyone in the Party has known that Long Way Liu may walk in a circle but he talks in a straight line."

Hua lowered his head remorsefully. It was inexcusable to make an elderly revolutionary leader lose face and stupid to risk alienating the man who controlled the southern armies. "Excuse me, honored friend. I did not mean to impugn your word. I would be pleased to have your troops in Peking and Xinjiang." Hua turned to Li. "Inform Ye of my decisions."

Li smiled as he stood up and left the room. He was glad that both sides seemed to be moving toward compromise.

"Perhaps we should take a break for a few minutes," Hua suggested. "I need a walk in the countryside to clear my head."

Deng waited until Hua had left the room. Then he sat down next to Liu. "What do you think of Hua?"

"He's stubborn and a little over his head," Liu replied. "But in time he'll come around."

"We may not have time. It will take your troops two weeks to mobilize and get in position."

"More like three days," Liu smiled. "They're already on the way."

"Without Hua's approval?" Deng's eyes twinkled.

Liu put his finger to his lips. "If Hua finds out, I'll tell him they went the wrong way. For me, that's par for the course."

"Then it's your troops against Jiang, the Red Guards, and Unit 8341," Deng said, calculating the odds.

"I'm not sure that Jiang can count on 8341," Liu replied. "Wang Dongxin is a member of the Wind Faction. If we can win over Hua, or at least Li and Ye, I think we can neutralize him."

Deng slapped Liu lightly on the back and laughed. "For two old codgers, one of whom can't hold a job and the other of whom can't find his way, we're not doing half bad."

Marc took a seat across the table. "What about the forged will?"

"Leave it to the long-nosed foreign devil," Deng joked, "to ruin our party."

"Humblest apologies." Marc bowed his head.

Deng stood up and paced to the back of the table. "We have to do something about the will, and we have to do it now. By the time Hua comes around, Mao could be dead, and Jiang, with her bogus will, could be, God help us, our new chairman."

As Deng walked off, Liu poured two cups of tea and offered one to Marc. "Old friend, tell me about this granddaughter of mine whom I've never met."

"I thought you knew each other," Marc said.

"Until a few years ago, I didn't even know she existed."

Marc smiled. "That explains why she was so insistent on bringing the information about the forgery of Mao's will to me directly."

"I'm sorry she did not," Liu said. "How did she find out about the forgery anyway?"

"That was an accident," Marc said, remembering the time they had gone jogging in Canton. "She bumped into Little Chang while running through Beihai Park."

"But she is working for your people, isn't she?"

"She's tracking the smuggling of arms and relics," Marc said. Though he had long suspected Linda's involvement, he had not learned the truth until this morning when he had talked to Kang Momin.

"How is she faring?"

"You would be proud of her," Marc said. "Last night she secretly substituted worthless copies for thirty million dollars' worth of Qin relics that Jiang was smuggling out of the country."

Liu laughed and clapped his hands. "I'm pleased to see my granddaughter has inherited my penchant for deception and misdirection. Tell me more about her."

Marc smiled as he recalled his first meeting with Linda at the Peninsula Hotel. "She's like you in many ways, old friend. She's stubborn, independent, determined, and very astute."

"Those sound like qualities of a man."

"In this case they belong to a very lovely woman."

"She gets her looks from her grandmother." Liu stared into space, remembering his lost love. "Margot was the most magnificent woman I have ever seen."

"You will not be disappointed in Linda."

"It sounds as if you like her." Liu winked at Marc.

"She's quite exceptional." A slightly embarrassed smile flashed across Marc's face. "She also saved my life on the train from Hong Kong."

"Then she is responsible for your future."

"A man could do far worse."

"Old friend, I hate to bring up painful memories"—Liu lit a cigarette—"but how would she compare with Meili?"

Marc walked to the back of the room as he thought about the young Chinese woman who had died in the quake. "That would be as difficult as comparing a delicate piece of carved jade to a large flawless diamond. They are completely different, but both very precious."

"Equally valued by a man like yourself?"

Marc smiled. "Are you trying to be a matchmaker?"

"I never even knew my son's wife. It is my duty to look after my granddaughter." The massive general smiled wryly.

"Doesn't she have any say in it?" Marc asked.

"Not in China."

"But she is American."

"Are you trying to wriggle out of this match?" Liu shook his fist at Marc in mock anger. "Aren't I good enough for you? In imperial times it would have been considered a signal honor for a foreign barbarian to be linked by marriage to one of the great generals of China."

"The honor is no less in Communist times," Marc said respectfully.

"The only difference," Liu joked, "is that we servants of the people cannot afford such large dowries."

"I am a man of humble needs," Marc said. "Just give me a pig and a few catties of rice and I'll live like a king."

"Good. Then it's settled."

Deng and Li walked back into the room. Their faces were bleached the color of dried husks of rice. "My friends," Liu called as he raised a glass of beer, "I have a marvelous announcement. For the cost of one pig and a few catties of rice, I have arranged to wed my granddaughter to the blue-eyed spirit who runs like the wind—if, of course, in accordance with the strange customs of the barbarians, they both fall in love and want to get married."

"We are pleased for you," Li said in a subdued voice. His eyes were red.

"You don't seem very happy," Liu protested in jest.

"We have some news of our own," Li said.

"Is it as good as mine?" Liu's eyes twinkled.

Deng walked up the aisle and placed his hands on Liu's shoulders. "I am afraid that it is very bad."

"Have a drink first. We will talk later of the troubles of China."

"This will not wait."

Liu drained his beer. "What is so important that it should disrupt old friends enjoying a drink?"

Li Xiannian dropped his tired body into a chair across from Liu. Lines ringed his eyes. His jowly cheeks sagged. "Our Helmsman is dead."

"What?" Liu looked up in surprise at the news he had long expected.

"Chairman Mao has left this world."

40: The Silks of Turpan

Frans Van Wyck paced the dirt floor of the mud brick hut in the village of Utu in the northwest corner of Xinjiang Province. Even with the shade from the grape arbors that were strung over the building, the heat of the desert was intense. Sipping a cup of lukewarm sun tea, Van Wyck turned to Avery Boswell. "I find your actions inexcusable," he said in a calm voice that belied his annoyance.

"You approved the kidnapping of Gateshead," Boswell replied.

"I approved an operation eight days ago in Peking, not yesterday in Urumqi."

"I really had no choice," Boswell said.

"Gateshead didn't even know you were there."

"It was only a matter of time before he found out," Boswell said, wiping his face with a damp cloth. "We were the only two Westerners in Kashi, we were at the same hotel, and I work for a company that bears his name. There was no way I could have kept my presence a secret."

"But you could have invented an excuse," Van Wyck said.

Boswell dipped the cloth into a porcelain bowl filled with water and dabbed it on his neck. "I didn't think Gateshead would believe me."

"So instead you kidnapped him and then sent those fool telegrams demanding the return of the New Territories as a ransom."

Boswell smiled like a child caught with his hand in the cookie jar. "I thought it would disturb Her Majesty's government."

"The only thing it has disturbed is my plans. Gateshead is a most unpleasant and unnecessary loose end."

"There won't be any more."

"There had better not be." Van Wyck poured another cup of tea.

Aziz Rahman, wearing blue cotton pants, a light corduroy jacket, and a gray Russian-style Kazak cap, stepped through the open door. A thick black stubble covered his face. "Please excuse the interruption." He bowed to Van Wyck. "Can we talk?"

"You can speak in front of Mr. Boswell."

"The Chinese have just exploded a hydrogen bomb at Lop Nor." Rahman referred to the atomic station in southern Xinjiang Province. "There is also evidence that they are preparing to launch a reconnaissance satellite."

"That's all we need." Van Wyck grimaced.

"Why are you concerned?" Boswell said. "It's just saber rattling."

"The bomb may be, but not the satellite," Van Wyck replied. "Once it's launched, they'll have a clear view of our troops in the Dzungarian Gate. We'll have no choice but to invade immediately or retreat. I would have preferred to wait until Mao had died and a civil war had begun." Van Wyck's voice trailed off as he stood staring silently at the mountains in the distance. Finally he walked to his desk and started to write. "Boswell, I want you to return to Peking. I'm giving you the names of five operatives and detailed instructions for one final operation."

"What is it?" Boswell asked.

"I want you to assassinate Hua Guofeng."

"What?" Boswell's mouth dropped open. "But why?"

"Because we need a civil war to cover our invasion. And nothing is going to happen until Hua is out of the way."

"But he is the premier of the People's Republic."

"For weeks you've been complaining that you haven't seen any real action." Van Wyck continued to write. "Now that I give you the opportunity, you start to vacillate."

"I'm not vacillating." Boswell strode to the desk. "I'm just confused as to why you selected me. I thought you were dissatisfied with my work."

Van Wyck glanced at Boswell without raising his head. "You are the only one I can send."

"When do you want me to leave?"

"I'd like you to be on tomorrow's plane from Urumqi."

Boswell looked at his watch. "That means I'll have to travel all night along nomad-infested camel tracks that pass for roads."

"Do you want me to radio Bulganov in Moscow and tell him that I've put off the invasion so you can have your beauty rest?"

"Ease up on me," Boswell protested. "I was only asking a question. If you want me to leave now, I'll leave. If you want me to shoot Hua, I'll shoot. I'm a good soldier, but I'm still entitled to ask a few questions."

"You're wrong, Mr. Boswell. None of my soldiers is entitled to ask questions. Isn't that correct, Rahman?" The Turk nodded. Van Wyck handed Boswell an envelope. "Here are the instructions. Don't be a hero. Just carry out my orders exactly as I've listed them."

After sending Boswell to Urumqi, Van Wyck and Rahman motored into the mountains. As they reached the first of the foothills, the land became greener and the air fresher. Fields of cotton lay tucked in narrow plains, while rugged stalks of marijuana grew wildly along the route. The narrow road was frequently blocked by camels pulling carts loaded with melons, or by flocks of goats. Turning into a green valley ringed by snowcapped peaks, the jeep drove over a rutted path until it reached a cluster of yurts.

Van Wyck walked to the largest of the circular tents that resembled giant mushrooms. More than forty feet in circumference and twelve feet high, this yurt was built with the same design that the nomadic Turks had used for thousands of years. Long flexible poles stretched from the ground to the rounded roof, where they were connected to a circular brace that formed a central skylight. A layer of tan felt cloth secured by sticks and leather ropes formed the outer layer. Although yurts could weather the intense storms of the mountains, they could be dismantled and packed up in a matter of hours.

Stopping at the entrance, Van Wyck peered inside. Lord Henry Gateshead, looking tired but otherwise unharmed, sat on an Oriental rug next to an iron cooking stove. "Good afternoon, Lord Gateshead," Van Wyck said as he stepped forward.

Gateshead stood up and brushed the dirt off his pants. He was dressed in a clean shirt, tie, and vest. "You have me at a disadvantage, sir."

"I am Frans Van Wyck," the Dutchman said, repressing a smile. Gateshead was undoubtedly the first person the natives had ever seen in such formal Western clothes.

"Well, Mr. Van Wyck, I hope you are here to resolve the injustice that has been perpetrated on me."

"I am sorry for whatever inconveniences you have suffered."

"Inconvenience? That's hardly an apt word for being kidnapped by a gang of Chinese lunatics."

"Turkic Nationalists," Van Wyck corrected. "I apologize for your abduction and for my incorrect choice of words."

"Apology accepted." Gateshead picked up his suit jacket. "Now can we return to Peking?"

"It's not that simple."

"What are you talking about?" Gateshead walked to the door. "You can drive me directly to the airport in Urumqi."

Van Wyck motioned for Gateshead to sit down. "I wish I could oblige you, but unfortunately you are in the midst of a most complicated situation. The Turks are threatening to revolt. There is the danger of a Russian invasion, and all the roads have been closed."

"How were you able to get here?"

"I traveled on back routes carved by the nomads."

"But you are a Westerner from . . ."

"The Netherlands. But I have spent so much time here that the Chinese and the Turks extend me special courtesies."

"I will do anything to get out of this wilderness," Gateshead said, with more bravado than he was feeling.

An old Turkic woman, wearing a red and white print dress and a long green cotton scarf over her head, came into the tent carrying a platter filled with flat, stone-ground bread, yogurt, goat cheese, and four types of fresh melons. Van Wyck dipped a piece of melon into the yogurt and took a bite. "I truly wish I could help you."

"Is it money? I will pay whatever you ask."

"Please, Lord Gateshead, this is not the time to take chances."

"When? Tomorrow? The next day?" Gateshead arched his eyebrows in frustration.

Van Wyck studied the Englishman. He was hardly an imposing figure, yet he did have an unmistakable pride. Even in the rustic surroundings of the Turkic yurt, he had retained his dignity. There was no reason to kill him. The kidnapping had not even been part of the plan. "Let's see if we can work something out," Van Wyck said, pondering a tempting idea.

"Say the word—I'll do anything."

The idea, Van Wyck knew, violated every professional principle by which he had lived. Yet it would not harm anyone. As long as his mission was not affected, why shouldn't he try to save the man's life and help himself as well? He would think of it as moonlighting. Bulganov would have made the same decision if he had the opportunity. "If you are willing to wait two more days, I may be able to get you back to Peking."

"Under what conditions?" Gateshead asked, pouring a cup of tea.

"You mentioned Turpan. I myself am a lover of Chinese art."

Gateshead smiled. "A connoisseur of art, a friend of the Turkic Nationalists, and a man who speaks English with an impeccably cultured accent—you are a strange one, Van Wyck."

"Things are often not what they seem." Van Wyck stared through the skylight. "If you want my help, I suggest you refrain from asking questions."

"As you wish."

"In Turpan, there is a Tang dynasty silk damask with a flower-and-bird pattern that I have long admired. I'd like you to purchase it for me."

"How do you expect me to do that?"

"I'll have the contracts brought here for your signature. The damask will be shipped to Hong Kong, and your agents will deliver it to me."

"How much does this damask cost?"

"Sixty thousand dollars, a rather modest sum for your safety."

"How do you know I won't renege on our agreement once I'm safe?"

"Because, Lord Gateshead, you are an English gentleman."

Gateshead nodded respectfully. He could never be a successful pirate like his grandfather, but in these times he was perhaps better off. He doubted whether anyone would have trusted George Alexander with such a bargain. "You have my word." He shook Van Wyck's hand.

41: The Sixteen Hours

Walking briskly from the conference room of the Yellow
River People's Commune to the helicopter that would take
him to Peking, Marc Slater was consumed with feelings of
shock and disbelief, but not of sadness. The most influential
leader of the twentieth century was dead. Mao Tse-tung, the
Great Helmsman, the man who had led the Long March,
built the Communist Party, and governed one-quarter of the
world for almost three decades, had died.

Marc had known Mao for more than forty years. As a
youth in Yan'an, he had idolized the Chairman. But Marc
did not grieve for Mao as he had for Chou En-lai. Over the
years, Mao had grown too large to be treated like another
fallible human being. It was not that Mao was perfect; few
had ever made more glaring errors—the Great Leap
Forward and the Cultural Revolution were two of the most
foolish escapades in history. But the Communist Party had
transformed Mao into a god. His successes were magnified
to excess, while history was rewritten to cover his failures, so

that now it was difficult to tell where the reality stopped and the myth started.

Marc was surprised that the others had reacted in the same way. There were no tears or overt signs of emotion, not even from Mao's oldest friends. Hua was Mao's protégé. He had served as the Party leader in Mao's home province. All his political success was based on Mao's support. Liu, Li, and Deng had served with Mao from the time of the Long March. They had lived together in the hills while fighting the KMT and the Japanese. For forty years they had worked together, building their vision of the future. Yet even for these men, Mao was a cold and distant Buddha.

Liu, Li, and Hua followed Marc to the helicopter. Deng had not been invited on the flight. It would have been unseemly for him to arrive at Zhong Nanhai on the night of Mao's death. It would also have needlessly alerted Jiang Qing to the possibility of his rehabilitation.

Pretending to read a magazine, Marc eavesdropped while the others discussed Mao's death. Dealing with a dead emperor was no less politically treacherous than dealing with a live one. They needed to stall for time while they developed a strategy. It was decided to delay the announcement for sixteen hours in order to give themselves some leeway.

Plans for the funeral and memorial service had to be made with great care. Issues such as the funeral clothing, the burial site, and the selection of pallbearers were of immense importance. The Chinese, who never saw their leaders, would carefully scrutinize the order of the mourners for a clue to the future composition of the government. Since he was the premier, Hua would have little difficulty maintaining his position, but Jiang would fight to place Zhang and Wang ahead of Ye and Li. If she succeeded, the people would take it as a sign of her ascendancy.

Another thorny political problem was how to bury Mao. Hua would have been happiest if, like Chou En-lai, Mao had asked to be cremated. But Mao wanted to be buried. He had selected a site in the Papaoshan Cemetery, next to one chosen by Jiang. Hua was worried that Jiang would use the neighboring plots as proof that she and Mao were united in death as well as in life. To foreigners, such a fact might seem trivial, but the Chinese would consider it a true indication of Jiang's status. "I don't know what to do about the gravesite," Hua said. "If we bury Mao in Papaoshan, it will be a great boost to Jiang's status. But if we try to move him elsewhere, she'll go crazy writing articles in the *People's Daily* and broadcasting programs on television calling us traitors. Either way we lose."

A wry smile tugged at the corners of Liu's lips. "Not if we transform Mao from a dead chairman into a national monument."

"A monument?"

"We can make Mao a national shrine. Picture this." Liu held up his massive hands. "We'll get the best taxidermists—like the ones from Vietnam who worked on Ho Chi Minh—to dress Mao in his finest Zhongshan suit and stuff him like an animal in a museum. Then we'll put him on exhibit in the Great Hall of the People and invite the entire country to pay their last respects. Hundreds of millions will trek to Peking. The mourning will last for years. Mao's body in death will remain the ultimate symbol of authority, and you"—Liu pointed to Hua—"will be the direct beneficiary."

"Jiang Qing will not allow it."

Liu laughed. "Jiang will have no choice. If she objects, she will seem petty and jealous."

"I don't know," Hua said. "It was not what Chairman Mao requested."

"To hell with Chairman Mao," Liu replied. "He's dead. If

we want to run the government, we can't let Jiang have the grave next to his or lead the mourners."

The butler opened the door of Kang's luxurious home. Marc hurried inside. Sam and Beatrice Tang were sitting in the living room while Sen Tailing nervously paced the floor. "How did it go?" Sam asked, rising to greet Marc.

"Hua didn't give us a commitment," Marc said, "but he's edging in our direction. However, there is something of much greater importance." Marc stepped to the kitchen door to make sure no one was there, and then turned back to the others. "Chairman Mao is dead," he whispered.

"We suspected as much," Sam said. "Kang received a call summoning him to an emergency meeting of the Politburo. We guessed it was Mao."

"We'd better get to work," Marc said. "There are sixteen hours until the announcement. After that, all hell is going to break loose."

"I convinced Defense Minister Ye to let me bring in the planes," Sam said. "They'll be here tomorrow."

"Good," Marc replied. "So will three battalions of Liu's men. We can use at least one in Xinjiang."

"I'm going there to help track down the Russians," Sam volunteered.

"Can you get a visa?" Marc asked.

"Ren Daoling of the China Travel Service has been transferred to Peking. He'll draw up the papers and then accompany me."

"Ren's a good man," Marc said. "You should also contact Kao Yangxu, Kang's man in Xinjiang. He's been following Rahman and the others."

"I'll do that." Sam walked to the window and poured himself a cup of tea. "There is one problem." He paused to sip his tea. "Linda Forbes has been arrested by the Red Guards."

Marc was stunned. "What happened?"

"I went to meet her at the airport last night," Sen said, "but Colonel Li and two Red Guards intercepted her and took her to a prison farm forty miles north of Peking."

"We've got to get her out." Marc pounded his fist on the table.

"We all want to help Linda," Sam said, "but with Jiang and the Russians ready to move, there may not be time."

"We have to do something," Marc said with concern.

"Our people will check out the situation," Sam advised, "but worrying will do you absolutely no good. We have other issues to consider, like removing the forged will from the National Archives."

Marc ran his hands through his hair. "How about giving me some easy ones for a change."

"You wouldn't like it if I did." Sam patted Marc on the back. "Didn't I read that your corporate slogan was P.O.R.—Push on Regardless?"

Marc shrugged and laughed. "That'll teach me not to give interviews."

The guard opened the door and ushered Linda into the dingy gray cell. She crimped her nose—the room stank of mildew and stale urine. She walked to the solitary window and tried to open it. It would not budge. Nails had been driven into the frame. She looked out into the circular dirt courtyard ringed by four barns. Dust from the Gobi Desert blew down from the surrounding hills.

Pacing the floor, Linda tried to figure out why she was being imprisoned. The only explanation that made any sense was that her arrest had been ordered by Alexandra Koo,

Linda could not believe that the Jade Empress had any hard evidence. She convinced herself that she was safe until the relics reached Hong Kong and were exposed as fakes. Then Alexandra would come in a fury. She had to find a way of getting out before that happened.

The guard opened the door and slid a tray of food into the cell. Dinner consisted of a bowl of noodles mixed with spinach and a few pieces of chicken, as well as a cup of tea. Linda had little appetite, but she forced herself to eat. She would need her strength for dealing with Alexandra and Colonel Li.

She had just finished when the door opened again. Colonel Li, dressed in a neatly pressed uniform, marched in, followed by his interpreter. "Did you enjoy your dinner, Miss Forbes?" he asked with an icy smile.

"I prefer the food at the Peking Hotel," Linda replied.

"The food here is much fresher. The chicken and the spinach come from our own farm."

"I'm a city girl," Linda said. "Fresh food means little to me."

"Then this will be an excellent learning experience." The colonel waited for the interpreter to translate. "I will instruct the cook to prepare a variety of Chinese vegetables. You will return to your country an expert in fresh Oriental cuisine."

The colonel's suggestion that she would eventually be set free gave Linda some hope. "When do you intend to let me go?"

"When I am authorized to do so."

"You can't still believe that I had anything to do with that woman you arrested two weeks ago. What was her name? Little . . ."

"Chang," the colonel replied. "What I believe is of no consequence. I am only following orders."

"Did they come from Alexandra Koo?"

The colonel stared at her in surprise as he listened to the translation of her words. "The source of my orders is irrelevant."

"Not if it's Mrs. Koo," Linda pressed. She had an idea. It was risky, but she had to take the chance.

"Why are you so concerned with Mrs. Koo?"

"Is she your friend?" Linda tried to keep her own voice steady.

"Mrs. Koo is a friend of the People's Republic."

"But is she someone who will help you in your future?"

"I'm tiring of your games." The colonel's voice was harsh.

Linda's legs shook. She was petrified that she was about to make a colossal mistake. She had defended herself against the accusations that she was in league with Little Chang by claiming she could not understand Chinese. Once she started to speak, Li would know she had been lying, but she saw no other way to get to him. Stepping in front of the colonel, she whispered in Chinese, "You are making a grave error trusting an overseas capitalist like Mrs. Koo." The colonel glared angrily. Linda's voice quivered. "Come back without your interpreter and I will give you some information of vital importance." She continued to stare at the colonel. She thought she detected a subtle change in his expression, but it could have been her imagination.

The colonel abruptly turned away. "What did the long-nosed foreign devil say?" he demanded of his interpreter.

"Excuse me, colonel." The man bowed obsequiously. "I did not hear her."

"There's no use throwing away spit on this barbarian whore." The colonel spun on his heels and stormed out.

Linda shifted nervously as she watched the door close. She had no way of knowing if he would take her bait. She was not even sure if she wanted him to. It was a long shot that could either set her free or ruin everything. If Colonel Li did come back, she would have to be careful. The colonel was no fool.

She lay down on the wooden platform that served as a bed. She was exhausted, but she could not sleep. There was a scratching noise on the wall at the other side of the room. She jumped, thinking it was a mouse. Nervously she turned on the ancient desk lamp. Its dim light cast eerie shadows through the room. She searched under the bed. There were no animals, but the scratching continued. It seemed to have a defined rhythm and be coming from the adjoining cell. Perhaps someone was trying to contact her. She walked to the wall and knocked twice. There was silence. She knocked again. A moment passed, then two knocks came in return. Her body trembled. Someone else was imprisoned with her. She did not know the identity of the person, but she had to communicate. "Is someone there?" she whispered.

"Sssh!" a muffled voice replied.

The scratching moved toward the corner. Linda lay down on the dank dirt floor and huddled against the musty wall. Something pricked the side of her arm. She looked down with a start. A piece of parchment protruded through a small hole. She pulled it into her room and unfolded it. Beautifully scripted Chinese characters, drawn like words of art, filled the parchment. She started to read. "Please do not speak. The walls have ears. Tap once on the wall if you can read this."

Linda knocked once.

"If you can write Chinese characters, tap three times."

Linda tapped three times.

"I am Comrade Rong Yi. I have been here for more than one month."

Linda crawled back to the chair and took a pen out of her purse. "I am Linda Forbes, an American. I was brought here this afternoon."

Linda slipped the paper under the door and pressed her

ear to the wall. She could hear the scratching of a quill pen. The parchment was slipped through again. "Your characters are excellent, especially for a foreigner. I am pleased to make a new friend. I would appreciate it if you could tell me of events in my country. How serious was the earthquake?"

Linda walked to the desk. She did not know who Rong Yi was but if he was a prisoner of the Red Guard, he was probably aligned against Jiang. She described her experiences in the earthquake. The characters flowed onto the page. It was a good emotional catharsis that kept her mind off Colonel Li and Alexandra Koo.

After filling the parchment, Linda slipped it through the crack. There was a noise in the hallway. Rong Yi scurried from the wall. She could hear the door of his cell open. She jumped up and hurried to the window, wondering if her neighbor was all right.

Thirty minutes later, there was another scraping sound. Linda hurried back to the wall. Rong Yi slipped a clean piece of parchment through the crack. "We must be careful not to alert the guards. Tell me what you know of Chairman Mao's health and of the struggle against the Gang of Four."

Linda wrote what she knew, omitting references that would reveal her mission. Rong Yi took the paper and moved to the far side of his cell. Perhaps he had another pen pal. More than two hours passed before he slid the paper back into Linda's cell. "Since you are an American, I am wondering if you know a friend of mine who works for an American company. His name is Sen Tailing."

Linda gasped. It could be a trap. Colonel Li was very clever. He could have put the man there to spy on her. Yet what would he have to gain by linking her to Sen? There had to be another explanation. Unless she answered Rong Yi's question, she would never find out what he had in mind. "I have met Sen several times," she wrote.

Rong Yi crawled to the other side of his room and quickly returned. Linda anxiously pulled the parchment into her cell and unfolded the note. Her heart pounded erratically. Every muscle in her body tensed. She could not believe the characters written on the paper. "Knock once if you have ever met a frightened Chinese woman in Beihai Park."

Linda steadied her arm and tapped one time. Another scrap of paper was slipped through the wall. "The woman in the next cell is called Little Chang. Knock once if that name means anything to you."

A tide of emotion welled up inside Linda. She had thought that Little Chang was dead. She knocked once. Then she scribbled one sentence and thrust the paper into the next cell. She had her answer in less than one minute. "I am," Rong Yi wrote in magnificently scripted characters, "the calligrapher for Chairman Mao Tse-tung."

Linda took a deep breath. She wished she could break down the walls and talk to Rong Yi and Little Chang face-to-face. They were the three witnesses to the forgery of Mao's will, and they were all in the same prison. If she could figure out a plan and gain their assistance, she might be able to retrieve the forged will. "If I could find a way to get out of jail"—Linda's fingers throbbed as she wrote—"would you be willing to help discredit Jiang Qing?"

"Comrade Chang and I will do whatever we can," Rong Yi responded.

Linda sat in the corner, trying to develop a plan. Three things were needed: a new will, a way to get into the National Archives, and a way to get out of prison. The calligrapher might be able to provide the first and Little Chang the second, but the third would be up to her. "Would you be willing to write another last will and testament?" Linda asked Rong.

"It is already written," read the note slipped back through

the wall.

"Ask Little Chang if there's a way to get into the archives."

Linda paced impatiently, awaiting an answer. She rushed to the wall when she heard the scraping sound and tugged the paper into her cell:

Dear friend Linda Fol-be:

There are three locks for the outside door of the archives. The padlock has the combination 10-1-19-49, in honor of the founding of our Republic. The others require keys. There is a set in the mattress in my apartment. Mao's private vault also has a combination. I don't know the numbers, but it is another symbolic date. To make the will look official, you will need Mao's chop. There is one in Comrade Rong's vault. The combination is 5-4-19-19, the date of the birth of nationalism in China. I pray the Red Guards have not found the chop and the keys and that you are able to escape. My heart and soul are with you.

Chang Shuli

Linda shook her fists triumphantly in the air. Everything was coming together. She had the evidence to stop Jiang Qing. Now all she needed was a way out of this hellhole. But time was short. If she could not convince Colonel Li to take action before Alexandra Koo complained about the forgeries, all would be lost. She just had to hope that the colonel took her bait and came back in the morning.

Sleep did not come. Feelings of imminent victory mixed with those of paralyzing fear as Linda stood watching the first rays of dawn. This was the day on which she would either stop Jiang Qing or find herself a permanent inmate in this Chinese prison. A guard placed a breakfast tray on the floor. The morning meal consisted of chicken congee and tea. It was no less spicy or greasy than dinner had been, but Linda wolfed it down.

The opening of the door startled her. She jumped up as Colonel Li strode into the room. He was alone. She nervously smoothed her skirt.

"Have you eaten rice today, Miss Fol-be?" the colonel said in Chinese.

Linda pressed her fingernails into her palm as she tried to remain calm. "I have eaten well," she replied.

"You have learned Chinese remarkably quickly." The colonel glared. "The last time you visited me, you pleaded, cried, and even threw away your face trying to convince me that you could not speak the language."

"You arrested me with that young woman. I never spoke to her, but if you had known I spoke Chinese, you wouldn't have believed me."

The colonel grasped Linda's arm. "Why don't we dispense with the nonsense. You mentioned that you had information that might interest me regarding Mrs. Koo. Let's hear it."

"Mrs. Koo controls the export of antiques and jewelry to the United States." Linda spoke deliberately. "She often cheats your country by paying very little for these products and then selling them for exorbitant amounts."

"I have little interest in an economic lesson," Colonel Li scoffed.

"Please hear me out." Linda nervously tugged on the wrinkled collar of her blouse. "Mrs. Koo has just smuggled thirty million dollars' worth of relics from the Qin Tombs out of the country and has sold them to Lord Henry Gateshead, the director of the English Museum. She is to use the money to purchase American weapons for the Red Guards."

"I am acquainted with these weapons," the colonel replied.

"This time there will be no delivery." As Linda spoke, she saw Colonel Li's eyes shift imperceptibly. She knew she had piqued his interest. "Mrs. Koo plans to cheat Comrade Jiang Qing and the People's Republic by claiming that the relics are fakes. She will complain that Jiang's people cheated her. Insisting that Lord Gateshead has rejected the fraudulent relics, she will refuse to advance the funds for the weapons. Your men and Jiang Qing's cause will be needlessly endangered by her greed."

"Where did you get this information?" the colonel asked.

"I overheard Mrs. Koo plotting her treachery when I was in Xian."

"Why should I believe you?"

"Because I'm willing to assume the risk. Let me repeat my story to others in position of power. If I'm wrong, I'll be blamed for the error and I'll still be your prisoner."

"And if you are right?"

"Then perhaps you could help me in the future."

Colonel Li smiled knowingly. "You want to grab Mrs. Koo's business."

"I only want a chance to do a little business on my own."

Colonel Li turned away. "We will see if your story has any merit."

Linda stepped in front of him. She almost had him hooked. "You can't wait. The relics are already in Hong Kong. By this afternoon, Mrs. Koo will start to complain about the forgeries. If our word is to have any impact, we must report our suspicions before Mrs. Koo does."

The colonel nodded, but Linda didn't know if he was agreeing or merely acknowleding her opinion. "We'll talk later," he said, stepping into the hallway.

*   *   *

Linda glanced at her watch for what seemed to be the hundredth time in the last hour. Patience was not one of her virtues. She was sure she had blown it. If Colonel Li had believed her story, he would have come back by now. The door opened. Colonel Li's interpreter smiled as he stepped into the room. "Colonel Li would like you to get ready for a short excursion," the interpreter said in English.

"Where am I going?"

"I am afraid I do not know." He bowed politely.

"Should I bring my luggage?" Linda probed for clues.

"The colonel would like you to look as dignified and presentable as possible. I will wait outside. We must leave in five minutes."

Linda put on navy-blue slacks and a conservative beige silk blouse. Fumbling with the buttons, she thought about the interpreter's words. It seemed likely that Colonel Li was taking her to see someone important. Why else would her appearance have been an issue? "Just relax," Linda lectured herself. "Pull this off and we'll be home free."

The black limousine approached the prison farm where Linda was being held. Marc Slater, wearing a Chinese worker's uniform and a Mao cap, motioned for Sen to turn onto a side road. "Let's go on foot and get a closer look," he said. He climbed out of the car and ran for the tall brush on the far side of the road. Sen followed closely behind.

Creeping through the furrows of a wheat field ready for harvesting, they approached the prison compound. On the far side were the single-story white mud-brick and wood buildings in which the inmates were detained. The other three sides were ringed with connecting whitewashed barns and silos. The solitary gate was protected by eight Red Guards armed with automatic weapons.

Marc stopped as the gates of the compound swung open.

A green Shanghai car pulled into sight. The driver paused to talk to one of the guards. Marc stared through his binoculars. "Colonel Li is the passenger in the front seat," he said. The car drove out. "My God, Linda's in the back. We've got to follow them," Marc said, crawling back toward their limousine.

"Wait!" Sen grabbed his leg. "There are too many people watching."

The green car turned onto the main road. "Come on!" Marc urged. "We'll lose them."

"There's no turnoff for three miles," Sen advised. "Unless they're heading into the middle of some farm, we'll catch them."

"I hope you're right."

Dipping a brush into the crimson polish, Alexandra Koo meticulously lacquered her nails. This was a day on which she could pamper herself. The relics were in the process of being inspected. Until they passed through customs and were delivered to Gateshead's people, she could not collect the thirty million dollars or purchase new weapons for Jiang Qing.

Alexandra waved her fingers in the air while the polish dried, thinking wistfully about Hong Kong. A few days in the air-conditioned comfort of the Peninsula would be lovely. She yearned for a massage, a long soak in an oversize tub, an elegant breakfast in bed, and, to celebrate her success, a bottle of French champagne. "Patience." She smiled at herself in the cracked mirror on the closet door. The luxuries would come soon enough.

She slipped a jade pendant around her neck and turned on the radio. "All people," the announcer blared, "are requested to listen at four o'clock for a special message from Premier

Hua Guofeng." Could it be Mao? Alexandra wondered. The last time there had been such a special announcement was when Chou En-lai died. She would call Jiang Qing. Her friend would need consolation.

She was about to lift the receiver when the phone rang. "Mrs. Koo," the operator said, "you have an overseas call. Please go ahead, Hong Kong."

"Mrs. Koo? This is Bing from your office."

"Yes, Bing." Alexandra waited anxiously for confirmation of the delivery of the relics.

"Your shipment passed through customs and was delivered to Mr. Cowley of the English Museum, but Mr. Cowley said he did not order the pieces."

"Of course he didn't." Alexandra tried to curb her annoyance. She suffered poorly incompetent underlings. "His employer, Lord Gateshead, did."

"Mr. Cowley has not talked with Lord Gateshead."

"I find that difficult to believe."

"Then you do not know that Lord Gateshead has been kidnapped by radicals in Xinjiang Province."

"That's ridiculous."

"I am afraid it's true. It was the lead story in every newspaper."

"Damn it!" Alexandra tugged at the pendant. "Talk to Cowley again. Gateshead was insistent that the English Museum wanted these relics from the Qin Tombs. He agreed to pay thirty million dollars."

"Excuse me, Mrs. Koo. I must have made a terrible error and delivered the wrong merchandise. This shipment had no relics, only cheaply made arts-and-crafts products."

"There were no pieces of jewelry, bronze bowls, gold figurines, or bolts of antique silk?"

"The pieces looked like that, but they were all copies."

"Are you absolutely positive?" Alexandra stammered.

"Mrs. Koo, I've worked for you for ten years. Don't you think I know the difference between relics and copies?"

"I packed the relics myself, flew with them to Canton, and then watched the plane leave. You met the shipment in Hong Kong and walked it through customs. How was it possible that priceless antiques could have been stolen and worthless forgeries substituted in their place?"

"I'm sorry, Mrs. Koo. I don't know."

"I suggest you start finding out!" Alexandra flared. "Check every movement made by those crates in Hong Kong. I'll do the same over here. Someone has my antiques. I don't intend to rest until I find them."

Alexandra's legs shook as she placed the receiver back in its cradle. She took a deep breath and tried to sort things out. The switch could have been made in Canton by one of Liu Teyu's people, or in Hong Kong. If she acted right away, she might be able to catch the culprits. It would be difficult to conceal such a large quantity of ancient relics.

She called Jiang Qing. Shen Mo answered. "Comrade Shen, this is Alexandra Koo. I heard the announcement on the radio. Is it the Great Helmsman?"

"I am sorry, Mrs. Koo, but I am not at liberty to say anything."

"I must see Comrade Jiang." Alexandra tried to cover the panic in her voice. "It is a matter of the greatest urgency."

"Comrade Jiang is in meetings. I am not certain she will have time."

"Trust me, Shen. This could have extremely dire consequences for us."

"Excuse me a minute."

Alexandra puffed nervously on her cigarette while she awaited Shen's reply.

"Mrs. Koo"—Shen returned to the phone—"Comrade Jiang will see you in two hours."

After hanging up, Alexandra filled a glass with Maotai and downed the potent, colorless liquid in one gulp. It burned all the way to her stomach. She would have to compose herself before facing Jiang Qing. Having to deal with the death of her husband and the theft of the relics on the same day would be difficult for even the most stable person, and Jiang Qing was far from that. If Alexandra was not careful, she could find herself the scapegoat.

Sitting in the back seat as the green Shanghai motored toward Peking, Linda Forbes opened her window and took a breath of the hot, dusty air. There was a black limousine behind them. She leaned back in her seat, closed her eyes, and started to review her lines. She felt like an aspiring actress preparing for a screen test. Everything depended on how well she acted.

The car turned onto Chang'an Avenue. They were still several miles from Tian'anmen Square. The limousine pulled abreast. Linda noted its massive size. It seemed strange to her that in a supposedly classless society, all bureaucrats had chauffeur-driven limousines, while many of the workers did not even have bicycles.

The limousine dropped back, pulled abreast, and then dropped back again. Stupid driver, Linda thought to herself. Why doesn't he just pass? The limousine again pulled even with the Shanghai car. Linda stuck her head out the window and stared at the two men inside. They were both wearing Mao caps. Her legs began to shake, but her eyes remained riveted on the men. She shivered, certain her mind was playing tricks on her.

"What are you staring at?" Colonel Li asked.

She pulled her head back into the car. "Ah—" she stuttered, "I was just marveling at the progress made since

521

the earthquake."

"When our people are organized," the colonel replied, "there is little we cannot do."

Shifting nervously, Linda waited for the colonel to turn back to the front. Finally she had her chance. She looked out the window. The limo was still there. The driver had removed his cap. It was not an apparition. It was Sen Tailing. But what of the passenger? How could it be? She gazed into his sky-blue eyes. He was alive! She wanted to reach out and touch him. She wanted to feel his arms embracing her. She did not know how, but she thanked God he had not been killed in the quake. Perhaps her grandfather had also survived. Marc doffed his cap and smiled. A charge of electricity surged through her body.

The limousine dropped behind them. Linda stared out the back window, no longer caring what Colonel Li thought. Marc was alive. That was all that mattered. The Shanghai turned right. The limousine continued along Chang'an Avenue. Linda watched until it was out of sight. She did not even notice that her car had entered Zhong Nanhai.

The gate to the compound closed behind them. "Where are we going?" she asked as the car approached a Ming dynasty pavilion.

"This is the home of the Great Helmsman," Colonel Li said proudly. The car parked between two bronze lions.

Despite the gravity of her crisis, Linda gazed at the magnificent palaces with the excitement of a tourist. Colonel Li ushered her up the marble stairs to the entrance of Chairman Mao's home. As she passed between the massive red pillars, Linda glanced over her shoulder. Marc and Sen were not there now, but she was certain they would find a way to get to her. She had to be ready for them. "Please be here," she whispered as she stepped through the door.

Shen Mo escorted Linda and Colonel Li through the entrance hall. Streams of light flooding through the windows atop the cathedral ceiling cast dazzling patterns on the silk watercolors hanging from the walls. Passing four antique screens, Shen motioned toward a cluster of couches and armchairs in the sparsely decorated living room. "Please be seated. Comrade Jiang Qing will be with you shortly."

Linda silently gazed around the room, trying to compose herself. Up until this moment, Jiang Qing had been only a name, a cardboard character against whom she was fighting. But now that she was standing in the imperial luxury of Jiang's home, Linda felt the weight of centuries of dynastic tradition pressing upon her. She was about to deal with the most powerful woman in the world. It might not be as easy as she thought.

Jiang Qing descended the stairs and entered the room. Far more attractive than Linda had expected, she was wearing a finely tailored, long black silk dress that showed off the still youthful firmness of her figure. A touch of makeup highlighted the sharp features of her face. Her dark, piercing eyes bore in on Linda as she greeted Colonel Li. "So this is the young woman you have told me about," Jiang said.

Linda trembled, wondering what was the appropriate way to greet the woman who thought herself to be the empress of China. Finding no better alternative, she bowed respectfully. "Comrade Jiang Qing, this is a great honor for such a humble long-nosed foreign devil."

"Not bad," Jiang laughed. "You have an excellent command of our language. I could use a young barbarian woman for one of my films. You're not an actress, are you?"

Linda shook her head and blushed. It was an ironic question because her life might well depend on her ability to act. "I am only a buyer of antiques for a department store in the United States."

"How is it that you speak such perfect Chinese?" Jiang asked.

Linda shifted her gaze, hoping she was not making an error in judgment. "My grandmother was named Margot Kappel."

Jiang Qing stared quizzically. "That names sounds familiar."

"She was an artist in Shanghai who worked closely with Chou En-lai. When Chiang Kai-shek crushed the Party in 1927, she was arrested and then deported. I have studied Chinese out of respect for her memory."

"That is excellent," Jiang Qing said. "You are a true *lao pengyou*. There were few who were with us during the twenties." Linda kept her head bowed. "I am sorry to be abrupt, but today is a very extraordinary day. Please briefly state the purpose of your visit."

"As I informed Colonel Li"—Linda clasped her hands together as she spoke—"I overheard a Chinese-American woman named Alexandra Koo speaking with one of her associates. Are you acquainted with Mrs. Koo?"

"I know her quite well," Jiang replied. "In fact, I intend to see her this afternoon. Please get to the point."

Linda repressed a smile. She had beaten Alexandra to the punch. Now all she had to do was create enough doubt in Jiang's mind to stymie the Jade Empress. "Mrs. Koo has sold relics from the Qin dynasty to Lord Henry Gateshead for thirty million dollars. She was supposed to use this money to buy arms that would help combat the capitalist-roaders."

Jiang's nostrils flared angrily. "What makes you think that?"

"Please excuse me," Linda said. "I am just repeating what I heard."

"How do I know you are not working for the American CIA?"

"Me?" Linda laughed and shrugged.

"Stop playing little Miss Cutesy!" Jiang pointed a finger at Linda. "Say what you have to say."

Linda placed her hands on her legs to stop them from shaking. "I can only repeat what I heard. Mrs. Koo said once Mao died, others would take control and you would lose your power. She alleged that she was owed vast sums of money and decided to keep the relics as collateral. She reached an agreement with Lord Gateshead. He would claim that the relics were fakes and refuse to pay for them. She would then fly into a fury and insist on going to Hong Kong to inspect the shipment. Once in Hong Kong, she would wait until she saw who was going to win. If you took control, she'd pay for the relics and return to China. If you lost, she'd keep the money and disappear."

Jiang glared angrily. "That's preposterous. Mrs. Koo is an old friend. I can't imagine why you would invent such a lie, unless, of course, you are a spy. And I can't understand how you, Comrade Li, could be such a fool as to believe this woman. I do not have time to waste with either of you."

"Comrade Jiang,"—Linda's voice cracked—"I swear that I am not a spy. I have long admired you. I thought I was doing something that would help."

"Stop talking such idiocy!" Jiang Qing scoffed.

Linda felt like bursting into tears. Her gamble had backfired, but she could not let herself fall apart. "Comrade Jiang, would you please at least remember what I have said when you talk to Alexandra Koo?"

"I will remember only that you tried to besmirch the reputation of one of my closest allies." Jiang waved her hand. "Get this woman out of here."

Linda's legs trembled as Colonel Li dragged her into the

courtyard of Zhong Nanhai. She'd been an idiot to think she could split Jiang Qing and Alexandra Koo. She was a foreigner, not a Chinese or even really a *lao pengyou*. Her word meant nothing. She should have realized her stupidity before she had dug herself so far into a hole. Now Colonel Li would never release her. She was no longer just a troublemaker or someone who had been seen with Little Chang. Jiang Qing had branded her a spy.

Linda searched for Marc and Sen. They could not leave her stranded in the clutches of Colonel Li. Her eyes scanned the buildings, wondering how and when they would appear. They would need a daring and ingenious plan to rescue her in such a public location. She stopped next to one of the brass lions. Once she was in the car, there would be no way to save her. "Marc, Sen," she whispered. "Please come out. Please!"

"We've had enough excursions for one day." Colonel Li grabbed her arm and shoved her into the back seat. Linda glanced wistfully out the window and wept.

Jiang Qing was already waiting as Alexandra Koo was escorted into the living room of Mao's home. This was the last hour in the lull before the storm. Soon she would officially be a widow. Four o'clock would mark the beginning of her time of mourning and the last phase of the struggle for power. Everything else was organized. Now she wanted to resolve Alexandra's problems so she could ready herself for her new role.

"Have you eaten rice today, old friend?" Jiang bowed politely.

"I have no interest in food," Alexandra said, responding literally to the figurative question.

"What is troubling you?" Jiang asked.

"I am greatly saddened by the death of the Great

Helmsman." Alexandra paid the appropriate respects, guessing correctly that Mao had died.

"Your thoughts comfort me," Jiang said. "But that is not why you are here."

"There has been treachery involving the relics." Alexandra spoke hesitantly.

Jiang remained expressionless. "Are these the relics that you sold to Lord Gateshead?"

Alexandra looked up in surprise. "How did you know?"

"Do you think I am ignorant of your business dealings?" Jiang smiled dryly.

"I am sure you are well informed." Alexandra nodded respectfully.

"I assume the relics have reached Hong Kong."

"They have."

"And you now have discovered"—Jiang paused, not wanting to believe that her friend was a traitor—"that all of the relics are fakes."

Alexandra ran a well-manicured hand through her long black hair. "How did you find out so quickly?"

"I have my sources."

"The real relics are either in Canton or in Hong Kong," Alexandra said. "One way or another, I will catch the thieves."

Jiang rubbed her eyes. Within the next three days, she would have to deal with the death of her husband, the reading of the will, the mobilization of her troops, and the fight for control of the Politburo. She could not worry about Alexandra, too. The problem of the stolen relics would have to wait until the others were resolved. "I do not think it would be appropriate for you to go to Hong Kong."

"How else can I recover the relics?" Alexandra asked.

"I have a house outside the city." Jiang sounded exhausted. "I'd like you to be my personal guest for the next two weeks."

"I don't understand!" Alexandra protested.

"I think you do. It will be beneficial for you to spend time in contemplation, away from your Western luxuries. We will talk in one week. Hopefully, by then we'll be able to find an answer to our mutual problems."

"If we don't act immediately, we may permanently lose the relics."

Jiang stood up and rang a bell. Two guards hurried into the living room. "Our discussion is now at an end," Jiang said. "Thank you for coming, Mrs. Koo." Without a word, she turned and walked to the stairs. It was time for her to become a grieving widow.

As the green Shanghai motored back to the country, Colonel Li tossed a cigarette out the window and lit another. He had lost his gamble. Jiang Qing was angry. He had built his position of trust by always doing exactly as she asked; he had been foolish to have acted on his own now. In the future, he would stick to attacking stated enemies, like Little Chang, or needed pawns, like the calligrapher. As for the American woman, he would deal with her at the prison farm.

Linda sat despondently in the back seat, taking little notice of Colonel Li. The day, which had begun so promisingly, had ended in disaster. There was little more that could go wrong. She closed her eyes and let exhaustion overtake her.

Ascending into the Western Hills, the car turned onto a twisting road ringed by steep cliffs. The driver rounded a bend and slammed on his brakes. A herd of pigs blocked the street while three farmers sat on a rock engrossed in conversation. The driver leaned on his horn. The farmers continued talking. "Move those pigs out of here!" the driver shouted.

"As soon as we finish our beers," a farmer called, holding up a half-empty bottle.

Colonel Li rolled down his window. "Get them out now!"

"Don't split a blood vessel," the farmer said. "We are waiting until our comrades arrive from our commune." He pointed up the dirt road.

The driver stepped out of the car. "We are in a great hurry. We do not intend to be inconvenienced by a group of rice-eating fools."

"Who do you think you are?" the farmer challenged.

Li jumped from the car. "I am a colonel in the Red Guard. And if you want to keep your pigs, you have ten seconds to move them off the road."

"Please excuse my foolish animals." The young farmer bowed deeply. "They are not as intelligent as most of your Red Guard troops."

A black limousine drove up the dirt road and edged onto a soft shoulder. Its driver impatiently honked his horn. A pig scampered out of the way. The limousine pulled parallel to the Shanghai. One of the men inside doffed his Mao cap. The man put his finger to his lips and unlatched the back door.

"Maybe we should move our animals," a farmer said, picking up a branch of a tree. "All right, pigs," he screamed, "let's get out of the colonel's way!" The pigs squealed as the farmers closed in from three sides.

The passenger in the limousine waved his hand. Linda jumped from the car and rushed into the limousine. She pressed her body to the floor as the driver pulled away from the intersection. The passenger leaned over and caressed her long blond hair. "You're safe now," he whispered.

Rounding a bend, the driver accelerated. It would take

Colonel Li only a few minutes to discover Linda was missing, but by then they would be gone. Linda looked up and smiled. "I'd begun to give up on you."

"On Lucky Slater?" Marc laughed and pulled her onto the seat next to him. "I'm glad to see you."

"You think *you're* glad?" Linda said. "Compared to the Red Guards and a few years in that prison farm, you look very good to me."

"Thanks for the compliment—I think." Marc clasped Linda's hand.

"Sen, why didn't you tell me Marc was alive?" Linda asked the driver.

"I was saving it as a surprise," Sen replied. "How did I know you'd run off with the Red Guard again?"

"I promise not to be so impetuous next time," Linda said.

Marc put his arm around her. "We're not letting you out of our sight."

"What about my grandfather?" she asked.

"A little the worse for wear, but otherwise fine," Marc said.

Sen turned on to a main road and headed for the center of Peking. "I hate to interrupt," he said, "but it's almost four o'clock."

"What happens at four o'clock?" Linda asked.

Marc placed his finger on his lips. The radio was playing "The East Is Red." When it ended, a funeral dirge began in the background. A somber announcer spoke over the sound of the music: "I have an announcement of utmost importance to all mankind. Chairman Mao has left the world."

42: State Farm 120

Samuel Tang stepped off the flight from Peking and followed Kang Xiaoma and Ren Daoling onto the tarmac of the tiny Urumqi airport. Although Urumqi was the largest city in an area of four million square miles, there were never more than six flights a day. Kao Yangxu, the manager of the Arts and Crafts Corporation, stepped forward and introduced himself. Sam bowed politely. "Have you been able to find out anything about the Turks?" he asked.

"Nothing concrete," Kao replied. "We think they're somewhere in the mountains near Utu."

"How far is that from the Dzungarian Gate?" Sam asked.

"Three hundred over the roads, but only eighty through the mountains."

"We have to stop the Turks before they stage another mock attack on the border."

"I have two jeeps waiting outside. We'll get reinforcements at State Farm 120," Kao said, escorting the others into the terminal.

531

As they reached the ticket counter, Sen tugged on Kao's arm and pointed to a Westerner, accompanied by a Turk, standing in line for the flight to Peking. "Isn't that Avery Boswell?" he asked.

Kao nodded. "The man with him is Ruzi, one of Rahman's men."

Sam herded his people to a corner. Finding Boswell might be a lucky break. He could not let him slip away. "We've got to get Xiaoma on board," Sam said.

"I'll handle it," Ren said. He led the others to the China Travel Service offices and presented his papers to the clerk on duty. The clerk snapped to attention, impressed by Ren's high ranking in the Travel Service. "I need a seat for Comrade Kang on the plane to Peking." Ren handed the clerk Kang's Party membership card.

The clerk bowed respectfully. "The flight is fully booked."

"Then bump someone," Ren ordered.

"I will arrange it immediately," the clerk said.

Ren and the others waited while the clerk made the arrangements. Then Xiaoma took his tickets and prepared to board the plane. "I intend to lodge an official protest when I get home," Xiaoma joked. "I traveled all the way to Xinjiang and didn't even make it out of the airport."

"When this is over," Sam smiled, "I'll treat you to an all-expense-paid tour of the Taklimakan Desert."

"On one of your jets?" Xiaoma asked.

"Of course not," Sam smiled. "The only way to see the Taklimakan is from the back of a camel."

The road to State Farm 120 wound through oblivion. For seven endless hours, each mile of desert was as monotonous as the one before. The wind picked up. Clouds of dust swirled around the jeep, choking the passengers and the carburetor. The sky was obliterated. The horizon disappeared. The world took on a strange, two-dimensional, monochromatic gray appearance that ended only when the jeep climbed into the foothills and reached the oasis on which State Farm 120 was located.

So named because it was a hundred and twenty miles from the border, State Farm 120 was an anti-Russian military project. Han Chinese had been sent to this and other neighboring farms to protect the frontiers. Continuing a two-thousand-year-old tradition, these colonizers were much like those who had defended China from the Mongols, the Manchus, and other invading enemies.

As the car drove through the gate, Sam noticed the sharp contrast with the rest of Xinjiang. The farm was green and prosperous. Irrigation ditches lined fields of cotton and melons. Instead of the camels and water buffaloes, State Farm 120 had tractors and other automated equipment. The workers were Han Chinese. Of the twenty thousand people, there was not one Turk.

In the main square, workers carrying rifles were practicing maneuvers. The director of the farm approached the jeep and welcomed his new guests. "I am Hong Guoqiang." His name meant Red Strengthen the Nation. "We are greatly honored by your presence."

Hong's greeting was interrupted by the loudspeakers that stretched throughout the commune. "There will be a special announcement in one hour," the radio blared. "All people are requested to listen."

"I wonder what it is?" Hong asked. Sam remained silent; he would choose his own time to reveal his knowledge of Mao's death. Hong escorted his guests past a cluster of barracks, into the central meeting room.

"I received instructions from Peking," Hong said, pouring tea for his guests. "We stand ready to help. There will be twelve thousand armed militiamen and an adequate supply of artillery at your disposal."

"Excellent," Sam replied. "We will also need a runway for our jets."

"That may be difficult," Hong said. "Our is suitable for only single-engine planes."

"It is essential," Sam said. "If we have to unload in Urumqi, we'll be too far from the border to be effective."

"I'll set my people to work. It should be ready within the week."

"We can't wait that long," Sam replied. "The Russians will invade within the next few days, and we must be prepared."

"What makes you so certain about the timing?" Hong asked.

Sam paused and stared at the others. This was the time to use his knowledge. "The special bulletin on the radio will be the announcement of the death of Chairman Mao."

Hong grasped his chair to steady himself. "But how do you know?"

"That's not important," Sam said. "What is critical is that we do everything we can to make that runway operable."

Hong flipped the switch to the loudspeaker system. "This is Comrade Hong Guoqiang." His voice echoed into every corner of the two-thousand-square-mile commune. "Everyone must assemble in the main square in two hours. No matter what you hear on the radio, do not delay your arrival."

Two hours later, all of the members of the commune, except for those working in the outlying sectors or serving guard duty, had arrived in the main square. Most were already wearing black armbands. Their faces reflected their shock. Mao Tse-tung had led the People's Republic since its inception. It was difficult to believe he was dead. Yet despite Mao's vast impact, many of the commune members did not mourn his death. They were people who had been wrenched from their families and sent thousands of miles to the forbidding wasteland of Xinjiang Province. They were border fighters, stranded in a desolate world. They loved their country and wanted to defend it, but they also wished that others could have been chosen in their places. Like Kao Yangxu, they wanted nothing more than to be transferred back home.

"This is a tragic day," Hong's voice echoed over the loudspeakers. "I know how much we all mourn our Great Helmsman, but we cannot permit his loss to overcome us. Word has reached me that the Russians, aided by the Turkic Nationlists, plan to invade our country. We must stop them. Defeating the enemy will be our lasting memorial to Chairman Mao."

Twenty minutes after Hong's speech, thousands of commune members descended on the decrepit runway. "The East Is Red" and other revolutionary songs were played as they set to work. As the hours passed, the expanded runway began to take shape. Women carried food so the workers could eat without taking a break. At dusk, torches were lit.

Samuel Tang watched the progress with grudging admiration. The workers were highly inefficient—a hundred Americans with bulldozers could probably have accomplished as much as the thirteen thousand Chinese. But the Chinese had never done anything the easy way. Without modern technology, they relied on the brute mass of their almost unlimited population to change the course of rivers, hold back the sea, and stand up against the major superpowers. Mao had once warned that his people could sink Albania "merely by pissing on it." With the Russians, it would not be as easy.

43: Where There's a Will, There's a Way

The sun had not yet risen when Liu Teyu, Beatrice Tang, Kang Moruo, and Sen Tailing gathered in a small meeting room in the Capital Airport. Outside, Liu's troops were arriving in transports from Canton. Half, under Liu's direct command, would continue on to Xinjiang. The other half would remain in Peking to help defend the capital.

"Did you talk to Hua?" Liu asked Kang.

"The meeting is set for tonight at Defense Minister Ye's Western Hills villa," Kang replied. "Hua, Ye, Vice-Chairman Li, Deng, and I will be there. The information you requested from the Americans is being relayed to us. If it arrives on time, Slater will bring it."

"We need those aerial photographs," Liu said. "If we can't convince Hua and the others tonight, we might not get another chance."

"I'll do what I can to make sure we get them," Beatrice said.

"Good," Liu replied. "Now we have to decide what to do about the forged will. Where do we stand at the moment?"

"We have a new copy of Mao's original will," Kang replied, "and we know where to get a copy of Mao's chop and the keys for the archives."

Liu looked at Kang with surprise. "How did we manage that?"

"We didn't," Beatrice replied. "Your granddaughter did."

A smile tugged at the ends of Liu's lips. "I'm going to have to meet this young woman."

Beatrice laughed. "I can guarantee that she won't leave the People's Republic without seeing you."

"Make sure she doesn't," Liu said.

"Even with the new will," Kang said, "we will have to steal the chop from Rong Yi's studio, get the keys from Little Chang's apartment, figure out the combination to Mao's private vault, and then break into the archives itself and switch the documents."

"None of those will be easy," Liu said, "but the last will be by far the most difficult. Do you have a plan?"

"Just a tentative one," Kang replied. "We will need four people. The first will lure the guard away from the door. Then the second and third will open the locks. After the second is safely inside, the third will relock the door. We can't take the chance of leaving it open. That's how Jiang Qing got caught. After the wills have been switched, the fourth person will create a diversion that will again lure the guard from the door while the third opens the locks and lets the second out."

Liu nodded. "It sounds like it could work. When do you propose that we attempt the break-in?"

"The only time we'll be able to get near the archives will be tomorrow afternoon during Mao's funeral when the entire building is closed," Kang said.

"That will limit our choice of operatives," Liu said. "All high-level ranking Party members will be on the podium, and even second-level cadres will have to be with their units."

"Then we'll just have to find someone of a lower rank."

"I don't like that idea," Liu replied. "Not only would we be trusting lower-level bureaucrats with the future of the People's Republic, but we'd be leaving ourselves open to blackmail. The four people who switch the will could turn on us at any time. I wouldn't like to give anyone that much power. The more people who know about the forgery, the greater the risk."

"How about some of our personal aides or family members?" Kang asked.

"They'd be the worst," Liu replied. "If they were caught, the blame would be laid on us. We need to find someone we can trust who can't be directly associated with our cause."

"Then why don't you stick with the people who already know about the forgery?" Sen asked.

"Whom did you have in mind?"

"Why don't you let Marc Slater, Linda Forbes, and me handle it with Kang's assistance."

Liu glared at Sen. "You can't be serious, suggesting that two foreign barbarians and one Chinese who works for a barbarian company should be entrusted with such responsibility."

Sen paused, realizing that he was gambling his own future. "I am completely serious. Slater and Linda would be perfect. We trust them and they're already involved, so we are taking no risk using them. To the contrary, if they take part in the break-in, they'll have to remain silent. Slater wouldn't risk his oil business, and Linda would do nothing to hurt you or Slater."

"What happens if they're caught?" Liu asked.

Sen smiled wryly. "We blame the break-in on the CIA.

The Americans make excellent scapegoats."

"But what about the wills?"

"Once the CIA is involved, it doesn't matter which document remains in the vault—everyone will believe that it has been doctored by the Americans. Even if Jiang's forgery is still there, we could claim that she had made a secret alliance with the capitalists. The only certainty will be that Mao publicly anointed Hua. Without a credible last will, Hua will retain control."

"Your logic is interesting, Comrade Sen," Liu said, "but why should we also include you? You are an ambitious young cadre."

"I am the most vulnerable of everyone," Sen replied. "I have worked in Hong Kong for a capitalist corporation and I have direct ties to the American government. If I step out of line, you can charge me with being an agent of the capitalists. Besides, I have a personal stake in this operation. Little Chang, the guardian of the archives who was branded a traitor by Jiang Qing, is my sister-in-law. Unless she is proved innocent, my relationship with her will doom my future in the People's Republic."

Liu hobbled to the windows and stared out at his planes. "Do you think my granddaughter is capable of handling such an assignment?"

"She was the one who learned of the forgery. She got a copy of the new will and found out about the chop and the keys. She escaped from the Red Guards on two separate occasions and even handled herself at a private meeting with Jiang Qing. You tell me. Do you think she's capable?"

"What do you think?" Liu asked Kang.

"I agree with Sen."

"All right," Liu replied, "I'm leaving it in your hands. I want you to supervise every aspect of the operation."

"I'll take care of it," Kang replied. "As soon as you leave

for Xinjiang, I'll take Sen and meet with Slater and Linda to lay out the first stage of the operation."

As the blue Toyota sedan drove through Tian'anmen Square, Marc Slater stared at the symbols of mourning that overnight had flooded the country. Flags flew at halfmast. The huge portrait of Chairman Mao that had hung in front of the Forbidden City had been replaced by a photograph trimmed with black and yellow silk. Funeral dirges and eulogies from leaders of the government blared through loudspeakers on every corner. Workers wore black armbands and white crepe-paper flowers. Young girls tied white ribbons in their hair, while the Chairman's most loyal supporters pinned on old-style Mao buttons that had not been seen for a decade. All photographs had been removed from sidewalk photo displays, while merchandise in shop windows had been replaced by pictures of the Great Helmsman trimmed with green wreaths, black silk, and white paper flowers.

The streets of the city were lined with people. Unlike the Americans, who would have remained at home with their families watching the news on television, the Chinese gathered in groups to mourn the death of their Chairman. They came out to commiserate and give each other solace. In the People's Republic, everything, including death, was a group activity.

Despite the millions milling about, there was an eerie quiet. Few spoke at all, and then just in a whisper. Only the funeral music from the loudspeakers disturbed the silence. Yet the mood was not one of personal grief. The mourning was proper but strangely emotionless. The feeling pervading the city was more fear than sadness. It was not just that the Great Helmsman had died, but also that the future of the

People's Republic had suddenly been cast in doubt. Without the man who had been their leader since the Liberation, the people were worried about what would happen next.

The blue Toyota stopped in front of a cold, rectangular, six-story building, constructed with intentional dullness by uninspired East European architects. It was an ironic home for the Peking Institute of Art. Marc, Linda, Sen, and Kang Pingnan, the son of Kang Moruo, presented themselves to the guard at the colorless cement entrance. "The school is closed," the guard announced. "This is a day of mourning for our Great Helmsman, or hadn't anyone told you?"

"Don't treat me like a donkey," Pingnan said, handing the guard his papers. "My orders come from the top of the pagoda." He used the slang word that workers had adopted to describe the often inefficient multilevel bureaucracy. "This man and his wife"—Pingnan pointed to Marc and Linda standing arm in arm behind him—"are American art collectors. They have more money than a black cloud has drops of rain. Their schedule is very exacting. They cannot wait until the mourning period ends."

"Who was the idiot who authorized this visit?" the guard asked.

"I think they are friends of Comrade Jiang Qing," Pingnan whispered.

"Damn long-nosed foreign devils get everything," the guard cursed as he studied the papers. "Wait here. I'll find someone to stand in for me."

The guard assigned one of his comrades to protect the front door, then reluctantly took his guests on a tour of the institute. Marc limped as they started down the first corridor, while Linda walked ahead, peppering the guard with incessant questions about new trends in Chinese culture. The sign at the entrance to the second floor read "Department of Calligraphy." The others waited while Marc caught up. Linda stopped in front of one of the offices. "What's inside this room?" she asked, even though she could read the Chinese characters on the door.

"That is the studio of Rong Yi, the director of the institute and Chairman Mao's personal calligrapher."

"I love calligraphy," Linda replied. "Can we see his work?"

"Comrade Rong is ill," the guard replied. "His studio is closed until he recovers."

Linda stared at the guard, wondering if he knew the truth.

They continued down the hall. "Is there a bathroom near by?" Linda asked. The guard pointed to a door. Inside were Chinese-style toilets, consisting of two porcelain foot guides astride an open hole, flush with the floor. The Chinese felt it was more hygienic to squat in the air than to sit on a seat. They also washed their hands before going to the bathroom rather than afterward, believing that their private parts should be kept cleaner than their hands. Linda stepped back into the corridor. She needed to lure the guard away. "I can't use those things," she protested. "Isn't there a Western-style toilet?"

"It's in the museum on the far side of the building," the guard said.

"Can we hurry?" Linda pointed to her stomach.

"I'll stay here," Marc said, massaging his leg. "I'm in great pain."

"It would be highly improper for me to leave you," the guard said.

"I'll wait with Mr. Slater," Pingnan volunteered. "You'd better go now before his wife busts her bladder."

The guard shrugged as he followed Linda and Sen, who had already started through the corridor. They turned down the stairs. After they were out of sight, Marc rushed toward Rong Yi's studio. He wedged a gold American Express card between the door and the frame and jiggled it. There was a click. The door popped open.

The safe was in the far corner underneath a pile of books. Marc's fingers worked quickly as he dialed 5-4-19-19. May 4, 1919, the date of the first mass intellectual demonstration in Peking, was considered to be the birth of revolutionary nationalism in China. The lock clicked. Marc pulled down the handle. The door creaked as it opened. Inside, the papers and parchments were in disarray. Someone else had ransacked Rong's personal possessions. Marc searched until he found a blue brocade box. He opened the ivory clasp. Inside, resting on a silk-covered bed of foam rubber, was the model for Mao's chop and a thin stick of red wax, Mao's official color.

Slipping the chop and wax into his pocket, Marc closed the safe and hurried to the door. Pingnan was still standing guard. Marc rushed to a chair in the hall and resumed rubbing his leg. Two minutes later, the others returned. Linda tenderly touched Marc's shoulder. "Ready for a little more touring?"

"I've had enough culture for one day," Marc replied. "Let's go back to the hotel and get a hamburger."

Sitting at her dressing table, Jiang Qing dabbed at her cheeks with a powder puff. She was now officially a widow, and would somehow have to summon the reserves not only to continue without her husband but also to assume his position as chairman. She had long ago prepared herself for his death. What was new and worrisome was that she no longer had his mantle for protection. In the past, no one had dared quarrel with her. But now her enemies would be seeking revenge, and she would have to fight them alone.

Applying dark mascara to her lashes, Jiang remembered the last words the Chairman had spoken to her. She and the

Gang of Four had been waiting in Mao's hospital room. After an hour of silence, Mao murmured, "Help Jiang Qing . . ." Then his voice trailed off. The end of the sentence was either "to carry the Red Flag," or "to correct her errors." No one had quite caught the words. The former would have indicated that Mao wanted Jiang to become chairman, while the latter was a deathbed rejection. The other members of her clique had assured her that Mao had said the former, but she was not certain. Whatever the truth, now it mattered little. Mao was dead and she would have to lead the country.

Jiang walked to her closet and lifted the black silk dress she had designed for the funeral. It had a beautiful mesh veil like those she had seen in Western films. She dangled the veil in front of her eyes, preparing herself for the public role she would soon play. There was a knock on the door. Shen Mo stepped into the room. "Comrade," Jiang said, "you're just in time to give me your opinion of my funeral outfit."

Shen stared at the ground. "I do not know if the veil is appropriate," she mumbled. "It looks very Western. I remember that Comrade Deng Yingchao wore nothing on her head after Comrade Chou En-lai died."

Jiang's jaw became taut. "Why must I always hear about Deng Yingchao? She was nothing but the wife of a weakling. There is an old Chinese proverb: 'If a woman marries a chicken, she should act like a chicken; if she marries a tiger, she should act like a tiger.' My husband was the emperor of the jungle. What other wives do is not my concern."

"Forgive my error," Shen said, nervously backing away. "Comrade Yuanxin is downstairs."

"Don't keep him waiting," Jiang replied. "He was the last person to see the Great Helmsman alive. We must keep him firmly aligned with us."

When Shen left the room, Jiang inspected the huge wreath of red and yellow orchids she had ordered. More than five feet in diameter, it was inscribed, "Deeply mourn the esteemed Great Teacher Chairman Mao Tse-tung—from your student and comrade-in-arms Jiang Qing." It would be the most impressive memorial placed beside Mao's casket. She did not care that Deng Yingchao had brought only small bouquets for Chou En-lai. She was about to become the next empress of China. A tribute on an imperial scale was appropriate.

"Good afternoon, honorable elder aunt." Yuanxin bowed politely.

"Honorable nephew, I am glad that you have come." Jiang motioned for him to sit down. "Have you talked to Zhang Chunqiao?"

"Zhang is on his way back for the funeral," Yuanxin replied. "He has organized the Shanghai garrison. By tomorrow morning, eighty thousand troops will be ready. Wang Hongwen has another twenty thousand, and there are six thousand in my three tank divisions. We feel that we should start to move as soon as possible."

"I'd like to be in military control of the capital within three days," Jiang replied.

"We'll be fine as long as Unit 8341 stays neutral," Yuanxin said.

"I'll talk to Wang Dongxin," Jiang said. "Once he sees that Chairman Mao has endorsed us, I'm sure he'll blow in our direction."

Jiang walked to her dressing table and ran an ivory-handled brush through her hair. "I am troubled by the presence of Zhang Yufeng." Jiang spoke bitterly of the beautiful woman who had been Mao's private secretary and mistress. She was jealous of the woman's youthful looks, and worried that Yufeng might try to trade on secrets she had learned from Mao in order to build herself a position of power. "When was the last time that wild pheasant"—Jiang used the slang term for "strumpet"—"saw my husband?"

"She was with him on the morning of his death," Yuanxin replied.

Jiang lifted a red rose from a vase and ripped the flower off the stem. "Then I think it would be wise to remove her for her own safety."

"I'll make the arrangements," Yuanxin replied.

"Did you bring the articles for the memorial edition of the *People's Daily*?"

"I have the proofs," Yuanxin said, handing Jiang a stack of papers.

Putting on her black glasses, Jiang started to read. There were four lead stories: a eulogy, a biography of the Great Helmsman, an editorial endorsing the Gang of Four, and an article purporting to be the last words of Mao himself. All had been written to her specifications. Jiang skimmed the biography, the eulogy, and the editorial, which attacked the capitalist-roaders and the vacillators of the Wind Faction. Finally she turned to Mao's article, which was short and to the point. Its warning, directed at Premier Hua, was spelled out in its final sentence: "Anyone who betrays Marxism, Leninism, and Mao Tse-tung thought, anyone who distorts my directives, or practices revisionism, splittism, or plotting, is doomed to failure." Jiang smiled as she studied the words. The people of China would read only what she wrote. It would be impossible for the impotent Hua to combat her powerful propaganda machine.

The blue Toyota sedan pulled to a halt in a *hutong* two blocks away from Little Chang's apartment. Although the apartment was empty, Jiang Qing had ordered that it be kept under continuous surveillance. Red Guards were stationed in front of the building and on Little Chang's floor. Breaking through their defense would require considerable luck.

Marc and Sen got out of the car. "Will you be all right?" Marc asked.

"I'll be fine." Linda squeezed his hand. "I have a doctor"— she pointed to Kang Pingnan—"and my own supply of blood"—she held up a pouch, the size of a bag of candy, filled with a thick crimson liquid.

"Give us five minutes to get there, then drive through," Marc said. "And remember, wait until Little Kam pulls out on the bicycle."

"There will be no difficulties," Pingnan replied.

Marc and Sen walked toward Little Chang's house. They reached a corner. Diagonally across was the modern, twelve-story, middle-class apartment building that looked as if it had been designed by a collection of first-year architecture students during the Cultural Revolution. Its decor was dingy, its facade was badly cracked, and nothing seemed to fit. Yet it was considered one of the city's best addresses, primarily because the apartments were unusually spacious. On the average, workers in Peking were allotted nine square feet of living space, the size of a large table. An apartment eighteen feet by nine feet would normally house six people, but in this building, middle-level bureaucrats were allotted ten times the usual space. With a studio measuring ten feet by twelve feet, Little Chang and her husband were the envy of virtually everyone they knew.

Marc and Sen crossed the street. A heavily dented red car pulled up next to them. The driver lit a cigarette and threw it out the window. Sen crushed it with his foot. A young boy on a bicycle nodded to Sen, who nodded back. They reached the entrance. Pingnan's blue Toyota drove toward them. The dented red car pulled slowly forward. The boy on the bicycle rode into the street. Suddenly he tottered and fell to the pavement. Pignan jerked the steering wheel of the Toyota.

The car swerved. The red car kept coming. Pingnan slammed on the brakes. The man in the red car did the same. It was too late. The Toyota sedan slammed into the dented red car. The driver fell forward on his horn.

People rushed to the accident. Two Red Guards opened the back door of the Toyota. Linda was lying on the floor, her head covered with blood. She looked badly hurt. The guards pulled her to the pavement. She was not moving. Marc turned into the building and followed Sen into the stairwell.

The front door of the Toyota was opened. Pingnan lay slumped on the seat. Blood poured from under his shirt. Two guards lifted him out. He seemed to be unconscious. The man in the red car stepped out onto the street. His legs wobbled and then he collapsed in a heap next to Linda and Pingan. People hurried to get bandages and water. Four policemen arrived and tried to control the crowd.

Marc panted as he followed Sen up eight flights of stairs. They reached the landing. Sen stepped into the hallway. A female Red Guard was standing in front of Little Chang's apartment. "There's been an accident involving a foreigner," Sen blurted. "I need to call a special doctor."

"The cadre at the end of the hall has a phone," the guard said.

"Show me the way!" Sen took her hand and pulled her down the corridor. The guard stared back at her post in the empty hallway as she opened the cadre's door. Marc waited until they were inside, then rushed from the stairwell. Little Chang's door was unlocked. The single room was a mess. Sheets, clothes, and books were strewn over the floor. The mattress was half off the bed, but it was still intact. Snapping open his stiletto, he ripped the center seam and pulled out a layer of cotton stuffing, then thrust his hand inside and searched feverishly. He touched something smooth. It was the silk purse that Little Chang had described to Linda. Clasping it, Marc felt the keys rattling inside. He shoved the purse in his pocket and hurried to the door. The hallway was still empty. He ran for the stairs and bounded down the eight flights, two steps at a time.

Reaching the entrance, Marc saw that the three bodies were still lying in the street. He restrained himself from rushing over to see if Linda was all right. Two ambulances had arrived, one from the local people's hospital and one from the prestigious Capital Hospital, where Pingnan was a surgeon. The doctor from the Capital Hospital produced his Party membership card and asserted his jurisdiction. Then he wiped the blood off Linda's face and bandaged her head. Her eyes remained closed, but her arms and legs twitched involuntarily. Two attendants lifted her onto a stretcher and shoved it inside the ambulance. Pingnan and the man from the red car were placed next to her. The doors closed. A siren blared. Marc inched forward and watched as the ambulance sped away.

After it was out of sight, he hurried back toward the *hutong*. There were footsteps behind him. He kept walking. The footsteps got closer. He did not look back. "Everything go all right?" Sen asked.

"Perfectly." Marc smiled.

44: The Dzungarian Gate

As the morning sun flooded across the cotton fields, Samuel Tang radioed his four C-45 cargo planes. Then he stepped outside and stared at the thousands of commune members still working on the runway. They were making progress, but there was little time left. No matter what the state of construction, the planes would have to land in two hours.

Hong Guoqiang, the director of the State Farm, summoned Sam to the administration building, where two hundred men were waiting to begin the search for the Turks. Hong had already divided them into fifty groups of four and assigned each a specific area, but locating the Turks would not be easy. They could be anywhere in thousands of miles of mountains and valleys, hidden in caravans of nomadic tribes. The best opportunity was to track Van Wyck and Gateshead. They were probably the only two Westerners in the region. Sam distributed photographs of the Englishman and instructed the men to exercise extreme caution. As the groups assembled by their jeeps, Sam hoped that one would get lucky.

He walked back to the communications shack and waited for the blips from his C-45 cargo planes to appear on the radar screen. He was not sure he had made the right decision. The C-45s were the largest and most modern cargo carriers in the world. Designed for military emergencies, they were supposed to be able to land on short runways in mountainous territory. Under normal load conditions, they needed thirty-seven hundred feet, compared to ten thousand for a smaller Boeing 747. Today they would have to make do with less. Despite the impressive efforts of the workers, the runway was barely twenty-eight hundred feet. As long as the wind stayed calm and there were no desert dust storms, they would have a chance. But there would be absolutely no room for error.

As the first of the C-45s approached, Sam nervously watched the plane he had spent four years designing. He felt like an expectant father. The C-45 touched down. It bounced twice on the choppy pavement. The pilot applied the brakes and steered to the middle of the narrow black strip. The plane roared past. There was less than fifteen hundred feet left. Sam's eyes were riveted on the wheels. The speed was decreasing. The pilot revved the engines in reverse. The plane stopped less than forty feet from a field of cotton. Sam ran back into the shed. "Move it to the taxiway," he ordered. "We've got three others waiting."

The sky darkened. Wind roared from the mountains as the second plane landed. Sand began to swirl. Sam finished one pack of cigarettes and started another. The third plane touched down safely. Crosswinds rattled the roof of the shed. Visibility was decreasing. The fourth plane approached. A violent gust of wind shook its tail. The wheels bounced. The pilot slammed on the brakes. The smell of burning rubber filled the air. The plane screeched as it

slowed. The pilot was running out of space. The plane
skidded. Sam clenched his fists. The plane thundered off the
end of the runway and plunged into the cotton field.

"Damn!" Sam cursed, running toward the crippled plane.
Something had to be done. If he was unable to move it, not
only would the airport be useless, but the ninety-two-
million-dollar plane and its two-hundred-million-dollar
military cargo could be permanently stranded near the
Russian border.

Brushing the sand from his eyes, Sam inspected the plane.
He felt like a man whose car has skidded off an icy road,
except that in this case the vehicle weighed eight hundred
and forty thousand pounds. All twenty-eight wheels, each
taller than a man, were buried in the sandy soil. Otherwise
the plane seemed unharmed. The C-45 had been built for just
such emergencies. It had been tested in the deserts of Nevada
and the snow-filled airfields of Wyoming. But this was rural
China and he was short of technicians.

"Is it ruined?" Hong asked.

"I'm hopeful we can move it." Sam tried to sound
confident.

"Perhaps if we tie ropes around the wheels and everyone in
the commune helps pull," Hong suggested, "we could drag it
out."

"Let's see what happens after we unload it." Sam
repressed a smile as he pondered the differences between the
American and the Chinese approaches. He radioed the pilot.
"Kneel her down."

The pilot turned on the hydraulic system. The fuselage
dropped to the ground. The plane rested on the sand. Sam
smiled; the hydraulics were one of the innovations that set
the C-45 apart from every other plane in the world. The crew
pulled open the doors to the cargo bays. Three American
tanks—an M-41, an M-48, and an M-63—rolled out of the

plane and drove through the neatly cultivated fields of cotton. Four trucks carrying rocket launchers and sixty antiaircraft missiles followed the tanks. "We're all empty," the pilot radioed.

"Back her out," Sam ordered, crossing his fingers.

The hydraulics lifted the plane to its normal height. The pilot revved the engines in reverse. The twenty-eight massive wheels spun through the sand, searching for traction. Clouds of sand filled the cotton field. The ground vibrated like it had just before the earthquake. The wheels gripped into the ground. The plane lurched backward and rolled onto the runway. Ten thousand people from the commune stood and cheered. Sam smiled. Nothing pleased him more than seeing his aircraft perform under seemingly impossible circumstances.

Frans Van Wyck wiped his brow as he gazed at a map of military emplacements along the border. The air in the dingy concrete railroad station in Druzhba was stifling and putrid. The temperature was above ninety and the room smelled as if a herd of camels had been living inside. The railroad station was a most unpleasant structure in which to work, but it was the only building suitable as a military headquarters.

Twenty years before, Russia and China had agreed to build the Friendship Railway, a line linking the two countries through the Dzungarian Gate, a mountain pass between Xinjiang and Turkestan. The Soviets finished their section in 1961 and founded Druzhba—"Friendship" in Russian. But then a rift erupted, and China stopped construction in Urumqi. Because a railroad terminating in the middle of a desolate mountain range was of little use to anyone, Druzhba remained an insignificant speck. For the last decade, it had been home to more camels and goats than people. But within the last week, it had come back to life as forty thousand Russian soldiers, equipped with tanks, missiles, and helicopters, arrived to prepare for the projected invasion of Xinjiang Province.

Van Wyck heard footsteps behind him. He turned and saw General Aleksei Bulganov, the deputy director of the KGB, approaching. "Comrade Van Wyck, so good to see you." The short, stocky Russian, dressed in a khaki army uniform, extended his hand in a viselike grip. His pale skin was tough and heavily calloused. Although Bulganov had not been on a horse in years, he carried a leather riding crop.

"Comrade General Bulganov," Van Wyck replied. "You look well."

"It's the mountain air and the camels," Bulganov laughed, holding in his rolling belly. "Vodka?" He poured the clear liquid into two dusty glasses before Van Wyck could reply. "Shall we drink to the demise of our old friend Comrade Mao?" He clinked the glasses together.

"Mao was once a great leader," Van Wyck said.

"That was a decade ago, before he turned on us." Bulganov drained his glass. "Tell me, my friend, do you foresee any problems with your operation?"

"With the Chinese I always foresee problems," Van Wyck said.

"I thought everything was perfectly planned."

"It is," Van Wyck replied, "but the Chinese are a strange and difficult enemy to subdue. Do you realize that in the last century they have fought three wars against the French, two against the British, two against the Japanese, and two against our people. And in all that time, not only have they not won a war, I don't think they've even won a battle."

"What's your point, comrade?" Bulganov said with a hint of impatience.

"The Chinese have lost every battle of every war, but they have never lost any territory. Their country is larger now than it has ever been."

Bulganov slapped Van Wyck on the back. "My friend, do you see our troops and armaments? Do you really think the Chinese have any hope of stopping us? You've been living in the Orient too long."

"Perhaps you're right," Van Wyck said, although he was not convinced by Bulganov's military bravado.

"After Operation Cossack is completed," Bulganov said, "I'm going to send you to the Black Sea for a vacation. That should be enough to wean you from your jaundiced thinking."

"I'd like that," Van Wyck said, realizing that it had been almost four years since he had been back to his homeland. The idea of painting in the magnificent resorts of southern Russia was very appealing.

Bulganov strode down the sandy street toward a new Russian tank. "Now, my friend, what remains to be done from your end?"

"Everything is set for the final attack." Van Wyck wiped his mouth with the damp handkerchief. "And to ensure that the Chinese are unable to respond effectively, I sent a team to Peking to remove Hua."

"Good thinking." Bulganov tapped his riding crop. "Whom are you using?"

"Yamaguchi."

"Perfect. I want Takamura to have blood on their hands."

"Bodo and Bator from Mongolia, the Hing brothers, and Avery Boswell."

"Boswell! That jerk! Why the hell are you using him?"

"He was the only one who could carry my orders back to Peking."

"He's an ass!"

"You approved his involvement."

Bulganov lit a cigar that smelled little better than the stench of the camels. "I never thought you'd listen. You never have before."

"Then why did you assign him to me?"

Bulganov ran his hands through his thick black hair, cropped flat on top. "Our friend Mr. Boswell has powerful friends at the highest levels of the Party."

"Who? Why?" Van Wyck asked incredulously.

"I think we should drop this discussion." Bulganov's tone was clipped and abrupt. "Contact Boswell. Order him to stop whatever he is doing. I just hope for both our sakes that idiot doesn't screw everything up trying to play soldier."

By four o'clock, Ren Daoling was very discouraged. He had searched most of his territory and talked with hundreds of people, but none had seen Gateshead or the Turks. The car entered a broad valley. Ren raised his binoculars. At the far end, tucked into a narrow canyon, was a small collection of yurts. A Turk on horseback rode through a mountain pass and galloped across the valley. It was Ruzi, one of Rahman's aides. Accelerating to full speed, the jeep pulled abreast. The Turk reined in his horse. "Have you seen this man?" Ren asked, showing him Gateshead's picture.

The Turk stared nervously at the four men. "What would a barbarian be doing around here?"

"Then you haven't seen him?" Ren asked.

"I already answered your question," the Turk sneered. He kicked his horse in the flanks and galloped away.

Ren climbed back into the jeep. "Did you believe him?"

"No way," the driver replied. "Let's check out the village."

The jeep moved ahead. The Turk wheeled his horse and approached from the rear. Ren turned to watch. The Turk pulled a submachine gun from under his blanket. Ren screamed a warning. It was too late. The first bullet ripped into the driver's neck. The jeep careened into a gully and flipped over. Ren and the others were thrown to the ground. The Turk continued firing. A second man was shot and killed. Ren grabbed the driver's gun and scampered behind a rock. The Turk turned his horse and rode back for another pass. The third of the men from the jeep raised his rifle and took aim. A hail of bullets from the submachine gun perforated his body. He toppled in a heap. His blood rained onto the ground.

Ren steadied his right arm with his left hand. It had been years since he had shot anything. Sweat poured from his hand as he grasped the pistol. Be calm! It's just like shooting a rabbit, he said to himself. The Turk circled around the rock, firing to keep him pinned down. Ren took a deep breath. He stood up and aimed at the Turk. A bullet tore into Ren's left shoulder. He tried not to flinch. His heart felt as if it had stopped beating. He squeezed the trigger. The Turk toppled off his horse.

Ren hurried back to the jeep. There was no way he could turn it upright. Trying to stay calm, he walked to the Turk's horse and grabbed the bridle. The horse reared. Ren pulled tightly. The bullet in his shoulder burned. He was losing blood. With all his strength, he yanked down on the reins. The horse stopped. He grasped the saddle and pulled himself up. The horse started to gallop toward the yurts. Ren dug his feet into the horse's flanks. The horse craned its head backward. Ren kicked the horse again. The animal shook its neck in the air and then grudgingly obeyed Ren's directions.

45: Know Yourself, Know Your Enemy

The People's Liberation Army officer ushered Marc Slater into the wood-paneled study in the Western Hills villa of Defense Minister Ye. Hua Guofeng, Deng Xiaoping, Ye Jianying, and Kang Moruo were already sitting around the rosewood conference table. "Good evening, Mr. Slater." Hua stood up and bowed politely. Despite the problems facing China, Hua's face remained placid and unlined. Only in the puffy bags sagging beneath his eyes could one see the intensity of his strain.

"Good evening, Premier Hua." Marc bowed in return.

"For a foreigner and a former corpse," Hua said, "you keep popping up in the strangest places."

Marc nodded politely, wondering what Hua would say if he knew about the plan to break into the archives. "I am just trying to help maintain the friendship between the People's

Republic and the United States."

"Fine, fine," Hua said, and then abruptly changed the subject. "I am told you have some photographs from one of your Scarecrow spy satellites."

Marc handed him the envelope filled with pictures of Russian and Red Guard military installations, photos he had received from Beatrice Tang. While Hua studied them, Marc made his way to a black leather chair at the far end of the table. Sitting down, he stared at the magnificent collection of Chinese watercolors hanging on the wall.

"These photographs are quite impressive. I wish those from our satellites were as good," Hua said, turning to Ye. "How many troops do you estimate the Russians have along the border?"

"About forty thousand, and they are exceedingly well armed." The aging defense minister pointed to the pictures. "You can see their concentrations quite graphically."

"It does not look promising," Hua said.

Ye glanced uneasily at Kang and Deng and then turned back to Hua. "We are not totally defenseless. We have four American cargo planes at a state farm a hundred and twenty miles from the border."

Hua looked flabbergasted. "Where did they come from?"

"Far West Aviation had scheduled a demonstration of its new products for the PLA," Ye replied. "I authorized them to go to Xinjiang."

"How could you do it without obtaining my approval?" Hua asked, trying to maintain the composure that was his trademark.

"You were in Tangshan. There was no time to contact you."

Hua crimped his nose. "That explanation is such crap that we could use it to fertilize a field of rice."

"I apologize for my error," Ye said, massaging his jowly cheeks, "but I felt we had to do something to stop the Russians."

"So you decided to take control of the government." The purple veins in Hua's neck throbbed as he spoke.

"I can order the planes back whenever you want."

"Do it now!"

Deng cleared his throat and hurled a wad of phlegm into a spittoon. "That's as intelligent as inviting a family of hungry tigers to eat dinner with your children. The Russians have a vast military superiority. You need all the help you can get."

"I can move troops and weapons from Peking."

"There is no time," the diminutive Deng replied. "Besides, you need your soldiers to defend yourself against Jiang Qing."

"Jiang poses no threat."

"Are you living in a dreamworld?" Deng said. "Jiang and her Red Guards are now as well equipped as your People's Liberation Army."

"I don't believe Jiang would violate the last wishes of her husband. You seem to forget that Chairman Mao appointed *me* his successor."

"And you seem to forget that Jiang Qing is as loyal as a bitch in heat and as greedy as a hungry crow in a field of grain. But don't take my word for it!" Deng shook the photographs in Hua's face. "Look at the evidence. Twenty thousand men in Fujian are being deployed toward Canton. Forty ships are sailing from the Yangtze Arsenal toward Qingdao and Tianjin. And eighty thousand men from Shanghai have moved to staging points from which they can attack Peking."

Hua studied the photographs. "What's your opinion, Comrade Ye?"

"I am"—Ye measured his words—"in agreement with

Comrade Deng."

"Do you think we can convince Jiang to support our government?"

"I do not."

Hua calmly poured a cup of tea. "Then unless we capitulate, we must simultaneously fight an internal and an external enemy?"

"That's the way I see it."

Hua walked to the window. "I don't think we can win on both fronts. Perhaps we should select the lesser of the two evils and sue for peace."

"How can you be so timid?" Deng challenged. "We have considerable strengths. We only have to decide how to use them. Whenever Mao faced a crisis, he turned to Sun Tzu's adage 'Know your enemy, know yourself. In a hundred battles, you will never be in peril.' For every situation there is always an appropriate strategy. In this case, since we face two strong enemies, the key is to defeat them without fighting."

Hua laughed. "And just how do you intend to accomplish that?"

"By understanding our strengths and weaknesses and those of our enemies," Deng said. "Look at the Russians. They could have taken our oil fields any time they wanted, so why are they still waiting? Because they don't want the world to think they would ruthlessly attack another country. That's why they set up the commando activities and formed an alliance with the Turkic Nationalists. My guess is that they plan to carry out at least one more mock attack on the border in order to justify their invasion." Deng marched nervously across the back of the room. "So our first move must be to stop the Turks. If we send Liu's troops to back up the men from the state farm, I think we've got a reasonable chance."

"Do you think that will stop the Russians from invading?" Hua asked.

"Not by itself," Deng replied. "To do that, we must convince them that the cost of their adventure will be exorbitant, that they will have to take on millions of Chinese along a four-thousand-mile front."

Hua stared incredulously at Deng. "We can't fight an all-out war against the Russians."

"I know that and you know that"—Deng smiled slyly—"but do the Russians?"

"I don't know if I want to bet my government on a bluff," Hua said.

"If the Russians attack, you won't have a government to bet."

"Just how do you see this bluff working?" Defense Minister Ye asked.

"First, we need a credible retaliatory force opposite the Dzungarian Gate." Deng gestured animatedly. "It doesn't have to be strong enough to defeat the Russians, but it does have to be able to inflict lots of casualties. We can bring men from Sichuan and Shaanxi into Urumqi, fly them to the state farm, and then shuttle them to the border in helicopters. Next," Deng continued in his rapid-fire speech, "we should move PLA units in Jilin, Heilongjiang, Inner Mongolia, Ningxia, and Gansu toward the nearest border points."

"The Russians have sophisticated spy satellites," Hua said. "They'll see the troops and think we really are planning to invade."

"Good." A gleam crept into Deng's eyes. "And so they don't misunderstand, you can inform Brezhnev that if he makes a move in Dzungaria, you'll launch an all-out attack. Tell him that Mao warned about Russian imperialism on his deathbed, and you intend to remain loyal to Mao's policies even if it requires killing one hundred million Chinese."

Hua stared quizzically at Deng. "But he'll think I'm crazy."

"That's what I'm hoping," Deng laughed. "If we convince him that we're prepared to fight at any cost, he'll back down."

"You lived in Russia," Hua said to Ye. "What do you think?"

"It just might work," the defense minister replied.

"All right," Hua said. "Let's send Liu after the Turks and order as many men as possible toward the border."

"I'll take care of it right now," Ye replied, "but we still have to deal with Jiang Qing."

"Handling Jiang will be a snap." Deng smiled like a Cheshire cat. "If we plan everything correctly, the Red Guards won't even have the chance to load their rifles."

"We'd be pleased if you'd enlighten us," Hua said in a monotone.

"The trick with Jiang Qing"—Deng strutted behind the table—"is to use her strengths against her. Jiang is conceited, self-centered, and completely absorbed in her own struggle for power. She and her three compatriots believe nothing can stop them. They think they hold the secret key to power, Mao's last will and testament. Jiang and her people forged a new will that names her as chairman. When it is read, she expects that the wavering members of the Wind Faction will follow Mao's wishes and side with her. Then the Gang of Four will take power, while the Red Guards will arrest leading moderates and clean up pockets of resistance."

"How can we stop her?" Hua asked.

"We have recovered the original will." The gleam returned to Deng's eyes. "By the time of the Politburo meeting, it will be the one in the vault."

"But how?" Hua asked.

While Marc shifted uneasily, Deng waved his arms.

"I'm not at liberty to tell you. It would jeopardize the lives of too many people."

"Must I remind you that I am the premier?" Hua asked.

"I recognize your position," Deng replied. "But you should realize that we are on the same side."

The men at the table stared at each other until the uneasy silence was broken by Ye. "How do you think Jiang will react when the will is read?"

"She'll probably fly into one of her well-known rages. She might even try to grab power right then and there."

"How do you suggest we handle her?"

"Until the meeting"—Deng lit a cigarette—"we must not make her suspicious. It might even be wise to give in on a few issues. For example, if you let Wang preside at tomorrow's funeral, Jiang's confidence will grow and she'll become careless. That's when we strike." Deng slammed his fist into the table. "We will take selected members of Unit 8341 and have them ready to arrest the Gang of Four as soon as they try to take control of the government."

"How can you be certain," Hua asked, "that Jiang won't attack with the Red Guards before the meeting?"

"Jiang is very concerned about her position in history," Deng replied. "Remember how she embarrassed herself in that biography with the American writer?" The others nodded in agreement. "She would never risk staging a military coup when she was certain that the Politburo would appoint her as the next chairman."

"You seem very confident of your judgment," Hua said.

"I have followed Sun Tzu's teachings," Deng replied, "and studied my enemies."

46: Attack on the Yurts

Sitting in front of his yurt, Aziz Rahman watched the sun setting over the majestic, snowcapped Heavenly Mountains. He loved the beauty and solitude of the valleys of Xinjiang. Despite the harsh temperatures and the lack of rain, it was his homeland. He and his people had struggled for years to overthrow the yoke of Chinese imperialism. Now the day for which he had struggled was in sight. Soon the Democratic Republic of East Turkestan would take its place among the nations of the world.

Nur Turdi galloped frantically into the village. Rahman jumped up and grabbed the bridle of Nur's horse. "Ruzi has been killed," Nur panted, trying to catch his breath. "It was the People's Militia."

"Bastards!" Rahman angrily kicked the ground. He and Ruzi had been friends since birth. "What happened?"

"I don't know," Nur replied, "but the three Chinese are also dead."

Rahman stared blankly into the valley. It did not seem logical that no one had survived the skirmish. "Are you sure there were only three men?"

"That's all I saw. Their jeep was wrecked, so I don't think anyone could have gotten away."

"What about Ruzi's horse?"

Nur shrugged. "It must have run away."

"Perhaps there was a fourth man who killed Ruzi and then escaped on his horse." Rahman placed his hands over his eyes and rubbed his temples.

"It's possible."

"Take some men and find the one who killed Ruzi. Then clear the jeep and the bodies from the valley. There can be no signs that point to us."

As Nur went to organize the men, Rahman stepped into his yurt and switched the shortwave radio to the frequency monitored by Van Wyck. "Kazak, Kazak," he called, "this is Turk. Come in please."

"Kazak here," Van Wyck's voice crackled. "What's the problem? Over."

"A few Chinese soldiers paid us a visit. Ruzi killed three, but then he was shot. It's possible a fourth man escaped. I've sent search teams, but he may already have gotten back to his people. Over."

There was a momentary silence. "Your news is quite disturbing." Van Wyck's voice was deliberate and measured. "It might be appropriate to step up the timing of our attack. I want you to organize your men and move immediately to the junction of the Kuytun River and Ebinur Lake. We'll attack at dawn, the day after tomorrow. Over."

"I'll have our camps ready to move in one hour," Rahman said. "What should I do with the Englishman? Over."

"I have plans for him," Van Wyck replied. "Keep him guarded. I'm holding you responsible for his safety. Over and out."

Rahman put down the microphone and called to Kamal, one of his aides. "Inform our camps that we are moving up the attack. Everyone is to leave at once, even women and children. We will rendezvous at the bend in the dry bed of the northern tributary of the Kuytun River."

"I'll take care of it at once," Kamal replied.

"My friend"—Rahman placed his arm on Kamal's shoulder—"I know how much you want to be with us, but I need you to guard the Englishman. I'm leaving you twenty men."

"But why?" Kamal asked. "That old man isn't worth anything."

"He is to the Dutchman"—Rahman shook his head— "and I'm not about to argue with Van Wyck."

Hong Guoqiang, the director of State Farm 120, sat behind his aluminum desk reviewing the reports from the teams that had been searching for Van Wyck. The door opened. Samuel Tang strode in. He looked drained and tired. His clothes were stained with grease. He had spent the day helping to unload and assemble the weapons from the cargo planes. "I was just going to look for you," Hong said. "You received a call from General Liu Teyu. His battalions have landed in Urumqi. They are making their way along the main road toward the Dzungarian Gate. He wants to use your cargo planes and helicopters to help speed the deployment of additional troops."

"They are at his disposal."

"I took the liberty of telling him that for you," Hong said.

"How's our search?" Sam slumped into a chair. "Any sign of the Turks?"

Hong shook his head. "They've melted into the mountains."

Sam stared at the map of the border hanging behind Hong's desk. "They have to be out there."

"We'll try again in the morning," Hong suggested.

"We may not have the time," Sam replied.

A man burst into the office. "Come quickly," he yelled. "Your friend, Comrade Ren, has been shot."

Following the man, Sam and Hong ran out the door and through the square to the hospital. Ren was lying on an examination table while a barefoot doctor removed the bullet embedded in his shoulder. The wound was superficial, but Ren had lost a lot of blood. The doctor applied bandages and then placed smelling salts under Ren's nose. Ren shook his head and slowly opened his eyes. "What happened?" Sam asked.

"We stumbled on the camp of the Turks," Ren murmured. "It's in a broad valley about forty *li* from here. We showed one of the Turks the photograph of Gateshead. He said he had never seen the Englishman. But then he turned and shot at us from behind with a machine gun. Our men were killed, but I was fortunate enough to shoot him."

Sam handed Ren a glass of water. "Do you feel well enough to show us the way to the valley?"

Ren grimaced as he sat up. "I'll try."

"I want one hundred men in jeeps ready to go as quickly as possible," Sam instructed Hong. After years of building weapons, he was feeling the excitement of being on a real military mission. "I also want all the helicopters to begin reconnaissance. The Turks may have already moved their base. I don't want to give them the chance to slip away."

It was well past midnight. Standing on a knoll overlooking the northern tributary of the Kuytun River, Aziz Rahman watched the lights of the caravans arriving from all directions. There were Uygurs, Kazaks, Kirgiz, Salars, and even Uzbeks. Some came on foot, some on camels and horses, and still others in jeeps. In all, there were more than two thousand Turks.

As Rahman silently inspected his troops, he was increasingly concerned that the Chinese might now know of his presence. He could not let them intercept him. He had to create a massive diversion using the women and children as decoys so that the men could reach Ebinur Lake without being detected.

Rahman divided his people into six groups. "I want groups one and two"—he pointed to the contingents of men—"to take the horses and go southeast and southwest along the river. Use no lights and stay close to the mountains. You had better leave now. I'll catch up with you." As Rahman watched, six hundred men gathered their horses, organized themselves into squads, and rode off into the night. Despite the darkness, they would be easy to spot unless other targets seemed far more compelling.

"The rest of you"—Rahman spoke to the women and children as well as to the few men who remained—"will serve as decoys. Group three is to go northeast, group four northwest, group five due west, and group six will remain here. Take all the jeeps and any spare animals. I want you to be as visible as possible. Use bright lights, burn torches, stay in the center of all valleys, and leave a trail of cooking fires. Make as much noise as you can. Your task is to distract the Chinese troops until our men reach the lake." Rahman paused. "The future of the Republic of East Turkestan depends on you. I know you will not let us down."

As the convoy of jeeps motored slowly along the main dirt road, Ren Daoling propped himself up in the back seat. His wound had left him weak and dizzy, but he could not let himself give in to his pain until he had found Rahman's camp. A winding camel path veered off to the right. Asking the driver to stop, Ren studied the markings of a massive boulder that rested incongruously at the intersection. "This is the entrance to the valley," he said. "The encampment of yurts is about six *li* dead ahead."

"How many men are there?" Sam asked.

"I wish I could tell you," Ren replied.

Sam paced across the camel path, trying to develop a plan. Although he now knew the location of the enemy's camp, getting there would not be easy. The Turks were natives of the region. They probably had Russian weapons as well as horses, which were well suited to the mountainous terrain. They also controlled the high ground. To offset these advantages, Sam had to find a way of penetrating the defenses in force without being spotted.

Hong Guoqiang called on the shortwave radio. "I have a report from the helicopters," Hong's voice crackled. "They have sighted four major squads of Turks. One is stationary in sector twelve, twenty miles west of you. Two are moving north in sectors two and five. And the fourth is heading due west toward the border."

"That doesn't make sense," Sam replied, studying his map. "The Russians are massed at the Dzungarian Gate, yet the Turks seem to be heading away from them. Are you sure there aren't any squads moving south?"

"The helicopters did not sight any."

"Something is wrong," Sam said, staring into the darkness. If the Turks were on the move, he could not afford to wait. He had to find answers. Perhaps the encampment at the end of the valley would yield some clues. There was only one way to capture it. He gave Hong a brief set of instructions. Then he assembled his men and described his plan.

While one driver and one gunner remained with each of the jeeps, Sam and the other fifty men set out toward the end of the valley. They walked silently, in single file, and used no lights. Secrecy was paramount. After almost thirty minutes, the outlines of the settlement became dimly visible. They continued until they were a quarter-mile from the yurts. There was no movement in the village. Sam motioned for his men to stop.

Twenty minutes passed. The silence was oppressive. Then Sam heard the first faint sound of motors in the distance. The noise became louder. Six helicopters flew through a narrow mountain pass and approached from the south. Passing over the yurts, they fired tracer flares that lit up the village like floodlights over a boxing ring. Although the yurts could easily have been destroyed, no bombs were dropped. Sam needed evidence of troop movements. Dead men and charred rubble would be of no help.

Kamal, Nur, and the other Turks awakened and grabbed their weapons. Retreating to the southwestern edge of the valley, the helicopters landed and discharged a squad of soldiers. The Turks mounted their horses and pursued the choppers across an open plain. Sam lit a flare. The twenty-five jeeps from his convoy motored in from the southeast, blocking the left flank of the Turks. Machine guns opened fire. Two Turks and six of their horses were shot. Kamal and his men circled to the east. The jeeps from the state farm closed in on them. The Turks were trapped. Seven men were gunned down.

Sam's men crept into the village from the north. The women and children were easily subdued. Ten members of the state-farm militia herded the villagers together. The rest advanced to block the retreat of the Turks.

Kamal and his men charged toward the jeeps, but the aim of the Chinese gunners was deadly. Three more Turks were killed. Kamal's men retreated toward the village. Sam's squad opened fire. Bullets rained in on the Turks from all sides. Then there was silence. Kamal, Nur, and all of their men were dead.

*　　　*　　　*

Lord Henry Gateshead, wearing a vest and tie, stood next to his yurt. Two of the Chinese pointed their guns at him. He raised his hands. "Please don't shoot! I am an Englishman."

The Chinese dragged him to where Sam was standing. Sam motioned for him to lower his arms. "Lord Gateshead, are you all right?"

"I am fine, but who are you?" Gateshead asked with astonishment.

"I am Samuel Tang."

"How do you know my identity?"

"I was sent here to rescue you," Sam said.

"Thank God."

"What happened to Rahman and the others?" Sam asked.

"They left about eight hours ago."

"Do you know where they went?"

"I'm not certain, but I believe there is a map in Rahman's yurt." Lord Gateshead showed Sam the way.

Tearing open the leather saddlebags, Gateshead searched until he found Rahman's map. The rendezvous point at the junction of the Kuytun River and Ebinur Lake was clearly marked. He handed the map to Sam, along with documents that listed the stores of weapons around the lake and the plans for the attack.

The evidence confirmed what Sam had suggested. The main force of Turks was heading south. The columns that the helicopters had sighted were just diversions. Sam now had the information he needed. The only problem was time. There was less than two hours until dawn. It would be impossible to get to the lake before Rahman. His only choice was to move as quickly as possible and hope he could intercept the Turks before they attacked the Russian border.

47: The Funeral

Marc Slater jumped up from the breakfast table in Kang Moruo's house and hurried toward the sound of voices coming from the front hall. He smiled broadly as Linda Forbes came toward him. In white linen slacks, a lilac blouse, and a magenta belt that accentuated her trim waist, she looked stunning. He wanted to throw his arms around her, but restrained himself. An overt display of emotion in front of his moralistic Chinese hosts would be highly inappropriate. "Are you all right?" he asked, reaching for her hand.

"I'm fine." Linda smiled with her soft green eyes. "My stay in the hospital did me a world of good."

"I'm sorry we had to strand you there overnight," Marc said, "but you must admit it was an improvement over the prison farm."

"Don't I have a choice of anything but a hospital or a prison?" Linda gave Marc a mock pout.

"What did you have in mind?" Marc asked, realizing that Linda seemed more appealing each time he saw her.

"How about a deluxe suite of rooms with an oversize Jacuzzi?"

"Alone, or with company?"

"It depends on the company."

"How do you feel about capitalists?" Marc whispered.

Linda laughed. "I like them sexy, rich, intelligent, single, and hopelessly in love with me."

Marc cupped her chin in his hands and smiled. "What happens if I find one who meets your requirements?"

"Have him send a résumé and I'll set up an interview."

"Suppose such a capitalist were to invite you for a week of sailing in Tahiti?"

"I could use a vacation. I guess a cruise could be pleasant."

"Pleasant!" Marc feigned anger. "It's every woman's dream."

"Every woman's dream, is it?" Linda smiled. "I couldn't live with myself knowing that I'd passed up such an opportunity."

Kang Moruo coughed intentionally as he entered the room. Marc looked up, edging silently away from Linda. "I hate to interrupt," Kang said as he straightened the collar of his light gray cashmere suit, "but we have to get to the building housing the National Archives before our people go off guard duty."

"Will we be back tonight?" Linda asked.

"That depends on what happens during the break-in," Kang replied. "But even if you're stranded in my office, you'll have Marc and Sen to protect you."

"And that's supposed to make me feel safe?" Linda winked at Marc.

"Come on." Marc grabbed Linda round the waist. "From what I've seen, you do a pretty good job taking care of yourself."

* * *

Avery Boswell paced in front of a map of Peking in the small administrative office of the single-story warehouse that the Chinese Hotel Corporation had leased to Royal Amsterdam Hotels. The five operatives sat in hard-backed desk chairs listening to the plan Van Wyck had devised for the assassination of Hua Guofeng. Two of the men were Mongolians, two were Russian-educated Chinese, and the sixth was Yamaguchi Yukio, the massive Japanese who was a director of the Takamura Corporation.

"Van Wyck's instructions are actually quite simple." Boswell tried to sound in control. "In addition to his home in Zhong Nanhai, Hua has a villa in the Western Hills." Boswell pointed to the map. "He goes there every day to get away from the pressures of work and indulge himself." The ends of Boswell's lips turned downward as he forced a laugh. "It seems the old boy leads rather a risqué life, if you get my drift." None of the Orientals smiled.

"We understand," Yamaguchi said. "Please continue."

"The attack will take place tomorrow afternoon, after the reading of Mao's will. You will wait on either side of the road, armed with machine guns. When Hua drives up, you will open fire. Once he is dead, you will scatter and the mission will be completed. Are there any questions?" Boswell shifted uneasily, waiting for a response.

"Why is this necessary?" Yamaguchi asked.

"What do you mean?"

"Why does Van Wyck want us to assassinate Hua?"

"The troops on the border are ready to move." Boswell spoke the words as he had been instructed. "But before our forces invade, Van Wyck wants to make one last attempt at fomenting a civil war. Hua is the only person holding the government together. If we kill him, the Chinese will be so busy fighting with each other that they'll pose no threat to us."

Yamaguchi's powerful body towered over that of the slim

Englishman. "It sounds like your people are losing their nerve."

"Van Wyck is just taking necessary precautions."

"I don't buy it," Yamaguchi said. "We've done everything Van Wyck has asked and more, but our deal says nothing about killing heads of state."

"My orders come directly from Van Wyck." Boswell tried to sound firm.

"I'd like to talk to the Dutchman myself."

"That's impossible. He's in the mountains. There's no way for you to communicate with him."

"I suggest you get him a message." Yamaguchi grabbed his briefcase. "If he wants our help, he had better be prepared to renegotiate our deal."

Boswell wiped sweat off his forehead. Yamaguchi was forcing him to lose face, a cardinal sin in the Orient. And the defection of the Japanese might cause the others to question his leadership. "You're making a serious miscalculation," Boswell said.

"I'll be at the hotel if your supervisors wish to talk with me." Yamaguchi turned and walked out of the warehouse.

Boswell marched across the floor, trying to maintain an authoritative front. As a foreigner, he could not permit any further weakening of his position in front of these Orientals. "What about the rest of you?" he challenged. "Are any of you frightened of carrying out this mission?" The others sat silently. Unlike Yamaguchi, who was a successful businessman, they were highly paid operatives who had no alternative but to follow orders. "Good," Boswell smiled. "Then we'll leave tomorrow at eleven."

The squad of forty-eight guards from Unit 8341, Mao's private security force, snapped to attention as the black

Hong Qi limousine pulled to a halt in front of the Great Hall of the People. Their commander bowed politely as he opened the back door. Mao Yuanxin climbed out, followed by Lina and Limin, the daughters of Mao and Jiang Qing. The commander waited. A woman's leg, draped with black silk, extended forward. The woman paused, almost as if she expected a roll of drums or a blare of trumpets to herald her arrival. When none was forthcoming, Jiang Qing pulled herself into the doorway. In her black silk dress and veil, she looked like a figure from a 1940s Hollywood melodrama. Grasping the side of the door, she glared imperiously at the guards. The commander offered his hand. She brushed it away and stepped regally to the pavement.

Another limousine drove up. Its back seat was filled with the huge wreath of orchids from Jiang Qing as well as with flower arrangements from Lina, Limin, and Yuanxin. Shen Mo distributed the funeral bouquets, while another woman snapped photographs with a Nikon camera. "I'd like a few minutes alone with my husband," Jiang instructed. "Then I want some pictures of myself laying the wreath in front of the casket."

Two guards held open the front door of the Great Hall of the People. Jiang shivered as she walked into the massive entryway. Although the hall, which could hold more than ten thousand people, usually teemed with life, it was now pervaded by an austere silence. Dim lights cast eerie shadows on the marble floors. All the furniture had been moved out, giving the room a hollow, cavernous feeling. The only object remaining was a solitary glass case at the far end of the floor.

Jiang trembled as she stared at the glass case. She felt nervous and ill at ease, like a sinner being summoned to an audience with the Lord. She was unsure how to act. She did not even know whether she was supposed to play the role of the grieving widow mourning a dead husband or that of the next chairman of the Communist party paying homage to her predecessor.

Her feet moved forward as if tugged by an irresistible force. Mao had become more than a man. He was a god, the Great Helmsman of one billion people. His passing was a public event. There had been no room for the private grief of the family. If Jiang had fought, she probably could have been with Mao at his deathbed, but she was no longer the docile wife waiting for her husband to die; she had become an imposing political figure on her own. She could not afford to let emotions distract her from attending to the political crisis in which she was the central figure.

For forty years she had been Mao's student. She had sat at his feet, studying and listening. He had taken a film actress with little formal education and promoted her to the highest levels of the Party. The strains of power had sometimes forced them apart, and she had made powerful enemies. Jiang did not regret the decisions she had made, but they had not been without their costs.

She was not sure she wanted to look, yet she knew that she had no choice. This was her first and undoubtedly last opportunity to be alone with her husband. Soon the doors would be thrown open and hundreds of millions of people would come to stake their claim on Mao's soul.

The base of the glass case was less than an arm's length ahead. Stopping, Jiang closed her eyes and took a deep breath. Then she looked up and gasped. Beneath the glass, like a stuffed animal in a museum, lay the body of Mao Tse-tung. He was smartly dressed in his finest uniform. His eyes gazed serenly at the ceiling, like a Buddha engaged in silent meditation. His hair was neatly parted in the center. His broad, pale, unwrinkled face had a healthy complexion. Only the mole on his chin seemed larger than it should have been.

Jiang felt faint. Reaching out, she steadied herself against the case as she gazed at Mao's puffy hands and pink, flat-topped ears. He seemed so alive. The taxidermists had worked wonders. They had mounted the Chairman so that he looked ten years younger than he had while alive. With their help, the Great Helmsman had become immortal, a person frozen in time.

As she stared at her husband, Jiang felt so distant and yet so close. She touched her fingers to her lips and pressed them against the glass above Mao's mouth. "I miss you so much," she whispered. "You were everything to me. My teacher, my lover, my friend. Whatever I am, I owe to you. I tried so hard to be the wife and student you wanted me to be. I tried to help you guide the country. I know sometimes I failed. Perhaps I was too weak to stand up against the enemies who tried to poison your mind against me. But I never stopped loving you."

Jiang choked on her words as she continued. "Those others, they don't care. They cried more for Chou En-lai than they did for you. They make speeches and say they honor you, but they are frauds. They want to lead China back onto the capitalist road. But I will never let them do that. I will keep your teachings alive. You will see that I am your true friend. I will never betray you. I will make you proud of me."

Jiang wiped the tears from her face. She opened her compact and stared at herself in the mirror. She looked old and tired, far worse than Mao lying placidly under the glass. She wiped the smudges under her eyes and powdered her face. Then she walked to the door to let the others in.

Yuanxin and Shen Mo placed the massive wreath in front of the tomb. Jiang motioned for them to step aside while the photographer snapped pictures of her beside the casket. Lina and Limin put bouquets honoring their father next to the wreath. Then they joined their mother for the family photograph. Finally Yuanxin was included for the last group of pictures.

The door of the Great Hall opened again. Hua Guofeng, wearing a simple cadre's uniform, strode deliberately across the floor to where Jiang was standing. "What do you think you are doing?" he demanded.

"I am paying homage to my husband."

"What is the purpose of the photographs?" Hua spoke in a monotone.

"They are family mementos."

"Why are you using a photographer from the *People's Daily*?"

"Comrade Liu"—Jiang Qing pointed to the photographer—"is a personal friend."

"Who, I am sure," Hua rejoined, "has been instructed to place the photograph of you standing in front of Mao's casket on the front page of her newspaper. Isn't that correct, comrade?"

"I have no say over what pictures are used in the paper," the photographer replied, stepping away from Hua and Jiang.

"But your friend, Comrade Jiang does, doesn't she?"

Jiang's nostrils flared. "Stop berating the poor woman. She's only doing her job."

"And what about you?" A hint of annoyance crept into Hua's voice.

"I am here to mourn my husband." Jiang turned away from Hua. "Aren't I entitled to a moment alone after forty years of marriage?"

"Of course, comrade," Hua said. "I am sure that Chairman Mao would be pleased that you have finally deigned to pay your last respects."

"What do you care about my husband's wishes?" Jiang

said, staring at Mao. "It was you who decided on the funeral arrangements. He would never have chosen to be exhibited like an animal in the zoo. You have made all the decisions without any concern for his personal preferences."

"Do I have to remind you that I am the premier and that Chairman Mao designated me as his successor?"

"And do I have to remind you that I am his wife? My husband's body is still warm and you are already viciously attacking me in front of my family. Look at my daughters, the daughters of Chairman Mao." A tear rolled down Jiang's cheek. "How can you make me lose face in front of them? Aren't they, too, entitled to mourn their father?"

"Please, comrade." Hua bowed his head. "I am sorry if I was abrupt. The stress of the last several weeks has been quite intense. For the sake of the memory of the Great Helmsman, we should try to cooperate."

"You have a strange way of demonstrating your friendship."

"Didn't I give in to your demands that Comrade Wang preside at the funeral?" Hua replied.

"You had no choice," Jiang said.

"There is always a choice. I could have sided with the moderates."

"But you are no fool," Jiang said. "You know the future belongs to me and my people."

"I am sure"—Hua's voice remained level—"that we can work together."

"Of course we can," Jiang replied, "just so long as you are willing to accord me my proper role."

"As long as you do not force me to lose face, we will have no difficulties," Hua said. He bowed to Jiang and strode out of the hall.

Jiang smiled as she watched Hua leave. He was an idiot and a weakling. Handling him would be even easier than she had thought. But she could not afford to be overconfident. She would have to be prepared to move quickly. As soon as she returned to Zhong Nanhai, she would order all of her Red Guard garrisons to begin to move their troops toward Peking. The reading of the will was scheduled for the next morning. Jiang smiled. Within twenty-four hours, she would be the new chairman of the Communist Party and the most powerful woman in the world.

Marc, Linda, Sen, and Kang sat around the conference table in Kang's office poring over stacks of books. They were reading histories of China and biographies of Chairman Mao, hoping to find a date that would unlock the Chairman's private vault in the National Archives. The tradition among the leaders of the People's Republic was to use the dates of important and symbolic events as the combinations to their locks. The most commonly selected was 10-1-19-49, the founding of the Republic, but people used everything from Chou En-lai's birthday to the date of one of Mao's purges.

The forty most likely dates had been culled from a list of five hundred, but none seemed the obvious choice. Marc had to hope that one would open the vault. He would have only a short time inside the archives. Unless he made the right choice, he would never be able to switch the wills.

Kang's private phone rang. "*Wei*," he answered tentatively.

"Honorable uncle, this is your fourth nephew, Xiaoma. I apologize for disturbing you, but I have news of considerable importance."

"Go ahead," Kang said, fingering a cloisonné vase.

"I've been following Boswell," Xiaoma said. "He has been

back to the warehouse of the Hotel Corporation three times in the last day. Two hours ago, five other men joined him. Two were Chinese, two were Mongolian, and one was Japanese. I suspect they are planning some type of operation."

Kang repeated the information. Marc motioned to another phone. Kang nodded. Marc lifted the receiver. "Xiaoma, this is Marc Slater. What did the Japanese look like?"

"He was elegantly dressed, extremely tall, and quite stocky, like a sumo wrestler."

"Damn! It's Yamaguchi." Marc tapped the end of a pencil on the table. "I was hoping he wasn't still working with the Russians."

"He may not be," Xiaoma said. "He left the meeting an hour before the others and returned to his hotel. He immediately called his home office."

"Do you know what the meeting or the phone call was about?"

"I'm sorry but I don't."

"Stay on top of Boswell," Kang said, "then call me tonight."

"As you request, honorable uncle," Xiaoma said, and hung up the phone.

This was the chance Marc had been waiting for. "It looks like there's a rift between Takamura and the Russians," he said to Kang. "Perhaps Yamaguchi couldn't accept Boswell's plans."

"The Japanese have no morals," Kang scoffed. He opened a drawer of his desk and poured two glasses of Suntory scotch.

Marc smiled. "But they do make good booze."

"And better television sets."

"It's possible the Russians are planning something so desperate that even the Japanese can't stomach it," Marc suggested.

Kang rocked back in his chair. "I lived under their occupation in Shanghai. It's difficult to imagine anything too extreme for them. But I guess that even the Island Dwarfs have their limits. They are, after all, Orientals." Kang winked at Marc.

Marc sipped his scotch. "Let's meet with Yamaguchi as soon as we can. With luck, we may be able to drive a further wedge between him and the Russians and find out what Boswell is planning."

"I'll call him," Kang said, "but I don't want to sound too obvious. If he thinks we're on the defensive, we'll never pry anything out of him."

"Wouldn't it be better," Marc asked, "to pressure him with the hard sell and make him think his trade in China is in jeopardy?"

"In the Orient," Kang said, "it is wise to rely more on the teachings of Sun Tzu and less on those of the Harvard Business School."

Marc smiled. "Is that an old Chinese saying?"

"No," Kang replied. "It's advice from a friend who has also lived in China and studied at Harvard."

"And did your years at Harvard teach you nothing?"

"To the contrary." Kang smiled wryly. "I learned two of life's most valuable lessons: to say 'incredible' instead of 'bullshit,' and to read the *Wall Street Journal* without moving my lips."

Marc laughed. "I'm sure that serves you in great stead in Peking."

While Kang set up the appointment, Marc stared out at Tian'anmen Square. An hour remained until the funeral, but half a million people had already gathered in the massive plaza. In front of the Forbidden City, workers were readying the platform from which the leaders of the government would pay their respects to the man who had guided the country since the Liberation.

Feeling uneasy, Marc lit his pipe and contemplated the task confronting him. Since arriving in China, he had worked primarily as a messenger. But now his role was about to change. He would be acting as an operative. The mission would be hazardous. If he was caught, there would be no one to protect him.

Marc tried to imagine how Americans would react if two Chinese were apprehended stealing secret documents from the White House. He could see the conservative ideologues indignantly calling for immediate military action against the People's Republic. The Chinese would be tried as traitors, relations between the two governments would be severed, and anti-Chinese paranoia would sweep the country.

If anything, the reaction to their breaking into the archives was likely to be even more extreme. Mao's will was a document of unparalleled importance. It spoke not to national security but rather to the future of the Republic. It would be as if an Englishman had stolen the only copy of the Constitution from the Founding Fathers. But the will was even more important because it had been written by a now deceased god. Any attempt by foreigners to violate his most personal writings would inflame public opinion and possibly instigate a new cultural revolution.

Marc glanced at Linda, lounging with a book on one of the pigskin sofas. He regretted that she had been included. He did not want anything to happen to her.

Linda walked to the window and placed her hand on the back of his neck. He shivered. "Don't worry about me," she whispered.

Marc looked up, shocked that she had read his mind.

"What makes you think I was worrying about you?"

Linda's green eyes smiled at him. "I'm sorry if I was wrong. But you can't kill me for hoping."

Marc caressed her cheek. "Perhaps I was a little concerned."

"That something would happen to me?"

"Of course not." Marc smiled. "That you'd leave me without a crew on my cruise in Tahiti."

"You're not going to slip out of your invitation that easily."

"Ssh!" Sen whispered loudly. He pointed to the hall. The guards were coming. The building was to be closed between 2:45 and 4:00 for Mao's funeral. Kang ushered the others into a closet. For the next ten minutes, they waited in the stuffy cubicle while the guards completed their rounds. Then Kang opened the door and crept back into the office. The building was deathly quiet. He waved to the others. The clock on the wall read 2:52. There were only eight minutes till the start of the operation.

Tian'anmen Square was now filled with more than a million workers, all wearing identical blue outfits. The leaders of the People's Republic had gathered on the podium in front of the Forbidden City. There, beneath the huge photograph of Chairman Mao, they stood, neatly arranged in order of importance with the most powerful in the center. Although Hua was to give the eulogy, Wang Hongwen had been selected to preside. Wang stepped to the rostrum and raised his arms to silence the crowd. Kang checked his watch. It read 2:57. "Good luck," he said. Then he opened the door and ran down the hall.

"Stop right there!" the guard in front of the archives ordered, shaking his gun at Kang. "This building is officially closed."

"I am aware of the regulations. I am Comrade Kang

Moruo, a member of the Politburo. I am supposed to be on the podium right now. I am humbly honored to give one of the eulogies for the Great Helmsman."

"Let me see your identification," the guard insisted. Kang handed him his Party membership card. The guard studied it and then bowed politely. "Please excuse me, comrade. I should have recognized you."

"Don't be concerned," Kang replied. "But I must have your help in getting out of the building. I can't spend the afternoon arguing with the guards on each floor. If I don't arrive at the podium soon, everyone will take it as an insult to our Great Teacher."

The guard shifted nervously. "I am not supposed to leave my post."

"There is no one in the building," Kang argued. "It will take you less than five minutes to get me to the side entrance. Nothing can happen in that short a time."

"It is my duty to follow my orders."

"And it will be my duty," Kang replied, "to take your name and tell Wang Dongxin that you stopped me from giving a eulogy to Chairman Mao."

The guard's legs trembled. "You can't do that. There's no telling what Comrade Wang might do to me."

"If you force me to miss my speech, I'll have no choice," Kang said. "But don't worry. All Wang can do is send you to Xinjiang."

"All right," the guard said, turning to the stairs, "I'll escort you out of the building, but let's move quickly."

Marc, Linda, and Sen waited for the official signal. At exactly 3:00, a deafening screech interrupted the quiet. Every siren in the People's Republic exploded in a high-pitched whine that was to continue for three minutes. Amplified by tens of millions of loudspeakers, it sounded as if the entire world had caught fire.

Marc dashed toward the archives. Sen followed on his heels. Grabbing the padlock, Marc twisted the dials. The numbers were indeliby etched in his mind: 10-1-19-49, the date of the Liberation. Sen unlocked the Fichet and the Medeco with Little Chang's keys. Marc pushed open the door and stepped inside. Sen reattached the locks. They could not take the chance that the guard would return before Marc was able to switch the wills.

As the sirens stopped, Marc hurried down the fifteen corridors lined with battleship-gray lockers and turned to his right. The private vault of Chairman Mao was in the far corner. Marc unfolded the sheets of paper that listed the possible dates. Then he laid the envelope containing the newly forged will on a table.

His fingers trembled as he twisted the dials of the padlock. The date of Mao's birth failed to unlock the vault, as did that of his mother's death, the birth of his eldest son, or his marriage to Jiang Qing. Outside, Hua was beginning his oration. There were only thirty minutes left. Marc counseled himself to be patient. He could not risk skipping one of the numbers. He forced all other considerations from his mind; if he dwelled on how naked and vulnerable he was, he would never be able to function.

The history of China flashed through his mind as he tried the dates marking the end of the Long March, the armistice with Japan, the commencement of the first Five Year Plan, and the beginning of the Cultural Revolution, as well as the start of the Hundred Flowers Campaign and the Great Leap Forward. But none of the combinations worked.

Footsteps echoed in the hallway. Marc dropped to the floor. The handle of the door turned. Marc's heart pounded so loudly that he was certain the man at the door could hear it. "Calm down. You're Lucky Slater," he told himself, but his words seemed hollow. He reached for the stiletto in his belt. He did not want to use it. He had never knifed anyone, but he would if he had to. He tried to steady his breathing as he waited. Then, as suddenly as they had come, the footsteps went away.

Marc's body was dripping with sweat as he grasped the padlock. His fingers felt swollen and arthritic. He forced himself to continue down the list: the battle at the Luding Bridge, the victory over Japan, the defeat of the Nationalists, and the armistice in Korea. With each failed combination, his hopes sank. There was only one number left, the entry of the People's Republic into the United Nations. "Please open," he whispered. He tugged on the lock. It would not budge. He clenched his fists in frustration. The vault was still locked, and he was out of options.

Marc fought the temptation to kick in the locker. The speeches were blaring over the loudspeakers. There were still a few minutes left. He could not give up. There had to be an answer. But if he was to find it, he could not panic. He had to place himself in Mao's position and try to figure out what numbers the Chairman would have selected.

He remembered Deng's advice drawn from the teachings of Sun Tzu, "Know yourself, know your enemy. In a thousand battles, there will be a thousand victories." It had been Mao's watchword. Perhaps it might also be the key.

"If I were Mao," Marc asked himself, "what numbers would I have picked?" It would not have been something obvious. Mao was too cautious and too devious. He had rarely trusted anyone or done what others had expected. But the answer could not be too obscure. Mao believed in symbolism. He would not have selected a meaningless combination.

"Know yourself, know your enemy," Marc recited.

Perhaps Mao had selected a date relating to an enemy. But which one? The United States? Since Nixon's visit, it would no longer qualify. The Soviet Union? It was now a political opponent, but Stalin and Lenin were still deities. Japan? It, too, was now a friend. Lin Biao? Liu Shaoqi? They were not important enough for such a symbolic honor.

There was only one other choice—Chiang Kai-shek. Mao could easily have picked Chiang as his quintessential enemy, but what date would he have selected? There were so many points of conflict: the split in their early alliance, the rape of Shanghai, any one of the six extermination campaigns, the sacrifice of the Eighth Route Army during the war, the Quemoy and Matsu crisis. All were possibilities, but Marc did not know their dates. Only one other choice came to mind—the kidnapping of Chiang in Xian, 12/11/1936. It was a date Marc remembered because it had been his eighth birthday. It was a farfetched alternative, but it was his last hope.

Marc took a deep breath. He had less than five minutes. His mouth was parched. His hands shook. Tentatively he turned the dials: 12-11-19. He did not expect anything, but he had to try. He positioned the last dial on 36 and jerked down. The lock clicked. Then it popped open in his hands.

Marc stood aghast, staring at the unhinged lock. He had done it. He had opened Mao's locker. Yet he was suddenly paralyzed. It was likely that no one besides Mao and Jiang had ever been inside. He was about to look into the most sacrosanct vault in the country. It was an awesome responsibility, one that he would have preferred to savor. But there was no time. The funeral was almost over.

Marc threaded the lock out of the loops on the door and pulled open the latch. He stood motionless, staring at the brown manila envelopes, pieces of parchment, and rice paper scrolls tied with black sashes. These were the personal writings of Chairman Mao. Some were inconsequential, but many had helped to shape the twentieth century.

Near the bottom, Marc found the envelope with the Chinese characters that read, "Last Will and Testament of Chairman Mao Tse-tung." He placed it next to his copy and smiled. The writing and the seal matched exactly. He shoved Jiang's forgery inside his shirt and placed the new document in the locker. Then he closed the door and snapped the lock shut.

In Tian'anmen Square, one million people faced the massive portrait of Chairman Mao and bowed three times. For a minute there was deafening silence. Then a band of five hundred musicians began to play "The East Is Red." One million Chinese raised their voices in the song, which ended by calling Mao the "people's great savior." Amplified by the loudspeakers, it sounded as if the entire country had joined in the singing.

Sen, dressed in the uniform of Unit 8341, waited in the stairwell for the first notes of the anthem. Then he lit the fuses to two stink bombs and dropped them to the floor below. Acrid smoke billowed up the stairs. Sen pulled his shirt over his mouth and ran toward the archives. "Fire!" he coughed.

"Where is it?" the guard asked, thinking Sen was a member of his unit.

"Fourth floor," Sen replied, covering his burning eyes.

The guard sounded the alarm. Sen staggered and dropped to the floor. "We'd better get you out of here," the guard said, pulling Sen to his feet. Supported by the guard, he walked to the staircase at the far end of the building.

When they were out of sight, Linda rushed to the archives. She had to work quickly; any second, someone could come into the corridor. Her hands trembled as she unlocked the Medeco and the Fichet. She twisted the dials on the padlock. The lock clicked.

Marc pulled open the door. Their eyes met. For an instant they stood motionless, staring at each other. An unspoken intimacy had developed between them. Marc patted his chest where the forged will was hidden. Linda grasped his arm and smiled. A man yelled something inaudible from the floor below. Footsteps thudded down the stairs. They had to hurry. While Linda closed the padlock, Marc fastened the other two locks. Then he grabbed her hand and ran back to Kang's office.

48: The Battle of Ebinur Lake

Shielding his head from the whirling blades of his helicopter, Samuel Tang rushed into the administration building. Liu Teyu, dressed in simple army fatigues, sat behind a desk reviewing intelligence data. Sam walked up and bowed respectfully. "You look well, my friend."

"It's the desert climate." Liu placed his hands on his chest and took a deep breath. "It does wonders for one's health."

"I'll stick with the dust of Peking and the smog of Los Angeles," Sam said as he poured water on a washcloth and mopped his face.

"Did you spot anything out there?" Liu asked.

Sam unfolded Rahman's map and laid it out on the metal desk. "The Turks are moving south along the Kuytun River toward Ebinur Lake. The sightings last night were just diversions. As we suspected, the real target is the Dzungarian Gate."

Liu limped across the room. His leg, broken in the earthquake, still had not fully healed. "Somehow," he said,

593

"we have to get between the Turks and the border without provoking the Russians."

"Why don't we attack now, before they reach the lake?" Sam suggested.

"We can't take the risk. Our forces are still too weak to discourage the Russians. Unless we have a credible deterrent, the Russians will ignore what happens to the Turks and roll right over us."

"We don't have much time," Sam advised.

"We won't need much. Your C-45s and helicopters are shuttling in men and equipment. Between my battalions, those from the state farms, and the PLA units from Shaanxi and Sichuan, we should outnumber the Russians by night-fall."

"What about weapons?" Sam asked.

Liu lit a cigarette. "As my father used to say, 'I gave you a bowl and chopsticks. You shouldn't be ungrateful just because there is no rice.' All we have are the test weapons that you brought, one hundred tanks from the Korean War, a couple of hundred mortars, and an assortment of other arms. It's enough to stop smugglers, but it's nothing compared to those of the Russians. At best we'll be like mosquitoes on the back of a bear: We can annoy the hell out of them, but there is no way that we can stop them."

"But they don't know that," Sam said.

"That's our only hope." The massive general slumped into a chair. "If we can get enough troops near the border and stop the Turks, we may be able to bluff the Russians into giving up their adventure."

Sam paced the floor. "It should be easy to stop a bunch of nomads."

"It's more difficult than it looks." Liu massaged his eyes. "The Turks are protected by the lake on the south and the border on the west. If we attack from the east or the north, they'll flee toward the border and set off the invasion. Our only hope is to attack from three sides at once, close the Turks in a vise, and then wipe them off the face of the earth."

"How are we going to get our men to the west without being spotted?"

"By creating a diversion of our own," Liu responded.

"Do you intend to march back into Tibet?" Sam joked, referring to Liu's two-thousand-mile detour during the Long March.

"The principle is the same," Liu smiled, "but the distance is a little shorter. We start by moving a thousand men, disguised as Turks, through the mountain passes. Then, after dark, our helicopters will attack a deserted valley about five miles to the east of the Turkic encampment."

"To what end?" Sam stared quizzically at Liu.

"While the Turks are watching the battle, we can sneak our troops past them. Once we are in position to the west, we can launch a three-pronged attack that leaves the Turks with no route of escape."

"It just might work." Sam smiled at Liu.

"It had better work," Liu replied. "If it doesn't, we will soon find ourselves guests of the Russian government in a Siberian prison camp."

Frans Van Wyck saw Aziz Rahman drive up to the main Turkic base near the junction of the Kuytun River and Ebinur Lake. Two miles behind him were the first four hundred of the more than one thousand Turkic recruits. Hurrying past huts filled with ammunition and provisions, Van Wyck greeted his ally. "Any problems, my friend?"

"One or two helicopters crossed our path," Rahman said, "but the women and children were shadowed by many more, so I think we're safe."

"Then let's get organized," Van Wyck said. "I want you to suit up your troops and send them to our satellite posts. The attack is still planned for dawn, but I want to move out by two A.M."

"My men will be ready," Rahman said. Then he turned away and set about transforming his nomads into fighting battalions of Chinese soldiers. PLA uniforms were unpacked and distributed. Chinese insignias were stenciled on the Russian jeeps and tanks, and Chinese flags were given to the squad leaders. In less than two hours, the first four hundred Turks had been organized into disciplined regiments that could easily have passed as part of the People's Liberation Army.

Hong Guoqiang, the director of State Farm 120, trotted cautiously into Xinchepaizi Pass. Directly ahead, wedged between towering snowcapped mountains and majestic sand dunes, was the scrubby green valley of the Kuytun River. Hong raised his right arm. Two hundred men riding behind him halted their horses. Hong surveyed his troops. All were dressed to resemble Turkic nomads. Instead of the neat blue uniforms of the People's Militia, they wore loose-fitting corduroy jackets and either black lamb's-wool Kazak hats or brightly colored and embroidered Moslem skullcaps. Hong nodded approvingly. Although his men were Chinese, from a distance it would be easy to mistake them for a caravan of Turks.

"Let's camp here," Hong ordered his men. "We'll move out at sundown."

Two soldiers removed the shortwave radio from a packhorse. Hong called his four lieutenants. Each had a squad of two hundred men positioned in other passes. When the helicopters attacked, they would move west. The operation would have to be handled with great care. They would have to position themselves within one mile of the Soviet border and fight with forty thousand Russians at their backs. If anything went wrong, it would be them and not the Turks who would be caught in a deadly trap.

After reviewing the plans with Liu Teyu, Samuel Tang climbed into the helicopter that would lead the attack. He did not really want to go. It had been more than twenty-five years since he had been involved in a combat mission. Although he tested all his new products, war was a young man's game. He would have preferred to supervise the arrivals of his C-45s, but the Chinese had been short of pilots.

Sam's helicopter lifted off the ground, hovered above the state farm, and headed toward the mountains. The other thirty-nine followed, flying south like a flock of migrating birds. After thirty minutes, they reached the Kuytun River and approached Ebinur Lake. Turkic cooking fires dotted the floor of the valley. Sam clutched the controls. He was anxious for the fighting to begin and yet he was apprehensive. Although he was a man used to taking chances, he hoped that this time he was not letting his bravado get the best of him.

At the first sound of the choppers, Frans Van Wyck jumped from his cot and stared through his binoculars at the small specks approaching in the distance. He could not believe that the Chinese were attacking by helicopter at night. His men were hidden throughout the valley. The choppers would be easy targets for his automatic weapons. It was a perfect example of inept Chinese military leadership.

"Distribute the arms and have the men take cover," he instructed Rahman.

Suddenly the squadron turned due east and flew toward the deserted corner of the valley. The forty choppers rendezvoused in midair, then swooped down, firing at the uninhabited valley floor. The flares, reflecting off the white sand, lit up the valley with the brightness of the noonday sun. Small bombs exploded in the foothills, shattering boulders and creating mammoth rockslides. The ground beneath Van Wyck shook.

Van Wyck was baffled. He prided himself on planning for all contingencies, but he could not understand why the Chinese would attack an empty valley when his camps were so close. It seemed that they had actually tried to stay away from his men. He radioed Bulganov. "I think we should move out now," he recommended after completing his report.

"I disagree," Bulganov replied. "The Chinese want to frighten you into acting prematurely. Once you've left your bases and assembled in strength in the open, they probably intend to attack in even greater force."

"No they won't," Van Wyck said. "It's too close to our airspace."

"The Chinese think they can stop you short of the border," Bulganov replied. "But we're not going to go for their bait. Keep your men hidden. The attack will take place as scheduled. I refuse to give the Chinese the satisfaction of dictating our strategy. You are to leave for the border at two A.M. and not a moment before. Is that understood?"

"It is understood," Van Wyck said. His voice was resigned.

As the helicopters began their bombardment, Hong

Guoqiang signaled his lieutenants and rode out of the mountain pass. Two hundred men followed as he galloped toward the Kuytun River. From four other passes, squads of Chinese dressed as Turks covered the same route. All had one goal in mind: to get to the hills in the west without being stopped.

Hong was thankful that the helicopters were putting on such a noisy display. Ordinarily the sound of gunfire, not to mention that of two hundred horsemen, would have echoed through the valley and alerted the Turks; but tonight, with the din of bombs and helicopter engines less than five miles away, it was very unlikely that anyone else would hear them.

Hong spurred his horse across the rocky floor of the shallow Kuytun River. The foothills on the far side of the valley were less than a mile ahead. The Russian border was only three miles away, but there would be room to hide. The ground started to ascend. Massive sand dunes towered above him. A narrow pass led out of the valley to the west. Galloping through at full speed, Hong raised his fists triumphantly in the air. He had made it. He had flanked the Turks. Now he and his men would wend their way south. In two hours, they would turn and destroy the Turkic troops. Soon he would be able to leave Xinjiang.

Liu Teyu waited while his helicopters were refueled and rearmed. It would be more than two hours until they were ready to return for the main battle. During that time other Chinese forces would be moving into place. In addition to Hong's cavalry to the west, Liu was positioning two other battalions east and north. Fifty additional choppers had also been ferried in from Urumqi.

Lui's voice blared over the loudspeaker as he briefed his crews. His plans seemed more than adequate, but to stop the

Russians a total victory was needed, and it might not be easy since the enemy had the advantages of terrain and darkness.

Finishing his instructions, Liu called Zhong Nanhai. He waited until Premier Hua came on the line. "Comrade Hua," he said, "we are about to attack the Turks. It might be useful if you could warn Comrade Brezhnev about Russian interference."

"I will call him immediately."

"You may guarantee him that we will not encroach on his territory," Liu said. "We expect him to do the same."

"I will tell him, but . . ." Hua paused.

"But what?"

"I just hope he listens."

"So do I, my friend," Liu replied. "So do I."

At 12:30 A.M., Liu Teyu signaled his troops. Two thousand Chinese riding in jeeps, tanks, and armored personnel carriers entered the Kuytun River valley from the north and east. Hong Guoqiang moved his cavalry into the passes in the west. Their primary duty was to block the routes of escape. Samuel Tang grouped his helicopters into ten clusters of nine and ordered them to fan out across the valley.

The troops from the north encountered the first of the Turkic bases. Four of Sam's helicopters circled and dropped flares. Tanks fired heavy salvos into the camp. Machine-gun bullets slaughtered the horses and camels. The Turks rushed for the hills. Illuminated by the flares, they made easy targets.

On the east, the Turks were more prepared. At the first sound of gunfire, one hundred men mounted their horses and began to ride toward the border. Nine of the helicopters circled to the west and laid down a barrage of bullets and small bombs. Forty Turks were killed. The rest fled. The Chinese tanks and personnel carriers fanned out in a broad arc, trapping the enemy inside. The Turks fired at the armored vehicles, but they were no match for the tanks. The Chinese moved in, narrowing the circle with heavy-arms fire until all the Turks were dead.

Samuel Tang and twenty-six other helicopters flew directly at the main base of the Turks. Circling once, he swooped toward the lake and dropped three bombs into the village. Sam flinched as bullets ricocheted off the metal fuselage. To his left, a helicopter sputtered, crashed to the ground, and then exploded.

Sam crossed the lake and raised his altitude stick. Bombs were dropping behind him. Two of his helicopters had been destroyed, but the village was in flames. The worst was over. He had handled the first pass. The next would be easy. He waited for his squadron to assemble. "Everybody ready," he signaled his pilots, trying to keep his voice firm. "Let's go," he called as he dived back for another attack.

Van Wyck could not believe what was happening. He was astounded at the strength and precision of the attack. Both here and at the satellite camps, large forces of well-armed Chinese were annihilating his men. He still could not understand how the Chinese had assembled so many soldiers and so much firepower. He had foolishly underestimated their ability. Now it was too late for blame. He had no choice but to flee to the west. Van Wyck stepped into his Quonset hut and radioed his orders. Machine-gun fire shredded the roof. A bullet rammed through the wall and plunged into the frame of his easel. He would have to call Bulganov from the jeep. He grabbed two antique snuff bottles from the desk and ran out the door.

Aziz Rahman was waiting in the command jeep. Van Wyck and he stared knowingly at each other. No words were necessary. They were professionals who accepted the possibility that something could go wrong, and yet they had worked so effectively together for such a long time that they had almost begun to believe in their infallibility.

The helicopters approached for another run. Rahman sped along the dirt road ringing the lake. Hundreds of Turks on horseback rode furiously toward the west. The tanks and armed personnel carriers of the Chinese forces approached from behind. Heavy bombardment trapped the stragglers. Three helicopters riddled the hill with bullets. Van Wyck could see his men falling. Short bursts from a machine gun hidden in the mountains killed a Chinese pilot. The chopper slammed into the ground in a fiery heap. A tank and a helicopter simultaneously fired powerful salvos at the Turkic gun emplacement in the mountain. The explosion tossed the gunners into the air like confetti in a hurricane. Van Wyck was furious. He should have argued when Bulganov urged him to stay put. If he had moved then, his men would now be safely in Russia.

Van Wyck stared toward the border, now less than half a mile away. The Chinese would never risk invading the Soviet Union. He and his men only had to make it to the passes at the top of the hill. The helicopters attacked again, firing flares. Van Wyck stared at the choppers in confusion. His men were about to escape into Russia. He could not understand why the Chinese would not make one last attempt to kill them.

Guns sounded ahead of him. Van Wyck turned. Suddenly he understood. Rifles fired from every mountain pass, chopping into the front ranks of his men. Rahman swerved onto a side trail. Chinese armored forces closed in from the north and east. The noose was getting tighter. Less than two hundred of his original thousand men were still alive. There was no way for them to reach the border in any semblance of force.

"Head for the lake," Van Wyck ordered as he untied his shoes.

Rahman nodded solemnly. There were no Chinese forces south of the lake. They would dump the jeep and swim for safety. There would be no mock attack, no Russian invasion, and no Republic of East Turkestan, at least not now. But if they were lucky, they might escape, as would some of the other Turks. Rahman had lost this battle, but he had thousands of countrymen on both sides of the border. He and his people would not just disappear, nor would they allow themselves to be absorbed by the Han. They would have their day, and he would be there to lead them.

49: The Wind Faction

The first rays of the sun flooded through the window of Kang Moruo's office. Marc Slater awakened with a start. He was lying on a couch. Linda was in his arms. He tried to inch away without disturbing her. She stirred. He stared at her asleep next to him. She looked breathtaking.

After returning from the archives flushed with the victory of having replaced the forged will, he had opened the suitcase Beatrice Tang had left for them. To his surprise, it contained not only changes of clothes but also a deluxe five-course Chinese dinner, three bottles of wine, and two candles. After sundown, when it became obvious they would be stranded for the night, they lit the candles, spread the food on the floor, and treated themselves to an elegant picnic.

They had talked well past midnight, enchanting each other with stories about their lives. There was so much they had in common. They touched, caressed, and held each other as if they had been lovers for years. It was not the instant passion he had experienced with Meili. It was instead

604

comfortable, sensitive, loving, and immensely satisfying. They laughed together and took great delight in bringing each other pleasure. Everything had been perfect. Marc leaned over and kissed Linda softly on the lips. "Good morning, bright eyes," he said, gently caressing her cheek.

She grasped his waist and cuddled next to him. "Good morning."

"Did you sleep well?"

"Like a lamb," she said. "I never knew an old leather couch could be so comfortable. You make a pretty good pillow."

"I'm available for a modest fee," he replied.

Reaching up, Linda held Marc's face in her hands and tenderly kissed him. "That's my first month's installment in advance."

"I like the way you do business," Marc smiled as he nibbled on Linda's ear. "Is there anything I can get you?"

"How about a glass of fresh orange juice, a bottle of champagne, and fresh Nova Scotia salmon and cream cheese on a bagel?" Linda smiled as she brushed her long blond hair over her shoulder.

"This is Peking, not Manhattan." Marc ran his hands along the creamy smooth skin of her back. "I'm afraid Beatrice's picnic basket is not that well stocked."

"But you're Marc Slater. You get anything you want."

"I can see I'm going to have to watch my step with you." Marc playfully patted Linda's rump as he slid away and stood up. The others would be there soon.

While Linda went to the closet to dress, Marc put on the light blue safari shirt and khaki pants from David's Tailors, then the Hermes shoes and belt, all of which Beatrice had flown in for him from Hong Kong. Since the earthquake, Marc had worn nothing but cadre's uniforms. It was nice to have his own clothes back. With his mission near an end and

Linda beside him, it seemed appropriate to revert to wearing Western clothes.

A door slammed across the hall. Footsteps approached. Marc grabbed the forged will and moved to the closet. Linda had put on only her maroon bra and panties. Stopping for an instant, Marc stared at the smooth contours of her slim, athletic body. The knob on the front door turned. Marc placed his finger to his lips and shut the closet door. Its rusty hinges squeaked.

"Is someone in there?" an old woman called in Chinese. There was no response. She stepped tentatively into the room. The empty bottles of wine and the remains of the picnic were in the middle of the floor. "Idiot cadres," she murmured as she started to dust the desk. "Even on the day of Mao's funeral, they never stop with their parties."

The old woman continued her cleaning. Linda reached for her blouse, but Marc shook his head; even the slightest movement might attract attention. The phone rang. Marc grasped the door. It was probably Kang calling him. He could not let the others think that he and Linda had been captured. Yet he also could not show himself.

The phone rang again. "*Wei*," the old woman answered. "Yes, this is the office of Kang Moruo. Who is this?" She rolled her "r's" in a thick Pekingese accent. "Are you really Liu Teyu?"

Linda grabbed Marc's arm at the mention of her grandfather. Liu was in Xinjiang and could only be calling on a matter of grave importance. They had to talk with him. Marc thrust open the door. The old woman was standing with her back to him. He lunged at her. The woman turned in surprise. "*Aiya!*" she screamed and dropped the phone. Linda followed Marc, still dressed in only her underwear. The woman stood paralyzed, staring at the half-naked foreign woman. "Long-nosed barbarians!" she shrieked.

Springing forward, Marc placed his hand over her mouth. "Don't be scared," he said in Chinese. "My wife and I were trapped here last night. Our friends will arrive soon to take us back to the hotel." The woman's eyes darted back and forth in panic. "It'll be all right." Marc tried to sound reassuring. "I'll take my hand away from your mouth if you promise not to scream." The woman nodded. Marc removed his hand.

"*Aiya!*" the woman screamed again.

Marc shoved his hand back over her mouth. "Be quiet until we have finished talking to the general." She tried to wriggle free, but he grasped her firmly from behind.

Linda buttoned her blouse as she picked up the phone. Her hands were shaking. She was about to talk with her grandfather for the first time. "Comrade Liu?" Her voice cracked.

"Who are you?" the general queried.

"My name"—her voice trembled—"is Linda Forbes." There was silence on the line. "Comrade Liu," Linda entreated, "are you still there?"

"Did you say your name was Linda Forbes?" Liu's voice was guarded.

"I did."

"Can you substantiate that?"

Linda tugged at the zipper of her skirt. Even though her grandfather was thousands of miles away, it seemed inappropriate to meet him while standing half-dressed. "My grandmother was named Margot Forbes. Her maiden name was Kappel. She was an artist who worked in France and China. She loved to paint pictures of the boat people in Shanghai. Perhaps you have seen her work." Linda paused, nervously awaiting Liu's response.

"Her art is with me always," the general said. His voice sounded distant and nostalgic. "It has comforted me since she left China. You sound very much like her."

Linda smiled. "People often said that we looked alike."

"Then you must be a very lovely young woman."

Linda blushed, pleased by her grandfather's flattery. "I am most anxious to meet you."

"As am I. But this is not the time for a reunion."

"I understand," Linda said, feeling disappointed.

"Where is Kang?"

"He'll be here soon," Linda said, looking at Marc, who was still trying to restrain the squirming old woman.

"Can you give him a message?"

"Of course," Linda responded, pleased that Liu would trust her.

"Tell him that we have wiped out the Turks. Now all we have to do is stop the Russians."

"I'm very pleased," Linda said as she repeated Liu's words for Marc. "The matter of the will is settled."

"Ssh," Liu replied. "The walls have ears."

Linda gazed dejectedly out the window. She wanted to tell her grandfather of her success. "Will I ever get a chance to meet you?" she asked.

"It is a day for which I will anxiously wait, my granddaughter," Liu said, and then hung up the phone.

A tear rolled down Linda's cheek. "Goodbye, grandfather," she said into the dead line. She wiped her face and turned around. Marc was still struggling to control the old woman. "Can I help?" she asked.

"No," Marc laughed. "I love wrestling with old Chinese cleaning ladies. It's good exercise."

"What do you want to do with her?" Linda asked.

"We can't take any chances. We'd better tie her up. Cut my jacket into strips." Marc motioned toward the stiletto. Seizing upon the distraction, the old woman bit his hand. He flinched and loosened his grip. She kicked his leg and slipped free. Fleeing to the door, she screamed, "*Aiya*! It's a long-nosed barbarian!"

Marc sprang after her. As she reached for the doorknob, his left arm chopped firmly into her neck. Gasping, she collapsed on the floor. Marc placed his finger to his lips while he and Linda waited to see if anyone would respond to the woman's cry. A minute passed. Then another. The building was quiet. "Some Boy Scout you make," Linda smiled as she bound the woman's legs.

Marc removed his Hermes belt and tied her hands. "You're in a good mood," Marc said, stuffing a gag into the old woman's mouth.

"Why shouldn't I be?" Linda replied, helping to carry the body into the closet. "I'm three for three. We took care of Mao's will. My grandfather acknowledged me. And I finally found a way to get you alone. Not bad for a day's work."

"Do you always get what you want?"

"I try."

Voices sounded in the hallway. Marc and Linda pulled the old woman into the closet with them. The office door opened. Pushing Linda back, Marc pressed his body against the wall. He had been lucky once, but that was with an old woman. This time there were three sets of heavy footsteps and they all belonged to men. Marc tried to quiet his breathing. He shoved the forged will into an empty box. He could hear one of the men walking toward the closet. He raised his arm to defend himself. "Is anyone in there?" the man called.

Marc sighed and dropped his arms as he recognized the voice of Kang Moruo. "We're in the closet," he said.

Peering inside, Kang saw Marc and Linda huddled over the prone body of the cleaning lady. "What happened?" he asked.

"She started screaming, so we had to tie her up," Marc

said, stepping out into the office where Kang, Pingnan, and Sen were standing.

"We'll take care of her later," Kang replied. "First I need the forged will."

Marc retrieved the document from the closet. Kang inspected the seal and the calligraphy and then handed it to his son. "Take it to Deng directly," Kang instructed. Pingnan bowed politely and left the room.

"Where is Deng?" Marc asked.

"At Hua's villa trying to convince the Wind Faction to come over to our side. The meeting of the Politburo has been postponed until two. The stated reason is that Hua wants to talk with Brezhnev about the situation on the border."

"My grand—" Linda stopped in midsentence. "Comrade Liu Teyu called. He said the Turks had been defeated."

"I know," Kang replied.

"Then what's the real reason for postponing the meeting?"

"The afternoon edition of the *People's Daily* is due out at noon," Kang explained. "Since Mao's will has not yet been read, Jiang Qing has two choices: She can either have the paper report that she is Mao's chosen successor, in which case she will incriminate herself, or she can put off saying anything until tomorrow, which will give us time to remove her and her henchmen."

"Then by midafternoon it will all be over," Marc said.

"So we hope," Kang replied.

"What's happening with our friends Boswell and Yamaguchi?" Marc asked.

"Boswell is in the Peking Hotel. Fourth Nephew Xiaoma is watching him. And Yamaguchi is at the airport."

Marc stared quizzically. "What's he doing there?"

"Trying to leave the country."

"You can't let him!"

"Relax, my friend," Kang said. "We won't let the Island

Dwarf get away that easily. We've canceled his ticket, and some of Liu's men are personally escorting him back here. In less than an hour, we shall have our opportunity to find out just what he is planning."

Avery Boswell passed through the front doors of the Peking Hotel and hurried down the driveway. He was concerned that he had not been able to confer with Frans Van Wyck. As a precaution, the Dutchman had wanted him to call before the assassination of Premier Hua. Boswell had phoned their contact in Urumqi, but the man had been unable to patch him through by radio. The Dutchman was probably preparing for the final mock attack, so Boswell had no choice but to proceed with the operation as planned.

Boswell glanced over his shoulder. A Chinese, dressed in a blue worker's uniform, was standing behind the stone gate of the hotel. It was the same man he had seen twice the day before. Turning onto Wangfujing Street, Boswell threaded his way through crowds of pedestrians and bicycle riders. He stopped at a small stand and bought a pack of cigarettes. The man from the hotel was standing in front of a store window. Boswell continued toward the Capital Hospital. An olive-drab ambulance motored past the massive green steel gates and turned the corner. Boswell quickened his pace. With the building obscuring the view of the man tailing him, Boswell started to sprint. The side door of the ambulance was thrust open. Boswell jumped in. The ambulance sped away.

"Did you have any trouble?" Boswell asked one of the two Chinese sitting in the front seat.

The driver shook his head. "We just turned the key and drove out. They're so confused at that damn hospital, they'll never know it's gone."

"Head for the Summer Palace," Boswell ordered.

"I thought we were going to Hua's villa," the driver said.

"We're early and I don't want to take the chance of stopping. In the People's Republic, you're always safe as long as you're moving." Boswell crawled into the back. The two Mongolians, wearing white hospital uniforms, were crouched on the jump seats. The guns and ammunition were packed on stretchers. Boswell checked his munitions and then changed into his own hospital uniform.

"Do you expect to pass as a Chinese doctor?" one of the Mongolians laughed, pointing to Boswell's blond hair and pale complexion.

Pulling a surgeon's cap over his head, Boswell rubbed tan dye on his face. "Don't worry about me," he said, trying to sound authoritative. "No one is going to get close enough to see us."

Jiang Qing sat in front of the television set in the dining room viewing a videotape of Mao's funeral. It gave her an opportunity to watch the reactions of other leaders and to study her own performance. Shen Mo stepped into the room. "Comrade Wang Hongwen is here to see you."

The tough young former textile worker, who had presided at Mao's funeral, bowed respectfully. "Good morning, Comrade Jiang." Wang smiled. "Or should I say Chairman Jiang?"

"Comrade will do quite well. Are you ready to be the president of the National People's Congress?" Jiang referred to the position Wang was slated to fill after the Gang of Four gained power.

"I am honored to serve my country," Wang replied, disappointed that Zhang Chunqiao and not he would be the new premier.

"To what do I owe the honor of this visit?" Jiang asked.

"There has been a change of plans," Wang replied. "The Politburo meeting has been delayed until two, and the location has been moved from the Great Hall of the People to the villa of Defense Minister Ye."

"They can't do that!"

"Of course they can. As long as Hua is still premier, he can schedule the meeting wherever and whenever he wants."

"What do you think they're up to?"

"Perhaps they think the three hours will give them extra time to organize, and Ye's house will provide a more conducive location in which to try to influence the Wind Faction."

Jiang placed two pills in her mouth and swallowed them. "It doesn't matter. Once the will is read, they'll be powerless to stop us."

"I still think we should take care to harvest our wheat before the first frost." Wang quoted the Chinese proverb.

"Have Yuanxin and Colonel Li move their troops into defensive positions around the Western Hills."

"Do you want them to take any action?"

"Not until they hear from us." Jiang smiled wryly. "But if something should happen to the telephone service, it wouldn't be a great tragedy."

"I'll contact them at once," Wang said, and left the room.

Jiang turned up the sound on the television. She would soon make her debut as chairman. She wanted her performance to be perfect.

Hua Guofeng drew ornate Chinese characters on a piece of paper while a voice on the other end of the conference phone conducted a long harangue in Russian. The voice paused while one of Hua's aides translated the words into

Chinese. Then it continued. Hua stared helplessly at Defense Minister Ye and Deng Xiaoping. "Let Brezhnev talk himself out," Ye whispered as he passed Hua a cup of tea.

Hua listened patiently while Brezhnev finished his tirade. "I can assure you, comrade," said Hua calmly, "that we would never encroach on your territory. We are brother Communist countries and should make every effort to cooperate."

"What about the ruthless and unprovoked attacks on our settlements?" Brezhnev asked.

"I deeply regret the incursions," Hua replied. "They are the work of Turkic Nationalists whose only interest is to pit our two republics against each other. Although some live in the People's Republic, fully half live in your country. Their leader, a man named Aziz Rahman, is a citizen of the Soviet Union." Hua paused while his words were translated.

"How do I know you are not just trying to shift the blame away from your own People's Liberation Army?" Brezhnev challenged.

"We have captured the ringleaders," Hua replied. "Evidence of their guilt will be made available to your diplomatic personnel. I am sure you will find it satisfactory. Until you have time to review it, I officially request that your people refrain from taking military action against our country. We cannot tolerate the presence of foreign troops on our soil."

"What guarantees do I have that you will not launch an invasion of your own?" Brezhnev asked. "I am informed that your soldiers are moving in force along the entire length of our mutual four-thousand-mile border."

"We will halt all troop movements," Hua said, "and begin a phased withdrawal if you will do the same."

"I will take your request under advisement," Brezhnev replied, "and give you my answer this evening."

"I appreciate your consideration," Hua said. "I hope this

will be the beginning of a renewed friendship between our two countries."

As Hua hung up the phone, the others in the room broke into broad smiles. Although Brezhnev might still want to press the invasion, they knew he could not. Their plan had worked. They had effectively deterred the KGB. Deng Xiaoping poured a round of Chinese brandy. "To checkmating the Russians," the diminutive leader said, raising his glass.

Defense Minister Ye sipped the liqueur. "Now we only have to worry about Jiang Qing and the Gang of Four."

"You can really put a damper on a celebration," Deng said.

"Wang Dongxin and Wu De are waiting outside." Ye referred to the two leaders of the Wind Faction. Wang, the director of Unit 8341, controlled Mao's thirty-thousand-man private security force, while Wu De, the mayor of Peking, managed the police in the capital. Though neither had taken sides, their support was essential to stopping the Gang of Four.

"We'd better see them now." Hua nodded to one of his aides. Both men had long been among his most loyal allies, but he was not certain he could count on their support in this, his most critical decision.

The sixty-year-old Wang entered the room and bowed politely to Hua. As short as Deng, with a broad nose, pointed chin, and thick fleshy lips, Wang vaguely resembled a duck. But he was a man of unusual determination and charisma, who, by studiously avoiding all political disputes, had become one of the most powerful figures in the country.

The hulking, sixty-five-year-old Wu followed. Wu's round, jowled face, graying temples, and horn-rimmed glasses gave him a benign, almost professorial look, but he was a consummate political opportunist who prided himself on his ability to survive. Less than six months earlier, he had led the movement to purge Deng. Before changing sides, he would have to be firmly convinced that Jiang Qing had no chance to win.

"The reason I asked you here"—Ye adjusted his black-framed glasses on the bridge of his nose—"is that we have learned that Jiang Qing and the Gang of Four are planning to seize control of the country. We have proof that Jiang forged Mao's last will and testament."

"That is a serious charge." Wang drummed his fingers on the table. "I'd like to see the evidence."

"It's right here," Deng said, slitting the red seal on the envelope. He removed the parchment and passed the forged will around the table. Wu put on his glasses and studied the document. "It looks real enough."

"Jiang captured Mao's calligrapher. Under threat of death, she forced him to write this document."

Wu eyed Deng suspiciously. "Then how did you get it?"

"We were able to retrieve the original," Defense Minister Ye said, "and exchange it for the forgery in Mao's vault."

"How do we know that your copy is real?" Wang asked.

"Do you remember Chairman Mao telling us that the contents of his last will were private and would not be read by anyone before his death?" Ye asked. "I'd like you to look at this article." An aide distributed a stack of papers. "This is from this afternoon's edition of the *People's Daily*. Do you notice anything interesting about the language?"

"It's the same as that in the forged will," Wang replied. The tone of his voice was grave."

"Perhaps it's a coincidence," Wu said.

"There's no coincidence." Deng leaned across the table and glared at the two members of the Wind Faction. "They were both written by Jiang Qing and Yao Wenyuan."

"The evidence seems incriminating," Wang said, "but I'm

not sure it's enough to move against Jiang."

"There is one way we can be certain," Defense Minister Ye interjected. "Assume for a moment that Jiang and her people did forge this will. What will happen when the other document is read?"

Wang laughed. "Jiang will fly into one of her tirades."

"And if she does?"

"We'll know she forged the will. But if she doesn't, we'll know that your will is the fraud."

"We'll take our chances," Deng said, pacing behind the table. "But unless we take precautions, this discussion will be nothing but hot air. Jiang's Red Guards are ready to attack. If you don't move the police and Unit 8341 into position, you're just handing her the government."

"Do you agree with Comrade Deng's position?" Mayor Wu asked Hua.

"I do, and so does Defense Minister Ye."

"If we go along, are we obligated to support this capitalist-roader?" Wu pointed to Deng.

"You most certainly are not," Ye replied.

Wang conferred quietly with Wu. "All right. We will mobilize our men. But I will order them not to move until they hear from me."

"That's all we can ask for," Defense Minister Ye said, praying that Jiang Qing would cooperate by incriminating herself.

"Mr. Yamaguchi, so kind of you to come to see us." Kang Moruo bowed with excessive politeness as three People's Liberation Army soldiers ushered the tall Japanese into the office. "May I introduce Comrade Sen Tailing and Mr. Marc Slater of the United States." Kang spoke in English. Protocol ordinarily demanded the use of interpreters, but

Kang was not about to allow Yamaguchi the advantage of conversing in his own language. "I believe that you and Mr. Slater are competitors."

"Only in some fields." Yamaguchi eyed Marc suspiciously. "I am pleased to see you in such good health, Mr. Slater. I had read you were killed."

Marc smiled. "The report of my death was slightly premature."

Kang motioned for everyone to sit down. Sen poured four cups of tea and then offered everyone Long March brand cigarettes. Only Kang accepted. Yamaguchi opened a silver case, took out a Marlboro, and lit it. "I'd like to know why I was pulled off my flight and brought here under armed guard." Yamaguchi spoke deliberately. His English was almost perfect.

"I apologize for the inconvenience"—Kang smiled smoothly at the Japanese—"but I received news that I thought would interest you."

"Your consideration is appreciated. What is the news?"

"The PLA has quelled a Turkic revolution in Xinjiang," Kang replied.

"I am pleased for your army, but that hardly concerns me."

"Doesn't your company have an agreement with the Russians to drill for oil in the Altay Mountains?" Kang asked.

Yamaguchi maintained a placid expression, but his eyes could not conceal his surprise. "My company has agreements throughout the world. I cannot be concerned about every incident."

"Of course you can't," Kang replied. "But I find these local revolts so fascinating. Do you know who was leading the Turks? It was a Dutchman named Van Wyck. Does the name mean anything to you?"

"The only Van Wyck I know is the director of a Dutch hotel company." Yamaguchi tried to sound nonchalant.

"It's the same man," Kang smiled. "Aren't you his subcontractor?"

"It's possible."

"This has certainly been a terrible day for Takamura. First you lose the Altay oil and then you find out that your Dutch partner is actually some sort of Turkic revolutionary." Kang poured a fresh cup of tea. "I wonder what can happen next."

"Perhaps you could tell me."

"We are trying to locate Avery Boswell," Kang said. "Since Boswell is an associate of Van Wyck's, we thought you might know him."

"I met him once in Canton, but I don't know where he is now."

"That's a pity." Kang lit a cigarette. "I'm in a most embarrassing position. Premier Hua was so incensed by the Turkic revolt that he ordered the termination of all contracts with companies having dealings with the Turks, the Russians, or with Van Wyck. I am afraid that Takamura qualifies in two of the three categories."

Yamaguchi shifted uneasily. "But that runs into billions of dollars."

"More tea?" Kang asked in his silky, cultured accent. "It really isn't fair. Your company is such an old friend. If only you'd been able to help us find this man Boswell."

"What does he have to do with anything?"

"Premier Hua authorized me to make special concessions to whoever could help us find the Englishman," Kang said.

"What are your concessions?"

"All of your contracts, except those for oil and hotel construction, would remain in effect."

"Are you prepared to put this offer in writing?"

"Old friends do not require written contracts." Kang

619

smiled wryly.

Yamaguchi lit another Marlboro. "I am not sure where you can find Boswell, but a Chinese who works for Gateshead and MacIntosh informed me that Boswell wanted to assassinate Permier Hua."

Kang looked up in shock. "Why didn't you report that to the police?"

"I thought the man was a crank."

"We cannot take threats like that lightly!" Kang thrust his finger at Yamaguchi. "Tell me everything you know."

"I'm not certain of the exact time or location," Yamaguchi replied, "but the attack is to take place this morning near Hua's villa. Boswell and his people will be riding in a Chinese ambulance."

"I am grateful for your cooperation, Mr. Yamaguchi." Kang pushed a button on the desk. Three PLA soldiers stepped into the room. "We would like you to remain as our guest until we find Boswell."

"But you promised my contracts would not be jeopardized," Yamaguchi said sternly.

"And they will not. We only need your services as a witness. As soon as we apprehend Boswell, you will be free to return home." Kang motioned to the soldiers, who surrounded Yamaguchi and escorted him from the room.

Kang dialed Hua's private line. There was no answer. Impatiently he checked the number and dialed again. "There are fifty people at the villa. Why doesn't someone answer?" he muttered. He called the People's Telephone Company. "I am trying to contact 88-34-61 in the Western Hills. Could you please check the line?"

"There is no phone service anywhere in the Hills," the representative of the phone company said. "An hour ago a gang of capitalist-roaders blew up the switching facility."

Kang hung up the phone and relayed the information to

the others. "Without phones," Sen said, "we can't warn Hua of Boswell's plan."

"Nor can we contact anyone in the Politburo." Kang massaged his eyes. "Half the members are at Hua's villa and the rest are on the way to the home of Defense Minister Ye. If the phones don't work, the entire government could be cut off from the rest of the country."

"Isn't there a shortwave radio at your house?" Marc asked.

"It's in the basement," Kang replied, "but I don't know if you will be able to raise anyone on the other end."

"It's worth a try."

"All right," Kang said. "Sen, you take Marc and Linda to my house. If you can't get Hua, try to get someone at Defense Minister Ye's villa. They are quite close."

"What about you?" Marc asked.

"I'm going to the Western Hills. With luck, I'll get through to Hua before Boswell does." ———

Mao Yuanxin pulled his jeep to a stop in front of the barricade blocking the main route from Peking to the Western Hills. Colonel Li strode out to greet his ally. "Are your men in place?" Yuanxin asked.

"Every road leading to the Western Hills is covered," Li said. "We have deployed two thousand men who are prepared to move as soon as we receive word from Comrade Jiang Qing."

"Very good," Yuanxin replied. "Let all members of the Politburo and their staffs through, as well as anyone else who will not interfere with our operation. We must be cautious, but we also must not needlessly alarm the people until we are ready to make our move."

"I understand," Colonel Li replied.

An ambulance from the Capital Hospital approached. The Red Guards surrounded the car. Colonel Li stepped briskly forward, anxious to demonstrate his leadership to Yuanxin. "State your business," he ordered.

"We have to bring a patient to the hospital," the driver responded.

"Who is it?"

The driver conferred with Boswell in the back of the ambulance. "He's an aide of Premier Hua. The hospital told us that he had a heart attack."

"What's his name?" the colonel demanded.

"We were not given that information," the driver replied.

Yuanxin paced around the ambulance and stared through the rear windows. The three men inside were hurriedly organizing drugs and medical equipment. Yuanxin could not see their faces, but they appeared to be working diligently. He nodded silently to Colonel Li. The colonel waved to his guards, who opened the barricades. "You can go," he said, "but come back on this road or you'll be stopped again."

"Thank you, sir," the driver replied, shifting the car into first gear.

Colonel Li watched the ambulance disappear in the dust. "Do you want to inspect the other barricades?" he asked.

Yuanxin checked his watch. "I have to be at Defense Minister Ye's house in forty minutes. I am confident that you are handling all matters with utmost competence."

Kang's limousine raced through the countryside until it reached the barricades of the Red Guards. A soldier approached. "State your business!" he ordered.

"I am taking Comrade Kang Moruo to the Politburo meeting," the driver said, handing the guard his papers.

The guard took the papers to Colonel Li and Mao Yuanxin. Kang climbed out of the car and moved to intercept the two men. He could not afford even a moment's delay. He had no way of knowing whether Marc and Linda had been able to get through to Hua. "Comrade Yuanxin, what is the purpose of this roadblock?"

Yuanxin bowed deeply. "Please excuse the inconvenience." Although he disagreed with Kang's moderate politics, he showed appropriate respect to the member of the Politburo. "We are looking for the capitalist-roaders who blew up the switching facilities of the People's Telephone Company."

Kang stared at Yuanxin. Perhaps he could use the Red Guards to stop Boswell. It would remove both of his enemies at the same time. Colonel Li and Yuanxin were not allies, but they were Chinese. Despite their political differences, no one wanted to see the leaders of the People's Republic assassinated. "May we talk in private?" Kang said to Yuanxin.

"Certainly," Mao's nephew replied, pulling Kang aside.

"Did an ambulance pass through your barricades?"

Yuanxin stared at Kang in surprise. "About half an hour ago. How did you know?"

"The men in that ambulance are Russian agents."

"What are they doing here?" Yuanxin asked.

"They are planning to kill all the members of the Politburo as a prelude to a Russian invasion."

"Are you certain?" Yuanxin shifted uneasily.

"I'm positive," Kang replied. "Our soldiers in Xinjiang captured a Russian who had plans for the operation. General Liu Teyu called me from Xinjiang. I tried to warn everyone, but there is no phone service."

"Do you know where they are now?" Yuanxin asked.

"I suspect they are on the road to Hua's villa. The premier

623

is to be their first target."

"Do you want to use my troops to hunt them down?" Yuanxin asked.

Kang bowed politely. "The People's Republic would be forever in your debt."

Yuanxin strode to his command post and radioed all of the Red Guard units in the area. Then he walked back to where Kang was standing. "I have sent more than two hundred soldiers to find the ambulance. I doubt that the Russians will have any chance of escaping."

"Thank you, Comrade Yuanxin," Kang said. "You are a true patriot."

50: The Last Will and Testament

Filing into the study in the Western Hills villa of Defense Minister Ye, the members of the Politburo milled around in small groups segmented by ideological alliances. Premier Hua Guofeng walked to the back of the room and rapped his fist on the table. "Comrades"—he spoke in a monotone—"we are ready to begin." The members moved quickly and silently to the table. Even Jiang Qing and the Gang of Four politely obliged. With Mao's will about to be read and the control of the Party so evenly split, no one wanted to risk alienating any votes.

Hua glanced around the table. Vice-Chairman Li and Defense Minister Ye, his two key supporters, sat on either side. Wang Dongxin, Wu De, and the other members of the Wind Faction were on the left, Kang Moruo and the moderates were on the right, while Jiang Qing and the Gang of Four sat at the far end. Hua shuffled a stack of papers as he stared at Jiang. He had made the right decision. He might have already mortgaged his soul to Deng, but at least he would have a chance. With Jiang, there could be no compromise. He only hoped he had taken the appropriate steps to stymie her.

"Comrades," Hua began, "this is a most solemn moment. We are assembled to read the last will of our Great Helmsman. I know his loss has deeply affected all of us, but I am confident that his testament will give us guidance for the future."

Hua rang an antique brass bell. The new guardian of the National Archives, accompanied by two guards, carried in a gray steel strongbox. The guardian put the box on the table and inserted a key in the first of the locks. Hua placed his key in the second lock and twisted it gently to the right. He paused before opening the box. He was about to read the most important words the Chairman had ever written. The sense of responsibility was almost overwhelming.

Hua removed the solitary manila envelope and held it up for the others to see. On the back was Mao's official chop. Hua studied Jiang's eyes as she nodded approvingly. There was a smug smile on her face. Hua split the seal and opened the envelope. An expectant hush settled over the room. He slid the parchment out and began to read. "'Last Will and Testament of Chairman Mao Tse-tung. Act According to Past Principles.'"

"What did you say?" Jiang exclaimed, sweeping her hand across the table.

"I said, 'Act According to Past Principles.'" Hua glared at Jiang as he read the phrase that indicated Mao's desire to continue the practice of having all Politburo members advance one position in filling vacancies. Using this principle, he, as premier, would become the new Party chairman.

"Don't you mean Act According to the Principles Laid Down?" Jiang insisted, using the phrase that everyone understood to symbolize Mao's support for the Gang of Four.

"Comrade Jiang, it may surprise you to know that I read quite well for a country bumpkin."

"I don't question your literacy," Jiang seethed, "just your words."

"I can only read what is written." Hua shook the parchment at Jiang. "Do you think I am so desperate that I would twist Mao's words?"

"I don't know what you'd do." Jiang petulantly stared at the ceiling.

"If you'll excuse me"—Hua nodded impassively—"I'd like to continue."

LAST WILL AND TESTAMENT
CHAIRMAN MAO TSE-TUNG

ACT ACCORDING TO PAST PRINCIPLES

Though I am about to die, the struggle between Marxism and the running dogs of imperialism must continue. We have fought the KMT and the revisionists, and have won every battle. But the fight is not over. We must continue to act according to past principles until the revolution of the proletariat has conquered the world.

To ensure a continuation of our revolutionary leadership, I designate my esteemed colleague, Premier Hua Guofeng, to lead the Party according to past principles. If we function as I have directed, the People's Republic will have a glorious future.

Mao Tse-tung
July 20, 1976
Peking

Jumping to her feet, Jiang thrust her finger toward Hua. "That will is a fraud!"

"It is written in Chairman Mao's hand and bears his official chop." Despite the intense pressures, Hua's voice remained level and controlled.

"I was Chairman Mao's wife and closest confidante for forty years," Jiang said. "I know my husband's dreams for the People's Republic. The words in his will are a lie."

"They coincide perfectly with the letter our Great Helmsman transmitted to me." Several months earlier Mao had written Hua, "With you in charge, I am at ease." It was universally accepted as Mao's endorsement of the premier.

"The letter was meaningless and the will is a forgery." Jiang shook her fist. "This treachery will not stand. I will inform everyone that you are trying to steal control of the government."

"Please, comrades," Defense Minister Ye said, "let us restore some decorum. This discussion is getting us nowhere. The issues are emotionally charged and we are all overwrought. I think we should adjourn until tomorrow. After a day of reflection, cooler heads will hopefully prevail."

"One minute." Yao Wenyuan waved his arm in the air. "I have three urgent motions that I wish to place before the Politburo."

"They are not in order," Hua said.

"Why not?" the baby-faced Yao protested. "This is an official meeting. I have the right to make a motion."

"Go ahead," Hua replied.

"Our Great Helmsman," the forty-five-year-old pamphleteer began, "labored for fifty years against the capitalists, the corrupt warlords, the imperialists, the right deviationists, the bourgeois intellectuals, and the incompetent bureaucrats—all of whom placed their own desires for wealth, position, and comfort above the needs of the people. While others strayed from the true line, our Great Helmsman steered the ship of state along the course of perfect socialism. Now that he is gone, we must remain true to his teachings. We cannot retreat nor allow the country to drift along the capitalist road."

"Are you making a motion or a speech?" Defense Minister Ye asked.

"I am coming to the motions," Yao replied.

"I hope you won't drag this on past dark."

Ignoring Ye's remark, Yao continued. "This country must not be allowed to fall into the hands of the capitalist-roaders. We must act according to the principles laid down by our Great Helmsman, we must have the proper leadership. Accordingly, I move that my esteemed colleague, Comrade Jiang Qing, be appointed chairman of the Chinese Communist Party."

A shocked murmuring rustled around the table. Given the explicit wishes in Mao's testament, the others could not believe that the Gang of Four was making such a barefaced grab for power. Hua stared uneasily at Jiang. "Is there a second?" he asked.

"Second," Wang Hongwen replied.

"I move," Yao said, "that Zhang Chunqiao be appointed premier."

"Second."

"And that Wang Hongwen be appointed president of the National People's Congress."

"Second."

A restless silence enveloped the room. "I'd like to speak in favor of my motions," Yao said. "Comrade Jiang Qing is the one person uniquely—"

Hua rapped his fist on the table. "Comrade, Yao, you have not been recognized. I call on Comrade Ye Jianying."

"But I had the floor," Yao protested.

"To make the motion, not to speak for it," Hua said. "Comrade Ye."

"I move"—the aged defense minister paused as he shifted his thick black glasses—"that we table this discussion until tomorrow."

"Second," Vice-Chairman Li said.

"You have no right to do this!" Jiang Qing protested. "There are three motions on the floor."

"The motion to table takes precedence," Hua said. "All those in favor?"

Defense Minister Ye and Vice-Chairman Li raised their hands. Kang and the moderates added their support. Wang Dongxin and Wu De whispered between themselves. Wang glanced at Jiang and then slowly raised his hand. Wu followed suit. The other members of the Wind Faction added their support.

"All those opposed?" Hua asked.

Jiang Qing kicked back her chair and stormed out of the room. Zhang, Wang, and Yao silently collected their papers and left the study.

"The motion is carried unanimously," Hua said, repressing a smile.

Mao Yuanxin rushed after Jiang Qing and the other members of the Gang of Four as they hurried to their waiting Hong Qi limousines. "What happened in there?" he asked.

"The goddamn will," Jiang grunted. "Somebody made a new copy of the original and put it back into the vault."

"How could they have managed it?" Yuanxin asked.

"There's no time to figure that out now. We must shut the gate before the rest of the sheep escape," Jiang quoted the Chinese saying. "Wenyuan"—she pointed to Yao. "Go to the *People's Daily*. Make sure the edition naming me as chairman is printed as planned. Then have the television and radio stations broadcast our appointments."

"I'll get to it right away," Yao said, climbing into his car.

"Hongwen," Jiang addressed Wang, "go to the base camp and take charge of the Red Guards. I want them ready to attack in one hour. Yuanxin, you organize the troops in the Western Hills. As soon as we are back in Peking, I want you to move in and arrest every member of the Politburo."

"I'll go with Hongwen," Zhang Chunqiao said. "I can use the base to coordinate the movement of my troops from Shanghai."

"How long will it take them to reach Peking?" Jiang asked.

"We'll have six divisions by nightfall and another ten in the morning."

"Excellent," Jiang smiled. "I'll show those old farts. They can't just walk in and steal the government from us."

Deng Xiaoping entered the study and herded Hua Guofeng, Ye Jianying, Wang Dongxin, and Wu De into a corner. "Do you need more evidence of Jiang's treachery?" Deng asked.

"I'm convinced," Wang Dongxin said. "As soon as I reach headquarters, I'll mobilize 8341."

"There's no time," Deng insisted. "If Jiang gets to her people, we'll be fighting the Red Guards in the street. You must order your troops now."

"How can we?" Dongxin questioned. "The phone lines are down."

"Follow me," Defense Minister Ye beckoned, leading the others down a flight of stairs. Two guards stood in front of a locked steel door. At Ye's command, they ushered the men into a brightly lit control room. A dozen soldiers sat behind computer terminals, radar consoles, and shortwave radios that kept them in contact with PLA headquarters throughout the country. "I've already ordered my men," Ye said. "They'll take care of the outlying provinces. We need 8341 and the municipal police to stop the troops of the Gang of Four that have already infiltrated the capital."

Wang Dongxin walked to one of the shortwave radios. "You'll have whatever help you need."

Stepping from the limousine, Yao Wenyuan hurried into the building housing the offices of the *People's Daily*. "Comrade Yao," a voice behind him called. He turned. Six men crowded in a circle around him.

"What do you want?" Yao asked.

"Comrade Wang Dongxin would like to see you," one of the men said.

Yao shifted uneasily. "Tell Comrade Wang that I'm very busy today."

"I am sorry"—the man bowed apologetically—"but I'm afraid I will have to insist that you accompany me."

"And if I choose not to?"

"My men have orders to use their weapons."

Yao searched impatiently for his guards. None was in sight. "What does Dongxin plan to accomplish?" Yao asked.

"You will find out when we reach the interrogation center."

The limousine in which Wang Hongwen and Zhang Chunqiao were riding slowed to a stop. A squad of guards from Unit 8341 surrounded the car. A guard stepped to the window. "What's going on?" Wang demanded.

"Please forgive the intrusion," the guard said politely,

"but there has been some difficulty at Defense Minister Ye's. Premier Hua would like to see you immediately."

"We will call him when we reach our destination," Wang replied.

"That would be difficult. There is no phone service."

"Then Premier Hua will have to wait."

"My orders are to take you to him," the guard said, aiming his gun at the driver. Wang shrugged and followed Zhang out of the car. Their attack would have to be delayed until he found out what Hua wanted. It never occurred to him that the moderates had struck first.

Mao Yuanxin and a regiment of his men motored back toward Ye's villa. They had easily dispensed with the ambulance, killing the men inside. Now Yuanxin was to arrest the members of the Politburo. It was a task he did not relish. Ye, Li, Hua, and the others were not only the leaders of the government, but were men he had known his entire life. But he knew he had to ignore friendships and look out for himself. His political future was completely dependent on Jiang Qing.

The regiment drove through a narrow valley. A barricade blocked the road. A small squad from Unit 8341 stood guard. Yuanxin could not understand what they were doing there. The jeep stopped. Yuanxin jumped out. "Move the roadblock," he called to the guards.

"I have been directed to stop you here," the guard said.

"I am Mao Yuanxin, the nephew of Mao Tse-tung. You have no jurisdiction over me."

"I'm sorry," the guard replied, "but I cannot allow you to proceed."

Yuanxin pointed to his heavily armed contingent of

troops. "Your ten men are greatly outnumbered."

"There are two regiments waiting in the hills," the guard replied.

"Of course there are." Yuanxin waved his arm toward the hills. Three of his tanks lobbed artillery shells. The shells tore into the mountain. The earth shook. Then there was silence. Yuanxin smiled. "What happened to your troops?"

The guard raised his hand over his head. Three hundred riflemen stood up from ditches on either side of the road and opened fire. The Red Guards fell like ducks in a shooting gallery. A bullet plunged into Yuanxin's forehead. He was dead before he hit the ground.

Hurrying into the Ming dynasty pavilion, Jiang Qing stared at the picture of Mao anointing her as the new chairman. She had ordered forty copies, but unless her people moved quickly, she would have no opportunity to use them. "Get me Comrade Yao," she told Shen Mo as she walked into Mao's study. "Then bring me herb tea, chrysanthemum leaves, and something bland to eat. My stomach is bothering me."

Jiang settled into Mao's chair and turned on the television. She did not want to be alone. An aide carried in a tray of tea and noodles. Jiang put a chrysanthemum petal on her tongue and sipped her tea. Then, pushing aside the chopsticks, she picked up a fork and started to eat. When in private, she preferred Western utensils.

Shen Mo steped tentatively into the study. "Is Yao on the line?" Jiang asked.

"No, but Comrade Wang Dongxin is here." Shen's voice cracked.

"I won't talk to that damn radish."

"Excuse me"—Shen shuffled her feet—"but I don't think

this is a courtesy call. Comrade Wang is accompanied by forty of his guards."

"In my house?"

"That's correct."

"What unmitigated gall!" Jiang jumped up and rushed to the entrance hall. "What is the meaning of this?" she demanded.

Wang bowed politely. "Comrade Jiang, please forgive the intrusion, but I would appreciate it if you would come with me."

Jiang pointed to the door. "I order you to leave my house this instant!"

Dongxin moved toward her. "I would like to spare you as much embarrassment as possible."

"From what?"

"Comrade Hua has asked me to place you in protective custody."

"You can't do that." Jiang's eyes flashed angrily. "I am Chairman Mao's wife."

"Our Great Helmsman is dead."

"His spirit is still alive."

"I'm sorry," Dongxin said, "but I have my orders."

Jiang whirled around and pointed to the painting of Mao anointing her. "The people will not stand for it. They love me. They know that I am Mao's chosen successor. You and the others are greedy old men, out of touch with the people, but I am the soul of the people. They watch my movies and my operas, read my books, and listen to my music. They hear what I tell them. They think what I want them to think. They and I are one." Jiang started to shout. "The people know that only I can stop the capitalist-roaders, only I can keep the country on the path to revolution. They will not let you do this. They will rise up in protest, demanding my return." Jiang thrust her hands into the air. "'Chairman Jiang!' they will shout. 'We demand Chairman Jiang!'" Suddenly she stopped. Everyone was staring at her. She dropped her arms and cast her eyes to the floor. A deafening silence enveloped the room. No one moved.

"Please, comrade," Wang Dongxin whispered.

Jiang looked up as if she had just awakened from a sound sleep. "Just give me a few minutes to pack my suitcase and put on a new dress."

Marc Slater jogged along Chang'an Avenue enjoying the tranquillity of the late-afternoon exercise. For the first time in weeks, there was nothing for him to do. It was too soon to talk about oil and too early in the day to contact his staff in the United States. Linda was at the airport awaiting the arrival of Liu Teyu. The government was in the process of reconstituting itself. Moderate leaders like Kang were being transferred to key posts formerly controlled by Jiang and the radicals.

Reaching Tian'anmen Square, Marc jogged toward the National History Museum. Crowds were already gathering. Even without public announcements, the news of the arrests of the Gang of Four had spread rapidly through the city. If the Chinese had greeted Chou's death with sorrow and Mao's with shock, they welcomed Jiang's arrest with jubilation. A New Year's spirit engulfed Peking. The usually reserved Chinese laughed, sang, and even danced in the streets. Wall posters with caricatures of Jiang and her cohorts were plastered everywhere. Marc had known Jiang for forty years. He disliked her flamboyant style and disagreed with her radical politics, but he never would have guessed the depth of the resentment against her.

Now Marc could get on with the rest of his life. He had already awakened his children and the secretary of state.

Tonight the people at M. H. Schaffer would learn that their president was still alive. The news would sharply increase the price of the stock. He enjoyed knowing that his exploits would be the center of attention at the White House and on Wall Street. As always, those who had bet against him would be badly squeezed.

He was anxious to return to his family and to his business. But before plunging into a new set of problems, he intended to take a week with Linda, sailing to Tahiti. He certainly had earned the rest, and they deserved a chance to spend some time together away from the constant series of crises that had beset them since their first meeting. It was difficult to build a relationship in the midst of attempted murders, kidnappings, earthquakes, Russian invasions, and coups. The tranquillity of the open ocean sounded very appealing.

Pausing at the entrance to the Forbidden City, Marc stared at the huge portrait of Chairman Mao. It was still difficult to remember that the Great Helmsman was dead. Without Mao and the radicals, the future of the People's Republic would be dramatically altered. China was not about to adopt capitalism or throw open its doors to hordes of foreigners. It was still the Middle Kingdom. Thousands of years of tradition could not be overcome in a single day. But now there was a chance for a change. It was not much, but at least it was a start.

A limousine with drawn curtains motored through the gates of Zhong Nanhai. The limousine stopped. A soldier in the front passenger seat rolled down the window and yelled, "Hey, long-nosed foreign devil, are you the blue-eyed spirit who runs like the wind?"

Marc smiled as he walked to the limousine. The soldier jumped out and opened the back door. "Need a lift?" Deng Xiaoping said.

Marc climbed into the car. "Are they letting you into Zhong Nanhai?"

"Officially I'm still purged."

"But unofficially?"

"Someone might just find a room for me."

"That's too bad," Marc said. "I was hoping for someone less formidable when it comes to negotiating oil contracts."

"I'll go easy on you," the diminutive Deng winked. "Who knows, we may need your help again. If I could rise from the dead, so could the radicals."

"I'm getting old," Marc laughed. "I'm not sure that I want to keep risking my life for a couple of million barrels of oil."

Deng opened the bar in the back of the limousine and poured two glasses of Maotai. "You know as well as I do, my friend, that oil has nothing to do with it. You may make noise like a capitalist, but I know you'd be here even if there wasn't a dime in it for you."

"Do you think I've taken leave of my senses?" Marc asked.

Deng raised his glass and clinked it against Marc's. "You are a *lao pengyou*." Deng drained his glass. "China is in your blood."

EXCITING ADVENTURES FROM ZEBRA